D1474236

Copyright © Peter Darman 2013

First Edition

I would like to thank the following people whose assistance has been integral to the creation of this work:
Julia, for her invaluable help and guidance with the text.
Dr Kaveh Farrokh, for his great knowledge of the Parthian Empire.
'Big John', for designing the cover.
Holly Martin, for the cover image.
Ardeshir Radpour, for his help regarding sourcing the cover image.

List of principal characters
Those marked with an asterisk * are Companions – individuals who fought with Spartacus in Italy and who travelled back to Parthia with Pacorus

The Kingdom of Dura
*Alcaeus: Greek physician in the army of Dura

*Byrd: Cappodocian scout in the army of Dura

Dobbai: Scythian mystic, formerly the sorceress of King of Kings Sinatruces, now resident at Dura

*Drenis: Thracian, former gladiator in Italy and now a senior officer in the army of Dura

*Gallia: Gaul, Queen of Dura Europos

*Godarz: Parthian governor of Dura Europos

Kronos: soldier from Pontus, commander of the Exiles in the army of Dura

*Lucius Domitus: Roman soldier and former slave. Commander of the army of Dura

Marcus Sutonius: Roman soldier captured by Pacorus, now the quartermaster general of Dura's Army

*Pacorus: Parthian King of Dura Europos

Rsan: Parthian treasurer of Dura Europos

Spandarat: Parthian lord in the Kingdom of Dura

Surena: a native of the Ma'adan and a soldier in the army of Dura

*Thumelicus: German soldier in the army of Dura

*Vagharsh: Parthian soldier who carries the banner of Pacorus in the army of Dura

The Kingdom of Hatra
Adeleh: Parthian princess, youngest sister of Pacorus

3

Aliyeh: Parthian princess, younger sister of Pacorus

Assur: High priest at the Great Temple at Hatra

*Diana: former Roman slave, now the wife of Gafarn and a princess of Hatra

*Gafarn: former Bedouin slave of Pacorus, now a prince of Hatra

Kogan: Parthian soldier, commander of the garrison of Hatra

Mihri: Parthian Queen of Hatra and mother of Pacorus

Varaz: Parthian King of Hatra and father of Pacorus

Vata: boyhood friend of Pacorus, governor of northern Hatra

Vistaspa: Parthian commander of Hatra's royal bodyguard

Other Parthians
Atrax: Prince of Media

Axsen: Queen of Babylon

Balas: King of Gordyene, killed fighting the Romans

Chosroes: King of the Kingdom of Mesene, committed suicide at Uruk

Farhad: King of Media

Mithridates: Parthian king of kings

Narses: King of Persis and Sakastan, Parthian lord high general

*Nergal: Hatran soldier and formerly commander of Dura's horse archers, now the King of Mesene

Orodes: prince of Susiana

Phraates: son of Sinatruces who became king of kings following his father's death

*Praxima: Spaniard, former Roman slave and now the wife of Nergal and Queen of Mesene

4

Silaces: soldier of the Kingdom of Elymais

Sinatruces: father of Phraates and king of kings who ruled the Parthian Empire for fifty years

Vardan: King of Babylon

Non-Parthians
Aulus Gabinius: Roman governor of Syria

Haytham: King of the Agraci

Malik: Agraci prince, son of Haytham

Noora: Agraci wife of Byrd

Rasha: Agraci princess, daughter of Haytham

Chapter 1

It had been three years now – many months spent preparing for an attack I was sure would come. While the trade caravans travelled east and west along the Silk Road transporting the precious material, ivory and spices from China through the Parthian Empire to fulfil the insatiable demand of Egypt and Rome, my army prepared. Every day the mud-brick forts that had been built north and south of Dura kept watch for an army that might attempt to approach the city by surprise; every day I received the same reports – there was no sign of any hostile forces. It had been over three years since the death of Phraates, the king of kings who had supposedly died of a broken heart, brought on by my having stormed the city of Uruk. This city was the capital of the Kingdom of Mesene and the residence of King Chosroes, the man who had marched an army to Dura and had attempted to storm it. But his army had been destroyed in front of my city and then I had captured Uruk and Phraates had supposedly taken his own life. The empire was now ruled by his son Mithridates, the man I had long suspected of being responsible for the death of his father. And ever since I had waited and prepared for the day when Mithridates would send an army against me. The days, weeks and months passed and nothing happened.

'Not this again,' barked my opponent.

Lucius Domitus came at me again with a thrust of his sword over the top of his shield aiming the blow at my own shield. Normally he would attempt to thrust his short sword – a straight, double-bladed weapon – into my neck or face. But as we were only practising and I was his friend he put aside the pleasure of killing me. Domitus, like many Romans, was shorter than me, by around six inches. Muscular, crop haired and uncompromising, he had been by my side since we had fought together under Spartacus in Italy all those years ago. He stabbed my oval shield – modelled on the Roman *scutum* – again with the point of his sword, forcing me back once more.

'It's a good job we're doing this for sport otherwise I would have killed you twice by now.'

I rested my shield on the ground. 'You're right, my mind's elsewhere today. My apologies.'

'Daydreaming about Mithridates again?'

I smiled. 'How did you guess?'

He sheathed his sword. 'It's written all over your face. Come on, you're no use to man or beast today.'

He began walking back to the camp, a sprawling collection of tents enclosed within a mud-brick wall half a mile from Dura.

My city was located on the west bank of the mighty River Euphrates and the dues raised from the caravans crossing the river were not Dura's only source of revenue, but they were crucial to the

6

kingdom's prosperity. When the animosity between myself and 'King of Kings' (so called) Mithridates had escalated into open warfare, he had decreed that no trade caravans were to travel through the Kingdom of Dura Europos. I had at first been greatly alarmed at this, but the royal order had been ignored by the merchants and had earned Mithridates the wrath of China's emperor and Egypt's pharaoh. No wonder – the route through my kingdom saved merchants around a month's journey time. Time was money and money was too important to be compromised by the arguments of kings.

After the humiliation of Chosroes' defeat and his father's death I had expected Mithridates to march against me but nothing had happened. Now, with the beginning of a new year, I again began to wonder if the king of kings would send an army against Dura.

'You waste your time dwelling on what will never happen,' said Domitus, handing me a cup of water as I sat in his command tent in the middle of the camp.

'He must come sometime. This kingdom's existence stands as a physical affront to his authority.'

Domitus shrugged and sat in one of the chairs opposite me.

'A man, and I use the term loosely when referring to Mithridates, thinks twice before going up against someone who has won as many victories as you have. In any case he prefers to let others do his fighting for him.'

I emptied the cup and then toyed with it, turning it round as I held it in my hand. What Domitus said was true enough. Mithridates had achieved the high crown probably through murder but every day that I ruled at Dura was a personal insult to him. And I knew that he would like nothing more than to see me dead and my kingdom destroyed. I placed the cup back on the small table beside me and stood up.

'Perhaps you are right. But when he does come I will be ready. Same time next week, Domitus?'

'Same time, same place. But don't bother turning up unless you are in the right frame of mind. It's no fun if you don't put up a fight.' I raised my arm in acknowledgement and left his tent.

I am Parthian and that will never change, but my time in Italy, first as a slave and then fighting in an army of slaves under Spartacus had given me the opportunity to see at first hand the military methods of the Romans. They had left a lasting impression upon me. Parthians were famed for their great armies of horsemen but these armies lacked discipline. Most kings in the empire had small retinues of professional soldiers, mainly mounted personal followers and palace guards. In times of war they would call upon the lords of their kingdoms to furnish them with thousands more troops, tens of thousands in some cases. But these soldiers followed their vassal lords, fighting around them in battle and doing their bidding. And when the fighting stopped they went with their lord back to the farms they worked on his lands. In Italy Spartacus had trained and organised his army along Roman lines, with the exception of his mounted arm, which I had commanded. We had beaten the Romans on many occasions but I had seen how effective Roman discipline and organisation had been and was determined to combine them with Parthian tactics. When King of Kings Sinatruces had given me my own kingdom, may Shamash bless his memory, I had the opportunity to put my ideas into practice. The result was the camp I was now strolling through, a giant rectangle that housed tents arranged in neat rows and blocks, workshops, stables, hospital, granaries and a parade ground. The oiled leather home of Domitus, the large and well appointed headquarters tent, stood in the centre of the camp. Either side of it were two smaller tents containing the legionary standards. Guards ringed these three tents.

As I made my way to the camp's stables I encountered one of the Companions. Gruff, burly and the veteran of many battles, Thumelicus was a German who had fought beside my friend Castus, a fellow German, now long dead, in Italy.

'How are your skills with the short sword progressing, Pacorus?' I may have been a king, but all the Companions were allowed such familiarity. Discipline in Dura's army was strict for all, but there were no ranks between those who had served under Spartacus.

'I think I might be getting the edge over Domitus,' I lied.

He raised an eyebrow at me. 'Really?'

I shook my head. 'No, not really.'

He looked round at a century of legionaries marching past us in its ranks, a centurion at its head barking orders at his charges. He raised his vine cane at Thumelicus in salute, for my German friend was the first spear centurion in the Duran Legion. This status was usually accorded to the bravest, meanest and most ruthless man in the legion. Thumelicus met all these criteria.

'Perhaps I should ask you to take my place and then we can determine who is the best swordsman in the army,' I said.

He looked at me with his pale blue eyes. 'We all know that Lucius Domitus is the best soldier in the army.'

I smiled at him. He was probably right but it was a close call. 'Well, I best get back to the city. Children to attend to.'

'How are your daughters?'

'Loud, full of energy and running rings round me.'

I was now the father of three children, all girls: Claudia the eldest now five, Isabella two, and the youngest Eszter, just six months old.

'I know how you feel. I have two of my own; both boys and both are bundles of energy. They live in the city with their mother. Future soldiers for your army.'

8

'Hopefully, Thumelicus, they won't see as much fighting as we have.'

He looked appalled at the notion. 'I hope they do. I'm raising them to be soldiers. No point in having the skills to use a sword and having no opportunity to show them off.'

'Well, let us hope that they won't have to do any fighting for the next few years at least.'

He smiled wryly. 'Have it you own way.'

He saluted and paced away to attend to his duties as I continued my journey to the stables. Once there I saddled my horse, a white stallion with muscular shoulders, thick neck and blue eyes called Remus. He was usually quartered in the stables in the Citadel, the city's stronghold perched atop a rocky escarpment overlooking the River Euphrates. The Citadel also housed the palace, the royal armouries, the treasury, Domitus' headquarters building which he rarely slept in, barracks, stables, granary and various other workshops. Like all the horses of Dura's army he lived a regal existence on the most nutritious fodder available and received the best care and attention from a host of farriers and veterinaries. When I visited the legionary camp he was fussed over by the grooms who worked in its stables, but just as when I had first owned him I always liked to saddle him myself.

Like all our mounts his saddle had been made especially for him. The hardwood frame was contoured to the shape of his back. It had four horns – two at the front and two at the back – to hold the rider in place. The front two horns were made so that they swept back to wrap themselves around the thighs of the rider and thereby anchor him in place. The rear horns were vertical but the joining arch between them was sloped to offer a curved feel to the rear of the saddle that also created a dip to form the seat. The entire frame was covered with felt for padding. Over the top of this were stitched pieces of rawhide leather. The leather was stained and finished with a polish containing a beeswax base to seal the material. Under his saddle Remus wore a white saddlecloth edged with red. Such equipment did not come cheaply, and neither did Remus' bridle, head collar, reins and the rest of his saddlery.

I had just finished tightening his straps when a mounted courier halted his horse in front of me and raised his hand in salute.

'Hail, majesty. Your presence is needed at the palace urgently.'

I was suddenly alarmed. 'Who has made this request?'

'Your sorceress, majesty.'

I had feared that one of my children had been taken ill, but if it had been so the queen would have summoned me. As I heaved myself into the saddle I felt more curious than apprehensive. I galloped from the camp and made my way to the city. The courier followed me as we galloped east along the road that led to Dura's main entrance – the

Palmyrene Gate. Over the gate was a great stone arch, on top of which was a large stone statue of a griffin, Dura's symbol and protector. The city had twenty-four other towers along its circuit wall and from each one flew my banner of a red griffin on a white background. I slowed Remus as we entered the city. The guards at the gates and on the walls snapped to attention as I passed them. As usual the city streets were thronged with tradesmen, citizens and beasts of burden and it took us a while to thread our way through the multitude to reach the Citadel.

Dura's Citadel could never be described as a beautiful or ornate place, with its thick walls, solid, squat buildings and its barracks, stables and armouries; but it was strong, built to withstand and defeat assaults and sieges. Perched high on the rocky escarpment on which the whole city was built, it radiated strength.

I dismounted and handed Remus' reins to a stable hand, then walked up the stone steps that fronted the palace. The courier bowed and left me as I walked through the entrance hall and into the throne room. At the far end, sitting on my throne – which in truth was nothing more than a simple high-backed wooden chair – was Dobbai. She had been the one who had foretold all those years ago at the court of King of Kings Sinatruces of my going to Italy and my return with Gallia my wife. Dobbai had made my city her home, and her gift of foresight and closeness to the gods had made her feared and respected throughout the kingdom. Now she was sitting on my throne as she regarded me with her black eyes. Queen Gallia was sitting next to her.

'May I know the reason you sent a courier to fetch me like an errant schoolboy?' I enquired.

'Do not be churlish, son of Hatra,' replied Dobbai, 'it does not suit you.'

'Then I will ask again. Why did you send for me?'

'Your life is in danger, Pacorus,' said Gallia.

My eyes went from Dobbai to my wife, from ugliness and old age to beauty and youth. How contrasting they were: Dobbai old and foul, her black hair lank, while Gallia's long blonde hair and beautiful face with its high cheekbones and slim nose were perfection.

'It is true, son of Hatra,' continued Dobbai. 'I was taking my afternoon sleep when a vision appeared to me, of a griffin limping and afraid, a blade in its belly and blood gushing from the wound.'

'Every time I fight on the battlefield I am in danger.'

Dobbai scowled. 'I did not mean that. I sense an assassin's dagger in your belly.'

I must confess a chill ran down my spine. The prophecies of Dobbai were not to be dismissed out of hand.

'You must have a personal bodyguard,' said Gallia, looking alarmed, 'soldiers who will be with you at all times.'

10

'At all times?' The idea filled me with horror. 'I have guards enough. They fill the Citadel and the city. There are also thousands of soldiers camped half a mile away. I do not intend to spend my life looking over my shoulder.' I smiled. 'Besides, the servants in the Citadel have been with us for years. I trust them.'

'With your life?' asked Dobbai.

'They have not poisoned my food or stuck a knife in my guts yet; why should they do so now?'

My words were met with stern countenances. Gallia started shaking her head.

'The risk is too great. We will have more guards in the palace.' She pointed at me. 'And you will not be riding alone in the foreseeable future. I shall organise an escort for you.'

Dobbai nodded approvingly at her. 'It is well that you take my words seriously, child.'

'I did not say that I did not believe you,' I reproached her, 'merely that I will not live my life in fear.'

'Perhaps the Amazons should protect you,' mused Gallia. 'At least I know I can trust them.' In Italy she had recruited a group of females that had served in my cavalry and named them Amazons. Now a queen of the Parthian Empire, Gallia retained her Amazons as a bodyguard. There were always one hundred of them but the idea that I would be protected by a group of females was ridiculous. It would lead to derision.

'I will not require the services of the Amazons,' I said curtly, then looked at Dobbai. 'Was it revealed to you when an attempt would be made on my life? What he or she will look like?'

Dobbai glowered at me. 'If I knew that then I could send someone to kill the assassin myself.'

'Well,' I said, 'let us keep this matter among ourselves. There is no need to burden others with something that may not occur.'

'It will occur unless we are vigilant,' insisted Gallia.

'Your queen speaks the truth, son of Hatra.'

'Nevertheless,' I replied, 'we will keep this our little secret. The matter is closed.'

I may have seemed untroubled by Dobbai's revelation, but for the rest of that day and the day after I was uneasy. I began to see danger everywhere and became a bag of nerves because of it. Gallia increased the number of guards both inside and outside the palace and had them stationed behind and beside the dais in the throne room when I received foreign embassies or heard the petitions of Dura's citizens. Dobbai took to attending all these gatherings and after a while I looked to her first to see her reaction when a visitor was presented to me. With each one I expected her to nod alarmingly to indicate that the assassin stood before me, but after examining each individual

11

carefully she just shrugged and shook her head. After a month of this I grew tired and stood down the extra guards. Things returned to normal. Perhaps not all Dobbai's dreams came true after all!

Shortly afterwards, at the weekly council meeting held in the headquarters building in the Citadel, the official home of Domitus, he brought up the subject of the additional guards. In attendance as usual were Godarz the city governor, Rsan the royal treasurer, and Prince Orodes a dear friend, now an exile from his homeland. Gallia also liked to sit in on these meetings, but today she and Dobbai had taken Claudia on a visit to the tiny harbour positioned at the foot of the escarpment directly under the Citadel. They had promised to take her fishing on the river, and as the day was clear and the waters calm they had left early in the morning, promising to return with a basket full of fish for our evening meal.

'So,' said Domitus, 'would you care to enlighten us about why the Citadel was suddenly filled with additional guards?'

'I had hoped to keep the matter discreet.'

Domitus laughed. 'No chance of that with your palace walls lined with soldiers.'

'Well, if you must know Dobbai had a vision and told me that I would be the target of an assassin's dagger.'

Rsan, who had taken to bringing a clerk with him to these meetings, a tall, pale youth with light brown hair, immediately instructed the boy not to make a note of that. My treasurer was an able, conscientious man but was prone to take alarm at the slightest provocation. It was so now.

'Assassin, majesty? That is grave news indeed.'

I raised my hand at him. 'I'm sure it is nothing. In any case I do not intend to go skulking round in my own kingdom.'

Domitus was frowning. 'You should have told me.'

'And what would you have done?' I asked.

'Tightened security.'

'Which means more guards.' I shook my head. 'No, that would not do at all. There are thousands of people who travel through Dura every year. They cannot all be stopped and searched. That would interfere with trade and soon the caravans would start to avoid us and we can't have that. Is that not correct, Rsan?'

Rsan began shaking his head vigorously. 'Yes, majesty. It is most important that trade is not interfered with.' He looked at his clerk. 'Make a note of that.'

Rsan regarded anything that threatened the kingdom's profits with abject horror.

'So that's an end to the matter,' I said. 'On another subject, I have been thinking for a while of establishing in the kingdom a breeding centre for horses.'

12

'Sensible idea,' remarked Godarz, 'at the moment we have to hire studs from your father's kingdom or further afield, such as Media and Atropaiene.'

'Exactly,' I said, 'it makes more sense if we can establish our own herds to supply the army. Cheaper as well.'

I could see Rsan nodding approvingly.

'Of course,' I continued, 'it will be expensive to start with.'

Rsan stopped nodding. 'Expensive, majesty?'

'Naturally, I'm only interested in the finest bloodstock. And I would prefer if we could have a herd of pure whites, such as the horses of my father's bodyguard.'

Godarz the governor of Dura and the city's father figure exhaled loudly. 'That will take a lot of time and a lot of money. Creating such a herd will not be easy, Pacorus.' Godarz lent back in his chair and ran his hands over his scalp in contemplation. 'It could take many years. Purchasing suitable studs will be very expensive, and even when you have them there is no guarantee they will produce pure whites.'

'Nevertheless,' I said, 'I want you to make a start, Godarz. Contact the breeders in Hatra, Media and Atropaiene.

'And the funds will be made available?'

'Pay whatever it costs.'

Rsan went ashen faced. 'I really must protest, majesty.'

'There's a surprise,' muttered Domitus.

'After all,' said Rsan, ignoring Domitus, 'surely one horse is much the same as another.'

I, Godarz and Orodes looked at him with horror. What he had said equated to sacrilege.

'I can assure you, Lord Rsan,' said Orodes slowly and purposely, 'there is a great difference between horse breeds.'

Orodes was a prince of Susiana, a kingdom in the centre of the empire. He was a brave and loyal friend to me, and that loyalty had cost him his crown for supporting me.

'What Prince Orodes says is true, my old friend,' added Godarz. 'The finest breeds of Parthian horses are the Przewalski, Karabair, Akhal-Teke and Nisean. Remus is descended from Carthaginian stock, of course. You wish to breed from him as well?' he asked me.

'I would like him to sire a line, yes.'

Rsan wore a blank look and I could tell that we might as well have been talking in a foreign tongue, but I was excited by the idea and so was Godarz.

'Well,' he said, 'I will get started straight away.'

Rsan cleared his throat, which was usually the signal that he had something to say but was hesitant to speak his mind.

'Spit it out, Rsan.'

'Well, the thing is, majesty, with the beginning of a new year there arises the matter of the annual tribute to Ctesiphon.'

'No tribute will be paid to Ctesiphon,' I replied. 'I will draw up a letter to that effect, inviting King Mithridates to come and take what is owed to him should he so wish.'

Every year I always hoped that when Ctesiphon was notified of my refusal to pay any tribute, Mithridates would take umbrage and send an army again Dura, but he never had, much to my disappointment. I would welcome the chance to defeat him and his lord high general, King Narses, the man who had once rebelled against King of Kings Phraates. I had defeated Narses in battle. But Narses and Mithridates had forged an alliance and whereas I had bested them both on the battlefield, they had triumphed over me when it came to intrigue. Thus it was that the Kingdom of Dura and its king were now outcasts from the Parthian Empire and Mithridates was Parthia's high king. I had once been the empire's lord high general but now I was viewed with contempt by those who held the highest positions within the empire. It never ceased to rile me.

'There is no point in sulking, Pacorus, nothing will happen despite your desire that it be otherwise,' said Godarz.

Rsan looked decidedly uncomfortable and Domitus laughed. Orodes appeared stern.

'You know he won't take the bait,' said Domitus. 'I don't know why you bother.'

'To annoy Mithridates, of course, and to goad him into action.'

'My stepbrother is full of malice, Pacorus,' said Orodes 'He will send Narses only when his enemies are weakened.'

'Dura will never be weak,' I growled, earning a murmur of approval from Domitus.

'Enough talk of that traitorous little bastard Mithridates,' said Domitus, 'let's talk about Godarz's wedding.'

'What?' I was most surprised.

I looked at my governor who was blushing. Orodes was smiling at him and Domitus gave him a hearty slap on the shoulders. Because of his age I had assumed that Godarz was happy being a single man, but it appeared that I was wrong. Rsan instructed the clerk to stop writing.

Godarz held up his hands. 'Domitus is exaggerating, I can assure you.'

'No I ain't. Byrd told me all about her. I had to work on him to get any information out of him, mind. We all know how tight-lipped he can be.' Byrd was a Cappadocian and my head scout. We had known each other for over thirteen years.

'So, Godarz,' I said, 'are you going to enlighten us further on your romantic adventures?'

'Certainly not,' he answered, and with that he folded his arms and said nothing further.

The meeting over, afterwards I managed to winkle a few details out of Godarz as I walked with him back to the governor's mansion just beyond the Citadel's walls. Apparently he had become acquainted with a woman who was the daughter of the head of one of the richest transport guilds in Anauon, a kingdom on the eastern edge of the empire. She and her father had arrived in Dura a few weeks ago and had presented themselves at the governor's mansion. Her father had rented a well-appointed house in the city and they had invited Godarz to dine with them on several occasions. I thought it odd that a transport guild from the eastern frontier of the empire should want to establish a presence in Dura, but Godarz told me that the woman's father was expanding the length of the route along the Silk Road that his guild controlled. This woman's father must have been very wealthy indeed to organise caravans that operated between Anauon and Dura and beyond, a distance of over a thousand miles. Godarz informed me with pride that her father's caravans could number up to a thousand camels and horses, each one had its own guards and they carried not only silk but also ceramics, bronze, spices and medicines. It was a most impressive summary.

By the time he had relayed all this information we had reached the gates of his mansion.

'I would like to meet this mysterious woman of yours,' I remarked casually.

'And I would like you to meet her, Pacorus.'

We strolled across the courtyard flanked by stables, storerooms, a small barracks and an armoury that held the weapons of the governor's guards.

'Perhaps you could bring her to the palace one evening.'

He paused at the foot of the mansion's steps leading to the columned entrance.

'I have a better idea, why don't you bring Gallia here and I can entertain you both.'

I smiled at him. 'That would be most excellent, my friend.'

Godarz smiled. He was clearly very happy and I was happy for him. He was extremely diligent in the execution of his duties as governor and his workload had increased substantially after Dura had become a major trading hub in the western part of the empire. At that moment a figure appeared at the top of the steps, a man I estimated to be in his mid-twenties with dark brown shoulder-length hair and a powerful build. He walked down the stone steps and bowed his head to Godarz.

'Ah, Pacorus, this is Polemo, my new headman. Polemo, meet your king.'

Polemo placed his right hand on his chest and bowed his head to me.

'Highness.' His voice was deep and severe. He was certainly an imposing figure, broad shoulders, thick chest and strong arms protruding from the short sleeves of his blue tunic.

'I assume my presence is required,' Godarz said.

'Yes, lord,' replied Polemo, 'the city's chief engineer is awaiting your presence, concerning the water supply to the caravan park.'

Godarz sighed. 'It seems a governor's work is never done. Thank you, Polemo. Tell him I will be with him shortly.'

Polemo bowed his head once more and disappeared up the steps and into the mansion.

'Well, duty calls,' said Godarz.

'What's the story with Polemo?'

'Oh he's been with me for a few weeks now. Turned up unannounced at the gates one day and asked for an audience. He used to work in the palace at Zeugma until old Darius took a fancy to him, so he ran away and pitched up here.'

I shuddered. It appeared Darius' tastes had now extended to more mature prey.

'He was a slave?' I asked. 'He looks like a soldier.'

Godarz shook his head. 'He's as gentle as a lamb. Reads poetry, would you believe? He's freeborn but his parents got him into the royal residence at Zeugma so he could learn to be a clerk. He can read and write Greek and Latin as well as Parthian. Darius' loss is my gain.'

Gallia was standing by the entrance to Remus' stall as I rubbed him down. It was a task that could have been performed by any one of the stable hands but I found that physical labour prevented me from dwelling on things, in this case Mithridates. I always took Remus out in the morning to the training fields where I put him through his paces, and afterwards rode him back to the Citadel's stables. Now I stood brushing his long white tail.

'I know that you think that your refusal to pay tribute will prompt Mithridates to march against you, but he will not and you know it.'

'Do I?' I unwittingly tugged on Remus' tail, causing him to grunt in protest and turn his head towards me.

Gallia shook her head. 'You shouldn't take it out on Remus. It's not his fault that you can't get what you want.'

I decided to change the subject. 'Where are our daughters?'

'Isabella and Eszter are with their nurses and Claudia is with Dobbai.'

'Claudia spends too much time with Dobbai. I shudder to think what she is learning from her.'

16

Gallia frowned. 'You know they are close. They like spending time together.'

'Too close. Dobbai is probably filling her head with nonsense.'

Gallia's expression hardened. 'The same nonsense that got you made king; that saved your crown and tells you the future? Is that the nonsense you allude to?'

I threw down the brush. 'All I am saying is that a young girl should not spend so much time with her; that is all.'

I began shovelling freshly produced dung into a wheelbarrow, just one of the treats I allowed myself each day.

'What do you know of this woman Godarz is seeing?' asked Gallia, changing the subject.

I wiped my sweating brow on the sleeve of my shirt.

'About as much as you do. Her father is a rich head of a trade guild based in Anauon.'

She raised an eyebrow at this. 'That is a long way from here. Why would she suddenly arrive in Dura?'

I shrugged. 'Same reason why all the other merchants and traders come here – to make money.'

I finished shovelling the dung and pushed the now full wheelbarrow out of the stall. It would be taken to the large tannery several miles south of the river and would be used in the process that turned animal skins into leather vests for the legionaries, belts and horse furniture for the cavalry and a host of other useful items.

'In any case,' I continued, 'we will be meeting her soon. Godarz has invited us to dine with them.'

'He should have said something to me,' said Gallia, 'we are his family, after all.'

I went to put my arms on her shoulders but she recoiled from me, seeing my sleeves smeared with dung.

'I think not.'

I walked over to a bucket of water on the floor opposite the stall and washed my hands in it.

'He has told us, or at least me. Besides, he has his life and we have ours. He doesn't have to explain himself to anyone.'

'I know that,' she snapped.

I was not entirely unsympathetic to her viewpoint. I suspected that she was disappointed that he had not confided in her regarding his new love.

'I am sure he would have told you himself once he became used to the idea,' I said. 'After all, he probably hasn't been in love in an age, and it was Domitus who brought up the subject at the council meeting, much to Godarz's discomfort.'

'Well he should have told me, that is all.'

I fastened the gate on the stall and looked at her.

17

'Does he need your approval?'

'Of course not.'

'Are you sure about that?'

She frowned deeply. 'I have better things to do than gossip to you.'

She didn't really, but I could tell that she had been stung by Godarz's secrecy and once her blood was up there was no chance of her seeing sense. She sighed, turned and waved her hand at me.

'Where are you going?'

'To see Godarz, of course. I might as well talk to Remus than you for all the sense you are making.'

With that she was gone. Poor Godarz, an afternoon being interrogated by my wife lay ahead of him. Truth be told the romantic life of my governor fascinated me not at all, however the affairs of powers beyond Dura's borders did, in this instance an invitation to Palmyra from King Haytham of the Agraci.

So a few days later I rode from the city with a small escort that included Orodes and fifty horse archers. We headed west and into the territory of the Agraci. They were a tribe of nomads who inhabited the northern part of the Arabian Peninsula; the tribe named the Bedouin populated the southern part. When I had first come to Dura open warfare had existed between my kingdom and the Agraci, but I had made peace with their king and ever since that time our two realms had prospered. The trade caravans passed through Dura on their way west through Agraci territory and then on to Egypt where they sold their precious wares. Of course Haytham charged them for the privilege of travelling through his domain, but in return he guaranteed their safety. He made a profit, they made a profit and everyone was happy, though many in the empire openly criticised Dura and its king for making peace with the accursed Agraci. Lord High General Narses had even boasted that he would rid the earth of the Agraci, but that had been over three years ago and since then neither them or I had seen hide or hair of him.

We rode at a steady pace, partly to spare the horses in the heat but mostly because the track west was literally heaving with traffic. Camels, mules, donkeys, carts and wagons stretched ahead as far as the eye could see. I smiled to myself. Most of the people on the road were Parthians – when there was money to be made people could always be relied upon to put their differences and prejudices aside.

Eventually we left the highway and rode parallel to it, a column of riders in white long-sleeved shirts and floppy hats, our helmets swinging from our saddles. Our bows were also hanging from our saddles while our quiver straps were slung over our shoulders. As usual I wore my Roman leather cuirass and the helmet on my saddle was Roman with a white goose feather crest. These items were gifts from a friend and were almost as dear to me as the sword that hung from my belt. This was also Roman, a cavalry sword called a *spatha*. Brown leggings and leather boots completed my appearance.

Orodes rode beside me, his leather cuirass covered in bronze and iron plates shimmering in the sunlight. He too wore a simple wide-brimmed hat on his head, his richly appointed helmet jangling on his saddle. I always felt extremely guilty about the circumstances that Orodes found himself in; made worse by the fact that he never complained or resented the ill hand that the gods had dealt him. I swore that one day I would make it up to him.

'I've never seen so much traffic on the road, Pacorus. So much for my stepbrother's orders that all trade through Dura should cease.'

'I heard that the Chinese emperor himself had complained to Mithridates about such a demand,' I replied.

'Even the king of kings thinks twice before interfering with the empire's trade.'

'He's not the king of kings,' I said, 'he's just a thief and murderer who occupies the high throne only temporarily.'

Orodes smiled at me and shook his head. 'Alas, my friend, I fear you are wrong. Mithridates is high king and is accepted as such by the other kings of the empire.'

'Not this one,' I retorted.

He laughed. 'No, not you, nor I for that matter, but we are in a minority, I fear.'

But Orodes was only half right, for I had the support of those kings who ruled the western part of the empire, plus the allegiance of the two kingdoms that guarded Parthia's northeastern border, Margiana and Hyrcania. On the other side of the Euphrates to Dura lay the Kingdom of Hatra between the Tigris and Euphrates – my father's kingdom. The waters of these two great rivers irrigated his land and grew the crops that were ripened by the great sun god Shamash, which meant that the people prospered. And He had blessed my father's kingdom further by ensuring that the great Silk Road ran through the middle of Hatra.

'We have many supporters across the Euphrates, Orodes. We are not alone.'

'None of the other kings will march against Ctesiphon,' he said. 'No one wants another civil war.'

It took us five days to reach Haytham's capital, a vast desert settlement of tents around the oasis of Palmyra. There was once a time when a column of Parthian horsemen would have been intercepted long before it reached Palmyra, but now our Agraci allies received us warmly enough. Haytham's soldiers, black-robed men with black tattoos adorning their faces, policed the Silk Road through his territory. A party had joined us not long after we had left Dura, more for the company than for reasons of security. Their leader was a wiry

19

man with a brown face and light brown eyes, his horse a magnificent grey mare.

'Do you have any problems on the road?' I had asked him.

He shook his head. 'No, lord, perhaps an argument when a collision has happened but nothing more serious than that.' He looked almost disappointed.

'A far cry from the years when your people and mine were at war.'

His eyes flashed with enthusiasm. 'Yes, lord. Then the desert ran red with blood when we raided Dura's lands.' He stopped, a mortified look on his face.

'Forgive me, lord, I did not mean...'

'It is quite all right,' I assured him. 'There was war and now there is peace. Let us hope it lasts.'

He looked away into the vastness of the desert. 'You have the friendship of my king and his children and the respect of my people. If someone had told me before you came that Agraci and Parthian would sit together round a fire and share a meal I would have thought them mad. But it is so and yet...'

He cast me a sideways glance, as if reluctant to continue. 'Speak freely.'

He nodded. 'But when you and my king have left this world, will Parthian and Agraci shed each other's blood once more?'

'Let us hope that will not be the case,' I replied.

He was right about the present, though. The only threats to the peace were the wretched caravan dogs that barked, growled and snapped at all and sundry. They were a menace to friend and foe alike. We said our farewells to our escort a day from Palmyra and made the rest of the journey unaccompanied. The landscape of the Tadmorean Desert is desolate, but the settlement of Palmyra in which it lies is green and lush, fed by the water that springs from the earth. Haytham's son, Prince Malik, met us at the outskirts. He was tall and lean, his face adorned with black tattoos; dressed in a black robe he presented a fearsome appearance. He halted his black stallion in front of us and beamed with delight.

'Hail Pacorus, hail Orodes.'

I reached over and shook his hand. 'It is good to see you again, my friend.'

Orodes greeted Malik similarly. It was a happy reunion of friends who had fought together many times. He rode beside us as we walked our horses through the heaving tented city that was Palmyra where the trade caravans, their personnel and animals were housed in a separate area to the south of the main settlement. After we had brushed the dust from our clothes and rested we were shown to Haytham's tent, situated in the middle of Palmyra. Our horses were taken from us and guards escorted us inside. Like King Haytham the tent was big and

20

imposing. The central section was cool and light, courtesy of a ventilation hole cut in the top of the roof. The king rose from the cushions on the carpet-covered floor and we bowed our heads to him. He looked in a relaxed mood in his baggy black leggings and white shirt, his black hair hanging loosely around his shoulders.

'Ah, you are here, good.'

He walked over and embraced me, then Orodes.

'You look well, lord king.'

'You do not have to call me lord, Pacorus. You are, after all, a king yourself.'

In truth I had never been able to put aside my sense of awe when in the presence of Haytham. He was the leader of the entire Agraci people, the man Parthian parents invoked when they wanted to frighten their children. Though he had proved a good friend and valuable ally, he still unnerved me somewhat. He turned to Orodes.

'Now you Orodes should be a king, and would be if Pacorus had killed your stepbrother when he had a chance.'

'How's Byrd?' I asked, changing the subject.

Byrd may have been the Parthian army's chief scout but he had made his home in Palmyra with an Agraci woman named Noora. Haytham gestured for us to sit on the cushions.

'He's well, as far as I know. Keeps himself to himself. Malik knows more than I do.'

Servants brought us water. 'He prospers,' said Malik. 'He seems happy enough.'

'Gallia wanted him to live in the palace with us; but I think the desert suits him better.'

More servants carried in bread that had been cooked on an open fire, mutton mixed with rice and vegetables, butter, yoghurt, cheese, honey and eggs.

'Rasha is well, lord?' I asked.

Rasha was Haytham's young daughter and was the chief reason that I was now sitting in the tent of my people's greatest enemy. When I first came to Dura I found Rasha a captive in the Citadel. Ever since their first meeting she and my wife had forged a close bond. We had subsequently returned Rasha to her father, and good fortune had favoured all of us ever since.

'Growing ever more the princess,' he replied. 'Gallia spoils her.'

Rasha had her own room in the Citadel at Dura, and I knew that Gallia had a tendency to treat her as one of her own children. 'I fear you are right, lord.'

'When she is at Dura there are five women to gang up on Pacorus,' said Orodes, shoving a piece of cheese into his mouth. 'He is outnumbered and outwitted at every turn.'

21

Haytham smiled. 'Three daughters and no sons. You should rectify that.'

I avoided his eyes. 'Alas lord, there will be no more children.'

Haytham looked solemn. 'I grieve for you.'

I looked up at him. 'Alcaeus, our Greek physician, told me after the birth of Eszter that Gallia would be able to bear no more children. Shamash has blessed me with my wife and three daughters. I can ask no more.'

Orodes fidgeted with his food and Malik looked uncomfortable.

'I am sure that you did not invite us here to discuss my children,' I said.

Haytham pointed at one of the guards standing by the entrance to the dining area where we sat cross-legged on the floor. He bowed and disappeared outside.

'No indeed,' replied Haytham. 'I have someone here whom you might find interesting.'

A few minutes later the guard returned with a man in tow, a figure of medium height and build with an untidy black beard and scruffy clothes. I estimated him to be in his early twenties. He eyed Orodes and me warily as he bowed his head to Haytham.

'This is Aaron, Pacorus, a Jew and a man who kills Romans. Is that not correct, Aaron?'

Aaron's eyes darted from Haytham to me. 'I have killed my enemies, it is true.'

Haytham nodded at me. 'This is King Pacorus, Aaron, a warrior who has won many great victories, most of them against the Romans. He has killed more Romans than you.'

Aaron bowed his head to me. 'Then it is an honour to meet you, lord.'

'Perhaps Aaron could sit with us,' I said to Haytham, 'so that we may be spared aching necks from having to look up at him.'

Haytham waved his hand at Aaron for him to sit with us. The way he tucked into the food before him indicated that he had not eaten properly for weeks. This view was confirmed by Haytham who told us his story while our guest tried to devour everything that was brought to us by the servants, in between taking large gulps of water and then wine. The son of a merchant, he had spent the last two years in hiding in Judea and fighting the troops of a Jewish king named Hyrcanus. Aaron had been in the army of another king named Aristobulus who had lost the civil war in Judea. The names meant nothing to me, but the end of Aaron's story did intrigue me.

'Ever since that bastard Pompey came to Judea my homeland is nothing more than a plaything of the Romans.'

I stopped eating. 'Pompey?'

Aaron also desisted his interpretation of a pig feasting. 'You know this name, lord?'

Both Orodes and Malik looked at me and at each other.

'Indeed,' I answered. 'With his army he thought to conquer my kingdom.'

Aaron was wide eyed. 'What happened?'

'I persuaded him that retreat was preferable to fighting.'

Haytham slapped his hands together. 'Not quite as I remember it.'

'Nor I,' added Orodes.

'Pacorus summoned the might of Parthia to his side,' said Malik, 'and then my father added his army to the strength of Pacorus. Pompey turned back and never returned.'

Aaron wiped his mouth with his sleeve. 'I would have liked to have seen that, lord. To have seen the Romans run.'

'I thought you may have a use for Aaron, Pacorus,' said Haytham.

'You are going to march against the Romans?' Aaron's eyes flashed with excitement.

'Not unless they march against me,' I replied.

His excitement disappeared. 'They will. There are two legions in Syria, and Judea sucks up to the Romans like a helpless lamb. They will swallow up Egypt soon enough, and then…'

He held out his arms in a forlorn gesture and spoke no more. I looked at Orodes and Malik. We knew the Romans and also knew that what Aaron had said was correct. Rome had an insatiable desire for lands and peoples to subjugate. The mood lightened somewhat when I questioned Aaron on his talents, of which he appeared to have many. His mother tongue was Aramaic but he could speak Greek, Agraci and Parthian well enough, though he said he refused to speak any Latin. His travels accompanying his father had taken him to Antioch, Jerusalem, Egypt and other towns and cities along the Mediterranean coast. Haytham was right, I could use such a man, or at least Godarz or Rsan could.

Aaron was delighted when I told him he would be welcome to accompany us back to Dura.

'One thing you should know, though,' I told him. 'The man who commands my foot soldiers is a Roman.'

Aaron's eyes opened wide in horror. 'A Roman?'

'A fine man,' said Orodes.

'And a great warrior,' added Malik. 'A man I am proud to call a friend.'

Aaron looked confused. 'I do not understand. King Haytham, you said that King Pacorus has fought the Romans.'

Haytham nodded. 'And so he has.'

Aaron then looked at me. 'Then how is it that a Roman leads your soldiers?'

23

'It is a long story,' I replied, 'but suffice to say that he is a man whom I trust with my life.'

'It is most strange,' mused Aaron.

'No stranger than some regarding King Pacorus as a messiah,' said Orodes.

'There is only one messiah,' snapped Aaron.

'Who is that?' I asked.

Aaron stared into the distance. 'The one who will deliver us from oppression.' He shot a glance at me. 'And the Romans.'

'Where is this messiah?' asked Malik.

'He has not come yet, but God will send him. It is written.'

'What god?' I asked casually.

'The god of Abraham, the one true god.'

'There are many gods,' I replied, 'what is his name?'

Aaron's eyes blazed with determination. 'No, there is only one.'

The next day Haytham took Orodes and me hunting. He also brought along his daughter Rasha. Now in her years just before womanhood, she had grown into a beautiful albeit wilful young lady. Her hair was as black as night, her eyes dark brown and her olive skin flawless. Like most of her people she was tall and lithe and had been raised to the saddle from an early age.

'One day, lord,' I told him as we rode into the rock and sand vastness south of his huge settlement, 'there will be great buildings and temples at Palmyra.'

He eyed me suspiciously. 'We have always lived in tents and always will.'

'Would you not like a palace to receive your visitors?'

'Palaces can be besieged and reduced to rubble. If I give the command Palmyra can vanish like a desert mirage.'

'Who would sack your palace, lord?' queried Orodes, riding on the other side of the king.

'The Romans,' he replied.

'Have you heard reports of the Romans making preparations for war?' I asked with concern.

'No, but with Romans in Syria and now Judea a Roman province in all but name I have potential enemies to the north and west. As Palmyra grows richer then it becomes a greater prize to possess for those with envious eyes.'

'We turned them back once, we can do so again,' I said.

'What do you think of Aaron?' he asked, changing the subject.

'He needs feeding up.'

Haytham laughed. 'He may look like a thief, but I think you will find him useful. Besides, if he stays here he will cause problems for us. We are too near to Judea I think, and if he foments trouble then the Romans will turn their attention to Palmyra.'

'What sort of trouble?'

'Aaron tells me that there are still rebels, freedom fighters he calls them, in Judea battling the Romans and their Jewish allies. He is one of them and burns to go back there.'

'Then why doesn't he?' I asked.

Haytham smiled grimly. 'He hopes to recruit others to his cause. He asked me whether the Agraci would support his friends.'

'What did you say?'

'I said no, of course. The fate of Judea does not concern me.'

'And you think it concerns me?' I asked.

'Of course not, but Dura is further from Judea than Palmyra. I think Aaron could be useful if his attention is turned elsewhere. And I wish to be rid of him. If you don't want him then I will have him killed. It is nothing to me.'

'I have offered him a place at Dura, lord, so let it be so.'

Rasha suddenly squealed and dug her knees into the sides of her horse as a gazelle broke cover from behind a collection of large boulders ahead and bolted for its life. She already had an arrow nocked in her bow as she galloped after her prey. We followed hard on her horse's hooves. I reached behind me and pulled my bow from its hide case then extracted an arrow from my quiver. Beneath me Remus powered ahead, straining to reach the gazelle as it tried to outrun us. I nocked the arrow in the bowstring as Remus caught up with Rasha's mount. Haytham and Orodes were immediately behind. Orodes shot his bow and the arrow cut through the air beside us as the gazelle suddenly darted right and then left. The arrow missed as Remus thundered across the baked ground in the wake of our prey. I brought up my bow so the bowstring was next to my face. I had done this a hundred times on the battlefield and on hunting expeditions. Keep looking at the target, lean slightly forward; let the bow become part of your body, as one with your soul. Time crawled as Remus closed on the gazelle and my breathing slowed as I aimed at the animal's hindquarters and released the bowstring. In the blink of an eye the gazelle changed direction once more and I missed him. Rasha pulled her horse right to follow the gazelle and shot her arrow, the iron head slammed into its side and caused the beast to stumble and roll over and over. She pulled up her horse and then lightning fast, shot another two arrows into the prostrate animal. It lay motionless, dead.

Elated, she leapt from her horse and ran over to the gazelle to stand beside it, raising her bow in triumph at her victory. I halted Remus in front of her.

'I'm glad all that time spent with Gallia and her women on the training fields did not go to waste, Rasha.'

She grinned at me. 'One day I will be an Amazon and will slay the enemies of your people and mine in battle.'

Haytham, Malik and Orodes rode up to join us.

'Did you see, father? I beat Pacorus, the greatest warrior in the Parthian Empire.'

She suddenly looked at Orodes. 'I meant no offence, Orodes.'

Orodes smiled at her. 'And none was taken, little princess. Well done.'

'Did your hand slip, Pacorus?' asked Malik. 'Perhaps we can invent a fiction that will save your face, for I fear that all Palmyra will soon learn that you have been bettered by a girl.'

'Thank you for bringing that to my attention, my friend.'

Haytham leaned forward. 'Well done, daughter. We shall eat your catch tonight in celebration.'

The king's entourage arrived, a score of warriors on horseback and attendants on camels. They slung the dead gazelle on one of the ill-tempered humped beasts and took it back to Palmyra. We continued with the hunt but came across no more gazelles, so Haytham ordered a halt at a small oasis surrounded by date palms. It was now blisteringly hot and we were glad of the shade and the opportunity to eat and slake our thirsts. After we had tethered our horses beneath one of the trees Rasha threw her arms around me and kissed me on the cheek.

'Will you tell Gallia about the gazelle?'

'Of course,' I replied, 'she will be delighted.'

'I have asked her if I can join the Amazons.'

'Really?' I looked at Haytham, who was frowning.

'She said I would have to ask my father. I was hoping you could speak to him on my behalf.'

'Oh, I see.'

She looked imploringly at me with her big brown eyes.

Haytham saved me. 'You should not pester Pacorus so. He is a king and has better things to think about than the fantasies of a young girl.'

Rasha stuck out her tongue at him and sauntered off to supervise the meal that was being prepared for us. I doubted that Haytham would allow his daughter to join my wife's band of women warriors, not least because she was a princess of her own people. The Amazons were mostly former slaves, runaways, prostitutes, thieves and the like, all united by a bond of sisterhood. And they were lethal. Gallia and her band were mounted on the finest horses, clothed in helmets and mail shirts and armed with bows and swords. I knew Rasha idolised them and they viewed her as a sort of younger sister, a lucky mascot. I also knew that her dream of being one of them was as her father had said, a fantasy.

26

Afterwards as we rode back to Palmyra, Haytham and I watched as Rasha and Orodes competed against each other in a series of short sprints on horseback.

'Rasha presents me with a problem.'

'How so, lord?' I replied.

'She is restless, Pacorus, she wants more than tents and the desert.'

'She is a princess of your people, lord.'

'But she has mixed with your people, has talked with merchants from distant lands and heard their tales of mythical beasts and strange tribes. More than that, she wants to be like your wife.'

'Gallia?'

'Of course, why not? Who would not want to be like the fabled warrior queen of Dura? To ride as well as any man, to fight as well as any man and be more ruthless than most? All these things she desires.'

'I had no idea that she was so besotted, lord. I apologise.'

He held up a hand. 'There is no need. Your wife, Pacorus, bewitches us all. Why do you think I let you live all those years ago when you and she came alone into my kingdom to return Rasha to me.'

He looked at me with his black, emotionless eyes then laughed aloud. He reached over and slapped me hard on the shoulder.

'And she shoots a bow better than you.'

But Haytham had been wrong about that day when we had brought his daughter back to him, for there had been another with us, a man who had made his home among the Agraci and had taken one of their women as his wife. Orodes and I went to see Byrd the next day. He knew we were in Palmyra, of course, but had no interest in hunting or the conversation of kings. He also knew that we were immensely fond of him and would call on him and Noora his wife. We found him shaking hands with a merchant over a dozen camels he had just purchased. He saw us and nodded, then continued with his conversation. The merchant became most intrigued by the two richly appointed individuals who dismounted and waited patiently behind Byrd as he conducted his business. There was no need for him to engage in such trade as he was given gold every month from the treasury in Dura. He had at first refused, saying that he had always earned his own keep. But I prevailed when I told him that it was unbecoming for the best scout in the Parthian Empire to be scratching a living in the desert. Gallia was always pestering him and Noora to come and live with us in the palace at Dura but he always refused. He was happy enough with his Agraci woman. But as he was also very fond of Gallia they both visited us often and as with Rasha, we had set aside a room for them in the palace.

The merchant pocketed his money, shook Byrd's hand once more, gave Orodes and me a curious look and then departed.

I walked up to Byrd and embraced him. 'Selling camels now, Byrd?'

Orodes likewise greeted him warmly.

'Just dabbling,' he replied. 'Always good to talk to those who pass through here. Pick up much useful information.'

He gestured to a youth, a boy of no more than twelve years in age, who gathered up the reins of the camels and led the beasts into a fenced-off area behind Byrd's large goatskin tent.

'And what is the latest gossip?' I enquired.

'I hear that three men rule Rome, two of them you have met: Crassus and Pompey.'

'Hopefully they will stay in Rome,' said Orodes.

'Who's the third?' I asked.

'A man called Caesar. This Romani general has won many victories, I have heard.'

Orodes slapped me on the arm. 'Not as many as Pacorus, I'll hazard.'

I laughed and then we went inside to share a meal with Byrd and his wife. Noora was a hardy woman who had been married before, though her husband had died many years before in an Agraci raid against my kingdom. That was in the time when there was open war between us. Noora had no children and the Romans had killed Byrd's family in Cappadocia, and now she was probably too old to give birth, but they were content with each other's company and for that I was glad. Once more I conveyed a request from Gallia for them to make their home in Dura and once more they politely refused.

'But we will all be together soon enough, lord,' Byrd said, 'when the Companions gather.'

Two weeks later he and Noora and the rest of those who had fought in Italy under Spartacus were gathered in the Citadel's banqueting hall. We called ourselves Companions because that is what we were; a band of warriors and survivors from many races and lands that had made the journey from Italy to Parthia. A motley collection of Greeks, Dacians, Spaniards, Germans, Thracians, Parthians and a woman from Gaul, my wife Gallia. Among the Companions there were no ranks, no hierarchy and no grades of social status. Just as Spartacus would have wanted we were all equal, free to call each other by our first names and to speak openly and without fear of recrimination.

The night was warm as the guests took their places at the tables arranged in parallel rows. There was no top table in the assembly of the Companions. I took my place next to Gallia, and beside her was Diana. Next to Diana was her husband Gafarn, by adoption a prince of the Kingdom of Hatra. Indeed Gafarn was now second in line to Hatra's throne and was also one of the finest archers in the Parthian Empire. Opposite us sat Nergal, a fellow Parthian from the Kingdom of Hatra. Tall, gangly, always optimistic and a fine leader on the battlefield, he was now a king himself, the ruler of Mesene, a land to the south that bordered the Persian Gulf. Mesene was not a rich kingdom and the people who lived in the marshlands to the south of Uruk, the Ma'adan, had been in open rebellion against Chosroes for many years. I had worried that they would continue their revolt against Uruk's new king but those fears had proved ungrounded for Nergal and his wife Praxima had proved to be good rulers.

Dobbai never attended the annual feast of the Companions, viewing it as too loud, boisterous and the venue for 'ruffians and boasters who should have grown up by now'. It was all those things but so much more – a reunion of old friends and the opportunity to forge new ties, for each Companion was allowed to bring his or her beloved, whether married or not. This year all eyes were on the guest Godarz brought, the mysterious woman from the east whom he had fallen in love with. I have to confess that I too was intrigued. Gallia, though, still smarting from not being taken into Godarz's confidence concerning this affair of the heart, professed no interest in the woman. But even her eyes were on the hall's entrance when the city governor entered. If he was intent on making a memorable entrance he succeeded, for the woman on his arm was truly stunning. Tall and slim, she wore a white low-cut dress that displayed her ample, perfect breasts. The sleeveless dress accentuated her toned arms. She had a narrow face, full lips, shaped eyebrows, long, dark eyelashes and high cheekbones. Gold hung from her ears and adorned her fingers. Her dark brown hair had been gathered behind her head and held in place by gold hairpins inlaid with jewels. Godarz walked over as I rose and held out my hand to him.

'Pacorus, may I present the Lady Nadira?'

Nadira means 'rare' and it was well chosen for she was indeed a rare beauty. She fixed me with her brown, almond-shaped eyes then averted her gaze and knelt before me. Any chatter that had been taking place when Godarz had entered the hall stopped as everyone stood up to observe the scene.

'Highness,' said Nadira, 'it is a great honour to meet you at last.'

I reached down, placed my hands on her arms and gently lifted her to her feet.

'Please, call me Pacorus, for we are all friends here.'

She dazzled me with a smile.

'You are most generous, highness. Lord Godarz told me that the greatest warrior in Parthia has a generous heart.'

She turned to Gallia standing beside me and bowed her head.

'And you must be Queen Gallia, whose name is known throughout the civilised world for beauty, courage and wisdom.'

Nadira knew how to flatter, that much was certain.

29

Gallia regarded her with a pronounced aloofness, though I could tell that she had been flattered by her words. 'You are too kind.'

'Well,' I said, 'Nadira, you must sit beside me and tell me more about how an old warrior such as Godarz managed to win the heart of such a beautiful woman.'

I led Nadira by the hand to her seat and embraced Godarz as he took his place beside his beloved. Domitus came over and bowed his head to Nadira and then slapped Godarz on the arm.

'You old ram.'

Nadira smiled politely at the muscular, crop haired barbarian standing beside her. The volume of noise in the hall increased again. The wine flowed freely and food was ferried from the kitchens.

Once everyone had been seated Godarz rose and held out his hands. The hubbub died again as all caught sight of the man of who had become the Companions' father figure, the sixty-year-old former slave who was now governor of Dura. He lowered his arms and as one we all rose to our feet and bowed our heads. The Companions had originally numbered one hundred and twenty but in the intervening years since our return to Parthia ten had died, all of them on the battlefield in my service. With great solemnity Godarz recited their names to the now silent assembly. In the courtyard outside each name was carved in granite on a memorial wall next to the gates of the Citadel so they would be remembered. He ended by asking the gods to care for their souls.

'We will see them again, for the bond between us can never be broken, not even by death.'

He picked up his cup and held it aloft.

'To Spartacus!'

We raised our own cups and toasted the man who had brought us all together, then returned to our drinking, talking and eating.

Gallia loved these occasions where she could reminisce about the old times in Italy and share jokes and tall tales with the surviving original Amazons. In my eyes she would always be the stunning blonde beauty I had first clapped eyes on in the camp of Spartacus on the slopes of Mount Vesuvius. But that was over ten years ago. Since then she had become a queen and had borne me three beautiful daughters. We both now had great responsibilities, to our children and to our subjects, but for at least one night Gallia could again be that carefree girl I had fallen in love with. She always had courage, but the years had hardened her to the greed and treachery of kings and I noticed that as the time passed she laughed and joked less and less. But tonight her blue eyes shone with excitement and she giggled and was happy among her friends.

'So,' I asked Nergal sitting across from me, 'how is Mesene?'

30

'It prospers,' he replied. 'I have given the marshlands to the Ma'adan to do with as they please.'

'Really?' I was shocked, for at a stroke Nergal had reduced the size of his kingdom by half.

'It is true, lord,' added Praxima, his Spanish-born wife who was now called Queen Allatu by the people of Mesene and revered as a god.

'You have halved your kingdom, then.'

Nergal shrugged. 'The marshlands belong to the Ma'adan, the people who live there. It has always been so. All I did was confirm what was already a fact. Besides, in return they have been most generous in supplying us with food and recruits.'

'They serve in your army?'

Praxima grinned. 'Of course! They know that a strong Mesene protects them also. They do not wish for another king like Chosroes.'

I was just about to converse with Nadira when the hulking figure of Thumelicus tapped Nergal on the shoulder and asked if he could sit in his chair.

'Shouldn't take more than a minute.'

Nergal winked at Praxima and duly surrendered his seat. Thumelicus ran a hand through his fair hair, his pale blue eyes wide as a result of too much wine. Every year I had to go through the same ritual with him at the annual feast. He placed his right elbow on the table.

'Best out of three then, Pacorus.'

I sighed and tilted my head at Nadira, taking care not to stare at her superb breasts.

'If you will forgive me, lady.'

In no time at all a small crowd had gathered round us as I rolled up my sleeves, placed my right elbow on the table and linked hands with Thumelicus. His grip tightened as he gaped at Nadira's chest, while Godarz's new love appeared to be bemused, confused and appalled in equal measure at the scene unfolding before her.

'So,' announced Thumelicus loudly, 'we all know the rules. Best out of three and the winner takes Queen Gallia, the crown of Dura and the contents of the royal treasury.'

Companions banged on the table and cheered in approval, while Thumelicus grinned at Gallia and winked at Diana.

Thumelicus looked at Godarz. 'On your signal, granddad.'

Godarz rested his hand on Nadira's arm. 'Your manners do not improve with the years, Thumelicus. Please begin.'

I like to think of myself as strong and physically fit, but Thumelicus was a brute who had fought as a gladiator in Italy many years ago and was now one of my best centurions, and as usual he almost wrenched my hand off as he forced it down onto the table. He

31

did the same with my left hand as the first round ended in my ritual humiliation. Thumelicus took a great gulp of wine and then slammed his right elbow down on the table once more.

'Come on, Pacorus, make a fist of it! An easy victory is no victory at all.'

I gripped his hand tightly and once more Godarz gave the signal to begin. I tried in vain to defeat the great German brute but to no avail and once more my hand was smashed down on to the table. Thumelicus screamed in triumph as he forced down my left arm to win the bout, though as he twisted my arm and I turned away in pain my eyes were confronted by Nadira's radiant breasts rising up and threatening to burst free from the confines of her dress. Rarely has the taste of defeat been so sweet!

Thumelicus banged the table with his fists, jumped up and raised his hands in the air. Those around him slapped him on the back.

'Behold,' he shouted, 'the new King of Dura.'

I rose from my seat and offered my aching hand to him.

'If I had a crown I would present it to you, you big German savage.'

He smiled and took my hand, then dragged me towards him and locked me in an iron embrace. He released me and grinned at Gallia.

'A kiss for your champion, my lady?'

Gallia blushed and offered her hand to him. Thumelicus hoisted himself on to the table and then slid across its surface to be in front of her, then embraced her and kissed her on the cheek. She pushed him away.

'Behave yourself Thumelicus, you have had too much to drink.'

He kissed her again and retreated back over the table.

Diana and Praxima squealed and clapped with delight and Gafarn was bent double with laughter.

As the evening wore on every Companion came over to Godarz and congratulated him on catching such a prize in Nadira. All of them were genuinely happy that he had found a soul mate in the autumn years of his life.

'She's half his age,' snapped Gallia as we took breakfast on the palace terrace the next morning. The Citadel sat atop a high rock escarpment overlooking the Euphrates, its sheer sides making it impregnable from the riverside. A large terrace surrounded by a stone balustrade had been created next to the rear of the throne room. It was extended so that each bedroom, ours included, that faced the river also had its own balcony.

'What difference does that make?' I replied as my two eldest daughters ran around us screaming at the tops of their voices. Little Eszter sitting in her raised chair cooed with delight. 'He is obviously happy and she seems very agreeable.'

She raised an eyebrow at me. 'Yes, I saw you gawping at her chest. Behaviour hardly becoming of a king.'

I told my daughters to sit down and eat their food in silence, but just as they had taken their seats Dobbai appeared and they began racing around once more, tugging on Dobbai's black robes.

'Can you calm them down?' I asked her.

Dobbai kissed Claudia, Isabella and little Eszter and then ushered the first two back to their chairs.

'Feeling delicate, son of Hatra?'

'Too much drinking and leering last night,' sneered Gallia.

'Ah, yes,' said Dobbai, 'grown men acting like small boys. It must have been excruciating for you, my dear.'

'Gallia is jealous of Godarz's new love.'

Gallia glared at me. 'I am not. I hope he is happy.'

'Just not with a beautiful woman half his age,' I replied mischievously.

'How pathetic are the carnal desires of men,' said Dobbai as she sat down in her wicker chair stuffed with cushions. She rarely left the palace these days, being content to amble around the palace and watch over our daughters.

'They love each other,' I said.

They both looked at me as though I had taken leave of my senses.

Dobbai picked at a date. 'She wants something from him that is all. If you had any brains you would see that.'

Gallia nodded gravely. 'That is what I think. I should tell Godarz before he gets hurt.'

'You will do no such thing,' I said. 'He is happy and deserves to be. We will leave well alone.'

'Ill omens are abroad in Hatra, you both would do well to take care.' Dobbai's face was blank as she relayed this news to us, as though speaking on behalf of another.

'Ill omens?' Gallia looked concerned.

Claudia put down her food and walked over to Dobbai and hoisted herself on to the old woman's knee.

'I saw an owl perched above the gates of the Citadel last night,' said Dobbai, stroking Claudia's long fair hair.

I felt a sense of dread. An owl was a sign that evil was present and was usually a portent of imminent death and destruction, or at the very least grave misfortune. Owls were believed to represent the souls of people who had died unavenged. I immediately became alarmed for the safety of my wife and children. Dobbai saw my look of concern towards the little ones.

'They are not in danger, son of Hatra. It is you that faces peril.'

She smiled at Claudia. 'Tell your father what happened to the smoke from the fire near the stables.'

Claudia looked very serious. 'The smoke did not disappear, father. It hung over the flames. It should have risen straight towards the heavens. But it did not. A bad omen.'

'What nonsense is this?' I asked Dobbai irritably.

'No nonsense, son of Hatra. It is an old Scythian ritual that can determine whether evil spirits are near.'

I pointed at Claudia. 'You should not fill her head with such foolishness.'

Then I turned to Gallia. 'This is just the sort of thing I was talking about.'

'What about that Jew you brought back with you from the desert?' asked Dobbai.

'Aaron? What about him?'

'He is an assassin,' she replied, 'I have seen his eyes. They are full of hate.'

'He will be arrested,' announced Gallia. 'Where is he now?'

'Wait,' I said. 'If Aaron is an assassin as you say, then he had plenty of opportunities to kill me on the journey from Palmyra.'

'You should kill him,' said Dobbai, 'just to make sure.'

'Kill him, kill him,' shouted Isabella, not knowing what it meant, or at least I hoped that she did not. Poor Aaron, Haytham was thinking of having him killed and now Dobbai wanted his head.

'Quiet!' I shouted. Isabella fell silent and then began to cry. Gallia walked over and picked her up.

'Now look what you have done.'

I held my head in my hands. 'Aaron is under my protection,' I said, looking at Gallia and then Dobbai. 'No harm shall come to him.'

'Let us hope the same can be said of you, son of Hatra,' quipped Dobbai.

I had suddenly lost my appetite, so I rose and walked from the terrace. The rigours of the training fields beckoned and were a welcome relief from the wittering of an old woman.

'You can turn a deaf ear to me if you wish, son of Hatra,' remarked Dobbai as I left them, 'but you are foolish not to heed the warning signs that the gods are sending you.'

Chapter 2

Gods! How they tormented us mortals! I worshipped and feared Shamash, God of the Sun, and respected the other deities that dwelt in heaven, but I sometimes despaired of their intrigues. It was well known throughout the empire that Dobbai was sent visions by the gods, but they were often so vague and shrouded in mystery as to be almost impossible to decipher. The movement of smoke over a fire did not bother me but the appearance of an owl perched on the Citadel's walls was not to be dismissed lightly. We had already increased the number of guards in and around the palace and there had been no new arrivals among the palace servants, most of whom had been with us for years, so I did not fear danger from that quarter. But then, any one of my soldiers could stick an arrow or blade into me at any time should they so wish. It all came down to trust. Did I trust them? Dura was different from many kingdoms in the empire in that it had a standing army. The Silk Road that passed through it paid for their weapons, equipment and wages. Each man was paid monthly for his services. The levels of pay were dictated by rank and length of service, with records diligently maintained and held in the headquarters building in the Citadel. Each man, and every woman in the Amazons, irrespective of rank or race received equality of treatment when it came to rewards and punishments. In return I demanded loyalty. In all the time I had been King of Dura I had experienced no mutinies or disloyalties. My soldiers had always obeyed orders unquestioningly. In the end that is all any commander can hope for.

A welcome diversion came with an invitation from Godarz for Gallia and me to dine with him and Nadira at the governor's mansion. It had probably been a mistake that the latter's first meeting with us had been at the Companions' feast, but what was done was done. At least this time there would be no raucous Germans present to humiliate me.

'Try to keep your eyes in their sockets this time, Pacorus.'

Gallia looked stunning on the evening we made the short journey from the Citadel to Godarz's residence, a score of legionaries acting as our escort.

My queen wore a blue, sleeveless dress with a gold belt around her waist, gold armlets and gold bracelets. Her long, thick blonde hair hung freely around her shoulders and over her breasts. Even among her curls were thin slivers of gold. She looked every bit the queen she was. I wore a simple white silk shirt, baggy brown leggings and red leather boots. As usual my Roman *spatha*, the gift from Spartacus, was worn at my hip. On the opposite hip was my dagger, a weapon taken from a dead Roman centurion.

The night was still and warm, the only noise the crunching sound made by the legionaries' hobnailed sandals as they marched beside us on the stone slabs. The road that led from the Citadel to the Palmyrene Gate was paved, though most of the streets in the city were dirt. I had instructed Rsan to embark on a programme to pave all the main roads inside the city to save us from the permanent cloud of dust that hung over Dura in the hottest months, especially over the tallest part – the Citadel – and the work was continuing apace. The Greeks had originally built the city and its roads and buildings were arranged like a giant grid with streets perpendicular to each other, the whole surrounded by a thick, strong circuit wall.

I held Gallia's hand as we walked to the governor's mansion. The odd citizen still abroad bowed to us as we passed. Dura had no curfew except in an emergency, though the city gates were shut two hours before midnight every evening and were not opened again until dawn the next morning. There was no danger of an Agraci attack against us, but Dura had always been a frontier city and its inhabitants slept sounder knowing that they were in a secure stronghold.

We arrived at the mansion within minutes, the guards either side of the gates snapping to attention as we walked past them into the courtyard. More guards flanked the stone path that ran from the gates to the foot of the steps leading to the mansion's entrance. We walked across the courtyard as Godarz and Nadira descended the steps to greet us. Nadira was wearing a yellow, figure-hugging dress with a diadem in her hair.

'Remember,' said Gallia in a whisper, smiling at our hosts, 'when you speak to Nadira, her eyes are in her head and not her chest!'

Godarz may have been the city governor but he always dressed modestly. It was the same tonight. The years spent as a slave in Italy had left their mark on him. In truth though, he had never been badly treated yet he had still been a slave. Tonight he was dressed in a simple long-sleeved beige shirt, white leggings and sandals. Though Parthian men wore their hair long, Godarz had had his hair shorn in Italy and had never let it grow back. As he and his new love bowed their heads to us he appeared truly happy, wearing the look of a man who had finally found contentment after years of loneliness.

'Welcome,' said Godarz, 'you are both most welcome.'

'We are glad to be here,' I replied.

Gallia smiled politely at Nadira and then embraced Godarz. She linked her arm in Nadira's and they walked up the steps together into the mansion. I embraced Godarz and slapped him on the back.

'Nadira is a beautiful woman. I am pleased for you, my old friend.'

His eyes were moist as he stepped back to face me.

'I never thought that I could be this happy, Pacorus. The gods have truly blessed me.'

36

We followed our women up the steps, Polemo bowing his head to us as we passed him at the top.

'You deserve to be happy, Godarz. We are truly happy for you.'

Godarz looked at Gallia and Nadira disappearing into the reception hall. 'Even Gallia?'

'Of course. Her nose has been put out of joint that is all. You know how it is with women, they get jealous.'

The meal was a most excellent feast. Though the mansion had a banqueting hall we ate in a smaller room just off the reception hall so as not to be dwarfed by our surroundings. I sat next to Gallia across from Godarz and Nadira. Servants brought us yoghurt, Parthian beans, fennel cooked with pine nuts and spices, roasted lamb, goat and chicken, steamed rice, crusty rice with cinnamon and pistachios, and meat balls. Other servants served us wine and water. As the wine flowed Gallia's suspicion of Nadira lessened somewhat. The latter was charm itself, engaging my wife in conversation and appearing interested in everything she said, especially the Amazons. Gallia was delighted to talk about her female warriors, which made Godarz overjoyed. I had been dreading any friction between my wife and Nadira, but Godarz's woman was adept at conversation and charm. She hardly spoke to me, knowing that the attitude of Gallia was the key to the success of the evening, and truth be told it was turning into a highly enjoyable occasion. I relaxed in my high-backed wooden chair and smiled at Godarz. He nodded and then stared lovingly at his gorgeous woman. He was truly blessed.

I drained my silver drinking vessel, a *rhyton*, and held it up to be refilled. Fashioned into the shape of a ram's head it was a beautiful piece, highly polished and delicately crafted. I turned the drinking vessel in my hand as a servant walked towards me with a jug of wine. I saw the reflection of a figure behind me in the polished surface of the *rhyton* and instinctively moved to my right. As I turned to see who it was, a sword blade directed at my head suddenly splintered the back of my chair. I instinctively rolled out of it and kicked it away as Polemo wrenched his blade free. I jumped to my feet and drew my own sword, then advanced to meet my would-be assassin.

'Godarz,' I shouted, 'get the women out of here. Sound the alarm.'

Polemo smiled. 'I have a message for you, slave king.'

He attacked me with powerful slashing blows directed against my head. I parried them with some difficulty and then tried to thrust my *spatha* into his chest. But he sprang back and avoided my sword point with ease.

Polemo grinned once more. 'King Mithridates sends his greetings.'

Then he came at me once more and again tried to behead me with his blade. His strength and speed forced me back. I caught his last slashing blow with my own blade, grabbed his sword hand with my left hand and head-butted his nose. He grimaced and staggered back, his nose broken.

I glanced behind me and saw with horror Gallia grappling with Nadira, who had a dagger in her hand and was trying to stab my wife. Godarz was standing, transfixed by what was happening in front of him.

'Godarz!' I screamed. 'Kill her, kill her now!'

I turned and saw the figure of Polemo charge at me once more. A servant ran at him but Polemo saw him, swung his blade to his left and sliced open the man's belly. A piercing scream came from the servant as he collapsed to the ground. Polemo raced over to the door that lead to the kitchen corridor and slammed it shut.

'Godarz,' I shouted again. 'In the name of Shamash do something!'

Godarz looked at me and then at Nadira and Gallia grappling with each other. He came to his senses and raced over to grab Nadira, who slapped Gallia round the face, pushed her to the ground and then swung round. Godarz was not stabbed by her dagger but rather ran on to its blade. Nadira grabbed his shoulder with her left hand and then stabbed him twice more before turning back to face Gallia. Another servant ran into the room from the hall.

'Sound the alarm,' I screamed, but Polemo was too quick and split the back of the man's head with his sword as he tried to run from the room. I ran at Polemo, my *spatha* grasped with both hands, and hacked at his head. He parried my blows but blood was now pouring from his shattered nose and he had difficulty in maintaining his defence. He tried to bar the door with a small table that had been positioned against the wall beside it, but another servant burst into the room and interrupted him. The servant looked at me and then died as Polemo nearly severed his head with a great swing of his sword. I screamed and ran at Polemo again, slashing at his neck and then whipping my blade back to thrust the point into his left shoulder. He groaned and winced in pain but still advanced and directed more blows against me. His strength was failing, though, and the sword strikes were becoming slower and easier to parry.

I looked behind me and saw Godarz lying on the floor. Gallia had sprung to her feet, grabbed a knife from the table and was facing Nadira.

'Come on, bitch!' she screamed.

Nadira glanced at me and then at Polemo, who was now bleeding from both the nose and shoulder. She spat at Gallia and ran over to Polemo.

'Come, we must go.'

Polemo raised his sword at me and then they fled from the room. Gallia ran to Godarz and cradled his head in her arms. Another servant rushed into the room and stared in horror at the scene that greeted his eyes.

'Sound the alarm,' I shouted. 'Go quickly!'

His mouth was open in terror and he shook his head like a demented man as he fled. I knelt beside Godarz. Tears were running down Gallia's cheeks as she held him. I looked at the blood oozing from the wound in his belly and knew he was dying. I heard the alarm bell ringing in the courtyard and shortly after a dozen guards raced into the room.

'Get a doctor,' I ordered.

Godarz was staring at the ceiling, a far-away look in his eyes. 'She said she loved me. I do not understand.'

'Don't speak,' said Gallia softly, 'Alcaeus will be here soon.'

Godarz looked at her. 'I loved her, you know.'

Her tears fell on his face. 'I know.'

Godarz's shirt was soaked with blood by the time Alcaeus our Greek physician appeared with his canvas bag over his shoulder. He ignored Gallia and me as he knelt down beside Godarz, reached into his bag and extracted a small knife. He cut away Godarz's shirt to examine the wound. I could see that it was deep, blood now oozing onto the floor. Alcaeus worked with skill and speed, cleaning the wound with vinegar and then applying a large honey-impregnated dressing on it. He then wound a large bandage around Godarz's belly in an attempt to staunch the flow of blood, but Godarz had already lost so much. He did not speak now, only stared unblinking at Gallia with a bewildered look in his eyes.

Domitus ran into the room followed by four of his officers and other servants. He stared at Godarz and I thought I detected a look of distress in his eyes, then his stern countenance returned.

'What happened?'

I stood up to face him, a wave of grief sweeping over me.

'That whore Nadira and Godarz's new headman were assassins sent by Mithridates. They fled but must still be in the city. They might try to escape using the harbour.'

The tiny harbour was reached via a small gate in the city's southern wall. Domitus turned to his officers.

'Turn out the garrison, seal the city and organise sweeps of all the buildings. Find them,' he ordered.

The men saluted and ran from the room.

'He's gone, I'm sorry.'

I turned to see Alcaeus had a finger at Godarz's neck to feel for a pulse. He shook his head at Gallia and then closed my governor's eyes. Gallia pulled up Godarz's head to her face and began sobbing. Domitus ordered everyone out of the room.

'I'm sorry.'

He placed a hand on my shoulder and also took his leave, as did Alcaeus. I knelt beside Gallia and we both wept for our dead friend.

The sweep of the city was carried out at once, soldiers hammering on every door to gain entrance. Soon word spread that the governor had been murdered and dazed and confused citizens, most in their night attire, flooded onto the streets. Many headed for the city's central square, perhaps thinking that a herald would inform them of what had happened and what measures I was taking. But the only thing I did was to assist Alcaeus carry the body of Godarz to his bedroom where it was washed and dressed. Most of his servants were in tears as they attempted to carry out their duties. Godarz had been a fair and gentle master, though like Gallia and I he had no slaves in his household, only paid servants. Those of us who had been slaves had no wish to be surrounded by others who lived in such misery. Afterwards I was numb as I held my wife and we made our way back to the palace. I found an ashen-faced Rsan on the palace steps. I merely nodded at him as we passed. There were no words I could speak that would ease his anguish.

We shuffled into the throne room where Domitus was pacing up and down. I looked at Gallia, her eyes puffy and red.

'Do you want to sleep?'

She shook her head. 'I cannot sleep tonight.'

She walked over to her high-backed chair on the dais and slumped into it. I sat down beside her. Domitus stopped pacing and stood before us. His face betrayed no emotion though I knew he must be grieving for his dead friend.

'Parties are sweeping the city now. All gates are sealed and no one can get in or out. The men are searching every home, business, temple and storeroom, and I've ordered more men from the camp.'

He glanced at Gallia. 'Most likely they will have rented a room or rooms and will be lying low until they make a run for it.'

'See to it that they don't escape,' hissed Gallia. She had Godarz's blood on her dress. Domitus noticed it but said nothing. He stood to attention, saluted and then marched from the room, leaving us alone with our grief.

Dura was a well-defended city surrounded by a circuit wall with a total of twenty-four towers, plus the Palmyrene Gate, spaced at regular intervals along the wall. Each tower had its own detachment of men who would be lining the wall to ensure no one scaled it from the city side. Five hundred men manned the walls and towers and a further five hundred garrisoned the Citadel. Added to these were the detachments of Dura's horsemen stabled in the city – more than enough to catch a pair of assassins, or so I hoped.

The new day began to dawn and still we remained on our thrones and waited for news. I had messages sent via carrier pigeon to

Palmyra to alert Malik and Haytham of what had happened, and to ask them for their assistance to track down the pair should they escape from Dura. Domitus organised searches of the trade caravans camped to the north of the city. All traffic using the pontoon bridges was stopped. Domitus even sent small boats north and south on the Euphrates to search for the pair.

Orodes came soon after dawn. He lived in his own house in the north of the city, a great walled residence that also housed his bodyguard – two hundred and fifty men from the Kingdom of Susiana. As soon as he heard the news of Godarz's murder he and his men had helped Dura's garrison search the city. Unshaven and looking tired, the first thing he did was embrace Gallia and kiss her on the cheek.

'You look tired, Gallia.' He noted her bloodstained dress. 'You should try to get some rest.'

She smiled faintly. 'Alas, lord prince, if I close my eyes all I will see is the murder of Godarz. I therefore prefer to keep them open.'

Orodes nodded grimly. 'Well, at least let us refresh ourselves. You too, Pacorus. You both look terrible.'

He organised fruit juices, bread, cheese and sweet meats to be brought to the palace terrace as Gallia and I changed our clothes and washed our faces. When we returned Dobbai was sitting in her chair. Orodes was speaking to her as a wan Gallia slumped into a chair beside her. In the east the sun was an angry red ball as it began its ascent into the sky. Dobbai said nothing to Gallia as I walked over to the table and helped myself to a cup of juice. I poured another and handed it to Gallia. I took my seat next to her and then all four of us sat in silence for a while. Dobbai spoke at last.

'So Mithridates shows his hand at last.' She turned to Orodes. 'Your brother has learnt patience, it would seem.'

'My stepbrother,' Orodes corrected her. He was always quick to inform all and sundry that he and Mithridates did not have the same mother, his being a concubine in the palace at Ctesiphon whom his father Phraates had fallen in love with. The mother of Mithridates, Queen Aruna, had had her poisoned, or so rumour had it.

'But why now?' asked Orodes despairingly.

'Is it not obvious?' replied Dobbai. 'Now he and his brother-in-evil Narses are ready to implement their plan.'

'What plan?' I asked.

Dobbai held out her hands. 'I do not know. But I do know that the death of Godarz will begin tumultuous events within the empire. He also knows this, though of course he would have preferred your death rather than your governor's.'

41

'I will march on Ctesiphon,' I announced, 'and bring back the head of Mithridates to adorn the entrance of Godarz's mansion. The head of Narses too, a fitting tribute to Godarz. This is my vow.'

'And that is exactly what they want you to do, son of Hatra,' said Dobbai, 'to march at the head of your army into their trap.'

'What trap?' asked Orodes.

Dobbai raised her face to the heavens. 'I have tried, I really have, to counsel you, son of Hatra, so you can carry out the wishes of the gods and keep the empire strong. But you have seen fit to ignore my advice.'

'That is unfair,' I replied. 'I have always respected your views.'

She fixed me with her black eyes. 'Have you? I told you years ago to kill Mithridates, yet you chose to ignore me. He will only be satisfied when you are dead and he is the unchallenged king of kings.'

'He is king of kings,' I said in exasperation.

'In name perhaps,' said Dobbai, 'but it is well known that you openly challenged him to march on Dura and take the city by storm. The longer you remain king here the more he is seen as impotent.'

'If he and his assassins had killed Pacorus,' said Orodes, 'he must have known that King Varaz, his father, would have marched against him. And Hatra has allies in Babylon and Media, to say nothing of Nergal at Uruk.'

Dobbai regarded Orodes with a bemused look. 'He knows all of that, but he and Narses have taken measures in anticipation of those events happening.'

'What measures?' I asked.

Dobbai pursed her lips. 'How should I know? I cannot see into the poisoned well that is the mind of Mithridates.'

'Mithridates must be punished,' said Gallia, staring into the distance.

'I agree,' I added.

'And so do I,' said Orodes.

Dobbai rose from her chair. 'Very well, I see that your minds are made up. So be it. Though take care, son of Hatra, not to underestimate your adversaries.'

She went over to Gallia and kissed her on the top of her head and then shuffled from the terrace. None of us said any more as we contemplated the future.

Six days later we burned the body of Godarz on a huge funeral pyre erected in the city's main square. I had paid a great deal of gold to an Egyptian embalmer to preserve it so that his friends from afar could witness his funeral. Gallia had shed all her tears by then and her face was an emotionless mask as the pyre was lit and the flames took hold and consumed our friend's body with a relentless ferocity. The square was packed with citizens for Godarz had been a respected governor who had administered the affairs of Dura with fairness, legality and commonsense. We stood in a line at the front of the multitude – I, Gallia, Orodes, Domitus, Diana, Gafarn, Nergal, Praxima, Byrd, Malik and a weeping Rsan. Poor Rsan. When we had first come to Dura he was the only one from the previous administration still alive. Rsan had been left to face us alone. He had subsequently proven himself to be a capable and above all honest royal treasurer. For those qualities he had become a valued and trusted member of the council. Rsan and Godarz had become close friends and now my treasurer was grief stricken. We could not criticise him; Godarz was a good man who deserved the shedding of an ocean of tears.

Behind us the Amazons were lined up in their mail shirts, swords at their hips. Diana and Gafarn had ridden hard from Hatra to be here and Nergal and Praxima had left their palace at Uruk to pay their respects to the man who had been like a father to them also.

The Companions remained motionless in their ranks among the soldiers who formed a cordon around the now blazing pyre. I watched the flames consume my friend, just as I had suffered with him many years ago in a green valley in Italy watching other flames devour the bodies of Spartacus and his wife Claudia. I prayed to Shamash that He would carry the soul of Godarz to heaven so he could be reunited with his friends. When the flames died down Domitus had his men clear the area and we remained at a loss as the legionaries used their shields to gently usher the citizens out of the square. As they did so I caught sight of Vistaspa, the commander of my father's army. He had been standing among the crowd unnoticed but now he came over to me. Lean, tall with a thin, bony face, Vistaspa was one of the most ruthless men I had ever encountered. He had once been a prince of the Kingdom of Silvan and Godarz had served under him. Vistaspa had been delighted when he had been reunited with one of his old comrades in the aftermath of my return from Italy. Godarz could have stayed in Hatra but I had asked him to become Dura's governor, and now Vistaspa had lost his friend for good. Although in his sixties, he still possessed the air of a ruthless warrior. He bowed his head and then regarded me with his cold, dark eyes.

'Have you caught the killers yet?'

'Not yet,' I replied, 'but be assured that they will not escape.'

But it seemed they had escaped. As the days passed I despaired that Godarz's killers would be apprehended. Gallia's mood darkened by the day and she lashed out at all and sundry. She spoke sharply to our daughters, argued with Domitus and Rsan and ordered that a servant, a girl barely out of her teens, be flogged for breaking a water jug. I immediately countermanded the order.

43

'I ordered her to be flogged!' Gallia stormed into the throne room as I was discussing sewage disposal with Rsan and the city's chief engineer.

She strode onto the dais and stood before me. Rsan and the engineer looked at each other and then stared at the floor.

'Thank you, Rsan, we will discuss this matter tomorrow.'

Rsan and the engineer bowed and left us.

'Well?'

'We do not flog young girls,' I said. 'And did you notice that I was in a meeting?'

She sneered at me. 'Sitting on your arse doing nothing, as usual.'

I stood up slowly. 'I know that you are upset my love, but do not test my patience.'

'Why?' she scoffed, 'what are you going to do? You should be out looking for Godarz's killers instead of sitting on your backside talking about disposing of shit.'

'That's enough!'

Her eyes were wild and I thought she was going to strike me, but then Domitus interrupted us.

'We've found them.'

Gallia's mood changed instantly as Domitus informed us that Polemo and Nadira had been caught and were on their way back to Dura under armed guard.

'They bribed a merchant and joined his caravan. Would have got away had it not been for the broken nose you gave the man,' said Domitus. 'They were picked up by an Agraci patrol just outside Palmyra.'

'What about the merchant?' growled Gallia.

'He is at Palmyra under Haytham's guard awaiting your decision.'

'Tell Haytham to execute him,' said Gallia. 'That is the penalty for helping assassins.'

Domitus looked at me.

'What are you looking at him for?' retorted Gallia. 'Do you no longer take orders from your queen?'

I nodded ever so slightly at Domitus, who came to attention before Gallia.

'It will be as you order, majesty.'

He turned, replaced his crested helmet on his head and marched from the throne room. Gallia sniffed and also marched away.

Malik himself brought back the pair who had been sent to kill me, handing them over to Domitus at the Palmyrene Gate. Gallia had wanted Nadira to be raped by a host of my soldiers but I instantly forbade such a torment. They would be executed for their crime and no more. Their deaths would take place in the main square so all could see that justice and law ruled in Dura. Gallia scoffed at what she called my high ideals, as did Dobbai, but I reminded them that I was the king of the city and my word held sway. Afterwards we held a meeting of the council, a mournful occasion at which we all found ourselves staring at the chair Godarz used to sit in. I should have had it removed but to do so seemed like a slight against his memory and we all wanted to have things around us that reminded us of him. So it stayed.

'You are governor now, Rsan,' I said. 'Godarz would have wanted that.'

Domitus and Orodes nodded in assent and the clerk recorded my decision.

I tried to lighten the mood. 'How is Aaron getting on, Rsan?'

'Quite well, majesty. He has a quick mind and a head for figures. His tongue is apt to take on a mind of its own but aside from that he shows great promise.'

Gallia began to drum her fingers on the table, causing Rsan to fidget in embarrassment. Orodes pretended not to notice and Domitus stared blankly at the table top.

'Is there something you wish to say?' I asked her.

'When are we marching against Mithridates?'

Domitus smiled and Orodes looked thoughtful. Rsan looked alarmed. The prospect of war always filled him with dread, not out of fear but because war meant a reduction in trade and an increase in costs, which meant his precious reserves of treasury gold would be called upon.

'In a month's time,' I replied.

She slammed a fist on the table, causing Rsan to flinch in alarm. 'That long? We can muster the army and be across the Euphrates in less than a week.'

She was right. Take the army across the river and then strike southeast towards Ctesiphon, the capital of the Parthian Empire. The residence of Mithridates was a large palace complex behind crumbling walls on the eastern bank of the Tigris. The distance was around two hundred miles as the buzzard flies.

'No,' I replied. 'I will not violate the territorial integrity of Hatra and Babylon by marching unannounced through their kingdoms.'

Gallia rolled her eyes in despair. 'Hatra and Babylon will not object to you crossing their lands. They are our allies, after all.'

'That may be,' I said. 'But I will have their agreement first before starting a war with Mithridates.'

'We could march down the western side of the Euphrates,' offered Orodes. 'Like we did when we campaigned against Chosroes.'

It was not a bad idea. The territory south of Dura for a hundred miles was my kingdom. Beyond that the Agraci ruled. Haytham was a friend and we had used that route when we had attacked Uruk to put

Nergal on its throne. But that would add another hundred miles to our journey and we would still have to cross Babylonian territory when we swung east to cross the Euphrates and then head directly for Ctesiphon.

'No,' I said. 'We would still need King Vardan's agreement to march through his territory. It is better to cross the Euphrates here, at Dura, and then strike for Ctesiphon.'

Domitus looked thoughtful. 'Mithridates will know by now that you are still alive. He might scarper from his palace and seek refuge further east, with Narses.'

'He might,' I replied, 'though even Mithridates will think twice before running from me. The eyes of the empire will be on him. He and Narses will have no choice but to meet us in battle.'

Mithridates was king of kings and in theory commanded the respect and obedience of all the other kings of the empire. In reality he could only rely on the eastern kings of the realm, including his lord high general Narses, King of Persis and Sakastan. In the northeast corner of the empire lay the kingdoms of Margiana and Hyrcania, and men who were friends of Dura ruled those two domains. And in the western half of the empire the kingdoms of Atropaiene, Media, Hatra, Babylon and Mesene were no friends of Mithridates. But that did not mean they would fight him.

'This is my fight,' I said. 'I have no desire to involve other kingdoms in my quarrel.'

'Narses will muster a large army, Pacorus,' said Orodes.

'I know that, my friend. But we have beaten Narses before and can do so again.'

'Except we had other kings with us then,' remarked Domitus grimly.

'Dura's army is strong, Domitus,' said Gallia,' you have made it so. And we can call on Haytham's help to swell our numbers.'

'I will ask Malik and his scouts to accompany us,' I said, 'but we will leave the Agraci out of it.' I looked at them all. 'It is no small thing that we embark on but if we do nothing Dura, and me for that matter, will appear weak and helpless. Mithridates has made the first move in what will be the final confrontation between us. There is no room in the empire for both of us, therefore let us end it now and rid the world of the villain. Domitus, muster your men!'

Dura's army was spread far and wide, not only in the camp west of the Palmyrene Gate but also stationed in the small forts that had been built to the north and south of the city. Each one held a garrison of forty men, whose duties ranged from policing the roads, maintaining the irrigation ditches and dams that controlled the flow of water from the Euphrates onto the land, to catching thieves and other criminals and sending them to Dura for punishment. They were also a visible symbol of Dura's strength. Other, larger forts had been constructed at the extreme ends of the kingdom. Each of these held a garrison of a hundred horse archers who patrolled the borders and ensured no undesirables wandered into Duran territory. There were three such forts at the northern extremity of the kingdom, for that was where Dura ended and Roman Syria began. The Romans had also constructed forts on their frontier so each side watched the other warily, though in truth there had been no trouble with the Romans. There had even been a degree of fraternisation between Dura's horsemen and their Roman counterparts. I had given orders that this was to cease – I did not trust the men of the Tiber any more than I would a cobra.

At the southern edge of the kingdom were two more forts, though there was never any problem there since south of them was Agraci territory. There were no forts along the long western edge of Dura's border as the entire length of the frontier also abutted Agraci territory.

Shamash had blessed Dura with the Silk Road and the duties that were levelled on this trade route financed the army. It was common knowledge throughout the empire that Dura possessed two legions modelled on the same formations found in the Roman army. In addition, there was a replacement cohort that recruited and trained new volunteers to ensure that each legion was kept at full strength. The Duran Legion had been the first formation and had been assembled even before we had arrived in Dura. The second legion, the Exiles, had originally been composed of soldiers who had fought in the army of Pontus against the Romans, and who had made their way south to Dura in the aftermath of their defeat.

These legions were trained, organised and equipped in the Roman fashion but they wore white tunics and their shields carried the griffin symbol of Dura.

As well as the foot soldiers there were three thousand horse archers. Originally Dura's horse archers had been equipped with helmets and mail shirts, but in recent times they had done away with the mail shirts and wore only loose-fitting white shirts with silk vests worn underneath. Each horse archer carried a quiver holding thirty arrows, but on campaign the horse archers were accompanied by a camel train equipped with tens of thousands of spare arrows. In battle it was the task of the horse archers to pepper the enemy with arrows, to harass and disorientate them, to weaken but not to fight them at close quarters. That was the task of the two legions that could cut their way through enemy foot soldiers and fight off opposing horsemen. But the jewels in the crown of Dura's army were its cataphracts.

The cataphracts were men on horseback who wore scale armour – thick hide coats covered in overlapping metal scales that protected their torsos – steel leg and arm armour and full-face helmets on their heads. They went into battle armed with the *kontus*, a long, thick lance that was held with both hands. They also carried swords, maces and axes for close-quarter combat. Their horses were also protected by scale armour so that man and beast were encased in thick hide and metal. Each cataphract was served by two young squires who cared for his horse, weapons and equipment. They in turn trained to be cataphracts themselves once they had served their apprenticeships, thus ensuring that Dura had a constant supply of heavy cavalry. But cataphracts were massively expensive to raise, equip and maintain, and it was a source of pride to me that Dura had a thousand of them. All the cataphracts were billeted in the city, along with their squires and horses. The camels that carried their weapons and armour were stabled outside the city.

Domitus organised the muster of the two legions while Orodes organised the assembly of the horsemen. I for my part sent messages to the lords to present themselves at the palace. In every Parthian kingdom there were vassal lords who owed allegiance to their king. Often men of great wealth and power themselves, they were granted lands in return for tribute and the pledge of soldiers in times of war. In Dura the situation was slightly different. Prior to my arrival there had been no king in Dura. It had been a frontier kingdom belonging to the aged King of Kings Sinatruces. He had used Dura as a dumping ground for malcontents, rogues, troublemakers and the like, granting them great swathes of land that they ruled as demi-kings themselves, providing they could stay alive. Most did not last six months, being either killed by their own mutinous supporters or by Agraci war bands. Those that did survive fought off the Agraci and stamped their iron will on the land, building great strongholds to protect their hard-won gains. They tamed the land and fought off the Agraci. When I arrived at Dura I did not demand their loyalty but treated them fairly and as equals. In this way I gained their trust and now their sons served me as cataphracts. They now answered my call and came to Dura to hear about the coming campaign.

They were full of fire and enthusiasm as they gathered before me in the throne room, each of the grizzled old rogues insisting that they kissed Gallia's hand before proceedings started. They loved her and she loved them back. They gave me obedience but she owned their utmost devotion. I suspect that many lusted after her, but all admired her courage and I sometimes wondered whether it was in fact she who ruled the kingdom and not me.

I rose from my chair and stepped down from the dais to address them as equals.

'My friends, I thank you for coming to Dura. You will know by now that I intend to make war upon Mithridates.'

'About time too,' shouted one. This was greeted with cheers and the stamping of feet. I raised my hands to still the commotion.

'We have fought many battles together,' I continued.

'And will fight many more,' shouted another, followed by more cheers and whistles.

'But I will not be asking you to accompany me on this campaign.'

There was stunned silence. Even Gallia looked at me with a perplexed expression.

'I know this may surprise and disappoint you, but I cannot leave the kingdom defenceless.'

'Defenceless against whom?' asked Spandarat, a one-eyed lord who had accompanied Gallia back to Dura when she had been pregnant with our first child while we were on campaign.

'The Romans in Syria,' I replied. 'I remember a time when the Romans took advantage of civil strife within the empire before, and then we lost a kingdom to them. I do not intend the same happening again.'

I was alluding to Gordyene, the land to the north that had been conquered by the Romans. I did not intend Dura to suffer the same fate.

'I have heard of no stirrings in Syria,' spoke one of the northern lords, a thickset man with a great bushy beard.

'When they learn that the forts that guard the northern frontier have been stripped of their garrisons they may be tempted to invade Dura. There are two legions in Syria and I do not trust the Romans not to take advantage of our army's absence. That is why your presence here is so important.'

They grumbled among themselves and looked unhappy but knew that what I had said made sense. Between them they could raise around forty thousand horse archers in addition to their personal bodyguards numbering another thousand men. It was enough to deter a Roman invasion, or so I hoped. Aside from their personal retinues their troops were drawn from the men who worked their lands: farmers and fishermen. They were not as disciplined as those who served in Dura's army, but they were frontiersmen who were hardy and knew how to shoot a bow from the saddle. As such they would delay any invading army long enough for me to bring mine back across the Euphrates after I had dealt with Mithridates.

After Gallia had flattered and flirted with them the lords went back to their estates. They may have been unhappy that they were missing out on a battle, but they were delighted to be entrusted with the safety of the queen and her children. I had told them that they would guard Gallia and the kingdom while I was away, and that they were to obey her in my absence. After they had gone I went out onto the palace terrace to lean on the stone balustrade and watch the activity below.

This was one of my favourite places where I could observe the traffic on the road flowing east and west and gaze at the blue waters of the Euphrates. The minutiae of life was fascinating: Rsan's officials collecting tolls from those crossing the pontoon bridges; legionaries ensuring that traffic flowed smoothly over the wooden bridges; and people from all corners of the empire on the road going about their business; fishermen in their small boats on the river. It was endless and fascinating.

'Daydreaming again, son of Hatra?'

Dobbai shuffled past me to sit in one of the chairs opposite.

'For a man about to embark upon great slaughter you seem remarkably calm.'

'Just one battle, Dobbai, and then it will all be over.'

She looked east across the river. 'Just one battle, to begin with.'

'To begin with?'

She turned to look at me. 'I will say it again. Do not underestimate Mithridates, or Narses for that matter.'

'I don't and won't.'

She pointed at me with a bony finger. 'You think that because you beat them before you will do so again with ease.'

She was referring to the Battle of Surkh, when I had been instrumental in defeating the combined armies of Mithridates and Narses. Afterwards I had been made lord high general of the empire by a grateful King of Kings Phraates. How long ago that seemed now.

I smiled at Dobbai. 'Have the gods revealed to you that they will defeat me?'

'You may mock me, but your smugness will disappear when you come running back to Dura with your tail between your legs.'

'Is that your prophecy or the gods?'

She waved a hand at me. 'I say again, do not underestimate your foes.'

She changed the subject. 'When are the executions?'

'Tomorrow.'

That was when Nadira and Polemo would die for the murder of Godarz. Vistaspa had stayed in Dura in the aftermath of Godarz's death and said he would return to Hatra once justice had been meted out. Haytham had also travelled to the city to witness the executions. There was a time when the visit of the Agraci king would have elicited horror among the city's residents but now no one batted an eyelid. Indeed, Malik visited us so often that many came to see him more as Duran than Agraci. He and Domitus were good friends, though Malik's agreeable nature meant that he got on well with most people. He was not like Haytham, who was hard, merciless and unyielding, much like the desert that had spawned him. Above all

50

Malik, though brave, lacked the ruthlessness, the utter indifference to suffering which Haytham possessed in abundance.

'Gallia has hired a headsman for the executions,' remarked Dobbai casually.

'A headsman, why? Dura has its own executioner.'

Dobbai rose and ambled away.

'Remember what I said, son of Hatra, do not underestimate your foes.'

Gallia refused to discuss the executions, saying that she was too upset to talk about the condemned as it reminded her of Godarz. When I asked her about the headsman she merely remarked that he had been recommended to her and that she wanted the task carried out properly. Further questioning of her was met by a stony silence so I gave up.

The day of the executions was overcast, the mood of the population sombre as the two prisoners were escorted from their confinement at the Palmyrene Gate. Notwithstanding Gallia's desires I had given orders that they were not to be mistreated in any way. Their quarters were to be functional and their rations adequate, and on no account were they to be abused by their gaolers, especially Nadira. Raping a woman had no place in Dura's army.

Just after dawn the pair walked from the Palmyrene Gate along the city's main street to the market place. Domitus had lined the route with guards to ensure that they reached their place of execution – Godarz had been a popular governor and many may have been tempted to exact their own vengeance upon his killers. Soldiers also lined the outside of the square and were posted around the wooden platform that had been erected in the centre of the square where the pair was to be put to death. Directly opposite and on the northern side of the square was a second platform of the same height. That is where we assembled to watch justice being administered.

Sullen, angry people were still filing into the square as Polemo and Nadira were escorted through the throng to their appointment with the headsman. He stood impassively as the murderers were manhandled up the steps and onto the platform. The executioner was tall, fat and completely bald. He held the handle of a large curved sword in his right hand, the point resting on the wooden boards. He watched Polemo and Nadira with piggy eyes, his stare fixed on Nadira's chest. Gallia had wanted her to be stripped naked before she was killed but I had countermanded this order as well, earning me a fierce rebuke from my wife. But I told her that I was not a barbarian. In these moments her wild Gaul side came to the fore and frankly unnerved me, but I was king in Dura. Even attired in a voluminous white gown Nadira's voluptuous figure was still apparent. Such a waste of womanhood.

On the platform the two were handed over to the executioner's assistants – half a dozen burly men dressed in black leggings and brown leather tunics. Two grabbed the arms of Polemo while two more stood either side of a now very pale Nadira. Polemo was stripped of his top and forced down onto his knees to face the executioner. Polemo looked up and spat at him. One of the assistants stepped forward, slapped him hard round the face and shoved his head down. The executioner hoisted his great sword onto his right shoulder and stepped to one side. He looked at me and I nodded. The crowd was silent and still whilst Nadira, wild-eyed, bit her lip and stared ahead. She was not looking at her accomplice kneeling a few feet from her.

With both hands the executioner raised the sword high above his head and then in one seamless movement brought it down on Polemo's neck. I stared in horror as the blade sliced Polemo's flesh but did not sever his head. The executioner once more raised the blade and sliced it down onto Polemo's neck. It cut flesh but again did not decapitate Polemo, who tried to lift himself up, blood gushing from his neck wound. Now terrified, he looked up at the executioner as the latter's blade once more sliced into his flesh. Polemo pitched forward, still alive, as the crowd groaned. The executioner gestured at his assistants, who stepped forward and yanked Polemo back onto his knees. Then they stepped away. The executioner wiped the blood off his blade with a cloth and then stepped forward and again aimed a blow at Polemo, this time slicing deep into his shoulder. Polemo shrieked in pain, his torso covered in blood. Nadira, now distraught at the awful spectacle unfolding before her, pissed herself. Orodes looked at Malik who shook his head, while Haytham remained impassive. Rsan, shaking, was covering his eyes with his hands.

Domitus turned to me. 'I'll finish this,' and made to leave our viewing platform.

'Stay where you are, Domitus,' commanded Gallia, who nodded at the executioner. He nodded back, raised his sword once more then finally severed Polemo's head. Blood poured from the headless torso as a weeping Nadira was forced down on her knees. No doubt she was being tortured by the thought of enduring the same treatment as Polemo. Domitus returned to his place as the executioner lopped off Nadira's head with a single blow. Thus was the grisly spectacle brought to an end.

The two lifeless bodies were dumped on a cart as the populace returned to their daily lives. Rsan walked over to the edge of the platform and threw up. Haytham regarded an iron-visaged Gallia and smiled. Orodes was most unhappy and Malik was frowning. Domitus stood and looked bemused as his soldiers ushered the remnants of the crowd from the square.

52

'There was no need for that,' I said to Gallia.

'If I had had my way,' she said slowly and loudly enough for everyone around us to hear, 'their deaths would have lasted for days. They got off lightly.'

With that she turned away from me and marched from the platform. Domitus slapped me on the arm.

'Perhaps you should stay here and let Gallia march against Mithridates. That way the war will be over in no time at all.'

I shook my head. 'I think not. There will be no one left alive from here to the Himalayas if I unleash her on the empire.'

The grisly episode was now over and it was time for the army to march east and spill some more blood.

Chapter 3

Standing looking at the large hide map of the Parthian Empire hanging on the wall in the headquarters building I shook my head. Couriers had arrived from Hatra, Media and Atropaiene informing me that parties attacking from Gordyene, Cappadocia and Armenia were raiding them. My father wrote that once again horsemen were attacking his northern towns and cities, including Nisibus whose governor was my childhood friend Vata. I was not unduly concerned about these reports as Hatra's army was more than capable of dealing with mere raiding parties. The same was true of Media and Atropaiene, ruled by Farhad and Aschek respectively. Still, if these raids presaged a general war with Rome, since Armenia was its client state and the Romans occupied Gordyene, then once again the empire would be under threat. I had comforted myself with the knowledge that to the east of these two realms were the kingdoms of Hyrcania and Margiana, both of which had alliances with Aschek and Farhad and both of which could raise sizeable armies. But then news reached us that the northern borders had erupted into violence and both Hyrcania and Margiana were also under assault. King Khosrou, the fierce ruler of Margiana, had written to me stating that the tribes that inhabited the great steppes to the north of his kingdom had attacked his frontier outposts and were marching against his capital, Merv. The entire northern border of the empire was in flames.

'What are the chances of the Romans, Armenians and the tribes of the steppes working in cooperation, do you think?' asked Domitus, leaning back in his chair with his hands behind his head.

I shook my head again. 'Almost nil.'

He jumped out of his chair. 'Exactly.'

'I thought Khosrou had peace with the northern tribes,' said Orodes.

'That is what he told me at Esfahan,' I replied, 'though that was a while ago. Perhaps relationships between the two have deteriorated since then.'

Domitus drew his dagger and used it to point at the map, moving the point from Hatra to the east towards the Caspian Sea and beyond.

'It cannot be a coincidence that all the kingdoms under assault are friends of Dura. I detect the hand of Mithridates in all this.'

I was confused. 'He sent assassins to kill me. If he wanted to harm Dura then he and Narses would lead their army against us. I suspect the Romans are behind this rather than Mithridates.'

'After all these years and after so much blood, you still act like a dotard, son of Hatra.'

Dobbai walked into the room accompanied by Gallia, who threw a despatch on the table. I picked it up.

'What is this?'

54

'An appeal from Gotarzes. His kingdom is assaulted by Narses.'

King Gotarzes was the ruler of Elymais, a land across the Tigris that lay to the east of Nergal's realm of Mesene. A valuable ally and trusted friend, Gotarzes had the great misfortune to rule a kingdom that had Narses' own kingdom of Persis to the south and Susiana, the domain of Mithridates, to the north. He had fought by my side against both of them and now Narses was attacking him.

'You can forget about the Romans, then,' said Domitus. 'This is the handiwork of Mithridates.'

'The Roman speaks the truth,' said Dobbai. 'I did warn you not to underestimate Mithridates.'

'We have to help Gotarzes,' said Gallia.

I looked at the map once more. That was easier said than done. It was over five hundred miles from Dura to the city of Elymais, the capital of Gotarzes' kingdom – it would take nearly four weeks to get there unimpeded, more if we encountered any resistance along the way.

'Gotarzes is beyond help,' remarked Dobbai. 'If he had any sense, which he doesn't, he would abandon his city and flee.'

'He would never do that,' insisted Orodes, 'he is a man of honour.'

Dobbai sat in one of the chairs around the table. 'Soon to be a dead man of honour.'

'The army is assembled, is it not?' asked Gallia.

'Yes,' I replied.

'Well, then, we can march to assist Gotarzes.'

I looked at her, then at Domitus and Orodes. They were thinking the same as me – we would be marching into a trap.

'No,' I said, 'we will stick to the original plan. We will strike for Ctesiphon first and then march into Susiana. Hopefully Gotarzes can hold out until we can organise his relief.'

'That is the best course of action,' said Domitus.

'It is sound strategy,' remarked Orodes.

Gallia was going to object but was stilled by Dobbai. 'What they say is correct, child. Gotarzes is the bait that Mithridates dangles in front of your husband's eyes. To take it would spell the end of the King of Dura and his army.'

Orodes folded his arms and looked very grave while Domitus went back to studying the map. Dobbai watched him like a hawk. At length he spoke.

'How does Mithridates benefit from inciting outsiders to attack his empire?'

Dobbai cackled. 'A good question, Roman, and one that has a simple answer.'

'Which is?' I asked irritably. Sometimes she sorely tested my patience.

She sighed. 'All of you,' she pointed at me, Orodes and Domitus with a bony finger, 'labour under the delusion that everyone thinks and acts the same as you. They do not. Mithridates and Narses desire above all to rid the world of the King of Dura.'

'Then why don't they march against me?' I asked.

Dobbai looked at me in exasperation. 'I sometimes think that Coalemus himself has rented your body.'

'Who is Coalemus' queries Domitus.

'The god of idiots,' replied Orodes, none too pleased at Dobbai's insolence. Gallia laughed aloud.

'You have, son of Hatra,' said Dobbai very slowly so I would understand what she was saying, 'beaten both Mithridates and Narses in battle, so they obviously see little merit in tangling with you again, at least not until they are certain of victory.'

'If Dura's allies are occupied dealing with threats to their own lands,' mused Orodes, 'then they cannot aid you, Pacorus.'

Dobbai's eyes narrowed. 'Leaving Mithridates and Narses free to concentrate their hatred on you, son of Hatra.' She really did revel in other people's misfortune and general misery.

'Then let them come,' I said grandly, 'and then I can destroy them.'

'They will not come to Dura,' said Dobbai. 'They are not idiots. They have seen what happens to armies that try to storm this city. As I told you before, as long as the griffin sits above the Palmyrene Gate no army shall take this city.'

'Then we shall go to them,' I announced.

Dobbai rose and held out her hand for Gallia to take. 'And that is precisely what they want. You must take care, son of Hatra; indeed all of you must take care not to underestimate Mithridates above all. Come child, let us leave them to their games of strategy.'

The proceeding days saw a flurry of letters between Dura and Hatra, Babylon and Mesene. I thanked Shamash that the empire had a reliable courier system that ensured that the kingdoms were in constant touch with each other. The postal system comprised hundreds of mounted couriers who rode from city to city via rest stations located every thirty miles. At these stations the couriers swapped their horses for fresh mounts that took them to the next station and so on. But even so it took several days for news to reach us of what was happening in other parts of the empire. Dura was around twelve hundred miles from the eastern edge of the empire. I sometimes forgot how large Parthia was.

I wrote to King Vardan of Babylon, friend to my father and me, asking if he could take his army east to aid Gotarzes while I marched Dura's army against Ctesiphon. In addition, I asked Nergal if he could reinforce Vardan and also strike at Susa, the capital city of Susiana. Uruk was only a hundred and fifty miles from Susa. Nergal could be there in around a week. I decided not to inform my father that I was striking at Ctesiphon and therefore marching across the south of his kingdom. He would learn of this after I had killed Mithridates. His anger would be a small price to pay for victory and peace in the empire. I also did not inform Vardan that I would be marching into the north of his kingdom. I would offer my apologies to him at the same time that I announced that Mithridates had been removed from power.

My father informed me that the raids Hatra was experiencing were inconvenient but not serious. However, they did require substantial numbers of troops to be sent north to patrol the border and deter any further incursions. Media and Atropaiene reported much the same.

'They are achieving their aim,' remarked Domitus as he sifted through parchments on his table.

The camp was heaving with men, mules and activity. Surrounded by a mud-brick wall, it was capacious enough to accommodate the Duran Legion and the Exiles plus all their wagons, animals and equipment, but it was a squeeze. Domitus had endured many sleepless nights overseeing the mustering of his men, but now the two legions were fully assembled and ready to march.

'We do not need Hatra's help,' I said.

'Mm, well,' he rose from his desk and grabbed his vine cane lying on the table, placing a weight on the parchments so they would not be disturbed. 'Let us hope you are right. Walk with me.'

Spring would soon be here and the temperature was already rising. It was pleasant enough inside the large tent but outside the atmosphere was becoming oppressive. The smell of sweat, leather and animal dung greeted me as I stepped into the open air.

'The horsemen are assembled?' asked Domitus.

I nodded. 'Twelve hundred cataphracts crammed inside the city and three thousand horse archers camped five miles south of it.'

'Ten thousand foot, four thousand horse,' he mused. 'You think that's enough to defeat Mithridates and Narses?'

I slapped him on the arm. 'As a Roman you above all should know that it is quality not quantity that makes the difference on the battlefield. What is troubling you?'

'Time to pay our respects.' He turned and walked to one of the two smaller tents that were located either side of the command tent. I followed. Guards stood at attention around the tent and more guards stood watch inside, for these shelters held sacred items – the legionary standards. The standard of the Duran Legion was a griffin cast from pure gold that was fixed to a silver plate atop a pole. When the legion marched the griffin would go with it. It was held upright in a rack next to the Staff of Victory, an old *kontus* shaft onto which had been attached silver discs depicting each of the army's victories. Domitus walked over to the griffin and stroked it gently. I did the same.

He turned to me. 'We could take the lords and some of their riders. There would still be enough men left in the kingdom to guard the northern border.'

'I can't risk it, Domitus. This army can beat anything Narses and Mithridates can throw at it. You know that. But I cannot fight them worrying about the possibility of the Romans launching an invasion from Syria.'

He bowed his head to the griffin and then ambled from the tent. I followed as he walked briskly to the other tent that held the standard of the Exiles, a silver lion also sitting on a silver plate. Again we touched the standard that was likewise ringed by guards.

'The Romans have tried to conquer Dura once,' I said. 'Forty thousand horse archers will hopefully make them think twice before they try to do so again.'

'Pity we don't still have the Margianans,' he sniffed.

He was alluding to the horsemen sent to Gallia as a gift by King Khosrou before we had faced the Roman Pompey. Originally numbering a thousand men led by an uncouth but brave warrior named Kuban, battle casualties had reduced their number to eight hundred. Essentially horse archers, they wore leather armour and also carried long spears in addition to bows and swords. But following the capture of Uruk I had sent them back to their homeland.

The legions were already on the march before the new dawn came. Ten thousand pairs of hobnailed sandals tramping east across the two pontoon bridges that spanned the Euphrates, their crunching sound resonating through the stillness of the early morning hours. I did not disturb our sleeping children as I dressed and made my way to the stables where cataphracts and squires were busy loading equipment on the backs of spitting and grunting camels. Remus had finished his breakfast by the time I entered his stall and placed the white saddlecloth on his back. Like all the saddlecloths of the army it had a red griffin stitched in each corner.

I threw my saddle onto his back and then fitted him with his bridle. His coat and hooves had already been cleaned and checked but I examined each one of his iron horseshoes anyway. Fresh on. He flicked his tail with impatience. He had been on too many campaigns not to know what was going on and was eager to be on our journey.

I stroked his neck. 'Easy, boy. You must save your energy. You should know all this by now.'

He turned his head and snorted. His blue eyes looked into my brown ones. The chief stable hand appeared, a tall, thin man with deep-set eyes.

'He is most impatient, majesty. Began kicking his door last night.'

I grabbed his reins and led him from the stall. 'Did he indeed. He picked up some bad habits during his time in Italy, I fear. Living in the open all that time made him think he was a wild horse.'

The man smiled. 'I fear it is so, majesty. He is wilful, but a fine horse nonetheless.'

We walked outside into the cold morning air and I vaulted into the saddle.

'He is indeed, and for that we must forgive him his idiosyncratic nature.'

The stable hand bowed his head. 'Shamash protect you, majesty.'

I nudged Remus ahead. 'You too.'

I walked him from the stables into the courtyard and halted in front of the palace where Gallia was standing at the top of the palace steps. I dismounted as one of the Amazons stepped forward to hold Remus while I said goodbye to my wife. Even though she was not coming with me she was dressed in her war gear of leather boots, leggings and mail shirt. The rest of the Amazons mustered behind her were similarly attired.

I walked up the steps and embraced her. There were no tears in her eyes, no emotion, just determination.

'Make sure you kill that toad Mithridates,' she hissed. 'Remember Godarz.'

I kissed her on the lips. 'I will endeavour to do what I should have done a long time ago.'

Unusually Dobbai was present. Now in her dotage she seldom rose until well after dawn but today was different. She grabbed my arm as I turned and made to descend the steps.

'Have a care, son of Hatra. Do not underestimate Mithridates or Narses.'

This was getting tiresome.

'I am always careful,' I replied.

She released my arm, turned and waved her hand in the air. 'I have warned you. I can do no more. Be gone and play the game of kings.'

I raised my eyes and walked down the steps and then vaulted into my saddle once more. I raised my hand at Gallia who nodded and then I wheeled Remus away and trotted from the Citadel. Behind me a company of cataphracts, a hundred riders, followed and after them came two hundred squires leading two hundred fully loaded camels. The commander of the company was a man named Surena, a native of the Ma'adan people who fell in beside me as we rode down the city's main street and headed for the Palmyrene Gate. The dour figure of Vagharsh, a Parthian and Companion, rode immediately behind us carrying my flag – a red griffin on a white background, the whole banner edged with gold. This morning it was safely wrapped in its wax-coated sleeve for the air was damp.

59

In the early hours I liked to keep my own counsel. Unfortunately Surena did not and this morning he was unusually talkative. No doubt the prospect of slaughter filled him with great anticipation.

'How long will it take before we encounter the enemy, lord?'

'We will know when we see them,' I replied.

'Hopefully less than a week, then I can be back in Dura in a fortnight. I have promised to take Viper to Palmyra.'

Viper was one of Gallia's Amazons, a woman who was lethal with a bow but who looked like a teenage girl. Surena was the exact opposite with his long black hair, square face, thin nose, broad shoulders and muscular arms. They had been married for over three years now.

'You expect the forthcoming campaign to be a straightforward affair, Surena?'

He looked at me. 'Of course, lord. All your campaigns end in victory.'

I laughed. Like most young men he only dreamed of glory and thought of victory. It never occurred to him that he might end up as a mangled corpse on the battlefield. But then we all comforted ourselves with the thought that we would be on the winning side and see our families again, Shamash willing.

'If we take much plunder I was thinking of purchasing a house for Viper and me,' continued Surena.

'We do not go to plunder,' I said sternly.

'No, lord, of course not. But if any happens to fall into our laps, all the better.'

In battle Surena was calm, brave and resourceful, though apt to take risks. In barracks he was a good officer to his men. Like many officers in Dura's army he was enrolled in the Sons of the Citadel scheme, an idea I had after I had first assumed power in the kingdom. The best tutors from Egypt, Parthia, China and even Rome had been hired to instruct the future leaders of the army. After spending the morning on the training field the best and the brightest in the army attended classes to learn about logistics, engineering, leadership, weapon making, the philosophy of war and languages. In this way they would know the ins and outs of what were called the military arts.

'There are some nice properties near the Citadel,' mused Surena, 'a bit of loot would go towards securing one.'

The reports from his tutors had stated that Surena was an excellent student – intelligent, inquisitive and eager to learn. He could also be extremely irritating.

I turned in the saddle. 'What do you think of Surena's grand plan, Vagharsh?'

Vagharsh shot a glance at Surena. 'I think he talks too much.'

We passed under the Palmyrene Gate and I drew my sword and raised it to salute the stone griffin sitting above the arch over the large twin gates. Surena did the same and so did all the men of his company. An insolent Greek sculptor named Demetrius who had also cast the Duran Legion's golden griffin had carved it. Dobbai had told me that the city would never fall as long as the griffin guarded the city. I believed her words and so did every man in the army and every citizen who lived in the city. As we exited the city and wheeled right to link up with the road across the river I looked behind me and bowed my head to the griffin.

Outside the city the air was even colder and the river was shrouded in a thick mist. Though this was not atypical for the time of year I prayed that it was not an ill omen for the coming campaign. Legionaries marching six abreast were filing over both bridges when we arrived at the river where Domitus was standing talking to some of his officers. He raised his cane to me, dismissed them and walked over.

'Glad you could join us, hope we didn't disturb your sleep.'

'Very amusing, Domitus. Where are Byrd and Malik?'

He grinned. 'You know them two. They left while Somnus was stilling entertaining me.'

'Is that a whore?' suggested a grinning Surena.

Domitus pointed his cane at him. 'Watch your mouth, puppy.'

I turned to Surena. 'Somnus is the Roman god of sleep, for your information. Now kindly be quiet.'

'Anyway,' continued Domitus, 'Byrd and Malik are across the river with their scouts just to make sure we don't have any nasty surprises.'

I doubted that. Directly opposite the bridges was Hatran territory, patrolled and garrisoned by detachments of my father's army.

Domitus continued. 'Orodes and the rest of the horsemen are waiting until my boys are over, then they will cross. It will be a while yet, though.'

I looked at Surena. 'You and I will ride over to the other side and see if we can catch up with Byrd and Malik. Bring a score of your men along. Vagharsh, you stay here with the rest and join Orodes when he crosses over.'

Vagharsh nodded. Surena ordered the first twenty men behind us to follow him as we walked our horses to the first bridge. The officers halted the legionaries marching onto the bridge to give us passage to the other side. And so, wrapped in our white cloaks for the chill and mist showed no signs of abating, we cantered over the bridge and into my father's kingdom and headed south, riding parallel to the great column of marching soldiers.

Two hours after I had left the Citadel the mist finally began to clear from the river. Orodes had brought over the cavalry and now parties of horse archers were sent into the east to cover our left flank and ahead to act as a vanguard. I was not overly concerned about being surprised, as we were still in Hatran territory and south of that lay the Kingdom of Babylon. Still, with Dobbai's warning ringing in my ears I was taking no chances. Soon the rays of sun had burnt off the last vestiges of the mist to reveal a cloudless sky. It would be a glorious spring day, ideal for marching, not too hot and with a slight northerly breeze. I had to confess that it felt good to be marching with the army again. At last I would settle things with Mithridates and Narses.

By noon most of the horsemen were walking to preserve their animals' strength. The only horsemen still riding were on patrol. Malik and Byrd rode back to the army, their clothes covered in dust and their horses breathing heavily from a long ride. They both dismounted and joined our small group of myself, Orodes and Domitus. Domitus always walked despite being general of the army and despite my efforts to persuade him otherwise.

'No enemy anywhere,' reported Byrd, 'land empty.'

'I'm sure my stepbrother has his spies watching us,' said Orodes.

'If they are, then they are very well hidden,' said Malik.

The land along the riverbank was highly cultivated and populated, but further inland the fields and irrigation ditches gave way to flat, barren desert until one encountered the cultivated land on the western bank of the River Tigris. There were few inhabitants of the land between the rivers apart from nomads.

'Mithridates will soon learn that we have left Dura,' I said. 'The disadvantage of being a city on the Silk Road is that the traffic is an efficient carrier of gossip as well as goods. It doesn't matter. After all, we want to goad him into action.'

Nevertheless Orodes shielded the army with a thick screen of patrols as we marched south along the Euphrates. As usual each night the army sheltered in a camp surrounded by an earth rampart surmounted by a wall of stakes, constructed after the Roman fashion. Each day the stakes were taken down and loaded onto mules for transportation to the next night's camp site. It was a time-consuming process to erect and then disassemble these camps, but it ensured that the army and its wagons and animals were safe from any night attack. Not that there was much risk of that – Parthians as a rule did not fight at night.

'I would not put it past my stepbrother to launch a night attack,' remarked Orodes as we relaxed in the command tent after another day's march.

'No army near,' said Byrd.

'I doubt he will even fight,' added Malik, his black robes matching the tattoos on his face.

'What was he like, as a child, I mean?' I asked.

'Pacorus wants to know if he had horns on his head and a forked tail,' said Domitus, cramming a biscuit into his mouth.

The biscuits that we took with us on campaign were called Parthian bread, though they were actually rock-hard wafers that reportedly lasted for years. Domitus said that they were excellent for patching shields.

Orodes leaned back in his chair. 'Cruel, I would say.'

'Nothing else?' I asked.

'Oh, he was spoilt and indulged by his mother, my stepmother, and by father. But then, there is nothing exceptional about that. But he was possessed of an evil nature. He made trouble just for the sake of it and inflicted injury on those who were helpless and could not fight back, slaves mostly. That is why he dislikes you, Pacorus.'

'Because Pacorus was a slave?' offered Domitus.

Orodes nodded. 'Yes. He could not accept that one reduced so low could rise up and become great. Made worse by you having taken the crown of Dura from him.'

'I did not take the crown from him,' I said bitterly. 'I found it lying in the gutter, such was the state he left my kingdom in.'

Domitus continued to munch on his biscuits. 'Most poetic. Hopefully we can track down the bastard, kill him and get things back to normal.' He looked at Orodes. 'No offence meant.'

'And none taken, my friend,' replied Orodes, 'the world will be a better place without Mithridates in it.'

Everyone agreed with him, though if we did end the reign of Mithridates then without a doubt Narses would seize the high crown for himself. But not if he too was dead. One battle at a time.

It took the army ten days to reach the spot that brought us parallel to where the Tigris and Ctesiphon lay fifty miles to the east, and still there was no sign of the enemy. Perhaps Mithridates had abandoned Ctesiphon and fled east to Narses' capital at Persepolis. I hoped not – it was five hundred miles from Ctesiphon to the capital of Persis. On the other hand, if he had then Narses would have to abandon the siege of Elymais and Gotarzes would be relieved. All these thoughts went through my mind as the army stocked up on its water supplies for the march east across the desert. Fourteen thousand soldiers, two thousand squires and their two thousand camels, over two thousand mules, the drivers of the wagons, a thousand camels carrying spare arrows and their riders and over six thousand horses consumed a lot of water each day. At least it was spring and not summer for the heat of these areas in the hottest months was fierce. Fortunately the camels and mules were hardy creatures. Indeed the mules were capable of tolerating extremes of heat and cold and surviving on sparse rations of food and water and only a few hours' sleep each night.

After a day of rest we set off east across the desert. Byrd, Malik and their scouts rode far ahead of the army and patrols of horse archers covered our flanks and formed a vanguard. I walked with Orodes and Domitus at the head of the army, the cataphracts leading their horses behind them, the squires tending to their horses and camels.

It was another glorious spring day with just a slight northerly breeze and a small number of puffy white clouds dotting the blue sky. Once again there was no sign of the enemy anywhere and I began to think that we would take the city of Seleucia, which lay on the west bank of the Tigris, unopposed. Directly opposite Seleucia, across the river, was the palace of Ctesiphon. It was a large palace complex filled with treasure but it was of no use to us. All I was interested in was confronting Mithridates. We covered fifteen miles the first day and another fifteen the next and once again we marched across empty desert. The army camped for the night behind its earthen rampart and wooden palisade, the men wrapping themselves in their cloaks as the temperature plummeted after the sun disappeared from the western sky.

Two hours after night had fallen Byrd and Malik rode into camp at the head of their scouts. They thundered up the main avenue that led directly to my command tent. As usual I was in attendance with Orodes and Domitus when the pair burst in, their faces unshaven and their clothes dirty.

'Mithridates' army approaches,' said Byrd.

'At last,' grunted Domitus, 'I was beginning to think that we would have to tramp for hundreds of miles to get our hands around his neck.'

'How far away is he?' I asked.

Malik walked over to a water jug on the table, filled a cup and handed it to Byrd. 'Twenty miles, perhaps less.'

Byrd gulped down some water. 'Many horse, no foot. There are more of them than we have.'

I smiled. 'There's always more of them than us, Byrd.'

Malik filled another cup and drained it. 'We saw the banner of Mithridates but there was no sign of Narses.'

'He must still be besieging Elymais,' said Orodes.

This was better than I expected. My enemies had made the fatal mistake of dividing their forces, allowing me to defeat each in turn. I began to feel very confident.

I walked past Malik and Byrd, clasping their arms in turn. 'I am in your debt, my friends. You bring good tidings. We should be able to see our opponents. Come.'

We all filed outside and stared into the east. Sure enough, the horizon was illuminated by a red glow – the campfires of Mithridates' army. At last we would finally settle the differences between us. I slapped Orodes on the arm.

'Well, my friend, by this time tomorrow your stepbrother will be dead and the empire will need another king of kings.'

'Narses will take his crown,' replied Orodes mournfully.

'After we have dealt with Mithridates we will march east, link up with Gotarzes and go after Narses. He will never wear the high crown.'

'And then?' asked Domitus.

'And then, what?' I replied.

'It is no small thing we do, Pacorus,' said Orodes.

I scratched my head. Orodes was a loyal and brave friend, one whom I held dear, but on occasion he could be insufferably correct. Even after all the treachery of Mithridates and Narses he still clung to his strict interpretation of protocol. I knew that he was appalled by the notion that we had as our objective the deaths of Mithridates and Narses. Perhaps a part of him still believed that bloodshed could be averted and we could all settle matters to everyone's mutual benefit. I knew this to be fantasy and deep down so did he, but he liked to think the best of everybody, including his vile stepbrother.

I laid a hand on his shoulder. 'I did not cross the Euphrates lightly, my friend, but the dagger thrust that killed Godarz began a course of events that can only have one end – my death or that of Mithridates.'

Orodes' black mood did not lessen my sense of satisfaction that we were about to fight Mithridates. I had disliked him ever since our first meeting at the city of Esfahan years ago, a loathing that had been instantly reciprocated. And now I had him. He may be king of kings but Mithridates was also a liar and a coward, and tomorrow all would be settled.

I rarely slept much before a battle and this night was no different. Domitus, Byrd and Malik wiled away the rest of the evening talking of past battles, Domitus as ever sharpening his *gladius* with a stone. Orodes retired to get some sleep and wrestle with his morality. He was probably the most upright individual in the empire. I excused myself and walked among neatly arranged rows of tents that each accommodated eight sleeping legionaries or a similar number of horsemen. Sentries stood guard and centurions stalked around with their trusty vine canes. The air was filled with the comforting aroma of leather, cooking fires, horses, mules, camels and animal dung. I stood for a moment and closed my eyes and was transported back more than ten years to when I was in Italy with Spartacus. After all this time I still missed him. I reached inside my shirt to touch the lock of Gallia's hair hanging on a chain round my neck. Together for all eternity.

I continued my tour of the camp, exchanging pleasantries with Companions and talking to other soldiers who were veterans of more recent campaigns. The horsemen were quartered with their animals in the northwest corner of the camp. Many of the Parthians in their ranks thought it most odd that they and their horses should be confined so. The camps of Parthian armies comprised an assortment of different-sized tents arranged in a random fashion. As it was the Parthian custom not to fight at night the notion of surrounding a camp with defences appeared a waste of time and effort. That may be, but no adversary of Dura would ever catch its army unawares by launching a night assault.

When I arrived at the quarters of the armoured horsemen their squires were still busy checking scale armour and helmets. If they were lucky they would get four or five hours sleep before they had to rise to get their masters ready for battle. I also found Surena with a group of his subordinates clustered round a brazier. They stopped their conversation when they saw me and bowed their heads.

'As you were,' I said. 'Surena, walk with me.'

We ambled among other groups of men gathered round fires, indulging in the idle chatter and boasting that most men partake of on the eve of battle. Tomorrow each one would fight secure in the knowledge that they trusted one another and that the man on either side of him in the battle line could be relied on not to desert him. It was no accident of speech that men were organised into companies, for at the end of the day men did not fight for causes, politics or gods; they fought for each other, their companions. And they preferred to fight and die among their friends.

'I want you to take care tomorrow, Surena. No recklessness on the battlefield, remember your training.'

He beamed at me. 'Of course, lord.'

His strong frame filled his white shirt and his well-groomed shoulder-length black hair gave him the appearance of a noble Parthian officer, but his eyes flashed with mischief. Despite all the training and education there was still a part of him that was that wild boy of the marshes I had first met years ago.

'I don't want you getting yourself killed and wasting all that expensive education I have lavished on you.'

He nodded solemnly. 'No, lord.'

We walked on in silence for a few moments, men rising to their feet as we passed them and bowing their heads, a few clasping Surena's forearm. He was a popular figure in the army, not least for saving my life in battle. He had also married an Amazon, one of the few men who had. That earned him much respect, though I never did tell him how close he had come to being hanged on the orders of Gallia for his pursuit of Viper.

'I was sorry about Godarz, lord, we all were. He was a good man.'

I nodded. 'Yes, he was.'

He cast me a sideways glance. 'The queen must miss him terribly.'

Gallia thought Surena cocky and arrogant, though grudgingly accepted that he was brave. Viper must have told him how much Godarz's death had affected the queen.

'She does, as do I.'

'I know what it is like to lose parents. The passing of time heals the wounds but the scars remain.'

He was speaking with a maturity that I did not know he possessed. He was talking of his own parents who had been murdered by the soldiers of Chosroes when he was a boy.

His visage hardened and he grasped the hilt of his sword, a *spatha* like my own. 'Mithridates deserves to die for what he has done.'

'Just make sure you don't die as well.'

As usual I slept for barely three hours that night and before the dawn announced the new day I was up and preparing for battle. I always slept with my dagger under my pillow. A most ridiculous habit considering I was in the middle of an armed camp and at Dura my bed was in a guarded palace surrounded by thick walls. It infuriated Gallia that our marriage bed had to accommodate a weapon, but as I reminded her she always secreted her own dagger under our bed. Like most of my military equipment, my dagger came from Italy and had once belonged to a Roman centurion I had killed on the night that Spartacus had rescued me. My scale armour hung on a frame at the foot of the bed. It was bulky and heavy but the metal scales and thick rawhide underneath became as light as a feather when the frenzy of combat gripped me. All Dura's cataphracts wore full-face helmets that covered all of their heads and necks, but I always wore my Roman helmet on the battlefield. It sat on the stool beside the scale armour.

I rose and knelt by the side of the bed, closed my eyes and prayed to Shamash that He would give me the courage to fight well this day. I held the lock of Gallia's hair in my hand. In that moment I felt a sense of supreme serenity. I opened my eyes and stood up. It was time to fight.

Though each cataphract had two squires to attend him I never bothered with servants, being content to enlist the assistance of anyone to hand. I had been raised a prince in the great palace at Hatra but during my time in Italy with Spartacus I had had no slaves or servants to attend to my every whim. I had become used to preparing my horse and equipment myself and the habit had stayed with me. First I put on my silk vest that felt cool next to my skin, then my leggings and boots. Finally I pulled on my long-sleeved white shirt and stepped out of the sleeping compartment and into the main section of the command tent. Domitus was already sitting at the table munching on some biscuits and salted meat. Did he ever sleep on campaign? The early morning was cool so his cloak was wrapped around him. Outside I could hear the blare of trumpets and officers hurling orders at their men.

Sentries brought us hot porridge from the field kitchens and after acknowledging each other we sat in silence as we devoured the thick, appetising stodge. There was nothing to say. Domitus was not one for idle chatter and on the morning of battle I always liked to mull over the coming clash in my mind.

Some ten minutes later Orodes, Byrd and Malik joined us. Byrd and Malik had already ridden out to reconnoitre the enemy's positions. I indicated for them all to join us at the table as more hot food was brought from the kitchens. The oil lamps hanging from the tent poles still burned to illuminate the tent's interior but outside the first rays of the sun were now lancing the eastern sky.

Domitus finished his food and pushed his metal plate aside. 'Well, what is your plan for today?'

I smiled at him. 'To beat the enemy, Domitus, as always!'

'It's too early to be a smart arse, just answer the question.'

I turned to Malik. 'You see, lord prince, how my subordinates disrespect me.'

'Alas, Pacorus,' replied Malik, winking at Domitus and shoving porridge into his mouth with his fingers, 'there is no respect left in the world, I fear.'

He and Domitus were good friends and would lay down their lives for each other, while Byrd had become like a brother to Malik. Indeed, all of us gathered at the table were brothers, having shared hardships and shed blood over the years.

'Guard!' I shouted.

One of the legionaries standing sentry outside the tent appeared and saluted.

'Go and find Marcus Sutonius and Surena and bring them here.'

He saluted and left. I turned to Domitus.

'The problem with you, Domitus, is that you have no sense of humour in the early morning.'

'And the problem with you,' he shot back, 'is that you talk too much. You should be more like Byrd, who says very little but what he does say is worth listening to. Isn't that right, Byrd?'

As ever Byrd cut a dishevelled figure in his scruffy robes, with long straggly hair and unshaven face. But his eyes were alert and his mind quick.

'Plenty of time to finish breakfast and beat enemy,' he sniffed. 'They in no hurry to leave their camp.'

Malik finished licking his fingers. 'It's true, we rode right up to the perimeter of their camp and saw very little activity.'

'Good,' I said. 'It appears that they anticipate an easy victory.'

'And they will have one unless Pacorus shares his battle plan with us,' said Domitus.

The tent flaps opened and Marcus and Surena entered. I invited them both to sit at the table as I rose and waited for them to be seated. The Roman Marcus Sutonius was the commander of my siege engines. He, the hundred men under him and their machines had been captured and enlisted into my service when a Roman army had invaded Dura. At first they served with reluctance but then enthusiastically when they discovered that life at Dura was pleasant enough and infinitely better than serving in the Roman army.

I ordered more food to be brought from the kitchens, which Surena and Marcus accepted greedily. Sitting side by side they presented very different appearances. Surena was tall and powerfully built with broad shoulders and muscular arms, while Marcus, nearly twice his age, was shorter and carried some fat mainly around the stomach on his wiry frame. His short hair was thinning on top.

'Very well,' I said, 'this is the plan. I intend to finish Mithridates and his army once and for all. Therefore our tactics today will be hammer and anvil.'

Orodes raised an eyebrow but said nothing while Domitus was nodding his head in agreement. Marcus was confused, as he did not understand what it meant. Domitus enlightened him.

'What the king means Marcus, is that my two legions will act as an anvil and the army's horsemen will be the hammer. In between the two will be the enemy, battered into fragments by a series of hammer blows.'

I continued. 'The foot will deploy behind a screen of horse archers who will advance and goad the enemy into launching an attack. Once they do the horse archers will fall back through the ranks of the legionaries.'

'What about your cataphracts, lord?' asked Surena.

'Pacorus was coming to them,' said Orodes.

'They are the hammer,' replied Domitus.

'Hammer?' Marcus was still confused.

'The cataphracts will be divided into two bodies,' I said, 'one deployed on the right and the other on the left. Each body will be positioned directly behind the two legions, so that when the enemy horsemen chasing our horse archers run into the locked shields of the Durans and Exiles, the heavy horsemen will advance forward to envelop the flanks and rear of the enemy.'

Marcus nodded in admiration. 'A most ambitious plan, sir. And the enemy will be willing participants in their own slaughter?'

'He has a point,' said Domitus.

'All we have to do is draw them in,' I replied, 'and when I dangle the bait in front of their noses they will fall into our laps easy enough.'

Orodes frowned. 'Bait?'

I smiled at him. 'Me, of course.'

Orodes looked most alarmed. 'You?'

'Of course. Domitus is always saying that everyone in the empire knows me on my white horse with a white crest in my helmet. Well then, it will be easy enough to lure the army of Mithridates into our trap if his soldiers see me riding in front of them. I will command the horse archers.'

Domitus had drawn his dagger and began toying with it. 'The plan has merits.'

'Prince Orodes will command the heavy horsemen deployed on the right, together with his own bodyguard.'

Orodes nodded solemnly. He would have seven hundred and fifty men under his command on the right, which left five hundred cataphracts on the left wing. I pointed at Surena.

'And you, Surena, will command the cavalry on the left wing.'

Surena stopped eating his porridge, wiped his mouth on his sleeve and beamed at me.

'Yes, lord, it will be an honour.'

Orodes looked at Domitus in alarm while Byrd and Malik seemed disinterested. It was Domitus who put into words Orodes' concern.

'That is a big responsibility for a junior officer.'

Surena shot my general a disdainful glance. Domitus respected Surena for his bravery and loyalty but thought him headstrong and reckless, and far too young to lead half a dragon of cataphracts. But I saw great promise in Surena.

'It is true that Surena is young for such responsibility, but his shoulders are broad and I believe that he will rise to the task.'

Surena stood up and bowed his head to me. 'I will not let you down, majesty.'

'Just make sure you don't. Now go and prepare your men.'

He beamed at me once more, bowed his head and then turned smartly and tripped over a chair leg to sprawl onto the floor. Blushing, he quickly jumped to his feet and raced from the tent. Domitus raised his eyes to the heavens.

'I hope you know what you are doing,' he said to me.

'Have faith, Domitus. You know he is a brave young man and a good officer.'

Domitus turned his dagger in his hand and examined the edges of the blade. 'I don't doubt that, but don't blame me if he tries to win the battle by himself and charges straight at Mithridates, leading half your heavy horse to their destruction.'

'What of me, sir?' enquired Marcus.

I walked over and laid a hand on his shoulder. 'You, my friend, will stay and protect the camp. I will place all the squires under your command, just in case some of the opposition attempts to storm the camp while we are occupied on the battlefield.'

It was doubtful that the enemy would detach a part of their army to attack the camp, though as it was led by Mithridates I would not put any underhand stratagem past him.

'I would join you with the archers, Pacorus,' said Malik.

'I would be glad of your company, my friend,' I replied.

Byrd was free to do as he wanted. He could not use a bow and carried no weapons aside from a long knife tucked into his belt. In all the years that I had known him I had never seen him fight, though I was mightily glad that he was part of this army for his abilities as a scout. Daylight was spreading across the desert as we made our way outside to take command of our men. The sky was blue and cloudless and the air windless, though still surprisingly cool.

I walked with Orodes to his tent where he would don his scale armour. Already columns of legionaries were marching out of the camp to head east to face the enemy, and around us squires were assisting their masters into their scale armour and encasing their horses in their armour protection. I would not be wearing my scale armour today, my Roman cuirass and helmet sufficing to lead the horse archers. We embraced each other and I left him to organise his men.

I strode to the stable area to collect Remus. When I arrived he appeared unconcerned by the frenetic level of activity surrounding him – he was always more calm living outdoors as opposed to being cooped up in the palace stables. He was now a veteran of many battles and campaigns and had seen it all before. He could still be feisty and stubborn but in battle he was brave and steady, a perfect Parthian mount despite his Roman heritage. He stood still as I threw the saddlecloth on his back and then strapped on his saddle and bridle. Around me some horses, sensing the nervousness of their riders, became skittish and had to be calmed, but Remus merely flicked his tail and waited for me to finish. I slid my bow into its hide case and fastened it to one of the rear horns of the saddle. I placed my helmet on my head, the large cheekguards protecting each side of my face. A farrier handed me my quiver whose strap I threw over my right shoulder so the arrows hung on my left side. Then I rode from the stables to where the senior officers of the horse archers were waiting on their horses.

'Well, gentlemen, today we will be the bait that hopefully entices the enemy into our trap. Prince Orodes has explained what your mission is?'

They all nodded their heads.

'Good, then may Shamash protect you all, and good luck.'

They bowed their heads and then wheeled their horses around to ride in a single file down the side of the camp's central avenue, which was now filled with legionaries marching six abreast to their battle positions. Marcus stood watching them go.

'I feel useless,' he muttered, clearly unhappy at being left behind to guard the camp. He had a *gladius* in a scabbard strapped to his belt and a helmet on his head.

'You are far from useless,' I replied. 'Just make sure the camp is secure. You and your engines will be needed when we reach Ctesiphon.'

He was far from convinced. 'If you kill Mithridates today then there will be no need to breach Ctesiphon's defences.'

I had not thought of that and it brought a smile to my lips.

'If we kill Mithridates today, then afterwards we will march on Persepolis. Then you can batter the walls of Narses' capital, I promise.' I raised my hand at him and he bowed his head in return, then I cantered from the camp to join the horse archers.

We were around twenty miles from the Tigris, too far away to be battling on cultivated land. The stretch of ground we would fight on today was hard, flat, featureless and arid – ideal cavalry country. Normally in such terrain it was customary for the horsemen to be placed on each wing with the foot in the middle but today would be different. In front of the foot would be the screen of horse archers, while behind the foot, on the extreme edges of their right and left flanks respectively, would be the cataphracts. There would no reserve. If everything unfolded according to plan there would be no need for one. If all went according to plan!

It took two hours for the legions to assemble in their battle positions, all the time the horse archers in front of them keeping a watchful eye for the enemy, and beyond them rode Byrd, Malik and the scouts. Domitus placed the Duran Legion on the right, the place of honour, and the Exiles on the left. Many Parthians derided Dura and its 'foreign' army made up of former slaves, exiles from foreign lands and what they saw as the scrapings of humanity. But Domitus had forged his two legions into fearsome weapons and they were as yet undefeated in battle. Many kings in the empire could raise larger armies than Dura's it was true, but they were comprised mostly of civilians, farmers in the main, who spent their lives growing crops and tending animals. All my men were full-time soldiers who spent every day on the training fields perfecting their skills. The Romans had taught me that discipline, endless training and the right equipment were the keys to victory, and I liked to think that Dura's army had all three in abundance. Above all, drill and discipline were worth far more than thousands of ill-trained levies. That was the reason I did not bring along the lords and their retinues. Fearless they might be but they were also a law unto themselves and uncontrollable once the fighting began.

Normally each legion was drawn up in three lines for battle but today Domitus had arranged them in two lines, five cohorts in the first line and five in the second. This was to extend the frontage of the army and also hide the presence of the cataphracts from the enemy, when the enemy appeared that is. Each cohort was made up of six centuries deployed side by side, each one composed of eight ranks, each rank made up of ten men. Each century had its own commander – a centurion – who stood in the front rank while his two second-in-commands were located at the rear. There was very little space between each century in the cohort but there was a gap equating to the frontage of a cohort between the cohorts in the first line. The cohorts of the second line were arranged in such a way that each one could march forward and fill the gaps in the first line, after which the legion would have a frontage of ten cohorts in a single line.

On the left flank the Exiles were arrayed so that the cohort on the extreme left of the second line extended to the left of the furthest left-flank cohort in the first line. This was done to allow it to deploy left to form a flank defence against any sudden enemy attack. With the Duran Legion it was the reverse, with the second line extending right to offer flank protection against an enemy assaulting that wing. It had taken years to perfect the drills that the legions would perform today, but I had every confidence that they would carry them out effortlessly, even in the white heat of combat.

The legionaries presented a magnificent sight as the sun began its ascent in the eastern sky and glinted off helmets and javelin points. Each legionary was dressed and equipped exactly the same as his comrades – helmet with cheekguards, neck guard, forehead cross-brace to deflect sword blows from men in the saddle, white tunic, leather vest over the tunic and mail shirt over the vest. On his feet he wore hobnailed sandals. His weapons were a *gladius* in a scabbard on his right hip, dagger on his left hip and javelin. Though the curved, oval shield is a defensive piece of equipment, comprising strips of planed wood laminated in three layers, faced with leather painted white and sporting red griffin wings and edged with brass, in battle it could also be used offensively. Held by the horizontal metal grip spanning the hole in the middle of the shield, over which is a round, bulging metal boss, a legionary could barge the shield into opponents and use the boss to unbalance or topple them. The clothing and equipment of the legions were sturdy and functional, though I did allow one indulgence in that every man had a white plume fastened to the top of his helmet. Domitus scoffed at such displays but it added to the impressive sight that the legions made on parade and in battle. It

73

also made the legionaries feel that they were not the poor relations of the cataphracts.

Once in position the legionaries grounded their shields, took off their helmets and laid their javelins on the ground to conserve their strength. It might be hours before they would be fighting. If they fought at all for the enemy was conspicuous by their absence!

Mounted on Remus I was behind the Duran Legion with Vagharsh behind me as more horse archers cantered past us to take up position in front of the legion. I saw Byrd and Malik riding in the opposite direction, both of them careering to a halt in front of me.

'Enemy come,' said Byrd. 'They five miles to east.'

'How many?'

Byrd looked round at the foot drawn up, the horse archers riding into position and the cataphracts making their way to their battle stations.

'Twice as many as you, maybe more.'

'All horsemen, Pacorus,' added Malik, 'we did not see any foot.'

'And did you see Mithridates?' I asked.

'Did not see him,' replied Byrd.

Domitus had strolled over to us. He nodded at Byrd and Malik.

'I assume that Mithridates is approaching.'

'His army is,' I said, 'but whether he is with it remains to be seen.'

'How long before our guests arrive?' asked Domitus.

'Half an hour,' said Byrd.

Orodes rode up dressed in his scale armour and helmet, behind him his bodyguard of two hundred and fifty men from Susiana and behind them five hundred Durans. Orodes' banner of an eagle holding a snake in its talons was carried behind him.

'I was beginning to think that you were going to miss the battle,' Domitus said to him. 'Then all that fancy armour and ironmongery would be wasted.'

'Very droll, Domitus.' Orodes never had much of a sense of humour on the eve of battle. In his eyes slaughter was far too serious for levity.

I pointed to the two legions drawn up in front of us. 'When you see the horse archers coming through their ranks, Orodes, that will be your signal to advance and attack.'

'And you had better be quick,' smiled Domitus, 'because my lads will have likely killed most of them by the time your horse boys arrive.'

Orodes frowned. 'I am fully briefed as to the battle plan.' He looked at me. 'I am concerned about Surena, Pacorus. Are you quite sure he is up to the task you have given him? If he fails you lose half your cataphracts.'

'He will not fail, my friend,' I reassured him.

74

'Well, then,' said Domitus, 'we had better get ready. The gods protect you all.'

He shook hands with all of us and then walked back to where a knot of his senior officers was waiting for him a couple of hundred yards away. I offered my hand to Orodes.

'Shamash be with you.'

He took my hand. 'You also, my friend.'

'I will go and impress upon Surena the importance of obeying orders, Orodes, to assuage your concern.'

Accompanied by Byrd and Malik I rode over to the left flank to where Surena and the rest of my heavy cavalry were waiting on their horses. Surena was surrounded by his five company commanders and like him their helmets were shoved back on top of their heads to save their brains being roasted. He was gesticulating to them with his arms. He stopped when we approached.

'Hail, lord,' he said.

'Greetings, Surena. Is everything in order?'

'Yes, lord,' he beamed, no doubt excited by the imminent promise of glory.

I turned in the saddle and pointed at the legions. 'When you see the horse archers withdrawing through their ranks, that is your signal to advance past the foot and swing right to take the enemy in the rear.'

'Right up their arses,' said Surena, producing grins from his officers, all of them in their twenties like him.

'Just keep your heads and keep your men under tight control,' I said sternly.

Actually I was being unfair, since most of them had fought for me against Mithridates and Narses before, as well as against the Romans. They were officers because they were good leaders and their men respected them. I indicated for them to go back to their companies. They bowed their heads and did so. I turned to Malik and Byrd.

'If you would give us a moment, please.'

They nodded and rode back to Orodes, leaving only Vagharsh, Surena and myself.

'Now remember, Surena, victory depends on you and Orodes fulfilling your roles.'

His smile disappeared. 'I will not let you down, lord.'

'I know that. I will see you after the battle. Stay safe.'

He saluted and then looked ahead as horn blasts came from the horse archers deployed in front of the foot. The army of Mithridates was here at last.

I rode forward to the first-line cohorts of the Exiles. Trumpet blasts alerted the men to the enemy's presence and thousands of men hoisted up their shields and javelins and dressed their lines as centurions and

75

officers barked orders and ensured that their formations were ready. In the distance the men of the Duran Legion did the same.

Train hard, fight easy. That is what my old tutor and former head of Hatra's army, Bozan, had taught me. Train hard so that in battle every drill becomes instinctive, performed without thinking. Train hard so that drills are bloodless battles and battles are bloody drills, nothing more. Train hard so that the hordes of enemy soldiers charging you, yelling blood-curdling screams, do not cause you to turn tail and run for your life; rather, you wait until they are within fifty paces before hurling your javelin into their densely packed ranks. Then you go to work with your sword as the enemy steps over the dead and dying javelin-pierced front ranks to get at you. Train hard so that it becomes easy, almost pleasurable to stab your short sword into enemy bellies and thighs, to thrust the sword point over the top rim of your shield into an enemy's face. To stab and stab without thinking, knowing that your blade will find the right targets as if by magic. But it is not magic; it is hours, days, months and years spent on the training fields to perfect your skills, to hone them to such a degree that your weapons become a part of you, living, breathing instruments that obey your will instantly and without question.

I turned to Vagharsh.

'Time to show them what they are fighting for,' and dug my knees into Remus.

He reared up on his hind legs and then raced forward. Vagharsh followed at a gallop as my griffin banner fluttered beside him. We rode from left to right along the front of the Exiles and then the Duran Legion, legionaries banging their javelins against their shield rims and shouting 'Dura, Dura' as we passed them by. Pure theatre but they loved it. We passed Domitus standing ahead of the Duran Legion, a solitary figure with a white crest on his helmet. He drew his *gladius* and clutched it to his chest as I thundered by. And behind him ten thousand men steeled themselves to earn another silver disc for the Staff of Victory.

I rode to where the horse archers were drawn up in two ranks five hundred paces in front of the legions and galloped to the centre of the line. I halted and walked Remus forward a few paces. There, filling the horizon, was the army of Mithridates –thousands of men on horses moving forward. There was no foot as Byrd said, only cavalry. I squinted and tried to make out what types of horsemen we faced. I could see spears and shields and the sun glinting off scale armour. They appeared to be a mixture of cataphracts and mounted spearmen. Their frontage was unbroken, suggesting they were deployed in one great mass.

I turned and called forward the senior officer of the horse archers as the enemy blew horns and kettle drummers banged their instruments.

Among the front ranks of the enemy I could now make out dragon windsocks and great banners displaying the symbol of Susiana – the eagle clutching a snake – the same standard that Orodes, the true heir to the throne of that kingdom, carried.

'On my signal we will advance,' I said to the commander. 'Your men are prepared?'

'Every man knows the plan, majesty,' he replied.

I nodded and he returned to his men.

'Time for you to retire, Vagharsh.'

The banner he carried had been a present from Dobbai before I had even taken up residence at Dura. When I was not on campaign it hung behind the dais in the throne room in the Citadel. To many in the kingdom it was a sacred object imbued with magical powers. As such I was also careful to ensure its safety on the battlefield, and the life of the one who carried it. Vagharsh rode through the horse archers and back to the Duran Legion as I pulled my bow from its case and held it aloft. To my left and right three thousand men replied in kind, raising their bows in the air.

The din from the enemy ranks increased as they got nearer. They were perhaps a quarter of a mile away now.

Moving at a steady pace I saw that the centre of their line was composed of cataphracts, the men bringing down their great lances to hold them with both hands by the sides of their horses. They were obviously going to charge us. It made sense. We were, after all, only lightly armed horse archers. I dug my knees into Remus' sides and he broke into a canter, then a gallop. The men behind me followed. The distance between us and the enemy narrowed as I nocked an arrow, drew back the bowstring and released it, then whipped another arrow from my quiver. I nocked it in the bowstring and released it. The enemy were around six or seven hundred paces from me now as I pulled a third arrow, shot it and then yanked on Remus' reins to turn him left and then left again. The enemy had broken into a gallop and I could hear their war cries as I yelled at Remus to move faster as I tried to outpace them. The other horse archers had also about-faced and were riding full pelt towards the legions as though demons were snapping at their heels. Remus, wild-eyed and straining every sinew in his powerful frame to outrun the enemy, thundered across the ground and headed towards one of the gaps between the cohorts. I prayed to Shamash that because the cataphracts and spearmen were heavily armed we would be able to widen the gap between them and us. But it would be tight.

I could see the cohorts now, a wall of white shields and shining helmets standing like great slabs of rock on the desert floor. I hurtled through one of the gaps with hundreds of others following me, then passed through the second line of cohorts. I should have run straight into a cohort that stood directly behind the gap between two cohorts in the first line. But the second-line cohorts had parted, the two halves of each one moving left and right to stand directly behind a cohort in the first line. This allowed the horsemen to pass through both lines unimpeded. That was the easy bit.

As soon as all the horse archers had passed safely though their lines, the legionaries of the second line had to race forward to fill the gaps in the first line. This was the hard part, for if they failed not only would the enemy be able to pour through the gaps where the second-line cohorts were supposed to be, they would also hit the men of that second line who were attempting to move forward. The result would be chaos and slaughter.

But they did not fail. As soon as the last horse archers had passed them by the men of the second-line cohorts rushed forward to fill the gaps in the first line and present a continuous front to the enemy. And as they reached their positions, like their comrades who had been in the first line the first five ranks hurled their javelins at the horde of enemy riders bearing down on them. Around three thousand javelins arched into the air as Mithridates' horsemen hit the front ranks of the legionaries. A sickening grinding noise reverberated across the battlefield as thousands of horsemen tried to turn their mounts aside to avoid hitting a solid wall of leather, wood and steel.

A horse, even when gripped by terror in battle, will not run at a solid object. He will either try to run through any gaps in front of him or turn aside to avoid hitting said object; others will attempt to stop dead, especially when a torrent of javelins is about to engulf them. Cataphracts and spearmen became a tangled mass of horse and human flesh as animals pulled up and catapulted their riders over their heads, while others somersaulted over and over, crushing their riders under them as they did so. Those behind smashed into the ones in front as others were hit and pierced by javelins.

The javelin rain had saved the front ranks of the legionaries from becoming entangled in the grisly drama as the first line of horsemen had careered into the missiles, which had killed their momentum. But it takes nerves of steel to stand in a tightly packed formation of men while thousands of horses' hooves are shaking the earth and coming closer at alarming speed. To not only stand but also still perform their drills – to throw their javelins and then draw their swords for close-quarter combat. They had practised for this day for years, sweating under a Mesopotamian sun and practising over and over again until they responded to orders and trumpet blasts without thinking. Train hard, fight easy.

The great charge of the enemy had been halted but the day was still young. I halted Remus and turned him around, horse archers kicking up dust as they too reformed behind me. To the left and right of us horns blasted as the army's two cataphract wings advanced to envelop the flanks of the enemy and attack them from behind.

I suddenly felt helpless. Orodes, Surena and their heavy horsemen would decide the battle. In front of me the front ranks of my legionaries were stabbing at the bellies of horsemen while the rear ranks hurled more volleys of javelins. A charging cataphract is a devastating and fearsome weapon; a stationary one is vulnerable. Those still mounted would have cast aside their great lances to use their close-quarter weapons – sword, axe or mace. But in the tightly packed mêlée it was almost impossible to manoeuvre their horses, and all the while javelins were striking them and their horses were being maimed by *gladius* blades thrust under their horses' scale armour. But there were still lot of horsemen hacking and slashing at the foot solders in front of them.

Vagharsh rode up to me and nodded.

'Domitus' men are taking a hard pounding.'

'The horse archers cannot aid them yet. We must have a reserve just in case he is forced back.'

I bit my lip nervously. I hated sitting here idle and helpless. I would much rather be hacking away by the side of Surena or Orodes. It was one of the disadvantages of being the commander of an army. I was sorely tempted to advance the horse archers so that they were immediately behind the cohorts. From there they could shoot over the heads of the legionaries into the seething mass of the enemy. But if Orodes and Surena had been successful then our arrows would be striking our own men as well. My feeling of helplessness magnified.

Then a chant echoed across the battlefield and a sense of elation swept through me. Above the cries of dying men, the squeals of lacerated horses and the clatter of steel against steel I could discern thousands of voices shouting 'Dura, Dura'. The hour of victory had come. The cohorts had withstood the great charge of men and horseflesh that had hit them like a thunderbolt, and now they were advancing, cutting though the enemy like a giant and remorseless saw. Then I spotted a man running towards me, a broad figure in a mail shirt adorned with metal discs, greaves around his shins and a white transverse crest atop his helmet. Domitus.

I rode over to meet him, his face streaked with dirt and sweat and his brown eyes alight with glee as his men chanted more loudly as they went about their grim work.

'They're breaking,' he panted. 'I can see your men in their rear. All that money you spent on plumes and pennants has proved useful in spotting friend from foe. Those that aren't dead or dying have lost the stomach for it and are retreating.'

I bent down and offered my hand. 'The victory is yours, my friend. I salute you.'

He shook my hand and spat on the ground. 'The boys are finding it difficult crawling over piles of dead horse and bodies. There's plenty that will get away unless you can deal with them.'

I nodded. 'Consider it done. Don't get careless, life can still be snatched away in the moment of victory.'

He raised his hand, turned and then trotted back to where his cohorts, slowly but purposely, were grinding their way forward. I rode back to where the officers of the horse archers waited on their mounts.

I pointed at the right flank of the cohorts. 'They're breaking. It is time to finish them. One dragon will come with me on the right, one dragon will advance on the left, and one dragon will stay here as a reserve.'

They nodded and rode back to organise their commands. Moments later horns blasted and I led a great column of horsemen to sweep round the right flank of the army. There was a mighty cheer as men spotted the griffin banner billowing behind me as we broke into a canter and then a gallop to pursue the fleeing enemy. I saw the banner of Orodes, or at least I thought it was his banner as Mithridates had taken the same banner to be his own. Where was he?

On we rode, a thousand riders deploying into line as we spread out across the desert floor. Ahead were riders fleeing for their lives, men in scale armour and others in leather cuirasses and helmets only – the remnants of the spearmen. I shouted at Remus to move faster and his powerful frame responded, his legs kicking up the earth as he closed on a man without spear, shield or spear who was clutching the neck of his horse. I pulled my bow from its case, drew an arrow from the quiver and nocked it in the bowstring. He turned round to glance at his pursuer as I released the string and the arrow shot through the air and hit him in the back. He yelped and then fell from his saddle. In front of me I spotted a large man in scale armour sporting a black horsehair crest in his helmet. His horse was lame. I raced past him, turned in the saddle and shot an arrow that pierced his eye socket. On we went, shooting at enemy horsemen and killing men who were on foot whose mounts had been killed in the mêlée. The companies fanned out to fell as many fleeing enemy horsemen as possible.

The army of Mithridates was finished; the last of his troops were being slaughtered in the final act of the battle. Already I was planning an assault on Seleucia and then Ctesiphon, whose garrisons would be scythed down like ripened crops in the fields. Mithridates would flee to Persepolis but I would follow him. My engines would batter down its defences and then I would put an end to him and Narses forever. There would be a proper king of kings on the throne and Dura would once more be a part of the empire. I raised my eyes to the heavens, stretched out my arms and gave a mighty cheer of triumph. Shamash had granted me a great victory and I vowed to build a grand temple in his honour in my city to rival the one that stood in Hatra.

I heard frantic horn blasts to my left and right and look around. My horsemen were slowing, some had stopped and were pointing ahead. I pulled on Remus' reins and also slowed him. I looked ahead and a chill went through my soul. It cannot be; it must be a mirage, a trick of the desert heat. The entire horizon was filled with black shapes: riders on horses and foot soldiers armed with spears carrying large shields. I slowed Remus to a halt.

There were thousands of them as far as the eye could see. In the centre of their vast line the sun glinted off scale armour – more cataphracts. The entire mass was moving at a steady pace, no more than a walk so the foot could keep up with the horsemen. It was as if a great black wave was rolling across the desert floor towards me. I sat, transfixed and appalled by the sight I beheld. And then the gods revealed their cruel nature, for in the centre of the approaching line, barely fluttering in the slight northerly wind that had now picked up, I saw a great yellow banner. And upon that banner was the symbol I come to loathe – the black head of Simurgel, the bird-god of Persis.

The army of Narses had come.

Chapter 4

Frantic horn blasts hastily assembled the horse archers and then we turned and galloped back to the rest of the army. I remained behind until the last remnants of Dura's riders had been located and ordered to withdraw, and then rode back in their wake. I kept glancing back, expecting to see parties of horsemen leaving the enemy ranks to pursue us, but they did not break their steady, remorseless advance. There was no need, they knew that Dura's army would be exhausted from having fought one battle, and there was no need for them to rush. I had walked straight into their trap. Narses must have known that even with greater numbers a straight fight between my army and his would probably result in him losing. So he had sacrificed one army; allowed it to be cut to pieces, safe in the knowledge that he had enough men to launch a second force against Dura's tired and weakened soldiers. Ruthless and very clever. As I shouted at Remus to move faster Dobbai's words were ringing in my ears. I had underestimated both Mithridates and Narses and now faced paying a heavy price.

The horse archers must have ridden five miles east from the army in their pursuit of the dregs of Mithridates' army, and by the time they got back to where the legions were gathered in their ragged ranks their horses were sweating and tired. Domitus had pulled back his men about a quarter of a mile from where the mêlée had taken place. A long, thick line of dead men and horses marked the spot where the fighting had been the fiercest. Hundreds of his men lay on the ground helmetless, others leaning on their rested shields, joking and talking with their comrades. I had stumbled upon a scene of near serenity, spoiled only by the carpet of offal that had been dumped on the desert floor. The air of calm was shattered as the horse archers retreated before the advance of Narses' army.

At first the men looked at each other in confusion, then put on their helmets and scrambled to their feet as I rode to find Domitus and Orodes. Soon trumpet blasts were coming from the ranks of the cohorts as officers and centurions joined their units and reorganised their men. Around two hundred paces behind the foot the cataphracts lay resting on the ground, squires busily unburdening their horses of the scale armour that had served them so well in the battle. Behind them were the beasts of the camel train loaded with spare arrows. They stopped and looked in confusion at each other and their masters as I halted among them when I spotted Domitus talking to Orodes, Malik and Byrd. Orodes, like many of the horsemen, had taken off his scale armour and had dumped it on the ground beside him. A squire was leading a camel to begin loading both his and his horse's scale armour onto the beast's back.

'What in the name of Jupiter is going on?' said Domitus, two of his metal discs having been knocked off his mail shirt in the fighting.

I halted Remus and jumped off his back. 'The army of Narses approaches. We have been well and truly duped.'

Byrd was appalled that his scouting skills had let him down. 'Impossible, we rode to the banks of the Tigris itself. There was no other army.'

'It is true, Pacorus,' added Malik. 'We saw no other enemy.'

I allowed myself a smile. 'My friends, of course you saw nothing because there was nothing to see. Mithridates and Narses are masters of deception. They allowed us to see what they wanted us to see. The second army was probably hidden on the eastern bank of the Tigris, or perhaps in Seleucia itself.'

'How many do they bring against us?' asked Orodes, who looked tired and drawn, though mercifully unhurt.

'Thousands,' I replied. 'The point is that we do not have the energy to fight a second battle.'

Domitus was nodding his head approvingly. 'Clever, very clever. They allowed you to slaughter one part of their force so you could wear yourself out, and then they come with fresh troops to finish you off.'

'When you have finished admiring the enemy perhaps you might like to get the legions back to camp,' I said.

'You are running from them?' Orodes was mortified by the idea of retreat.

I walked over to him and laid a hand on his shoulder. 'My friend, much as I would like to fight your brother....'

'Stepbrother,' he reminded me.

I continued. 'As much as I would like to fight him, and Narses, if we do we die. He has held back his horse archers and they bring more cataphracts and thousands of foot.'

'Tired men cannot fight another battle and win,' added Domitus.

Orodes looked dejected and said no more.

'Well, then,' said Domitus, 'I'd better get the camp organised.'

He took a swig from his water bottle, replaced the cork and then strode off.

'Domitus,' I called after him, 'ensure that no water is wasted. We will need every drop.' He raised his hand in acknowledgement and then was gone.

At that moment Surena rode up. His helmet was pushed back on his head although he was still wearing his scale armour. His horse was still similarly protected. 'I have just heard, lord. Let me take my half dragon to disperse them.'

Orodes rolled his eyes in despair and Malik laughed. Byrd stared at Surena in disbelief.

83

'As much as a glorious death may appeal to you, Surena,' I said, 'I still have need of you. Get your men and their squires back to camp and wait for further orders.'

He looked towards where the din of kettledrums and horns was getting louder and then at me in frustration. Finally he snorted loudly and then rode back to his men.

'He fought well today, Pacorus,' said Orodes. 'But he doesn't know when to stop. He will over-reach himself one day, I fear.'

'But not today,' I replied.

Orodes' squire had finished packing his armour onto the camel and now held the reins of his and his master's horse. Orodes nodded to me and then vaulted into his saddle and rode away to his men mounted and waiting a couple of hundred paces away. I turned to Byrd and Malik.

'My friends, though you are tired I would ask a favour of you both.'

They both nodded.

'Byrd, I would like you to ride to King Vardan at Babylon and tell him what has happened here. Tell him that we are marching back to Dura. Warn him that Mithridates may strike at Babylon then make your way back to us. Malik, I would ask you to ride straight to Dura and convey the news of our predicament to Gallia. She will take it better if it comes from a friend. And convey my love to her also.'

He bowed his head to me. 'You can tell her that yourself when you return home.'

I embraced him and then Byrd and then they were away, riding back to camp to get food and fodder before leaving us. Byrd would head southwest towards the Euphrates, taking him away from the enemy and allowing him to get water for both him and his horse. The great river lay around thirty miles in that direction, and Babylon another eighty travelling southeast and following the course of the waterway.

Malik would ride west, following the same route that the army had taken to get to this place. After travelling fifty miles he and his men would reach the Euphrates, thereafter riding another two hundred miles north before arriving at Dura. We were in Babylonian territory, but sixty miles north lay Hatra's border, and once Malik reached my father's kingdom he would make contact with one of the mud-brick forts that littered the realm. Each one held carrier pigeons that could convey messages faster than a horse. With luck news of my predicament would reach Dura in a week. I prayed that any subsequent news that reached my wife's ears would not tell of my bleached bones lying in the sun.

The horse archers acted as the rear-guard of the army as the legions, cataphracts, squires and camels retreated back to camp. I stayed with the rearmost units as I watched the army disappear into the vast rectangle that we had created in the desert, and then cast my eyes to the east. The army of Narses was visible now, a black line of foot and cavalry filling the horizon. I gave the signal to fall back as a party of enemy horse archers, dressed in baggy long-sleeved yellow shirts and blue leggings, halted around five hundred paces from me. About a hundred in number, they gave no indication that they were going to attack. They merely spread into a long line and pulled their bows from their cases and observed us retreating. They advanced as we fell back, but when I ordered a halt and about-face they stopped. More of their comrades joined the end of their line until there were around five hundred horsemen facing us. We fell back another five hundred paces and they followed, but when we wheeled round to face them as before they again halted. They were obviously under orders not to provoke a fight. I was tempted to launch my own assault, but more and more horse archers were now joining them and any combat would have been a very one-sided affair. And so, as the final units of Dura's army filed back into camp, the rear-guard and I followed them. What had started as a most propitious day had ended very badly.

I thanked Rome's gods that they had revealed to me the mysteries of the Roman military machine, its organisation and encampment procedures. For if Dura's army had been run along Parthian lines then we would surely have been carrion for the crows by the morning. But at least we had a ditch, rampart and palisade surrounding us. Those defences gave me time to think of a plan for the morrow. I also breathed a huge sigh of relief that it was not the Parthian way to fight at night; otherwise we would be fending off attacks during the hours of darkness.

When word had reached Marcus of what was happening, after they had arrived back in camp he had ordered the squires to man the rampart with their bows in case the enemy tried to storm the camp. The squires had taken no part in the battle and they were thus fresh and rested, and eager to fight. They may have been boys, mostly between fourteen and sixteen years of age, but they were well versed in using a Parthian bow. To curb their youthful enthusiasm Marcus gave each boy a full quiver and said he would increase his fatigue duties if he wasted any arrows.

As well as the squires and the fighting men there were farriers, veterinaries, blacksmiths, the riders of the camels of the ammunition train and the wagons, Marcus' men and Alcaeus' medical personnel in camp – over three thousand men.

Domitus organised parties to reinforce the rampart defences as the enemy slowly surrounded the camp. Despite my general's fears that they would launch an immediate attack from all sides they actually showed no signs that they would assault us. They were content to deploy on all four sides of the camp and then stand in their ranks. The camp's main entrance was on the western side and that was where Narses placed his foot, thousands of spearmen dressed in yellow tunics and blue leggings. They carried long spears topped by leaf-shaped points and wore helmets on their heads. Their large rectangular shields were made of wicker covered with leather painted yellow. They also carried what looked like long daggers in scabbards fixed to their belts. They wore no body armour. In the centre of the line stood Narses' élite foot soldiers – his palace guard, or at least that is what I assumed they were. They wore bronze helmets with large cheekguards to protect the sides of their faces and had leather cuirasses over their torsos. Their tunics were yellow like the other foot soldiers and they too were armed with spears that had leaf-shaped blades. However, their shields were round and faced with bronze after the Greek fashion, with the symbol of the bird-god painted on each one. There were around two thousands of them.

To the north of our camp Narses deployed his horse archers, thousands of men in helmets, yellow shirts and red leggings. Some of them wore armour on their bodies. On the south side of the camp were yet more archers similarly attired, a great mass of men and horseflesh intended to awe us. Last but by no means least to the east of the camp came Narses himself, accompanied by around five thousand or more armoured horsemen.

I stood on the rampart with Orodes, Domitus and Surena as they rode towards our camp and then halted around four hundred paces away; a horde of heavy cavalry, each man holding a *kontus*. I estimated that we were surrounded by at least thirty thousand enemy soldiers.

Narses, the King of Persis and Sakastan, had always cut a dashing figure, adorning every inch of his powerful frame with expensive clothes and armour. Today was no different. Mounted as ever on his magnificent black stallion, whose immaculately groomed coat shone in the late afternoon sun, he and his horse wore no scale armour. Instead he wore a cuirass made up of overlapping rows of silver segments and on his large head he wore a helmet inlaid with gold. Its cheekguards were also inlaid with gold and silver and from its crown streamed a long black horsehair plume. Next to him, also seated on a black stallion, was King of Kings Mithridates. I spat over the palisade stakes in his direction, hoping he would see my insult. Perhaps he would be enraged and launch an assault. I gripped the hilt of my *spatha*.

'You are wasting your spit,' growled Domitus. 'He's got us where he wants us. The last thing he'll do is make any rash moves.'

86

'Give me some men, lord,' said Surena, who appeared remarkably fresh despite his participation in the battle. 'I can launch an attack against them. They are very close.'

Domitus looked at him and shook his head, prompting a scowl from Surena. Domitus had always regarded Surena as volatile and reckless. For his part Surena believed Domitus to be far too cautious.

'No, Surena,' I replied. 'For the moment we conserve our strength.'

Domitus looked up at the sun descending on the western horizon.

'They won't attack today.'

'Knowing my stepbrother,' added Orodes, 'he would prefer to starve us into submission rather than offer battle.'

Narses was obviously bored with watching us as he wheeled his horse away and rode back to the camp that was being established to the south of our position. His many cataphracts and Mithridates followed the lord high general of the Parthian Empire. To the east where the earlier battle had taken place, smoke was billowing into the sky. The enemy was cremating the dead on great pyres rather than burying them. Perhaps Orodes was right – the enemy intended to starve us into submission rather than assault our camp. No general would want piles of bodies and rotting carcasses near his army. Already the flies would be swarming over dead flesh, and where there was dead flesh there would soon be plague and sickness. At least there was still a slight northerly wind that carried the stench of burning flesh to the south rather than over our camp. To the west the sky was a mass of blues and purples streaked with orange and yellow. It was a beautiful spring evening. I hoped it would not be our last.

I turned to the others. 'Get something to eat. Council of war in an hour.'

With due reverence the griffin and lion standards were returned to their tents and guards placed around them. Officers reported to Domitus and Orodes in my command tent and clerks recorded the number of dead and wounded. When we returned to Dura, if we returned to Dura, those killed who had families would be informed of the pensions they were entitled to. Any children of the deceased would be entitled to free education and any males could be enrolled in the Sons of the Citadel scheme should they be suitable. When I had first come to Dura Domitus had insisted that his legionaries should be forbidden to marry, as was the rule in the Roman army. However, after a while many legionaries had formed relationships and had given their women part of their wages so they could rent rooms in the city. They were de facto man and wife. And when men among the cavalry began to enter into marriages it was clearly impractical and unfair to insist that the legionaries should be treated differently. Domitus grumbled but acquiesced. I suggested that he too should take a wife but he had scowled and grumbled some more so I let the matter rest.

Before the council meeting I walked round the camp and talked with as many men as possible. Despite being outnumbered and surrounded they were in remarkably good spirits, but then victory has a habit of intoxicating the soul and diminishing the size of the enemy. Walking back to my tent I threaded my way through the neat rows of eight-man tents in which the legionaries and horsemen slept. I came across one of the Companions, a Thracian named Drenis who had been a gladiator in Capua, in the same school as Spartacus. I had absolutely no idea how old he was but judging by the scars and lines on his face he must have been a veteran of a hundred battles! His arms and legs were similarly adorned with scars and marks, further mementoes of his time in the arena and on the battlefield. He had started out as a slave before becoming a gladiator, then served in the ranks of the slave army in Italy before becoming a centurion in Dura's army. He now commanded two cohorts, the equivalent of a Roman tribune, though he would never countenance accepting a title used by his enemies. He was standing next to a brazier holding forth to a group of his centurions sitting on stools round it. They all stood up when they saw me. I indicated to them to regain their seats.

'Ah, Pacorus,' all the Companions were allowed such familiarity with each other, 'I was just telling them about when that bastard Crassus had us boxed in at Rhegium, do you remember?'

'I do indeed, I also remember it being very cold.'

I was taken back to the southern tip of Italy, to when Spartacus had led the army to the port of Rhegium prior to embarkation aboard ships of the Cilician pirates for transportation to the island of Sicily. But the pirates had betrayed us, and Crassus had built a line of earthworks and wooden forts across the land to trap the slave army with its back against the sea.

Drenis put his arm round my shoulder.

'So the Romans thought they had the war all done and dusted and were planning their victory parade when Pacorus and his horsemen smashes through their lines and allowed us to escape. We gave one lot a beating today and tomorrow the ones that turned up late for the show will get the same treatment. I was telling them that there's nothing to worry about.'

'Perhaps we might negotiate our way out of here, Drenis.'

He laughed aloud. 'You've been a king too long. Besides, someone told me that Mithridates is present.'

'He is.'

Drenis pulled his *gladius* from its scabbard. 'Well he can negotiate all he wants to; he's not going anywhere. He has to pay for what he did to Godarz.'

They all cheered at this. I clasped Drenis' forearm and left him to his tall stories. I suddenly felt more confident that we would all live to see Dura again.

Back at the command tent Domitus and Orodes had dismissed the clerks and were seated at the table in the main compartment. They too appeared to be in good spirits.

'What is the damage?' I asked.

'A hundred dead legionaries and another hundred wounded,' replied Domitus.

'Forty cataphracts were killed, another thirty-five wounded, two score horse archers also,' added Orodes.

They were remarkably light casualties considering the size of the opposition, and had we faced but one army we would have been able to march on Ctesiphon in the morning. As it was we were penned in like a herd of pigs.

I unbuckled my sword belt and laid it on the table.

'Are you hungry?' asked Orodes.

'No,' I replied, staring at the polished surface.

'You'd better get some food inside you, it's going to be a long day tomorrow.'

Outside the enemy's kettledrums started drumming, a low thumping noise that had no interruption.

'Looks like it is going to be a long night as well,' added Domitus.

'Guard,' I shouted. One of the two sentries standing outside the entrance pulled back the flap and entered, standing to attention once inside.

'Go and find Surena, Marcus the Roman engineer and Alcaeus.'

He saluted and disappeared. Outside the racket made by the kettledrums got louder. The enemy was obviously trying to unnerve us and deny us any sleep, not that I would have been able to sleep much anyway. Thoughts, some good, most bad, raced through my mind, foremost among them the realisation that Narses and Mithridates had duped me. Orodes sensed my unease.

'It is not your fault, Pacorus.'

I looked at him. 'Isn't it? Dobbai warned me not to underestimate them and that is exactly what I have done.'

Domitus began his usual habit of toying with his dagger. 'You had to do something. After the assassination attempt on your life you could not have carried on as if nothing had happened, otherwise you would have appeared weak.'

'Better weak than dead,' I mumbled.

Orodes looked most concerned but Domitus merely stretched back in his chair. 'You know what he's like, Orodes. Pacorus always gets morose on the eve of battle. I take it as a good omen.'

Those whom I had summoned arrived soon after and I told them to sit at the table. I rose from my chair and walked over to a smaller table nearby, grabbed the hide map that lay on it and unrolled it before them. It depicted the western half of the empire, specifically the area between the Tigris and Euphrates rivers.

I looked at the circle of faces illuminated by the oil lamps hanging from the tent poles. There was no concern or fear in their eyes, only an expectation that I would reveal to them a plan that would get us out of the predicament we were in. As ever in these situations I felt the loneliest man in the world at that moment. The burden of command bore down heavily on my shoulders. Outside the annoying drone of the massed kettledrums of the enemy continued their tuneless racket. I pointed at the map.

'We are around twenty miles west of the Tigris and eighty miles east of the Euphrates and, as you will all have gathered, currently surrounded by the enemy. I had toyed with the idea of offering battle tomorrow.'

I saw Orodes nodding in agreement, his high sense of honour sometimes overruling sound military sense.

'However,' I continued, 'to do so would only invite defeat and possible destruction. Therefore I intend to withdraw back to Dura.'

Orodes frowned but said nothing while Domitus continued playing with his dagger. He stopped and looked at me. He tilted his head to the sound outside.

'They might have something to say about that.'

'I will keep them occupied while Orodes and Surena make good their escape with the horse.'

Orodes looked confused. 'I do not understand, Pacorus.'

'It is quite simple,' I replied. 'If we offer battle tomorrow we will either lose and be forced to crawl back into camp once more, after which we will be in a more dire state than we are currently in. However, if you and Surena lead the horsemen to safety then I will have saved at least half the army.'

The significance of what I was saying suddenly dawned on Orodes.

'You intend to divide the army?'

'That is correct, my friend,' I said. 'The horse can break through the enemy while I keep Mithridates and Narses occupied. If they know that I am still in camp they will let you go.'

Orodes folded his arms. 'I will not desert the army.'

'Neither will I,' added Surena, earning him a scowl from Domitus.

I pointed at Surena. '*You* will obey orders.'

I looked at Orodes. 'I cannot order you to do anything, my friend, and nor would I attempt to. But as a friend I ask you to do this. With you leading them the cavalry stands a good chance of getting back to Dura.'

90

Orodes said nothing, which I took to mean that he accepted the charge, though he wore a deeply unhappy expression.

'And after the horse have left, what then?' enquired Domitus.

'If the legions stay here they will be destroyed,' I said. 'Our only option is to march northwest across the desert towards Hatran territory.' I traced my finger from where we were presently trapped to the southern frontier of my father's kingdom. 'The distance is around eighty or ninety miles.'

'Four days' march,' said Domitus.

'I fear it will take longer than that,' I replied. 'Marcus, what is the situation regarding our water supplies?'

Marcus stroked his chin as he stared at the map, then he looked up. 'The water wagons are nearly full, though they will be emptied soon enough if we stay here.'

'And if all the horses and camels are removed from camp?' I asked.

He weighed up the figures in his mind, gently moving his head from side to side. 'If that is so then we have enough water to last for ten days, though it will have to be rationed strictly.'

'Thank you, Marcus.' I looked at Orodes. 'You see, my friend, how it is impossible for the horses and camels to remain. Our only chance is for you to take the cataphracts, horse archers, squires and camels and strike west for the Euphrates.'

'That still leaves over twelve thousand men and thousands of mules,' remarked Domitus.

'Over twelve thousand plus one, for I shall be staying,' I said, attempting levity. Domitus' narrowing eyes told me I had failed.

I looked at him. 'You know that mules are hardier than horses, can endure extremes of heat and cold and can survive on limited amounts of water. Without the mules we lose the tents, tools, spare weapons, armour, supplies and Marcus' siege engines.'

'To say nothing of the wounded,' said Alcaeus, speaking for the first time.

'What is the position regarding the wounded?' I asked him.

He leaned back in his chair and ran a hand through his wiry black hair. 'Half are walking wounded and can hobble out of here, but the rest will have to be put on wagons if they are to survive.'

'It's decided then,' I said. 'We will leave no one behind to fall into the hands of Mithridates.'

'When will the horse break out, at dawn?' asked Domitus.

I shook my head. 'No, I will request a meeting with Mithridates first. That will give Orodes time to organise his breakout attempt.'

Orodes looked at me and was about to protest but I froze him with a glare. I esteemed him one of my closest friends but we were fighting for our very existence and I had no time for ridiculous notions of honour, especially not when it came to creatures such as Mithridates.

91

It was now past midnight and there was nothing else to say. There would be no sleep for any of us, though, as we all still had work to do. Alcaeus and Marcus would have to construct wooden roofs over the wagons that would carry the wounded, because once we were on the march we would be constantly harassed by the enemy's horse archers. I understood now why there had been none when we had fought the battle earlier. Narses was many things but he was no fool. He had clearly developed a strategy for dealing with us and thus far it had worked perfectly. But his war was only half won.

Before I dismissed the council there was one more thing to attend to.

'Surena, you are no longer an officer in the cataphracts.'

The colour drained from his face at my words. His mouth opened but no words came, his eyes filled with hurt.

'Orodes will lead the cavalry tomorrow but you will command the horse archers. Don't let me down.'

Where there was despair there was now triumph in Surena's eyes, plus a certain amount of smugness. Domitus looked at me, raised an eyebrow but said nothing.

'Remember, Surena,' I added, 'that you take orders from Orodes. I am entrusting you with three thousand men. Your task is to get them home safely.'

His cockiness disappeared, for the moment. 'Yes, lord.'

The others filed out of the tent back to their commands. Domitus cornered me before I returned back to making my rounds of the camp.

'You sure about promoting the puppy?'

'He's brave and well liked by the men. Besides, he'll be useful directing a rear-guard.'

'You are taking a risk.'

I shrugged. 'The position we are in, I have no choice.'

I returned to walking round the perimeter of the camp, which by now was guarded by legionaries as well as squires armed with bows. The camp was ringed by a multitude of campfires spreading far into the distance. All of the enemy's foot soldiers would be sleeping on the ground round their fires, the horse archers too. Only the cataphracts and the senior officers would sleep in tents on carpets and soft pillows, with the royal pavilions being the most luxurious. As I stood on the southern rampart staring at the two large pavilions that housed Mithridates and Narses I toyed with the idea of launching a large-scale night attack against them, but the ground between us and them was carpeted with sentries and sleeping soldiers. Even if we got to the pavilions there would be more troops to tackle. I dismissed the idea.

I saw a movement ahead and instinctively gripped the hilt of my sword. Was the enemy making a night assault? The squire next to me, a tall, skinny youth, brought up his bow and drew back the bowstring, which was nocked with an arrow. A hare ran towards us and then bolted right along the ditch and disappeared. I relaxed and laid a hand on the squire's shoulder.

'You can put down your bow, now.'

So focused had he been on scanning the ground in front of the ditch that he had not realised that I stood next to him. He grunted and released the strain on his bowstring. His eyes opened wide when he recognised me.

'Apologies, majesty, I did not realise…'

'No need to apologise for being a good sentry,' I reassured him. 'How long have you been a squire?'

'Eighteen months, majesty,' he said proudly.

It normally took four years before a squire was fully trained and old enough to become a cataphract, usually when he turned eighteen years of age. They began their training at fourteen and not all of them made it; the lazy, stupid and untrustworthy being weeded out in the first year. This youth had obviously been assessed as being capable of achieving membership of Dura's horsed élite.

'What are your ambitions?' I asked him.

'To become a cataphract and marry an Amazon,' he said proudly.

'Noble aims,' I replied, 'I'm sure you will fulfil them.'

At least he would be riding with Orodes and Surena tomorrow, and would have a chance of seeing his home again. I prayed to Shamash that He would also grant me the same privilege. But I was sure that I was making the right decision regarding sending the horsemen away.

And still the wretched kettledrums kept playing.

Dawn came all too soon. I had slept for perhaps two hours at the most when I rose and stretched my legs outside the tent. The sky was overcast and grey, the temperature cool. I went back inside to retrieve my cloak and then walked over to the stable area. The stables themselves were made of canvas stretched over wooden frames making up the stalls. Wicker panels had been fastened together to form a slanting roof over them and the horses. Thus on campaign they were sheltered from the elements. The camels and mules were corralled in a separate area but had no individual stalls. Already there was a great bustle of activity in and around the horses as squires, their masters and horse archers checked their mounts. Whether king or squire the routine was the same each morning: the horses were watered and fed and then checked for scrapes, cuts, bruises and puncture wounds on their legs, heads and bodies. Each of the hooves was then checked to see if the iron shoes had worked themselves loose, especially after the exertions of battle. Finally their coats were groomed. This is especially important for horses that are saddled most of the day to keep their coats healthy. Horses that required shoeing were taken to farriers while veterinaries attended to those that were wounded.

After I had ensured that Remus was fit for duty I searched out Orodes, finding him mucking out his brown mare. I stood at the entrance to the stall as he heaped fresh dung into a wheelbarrow.

'I'm sure your brother does not undertake such duties.'

He looked up. 'Stepbrother,' he reminded me.

'I would ask a favour of you.'

He leaned his spade against the wheelbarrow. 'If it is within my power, consider it done.'

'I want you to take Remus with you when you strike out for the Euphrates. I know you will take care of him.'

His concerned look resurfaced. 'What will you ride?'

'Nothing. I intend to walk like the rest of the men.'

He walked over to face me, whispering so no one else could hear our conversation. 'Are you sure about your plan, Pacorus? We could always fight the enemy today, here.'

'We cannot afford to suffer losses whereas Narses can always send for more reinforcements from Ctesiphon. We have to retreat, distasteful though it may be.'

He voiced no protest and I hoped that he saw the merits of my plan. He cocked his head.

'Do you hear that?'

'I can't hear anything,' I replied.

'Exactly, those wretched kettledrums have finally stopped.'

He was right. At least that was one thing to be thankful for. I returned to the command tent where Domitus was chewing on salted beef.

'It's very quiet,' he said.

'Yes, peace at last.'

Outside the camp was coming alive as men formed up for morning assembly and to relieve the sentries posted around the perimeter. The main entrance to the camp was on the western side, the exit from which Orodes would lead the cavalry, but there were other minor exits at the other three points of the compass. They were all blocked by sharpened stakes driven into the ground and pointing towards the enemy at an angle of forty-five degrees, while immediately behind them was a line of wagons.

A sentry walked in and saluted.

'The enemy have sent a courier under a flag of truce to the southern gate, majesty.'

'Courier?'

'Yes, majesty. King Mithridates requests a meeting with you.'

'Perhaps he wants to surrender,' said Domitus.

94

I laughed. 'Perhaps he does.' I rose from the chair and stretched out my arms. I felt tired, stiff and dirty.

'Send a message back that I will meet with the king in one hour.'

The guard saluted and left. I filled a cup with water and drank it. The liquid was tepid and unappetising.

'I wonder what he wants?' mused Domitus, who was now sharpening his *gladius* with a stone, running it along each of its edges and then admiring his handiwork.

'To gloat I would imagine. Still, an hour will give Orodes more time to prepare his men.'

I informed Orodes that his stepbrother had requested a meeting and asked whether he wanted to accompany me. He declined, stating that he might be tempted to break the rules of parley and kill Mithridates, and such a breach of the code of honour would be intolerable for him to endure. Same old Orodes. So I took Surena along, who borrowed Orodes' shimmering cuirass of silver scales and a helmet from a horse archer, with cheek guards but no face covering. He had also cadged a pristine long-sleeved white shirt off someone as his own was filthy from yesterday's battle. Red leggings and brown boots completed his appearance. I had to admit that Surena looked every inch a senior officer as we rode from the camp to meet my nemesis. We both carried our bows in cases dangling from our saddles and like me Surena was also armed with a *spatha*. Like my own it had been taken off a dead Roman; mine from a fallen foe in Italy, his from a slain cavalryman in Parthia.

I wore my usual attire of Roman helmet with its white goose feather crest, Roman cuirass, white shirt, brown leggings and leather boots. I took an escort of a dozen horse archers. Orodes said I should take more but I saw little point. Mithridates was a murderer and liar it was true, but he would be confident that he had me where he wanted me. He would be interested in torturing me with his words and nothing more, at least for the moment. So we rode from the southern entrance under a mournful grey sky with the army of the king of kings arrayed before us. Mithridates and Narses were obviously keen to taunt me as they already waited on their immaculately groomed black horses, surrounded by at least a hundred cataphracts. Members of Narses' foot guards stood in two blocks either side of the heavy horsemen and behind the two kings their standards hung limply from their poles, not a sniff of wind to disturb them. Servants held the reins of the kings' horses, young boys no older than sixteen years dressed in red silk shirts and baggy yellow trousers, gold earrings dangling from their ears.

We walked our horses to the meeting point halfway between our ditch and the enemy camp, or at least the southern part of it. Surena was eager to gallop across the barren ground, no doubt to clap eyes on the king of kings and his lord high general. He rode on my right and fidgeted in his saddle.

'Calm yourself, Surena, it is unbecoming to act like an excited child during a meeting of kings.'

He had heard much about Mithridates and Narses over the past few years and had even visited the palace at Ctesiphon following my abortive campaign in Gordyene. But he had never actually laid eyes upon either of them. I could tell that he was most curious to see them up close.

'And keep your tongue in check,' I reminded him. 'They may be our enemies but we must retain our dignity and manners even in the face of provocation.'

'Yes, lord.'

'And don't provoke them,' I added. 'I know your propensity for acting rashly. Just remember they are kings and you are not. Listen and learn, Surena.'

'Not much chance of that,' said Vagharsh from behind us, as ever carrying my griffin banner.

When we were around fifty paces from Mithridates and Narses they both waved away the boys holding their mounts and nudged their horses forward. I signalled to Vagharsh and the horse archers to halt as Surena and I continued to walk our horses forward. We halted around ten paces from Mithridates and Narses and I brought my hands forward in front of my body and rested each one on the two front horns of the saddle. Thus could my enemies see that my hands held no weapons. I scowled at Surena when I saw that his left hand was resting on the hilt of his sword, and nodded down at my own hands, then his for him to do the same. Mithridates and Narses looked on in contempt as he finally worked out what to do and removed his hand from the hilt of his sword.

There were no greetings or smiles as I looked at Mithridates and then Narses, the latter a more imposing and authoritative figure than the high king; indeed, Mithridates could have been mistaken for one of Narses' junior officers. As usual he was dressed in a black long-sleeved tunic, over which he wore a cuirass of silver scale armour, black leggings, black boots and at his left hip a sword held in a black scabbard decorated with silver leaf. He wore a richly adorned helmet on his head that fully encompassed his narrow, reptilian face. He hadn't changed in all the years since I had first encountered him at Esfahan where the kings of the empire had elected his father to the high crown. His beard was still neatly trimmed and his eyes were still black and devoid of feeling. I also had no doubt that he was positively gloating over my predicament.

The King of Persis and Sakastan had also changed little since the last time I had the misfortune of meeting him. His pale face showed no signs of ageing and his shoulders were as broad as ever. Like Mithridates, Narses had a well-groomed beard and his brown eyes were as calculating and condescending as ever. His powerful frame contrasted sharply to the slim build of the high king, as did his big round face with its broad forehead compared to the narrow face and long, pointed jaw line of Mithridates.

Mithridates curled his lip at Surena. 'Who's this, another one of your slave soldiers?'

I did not rise to the bait. 'This is Surena, a trusted and loyal subordinate.'

Mithridates smiled maliciously. 'Where is my brother, has he seen sense and deserted you?'

'Your stepbrother is in camp. He ate something last night that disagreed with him and feared that seeing you might make him feel worse.'

Surena laughed and Mithridates glowered at him. His eyes narrowed as he regarded Surena, no doubt making sure he remembered him.

'What do you want, Mithridates?' I asked, already growing tired of his company.

'I called this meeting,' he replied grandly, 'to save further bloodshed.'

Now it was my time to laugh. 'I would have thought the spilling of Duran blood would fill you with relish, especially mine.'

'Parthians do not engage in killing each other,' he replied haughtily, 'or at least they should not.'

He was obviously alluding to my having been responsible for the deaths of King Porus of Sakastan and King Chosroes of Mesene. The former had died fighting me in battle and the latter had taken his own life when I had stormed his city of Uruk.

'I fight only those who declare themselves to be my enemies,' I said, 'and seek to settle our differences on the battlefield. I never send assassins to do my work.'

I detected a fleeting look of alarm in Mithridates' eyes, to be instantly replaced with icy disdain. He turned to Narses.

'I told you this would be a mistake.'

Narses sighed loudly. 'He is testing, I agree. But he should hear the terms.'

Mithridates nodded and looked away from me.

'King Pacorus,' said Narses without emotion. 'You are surrounded and far from home. You must know that your position is hopeless. No one is coming to your aid. Hatra is preoccupied to the north and King Gotarzes is besieged in his city.'

'I am fully appraised of the current situation,' I said.

Narses continued. 'If you lay down your arms now we will allow you to go back to your home unmolested.'

'Back to Dura?' I enquired.

'Back to Hatra,' snapped Mithridates. 'Dura will be taken back into the empire, to be ruled directly from Ctesiphon. A loyal satrap will sit on its throne.'

I glanced at Surena, who was looking at Mithridates with venom in his eyes. 'And what of my army?'

'They will becomes slaves in the service of King of Kings Mithridates,' replied Narses. 'You, and your wife, though, will be allowed to return to your father's kingdom.'

'All except the Roman,' said Mithridates.

'The Roman?' I enquired. I knew he was talking about Domitus, but I thought I would let him talk some more. Anything to waste time.

'Yes,' leered Mithridates, 'the one who insulted me at Esfahan and who has been responsible for the deaths of so many innocent Parthians.'

Whether Mithridates had been responsible for more deaths was a moot point, but his words confirmed that he had an unending capacity for bearing grudges and hatred. He was referring to Domitus having placed his blade against the throat of one of Mithridates' companions after I had had the misfortune of meeting him in the mausoleum to Arsaces, the first Parthian king, at Esfahan many years before.

'He is the general of my army.'

'He will not be allowed to live,' said Mithridates, 'but will be put to death in the Roman fashion. You see how merciful I am, to allow him to die according to his own customs.'

'You really think I will agree to this?' I answered with incredulity.

'You might,' remarked Narses casually, 'if you knew that it would ensure that Gotarzes lives.'

What trickery was this? 'I do not understand.'

Mithridates was relishing my uncertainty. 'It is quite simple. Agree to the terms and Narses will withdraw the army from before the walls of Elymais and I will forgive Gotarzes his treachery.'

How many soldiers did they have? I had destroyed one army, only to see another spring from the desert. And now there was a third still besieging Gotarzes.

'You may yet still save your ally,' said Narses.

There followed a deafening silence as I weighed up what they offered. They knew that I would never agree to my army being disbanded and seeing its members go into slavery, much less sentence my friend and general to death. Or perhaps they thought that I was like them: calculating, ruthless and devoid of any notion of right and wrong.

'I need time to think about your offer,' was all I could say.

'You have one hour,' snapped Mithridates.

The parley was over and we returned to camp.

'Well, Surena,' I said as we walked the horses back to the entrance, the sky still showing no signs of clearing, 'what do you think of the king of kings and his lord high general?'

'They are liars, lord,' he spat with contempt. He looked at me, concern etched on his face.

'You are not going to surrender the army, lord?'

I smiled. 'No, Surena, I am not.'

Back in camp Orodes was also dismissive of his stepbrother's offer.

'He intends to starve Gotarzes into surrender anyway. There is nothing you can do.'

'Most likely he is dead already,' added Domitus, now dressed in his helmet, mail shirt and greaves.

I was toying with the idea of offering battle instead of running. Perhaps we could still be victorious, march on Ctesiphon and relieve Gotarzes. I voiced my opinion to the others. Surena thought it an excellent idea, though Domitus, Marcus and even Orodes had grave misgivings.

'Even if we beat them,' said Domitus, 'there is no guarantee that there isn't another army waiting on the other side of the Tigris.'

'You may offer battle,' added Orodes, 'but there is no guarantee that my stepbrother and Narses will accept. Most likely they will sacrifice their foot and fall back with their horse, but they could still harry us as we marched east.'

'Another battle will use up most of our water supplies, sir,' said Marcus.

By now the enemy army had moved into its positions around the camp, the foot to the west, horse archers to the north and east and the cataphracts in the south with Mithridates and Narses. There were nearly forty thousand soldiers surrounding us now. I knew that my two legions were worth three of four times the number of the enemy's foot, but I only had four thousand horsemen against nearly five times that number of enemy cavalry. I had over a thousand cataphracts and the enemy had around five thousand, to say nothing of outnumbering us five to one in horse archers.

I looked at each of their faces. I knew that if I gave the command to deploy for battle they would obey without question, and no doubt would be dead by the end of the day. I could not have that on my conscience.

'Very well,' I said, 'we stick to the plan. To your positions.'

Surena, Marcus and Domitus scurried away back to their men, though I asked Orodes to stay behind. As ever before combat he looked very serious. He was not like Surena, who regarded battle as another opportunity to acquire more glory and viewed it like a game with a few risks. Orodes drew his sword reluctantly, though in the midst of battle he was as expert at killing the enemy as the rest of us. But he always ensured that his conduct was beyond reproach at all times, even in the cauldron of combat.

'I would ask one more favour of you, my friend.'

'Anything,' he replied.

'Keep an eye on Surena. Above all do not let him do anything rash. I want him to become a good commander rather than an heroic dead one.'

'Very well,' he said quietly.

We embraced and then he went back to his men. Mithridates' 'generous' offer of an hour to resign ourselves to our fate did at least give the horsemen the opportunity to finalise their arrangements. While Surena and I had been in his company, Orodes, Marcus and Domitus had drawn up the legions and the horsemen ready for the breakout. The plan was for the two legions to charge the enemy foot drawn up beyond the western entrance to the camp while I organised a diversion at the southern side. The latter was to deceive Narses and Mithridates into thinking that I was launching an attack upon their own persons and they would hopefully rally their forces to them. That was the theory at least.

Orodes charged one of the best men in his bodyguard to take care of Remus, standing now with his scale armour covering his body, neck and head. Even his eyes had wire grills over them as protection against enemy arrows. I stroked him under his chin.

'Orodes will take care of you, and when you get back to Dura Gallia will ensure your needs are met. May Shamash protect you my faithful friend.'

I nodded to Orodes' officer who bowed his head and led Remus away towards the camp's western entrance. It was the first time that I would not ride him in battle.

Though they had been deployed to the west of the camp yesterday, today Narses' palace guard were drawn up around their king and Mithridates. This meant that the foot soldiers the legions would be attacking would not be élite troops. I thanked the gods for that.

A hundred horse archers had volunteered to remain with the legions and it was they who accompanied me on foot as I ran from the southern entrance across the open ground towards where Narses, Mithridates and their soldiers were grouped. Their cataphracts were drawn up in a long line of two ranks either side of the two kings who stood with the best foot soldiers in Persis, their bronze-faced shields presenting a wall of metal in front of a forest of spears. As we ran in one rank towards the enemy, to my right I could hear trumpet blasts coming from the camp – Domitus was attacking. We rushed across the

100

ground to within five hundred paces of the enemy, horns and kettledrums answering our trumpets.

We halted, strung arrows in our bowstrings and released them, then kept on shooting at the enemy ranks. Our arrows arched high into the sky and then dropped onto the densely packed ranks of the enemy foot. We shot at least four volleys – sixteen hundred arrows – before groups of armoured riders from each flank on either side of the foot began trotting towards us.

'Back to camp!' I screamed. Then we were running as though all the demons in hell were snapping at our heels. Behind us the cataphracts broke into a canter and lowered their lances. Perhaps Narses himself was leading them. I saw the camp's entrance ahead, my heart pounding in my chest. Don't look back; keep moving; run faster! I heard the thunder of iron-shod hooves getting closer and the shouts of men on horseback closing on their quarry. We dropped our quivers as we neared the wide gap in the earth rampart and ran into the camp with only seconds to spare. As we did so groups of legionaries either side of us and on top of the rampart next to the entrance hurled caltrops into the gap. These comprised three stakes that were ordinarily used to construct the palisade around the camp lashed together with wire to form a three-headed stake. Where only half minute before there had been a gap wide enough for twelve men to march through abreast, there now stood a thick carpet of caltrops.

The enemy's horses panicked and either tried to veer aside or pull up sharply to avoid crashing into the caltrops. Those behind smashed into the front ranks as dozens of horses and their riders were caught up in a giant, tangled press. Some horses reared up on their hind legs and threw their riders to the ground, to be trampled by other animals behind. It was chaos and I wished that I had fresh archers to shoot arrows into the faces of the horsemen and the unarmoured bellies of horses as they reared up, but all I had was a hundred men who stood panting and slapping each other on the back at their escape from the clutches of the enemy. More legionaries ran onto the rampart and hurled their javelins at the disorganised mass of horsemen. Most glanced off scale armour harmlessly; a few found flesh. Finding their way barred, the enemy officers reasserted control and began to pull their men back. They retreated out of arrow and javelin range and re-dressed their ranks. There were few empty saddles but, more importantly, we had created a diversion and given the army at the camp's western entrance time to carry out its attack unhindered.

The Romans call it *cuneus*, meaning 'wedge', and as the attention of Mithridates, Narses and the cream of their horsemen was focused on what was happening immediately to their front, the Duran Legion and the Exiles were pouring out of the western entrance of the camp, straight into the enemy's foot. Each legion charged at the enemy in one long column, each one made up of dozens of ranks of six men.

Immediately before they charged at the enemy a barrage of missiles was unleashed by the ballista operated by Marcus and his men. These had been placed on the ramparts either side of the western entrance. The smaller ballista were essentially over-sized and over-powered bows fixed horizontally on wooden stands that shot bolts, stones and solid metal balls over great distances.

The charge of the Durans and Exiles was a foregone conclusion, made quicker as the enemy actually advanced towards the camp and then stopped abruptly when ballista ammunition began tearing into their tightly packed ranks, some bolts and balls taking heads off and showering those around with bone and gore. Soon the ranks faltered and then fractured as some men attempted to turn around and run from the horror that was being visited upon them, while others tried to press on with their attack. And then they were hit by the legions.

Two great columns of men resembling a pair of great armoured serpents slithered out of camp towards them, the front two ranks gripping their lethal short swords tight to their bodies while those behind held their javelins at the ready. The ballista stopped shooting as the head of each column reached the enemy's battered front rank. And then the slaughter began.

As the front ranks of the enemy stood transfixed by the snarling and screaming legionaries running at them, the sky was suddenly filled with other missiles as the men behind the front two ranks hurled their javelins forward. Ever since I had first encountered them in Italy I had been fascinated by the Roman javelin, a spear that bent upon impact, making it impossible for an enemy to throw it back. And now dozens of javelins embedded themselves in enemy flesh, felling dozens. And then the legionaries went to work with their swords, stabbing upwards into thighs and bellies and over the rims of their shields into faces.

I was told later that the two columns went through the enemy like a *gladius* through a linen shirt. On the legionaries went and the enemy was glad to get out of their way, fleeing left and right before them. So the Durans and Exiles prised apart the enemy, herding them into two disorganised and dispirited blocks, one to the north and the other to the south. In the middle the two columns of legionaries pushed their way forward until they had broken clear through the enemy. And then they stopped. Trumpets blasted and the Durans and Exiles halted as one. Whereas the enemy foot was a mass of frightened and confused men, the Durans and Exiles retained their discipline and cohesion. Train hard, fight easy.

The Duran Legion formed the northern column and the Exiles the southern one. The trumpeters of both formations now sounded again and as one the Durans faced right to present a wall of shields to the enemy that had been barged aside and herded in a northwards direction like a flock of sheep. At the same time the Exiles faced left to prepare to advance against the second mass of enemy soldiers. Different trumpet blasts signalled a general advance, followed by another hail of javelins as both legions once more hurled their missiles at the enemy, the squeals and cries announcing that the latter's ranks had been culled once more. Then the legions advanced north and south respectively, literally herding the enemy before them and creating a wide corridor behind them. Then Orodes led his horsemen out of the camp.

The corridor that had been created by the foot was wide enough to allow the Prince of Susiana to deploy his cataphracts in a great wedge formation, he and his bodyguard forming the point, the banners of Susiana and Dura fluttering behind him as he led the horsemen into the desert. Behind the cataphracts came the squires leading camels loaded with food, fodder, full water skins, spare arrows, weapons and clothing, plus the camels of the ammunition train. Either side of the squires, providing flank protection, rode two great columns of horse archers, each one riding parallel to the rear of the legions. As they did so they shot volleys of arrows over the legionaries into the ranks of the enemy foot soldiers, causing them to fall back further. Surena came last with the rear guard – a thousand horse archers following in the wake of the other riders.

The enemy's attention had been first focused on what was happening at the southern entrance to the camp, especially after I led a hundred archers to pepper the enemy with missiles. The great number of horse archers deployed to the east and north of the camp remained immobile when the legions attacked from the camp's western entrance. Now, as I ran with the other archers and those legionaries that had been detailed to support us to join the departing legions, the enemy horse archers began to move. Those to the north of the camp, obviously alerted by couriers to what was happening to the west, endeavoured to assault the Duran Legion. Fortunately for the Durans the enemy foot soldiers that had been herded north acted as a barrier between them and the horse archers.

By the time Narses had realised what was happening Orodes and the cavalry and camels were galloping west into the desert, leaving the legions to redeploy into a giant hollow square as it inched its way northwest, towards Hatran territory. I caught up with them as enemy horse archers forced their way into the empty camp via the eastern entrance. Everything had been packed into the wagons and on mules, which were now positioned around the inner sides of the hollow square.

The enemy cavalry had ridden out into the desert to try and catch Orodes, but had been recalled. The first part of the plan had worked –

my horsemen had been saved. But then the grim realisation dawned on me that I plus thousands of others were now surrounded by around forty thousand enemy troops. Orodes may have escaped but our ordeal was only just beginning.

Chapter 5

I watched the great dust cloud thrown up by Orodes and his horsemen and camels grow smaller as they rapidly disappeared into the west. By contrast the pace of our great hollow square was painfully slow, literally inching its way to the northwest like an injured crab. I took up position on the southern side of the square, the men on all four sides having adopted what the Romans call a *testudo* formation. Derived from the Latin word for 'tortoise', it refers to the legionaries locking their oval shields together to the front and overhead as a protection against enemy missiles. So our massive tortoise crawled across the desert, five cohorts on each side of the square presenting a solid and impenetrable wall and roof of shields all the way round.

I felt like an unwanted guest at a banquet. I had no shield, no *gladius* and no use as I walked behind a wagon of cooking utensils with the other archers. All the wagons had been arranged so they 'hugged' each side of the square, which meant that there was a massive empty space in the centre of the square. Already the pungent smell of mules and their dung filled the warm air. I looked up and saw that the sun was finally breaking through the clouds. It was now mid-morning and the temperature was rising. It was going to be a long day.

Centurions and officers stalked around like hungry wolves, cajoling and encouraging their men. I saw Domitus strolling down the western side of the square, occasionally stopping and sharing a joke with some of the men and encouraging others. Alcaeus joined him as they made their way over to me. Thus far our progress had been relatively straightforward and unimpeded.

'Orodes made good his escape, then,' said Domitus.

'It would appear so,' I replied. 'Did we lose many men in the fight earlier?'

He spat out a fly that had flown into his mouth. 'A dozen killed, five wounded. The ballista shattered their morale before we even hit them.'

'How are the wounded?' I asked Alcaeus.

'Those who can walk are accompanying the wagons that are carrying those too sick to use their legs.'

He had no helmet or mail shirt and carried only his medical bag slung over his shoulder.

'You should get a mail shirt and helmet,' I told him. 'It's quiet now, but soon the enemy will send their horse archers against us.'

'In which case,' he replied, 'I shall shelter under the shield of a legionary.'

'I would take Pacorus' advice,' said Domitus. 'When they begin shooting the air will be thick with arrows.'

'In that case, Domitus,' quipped Alcaeus, 'I shall be able to work in the shade.'

'I could order you to wear a helmet,' I said.

He screwed up his face. 'And I could refuse, but I am touched that you are both so concerned about my welfare.'

He smiled and then walked off back to his medical wagons.

'He's impossible,' grumbled Domitus.

'But a good doctor,' I replied.

It was as if the enemy had disappeared as thousands of hobnailed sandals tramped across the barren ground. The thousands of mules grunted and the oxen pulling the wagons containing Marcus' siege engines lowered. Only a few puffy clouds filled the sky now and the sun was beating down on us and heating the earth. I was beginning to think that our trek would be unmolested when from the south I heard the infernal din of kettledrums and the sound of horns. Then the earth began to shake and I knew that we were under attack.

Narses sent in his horse archers first, a great torrent of horseflesh that swept around us and unleashed volley after volley of arrows against the square. The drivers of the wagons dived for cover under their vehicles, while the walking wounded sought shelter beneath the shields of the legionaries. Parthians use a variety of arrowheads, ranging from leaf-shaped to those with grooves for the application of poison, but the most common variety is the bronze three-winged arrowhead. And it was these that were loosed against the edges of the square.

At first horsemen rode parallel to each side of the square, shooting arrows as they did so. Discharging up to five arrows a minute, each side of the square was peppered with thousands of arrows in a matter of minutes. For those on the receiving end of this barrage it was truly nerve-wracking, arrows slamming into shields like raindrops hitting a tile roof in a thunderstorm. It was an impressive display of mass archery and against typical Parthian foot soldiers would have been devastating. Unfortunately for Narses he had sent his horse archers against men who knew how to counter his tactics. Before the first charge of his horse archers had been made the trumpets had sounded a halt and then signalled to defend against arrow attack. The men deployed on each side of the square as one all knelt down. The first rank formed an unbroken shield wall while those behind lifted their shields above their heads to form a forward-sloping roof of leather and wood to counter the arrow rain that fell on them. The front ranks also rested one end of their javelins on the ground and held them at an angle of forty-five degrees to present a line of points to deter the enemy horsemen from getting too close.

We all knelt and prayed as whooping, cheering and screaming horse archers emptied their quivers against us. Each shield weighs over twenty pounds and it was testimony to the strength and stamina of the Durans and Exiles that they were able to hold them in place while the horse archers lapped around the square. Each leather-faced shield was identical – three layers of wood glued together with the grain of each layer fitted at right angles to the preceding layer to make it harder to cut through. Wooden reinforcing strips added to the back further increased its defensive capabilities.

The first attack was noisy, frightening and largely ineffective and covered us all in choking dust. There was little time to celebrate, however, as more horns calls announced a second assault against us. This time the horse archers ignored the wall and roof of shields on each side of the formation and shot their arrows high into the sky so they fell inside the square itself. The central area of the square was empty but around its edges were grouped the wagons and the mules pulling them. Once more arrows thudded harmlessly into shields but others hit mules and caused a dreadful carnage. We lost four hundred animals in that second attack, some killed outright and others being grievously wounded as they were struck by a number of arrows. Some went mad with the pain and bolted in a vain effort to escape their tormentors, succeeding only in colliding into wagons in front of them and suffering more wounds. A few ran into the rear of the cohorts and nearly caused the formation to rupture. Only a few quick-thinking centurions saved the day, using their swords to kill the beasts outright and stop their rampage.

The square held but it required great efforts on the part of the drivers, those who hadn't been crushed under the wheels when their beasts bolted, to get their animals under control.

The enemy horse archers retreated to regroup and fill their quivers, giving us time to take stock of the situation. I called a meeting of the senior officers to ascertain whether we could continue the march. Domitus was not optimistic.

'As soon as we start marching again they will be back.'

'We can't stay here forever,' I said.

'Perhaps we may march through the night, majesty.'

Kronos, the man who had spoken, was the commander of the Exiles. Having just entered his forties, he had spent fifteen years fighting under King Mithridates of Pontus against the Romans and had been one of the first to present himself at Dura following Rome's victory over that land. Thereafter thousands of his countrymen had made their way south from their homeland, through Armenia and into my father's kingdom. Many made their way south on hearing that the King of Dura, the man who was the enemy of Rome, was raising an army and needed veteran soldiers.

'That is not a bad idea, Kronos,' I replied. 'Parthians do not like fighting at night. Perhaps we can steal away under cover of darkness.'

Domitus was not convinced. 'Except that Narses will surround us with his army. As soon as they realise we are on the march they will be alerted and will be standing to arms, regardless of whether it is night or day.'

Such was the contempt that everyone had for Mithridates that no one mentioned his name, despite the fact that he was technically in command of the enemy horde. No one liked Narses but they at least respected his military ability.

'If they try the same tactics as the last attack,' said a concerned Marcus, 'we will undoubtedly lose more mules and oxen, which means we will not be able to move all the wagons.'

'Our priorities,' I told him, 'are the wounded, water and food. After that, your siege engines and the spare weapons. The tents, tools and spare clothing we can do without if need be.'

'How much water do we have?' Domitus asked Marcus.

'Enough for five more days.'

We all looked at him. Unimpeded we could march a hundred miles in that time. Surrounded and under constant attack we would be able to cover barely half that distance, probably less.

'It would be best to drain the dead mules of their blood so we can drink it,' remarked Kronos.

Compact and muscular, Kronos was actually shorter than Domitus but his lack of height did not detract from his martial bearing nor his great intelligence.

'A veritable feast for us all,' remarked Alcaeus dryly. 'Unfortunately I will need additional water to keep the wounds of the injured clean, Pacorus.'

I drew the meeting to a close. 'Very well, we will drink dead mule blood and cook their flesh tonight. Keep the situation regarding the water supplies to yourselves but enforce strict water discipline.'

There were no more attacks that day, the enemy content to make camp at a distance of a mile all around us. The blood drained from the mules tasted disgusting though their cooked flesh was palatable enough. The men rested and slept where they had fought in their ranks earlier that day. Sentries were posted every ten paces a hundred paces beyond the outer edges of the square and were relieved every hour.

The mood among the men was subdued but not bordering on despair. To date they had tasted nothing but victory, and though they had been forced to retreat they had still beaten off the enemy. I walked among as many as I could, clasping arms and sharing stories. All of us were aware of the glow of the opposition's campfires that seemed unending as they stretched into the distance, and which indicated the enemy's great strength. I wondered if Narses had received reinforcements during the day – he must have emptied the whole of Persis and Sakastan.

An hour after midnight I stood with my arms folded staring south at what I assumed to be the camp of Mithridates and Narses. They had played their hand expertly. I thought of Gotarzes and my stomach turned. How could I assist him now? I prayed that he could hold out until… Until what? I felt wretched.

'Spartacus used to do that.' I recognised the deep voice of Domitus. I turned to see him standing beside me. 'Do what?'

'Stalk around the camp like a wraith and stand in the dark with his arms folded. You do a good impression of him.'

'I'm glad I amuse you, Domitus.'

'All right. What's the matter?'

I kicked at the earth. 'I feel helpless.'

'Ah, I see. You find the new sensation distasteful.'

I had no idea what he was alluding to. 'What sensation?'

'The sensation of having to dance to the enemy's tune. Up to now you have dictated what happens on the battlefield, more or less, now the sandal's on the other foot.'

'Nonsense,' I snapped.

He placed his hand on my shoulder. 'It is not nonsense. Just because you have been out-manoeuvred does not mean that you have lost the war. You have saved your horsemen and we are in good order.'

'Far from home and surrounded,' I added bitterly.

'All we have to do is hold our nerve, Pacorus. There is an old Roman saying: it doesn't matter how many battles you lose as long as you win the final one.'

The next day we marched before dawn and before the enemy was in the saddle. Of the enemy foot we saw nothing and I suspected that they had been sent back to Ctesiphon and then probably Elymais. We managed to march five miles before the enemy horse archers attacked once more and again they caused few casualties but did manage to kill a couple of hundred mules. We adopted the same tactics and presented a continuous wall and roof of shields to the enemy, against which their arrows had little effect. Nevertheless, once again we were forced to halt and stand under the spring sun.

Night came and once more the enemy's campfires illuminated the darkness. I was comforted by the thought that Orodes would have reached the Euphrates by now and would be riding north back to Dura. Once more we drank mule blood and ate their roasted meat. We set off northwest again before dawn.

The enemy showed no great desire to launch their attacks during the early part of the day, being content to allow us to cover around ten miles before sending their horse archers against us. But Narses knew that we were using up our water supplies and he was doing enough to slow our rate of advance.

'Narses is a clever bastard, I'll give him that.' Domitus smiled at me. He looked as bad as I felt, his face unshaven and his arms and tunic smeared with dirt. We sat on stools next to a wagon that had a number of arrows sticking in it. I pulled one out and began turning over the bronze head in my hand.

'I still think a night march might be advantageous, majesty,' urged Kronos.

'Perhaps not a night march but a night attack,' I replied.

'The boys are tired,' said Domitus. 'They can't fight all day and at night as well.'

'You are right, Domitus. But I only need a dozen.'

He looked at me in confusion. 'A dozen?'

I stood up and pointed at him with the arrowhead. 'What did you say about me having to dance to Narses' tune? Well, I think it is time that he danced to mine.'

Half an hour later I was squatting in a circle with a dozen volunteers, including Thumelicus and Domitus, each of us having smeared our faces and tunics with charcoal from the ashes of a fire. Even our sword blades had been blackened with charcoal and we wore nothing on our heads. We looked like a bunch of filthy miners. It was now an hour past midnight.

Domitus looked at each of them.

'Before we leave make sure you are wearing nothing that jangles when you move.'

The pavilions of Mithridates and Narses had thus far always been positioned to the south of our position, and I gambled that tonight they would be in the same spot. That was the direction we would head to sow a little terror in the hearts of the enemy. As we exited our square, crouching low, we scampered across the featureless terrain towards the enemy camp. I prayed to Shamash that our efforts would not be wasted.

A massive moon illuminated the landscape, its great pale surface smeared with grey blotches and filling the cloudless night sky. We advanced in two files. Domitus led one and I the other. The night was cool but I was sweating as we neared the enemy sentries. I slowed and then eased myself onto my belly to crawl forward. I glanced at Domitus who was likewise prostrate on the ground, those behind us following our example. There were two sentries standing directly ahead. I looked right and left and saw the figures of two other sentries perhaps a hundred paces away. The two ahead were wrapped in their cloaks and seemed to be deep in conversation.

We crawled to within fifty paces of the sentries ahead and stopped. My heart pounded in my chest so loudly that I thought the sound might alert the guards. As yet we were undiscovered but the night was so still and bright that it would be only a matter of time before we were spotted. I looked over at Domitus and pointed at him, then at the guards and then drew my finger across my neck. He nodded and assumed a crouching position. I did the same. Then we rushed them.

We did not run but rather adopted a quick scuttling pace as we neared our prey, clutching our swords as we did so. They were still wrapped tightly in their cloaks, deep in conversation when we reached them. One opened his mouth in surprise as Domitus rammed the point of his *gladius* into his throat. I grabbed the other's neck from behind and thrust my sword through his back. He thrashed wildly around for a few seconds as his life ebbed away, blood sheeting from the wound.

'Take off his cloak,' I whispered to Domitus as I pulled the cloak off my dead sentry.

Domitus did so and then used his free arm to beckon the others over. We left two behind wrapped in the dead men's cloaks so as not to arouse suspicion when the other guards on duty looked for their companions, then continued on towards the enemy camp. I did not know when the guards would be relieved, perhaps an hour, perhaps less. Perhaps in a few minutes' time. In which case our little venture would be compromised.

There was no order in the enemy camp, no neat rows of shelters with sentries patrolling in between, just a huge collection of round tents of various sizes stretching as far as the eye could see. Beside some of them were large corrals holding horses, others containing camels. We moved in the shadows cast by the tents as we ventured deeper into the enemy compound. A guard stood urinating against the side of a tent. Servants, slaves most likely, huddled in groups round fires at the entrance to the animal pens, while others slept on the ground outside a great field kitchen. Suddenly, around a hundred paces away in front of us, a massive pavilion appeared.

The front entrance of the pavilion was illuminated by a row of small, lighted braziers perched on stands extending out from the ornate canopy. Sentries were standing on guard in front of them. They wore helmets, were armed with long spears and their hide-covered shields sported the symbol of an eagle clutching a snake. This was the tent of Mithridates, not Narses. The King of Persis must be located elsewhere in the camp, or perhaps he had returned to oversee the siege of Elymais. I dismissed the notion; he would ensure that we were defeated before he left the area.

Thus far we had penetrated the enemy's camp unseen but I knew that the chances of remaining invisible would diminish the longer we remained. We had to act fast. We huddled in the middle of a host of large four-wheeled wagons positioned near the pavilion. No doubt they were used to carry the great tent and its furnishings when the army was on the march.

The others kept watch as I knelt on the ground and whispered to Domitus.

111

'The guards have the symbol of Mithridates on their shields,' I said. 'He must be inside.'

'All nicely tucked up in bed, no doubt,' grinned Domitus. 'What do you want to do?'

'We can't waste any more time wandering around looking for Narses. We go after Mithridates.'

A couple of minutes later we were moving very stealthily around the pavilion to access its rear. Guards were posted at regular intervals all the way round its edge, forcing us to take a wide detour into a corral holding sleeping camels. The pavilion was on our right now as we crawled through the animal enclosure, the beasts grunting in annoyance at our presence but otherwise letting us pass. I reached forward and put my palm into a pile of dung and dunked my knee in the same pile of filth as we left the animal pen and crawled to the rear of the pavilion.

Like all the great pavilions of Parthian kings this one was oval shaped. The main entrance opened into a reception area where guests and dignitaries assembled before being ushered into the dining area, usually a vast space housing couches, cushions and carpets. Next came the throne room, always separated from the dining area by curtains. Here on a dais the king presided on his throne. His commanders, advisers, courtiers and priests would gather around him. Finally, to the rear of the throne room, were the private chambers where the king slept, his concubines, friends and most trusted guards being quartered around him.

We grouped together as I stared at the rear entrance to the pavilion, which was also heavily guarded. How to get in? I wiped my nose on my sleeve and caked my face in camel dung. Damn! Of course, the camels.

'Wait here,' I hissed at the others then went back to where the camels were sleeping. The fence that surrounded the pen was a makeshift affair of wooden posts hammered into the ground with two horizontal poles slotted into holes in their sides. I pulled out the horizontals in between two posts to create a gap through which a camel could just about squeeze through. I grabbed the bridle of one of the mangy beasts and pulled him forward. He grunted, spat at me and then got to his feet. I led him through the gap in the fence towards where Domitus and the others were crouching. I pulled my *spatha* and prodded his rump with it whereupon he bellowed and raced forward towards the tent.

As the beast neared the tent he suddenly veered to the right to avoid crashing into it. Immediately several of the guards left their posts and chased after it.

'Now,' I shouted and ran across the ground to reach the unguarded side of the pavilion.

Royal pavilions are made from canvas, a durable and waterproof material that is also easy to cut. Domitus and I slashed at it with our swords to create an entry and then we threw ourselves inside into a space packed with musical instruments. I glimpsed a throne on a dais. Outside I could hear shouts and curses as the guards chased after the runaway camel. We moved along the canvas wall to a yellow curtain barring the entrance to the private apartments. I eased it aside slightly to spy behind it. Clutching my sword in one hand I gestured to the others to follow me. We did not have much time now, as the rip in the pavilion's sidewall would soon be discovered.

I pushed the curtain aside and stepped into a small area that smelt of incense and roasted meat. Ahead were more curtains, these ones blue edged with gold.

At that moment the curtains parted and two male servants appeared dressed in red tunics and baggy blue leggings carrying silver wine jugs. They froze when they saw us – ten filthy, wild men with swords in their hands.

It was at times like this that I thanked Shamash for the wits of Lucius Domitus, for without thinking he raced forward and plunged his *gladius* into the chest of one of the servants, yanked it free and then slashed it across the throat of the other in a great scything movement that sprayed blood over the luxurious red carpets. He turned, fire in his eyes. 'Move!'

We ran at the curtains, pushing aside the flimsy linen material to enter the private reception area of the king of kings. Oil lamps were hanging from four parallel lines of tent poles. We saw a large table in the centre and couches at the far end. I could hear moaning and shouts.

The two guards that had allowed the servants to pass through the curtains were the first to die as we burst in. We ran at the other guards who were standing by the poles, each one armed with a short spear with a great burnished blade at its tip. They held hide-covered shields painted white, the motif of an eagle clutching a snake decorating them. These were the élite palace guards of Ctesiphon and they knew how to handle their weapons.

There were a dozen of them in total and after the initial shock of our appearance, during which two more had died on our sword points, they came at us with shields held close to their bodies and spears levelled. One stood before me and jabbed his spear at me, attempting to skewer me on its point. He was as tall as me, broader but very light on his feet, pouncing to and fro and attacking me like a wildcat. He jabbed at me again, thrusting the spear point at my chest. I brought my sword arm up and across my body and then slashed it down, the metal cutting through the spear shaft and severing the head. He threw the broken shaft at me and attempted to draw his own sword. But I was too fast for him, thrusting my sword forward at his chest. His reflexes were also quick and he managed to stop the blow with his shield. In the instant when the point went into the hide and wood underneath I pulled my dagger from its sheath and rammed it hard into his face, the point going through his right eye socket. I withdraw it and yanked my sword free as he slumped to the floor. I ran forward as one of my men was impaled on an enemy spear in front of me. As he fell I ran his killer through with my sword.

I looked round and saw Thumelicus finishing off the last surviving guard with ease, dumfounding him with a series of lightning-fast sword attacks that finished with his *gladius* slicing deep into the man's belly. I nodded to him and he returned the gesture. We had lost two dead but had at last found our prey.

I ran forward and ripped aside one of the two silk curtains barring the entrance to the bedroom of the king of kings, the ruler of the mighty Parthian Empire. And stopped dead in my tracks. Standing ahead, naked and sweating profusely, was Mithridates. I say standing but I could not properly tell since he was behind a naked slave girl down on all fours. He was holding her long hair tightly as he rammed his manhood hard into her from behind. He was obviously performing an unnatural act upon her young body as her face was contorted with pain and tears were running down her cheeks. Two young men, both oiled and naked, were kneeling either side of Mithridates, one of whom was licking his chest. All around naked couples were writhing in ecstasy on the plush carpets covering the floor and on the giant circular bed. And then the screaming started.

While I stared in disbelief at the orgy before my eye, Domitus raced forward tripping over one of the couples on the floor. Both young boys started to screech at this dirt-encrusted demon sprawling onto the floor beside them. Domitus sprang to his feet and slit both their throats without further ado. The room erupted in screams and wails as teenage boys and girls, all naked, ran around as though they were demented. Mithridates stopped his act of depravity and for a few seconds stared at me in disbelief, unable to comprehend that anyone, not least his greatest enemy, would dare to violate his inner sanctum.

Whistles blew behind us and I knew that the game was up. More soldiers were coming to save their king.

'Kill the bastard,' screamed Domitus.

Thumelicus hurled one of the dead guards' spears at Mithridates, but he grabbed the long hair of one of the boy lovers next to him and thrust his young body in front of his. The spear blade went clean through the youth's chest, killing him instantly. One of the girls, completely naked and completely hairless, sprang at Domitus like a demon from hell, scratching at his eyes and shrieking as she did so. He head-butted her and split her nose, causing her to collapse on the

114

floor. Another of my men tried to spear Mithridates but he was again too quick and threw himself to the floor. The young girl he had been violating, still on her knees, looked up as the spear went through her mouth and out through the base of her skull.

I heard screams behind me and saw two of my men being run through by enemy spearmen.

'Time to go,' shouted Domitus.

We ran across the bedroom and slashed at the silk drapes behind the bed as more soldiers flooded into the room.

'Kill them, kill them all,' screamed Mithridates, standing naked with two dead bodies at his feet.

Fortunately the hysterical boys and girls were still behaving like possessed beings and got in the way of the guards chasing after us. Six of us cut our way out to exit the rear of the pavilion.

Mithridates was screaming at us as we left. 'You are dead, filth. You hear me. Either tonight or tomorrow all of you will be dead. And then I will raze that rat-hole Dura to the ground. You are dead, Pacorus, and so is your whore wife and your children. Kill them!'

We killed the guards standing outside the part of the pavilion side we had cut through and then skirted the camel pen before heading north back to camp. Whistles, shouts and horns were now sounding the alarm and causing hundreds of men to rush to their assembly points. Horses whinnied and camels grunted as we threaded our way through the gathering throng. The general chaos was to our advantage because in the dark we were just another group of bleary-eyed soldiers endeavouring to form up.

The guards who had come to the aid of Mithridates were still on our heels however, and as we left the perimeter of the camp I glanced behind to see at least a score of them coming after us. The two men we had left at the perimeter saw us coming and prepared to face our pursuers.

'Get back to camp,' I screamed at them. There was no need for them to die this night. They did as they were ordered.

The sentries to our right and left saw what was happening and responded to the orders being yelled at them by our pursuers and headed in our direction, hoping to cut us off. Two were running at us from the right and another two from the left, and then I heard a hissing sound in my right ear, then another. Arrows!

We were beyond the camp's furthest sentry line now and I could see the glow of our own braziers ahead. Arrows whistled past me and others hit the ground with a phut. Then I heard a shriek and turned to see one of my men tumbling to the ground. I stopped immediately and went to his assistance. Domitus also halted and came to my side. The man had an arrow in his hamstring. We were now around a hundred paces or so from our own camp and I could see the sentries standing and pointing at us. I put my left arm around the wounded man's back and heaved him onto his feet. Arrows felled another two of my men as they turned and came to stand by Domitus and me. Then the enemy archers stopped their shooting for fear of hitting their own men as they bore down on us from three directions. I had to drop the wounded man as we prepared to receive their attack.

I heard grunts and saw the sentries on our flanks pitch forward onto the ground, and then saw more enemy soldiers to our front fall as arrows hit them. I turned to see two centuries running towards us.

'Are you going to stand there gawping or are you going to get behind us?' the voice of Drenis bellowed at us.

'Back,' I shouted. Thumelicus and I helped the wounded man to his feet once more and then we fled as the centuries parted and then closed behind us. Their shields then locked to form a wall and roof of wood and leather. We crouched behind the last rank as Drenis came to our side. Behind us the hundred archers who had stayed with the legions walked back to camp.

'Very thoughtful of you, Drenis' said Domitus calmly, 'to organise a reception party.'

Drenis winked at me. 'I knew you would stir up a hornets' nest. Do you want us to finish them off?'

'No,' I replied. 'Let's get back to camp.'

'Fall back! Fall back!' shouted Drenis and he and his men inched their way rearwards.

A few arrows thudded into our shields but the enemy, now greatly outnumbered, lost heart and trudged back to their naked king.

When we reached the safety of our lines a crowd quickly gathered round us, eager for news. Domitus wasted no time in telling how we had reached the sleeping quarters of Mithridates.

'Not that he was doing much sleeping. He was humping everything in sight. Pacorus was worried that he might pounce on him, you should have seen the fear in his eyes.'

Riotous laughter. Drenis handed him a water bottle to slake his thirst, then Domitus continued.

'I've never seen so much naked flesh and Mithridates was using his pork lance to spear it all.'

He put an arm round my shoulder. 'He must have thought Pacorus was another pretty young boy come to satisfy his needs.'

Wild cheering.

I raised my arms to still the commotion. 'Thank you, Domitus, for your most graphic account of the raid. Unfortunately Mithridates still lives and will send everything he has against us later today.'

'Let's hope he remembers to get dressed before he does,' shouted Thumelicus. More cheering and laughter.

116

I smiled. Their morale was still high despite us being many miles from home, almost out of water and surrounded and outnumbered by the enemy. I looked to the east and saw the first shards of light on the horizon. Dawn would be breaking soon. There would be no time for any rest or sleep now. Domitus dismissed the men and Alcaeus attended to the wounded man we had brought back. The wagons that he had commandeered for the injured were grouped in the southeast corner of the camp. Those men who were too sick to walk had been carried in them under protective wooden roofs. At night they were moved to tents that they shared with the walking wounded. Despite the care of his medical staff a few had succumbed to their wounds and Alcaeus feared that with each passing day more would die.

'I have lost fifty thus far and another ten or so won't see tomorrow's dawn.'

'What about the man we brought back tonight?' I asked.

'He'll live. I gave him some sarpagandha to make him drowsy and I extracted the arrow and bound the wound.'

As the dim pre-dawn light began to engulf the camp Alcaeus yawned and stretched his aching limbs. Like all of us he was unshaven and had black rings round his eyes. His tunic, usually immaculately white, was torn and smeared with blood.

'So,' he asked me, 'how do you rate our chances?'

'Well, if Malik has reached Hatran territory then he would have sent a message to Dura and hopefully the lords will come. If Byrd got to Babylon safely then perhaps Vardan will send troops to aid us. And if Babylon has been alerted then Nergal at Uruk will not abandon us.'

He had a bemused look on his face. 'That's a lot of ifs.'

I slapped him on the arm. 'You should have more faith, Alcaeus.'

'I use to pray to Zeus every day when I was young, asking him to protect my parents and my city. But my parents were killed and the Romans enslaved me and I stopped asking the gods for anything. I'm not sure they even exist.'

'Of course they exist, Alcaeus. How else can you explain all that has happened to us, of our time in Italy and our journey back to Parthia? Then making Dura strong? There must be divine guidance involved.'

He smiled at me. 'Or it could be that you are a great warlord who has done all these things on your own. But if it comforts you to believe that there is a god smiling down on you, then that is good.'

He suddenly looked very serious. 'In case the opportunity does not arrive later, I want to thank you, Pacorus, for my time in Dura. It has been a privilege to be your friend.'

I had the feeling that he was saying goodbye. 'None of that, Alcaeus, we are not dead yet.'

117

He looked around at the tents where the wounded were sleeping and the wagons standing ready to carry the seriously hurt. The sun was beginning its ascent in the eastern sky. The new day was dawning.

'You know what gives this army strength, Pacorus?'

'Ten thousand foot and four thousand horse?' I replied.

He shook his head. 'No. It's pride. Every man is proud to be a part of your army. Numbers are irrelevant. Each man stands tall in the ranks beside his comrades, knowing that you will never be careless with his life, will never ask him to do what you yourself would not attempt. That is why this army is strong, because you treat your soldiers like men, not slaves. They are proud to serve in Dura's army.'

'Well, then, we have nothing to worry about. You said it yourself – numbers are irrelevant.'

A wry smile crept over his face. 'Even men of iron need water, Pacorus.'

He offered me his hand and we clasped each other's forearm.

'They will not break us, Alcaeus. I swear it.'

But they tried. An hour later the enemy attacked us on all sides. First they sent in their horse archers, who once again rained arrows down on us. Yet again they did not shoot at the ring of shields but instead loosed their missiles in a high trajectory that fell behind the cohorts. And once again they slaughtered dozens of mules, the animals crying pitifully after they had been hit. We could do nothing but stand and listen to their squeals and moans. After a while the horse archers mercifully withdrew and a lull descended over the battlefield.

I was kneeling with the other archers in the rear of the cohorts deployed on the southern edge of our hollow square, holding a shield over my head. Its top edge was tucked under the shield of the man in front of me. Trumpets blasted to order the men to stand easy and a great clatter signalled thousands of men resting their shields on the ground. They had had their meagre ration of water earlier and there was none to spare until they wet their lips in the evening. Those that lived.

Domitus and Kronos came over to where I was standing, my shield lying on the ground. Domitus pointed at it.

'Please pick it up and rest it against your body. It has just saved your life so treat it with some respect.'

I felt myself blushing as I bent down and did as I was told, resting the edge against my body. Around me other legionaries were nudging each other and grinning at my being rebuked.

'That was short and sweet,' said Domitus.

'Yesterday they spent hours showering us with the bloody things,' added Kronos, freezing the grinning soldiers with his iron stare. They quickly faced front.

I slammed the rim of my shield with my palm. 'They've run out of arrows.'

'What?' Domitus was most surprised.

'They have run out of arrows. That is the only reason they have pulled back the horse archers.'

In Dura's army a great camel train carrying tens of thousands of spare arrows always accompanied the horse archers. But most Parthian armies save my own and Hatra's did not bother to supply its archers with spare ammunition. After all the main striking power of an army was its cataphracts. The role of the horse archers was to weaken the enemy before the heavy horsemen attacked.

'They will send in their heavy horsemen next,' I said. 'If they had not run out of arrows then they would have spent more time softening us up.'

'There aren't enough arrows in the world to soften up my boys,' growled Domitus, prompting Kronos to smile in approval.

Their little mutual admiration society was interrupted by the sound of kettledrums to the south. Trumpets blasted and once again the legionaries dressed their ranks and stood facing outwards. With Domitus and Kronos I pushed my way through the ranks to see what was happening. Men were twisting arrows from their shields and the ground in front of the first rank was littered with missiles. I peered ahead and in the early morning light saw the horizon filled with horsemen riding knee to knee. Cataphracts!

Narses and Mithridates did not have enough heavy horsemen to assault our square on all four sides, so they were gambling on one large attack against one of its sides. If they broke through then they would destroy the army, for behind them would come thousands of horse archers. Domitus realised this also.

'So,' he said, 'it all comes down to us holding off their heavy horsemen.'

'Do you want me to reinforce this part of the line with some of my lads?' asked Kronos.

Domitus shook his head. 'No, if we weaken one part of the line they might throw in any reserves they have at it. We wait until they hit us and see what happens.'

He slapped me on the arm. 'I wish we had Orodes with us.'

'Me too,' I said.

We went back through the ranks as the legionaries stood up and locked their shields together to present a wall of white shields once again. The horsemen became more widely spaced as they trotted towards us, each man bringing down his *kontus* on his right side and grasping it with both hands. The charge of thousands of cataphracts is a magnificent sight; the sun glinting off lance points, scale armour and helmets and the ground shaking as tens of thousands of iron-shod hooves race across the earth. It is also terrifying for those standing in its way. Ordinary Parthian foot soldiers would have crumbled long before the horsemen reached them. But the men standing in the path of the cataphracts were not ordinary soldiers. They had spent years training not only in perfecting their own drills but also working with horsemen, and they knew what it was like to face a charge of heavy cavalry.

At least once a month the whole army was taken out into the desert to the west of Dura to train in massed formations. At the end of the exercise the legions had been drawn up in battle array and had been charged by a thousand cataphracts. The charge had not been pressed home of course, but it had acquainted the legionaries with the sights and sounds of heavy horsemen hurtling towards them. So it was today, as upwards of five thousand armour-clad horsemen broke into a gallop to charge and thunder towards them. The enemy screamed and urged their horses to move faster as thousands of javelins were hurled at the oncoming horsemen.

In their defensive formation each cohort had a depth of four ranks, each rank made up of twenty men. It was the rear two ranks that threw their javelins as front ranks of the cataphracts tried to batter their way through the legionaries. Batter was the correct word for the charge, magnificent though it was, had already begun to falter before it had even reached the foot soldiers. No horse will run blindly into a solid object. Unable to turn aside or wheel about, the horses either tried to stop or slowed and reared up on their back legs. Some lost balance and somersaulted into the ranks of the packed legionaries, causing dreadful carnage. In those few seconds the Durans lost more men than they had in the first battle or in the previous few days. The javelin storm further interrupted the momentum of the charge but caused few casualties, the points mostly glancing off scale armour.

So a desperate mêlée began, cataphracts either trying to jab their lance points into the faces of legionaries or, abandoning the shafts, going to work with their maces, axes and swords. But the legionaries kept their discipline and fought back, the front two ranks keeping their shields tight to their front and jabbing at the horses and riders with their javelins. The gaps that had been created by the careering and thrashing horses had been sealed by reinforcements sent from the cohorts drawn from the other sides of the square, and those thrown riders who had not been killed when they had been crushed by their own mounts were quickly dispatched.

'Archers!' I screamed. I threw my shield to the ground and picked up my bow and the two full quivers lying at my feet. The other archers deployed in a single line either side of me did the same.

'Shoot at the faces of the riders,' I shouted.

I nocked an arrow in the bowstring and searched for a target. Dura's armoured fist wore full-face helmets but most heavy horsemen in the empire sported open-faced helmets. They gave a rider a wide field of view and were not as hot to wear for hours on end in battle. The disadvantage was that they left the face exposed. I saw a rider stabbing at legionaries with his *kontus* and released my bowstring. I watched the arrow hurtle through the air to strike the man's eye socket. He yelped and clutched his face with his hands, as he was pulled from his horse by a group of legionaries and disappeared from view beneath a flurry of *gladius* blades. I loosed another arrow that missed a rider who was hacking right and left with a mace. Then I shot three more arrows, one of which went through a rider's mouth. I quickly used up my arrows as the rest of my archers also emptied their quivers.

'Arrows,' I shouted. The others also held up their bows to signal that they too required more ammunition.

In front of us riders were still trying to cut their way into the Duran ranks, flailing their weapons with frenzy. But our line was holding and it was becoming obvious that the enemy horsemen had been stopped. Domitus stalked immediately behind the rear ranks, *gladius* in hand, shouting encouragement. Wounded men were hauled from the ranks and attended by members of Alcaeus' medical corps. The seriously injured were placed on stretchers and taken to where Alcaeus had established his hospital area.

Panting legionaries, Exiles sent to us as reinforcements by Kronos, ran along the line and dumped full quivers at our feet, no doubt enemy arrows they had picked up. We began shooting again. I saw a mounted enemy officer directing his men against us, calmly issued orders within feet of our front line. He was around a hundred paces from where I stood as I drew the bowstring back so the three flight feathers were by my right ear. I did not look at the arrowhead, only the target. The sounds of battle disappeared as I concentrated. My breathing slowed as I exhaled and let the bowstring slip from my fingers. The arrow sliced through the air over legionary helmets and hit the officer's right eye socket. His arms immediately dropped by his sides and his head slumped forward. He remained in his saddle, just another dead man on the battlefield.

Above the clatter of weapons striking helmets and shields and the roar of men cursing and crying out in agony came the shrill sound of horn blasts. Slowly the cataphracts disengaged and retreated from our front line. The legionaries began cheering and banging their swords and javelins on their shields, chanting 'Dura, Dura'. The enemy's heavy horsemen reformed their line and then about-faced and withdrew. We had beaten them. Domitus came rushing over and we embraced each other like small boys who have just discovered a heap of freshly baked cakes.

All around men fell to their knees and gave thanks to their gods while others, racked with pain from wounds now the frenzy of bloodlust had left them, winced and leaned on their shields or their comrades for support. Others fainted from exhaustion, for they had been standing and fighting in the sun for hours now. We had been fortunate that the enemy had assaulted only one side of the square. If we had been attacked on all four sides then perhaps they would have broken us.

'They knew their foot and horse archers couldn't break our line,' said Domitus, who had taken off his helmet and was wiping his sweat-covered scalp with a rag. 'They gambled that their heavy horse could break through and they lost.'

He glanced at the sun and squinted. 'What I wouldn't give to dunk my head in the Euphrates right now.'

'That, my friend,' I said, 'is our Achilles' heel.'

My fears were confirmed by Marcus who reported to me as I lay on the ground, my right forearm across my eyes to shield them from the sun. I was exhausted from the exertions of battle and from having no sleep on account of the night raid on the enemy camp.

Domitus kicked the sole of my boot.

'You awake, Pacorus?'

'If I wasn't before I am now.' My limbs ached and with difficulty I sat up.

'Begging your pardon, sir,' said Marcus. 'But the water situation is most dire.'

'How dire?' I asked.

'Enough in the wagons for only half a day.'

I held out an arm to Domitus who hauled me up. I picked up my helmet and bow.

'Very well, I said. 'Council of war in ten minutes. Assemble all the senior officers.'

As our precious water supplies were allocated in order or priority – to those who had been fighting, to the rest who had been standing in the ranks, and lastly to the wounded – Domitus, Kronos, Alcaeus, Marcus and the cohort commanders gathered in the centre of the camp. They sat down on stools arranged under a temporary awning Marcus had rigged up between two wagons, though it was now late afternoon and mercifully the sun's heat was abating.

'You and your men did well today,' I told them. 'There are very few soldiers who can hold their ground against the empire's finest cataphracts, but they did and more.'

'I thought Dura had the finest cataphracts in the empire,' said Drenis, the others cheering at his words.

122

'But we are still surrounded and far from home,' I continued. 'Marcus informs me that our water supplies will last only one more day. We cannot remain here if we are to live.'

'We could always strike for the Tigris,' suggested Kronos. 'It is only two or three days' march from here.'

'Without water the mules and oxen will quickly expire,' said Marcus.

'To say nothing of the wounded,' added a grim-faced Alcaeus.

'We cannot do that,' I answered. 'Even if we reach the river we will be nearer the enemy's homeland and will face certain destruction, even if our thirst has been quenched.'

'What, then?' asked Domitus.

'We attack the enemy. Tomorrow. At dawn. We will advance on the camp of Mithridates.'

Domitus rubbed his nose and looked into the distance.

'You disapprove?' I said.

'The boys are tired and thirsty. If they form into a battle line and advance there is nothing to stop the enemy from hitting us behind and on our flanks.'

'Ordinarily,' I replied, 'I would agree. But these are not ordinary circumstances. We are being ground down here. We cannot shake off the enemy and we will not be able to outrun them. They have time on their side; we do not. They won't be expecting an attack.'

'Well,' said Kronos, 'at least we won't have to stand around being pelted with arrows and charged by horsemen.'

'Very well, then,' I said. 'Organise your men. We attack south at dawn.'

The meeting broke up and the officers returned to their commands. I suddenly felt a sharp spasm of pain in my left leg and stopped until it eased. I rubbed my left thigh with my palm. Alcaeus spotted my pained expression and came over to me.

'Are you hurt?'

'No. It's the old wound I picked up at Dura when the city was besieged.'

That was nearly four years ago, when Chosroes had brought his army to besiege my city and I had defeated him, suffering an arrow wound to my leg in the process.

'Alas, there is little I can do. Being on your feet all day long has inflamed it. I would advise rest and keeping the weight off it but that hardly seems appropriate.'

'I shall have to wait until we get back home.'

The air was suddenly filled with trumpet blasts and I knew that we were once again under attack. As tired legionaries reformed into their ranks and hoisted up their shields once more the enemy assaulted us on all four sides. The pain in my leg disappeared as excitement heightened my senses and the stamina of an immortal filled my being. I rushed over to the south side of the square, thinking that the enemy might be trying to break our line there once more. The other archers formed a long line behind the ranks of the cohorts as the clatter of metal against metal filled the air.

The light was beginning to fade as the level of noise rose but I could see no enemy horsemen. Most strange. Domitus ran back from his men to report. Behind him the rear two ranks of two cohorts hurled their javelins at the enemy.

'It seems that they are throwing the dregs against us now. All foot soldiers, mostly ill armed and acting in small groups. Some have no weapons at all.'

Kronos reported the same thing. On all four sides of the square small groups of poorly armed men would charge us in an attempt to break our line. But they either died before they got within striking distance of the front ranks, felled by javelins, or were literally cut to pieces when they came within *gladius* range. They would fall back, reform then charge again, only to meet the same fate. As the sun set the desultory affair continued, the piles of enemy dead getting larger by the hour as dusk gave way to night. Some of the enemy wore only tunics, no armour or helmets. Their only weapons were stones that they hurled at legionaries in a vain attempt to split a skull encased in a helmet. Some had to be whipped forward by their own officers before they would fight, only to have their bellies sliced open by the waiting legionaries. After a while they stopped attacking and stood out of javelin range, hurling insults at us. So I moved the archers forward and stood with them beyond the front rank of the legionaries. And as the moon once again filled the night sky to illuminate the enemy in a ghostly glow, we shot at them. Legionaries ran back to the wagons to pick up bundles of enemy arrows that had been shot at us earlier. They had been meticulously collected by details of men under the command of Marcus. They were dumped at our feet as we shot arrow after arrow at the enemy.

At first we were content to stay close to the front ranks, especially when a group of the enemy made a half-hearted attempt to rush us. But after a while there was nothing left living in front of us, just heaps of dead that stretched left and right and into the distance. I rested the end of my bow on the ground. The fingers on my right hand hurt and my right shoulder ached. I had no idea how long I had been shooting at the enemy or how many arrows I had used.

Domitus came through the ranks of his men to join me. In his mail shirt, white tunic, greaves and helmet with its white crest he looked like a phantom in the moonlight.

'What's happening on the other sides of the square?' I knew that there were no archers to support the legionaries on the other three sides of our formation.

'They are holding the line with ease. Kronos sent a message that a load of unarmed slaves or such like attacked from the east. Most were cut down by javelins, the rest died easily enough on our swords.'

'I don't understand,' I said.

He looked up and down the line with a grim smile on his face.

'I do. Narses and Mithridates are keeping us occupied while they go about their purpose.'

'What purpose?'

'They're either scarpering or they will hit us again when it's light and roll right over us.'

I suddenly felt very tired and every limb in my body ached with a fury as the awful realisation dawned on me that the last reserves of our strength had been used up on slaughtering the scrapings of the enemy army.

The men were spent. They had been fighting almost non-stop for over twenty-four hours. Dehydrated, tired, hungry and filthy, they had surpassed themselves in maintaining their discipline, morale and fighting spirit. But even men of Dura's army now needed rest.

When the dawn came there were no longer any enemy soldiers attacking us, only heaps of dead and dying in front of the first rank of legionaries. These stood leaning on their battered shields like ghosts, staring blankly ahead at the twisted mounds of men that they had made dead flesh. There was no water left to slake their thirsts now. With parched mouths and fatigued limbs they remained silent and waited for the next enemy assault. The final assault that would destroy them. Except that there was no assault, and as the red and yellow rays of light lanced the eastern sky and Shamash returned day to the earth once more we realised that there was no enemy. Narses and Mithridates had gone and taken their army with them.

An hour after dawn had broken and as the sun began its accent in a cloudless sky, Kronos and Domitus joined me as I left the ranks and walked south. My left leg was screaming at me to stop and lie down. It was with difficulty I ignored the torment, enduring a stab of pain with every step. We halted a couple of hundred paces from our lines and stared at the empty space previously occupied by the enemy camp.

'So, they've gone,' mused Kronos.

'All that fighting last night was to cover their retreat,' said Domitus, smugly.

'You were right,' I replied. 'But why? They had almost finished us off. One more day and we would have been meat for crows.'

'Perhaps that god of yours took pity on us,' suggested Domitus.

'Well if he did,' said Kronos, 'he only did half a job because we still have no water.'

Our good fortune with regard to the enemy vanishing was forgotten as I gave orders for the army to continue its march northwest, if only to escape the stench of dead flesh that permeated that air. We broke up some wagons to make a pyre on which to burn our own dead, but the thousands of opposition slain and dozens of mules that had been killed by arrows we left to rot. In no time corpses were swarming with large black flies gorging themselves on decaying flesh. As the black smoke of the funeral pyres drifted upwards into the vivid blue sky those still living trudged from the scene of horror.

We maintained our hollow square formation but had not gone half a mile before trumpet calls signalled the alarm. Reflexes honed by countless hours on the training fields commanded tired bodies to once again close ranks, shields forming a wall and roof around our battered formation. I hobbled over to the northern side of the square to join Domitus and Kronos who were standing beyond the front rank peering into the distance.

'What is it?' I asked.

Domitus pointed his vine cane directly ahead. 'Riders.'

My heart sank. 'The enemy?'

'Looks like,' he replied.

I strained to identify the shimmering black shapes on the horizon that were getting larger, albeit agonisingly slowly.

'Why are they approaching from the northwest?' asked Kronos. 'It makes no sense. They should be coming from the south or east.'

I did not care from which direction they were coming, only that once more the enemy was approaching. I knew that this time they would succeed in breaking our square, and after that... There would be no after that for us. With a macabre fascination I watched the figures grow larger as they approached. Oddly they did not fill the horizon in a line but seemed to be riding in a column. Black shapes on black horses. I could now make out spears, the sun catching the tips of the whetted points, presaging our slaughter.

The silence was unbearable as we watched, unable to take our eyes off the black demons approaching with the intent of sending us into the next life. There were a lot of them that much was certain, for they were kicking up a large dust cloud.

'They are Agraci.'

All three of us turned to stare at the legionary behind us whose eyes were obviously keener than ours. In his relief and joy he momentarily forgot that he was speaking to his king and general as he smiled at me and said the words again.

'They are Agraci. It is Prince Malik.'

We snapped our heads back to the front once more to see with our own eyes the miracle that was unfolding. Ahead, swathed in black robes and riding a black horse, was the son of King Haytham, my friend and Dura's ally. But he was not alone. Beside him, galloping towards me on her faithful mare, rode Gallia, her face covered by the cheekguards of her helmet. Behind her came Vagharsh carrying my griffin banner and behind him rode the Amazons, while on Gallia's other side was Orodes.

As the low rumble of horses' hooves filled the air the ranks behind me were silent. Then they erupted into wild cheering, the sound reverberating along each side of the square as the word was passed that our salvation had arrived. Domitus slapped me hard on the arm and Kronos locked me in an iron bear hug. With difficulty I fought back the tears as I fell to my knees and bowed my head in thanks to Shamash, who had surely woven this miracle.

Domitus helped me to my feet as Malik, Gallia and Orodes pulled up their horses in front of us and my wife leapt from her saddle and wrapped herself around me. Both of us sprawled in the dirt. This brought whistles and hoots from the men behind as Gallia stood up, untied the straps on her helmet and threw it on the ground. I hauled myself onto my feet once more and she grabbed my face and kissed me long on the lips.

'I came as fast as I could,' she said, running a finger tenderly down the scar on my left cheek. 'I would ride into hell if need be to save you.'

My eyes misted as I looked at her flawless face and blue eyes.

'Orodes must have ridden like the wind to reach Dura in so short a time.'

She reached down to hold both my hands. 'No, my love. We left Dura before Orodes had time to reach the city.'

She smiled her most beautiful smile as Orodes came up and embraced me. He stood back seeing my haggard appearance, my torn and filthy tunic, my battered cuirass and unshaven face.

'You look terrible.'

He, as ever, looked immaculate in his scale armour cuirass, well-groomed hair and clean-shaven face.

'I have been entertaining Mithridates and Narses these past few days. Alas, I have had no time to wash and change.'

Malik, face adorned with the black tattoos that were the hallmark of Agraci men folk, embraced me warmly.

'It is good to see you, my friend,' he beamed.

'You too, Malik. Never has a Parthian king been so glad to see an Agraci prince.'

127

There followed a series of happy reunions as Malik's warriors, who must have numbered over a thousand, flanked the square and rode south and east to ensure that we were not surprised by a returning foe. 'There is little chance of that,' said Orodes as we all retired to my command tent that had been hastily assembled in the centre of the square. 'Their scouts will have reported that a great number of horsemen are riding to your relief.'

I was surprised. 'Really?'

'Of course,' added Gallia. 'Your father brings the army of Hatra to your aid.'

'Your horsemen are accompanying your father, Pacorus,' said Orodes.

'And with him rides my father and ten thousand of his warriors,' added Malik.

'King Haytham?' I could scarcely believe it.

'Of course,' continued Malik. 'When Queen Gallia issues a summons, men obey.'

This was most excellent news and I had difficulty in maintaining my composure. I embraced Gallia once more and then Orodes. But then I noticed that someone was missing.

'Where is Surena?'

'I sent him east with a thousand horse archers,' replied Gallia.

I stared at her, unsure whether my hearing had been damaged during the fighting. I smiled.

'Very droll. I assume he is with the rest of my horsemen.'

'It is true, Pacorus,' said Orodes. 'He was sent to the Tigris with a thousand riders and ordered to ride south.'

I looked at him and then Gallia.

'What madness is this?'

'No madness,' replied Gallia. 'Dobbai told me that Surena would reap a rich harvest east of the Tigris so that's where he is heading.'

I was so relieved and tired in equal measure that I asked no more questions about Surena. But I felt certain that he and a thousand of my horse archers were riding to their deaths.

Chapter 6

My father, his red banner with its white horse motif carried behind him, arrived two hours later with Gafarn in tow. He was accompanied by his five-hundred-strong bodyguard, a thousand other armoured riders, five thousand horse archers, three thousand squires in full war gear leading the same number of camels and a further thousand camels carrying spare arrows, tents, food and waterskins. My two legions had been drawn up in battle order to salute their arrival.

The army of Hatra was a sight to behold. Each cataphract was encased in scale armour, legs and arms in steel circular armour similar to that worn by my own heavy horsemen. White plumes were fixed to the top of every helmet and white pennants fluttered from every *kontus*. The horses wore armour from head to thigh, their eyes covered by metal grills to protect them from sword and spear thrusts and missiles.

My father's bodyguard, recruited from the sons of the kingdom's nobles, were the finest of all, each man wearing scale armour of overlapping polished steel plates riveted onto the thick hide undercoat. The sun glinted off their armour and whetted *kontus* points. For additional armament each man carried a sword, mace, axe and dagger – they were truly fearsome killing machines.

Only Hatran nobility could serve in the ranks of the royal bodyguard, a notion that I scoffed at. But I had to admit as they halted behind my father and Vistaspa they presented a magnificent sight.

The same could not be said for the horse archers brought by Dura's lords: men in varying shades of brown, yellow and white shirts and leggings, wearing no armour and riding horses of different colours. Every horse in my father's bodyguard was a pure white to complement each rider's white shirt and leggings. But to amass such a contingent took time and a great deal of wealth, attributes that Hatra had in abundance. Dura's lords, though men of some wealth in their own right, did not have the means to raise and equip such immaculately attired soldiers. But my lords had carved out their lands with blood and hard graft, often fighting the Agraci in the process before the time of peace between our two peoples. The farmers who worked their lands were also hardy individuals who knew how to fight their way out of a tight spot if need be. Gallia had brought twenty thousand of them. The lords had elected Spandarat to be their commander for the duration of the campaign. One-eyed, brusque and having the appearance of a shabby carpet salesman, he had been the one who had escorted the queen back to Dura when she had been pregnant with Claudia when I had marched to fight King Porus of Sakastan and his elephants. How long ago that seemed now!

Trumpets and horns blasted as the legions stood to attention and I walked to greet my father from where Gallia, Orodes, Malik, Domitus and Kronos were standing beyond the front rank of legionaries. Vistaspa held the reins of his horse as he dismounted and paced towards me, Gafarn next to him. We embraced and he stepped back to examine me. He wore a sleeveless leather cuirass overlaid with silver scales and a gold crown atop his silver-inlaid helmet. His spotless long-sleeved white shirt contrasted sharply with my own filthy shirt and leggings. Gafarn was similarly dressed but wore no crown on his helmet.

'It would appear that we have arrived just in time, my son.'

'It would appear so, father.'

He looked at the lines of filthy, tired men drawn up behind me.

'Your soldiers look as though they have taken a battering. It is fortunate for you that you have allies to come to your aid, for otherwise the buzzards would have been picking at your bones by now.'

'There are worse ways to die,' I replied casually.

His brow furrowed. 'Are there?'

'Better not to die at all,' suggested Gafarn. 'You and Mithridates didn't kiss and make up then?'

'Grovelling to snakes has little appeal, brother,' I said.

My father was going to say more but at that moment a great rumbling noise heralded the arrival of more reinforcements – Haytham's warriors. Like a great cloud of locusts the black-clad Agraci warriors filled the horizon, and my father kept his council as Haytham and his desert lords rode up to where we stood. I smiled as the Agraci king dismounted from his shining black stallion and strode over to me. He nodded curtly at my father who nodded back but said nothing. I bowed my head to Haytham.

'Welcome, lord,' I said. 'I am in your debt.'

My father folded his arms and glanced at the long line of Agraci warriors who now waited on their horses and camels on the right flank of Hatra's army – a stark contrast to the white-uniformed Parthian riders.

'I had no say in the matter,' replied Haytham, his black eyes studying my father. 'Your queen sent for me and told me to bring my warriors.'

This was nonsense, of course, but Haytham was obviously at ease and enjoying himself. No wonder, for no Agraci king had ever crossed the Euphrates to venture into the empire. I could see that my father was most uncomfortable by the presence of both him and his warriors. But I gave thanks to Shamash that they had come for it signalled that Haytham valued our alliance and my friendship.

The awkwardness was shattered by the appearance of Spandarat, who walked over to us. He bowed to my father and Haytham, muttering 'majesty' as he did so, then slapped me on the arm.

130

'Nearly got your arse kicked, then? I reckon that sorceress of yours must have been working flat-out weaving spells to protect you.'

My father was appalled at his behaviour but I had never insisted on a strict adherence to protocol at Dura, preferring loyalty and honesty to sycophancy and faithlessness.

'Perhaps we should make camp,' said my father brusquely, 'then we can discuss matters more fully and Pacorus can change his clothes to look more like a Parthian king.'

He nodded stiffly to Haytham and then went back to his bodyguard.

Gafarn smiled and bowed his head to Haytham. 'Until later, lord king. Diana sends her love, Pacorus.'

He walked back to his officers assembled on their horses before Dura's horse archers. It was appropriate that Gafarn, one of the finest bowmen in the Parthian Empire, commanded some of the empire's finest horse archers.

Malik came forward to speak to his father while Gallia told Spandarat to distribute the extra full waterskins that had been brought by each of his riders. At least the legionaries would be thirsty no more.

Domitus stood the men down as a multitude of tents sprang up around the hastily erected royal tent of my father. Domitus ordered that the legions dig a ditch and rampart to surround their camp, in which the lords would also shelter. The men grumbled but to no avail. We may have lost our wooden stakes and most of our tents but Domitus was determined to maintain proper procedures.

'The enemy might come back,' he growled as hundreds of men sweated and cursed as they wielded entrenching tools to dig the ditch and erect the rampart.

When they had finished both legions were allowed to rest for the night, security provided by a screen of horse archers five miles away in all directions from the camps of the allied armies. Malik threw parties of Agraci scouts out even further. In the late afternoon he himself rode east with a large group towards the Tigris. My father camped his army to the north of our own tents and east of Haytham's warriors. As dusk was enveloping the land he sent a rider to my tent inviting me to dine with him. But I sent a message back that I was too exhausted to be good company and if I did attend him would probably fall asleep at his table. No doubt my absence fuelled his ill ease further. Domitus and Kronos were also listless as they sat down with me at the table in my tent. Orodes and Gallia tried in vain to engage us in conversation. After we had eaten a meal of salted Hatran mutton and dried biscuit washed down with tepid water, Orodes, Domitus and Kronos made their excuses and left to get some sleep. Fortunately we had managed to save the blankets in our flight from Mithridates, and in the darkness row upon row of legionaries lay on the ground

131

wrapped in them as they slept like the dead, the Amazons and the lords' horse archers standing guard over them.

In my sleeping quarters I lay next to Gallia, her head on my chest, her hand caressing my scalp. It was sheer heaven. Her voice was soft and soothing.

'Soon after you left Dura Dobbai had a dream in which she saw a griffin with one of its wings pinned to the ground. It was all alone and squealing in agony and she knew that you were in danger. So I mustered the lords and sent a message to Haytham, asking for his help.'

'So Orodes never made it back to Dura.'

'No, we met him and his horsemen on the east bank of the Euphrates.'

'And my father?' I asked, finding it difficult to stay awake.

'I sent a message to Hatra at the same time as the request to Haytham, saying that you faced defeat if your father did not bring his army south.'

'Perhaps you should command the army and I will stay at Dura to raise our daughters.' I never heard her answer as I drifted off into a deep sleep, my beloved wife beside me.

The morning came soon enough. When I awoke I found Gallia gone. I dressed and donned my cuirass and left my bedchamber, buckling my sword belt as I walked into the tent's main area to find Byrd pacing up and down while Domitus and Orodes were seated at the table.

'Ah, the sleeping hero comes at last,' remarked Domitus sarcastically.

I ignored him. 'Byrd, you are a sight for sore eyes.'

He stopped pacing and nodded at me. 'I ride in earlier. Vardan comes with his horsemen.'

I picked up the jug of water on the table and poured myself a cup.

'That is excellent news. We may yet bring this campaign to a happy end.'

'Vardan also sent a message to Nergal at Uruk to let him know situation,' continued Byrd.

'It will take him a few days to get to us,' said Orodes.

He was right about that. Uruk was over a hundred miles south of Babylon and Babylon lay eighty miles at least south of where we were camped. Still, I knew that if Nergal learned that we were in peril he would also bring his army to support me. Except that we were no longer in peril.

When Vardan and his horsemen arrived two hours later a council of kings was held in my father's camp. Gallia returned from her early morning ride with her Amazons as did Malik and his men, and she and Orodes joined me as I journeyed to the tent of my father in the middle of the Hatran army's camp. Gallia had brought Remus back with her and it was good to be in the saddle again, albeit only for a short time as I rode with them through my father's camp to his pavilion. As is the Parthian custom the king's marquee was located in the centre of the camp, with the king's horse and those of his bodyguard stabled immediately behind it. The tents of the royal bodyguard's officers were pitched around the royal pavilion, the smaller tents of the rest of the royal bodyguard positioned beyond them in an outer circle. Further out still were the tents of the horse archers, with stable areas for their horses dotted among the tents. The camel park was usually located anywhere as long as it was downwind and far away from the royal pavilion. The banners of Dura and Susiana fluttered in the light breeze behind us as we rode. At my father's tent our horses were taken from us and we were escorted inside.

Already the legions were marching west to the Euphrates. I had told Domitus that he was to take them to the river and then north back to Dura. They would be of no further use here and it was imperative that the wounded were taken back to the city where they could be properly cared for. In the fighting with the enemy we had lost only one hundred and fifty killed but over four hundred more had been wounded, mostly by arrows. Of those fifty were expected to die before they reached Dura. We had also lost four Companions killed.

Before the meeting with my father Haytham and Malik had ridden over to my tent to tell me that the King of the Agraci was going back to his lands.

'My presence within the Parthian Empire is not welcome, I think,' King Haytham explained.

'Your presence is very welcome, lord,' I reassured him.

'To you, perhaps. But you are different from other Parthian kings. I will accompany your foot soldiers back to Dura.'

'I am in your debt, lord.'

He smiled. 'When I am in danger, then perhaps you will bring your army to assist me.'

'You have only to ask,' I said.

He walked over to Gallia who bowed her head to him. He then leant forward and kissed her on the cheek.

'Do not leave it too long before you visit Palmyra, Gallia.'

She dazzled him with her smile. 'Tell Rasha I will see her soon.'

Malik embraced us both and then we all followed Haytham outside where a score of his mounted warriors waited for him.

When he was in the saddle he raised his hand to us and then departed.

'He is a good man,' I said.

'Yes he is,' agreed Gallia. She turned to look at me. 'You may find that your father is not as agreeable.'

She was right about that. The reception I received from him was icy to say the least. When we were shown into his marquee my father was seated on a great couch discussing matters with Vistaspa. Both of them were dressed in white flowing robes, not their war gear. When we entered Gafarn rose from the couch next to my father and embraced Gallia and then me. He too was dressed casually.

'Our father is spitting blood,' he whispered to me.

Vistaspa also rose when I entered with Gallia and Orodes and bowed his head to us. My father raised his hand to me and smiled at Gallia, who stepped forward and kissed him on the cheek. On another couch, dressed in a rich purple tunic and yellow silk leggings, his feet encased in red slippers studded with silver, sat King Vardan of Babylon. I bowed my head to him, as did Gallia, while Orodes, being a prince, went down on one knee before him and my father.

Vardan had not changed much in the years since I had last seen him. A short, broad-shouldered man, he had a round face and a long nose. His full beard and moustache were brown, though I noticed that, like my father's hair, they now had flecks of grey in them.

'Greetings father, lord king,' I said to them.

Gallia walked over to Vardan and likewise kissed him on the cheek.

'Greetings, lord king. I hope Axsen prospers.'

Princess Axsen was Vardan's daughter. Unfortunately she had inherited her father's physical attributes and was a rather short, stocky woman, though possessed of an agreeable nature and great charm.

Vardan smiled at Gallia. 'She sends her love to you both and wonders why you have not visited her at Babylon.'

'We have been remiss, lord,' she said. 'I promise that we will visit her soon. Is that not so, Pacorus?'

'Mm, yes, of course.' I was watching my father during this interlude between my wife and Vardan. He had a face like thunder and clearly wanted to get something off his chest.

'Be seated, all of you,' he snapped. 'And get off your knees, Orodes.'

I unbuckled my sword belt and rested it against the couch opposite my father that Gallia and I sat down on. His servants offered us wine and pastries. Orodes reclined on another couch opposite to Vardan, the King of Babylon smiling at Gallia though ignoring me. I felt like a chastened child.

'Haytham has left?' asked my father.

'Not two hours ago,' I replied. 'He and his men escort the legions back to Dura.'

My father turned the silver cup he was holding in his hand, staring at it as he did so.

134

'Probably just as well. The presence of a large group of Agraci east of the Euphrates will not sit well with many people.'

'And what people would they be, father?'

He stopped turning the cup and looked at me with narrow eyes. 'Most of the Parthian Empire. It was a mistake enlisting Haytham's help. It is one thing having him as a friend and ally on your western border, quite another inviting him and his army into the empire.'

'It is my fault, lord,' said Gallia apologetically. 'I was the one who requested King Haytham's aid.'

My father smiled warmly at her. 'It is not your fault, daughter. You were only trying to save your foolish husband.'

Now we were coming to the kernel of the matter.

'Foolish, father? Is it foolish to seek justice from those who attempted to murder me, who did succeed in murdering my governor?' I pointed at Vistaspa. 'A friend of the commander of your army, no less.'

My father placed his cup on the table beside his couch. 'Perhaps you mistake revenge for justice.'

I could feel my temper rise within me. 'Mithridates needs to be punished for his failed assassination attempt.'

Vardan took a sharp intake of breath while my father rose to his feet and began pacing in front of me, turning his head as he spat words in my direction.

'You take it upon yourself to march against Ctesiphon, in the process violating the territorial integrity of both Hatra and Babylon. You march your army through our kingdoms without even the courtesy of asking for our permission. Then you bite off more than you can chew, nearly get yourself killed and then have to rely on Vardan and me to get you out of trouble. I did think, once, that you would make a good king, but the events of the last few days have disabused me of that notion. With the Armenians raiding my northern territories the last thing I want is a war on my southern border.'

'I fear Varaz is right,' added Vardan. 'The empire needs internal stability in the face of external threats. All of the northern borders are aflame.'

'You are right, lord king,' I replied, ignoring my father who had regained his couch. 'That is why we must grasp the opportunity that has presented itself.'

'Opportunity?' Vardan looked at me with a confused expression.

'Nergal will arrive within the next two days, and with his horsemen combined with our own we may yet strike at Ctesiphon and destroy Mithridates.'

Vardan's eyes widened with shock. 'Strike at Ctesiphon?'

'Of course,' I replied. 'Mithridates will not be expecting that. And with the horsemen of Babylon, Hatra and Mesene combined with my own we will surely destroy his army.'

Vardan said nothing, his mouth opening and closing like that of a fish out of water. Gafarn buried his head in his hands and Orodes and Vistaspa both stared at the red carpets spread on the floor.

'Hatra's army will not be marching against Ctesiphon,' said my father slowly and forcefully. 'I will not be dragged into your war, Pacorus.'

'Nor I,' added Vardan. 'For good or ill, Mithridates is the king of kings. We cannot have another civil war in the empire, Pacorus, not at all. The Romans, Armenians and the tribes of the northern steppes will take advantage of our weakness.'

'Exactly,' said my father. 'There will be no empire left if we fight among ourselves once more.'

'And Mithridates and Narses are allowed to go unpunished for their crimes?' I said.

'The only proof that it was Mithridates who sent those assassins was the word of the killers themselves,' replied my father. 'Perhaps it was someone else who sent them. After all, you have made many enemies since you became King of Dura.'

'I thought Hatra and Babylon were friends of Dura,' I said.

'You abuse our friendship, Pacorus,' replied my father. 'This is the second time that Vardan and I have brought our armies to help you.' He was referring to the time when I had faced the Roman Pompey on Dura's northern border. 'But instead of being grateful you want to embroil us in another war. Well not this time. This time we are going home.'

'I have to concur with your father,' added Vardan. 'Babylon cannot afford to fight a war against the might of the eastern kings.'

'Pacorus is grateful for your support,' said Gallia to my father, 'to both of you.' She smiled at Vardan. 'Is that not correct, Pacorus?'

I said nothing, which earned me a look of fury from my wife. I held my father's iron gaze, not blinking.

'I see my words are wasted on you, Pacorus,' he said at length. 'I leave for Hatra tomorrow.'

'I will also be taking my men home,' said Vardan. 'I am sorry, Pacorus.'

There was nothing else to say. I bowed my head perfunctorily to my father and Vardan and then left. Gallia took her leave by again kissing the cheeks of the two kings. Orodes was the last to depart, as ever endeavouring to smooth troubled waters with his diplomatic tongue. As I waited impatiently for Remus to be brought to me Gafarn came to my side.

'Do not be too disappointed, Pacorus. Our father is preoccupied with securing our northern border.'

'Hatra has enough strength to deal with the Armenians and help me defeat Mithridates.'

A servant, a boy dressed in the white livery of my father's kingdom, brought Remus to me.

'I have been remiss,' I said to Gafarn. 'How is Diana?'

He smiled. 'She is well and sends her love.'

'And your son?' Diana had given birth to a boy two years ago. They had named the child Varaz after his grandfather.

'He thrives. Diana and your mother want to know if Hatra will see you and Gallia soon.'

I shrugged. 'I have to deal with Mithridates and Narses first.'

'Not for a few years, then,' he quipped.

I took Remus' reins and vaulted into the saddle. Epona was brought to Gallia and Orodes was provided with his brown mare.

'And young Spartacus?' I asked.

'Big and strong, just like his father was,' said Gafarn approvingly.

'How old is he now?' asked Gallia.

'He has seen eleven summers,' replied Gafarn.

We had brought the infant son of Spartacus back with us from Italy. Eleven years. It had passed in the blink of an eye.

'Farewell, Gafarn,' I said. 'Convey my love to Diana.'

I dug my knees into Remus' sides, causing him to snort in annoyance before he broke into a canter. I would not be visiting my father again before he took his army north, and with it any chance that I had of seeking a decision against Mithridates. By now he and Narses would be back across the Tigris with their troops. Meanwhile Gotarzes was still besieged in Elymais with no hope of relief. It was obvious to me that Mithridates was intent on destroying Dura and all its allies, and if he did he would have an iron grip over the empire. I shuddered at the thought.

'There is nothing to be done, Pacorus,' said Gallia later as we sat at the table in my tent with Orodes for company.

'Your father is a wise king,' added Orodes. 'He knows that there is no willingness to fight a campaign in the east of the empire, beyond the Tigris. For that is where we shall have to go if Mithridates and Narses retreat further east.'

'But if they do,' I said, 'at least we will have saved Gotarzes.'

'How long can he hold out in his city?' asked Gallia.

'Not long, I fear,' replied Orodes.

'Perhaps we do not need Hatra and Babylon,' I mused.

Orodes wore a perplexed expression. 'I do not understand.'

I smiled at him. 'Vardan and my father may be hesitant to resolve matters, but Nergal will not be so reticent.'

Gallia raised an eyebrow at me. 'What plot are you hatching now?'

I clasped her face with my hands and kissed her on the lips.

'All will be revealed when our friend and ally arrives with his men, my sweet.'

'Does this mean we are not returning to Dura?' asked Orodes.

I jumped up and clapped my hands together. 'Dura will have to wait, my friend, for we have unfinished business across the Tigris.'

Gallia, tired from her rapid journey from Dura, retired soon after, leaving Orodes and me alone. I spread the hide map of the empire that I always took with me on campaign across the table. I took one of the oil lamps hanging on a tent pole and placed it next to the map so we could see its details better. I placed a finger on our present position.

'We are less than a hundred miles from Babylon,' I said, moving my finger over the map to take it past Babylon and towards Uruk. 'Another fifty miles south is the northern border of Mesene.'

Orodes yawned. 'What of it?'

'If we accompany Vardan and then continue our journey south, with Nergal's permission we can strike southeast towards Elymais. We may yet aid Gotarzes.'

He stretched out his arms, clearly thinking about his bed more than my plan.

'But your father and Vardan have no interest in attempting to help Gotarzes.'

'We do not need their help, my friend. We have Dura's horsemen and whatever Nergal can muster. It will be enough.'

I was bluffing, of course. Even with Nergal's forces – I had no idea how many men he would bring – we would probably be inferior in numbers to the enemy. But the thought of abandoning Gotarzes gnawed at me incessantly like a toothache.

Orodes looked at me and then at the map.

'Have you thought that laying siege to Elymais might be a ruse to lure you to a place of the enemy's choosing, Pacorus? Perhaps my stepbrother and Narses know you better than you think.'

In truth I had not thought of that possibility.

'Gotarzes came to my aid when I faced Pompey, Orodes. For that reason alone I must attempt to aid him.'

I looked into his eyes.

'I have no right to ask you or your men to hazard such an undertaking.'

A hurt look crept over his face. 'I would be offended if I was not included in your plan.'

I smiled. 'Well then, let us await the arrival of our friend, the King of Mesene.'

The new day dawned cool and overcast, grey clouds filling the sky to block out the sun and making everything appear dull and drab.

Squires scurried around preparing meals for their masters and providing fodder for the horses. With the legions gone there were no tools to dig a ditch and erect a rampart. In any case we had lost all our wooden stakes that were used to make the rampart, so I commanded that the squires and their masters form a cordon around the camp. They complained that it was not their task to be sentries but to no avail. They may be cataphracts but they enjoyed no special dispensations when it came to the mundane tasks of military life.

It was mid-morning when Byrd, accompanied by two of his Agraci scouts, rode to my tent. He had taken to wearing the clothes of his adopted people: his head was wrapped in a black turban that covered the lower half of his face and he wore black leggings and a long-sleeved black tunic. His horse was also a black beast, its black leather harness, straps and reins giving it a forbidding appearance. The sentries outside had alerted us to his arrival so we were outside the tent as he slid off his horse and bowed his head to me and then Gallia and Orodes.

'Nergal come,' he said, handing the reins of his horse to one of the scouts, who then wheeled away to find the field kitchens.

'And Praxima?' asked Gallia.

'She too.'

I put an arm round his shoulder. 'Come inside and tell us your news.'

As the day was cool I ordered one of the two sentries, both squires, to fetch us some warm wine to drink and hot porridge for Byrd. He had probably been in the saddle since before dawn judging by the black rings round his eyes. He slumped into one of the chairs at the table and stretched out his legs. Byrd was reserved at the best of times, sullen some would say, but this morning he seemed more withdrawn than usual. I caught his eyes and a finger of ice went down my spine.

'You look troubled. What is the matter?'

He looked at Gallia and then Orodes.

'Gotarzes is dead,' he said blankly.

'What?' Orodes was appalled.

I closed my eyes. 'How?'

'We encountered refugees from Elymais on the road,' said Byrd. 'They told of great battle between Gotarzes and the forces of Mithridates and Narses. Gotarzes lost.'

'I thought he was besieged in his city,' said Gallia. 'Was Elymais stormed?'

Byrd shook his head. 'Gotarzes ride out of city to give battle but underestimate number of his enemies. He heard...'

Byrd halted his words and looked down at his feet.

'Heard what?' I pressed him.

He looked up at me. 'He heard that you were coming to help him. That is what men I speak to on road say.'

I felt sick and held my head in my hands. I had been played by Mithridates and Narses and had danced to their tune like a performing bear. I had walked into their trap and now because of me, Gotarzes was dead and his kingdom lost.

'It's not your fault, Pacorus,' said Orodes.

'Isn't it?' I replied. 'If it had not been for me Gotarzes would never have hazarded a battle.'

I could have wept at that moment, wept for a dead king and the thousands of his soldiers who had perished on the battlefield and the thousands of his people who would now be ruled by the tyranny of Mithridates. Gotarzes had been my ally and friend and now he was dead. Godarz was dead, also killed by Mithridates. I looked at Gallia, Orodes and then Byrd and feared for their lives also.

Gallia smiled at me. 'You did your best.'

'Only it was not good enough.'

'What will you do now?' asked Orodes.

In truth I did not know. With Gotarzes gone and Elymais fallen there was no purpose in striking across the Tigris. An attack on Ctesiphon was still tempting, but the enemy would merely retreat further east beyond our clutches. I was not interested in the palace of the king of kings; it was Mithridates that I wanted.

I sighed. 'We go home, Orodes.'

I suddenly felt very tired and bereft of hope. Mithridates had won and my reputation, such as it was, had suffered a grave blow. The army of Dura had previously never suffered a defeat but now it had been stopped in its tracks and forced to limp back home. Mithridates would be emboldened by recent events and he and Narses were probably planning an assault on my kingdom now. It was all too depressing to think about.

I wrote letters to Vardan and my father and sent couriers to deliver them. I would have ridden over to my father's camp myself, but he would undoubtedly blame me for his friend's death and I was in no mood to endure another of his lectures. I also had to inform Nergal when he arrived that his journey had been in vain – a ride of two hundred miles for nothing. It was all too much to bear.

Nergal and his men duly arrived the next morning, five thousand horse archers with a large camel train in tow. I rode out of camp with Gallia, Byrd and Orodes to greet my friend and fellow king. This was the man who had been my second-in-command in Italy and when I had first gone to Dura. A year older than me, Nergal was a fellow Hatran who had fought by my side for over ten years before gaining the crown of the Kingdom of Mesene. Brave, loyal and possessed of an optimistic nature, out of the saddle his long arms and legs gave him an awkward, gangly appearance. It was that appearance that had convinced Rahim, the high priest of Uruk, that Nergal was the reincarnation of the god of the same name. His coming had been foretold thousands of years before on sacred tablets held in the great ziggurat in Uruk, a massive structure that was the residence of the sky god Anu. The banner that now flew behind my friend was the symbol of the god Nergal – a great yellow banner embossed with a double-headed lion sceptre crossed with a sword. It was a happy reunion of old friends who had shared many hardships and also great victories. After we had all dismounted and embraced each other, Gallia and Praxima with an emotional greeting, Nergal's horsemen were ordered to pitch camp next to the army of Dura.

Mesene is not a rich kingdom. Located south of Babylon, it lies between the Tigris and Euphrates whose southern border was formerly where these two mighty rivers empty their waters into the Persian Gulf. But Nergal had granted his southern marshlands to the area's inhabitants, the Ma'adan – Surena's people. In the process he had given away a sizeable proportion of his kingdom. No longer did Mesene's warriors wage war against the Ma'adan, though, and in place of strife there was now trade. This allowed the kingdom to prosper and provided Nergal with the revenues to raise and maintain his army. Dura and Hatra were unusual in having permanent armies staffed by full-time soldiers, equipped and paid for by the crown. Such armies were prohibitively expensive to maintain, their existence made possible only because of the profits raised from the Silk Road. But the Silk Road did not run through Mesene so Nergal had to cut his cloth accordingly.

There were no armoured horsemen among the riders who trotted past us on their way to their campsite, no squires pulling camels loaded with scale armour, lances, tubular arm and leg armour, tents and spare arrows and weapons for their masters. The horse archers of Mesene wore a simple woollen kaftan dyed red known as a *kurta* that opened at the front and was wrapped across the chest from right to left. It was loose fitting like their leggings called *saravanas*. Each man wore leather ankle boots called *xshumaka*, tied in place by leather bands that passed around the ankle and under the sole. Over the kaftans the archers wore scale-armour cuirasses, short-sleeved garments that reached to the mid-thigh, slit at each side up to the waist to facilitate riding. On the leather cuirasses were attached horizontal rows of rectangular iron scales, each row of scales partly covering the layer below. On his head each man wore a helmet made from curved iron plates attached to an iron skeleton of vertical bands, complete with large cheekguards and a long, leather neck flap. They were an impressive sight.

'I like your horsemen, Nergal,' I said approvingly.

'It is their first campaign,' he replied. 'They are looking forward to being tested in battle.'

'Alas, my friend, I think they may have to wait a little longer.'

Later, as we all sat relaxing in my tent, I told Nergal the news that Gotarzes was dead and Elymais in the possession of the enemy.

'That is grave news indeed,' he said. 'We have lost a valued ally.'

'Will Mithridates make war upon Mesene, Pacorus?' asked Praxima with concern.

'I hope not,' I replied.

In truth I did not know but suspected that my nemesis would strike against Mesene. Susiana, Mithridates' own kingdom, lay next to Mesene, the Tigris demarking their eastern and western borders respectively. With Elymais laid low Mithridates and Narses could now turn their attention against Mesene.

'Dura stands with you, Nergal,' said Gallia. 'Mithridates will think twice before he tangles with our combined forces.'

'It is as Gallia says,' I said, causing Praxima to grin with delight.

Orodes said nothing but he knew, as did I, that Dura lay two hundred miles from Mesene whereas the forces of the enemy were within striking distance of Nergal's kingdom. I would have to take my horsemen south to reinforce Mesene.

'How is your high priest, Nergal?' asked Orodes, diplomatically changing the subject.

'Agreeable I am glad to say,' he replied.

'You two are still gods, then?' I teased them.

'Gods given human bodies,' said Praxima sternly before breaking out in giggles.

The sacred tablets that were held at Uruk spoke of Nergal, the god of war, with his wife the goddess Allatu, the queen of the underworld. Allatu was represented on the tablets as having the head of a lion, the red mane of Praxima confirming to the priests of Uruk that she was indeed the goddess. But there was more that confirmed that the wife of Nergal was an immortal. She had arrived at the city at the head of an army – Dura's army – and was dressed as a warrior. That she fought as an Amazon and took life corresponded to the ancient tablets describing Allatu as ferocious and warlike, whose anger knew no bounds. One of the tablets held in the ziggurat at Uruk showed Nergal with his symbol of a lion, with Allatu seated on a horse beside him. Praxima had arrived at Uruk mounted on a horse and dressed as a warrior. All these things convinced Rahim and his priests that Nergal and Praxima were gods made flesh. When I had taken Uruk I was determined that they would become the new rulers of the city to replace the treacherous Chosroes, who had obligingly committed suicide after my soldiers had breached the city walls. I had anticipated difficulties in imposing a new regime on the populace, but the happy coincidence that Nergal and his wife resembled gods removed all obstacles to their accession to power.

'Rahim obligingly opened the temple vaults to me,' said Nergal casually. 'They were full of gold, which was more than could be said for the palace treasury. That was bare.'

'Chosroes had no gold?' asked Orodes.

Nergal shook his head. 'Chosroes was a cruel lord who bought the allegiance of his lords, and his expensive tastes were too much for his kingdom to bear.'

I thought of the rabble that was Chosroes' army, the ragged foot soldiers and the inadequately armed horsemen on their threadbare mounts. He certainly did not lavish money on his troops.

'Why didn't Chosroes empty the temple vaults?' I asked.

'Because Rahim wields much power within the city and kingdom,' said Praxima.

'One does not make an enemy of such a man,' added Nergal. 'He can make much trouble.'

'But not for you,' said Gallia.

Nergal smiled. 'No, not for me, for I am careful not to abuse the exalted position my people accord me.'

'We gave back to the Ma'adan their homeland and justice to the people of Mesene,' added Praxima with pride.

'And in return,' continued Nergal, 'they give us their sons to serve in my army.'

'And the Mesenians, the people who have waged a war of annihilation against the Ma'adan,' I asked, 'they do not object to welcoming the marsh people among them?'

'They have no choice,' said Nergal sternly. 'Besides, it is amazing how the allure of profit lessens the hatred that the Mesenians have for the Ma'adan.'

Orodes looked perplexed. 'I do not understand.'

'It is quite simple,' said Nergal. 'The villages, previously deserted and derelict, situated near the marshlands have been rebuilt and repopulated. The Ma'adan barter their goods with the villagers, mostly fish, rice and water buffaloes, and the villagers sell the hides of the slaughtered animals to the royal armouries in Uruk to make scale armour. It is a lucrative trade.'

'You have done well, Nergal,' I said, smiling at Praxima, 'both of you.'

'Do you pay the annual tribute to Mithridates?' asked Gallia.

Nergal drained his cup of wine. 'No ambassadors from Ctesiphon come to Uruk and I send no word to Mithridates. The Silk Road does not run through Mesene so I suppose that the high king hopes that my kingdom will wither and die if he ignores it.'

'Except it will not,' said Praxima with fire in her eyes. 'It grows stronger and waits for the day when Dura and its allies summon us to march against the false king in Ctesiphon.'

Gallia lent across and placed her hand on her friend's arm, grinning as she did so.

'Always an Amazon,' she said.

I had always liked Praxima, this fierce, wild Spanish woman who had been enslaved by the Romans and forced to work as a whore before she had escaped her bondage. In northern Italy I had seen her shoot down her enemies without mercy and kill Romans with her dagger. Now, ten years later, she was sitting in my tent looking exactly the same as she did all those years ago. She appeared ageless, dressed in her scale-armour cuirass, her long red hair cascading over her shoulders, with her brown eyes full of vigour. I had often lamented that she and Nergal had not yet been blessed with children. Gallia had always assured her friend that she would know the joy of offspring, but Dobbai had told me that Praxima probably would not be able to conceive on account of the hard usage her body had been subjected to at the hands of the Romans.

I rose from my chair and kissed Praxima on the cheek.

'That day will come but not yet. For the moment, my friends, we return home and plan our next move.'

'We are all outcasts,' said Orodes thoughtfully, a note of sadness in his voice.

Always a deep thinker, Orodes was prone to bouts of melancholy when reminded of his exile from his homeland. By rights he should be the prince and de facto ruler of the Kingdom of Susiana, his stepbrother's realm. Though technically the king of kings ruled both the empire and his own kingdom, in reality the day-to-day affairs of the empire soaked up the high king's time and it was customary for the next-in-line to the throne to rule the high king's homeland in his absence. But being friends with me had cost Orodes his position and his homeland, a burden that he shouldered without complaint. But he was right, my kingdom and I were outcasts from the empire and it would appear that Nergal and Mesene had been similarly cut adrift. It was a truly sad state of affairs.

'Nothing lasts forever, my friend,' was all I could muster as a reply.

We then sat in silence staring at the cups we held in our hands. The silence was becoming oppressive but then the flaps of the entrance opened and one of the sentries entered escorting a soldier dressed in the purple uniform of Babylon – baggy leggings, long-sleeved tunic and purple cap on his head. He bowed deeply and then handed me a letter with a wax seal. The seal bore the symbol of the *gauw*, the horned bull of Babylon. It was a message from Vardan himself. I broke the seal and read the contents. I stood up and pointed at the messenger.

'Tell King Vardan I will attend him at once.'

He bowed and then turned on his heels and walked briskly from my presence. The others looked at me in anticipation.

'Well, it would appear that Mithridates and Narses intend to deal with their enemies sooner than we thought. They have laid siege to Babylon.'

Orodes and Nergal jumped up.

'Babylon?' Orodes was shocked. 'They would not dare.'

Babylon was a city of great age and glory. Though it no longer had a major say in world affairs, the city and its rulers were still accorded great esteem by the other kings of the empire. And the King of Babylon had always enjoyed close and amiable relations with the court at Ctesiphon, the two palaces being only around seventy miles from each other. But now the army of Mithridates and Narses were laying siege to the ancient city.

I rode to the Babylonian camp in the company of Gallia, Orodes, Nergal and Praxima. It was late afternoon now and the weather was still overcast and gloomy, made worse by Vardan's news. Our horses were taken from us at the entrance to the royal pavilion and we were escorted inside the cavernous structure by purple-clad guards carrying wicker shields and spears with leaf-shaped blades that were the height of a man. Such weapons were useless in battle but were ideal for wielding in the confined and often cluttered spaces inside royal tents. We found an agitated Vardan in the throne area of the pavilion pacing up and down in front of his senior officers. His commanders were dressed in the same dragon-skin armour worn by Vardan's royal bodyguard – a leather vest covered with overlapping silver plates that protected the chest and back. They all held richly embossed silver helmets in the crooks of their arms and wore swords in purple scabbards decorated with silver adornments at their hips. They looked nervous as their liege paced up and down.

Vardan stopped moving when we entered.

'Ah, Pacorus, thank the gods you are here.'

I bowed my head. 'At your service, lord king.'

'Yes, yes.' He pointed at a servant. 'Fetch us refreshments. Have you eaten, are you hungry? And wine, we must have wine.'

He became aware of the others with me and walked over to Orodes and embraced him.

'Forgive me my lack of manners, lord prince.'

He turned to Nergal and embraced him too. 'And my thanks to you King Nergal, the sword that guards Babylon's southern border.' Nergal, unaccustomed to the etiquette of kings, was momentarily

145

surprised by Vardan's show of affection but quickly recovered. 'It is an honour, lord.'

Vardan kissed Gallia and Praxima, hailing them as close friends of his daughter, Princess Axsen. His complexion became ashen at the thought of his only child in peril.

Slaves brought in silver jugs, poured wine into jewel-adorned silver cups and served them to us from gold trays. If only Vardan spent as much on his army as he did on his rich living! A blast of trumpets signalled the arrival of my father as more slaves positioned a large rectangular table with ornately carved legs in front of us. It was at least six feet wide and over double that in length. Upon the table was unrolled a beautiful tapestry that depicted the entire Parthian Empire. The base colour was a rich yellow, with the course of the Euphrates and Tigris rivers depicted in blue and cities and towns marked with black thread. It must have taken months to create such a masterpiece. But awe-inspiring as it was, the money and resources devoted to creating it would have been better spent on soldiers and weapons for Babylon's army.

My father was shown into the throne area and he embraced Vardan. He had brought Vistaspa, who bowed stiffly to the King of Babylon. Gafarn, who accompanied my father, smiled and laid his hands on the king's shoulders, assuring Vardan that we were all here to help him and he should not worry. My brother's words seemed to have a calming effect on Vardan, if only for a while. My father pointedly ignored Nergal and me. I had heard from Gafarn that my father had taken a dim view of my placing Nergal, formerly an officer in Hatra's army, on Mesene's throne. He thought even less of Praxima, a former whore, becoming Parthian royalty. I did not care; they were my friends and I trusted them both, which is more than I could presently say of Hatra.

More slaves brought silver platters heaped with pastries, sweet meats, yoghurt, dried fruit and bread as we all gathered round the table. At its head Vardan stood with arms folded, staring glumly at the map of the empire. His eyes were fixed on his city of Babylon. My father stood halfway down the table, resting his hands on the edge, flanked by Vistaspa on his right and Gafarn on his left. I stood across the table, directly opposite my father, Orodes on my right and Nergal on my left. Praxima stood next to her husband with Gallia on her other side. Thus four kings, two queens and two princes stared at the map lying before them. Vardan looked at one of his officers.

'General Mardonius, you will be our guide.'

A man in his late fifties with thick grey hair handed a slave his helmet and walked to the table, a long cane in his right hand. He bowed his head to Vardan and pointed the end of the cane at where Babylon was marked on the map.

Vardan sighed deeply. 'My friends, word reached me earlier that Babylon is now encircled by the forces of Narses and Mithridates. Axsen managed to send a messenger alerting me to her peril before the city was closely invested. It appears that the enemy has also destroyed many villages on their march south from the Tigris to Babylon. As well as being encircled by the enemy the city is awash with refugees from the surrounding area.'

'It grieves me to hear such news, my friend,' said my father. 'Hatra's army is at your disposal.'

'As is Dura's,' I announced.

'And Mesene's,' added Nergal.

Vardan's mouth showed a slight smile. 'I thank you all. I shall be marching south at once along the Euphrates.' Mardonius moved the end of the cane from our present position, approximately eighty miles north of Babylon, down to the Euphrates and then along the river to Babylon. Three days' march, more or less.

'Sensible,' agreed my father.

I looked at the map and saw another possibility present itself.

Vardan looked at my father. 'Thank you, my friend.'

I looked at the map, to where Dura was marked on the western bank of the Euphrates. From my city the great river travels south for a distance of around fifty miles before changing direction to run directly east for nearly a hundred miles. The waterway then changes course again, this time southeast for another hundred miles, before resuming its southerly course once more. Our present location was near where the river changes direction from southeast to directly south. We were within a day's march of the Euphrates and two days away from the Tigris.

'May I suggest another strategy, lord?' I said at length.

My father folded his arms and stared at me disapprovingly.

Vardan was confused. 'Another strategy?'

I held out my palm to Mardonius for his cane. He handed it to me. I used it to point to where Ctesiphon was located.

'You mean to march down the east bank of the Euphrates?' I asked Vardan.

'Naturally, it is the quickest route to Babylon.'

'Indeed,' I said. 'But if we strike southeast we would be able to march along the west bank of the Tigris.'

Vardan wore a furrowed brow. 'The Tigris?'

'Yes, lord,' I continued. 'The enemy retreated across the Tigris when the armies of Hatra, Babylon and Mesene came to my aid.' I traced the end of the cane from Ctesiphon to Babylon. 'But then recrossed the Tigris to march southwest when news reached them that you had left Babylon to be here.'

'All this I know,' snapped Vardan.

147

'Yes, lord,' I said, 'but if we strike for the Tigris and then march southwest we can trap the enemy between ourselves and Babylon.'

My father slowly placed his hands on the edge of the table once more. 'We go to relieve Babylon, not to fight a battle. I would have thought that much was obvious.'

I handed the cane back to Mardonius. 'The enemy has struck at Babylon believing they can take the city. But Babylon has not fallen.'

I looked at Vardan. 'It has high walls and an adequate garrison, lord?'

'It has a garrison, or course,' replied Vardan. 'But it will be hard pressed if the enemy attempts an assault.'

I shook my head. 'They have no means to breach the walls, lord, so any assault will come to grief.'

Only I among all the kings of the empire had siege engines that could breach high and strong walls.

'The refugees within the city will soon consume the food supplies, majesty,' said a concerned Mardonius.

'It is as Mardonius says,' said Vardan to me.

But I was not to be put off by incidentals. 'If we leave at dawn and march to the Tigris we can reach Babylon in four days. More importantly we will have severed the enemy's line of retreat. Mithridates and Narses will be forced to give battle.'

Vardan stared at the map once more, seemingly torn between wanting to reach his capital as soon as possible and the thought of dealing with Mithridates and Narses, who had invaded his kingdom.

He sighed deeply. 'I came to your aid, Pacorus, because you are a valiant and honourable man and also the son of my friend, Varaz.'

My father bowed his head at Vardan.

'And Mithridates has insulted me by bringing his army into my kingdom without my permission, and has insulted me further by laying siege to my capital. But your objectives are not mine. If we march to Babylon then Mithridates and Narses will withdraw, I have no doubt of that.'

'And after that?' I asked.

'After that,' continued Vardan, 'I will request that Mithridates pays me compensation for the ruin he has visited upon my kingdom.'

I drummed my fingers on the table, causing my father to frown some more.

'Mithridates will never agree to that, lord. It would be better if the empire was rid of him once and for all.'

Vardan and Mardonius behind him appeared horrified at my suggestion, while my father's face was like thunder.

'Your quarrel with Mithridates is not mine, Pacorus,' said Vardan at length. 'Have you forgotten the chaos and bloodshed that followed the death of Sinatruces? The empire cannot afford another civil war, not with the Armenians and the nomads of the northern steppes causing trouble on our borders. To say nothing of the Romans.'

'I concur with Vardan's thoughts,' growled my father. 'You will not drag us into your own private war.'

I laughed. 'How short is your memory, father. Cast your mind back to when we fought Mithridates and Narses at Surkh, or should I say when I fought them.'

The Battle of Surkh was fought east of Ctesiphon, when Narses had attempted to become king of kings by force. Phraates, the son of Sinatruces and father of Orodes, had been elected to the high crown at the Council of Kings held at Esfahan. But Narses had disagreed with the decision, believing that he should rule the empire. He had enlisted the aid of the eastern kings of the empire, plus Mithridates, who had turned against his own father, and had brought a great army to fight those who abided by the decision taken at Esfahan. The two armies met at Surkh. Domitus and the Duran Legion, supported by the Babylonian foot, had destroyed Narses' foot soldiers, while I commanded my cavalry on the army's right wing and had led them to victory over the enemy horsemen opposite them. The army of Hatra had been positioned on the left wing of the army and had done nothing that day but stand and watch the enemy being routed and escape to safety.

My father looked at Vardan in confusion. 'Surkh, what nonsense is this?'

My blood was up now. 'If you had attacked that day Narses and Mithridates would not have escaped, Phraates would not have been murdered by his own son and we would not be standing round a table arguing how to relieve Babylon.'

My father jabbed a finger at me. 'Have a care, Pacorus. The support of Hatra and Babylon, so freely given, can be just as easily withdrawn. How short is your memory? Just a few days ago you were surrounded and half-dead in the middle of the desert. Do not add ingratitude to your list of failings.'

Nergal and Praxima were squirming with embarrassment at this exchange, and even Gafarn appeared to be lost for words. Vardan looked very serious and Mardonius fiddled nervously with his pointing stick. Gallia gave me a look of disapproval, willing me to cease talking. But I could not let it rest.

'I am grateful of course that you brought your army to this place, father.' I smiled at Vardan. 'And I esteem Babylon my most valuable and trusted ally.' Out of the corner of my eye I saw Vistaspa bristle at the veiled insult to Hatra. 'But eventually matters will have to be settled with Mithridates and Narses. I say better sooner than later.'

'Hatra's army will be marching south with King Vardan to relieve Babylon,' said my father coolly. 'If you do not wish to support us then

I suggest you take your soldiers back to Dura. But I tell you this, Pacorus, I will not be seeking a battle with Mithridates.'

'Nor I,' added Vardan.

'And if Mithridates marches north to meet us?' I asked.

My father's nostrils flared. 'Then you will have your battle, Pacorus. And if you kill Mithridates then the empire will have need of a new king of kings. And that man will be Narses no doubt. And then the whole process begins again and we will have civil war in the empire once more.'

'Not if Narses also dies,' I remarked casually.

Orodes and Vardan stared at me in horror. My father held out his hands.

'Just how many kings do you intend to kill, Pacorus?'

'None that do not deserve to die,' I retorted.

'Perhaps you wish to be king of kings yourself,' he remarked with sarcasm.

'Why not?' I answered. 'At least then justice would rule the empire in place of tyranny.'

'You aspire to the high crown?' asked Vardan, his brown eyes full of anxiety.

'No, lord,' I said. 'I was merely making the point that the empire would be a better place without Mithridates.'

'That is not your decision to make,' said my father. 'Whether you like it or not, Mithridates is king of kings.'

There followed an angry silence as we all stared at the table and avoided each other's eyes. The tension was unbearable. Eventually my father spoke to Vardan.

'It would be best if we marched at dawn, Vardan, along the eastern bank of the Euphrates.'

Vardan looked up at him and nodded. My father nodded back, turned on his heels and left without acknowledging me, Vistaspa and Gafarn following. I stood back from the table, bowed my head to Vardan and also departed. Gallia, Orodes, Nergal and Praxima trailed in my wake. It had been a most unpleasant meeting and resentment against my father began to rise within me.

In my tent later, in the company of Gallia, Nergal, Praxima and Orodes and with several cups of wine inside me, I began to pace up and down in a temper.

'We have Mithridates where we want him and my father refuses to see it. This is an opportunity sent by the gods and we ignore it.'

'Vardan just wishes to see his daughter safe, Pacorus,' said Gallia, 'and so do I.'

'Praxima and I feel the same way,' said Nergal. 'We are very fond of Axsen.'

I stopped and clasped a palm to my chest. 'I love Axsen too, but no one is safe in this world while Mithridates lives. I'm half-tempted to strike for the Tigris myself and leave Vardan and my father to relieve Babylon.' I emptied my cup and walked over to refill it from the jug that sat on the table. I did so and held it up to Nergal.

'Are you with me, my old friend?'

Nergal looked at me and glanced at Praxima. Before he could answer Gallia stood up.

'You have had too much to drink, Pacorus. Even I, a mere woman, know that it is foolish to divide one's forces in the face of the enemy. Nergal is too polite and loyal to point out that to divide an army would be the height of folly.'

'The height of folly?' I said. 'I think sending Surena and a thousand of my horse archers across the Tigris is more idiotic. You have, my sweet, condemned him and them to death by doing so. Surena was one of my most promising commanders and now he almost certainly lies dead in the desert, vultures picking his bones clean.'

My wife had the most beautiful eyes of any woman, their shade of blue purer and more striking than the surface of the Euphrates on a high summer's day, but now they bored into me like two thunderbolts.

'This *idiot* saved your arse a few days ago,' she shot back at me.

Orodes jumped up and placed an arm round my shoulders.

'My friends,' he implored, 'let us not bicker thus. Let us instead thank the gods that we are safe and all together. If we argue among ourselves then the laughter of my stepbrother will be our only reward.'

He was right, of course. I apologised to Nergal and Gallia and the day ended better than it had begun. Later, when we were alone, Gallia rebuked me for provoking my father. On one level she was right; it was not appropriate for a son to criticise his father, much less in public. But it irked me that he and Vardan could not see the logic that was staring them both in the face, that Mithridates and Narses intended to deal with all their enemies and that Hatra and Babylon, along with Dura, were all in that category. With Gotarzes gone Mithridates now ruled unchallenged from the Tigris to the Himalayas and south to the Persian Gulf and Arabian Sea. In the north the kingdoms of Hyrcania and Margiana, whose rulers had both pledged their allegiance to me, were under assault from the nomads of the northern steppes. If they too fell then Dura would lose two more allies.

As I lay in my cot in the early hours of the next day staring at the roof of the tent, Gallia sleeping beside me, I burned with a desire to seek a battle with the enemy. If I killed Mithridates then his malice would be gone from the world. He had no sons to carry on his line. But then, his demise would allow Narses to seize the high crown. But if he too was killed; what then? No doubt his sons would swear blood vengeance against me. But they too were probably with his army. It was not unconceivable that they might also fall, in which case all would be settled. No, not all, for the empire would then need a new king of kings. Years ago his friend Balas, King of Gordyene, had proposed my father as a suitable candidate following Sinatruces' death. My father had been obstinate in his refusal to be put forward for the position. But now? Perhaps he could be persuaded to take the high crown in the interests of preserving the empire. Hatra was rich, her army strong and my father was widely respected as a wise and just king who had the empire's best interests at heart. I smiled to myself. It all suddenly made perfect sense.

Chapter 7

The next day we broke camp and headed south along the Euphrates, though not actually along the eastern bank of the river itself. We were less than a hundred miles north of Babylon. Inland from the river for a distance of around two miles was a continuous belt of land dotted with villages and fields. This was Mesopotamia, which in Greek means 'land between the rivers', the fertile area that had for thousands of years produced food, building materials and clothing in abundance for its people. In the spring the Euphrates, which began its long journey in the great Taurus Mountains in the north, was swelled with melt waters that threatened to engulf the towns and villages along its length with flooding. But the ancients had learned long ago to tame the great river with dams, dykes and irrigation canals. When the level of the river rose the dams and dykes prevented the land from being flooded, while the canals channelled the water inland where it could be stored and used to irrigate crops and water livestock.

Each Babylonian village was home to between a hundred and two hundred people and was surrounded by fields and orchards that produced barley, dates, wheat, lentils, peas, olives, grapes, pomegranates and vegetables. There were also fields of flax, which once harvested, cleaned and combed was woven into linen to make clothing. It was also used to make fishermen's nets. The villagers also kept goats, sheep and cows in pens next to their homes to produce milk, cheese, meat and leather.

This stretch of the river was densely populated and farmed, and the last thing the villagers needed was an army marching across their fields. Therefore we marched in three great columns inland from where the fields and farms ended and the desert began. Vardan and his Babylonians formed the right-hand column as we rode south, the villagers stopping their work and cheering him and his senior officers as they passed by their homes. No doubt many who rode in the ranks of his horse archers were recruited from these same villages, and would return to their farming once the campaign was over – those who still lived. My father rode with Vardan as it was the custom for the kings to travel in each other's company when on campaign. In his place Vistaspa commanded Hatra's army that made up the central column.

Dura's army and Nergal's horsemen formed the left-hand column of our combined forces and I rode at its head. I was still annoyed with my father and so preferred to avoid his company.

'You are being childish,' Gallia rebuked me as walked beside our horses across the parched ground. Like yesterday the sky was heaped with sullen grey clouds that threatened to burst but withheld their rain, creating a humid and uncomfortable atmosphere, rather like that which had existed in Vardan's pavilion the day before.

153

'I prefer the company of my friends to that of kings,' I replied.

Orodes held the reins of his horse as he walked beside me, while on my other side the long, gangly legs of Nergal paced the ground. Behind us Gallia and Praxima led their mounts.

We had ridden hard during the morning, covering around fifteen miles, and then the whole army had dismounted so as not to tax the horses unduly. We would soon halt for an hour or so before resuming our ride south. The day after tomorrow we would be at Babylon, unless Mithridates chose to march north to meet us.

'This continual bickering between you and your father is tiresome Pacorus,' continued Gallia.

'A father and son should not quarrel so,' said Orodes sternly.

'Orodes is right,' added Nergal.

'I have no wish to argue with my father,' I said.

'As long as he agrees with you,' interrupted Gallia.

'As long as he sees Mithridates for what he is,' I corrected her. 'I don't want to see my father's head split open by an assassin's sword like mine nearly was.'

'Surely he would not attempt to murder your father?' said Praxima.

'Why not?' I replied. 'He has already killed his own father and now Gotarzes.'

I glanced at Orodes who stared ahead with unblinking eyes.

'I am sorry, my friend,' I said.

He managed a weak smile. 'You are right in what you say, Pacorus, but my stepbrother is clever as well as malicious. I have no doubt that he has sent many messages to your father professing his friendship and allegiance. For your father it is no small thing to take arms against the king of kings.'

'And in truth it is no small matter for Mesene,' said Nergal.

'I know that, Nergal, and I appreciate your presence here. You are a loyal friend.'

'And we are glad to be by your side, Pacorus,' added Praxima.

Brave and fearless Praxima. She was as good as any man on the battlefield but beyond the bravado I knew that she and her husband were in great peril. Like Babylon Mesene occupied land between the Tigris and Euphrates, and directly opposite Nergal's kingdom, across the Tigris, lay the Kingdom of Susiana, Mithridates' domain. Its capital Susa was only a hundred and fifty miles from Uruk. At least while Gotarzes still lived the Kingdom of Elymais acted as a counterweight to Susiana, but now Mesene potentially faced the full might of Mithridates' wrath. That is why he must be dealt with quickly. If Mithridates and Narses were allowed to turn their full strength against Mesene, Nergal's kingdom would crumble.

'How many troops can you raise, Nergal?' I asked.

'Five thousand horse archers I have brought with me,' he replied. 'These are my professional troops, men who are paid by me to be full-time soldiers. Uruk has a garrison of a further thousand men, trained and equipped after the Greek fashion, each man with bronze helmet, leather cuirass, bronze-faced shield, spear and sword. In times of emergency I can muster a further ten thousand horse archers at most.'

'It is a credit to you that you can raise such a force,' remarked Orodes.

And so it was, for Mesene was a poor kingdom and the campaign that Chosroes had waged against me had cost him his army, his city and ultimately his life. A fair number of the kingdom's lords and their men had also died before the walls of Dura and later in the defence of Uruk.

'How many Ma'adan have you recruited?' I asked.

'A third of my horse archers are men from the marshes,' Nergal replied. 'They are good warriors, used to living off their wits and unafraid of hardships. Much like Surena.'

'Ah, yes,' I said. 'Surena. You heard that Gallia sent him and a thousand of my horse archers, men you used to command Nergal, into the heart of enemy territory. I had great hopes for Surena and now he lies dead in the desert.'

Nergal was shocked. 'Surena is dead?'

'Of course he isn't,' snapped Gallia. 'Pacorus whines like an old mule. Surena is perfectly capable of taking care of himself. He fought the soldiers of Chosroes for many years with only a long knife and a ragged band of feral youths for company.'

'I did not know you took such an interest in him,' I said.

'I don't,' she replied irritably, 'but Viper is forever talking about him and as I am very fond of her I listen to her words.'

I tried a clever riposte. 'And soon you will have to tell her that she is a widow.'

'Don't be an idiot, Pacorus. Do you think I would willingly send him and a thousand of Dura's soldiers to their deaths? Do you think I am so stupid, that I know nothing of war even though I have fought by your side these past ten years?'

'Of course not, I merely meant…'

Her voice rose in anger. 'I have saved your life on more than one occasion, when your short-sightedness nearly got you and the men you led killed. And now you mock me in front of our friends.'

'Gallia, I would never…'

Her tone got sharper. 'Shut up! I grow weary of your voice.'

We walked on in silence for another few minutes, the only sound being the jangling of the horses' bits and the tramp of our boots on the ground. At length Gallia spoke once more, her voice calmer and more measured.

155

'As I have told you, Pacorus, before we left Dura Dobbai told me to send Surena across the Tigris. She said that if I did do so he would reap a rich harvest.'

I mumbled an acknowledgement of her words but said no more. I was still annoyed that she had sent a third of my horse archers to God knows where. That said, the visions and advice of Dobbai were not to be dismissed lightly so I let the matter rest. I still believed Surena to be dead, though.

That night the armies of the kings camped inland from the Euphrates. The logistics of watering over forty thousand horses and ten thousand camels were huge, and so bad-tempered quartermasters scurried around like demented wildcats as they allocated companies to the dozens of small reservoirs that dotted the landscape. Fed by canals that extended inland from the Euphrates, these reservoirs in turn fed a myriad of irrigation channels that delivered water to the fields. In this way crops were irrigated, the bellies of the villagers were filled when they were harvested and the surpluses were sent to Babylon as taxes. The canals, dams and irrigation ditches were so crucial to the life of the kingdom that each village was charged with the responsibility for the upkeep of the irrigation system surrounding it. Each village's headman was paid by the treasury in Babylon to ensure that the system functioned smoothly, on pain of death. This appeared harsh, but the lives of the villagers depended on the fields being irrigated. If the crops failed, they starved.

The weather had not broken and so the early evening was still humid as the squires put up our tents. The horses were quartered in stables made from wooden poles and linen sheets and the camels were confined to corrals. I had sent Byrd and his scouts south the day before. He returned two hours before sundown with his black-clad companions. His horse and those of his men stood sweating with their heads bowed as he slid off his mount in front of my tent. Gallia was standing beside me.

'You men take your horses to the stables to be watered and fed,' I ordered, 'then get some food inside you.'

I pointed at a waiting squire who walked over and took the reins of Byrd's horse from him. I grabbed Byrd's elbow.

'Come inside and take the weight off your feet.'

Inside he slumped into a chair and stretched out his legs. Orodes handed him a cup of water then sat beside him. Gallia and I likewise seated ourselves.

Byrd drained his cup and unwrapped the turban from his head. His swarthy features matched the black shadows under his eyes.

'Babylon still under siege,' he said at last.

'You rode all the way to the city?' asked Orodes. No wonder his horse and those of his scouts looked done-in.

Byrd shook his head. 'No need. Many enemy tents pitched all round city. No smoke or fire coming from Babylon, so it holds out.'

'We had better get word to Vardan,' said Orodes, 'to let him know that his daughter is safe, at least for the present.'

He stood up and shook Byrd's hand, much to the amusement of my chief scout.

'I will ride to Vardan's camp myself.' Orodes bowed his head to Gallia, then me and left.

Gallia smiled. 'You would think that after all these years Orodes would be less formal in our company.'

'Manners and protocol are important to him,' I said. 'Perhaps more so now he no longer has a kingdom to go back to.'

'If ever there was a man who would make a just and great king, it is Orodes,' she mused.

'He will be a king one day,' I said. 'That I promise.'

'We see many people fleeing north on road,' said Byrd. 'Men, women, children, some driving goats and cattle before them. They flee from enemy. Tell of much killing.' He glanced at Gallia. 'And raping.'

'And if ever there was a king that deserved to be deposed,' said Gallia dryly, 'it is Mithridates.'

I stood and slapped Byrd on the shoulder.

'Well done, my friend. Get some food inside you.'

Later, after we had groomed our horses, Gallia and I led Remus and Epona out of camp to one of the reservoirs allocated to Dura's army by the Babylonian commissariat. We walked them out of camp and across the arid ground that led to the large high-banked, stone-lined irrigator that was full to the brim with water. Sluiceways extended out from the reservoir across the fields, but men were leading their horses up the banks to allow the animals to drink directly from the reservoir itself. On the western side of the reservoir was a wide canal that brought water directly from the Euphrates, some two miles distant. As we neared the reservoir, the Amazons leading their horses behind us, I caught sight of a figure standing on the top of the bank gesticulating with his arms. As we neared the eastern side of the reservoir I heard his voice.

'You're at the wrong waterhole, you sons of whores. Second company of cataphracts is allocated to the reservoir in the next village. So bugger off and take your horses with you. What's the point of having a system if you ignore it.'

He was a large man with a round face and long dark hair, his leggings and shirt dirty and torn. He could have been mistaken for a local beggar but he happened to be one of my best quartermasters.

'Strabo,' I called out. 'That's no way to address the best horsemen in the empire.'

157

He squinted in my direction with his piggy eyes and then they bulged wide.

He turned to the men who were causing him much anxiety.

'Here's the king and queen, so you'd better clear off quick otherwise they'll have your balls on the end of a spear.'

Gallia frowned and I laughed as the men of the second company bowed their heads to me and my queen, led their horses down the bank and then rode to where they should have been watering their horses.

Gallia and I led our horses up the bank and let them drink from the cool water, the Amazons doing the same. Next to Strabo was a tall, wiry man in his fifties with thinning hair and sinewy arms. He wore a simple linen tunic, frayed knee-length leggings and sandals on his feet. He bowed deeply to me.

Strabo wiped his nose on his sleeve and belched. 'This is Teres, majesty. Headman of the village whose little lake this is.'

'Welcome, highness,' said Teres, who was staring in amazement at Gallia's long blonde hair. Parthian women have olive complexions and dark hair; he had probably never seen a light-skinned, blue-eyed woman in his life. And he stood transfixed as the mail-clad women warriors beyond us stood and watched as their horses drank the water.

'Well, Strabo,' I said, 'is everything going according to plan?'

He shrugged. 'Mostly, although your cataphracts think they are God's gift and do as they like. They need their arses tanning if you ask me.'

'I didn't, but I'm sure you have everything in hand.'

Strabo grinned at Gallia. 'I trust the queen is well.'

Gallia observed him as an eagle would a field mouse, curling up her lip at him. Strabo jabbed a finger into Teres' ribs.

'My queen is from a land far away from here, from a place called Gaul. Never heard of that, have you?'

Teres, still transfixed by Gallia's looks, shook his head.

'Well,' continued Strabo, his eyes walking all over my wife's body, 'it's a place that breeds fierce women warriors.'

He nodded at the Amazons standing beside their horses taking water from the reservoir.

'Pretty to look at, aren't they? And about as friendly as a nest of cobras. They'll slice off your balls as soon as look at you.'

But Teres was not looking at the Amazons but Remus, nodding his head slightly while Strabo continued to admire the contours of my wife's body.

'You know it is death to touch the queen's person, Strabo,' I remarked casually.

Strabo flushed and clasped his hands in front of him, a look of innocence on his face.

'I didn't, wouldn't, touch her majesty, majesty. Of course not.'

'Even impure thoughts could be construed as a form of molestation,' I said sternly.

Strabo became nonplussed. 'I, er, well. I must be getting along, majesty, many things to do before I turn in.'

He bowed awkwardly and then turned on his heels, scurrying down the bank and leaping into his saddle.

'I don't know why I tolerate you, Strabo,' I called after him.

'Because I keep your horses shod, fed, saddled and ready for your wars, majesty,' he replied, then whooped for joy, dug his knees into his horse and galloped off.

'You should have him flogged for his insolence,' sneered Gallia, who had noted Strabo's lecherousness.

'He's my best quartermaster,' I replied. 'If I flog him he'll only be more bad tempered and offensive, and probably less efficient. Besides, having been flogged myself once, I will not visit the same punishment upon someone unless they truly deserve it.'

'His eyes were all over me,' said Gallia.

I dropped Remus' reins and went to her side.

'Can't blame him for that,' I whispered in her ear.

She dug a finger in my ribs.

'You are impossible.'

Teres had picked up my horse's reins as Remus drank from the water, the headman stroking his neck. Remus didn't flinch as a stranger petted him.

'He likes you,' I said to Teres, who blushed and bowed to me.

'Forgive me, highness, I meant no offence.'

I laid my hand on his arm. 'Of course not. Be at ease. We are grateful for your help.'

'You have enough water to grow your crops?' asked Gallia.

'Yes, highborn,' replied Teres, 'Tishtrya has been kind to us.'

'Tishtrya?'

Teres then explained that he and his villagers worshipped Tishtrya, the god of rain who had created the world's lakes and rivers and who now gave water to the earth so that his followers could grow the crops that fed them. As well as providing rains that feed the rivers and lakes, Tishtrya also patrolled the heavens and kept evil away from his followers.

'When danger threatens,' he continued, admiring Remus, 'he takes the form of a great white stallion to defeat it.'

Gallia was most interested in his words. 'A white stallion?'

'Yes, highness. The legend has been handed down to us through many generations of our people. Before there were any cities on the earth, when Tishtrya was spreading rains over the land, the dread demon of drought, Apaosha, suddenly appeared to suck the land dry and kill thousands of men and animals. So Tishtrya took the form of a mighty white stallion that reflected the purity of his purpose and the strength of his will. Apaosha, reflecting his dark nature, transformed himself into a terrible black stallion and the two did battle in the middle of a vast plain. After three days and three nights of battle neither could overcome the other and men began to lose faith in Tishtrya and stopped praying for him and offering their libations. And so Tishtrya grew weaker and weaker until it appeared that he would be defeated. But then Ahura Mazda, the supreme god, the creator of heaven and earth, offered his own prayers in support of Tishtrya, who was strengthened and thus able to overcome Apaosha, who was finally banished from the earth.'

I thought of Narses mounted on his black stallion and took Teres' words as a good omen.

Gallia smiled at him. 'That is a beautiful story. I pray that Tishtrya continues to smile on you and your people.'

The next day, as we continued our march south to Babylon, the clouds at last burst and the land was drenched by a great thunderstorm. Any depressions quickly filled with water and the ground was transformed into a sea of mud that slowed our advance as horses and camels struggled to find their footing in the deluge. Flaps on quivers and bow cases were fastened shut to keep bows and arrows dry, and scale armour carried on the camels was wrapped in waxed covers to keep the rain off it. Mail armour can rust after a good dousing with water and so the Amazons also stashed their mail shirts on the camel train. Gallia rode on Epona with her arms outstretched, laughing as she held her face up to the heavens and drank from the raindrops. Her drenched shirt clung to her lithe body, highlighting the contours of her breasts and arms, her silk vest maintaining her modesty. She was deliriously happy.

'You see, Pacorus, how Tishtrya smiles on us. Are you not joyous that he gives us his blessing'

I looked at Orodes sitting in his saddle beside me, his hair matted to his skull, his clothes sodden, and felt water coursing off my nose, ears and running down my back.

'Delighted, my sweet.'

Vagharsh sitting behind us, holding my banner in its waxed sleeve, laughed aloud.

Eventually the rain ceased and the temperature dropped rapidly with the onset of the evening. We warmed ourselves round great fires that appeared as numerous as the stars in the night sky. Darkness fell and the armies camped on a stretch of land that extended for over ten miles. We were now less than half a day's march from Babylon. Tomorrow we would be locked in battle with the enemy.

160

After we had changed our clothes and eaten I sent Byrd and his scouts south to reconnoitre the enemy's position, instructing him to retreat immediately if he encountered enemy patrols. I did not want him or any of his men falling into the merciless hands of Narses or Mithridates. I watched them ride out of camp. At the same time a rider came from the camp of Vardan requesting my presence at the king's pavilion. I took Orodes and Gallia along with me, the Amazons acting as our escort.

We arrived at the pavilion and were shown into the throne room where, once again, Mardonius stood before a table with his pointing stick, the Babylonian high command standing to one side. Also at the table were my father, Gafarn, Vistaspa, Vardan, Nergal and Praxima.

We bowed our heads to Vardan and I acknowledged my father but said no words to him. Servants brought us warm wine to drink and we once more gathered for another lecture. The new map spread out before us showed the city of Babylon and the surrounding area. I had never visited the city and was in truth fascinated by its layout and history. I knew that there had been a settlement on its site three thousand years ago, and that seventeen hundred years ago one of its kings, Hammurabi, had established the first codes of laws in human history. Thereafter Babylon had increased in size and influence, King Nebuchadnezzar building great inner and out walls around the city to make it an impregnable fortress. That was over five hundred years ago, though, and since then Babylon's power and influence had been in decline. It had been captured by the great Alexander, the warrior king of Macedon, two hundred and seventy years ago, and thirty years afterwards the city's outer walls had been demolished, the bricks being transported north to construct the city of Seleucia, which stood opposite the palace complex of Ctesiphon.

Vardan's words brought me back to the present.

'Tomorrow we will advance to the walls of Babylon and relieve my city. The latest intelligence that I have received indicates that the enemy have not left their siege positions.'

I felt a tingle go down my spine. This meant that we would get the chance to fight the enemy. Good. I smiled to myself and then felt my father's eyes upon me across the table. He said nothing and made no gesture, but he knew what was going through my mind.

Vardan continued. 'This being so, our joint forces will march directly south to enter the city via the Ishtar Gate.'

Mardonius used his pointer to indicate the aforementioned entrance that stood on the city's northern wall.

'The city's strongest bastion,' continued Vardan, 'the Northern Fortress, stands adjacent to the Ishtar Gate, and the archers on its high walls will be able to provide cover to our soldiers as they enter the city.'

161

Looking at the map I could see that the Euphrates ran right through Babylon, effectively cutting it in half, though the largest part – the old city I assumed – stood on the eastern bank of the river. The map also showed that the river was used to fill the great moat that surrounded all four sides of the city. It was undoubtedly still a formidable fortress. In addition to the Ishtar Gate there were nine other entrances into the city.

'It is most important that we get our soldiers inside the city,' said Vardan. 'The enemy has already tried to infiltrate Babylon north and south via the Euphrates, using rafts carrying troops, and they were beaten off with some difficulty.'

Vardan's plan made no sense. What was the point of trying to get horsemen into a city under siege when they could be used to destroy the besiegers outside the walls?

'Your pardon, lord king,' I said.

Vardan looked up at me. 'Yes, Pacorus?'

'Surely, lord, it would be better to destroy the enemy in battle and afterwards take our forces into your city.'

Vardan nodded knowingly at me. 'I have discussed this with your father and we are in agreement that the enemy will retreat before our forces arrive at Babylon.'

So, they had agreed on the plan for tomorrow without consulting Nergal or me. I saw the look of triumph on my father's face.

'Can you be certain that the enemy will retreat, lord king?' I said to Vardan.

'They will fall back,' said my father. 'They tried to take Babylon in Vardan's absence. Now he has returned at the head of over forty thousand men they won't let themselves be trapped between us and the city's garrison.'

My father made a good point but I resented not being consulted on matters of strategy.

'As it is Dura who fields the largest portion of the army, over half by my reckoning, it would have been good manners, father, to have sought my advice on the plan for tomorrow.'

My father folded his arms across his chest.

'You have already dragged Vardan and myself into your private war with Mithridates and Narses, which has led to Babylon being besieged. It is fortunate for you that the city has thick walls and strong defences, otherwise the blood of its inhabitants would be on your conscience. As I have told you once before, I do not wish to plunge the empire into another civil war.'

'Neither do I, Pacorus,' said Vardan. 'Further war will be the ruin of the empire and of us all, I fear.'

I held out my palms to Vardan. 'I am in your service and debt, lord king.'

To my father I said nothing. Nergal appeared to be squirming with embarrassment while Gafarn merely looked at me with sympathetic eyes and shook his head.

'Good, well, let us continue.' Vardan nodded at Mardonius who pointed his stick at the Ishtar Gate. 'Tomorrow we will advance to the city with the army of Hatra on the right flank, the place of honour.'

Vardan nodded at my father, who smiled back.

'My own Babylonians,' continued Vardan, 'will occupy the centre of the line, with the Durans and Mesenians deployed on the left wing.'

This arrangement made sense in that it placed fifteen hundred cataphracts on the right under my father and a thousand of my own armoured horsemen on the left wing, though the army would be rather lopsided with my lords and their twenty thousand horse archers grouped on the left flank.

'My lords and their men could be used to strengthen our centre,' I suggested. 'In that way we can extend our frontage and thus have a better chance of enveloping the enemy.'

'Poor farmers on ragged mounts,' sneered Vistaspa, to which my father laughed.

Vistaspa was a great warrior, a man who had helped to forge Hatra's army into a fearsome weapon, but his blind loyalty to my father and his callous nature made him a difficult man to like, though one could certainly admire him for his achievements. But at this moment I despised him. What was the bulk of Vardan's army but horse archers who were also farmers and townsfolk?

'At least my farmers have fought in battle, Lord Vistaspa. Remind me, when was the last time Hatra's army crossed swords with the enemy, I forget?'

Vistaspa's nostrils flared at the insult but it was my father who spoke.

'A kingdom's army is a resource to be used wisely, to preserve its safety and prosperity, not as a tool for a reckless king.'

Mardonius glanced anxiously at his fellow officers.

'Father,' I said slowly, 'when I think of all the blood that has been shed these last few years, I cannot help but think that if you had listened to the words of your friends and had become king of kings then we would not be standing at this table arguing thus.'

My father let his hands fall by his sides.

'So it is my fault that Mithridates is king of kings, that Narses is his lord high general and that Babylon is under siege, is it? Would you admit that perhaps some of the blame for the empire's current problems can be attributable to the King of Dura?'

'I have only responded to threats, never made them.'

He rested his hands on the side of the table and leaned towards me.

'Do you deny that you wrote a letter to Mithridates following your capture of Uruk, stating that you would never rest until he was gone from the world.'

'It is common knowledge that I did so,' I replied.

'And did you expect that the high king would forget such an insult?'

'I do not care what Mithridates thinks.'

He gripped the edge of the table. 'Of course not, and in so doing you condemn your allies to a state of perpetual war.'

'What would you have me do, father, beg Mithridates for forgiveness?'

'Why not?' he said. 'You might find that he is more accommodating than you think.'

I thought of the sneering visage of Mithridates, the blood-soaked body of Godarz lying on the floor of his residence and the way he had insulted me at Esfahan during the Council of Kings.

'There can be no accommodation with Mithridates,' I replied.

My father then tried a different strategy. He looked at Nergal.

'What does the King of Mesene think on this matter? Your kingdom lies next to Susiana and your presence at this table may condemn you to face an invasion from the east.'

My father had articulated my own fears, for whereas the kingdoms of Babylon and Hatra lay between Dura and Susiana, Nergal's lands were adjacent to Mithridates' kingdom.

'It is as you say, lord king,' replied Nergal. 'Mesene would not be able to defeat the wrath of Susiana and Persis. But I have fought beside your son for ten years and everything I now have,' he put his arm round Praxima. 'Everything *we* have, is all down to him. But more than that, lord, he is our friend and we will not desert his side.'

'You must understand, father,' said Gafarn, 'that those of us who fought beside Spartacus in Italy have an unbreakable bond. We stand and fall together.'

'It is the falling that I worry about,' remarked my father grimly. 'But regarding the plan for tomorrow, it stands. Our main priority is to relieve Babylon, nothing more.'

I was tempted to raise the issue of the enemy burning Babylonian villages and killing and raping their inhabitants, but this would have provoked more argument to little effect. Thus the meeting petered out and we said our farewells to Gafarn, Vardan and Mardonius. I ignored Vistaspa and bade an icy good night to my father, though Gallia embraced both him and Gafarn warmly.

It was late when I assembled the lords and the senior officers of my cavalry in my tent. They all stood before me as I explained to them the dispositions they would adopt tomorrow. I told them that we had

164

Mithridates and Narses where we wanted them and that the coming battle would be a chance to settle things once and for all.

'We go to kill Mithridates and Narses,' I told them, 'to avenge Godarz and Gotarzes and rid the empire of the false high king. Only when we have a new king of kings sitting at Ctesiphon will we have peace and justice in the empire instead of tyranny and lawlessness.'

They cheered and slapped each other on the back and left in high spirits. When they had all filed out into the night Orodes came to my side.

'That was not what was agreed earlier in Vardan's pavilion,' he said.

I smiled at him. 'I am aware of that, my friend. But you know as well as I do that your stepbrother will not rest until I and my family are dead. He probably wishes your death as well. That being the case, I would rather the vultures were picking at his bones than mine.'

The day of battle is like any other for the army of Dura. The men rise, dress, eat breakfast and then form up in their companies or centuries. Roll calls are taken and inspections carried out. For the horsemen the morning routine also includes mucking out, watering, feeding and grooming their horses, before saddling them to ride out to battle. The squires help to dress and arm their masters but they also have their own horses to attend to, plus the two camels allotted to each cataphract, and so even my heavy cavalrymen can be found in the early morning light shovelling horse dung. I knew that in the army of Hatra the cataphracts were spared such duties, the city's aristocrats and their sons considering such tasks beneath them. Indeed, in the city's royal barracks even the squires were saved such tasks, an army of slaves being used for menial duties. In Dura's army there were no slaves and I considered it good practice for every man to acquaint himself with physical labour. On campaign the legionaries dug ditches and ramparts and the horsemen shovelled dung and groomed horses. It was a most satisfactory arrangement.

I went through the usual routine on the eve of battle. I had no squire of my own now that Surena had risen in the ranks but it mattered not. Orodes was always haranguing me about the necessity of maintaining appearances in having at least two squires, especially as I was a king, but I did not see the need. On campaign there was always someone to assist me, be it Gallia, the Amazons or Orodes himself after he had been dressed in his scale armour.

Gallia usually stayed with her Amazons the night before battle and last night had been no different. I myself rarely slept for more than two hours before a fight, rising before dawn to kneel by my bed to pray to Shamash. The prayers were always the same – that He would give me courage in the coming fight, that Gallia's life would be preserved, even if the price was the end of my own life, and that my conduct on this day would make my friends and family proud of me. As I closed my eyes and said the words I clutched the lock of my wife's hair that I always wore on a chain round my neck. Then I put on my silk vest, white long-sleeved shirt, leggings, boots and strapped on my sword belt. The scabbard was on my left hip and on the right I slipped my dagger into its sheath. It had formerly belonged to a Roman centurion who had been my jailer and tormentor. I had killed the centurion on the night Spartacus had freed me on the slopes of Mount Vesuvius. Gafarn had retrieved the dagger and had given it to me afterwards as a present. I had carried it ever since, as I had the Roman *spatha* that had been a gift from Spartacus himself. Even my helmet and leather cuirass were Roman. Today, though, I would be wearing the suit of scale armour that hung on a wooden frame beside my bed.

After attending to Remus' needs I ate with Gallia and Orodes. We shared a light breakfast of fruit, dried apricots and dates, bread and cheese, washed down with water. Outside the tent the air smelt of camel and horse dung, leather and campfires. Gallia sat at the table in her mail shirt, her helmet and sword resting on the surface. Orodes was dressed in a rich blue shirt, white leggings and red leather boots, his hair immaculately groomed and his beard neatly trimmed.

'Seems strange not having Domitus here with us,' he said, nibbling on a piece of cheese.

'I would rather he were here than the Babylonians,' I mused.

'You do not like King Vardan's soldiers, Pacorus?' asked Orodes.

'I like them well enough, I just don't like the idea of them on my flank. If today's fight is a hard one they might give way.'

'Not with your father's army on their other flank they won't,' said Gallia.

I smiled at her. 'Let's hope not, my sweet, let's hope not. It all depends on what the enemy does and how many of them there are.'

Those two questions were answered half an hour later when Byrd and his scouts rode into camp and he made his report in my tent. He looked tired and his robes were covered in dust. He flopped into a chair and drank greedily from a cup filled with water offered to him by Orodes.

Byrd looked at me. 'Mithridates not with enemy army. We saw no eagle banners.'

The banner of Susiana was well known to Byrd and his scouts for it was the same standard carried by Orodes, who was the rightful prince and heir to the throne of the kingdom.

I could not hide my disappointment. 'This is grave news indeed. You are sure, Byrd?'

I knew the answer before he nodded his head.

166

'The enemy host still very large, though,' he added. 'Their campfires filled the night.'

I slapped Byrd on the arm. 'Numbers aren't what count, Byrd. You should know that by now.'

At that moment a sentry opened the tent flap, stepped inside and saluted.

'Messenger from your father, majesty.'

I indicated for him to let the man enter. By his appearance – cuirass made of leather on which were fastened overlapping steel and bronze scales – I knew he was a member of Hatra's royal bodyguard. He held his burnished helmet in the crook of his right arm, a white horsehair plume fitted to its top ring, his white shirt edged with silver and his sword belt and scabbard also decorated with silver. He was obviously Hatran nobility.

He held out a wax-sealed parchment to me with his left hand.

'I send greetings from the king, your father, majesty. These are your battle orders.'

I looked at Gallia and then Orodes. 'My what?'

'King Vardan has appointed King Varaz as general-in-chief for the day and these are his orders. I am also to instruct you that the march south will commence in two hours.'

I snatched the letter from his hand and broke the seal. Another courier would have been nervous in our company but this one merely stood and waited for any message I might have for my father. Hatra's royal bodyguard was lavished with the best horses, the finest weapons that money could buy and stabling and quarters that would not shame kings and princes. Their reputation as great warriors was known throughout the empire, but looking at this fine young man standing before me I realised that arrogance and haughtiness were also part of their nature. I began to wonder how good they actually were.

I read the letter and then handed it to Orodes.

'My father obviously intends to fight the battle his way. He forgets that I too am a king.'

'This is merely confirmation of the dispositions that we discussed yesterday in King Vardan's pavilion,' said Orodes, trying to be the diplomat as usual.

'You mean the orders that we were given.'

'Don't start all that again, Pacorus,' said Gallia. 'You are like a dog with a bone, constantly gnawing away.'

'Perhaps we should go home, seeing as my father has obviously reduced us to bit-part players in his grand drama.'

'We must relieve Babylon,' said Orodes severely.

Gallia smiled at him. 'Ignore Pacorus, Orodes, he is aggrieved that it is his father and not he who is chief general for the day.'

The courier cleared his throat.

167

'Well?' I snapped.

'Is there any message you wish to convey to your father, majesty?'

I grinned at him mischievously. 'There is, but he would have your head if you spoke those words to him. So no, there is no message. You may go.'

Gallia rolled her eyes as he bowed his head and left us.

More agreeable company was Spandarat who appeared shortly after, his wild hair and beard matching his unruly appearance. He winked at Gallia with his one eye and sat himself down without asking permission, then helped himself to a cup of water.

He grimaced as he tasted the liquid. 'No wine, then?'

'I find that wine dulls the senses,' I said sternly. 'It is best to have a clear head in battle.'

He roared with laughter. 'Nonsense, a man fights better with a belly full of wine or beer inside him, ain't that right, princess?'

He winked at Gallia again who stuck out her tongue at him. She liked Dura's lords and they liked her. It was a sort of unholy alliance between them: the rough-and ready frontiersmen who lived hard lives and their queen who tolerated no nonsense.

'Are you and your men ready, Spandarat?' I enquired.

He shoved a great lump of cheese into his mouth. 'Me and twenty thousand others itching to get to grips with the enemy.'

I nodded. 'Excellent. You and the other lords will take up position behind my horse archers.'

A hurt look spread across his face. 'Behind them?'

'Don't worry,' I assured him. 'You will get a chance to empty your quivers.'

My lords were fearless in battle but totally undisciplined. They were like a bee. They had a powerful sting but could only sting once. On the battlefield each lord led his retainers oblivious to what was happening around him. Once committed the lords would charge headlong at the enemy in a great disorganised mass; their commitment thus required expert timing.

With Surena still absent, no doubt long dead, the command of the horse archers presented something of a dilemma. Ideally Orodes would lead the cataphracts, leaving me free to direct the whole army.

'I would esteem it an honour if you would command Dura's horse archers this day, lord prince,' I said to Orodes.

Before he could answer Gallia spoke. 'I will lead the horse archers so that Orodes may command your cataphracts.'

I looked at her and then Orodes, who said nothing.

'Makes sense,' said Spandarat with a mouthful of cheese, who then stood and nodded to me. 'I will go and inform the other lords. They will be as chuffed as a bull in a herd of young cows.'

168

After he had left Orodes and I put on our scale armour. The short-sleeved, thigh-length hide coats were thick and heavy, made more so by the iron scales riveted onto them. Split up to the waist to facilitate sitting in the saddle, the hide itself was thick enough to stop a glancing blow from a sword or spear. The best hide for scale armour was made from the skin of a water buffalo. This being the case, Nergal's officials in Uruk purchased these animals from the Ma'adan. They were then slaughtered and the skins sold to the armouries in Dura, Media, Atropaiene and even Hatra.

Next came the leg and arm armour – overlapping steel rings that extended from the shoulders to the wrists and from the thigh down to the ankles. Orodes wore an open-faced helmet with cheekguards and a neck flap and I wore my Roman officer's helmet with its goose feather plume.

We walked outside to where Orodes' squires held his horse and Gallia held Remus' reins. Both animals wore their own suits of scale armour that covered their bodies, necks and heads, with metal grills over their eyes. The squires assisted the Prince of Susiana and myself into our saddles and then handed us our lances, the hafts as thick as our wrists and tipped with a long spearhead at one end and savage butt spike at the other. My own *kontus* sported a pennant showing a red griffin on a white background, that of Orodes an eagle clutching a snake.

I rode with Gallia and Orodes at the head of the army as it made a leisurely march south towards the enemy. We were approximately ten miles from the walls of Babylon and roughly the same distance east of the Euphrates. We were riding across the hard-packed earth of the desert but Vardan and my father were travelling over the cultivated ground north of Babylon, fed by the waters of the great river, which had now been despoiled by the enemy. The mud-brick homes of the villages in the immediate vicinity of the city had been destroyed and their inhabitants no doubt dragged off into slavery. Babylonia had no fortified outposts such as existed in my own land or the Kingdom of Hatra. It would have thus been easy for enemy riders to appear as if by magic to pillage the villages.

I took no chances when it came to our own security, sending parties of horse archers ahead and into the desert on our left flank to ensure we were not attacked from those directions. After snatching a couple of hours' sleep, Byrd and his men were again in the saddle and scouting far and wide. My fears were allayed somewhat when the army of Mesene – five thousand horse archers – flooded the eastern horizon and provided security for my left flank. Nergal had been camped further north of our position and it had taken him and his men longer to assume their battle positions. With the Babylonians on my right flank and the Hatrans beyond them, the combined armies of four

169

kings made an impressive sight and numbered over two thousand, seven hundred cataphracts, thirty-eight thousand horse archers, a thousand Babylonian mounted spearmen and Vardan's royal bodyguard of five hundred men. And in the wake of my own army came a thousand camels carrying spare arrows; my father had a similar camel train transporting spare ammunition. Nergal had informed me that he also had a thousand camels for the same purpose.

The day was mild and sunny with only a few white, puffy clouds dotting an otherwise clear blue sky. There was a slight westerly breeze that barely troubled the banners of Dura and Susiana carried behind us as we trotted southwest so as to close up on the Babylonians. I deployed my cataphracts on the left of the Duran line, with the horse archers to their right and the lords and their men directly behind the latter. It would have been better if all the kings' heavy horsemen were grouped together so they could deliver the killer blow against the enemy when the time came, but my father would never have agreed to this unless he, or Vistaspa, was given command over all of them, something that I would never accept.

When Nergal's companies had dressed their lines on our left he and Praxima rode over to be with us, his banner fluttering behind them. As Nergal had formerly been my second-in-command and had raised and trained my own horsemen I had no fears that his Mesenians would not perform well this day.

'Do you think Narses will give battle?' asked Gallia.

'He has no choice,' I answered, 'unless he wishes to give himself up and submit to our mercy.'

'I doubt that,' said Orodes. 'But he may request a parley.'

'To what end?' asked Nergal.

'To attempt to sow disharmony within our ranks.' Orodes looked at me. 'He already knows that the kings of Babylon and Hatra do not share Dura's desire to see him destroyed.'

'I shall not speak to him,' I announced. 'I have no interest in hearing his voice.'

'He should be killed,' said Praxima.

'Some sense at last,' I replied.

Orodes was most unhappy. 'It is custom for all parties to be present at a parley, in the hope that bloodshed can be avoided.'

'If we avoid bloodshed this day,' I said in irritation, 'then that will mean that Narses and his army will have escaped, which means that he and it will be free to attack another Parthian kingdom. Have you forgotten Gotarzes so quickly, Orodes?'

Anger flashed in his eyes. 'Of course not!'

'You forget yourself, Pacorus,' said Gallia in rebuke.

I held up my hand to Orodes. 'Forgive me, my friend, I did not mean to offend you.'

His amiable disposition returned. 'No offence taken.'

We rode on in silence, but the thought of Narses slipping through our fingers was like a knife being twisted in my guts.

My mood was further darkened when a rider came from my father with a letter reminding me that our objective was to secure entry to Babylon via the Ishtar Gate and that I was to support the attack by ensuring that the left flank of the army was secure. I sent him back to my father with the reply that I was quite capable of securing his flank.

An hour later we were half a mile from the walls of Babylon, which rose majestically from the desert floor to a height of at least seventy feet, defensive towers at regular intervals all along their circumference. Once there had been outer walls that gave the city even greater protection. They were so high and wide that it was reputed that two chariots travelling along the top of them in opposite directions could pass each other without difficulty. These walls had long since gone, the only remnant being the paved road that linked where the outer wall had once stood to the Ishtar Gate. It was called *Aibur-shabu* – 'the enemy shall not pass' – and was built by King Hammurabi when Babylon had ruled the world.

Even from this distance the walls looked imposing and impregnable. I knew that they were constructed from large mud-bricks cemented together with bitumen, and that the moat that surrounded the city was also lined with bricks. Without siege towers and engines such as Dura possessed the enemy would have no chance of breaching those walls. But with the city surrounded the chance of starving a Babylon filled with many hungry mouths into surrender was a very real possibility. At least it was! Now relief had come.

Narses had scorned the chance of flight, obviously believing that even without Mithridates he had every chance of defeating us. He would have known that my legions had limped back home, for information was easily bought and word would have spread down the Euphrates that my foot soldiers were on their way back to Dura. He would have also known that the armies of Hatra, Mesene and Babylon had joined with my horsemen to make a formidable force. That said, he would have assumed, not unreasonably, that the Babylonians were second-rate compared to his own forces and would have assumed that Nergal's soldiers were also inferior. Mesene had always produced ragtag armies composed of ill-equipped soldiers. He would have thus also discounted them. In his mind the only formidable troops he faced were my own and those of my father. That my father had brought only six and a half thousand horsemen with him must have filled Narses with confidence, the more so as we approached the city and it became apparent that we were greatly outnumbered by his own forces.

Narses had drawn up his army in three sections. On his left flank, occupying the space between the walls and my father's Hatrans, was a

171

great body of horsemen armed with lances and carrying round shields. They wore helmets on their heads and armless leather cuirasses on their bodies. Interspersed with these lancers were bodies of horse archers. Riders sent from my father and Vardan reported that they could see no cataphracts among these horsemen.

In the centre of the enemy's line was a great mass of foot that must have numbered thirty thousand men or more, and which faced the horsemen of Babylon and extended right to face my own cavalry.

Officers barked orders at their men as the troops of both sides dressed their ranks and lines before the first clash. I clasped arms with Nergal as he and Praxima rode back to their horsemen that faced the mounted spearmen of the enemy's right wing. I reached over and kissed Gallia on the lips before she took up her position in front of Dura's horse archers.

'Shamash be with you, my sweet, and remember not to unleash the lords until the enemy is breaking.'

'God be with you, Pacorus.' She closed her helmet's cheekguards, tied the leather straps together under her chin and then pulled her bow from its hide case attached to her saddle. She held it over her head, a gesture reciprocated by the Amazons grouped behind her, and then dug her knees into Epona and galloped away to take command of the horse archers.

I rammed the butt spike of my *kontus* into the earth.

'Come, Orodes, let us take a closer look at the enemy.'

He did the same and we trotted across no man's land to with five hundred paces or so of the enemy's front ranks. I kept an eye over to the left to where the enemy's horsemen were grouped but in truth did not think they would charge us. The foot opposite us was firmly routed to the spot – it seemed that Narses would fight a defensive battle.

We edged our horses closer to the front ranks of the enemy, a long line of large wicker shields, rectangular in shape and almost the height of a man. Covered in thick leather and painted yellow, with the bird-god symbol of Persis painted on each one, they were held by Narses' royal spearmen. Looking up and down their line I estimated that there were at least five thousand of them standing in three ranks or more. Each man wore a plumed, bronze helmet and probably wore leather armour. Reflecting their Persian heritage they most likely were armed with light battleaxes and daggers, in addition to the long spear each man carried. The shield was thick enough to stop arrows, though too large and cumbersome to form a roof under which the men could take shelter in an arrow storm. The front rank held their spears towards us at an angle of forty-five degrees, the ranks behind holding their spears upright. These soldiers were not a rabble but among the best that Persis could field. That Narses had brought mostly foot soldiers before

172

the walls of Babylon did not surprise me. Horsemen are mostly useless in sieges but their mounts consume fodder that can easily exhaust the resources of the surrounding areas. In addition, Babylon lies only fifty miles from the Tigris and the Kingdom of Susiana, close enough to get an army of foot soldiers to the city within four days.

A group of arrows suddenly arched into the sky from behind the ranks of the spearmen to land harmlessly a few paces in front of us. No other volley followed but I thanked Shamash for this lack of discipline, for the enemy had revealed to me that there were foot archers standing behind the spearmen.

'Time to retreat,' I said to Orodes and wheeled Remus around.

I heard a thud and he suddenly bolted forward. I managed to bring him under control as Orodes galloped up to me.

'They have slingers as well, then,' he said, grinning at my temporary discomfort.

We rode to where Gallia waited in front of her Amazons with a knot of officers from my horse archers around her.

'Don't get too close to the foot opposite,' I told them. 'They have archers and slingers behind the spearmen.'

'Don't give them any cheap victories,' I said to Gallia. 'Just annoy them. Shoot high so your arrows fall on the heads of the front ranks. You will be able to thin them out but that's about all.'

'And your cataphracts?' she asked.

I smiled at her and pointed to where the horsemen of the enemy right wing were standing.

'That is where the key to the battle lies, my sweet.'

I smiled at her again and then dug my knees into Remus' flanks to take me back to my cataphracts. It appeared that the enemy had no heavy cavalry, which evened the odds greatly. In my mind I quickly formulated a plan: shatter the enemy's right wing with my heavy horsemen to allow Nergal's horse archers to sweep around the enemy foot to attack their exposed flank and rear. Once that had been achieved Narses' foot soldiers would be peppered with volleys of arrows that would both demoralise and decimate them. I did not worry about what would be happening on the enemy's left flank where Narses faced the combined horsemen of Hatra and Babylon. The enemy's mounted spearmen would be no match for my father's cavalry. Orodes looked at me with concern as I began to whistle to myself. We had Narses cornered like a rat. So much for the lord high general of the Parthian Empire. Victory was so close I could taste it.

173

Chapter 8

As both sides eyed each other warily across the featureless stretch of desert that would soon become a blood-soaked killing ground, an eerie silence descended over the battlefield. Horses scraped at the ground impatiently, chomped on their bits and flicked their tails to swat away flies. Men pulled on their bowstrings to test the draw weight, others checked their quivers and the cataphracts rested their great lances on their shoulders, their helmets pushed back on their heads. The breeze ruffled windsocks and banners and offered slight relief to men sweating in armour. Most of the clouds had disappeared by now to leave a clear blue sky. It was a beautiful spring day, and for many their last one on earth.

I was suddenly gripped by a fear that Narses would request a parley and escape our clutches, but my concern was allayed when a great noise suddenly erupted from the enemy ranks. The accursed kettledrums began to beat and then the shrill sound of horns pierced the air. Horses whinnied and some reared up in alarm but Remus merely stood unconcerned. He had heard these sounds many times before. Behind me men pulled their helmets down and wrapped their reins round their left wrists. Orodes offered me his hand.

'God keep you safe, Pacorus.'

'And you too, my friend.'

In front of us the foot soldiers of Narses were beating their spear shafts against their wicker shields, producing a great rattling sound that mixed with the noise of the kettledrums and horns to produce a dreadful din. How I regretted that Domitus was not here – his legions would reduce those wicker shields to wood shavings!

'The enemy is moving,' shouted Orodes, pointing over to the left to where the enemy's right wing of horsemen appeared to be shifting further right. Were they fleeing?

Closer inspection revealed that the horsemen were actually moving in an ordered fashion and not in flight. I glanced at the mass of enemy foot. They were still rooted to the same spot. As the right wing of enemy horsemen continued to shift right more riders appeared to fill the gap that had appeared between the foot soldiers and the horsemen on the enemy right wing. Now our own left wing was greatly overlapped by the enemy opposite that began to advance against Nergal's outnumbered horse archers.

It suddenly became horribly clear that the enemy had also been closely observing us just as we had been scrutinising them. Narses would have seen the banner of Mesene and would have also spotted my heavy cavalry positioned near the centre and not on the flank. He therefore believed our left wing to be weak and would throw his mounted spearmen and horse archers against it. If he succeeded then he would be able to drive back or even rout Nergal's men and get his riders behind our army. A potential disaster was unfolding before my eyes.

I looked to my right to see Gallia leading Dura's horse archers against the enemy foot. The companies rode towards the enemy in single-file columns, twenty in all, each rider at the head of the column loosing his arrows high into the sky at a distance of around four hundred paces from the front ranks. He then wheeled his horse to the right to return to the rear of the column. In this way a withering rain of arrows was directed at the enemy, while Dura's horsemen stayed out of the range of enemy arrows and slingshots. I did not have to worry about the centre.

Meanwhile the enemy horsemen were now moving at a canter towards Nergal's men, arrows arching into the sky from the horse archers behind their front ranks of spearmen. There were frantic horn calls coming from Nergal's ranks as the Mesenians about-turned and began to retreat, the rear ranks turning in their saddles and shooting their bows over the hind quarters of their horses. Many enemy spearmen were felled as Nergal's men loosed arrow after arrow at the oncoming enemy. He had obviously trained his men well.

'Wedge, wedge. Follow me!' I shouted and pulled my *kontus* from the earth. I dug my knees into Remus' flanks and shouted at him to move forward. He reared up on his back legs and broke into a canter, then a gallop. In seconds Orodes was next to me and behind us over twelve hundred riders followed.

A cataphract is the most expensive soldier on earth, a man dressed in the finest and most effective armour and armed with an array of weapons made from the finest materials. As well as his *kontus* his weapons included a sword, mace, axe and dagger. He and his horse were encased in scale armour, steel leg and arm armour and a helmet that offered protection to the head, neck and face from arrows and blades. Yet all this lavish equipment counts for nothing if the man wearing it is not thoroughly trained.

Just as Domitus had honed his legions into fearsome machines, so had I, assisted by Orodes, moulded my cataphracts into a battle-winning force. As hundreds of iron-shod horses thundered across the ground the ten companies that made up the dragon, plus Orodes' men, instinctively adopted the wedge formation. The first company formed up behind me, a hundred men forming the tip of the wedge widely spaced in two ranks, and behind them a second company and Orodes' men mirroring the wedge arrangement of those in front. Either side of these companies, each one riding behind and in echelon of the one in front, were four companies to make the rest of the wedge. Years of practise on the training fields came down to these few moments on the field of honour, when twelve hundred horsemen can be transformed into a battle-winning instrument seemingly in a blink of an eye.

The scale armour, bulky and uncomfortable before battle, becomes as light as a feather in the cauldron of combat. I screamed my war cry and brought my *kontus* down on the right side of Remus, clutching it with both hands as we galloped headlong into the dense ranks of the enemy horsemen.

When we hit them a sickening scraping noise was heard as the cataphracts ground their way into the enemy's left flank. They were still moving forward to get to grips with Nergal's men when we struck, driving into the packed ranks of their horse archers and skewing horses and men with our lances. The horse archers wore no armour and had only soft caps on their heads. Ordinarily they would have fled before a cataphract charge, but though many did try to turn their horses away from us, there was nowhere for them run to. The packed ranks of their comrades were to their front, right and rear, and so they were forced to face the armoured monsters that had suddenly appeared in their midst. And then the killing began.

Remus galloped into a gap between two ranks of enemy horse archers and I buried my *kontus* in the first target that presented itself, a bowman dressed in nothing more than a beige kaftan and leggings. He turned in the saddle and stared wild-eyed as the metal tip of the *kontus* went into his sternum and out through his back. Whether he was alive or dead when I released the shaft that had penetrated his body up to half its length I did not know, but in the mêlée there is no time to sit and make judgements. Quick reflexes and speed are the keys to survival. I drew my sword and slashed at the head of a rider who appeared before me, inflicting a deep gash in his jaw. I screamed at Remus to move forward as I advanced deeper among the enemy, hacking left and right with my sword at heads and torsos. Orodes clung to my side like a limpet on a piece of rock, swinging his mace in his hand, the horsemen behind us using their maces and axes against the cloth caps of the enemy horse archers. It was carnage. Skulls were split like a grapes being stepped on as mace blows were rained down on hapless victims. The enemy spearmen had stopped their attack against Nergal's men and had about-turned to get to grips with us, but between us and them was a great press of horse archers trying to flee for their lives.

After what seemed like only a few seconds but was probably half an hour, as if by magic the enemy horse archers disappeared. We then faced a charge by the enemy spearmen but it was not pressed home with any great vigour. Having seen the remnants of the horse archers flee into the desert, only small groups of spearmen attempted to charge us. Orodes rode up and down the line waving his mace in the air, shouting orders for the ranks to reform to face north where the bulk of enemy spearmen sat on their horses. I rode to the centre of the line, Vagharsh holding my banner and the standard of Orodes being

176

held by another rider beside him. I tried to make a quick tally as officers arranged their companies in two ranks. It appeared that our losses had been slight, which was more than could be said for the enemy. The ground was carpeted with their dead as far as the eye could see, with dozens of slain horses also lying on the ground.

My own and Remus' scale armour was smeared with blood but it was not my own, and a closer inspection of my cataphracts revealed that they too were daubed with enemy gore. It had been one of the most one-sided victories that I had taken part in. All that remained were the disorganised and no doubt dispirited enemy spearmen who were now grouped to our front. Their officers were riding to and fro, cajoling and threatening their men to move forward. But then arrows began falling among their ranks and many saddles were suddenly emptied. This was the final straw for the demoralised spearmen who suddenly broke and fled east into the desert in the wake of the surviving horse archers.

My men whooped and cheered as the enemy ran, pursued by companies of Nergal's horse archers. Seeing the charge of the enemy horse stopped and then their whole wing largely destroyed, he had halted the retreat of his horse archers and brought them back onto the battlefield. He and Praxima now rode over to where we stood among the enemy dead and dying. I clasped his forearm when he arrived at our position.

'My thanks, Pacorus,' he said, grinning.

'My thanks to you, my friend,' I said.

'You have won a great victory, lord,' said Praxima, which elicited cheers from those men within earshot.

Nergal looked east to where his men pursued the enemy.

'Not many will get back across the Tigris,' he said with satisfaction.

'Our men are under orders to take no prisoners,' said Praxima sternly. I smiled at her. Even after all these years she still had the power to unnerve me.

'That's one part of Narses' army dealt with,' I said. 'Let's hope my father and Vardan have broken through to the Ishtar Gate.'

I saw Praxima pull an arrow from her quiver and nock it in her bowstring. Around fifty paces from us a wounded enemy soldier had staggered to his feet and was limping away east, into the desert. His right leg was obviously injured as he could barely put any weight on it. Just a few feet away, men on their horses watched him making his escape. They could have ridden him down with ease but saw no honour in killing such a pathetic figure. Sweating profusely from their exertions in battle, most had pushed their helmets back up on their heads. I saw their expressions change from unconcern to horror as Praxima's arrow hit the poor wretch in the right leg, causing him to yelp in pain and collapse on the ground. He groaned in agony for a few seconds then, with great effort, managed to get back on his feet, almost hopping as his right leg hung uselessly. There was another twang and a second arrow hit him square in the back, pitching him forward face down on the ground. He made no further movement as Praxima calmly replaced her bow in its case.

She spat on the ground. 'No pity for the soldiers of Narses.'

Suddenly the ground shook and I heard a deep rumble – the sound of thousands of horses charging. I gave the order to wheel left and face the direction of the sound, hoping that it was not more enemy horsemen mounting another attack against us. Within minutes we had reformed our line facing west and moved forward. Nergal, meanwhile, had brought his horse archers forward and deployed them either side of my cataphracts to provide missile support should we need it. We did not, for ahead I saw a most imposing sight – the lords were leading their men against the now isolated enemy foot soldiers.

A rider, one of Dura's horse archers, arrived at my position with a message from Gallia that she had committed the lords and their horsemen against Narses' foot soldiers. She had received news that the Babylonians and Hatrans had routed the enemy horsemen in front of them and had pushed back the remnants to the Ishtar Gate. The battle was as good as won and all that remained was the destruction of the enemy's foot. Twenty thousand horse archers were now enveloping those troops as the lords and their horse archers emptied their quivers against them. The air was thick with arrows as Narses' men were assailed from all directions.

I rode over to where Gallia had halted with her Amazons observing the scene unfolding before her, a great cloud of dust now obscuring the distance as Dura's lords directed their assaults against the enemy. I reached over and kissed her on the cheek, my vest and shirt drenched with sweat. In comparison she looked as though she had just washed and dressed. There wasn't a speck of dirt on her or Epona and her bow was still in its case. Behind her the Amazons appeared just as fresh and unruffled.

She smiled warmly at Nergal and Praxima as they joined us. She laid a hand on Orodes' arm.

'It warms me to see you all unharmed, especially you, lord prince.'

He took off his helmet and bowed his head solemnly. 'Your servant, lady.' Ever the gallant knight.

I also took off my own helmet, my sweat-soaked hair matted to my skull.

'Spandarat insisted on getting involved, then,' I said to Gallia, observing horse archers riding towards the enemy mass, shooting their bows and then wheeling sharply away.

'I ordered him and the rest of the lords to attack,' she replied. 'Word reached me from your father that the enemy horsemen in front of him had been dispersed, and with you and Nergal scattering those on the other wing, it seemed an opportune moment to unleash the lords.'

'You have impeccable timing, lady,' remarked Orodes, wiping his brow with a cloth.

'Now we can watch them being slaughtered,' said Praxima with relish.

Dura's horse archers were now reforming in their companies behind the Amazons, having retreated to the camel train stationed in the rear to obtain fresh quivers of arrows. To our left the tired cataphracts and their blown horses were forming into line, and beyond them the Mesenians. We had returned to our original positions.

'Do you wish me to commit my men?' asked Nergal.

I smiled at him. 'Your troops are yours to dispose of as you see fit, lord king.'

Gallia swung round in her saddle. 'Nergal is offering you assistance, Pacorus, don't get all high and mighty with your royal talk.'

'Why don't we take the Amazons forward, Gallia,' suggested Praxima. 'Lop off some heads and balls just like in the old days.'

Nergal laughed and Orodes looked most uncomfortable.

'Wait,' I said. I turned and beckoned forward one of the commanders of my horse archers.

'Send some of your men forward and inform the lords that I command that they desist their attacks.'

He saluted and rode back to his waiting officers.

'What nonsense is this?' asked Gallia.

'No nonsense, my sweet,' I replied. 'Rather common sense.'

Praxima looked perplexed as a detachment of officers rode forward and searched out Spandarat and the other lords in the dust storm that was engulfing the horsemen and foot soldiers as thousands of hooves kicked up the dry earth. I sent other riders to the Ishtar Gate to see if Vardan or my father wanted assistance, and while I waited for a reply the shrieks, cries, shouts and screams of horses and men in front of us gradually died down as the lords disengaged from the battle.

A most unhappy Spandarat brought his horse to a halt in front of me.

'If you weren't my king, if my sons didn't serve in your army and if I didn't love your wife I would tan your arse.'

'A most eloquent speech, Spandarat. Can I assume that you disagree with my orders,' I said calmly.

He pointed excitedly at the enemy foot still standing in their ranks.

'We have the bastards. They are surrounded and short of missiles and they can't go anywhere. They are helpless.'

'That is precisely the point, Spandarat. Everything you say is true and I am sure that they are even more aware of their predicament.'

He threw out his arms. 'So?'

'So I would speak to them first.'

He dropped his arms to his sides. 'Speak to them?'

'Yes, Spandarat. And I can't do that if you and your men are shooting arrows at them.'

He looked behind him, scratched his head and rode to the rear muttering to himself. During the next few minutes parties of horse archers, most with empty quivers, filed past us to muster once more around the banners of their lords.

I asked Nergal to take his men and form a cordon around the enemy's foot, supported by the resupplied Duran horse archers, telling them to stay out of bow and sling range.

Orodes was impressed. 'You show mercy in victory, Pacorus.'

'Mercy has nothing to do with it,' I grunted in reply.

Men on foot, surrounded and with no hope of relief, would be more amenable to surrendering than fighting on, and that meant Duran and Mesenian lives would be saved. The battle had gone better than expected, our losses had been light and the enemy had been routed. As Nergal's horse archers cantered south to form a cordon around the enemy foot soldiers, I began to formulate a plan that could yet salvage the whole campaign and avenge Gotarzes.

The army of Narses was on the verge of being destroyed and once that had happened the road to Ctesiphon would be open. Mithridates himself had suffered great losses when they had engaged my legions near the Tigris, notwithstanding our own brush with calamity, and now the enemy had tasted yet another defeat. Mithridates had clearly fled the scene, no doubt scurrying back to Ctesiphon to seek solace from his poisonous mother, Queen Aruna. If we finished Narses' forces here, today, then Susiana and perhaps Persis would be open to attack. Once they had been rested and refitted the legions could be recalled to join with my horsemen. I could field ten thousand foot and twenty-three thousand horsemen, more if I could persuade Nergal to help us. My father would not be a part of any plan, I knew that, but Vardan might be willing to lend me some horse archers at least, if only to repay Narses and Mithridates for the destruction they had visited on his kingdom. I closed my eyes and took a deep breath. It all seemed perfectly achievable. Then I opened my eyes and saw Byrd and half a dozen of his scouts riding towards us, and my plan began to disintegrate.

Dobbai had once told me that the gods cared nothing for the lives of men and that our prayers to them were wasted words. She said that they sent plagues, drought and famine to torment men to alleviate their boredom for it amused their cruel natures to see humanity suffer, much as a small child delights in pulling the wings off a fly or the legs off a spider. She said that some men were beloved of the gods, and included me in that number, but only because such individuals were warriors or tyrants who inflicted pain upon others and washed the land with blood. She said the notions of peace and prosperity, which most men craved, were anathema to the gods. They loved only chaos, despair and bloodshed, for in such tumults men fell on their knees in front of idols of their gods and begged for deliverance, and the divine ones responded by heaping more misery upon them to satisfy their cruel natures. And men wept and the land bled. And so it was now as Byrd brought his sweating horse to a halt before me.

'Vardan dead at Ishtar Gate. Narses reveals his hand.'

I heard the words but did not believe them.

'Dead?' said Orodes incredulously.

Byrd nodded nonchalantly. 'Great number of enemy horsemen attack from south. Narses leads them. I see his great banner.'

I felt sick to my stomach. How can this be?

'We must aid your father,' said Orodes.

I looked at him and then Byrd, unsure of what to do.

'Pacorus, decide!' shouted Gallia.

My cataphracts were tired, their horses blown, and my horse archers and those of the lords had already fought their own battle. Only Nergal's men were relatively fresh. I looked at the expectant faces around me.

'Very well,' I said. 'We must ride to the Ishtar Gate immediately. Nergal, will you ride with us as your men are the least tired among our forces?'

'It will be an honour, Pacorus,' he replied.

So I took my heavy horsemen, my own and Nergal's horse archers, plus half the lords and their riders to the Ishtar Gate. Spandarat and the remaining lords were left behind to guard the enemy foot soldiers. We rode in haste across the battlefield to the blue-painted bricks of the Ishtar Gate, to find a scene of grim carnage but no Narses. Dead horses lay scattered all around, their guts ripped open and their legs twisted and broken, staring with lifeless eyes. Bones protruded from shattered ankles and blood oozed from gaping neck wounds. Some animals, still alive, groaned pitifully as pain shot through their punctured bodies. As we halted and slid from our saddles I could see that the path of dead and dying began around a hundred paces from the Ishtar Gate and led directly north.

Dead riders lay alongside their slain mounts and I saw that most of them wore the purple of Babylon. Some of Vardan's soldiers were walking among the dead horseflesh, putting wounded animals out of their misery and retrieving any men still alive. Smashed shields and broken lances lay scattered on the ground along with abandoned swords and helmets.

As we led our horses in the direction of the Euphrates we came across a knot of officers from Vardan's royal bodyguard, and among them my father and Vistaspa. Relief swept through me. I left Remus with my men and went to his side. We embraced and I thanked Shamash that he was safe and unhurt. I nodded to Vistaspa who bowed his head, and then saw Mardonius kneeling by the side of his dead lord. Vardan looked serene and untroubled in death, his eyes closed and not a mark on his face. His body was covered with a rich purple cloak edged with gold. There were a great many dead soldiers of the royal bodyguard in this particular spot, no doubt where fierce fighting had taken place. I also saw a number of slain cataphracts dressed in short-sleeved scale armour cuirasses, yellow shirts underneath – the colours of Persis. My father's bodyguard waited on their horses two hundred paces away, their heads bowed with exhaustion.

I took off my helmet as Gallia embraced my father and Orodes bowed to him.

'What happened?' I asked.

My father, ashen faced and looking tired, shook his head.

'What happened? I will tell you what happened. We advanced and engaged the enemy horsemen deployed in front of the Ishtar Gate, my soldiers on the right and Vardan's men on the left. We cut our way through their spearmen and horse archers and reached the Ishtar Gate. That was easy enough. And in the moment of victory, when the soldiers of Hatra were finishing off the enemy and filling the city's moat with their dead, Narses appeared at the head of a multitude of horsemen and hit the Babylonians in the flank.'

I could scarce believe it. 'Appeared from where?'

'From the Marduk Gate,' answered Mardonius with a quivering voice as his lord and master, lifted onto a stretcher fashioned from lances lashed together, was carried into his city. Still wrapped in the purple cloak, his arms had been crossed over his chest and his sword lay on his body. The remnants of his bodyguard followed their lord on foot.

'Narses kept his heavy cavalry in reserve near the Marduk Gate,' continued Mardonius, 'the main entrance into the city from the west, and led them against us when we and the Hatrans were disorganised following our first attack.'

'It was clever,' added my father, 'very clever. He struck the Babylonians in the flank when they, just like us, were disorganised and compressed into a small area in front of the city walls. His men hit the Babylonians who had no time to turn and face them, herding them towards the river and preventing me from deploying my men.'

'He used the Babylonians as a wall of flesh between them and us,' said Vistaspa undiplomatically.

'Their first charge inflicted many casualties, including the king,' said Mardonius.

'Where is Narses now?' I asked.

'Fled north,' replied my father. 'I sent my horse archers after him but he will be miles away by now.'

It was a catastrophe. Two of the empire's kings, both of them allies, had been killed in the space of two weeks. My plans evaporated and the gods laughed. On the heels of Vardan's death came more grievous news when a rider came from Spandarat informing me that the enemy foot that I had left him to guard had escaped and were marching towards the Tigris.

When I rode back to my lords and demanded an explanation I learned that not all of Narses' reserves had been committed at the Ishtar Gate. I found Spandarat sitting on the ground when we arrived, his dead horse laying a few paces away, a lance through its body, and one of his men bandaging a nasty gash to his scalp. After the bandage had been tied off he was hauled to his feet. I slid out of my saddle and stood before him. Gallia did the same.

'Are you hurt, Spandarat?' she enquired with concern.

'Nothing a bellyful of beer won't cure,' he replied, blood already seeping through the bandage.

I looked around and saw more than a few dead Durans on the ground. Spandarat saw my concerned look.

'A great load of horsemen, men armed with shields and spears, came from the south and charged us. We emptied a few saddles with our bows but there were a lot of them, we had empty quivers and they were fresh. They charged us a couple of times and I was nearly turned into a kebab,' he nodded at his dead horse. 'They kept us occupied long enough for the foot soldiers to escape. I reckon they are about five miles away by now.'

'They are falling back on Kish,' I sighed. Kish was a city less then twenty miles northeast of Babylon that had been captured by Narses. I laid a hand on his shoulder. 'You and your men did well today. Take them back to camp and get that wound stitched.'

There was nothing to do except consign our dead to the flames, tend to the wounded and recover our strength. By the position of the sun in the sky I estimated that it was now late afternoon. I gave the order to retreat back to camp and thousands of tired, thirsty and hungry horse archers led their exhausted horses on foot back to their tents. In the elation and frenzy of combat scale armour and steel leg and arm armour feels as light as a feather; in the aftermath of battle they feel like they are made of lead. Every sinew and muscle in my body ached and it required two of Spandarat's men to get me back in the saddle, so weak did I feel.

Remus, still in his scale armour, plodded back to camp like the rest of the horses carrying cataphracts, each man sitting listlessly in his saddle. It was a most curious thing, this afterglow of slaughter. It was as if each man was filled with a fire that gave him god-like strength in battle, but as soon as the fighting stopped it disappeared like the flame of a candle when it is snuffed out. In its place is lethargy and slow-wittedness. As we trudged back to camp Narses himself could have galloped among us and not one man would have had the strength to raise his sword against him.

In fact I learned later, when two farriers were unstrapping Remus' scale armour, that Narses' column of horsemen had ridden directly north and through the Babylonian camp, firing the tents, scattering camels and killing most of the camp guards and the small army of servants and hangers-on that always accompanied Vardan on campaign, before swinging east to head for Kish. It was a blessing that Vardan had not brought the half-naked teenage slave girls who served his guests food. Their lives had at least been spared. My own camp escaped any destruction, as did those of my father and Nergal.

There was no pursuit of Narses.

The next morning's roll call revealed that the heaviest of our losses had been among the lords' retainers: five hundred killed, three hundred wounded and a hundred and fifty horses slain. The cataphracts had suffered fifteen dead and forty wounded with no losses among their horses. A fair amount of leg and arm armour was dented and many iron scales had been dislodged from scale armour but that was a small price to pay for so few casualties. When we got back to Dura the armour could be repaired and squires would be busy over the next few days fixing iron scales back on rawhide. The horse archers had suffered a score killed and fifty wounded.

During the morning I received an invitation from Princess Axsen to attend her at her palace in Babylon and at noon rode with Gallia and Orodes and an escort of a hundred Babylonian horse archers to the city.

The signs of the previous day's battle were all around as we rode to the city. The area in front of the Ishtar Gate and east of the city was filled with carts being piled high with the slain for transportation to great funeral pyres that were already roasting dead flesh. The sickly sweet smell of burning carcasses entered my nostrils and made me feel nauseous. I saw slain horses being hauled by their legs towards the raging fires and soldiers with fishhooks pulling bodies from the city's moat. The buzzing of a plague of flies added to the horror of the scene as we trotted over the wooden bridge that spanned the moat and entered Babylon via the Ishtar Gate.

The gate itself, now over five hundred years old, was a most wondrous thing. More than forty feet high, it was made of bricks fronted with a copper turquoise glaze alternating with unglazed bricks covered with gold leaf. Either side of the arch itself were base reliefs of animals – lions, the symbol of the goddess Ishtar, horned bulls – *gauws* – and dragons, the symbols of the god Marduk, the deity whose city this was. There appeared to be no damage to the gate itself or the surrounding walls, which suggested that either Narses intended to starve the city into surrender or he had attempted an assault against another sector of the walls.

We rode through the gate and onto a paved road that the commander of our escort informed me was called the Processional Way. In the centre of the road were laid great limestone flagstones, either side of them smaller red flagstones. The way itself was lined with the statues of one hundred and twenty lions made from glazed bricks.

We turned off the road when we reached the gates to the royal palace and entered the huge compound, which was surrounded by a wall of great height and strength with guard towers positioned along its circumference every fifty paces. We rode into a great paved square surrounded on two sides by barracks and stables. The large gatehouse behind us filled another side and a second gatehouse occupied the fourth side. We made our way across the square and through the second gatehouse to reach a second square that fronted the palace.

The palace guard stood to attention on the square to receive us, at least five hundred purple-dressed warriors armed with thrusting spears, wearing bronze helmets and carrying round wooden shields faced with bronze and bearing Vardan's *gauw* symbol. We dismounted and Mardonius walked over and bowed his head to all three of us as slaves took our horses to the stables.

'Greetings King Pacorus, Queen Gallia and Prince Orodes,' he said formally. 'Princess Axsen awaits you in the palace. If your majesties would follow me.'

He strode purposefully in front as a guard of honour fell in behind us and we walked to the steps of the royal palace. There, standing at the top of the steps at the entrance to the palace, stood Axsen. About my age and shorter than me, she had always been a sturdy girl having inherited the physical characteristics of her father. Usually of a cheerful disposition, she mostly wore her long brown hair in two plaits. Today, though, she wore it free with black ribbons tied in it. Her round face was full of sorrow and her brown eyes were puffy from weeping over the death of her father. She looked like a lost and lonely child despite being surrounded by priests, slaves and her father's commanders and advisers. My heart went out to her. Ignoring all protocol and royal etiquette, Gallia raced up the steps and threw her arms round her friend. The tall severe-looking priests, sporting thick, long black beards and adorned in red robes, frowned and mumbled disapprovingly among themselves, but Axsen hugged her friend and thanked her for her show of affection.

I bowed my head to Babylon's princess, then stepped forward and embraced her.

'I am truly sorry for your loss, lady.'

She managed a thin smile. 'Thank you, Pacorus, your presence here is most welcome.'

Her voice was faltering and I could tell that she was having difficulty maintaining her royal composure. Alas, she had no husband or siblings with whom to share the burden of grief, only a multitude of servants and subjects.

Orodes stepped forward and went down on one knee before her. It was the first time that they had met.

'Dear lady, I am but an impoverished prince and yet I pledge my sword to your service in honour of your father, a valiant and great king who has been taken from the world too early.'

They were fine words well spoken and touched Axsen, who extended her hand to Orodes so that he could kiss it. She stepped forward and gently lifted him to his feet.

'Thank you, Prince Orodes. I have heard of your charm and great courage. Babylon is honoured to receive you.'

My father arrived with Gafarn moments later and behind them Nergal and Praxima. Like Gallia the wife of Nergal dispensed with royal protocol and embraced her friend warmly, again to the consternation of the assembled priests and advisers.

The palace's throne room was vast, the intricately painted ceiling depicting the stars and moon and supported by a dozen thick stone pillars. The central dais on which two gold-inlaid thrones stood was fashioned from smooth slabs of sandstone and *gauw* banners hung on the walls behind it. Sunlight flooded the room from square windows cut high in the walls and fires burned on great metal dishes on stands for the chamber was cool despite the bright sunshine outside. Guards stood at every pillar and around the dais.

Axsen led us across the throne room to a small antechamber behind the dais, guards opening the plain wooden doors to allow their princess and her guests to enter. The room was airy and bright, the walls painted white and the interior furnished with plush white couches piled with cushions. Axsen sat in a great cushioned chair and bade us sit on the couches opposite her. Mardonius stood on her right side. A stern-looking priest with a black beard stood on her left side.

186

Next to him was a woman with a very low-cut white gown and bare arms adorned with gold jewellery.

Slaves bought us fine wine to drink and fruit, honey cakes and pastries to eat. The slats in the windows had been opened fully to allow air to enter as the doors to the room were closed. Axsen waved away a slave who offered her wine.

'My friends,' she said, 'I thank you all for being here, especially you, King Varaz, whose army is the mightiest in the Parthian Empire.'

My father bowed his head to her.

'I am only sorry that we should meet in such unhappy circumstances. Be assured that Hatra is first among the allies of Babylon.'

Axsen smiled and I saw a look of relief appear on Mardonius' face.

'Lord Mardonius you all already know,' said Axsen, then gesturing to the priest and woman standing near her. 'These are my father's other chief advisers, who now serve me. Nabu, high priest of the Temple of Marduk, and Afrand, high priestess of the Temple of Ishtar.'

The pair bowed their heads to us as Axsen nodded to Mardonius.

'Thank you, highness,' he began. 'We have made a tally of the losses suffered before the city yesterday. We have counted eight thousand enemy dead and two thousand Babylonians slain. Of our valiant allies, I believe that the losses of Hatra, Dura and Mesene are light in comparison.'

'Two hundred dead,' reported Nergal.

'Seven hundred dead,' remarked my father grimly, 'most of them suffered when Narses attacked with his reserves.'

'Most of my losses were suffered in the same way,' I added. 'What news of Narses?'

'We received reports earlier that he and his forces had left Kish and are now falling back on Jem det Nasr,' replied Mardonius.

The latter place was a small town near the Tigris.

'Most likely,' continued Mardonius, 'he will retreat back over the Tigris.'

My father looked at me, no doubt thinking that I would urge a pursuit of Narses, but I said nothing. For one thing the funeral of Vardan had to take place first, and then Axsen would have to be made queen of Babylon. So I stayed silent.

'Babylon has suffered grievously at the hands of Narses and Mithridates,' said Axsen. 'Many villages have been destroyed and their inhabitants killed or carried off into slavery. In addition, irrigation systems have been destroyed and livestock slaughtered. It will take many months before the kingdom returns to normal. Therefore I have no alternative but to seek to make peace with Mithridates. I am sorry, Pacorus.'

187

I smiled at her. What else could she do? Babylon had lost thousands of its citizens as well as its king, and Babylon also bordered Susiana.

'You follow the course of wisdom,' I replied. 'It would be foolish to impoverish your kingdom further.'

Mardonius closed his eyes with relief and my father nodded approvingly. Mithridates and Narses would have to wait, though how I would be able strike against them now was beyond me. I toyed with my drinking cup, a delicate silver vessel inlaid with gold. If only Vardan had used his wealth to raise a larger army then perhaps he would not be lying in his private chambers being washed and prepared for his funeral. In the silence I thought I could hear the gods mocking me.

The next day dawned crystal clear and windless, the vivid blue of the sky a fitting backdrop to Vardan's funeral. The whole of the city, which also contained the refugees from the countryside, turned out to see their king's last journey on earth. He had ruled them for nearly forty years, most of them alone as his wife had died giving birth to Axsen. We slept in the palace the night before the funeral but I spent most of the night on the bedroom balcony staring across the city at the mirror-like waters of the Euphrates that were illuminated by a full moon.

Earlier in the day I had assembled Spandarat and the rest of the lords and told them to take their men back to Dura. Nearly twenty thousand men and their horses would soon denude the locality of provisions and I did not want to impoverish Axsen's kingdom any further. My two thousand horse archers went with them. I watched them file out of camp before we visited Axsen: a long line of horses and camels winding its way north. Nergal likewise sent most of his horse archers south back to Uruk and Vistaspa ordered Hatra's cavalry back to their homeland, he himself staying with my father's bodyguard that had suffered no losses during the recent battle. Indeed, I heard that even in the fight with Narses' reserve at the Ishtar Gate they had formed a cordon round my father but had even then seen no fighting. The Babylonians and Hatra's other cataphracts were between them and Narses' men.

'What's the matter? It's late, come to bed.' Gallia shook me out of my daydreaming.

'I cannot sleep,' I answered. 'It's all my fault.'

She sat down in the chair beside me.

'What are you talking about?'

'Gotarzes, Vardan. They are dead because of me. If I had not made an enemy of Mithridates and Narses they would still be alive.'

She regarded me with narrowed eyes. 'Do you really believe that? That if you had grovelled at their feet that Phraates would not now be dead, or Gotarzes for that matter?'

'Vardan came to my aid and the price he paid was his own life,' I said.

'Oh, Pacorus. He aided you of his own free will, just as your father did.'

I was not to be consoled, though. 'Dobbai was right. I underestimated them and Babylon has paid a heavy price.'

She laid a hand on my arm. 'You cannot take on the troubles of the whole world and nor can you give up and allow Mithridates and Narses to win.'

I rose and kissed her on the forehead. 'What would I do without you?'

'Get yourself killed in battle. Now come to bed.'

But I slept little and my heart was heavy the next day as we accompanied Axsen and her priests, advisers, commanders, courtiers, aristocrats and their wives to Vardan's funeral. My education as a prince had acquainted me with the rituals and religious beliefs of the different kingdoms in the empire. I knew, for example, that to Babylonians proper funerals were important to prevent the disgruntled dead from returning from the afterlife to haunt their relatives.

The great funeral procession began its journey in the royal palace and then headed for the Temple of Marduk in the centre of the city. Guards lined the route to keep back the multitude of wailing and weeping citizens who threw flowers at the coffin resting on a four-wheeled cart pulled by four black bulls whose horns were covered in gold leaf. A soldier of the palace guard led each animal by a gold chain attached to the bull's nose ring. Even their tails were adorned with gold. These beasts would later be slaughtered to accompany Vardan on his journey into the afterlife.

Immediately behind the cart walked Axsen and behind her Mardonius and her senior advisers. After them came the visiting royal guests. I walked beside Gafarn, my adopted brother who had once been my slave but who now was a prince of the empire.

'By the way,' he said to me in a hushed voice, 'I meant to tell you that Vata is to marry your sister.'

I had always thought that my younger sister, Adeleh, would end her days as a spinster. Happy and carefree, she had been pursued by a number of sons of Hatra's richest aristocrats but had always declined their offers of marriage.

I was shocked. 'I had no idea.'

Vata was my childhood friend and was the son of Bozan, formerly the commander-in-chief of my father's army. He had led the expedition into Cappadocia that had resulted in his death and my

189

transportation to Italy. Now Vata held the north of my father's kingdom against external threats.

'He visits Hatra often,' said Gafarn, 'and Diana always arranged that he and Adeleh would see each other when he did. She said they were both lonely souls and should be together. So she insisted that they both eat with us at every opportunity. You can only imagine the amount of food I had to consume to encourage their friendship to turn into love.'

'It must have been torture for you,' I grinned.

On this sombre day to receive such news was welcome indeed.

Behind us came Babylon's aristocrats and their wives, the women wearing brightly coloured robes and headdresses inlaid with lapis lazuli, silver and gold. Many of them also wore bell-shaped amulets to ward off evil spirits. A small army of musicians accompanying us played harps and lyres and sang songs about Vardan and his greatness.

At the temple itself the coffin holding the body of Vardan was carried by soldiers of the royal bodyguard into the inner sanctum at the rear of the chamber that contained the statue of Marduk. We stood as Nabu prayed to Marduk that Vardan would be allowed to enter heaven. A great purple curtain separated the statue of the god from those assembled in the temple.

'Who's Marduk?' whispered Gallia.

'The creator of the world,' I answered. 'He defeated the evil goddess Tiamat in single combat then spilt her body in two. One half he used to create the heavens and the other to create the earth. He also created the Tigris and Euphrates from her eyes and made mountains from her udders.'

'Why can't we see the statue?' she pressed me, clearly unimpressed that we stood in the house of a powerful god.

'It is considered ill manners for mortals to gawp at his statue. I have been told that he has four eyes and four ears so that he may see and hear everything, including you, my sweet.'

She curled her lip at me as the coffin containing Vardan's body was carried from the holy of holies to be placed once more on its carriage. As the funeral cortege made its way back to the grounds of the royal palace the crowds who stood packed either side of the route stood in silent reverence as their king passed by. Many were weeping and their tears appeared genuine, for I knew that at funerals professional mourners were hired to impress guests. Vardan had been a good king in the tradition of Babylonian rulers. One of the reasons that Babylon was accorded great status in the empire was that its rulers stressed goodness and truth, law and order, justice and freedom, learning, courage and loyalty. Indeed, the city had always accorded special protection to widows, orphans, refugees, the poor and the oppressed. Just as well – the ravages of Narses had created many of each group.

190

As I walked with my wife to the royal tomb, – a vaulted chamber underneath the palace and approached from the outside by a ramp – I knew that Axsen would not be swearing vengeance against the killers of her father. Babylonians believed that immoral acts were crimes against the gods and would be punished by them. I could hear the laughter of Dobbai in my ears at such a notion.

Only Axsen, Nabu, half a dozen of his priests who carried the king's coffin from the cart at the top of the ramp and the soldiers pulling the bulls entered the tomb itself, the latter departing once the throats of the bulls had been slit.

'Poor bulls,' said Gallia as the soldiers walked back up the ramp.

'They used to kill slaves to attend the king in the next life,' I said, 'and I have heard that even aristocrats who were close to the king took their own lives in the tomb so they could be with him always.'

Gallia screwed up her face. 'That is disgusting.'

'We live in more enlightened times,' I answered. 'Now only the bulls and precious objects will accompany Vardan into the afterlife.'

She was still curious, though. 'What objects?'

'His clothes, games, weapons, treasure and vessels filled with food and drink. Everything he needs to maintain his status in the next life.'

She ridiculed the idea. 'The dead do not need objects.'

As an ashen-faced Axsen came from the tomb and walked with faltering steps up the stone ramp, I whispered into Gallia's ear.

'Perhaps not, but we must respect the beliefs of others just as we expect them to respect our own.'

The tomb was sealed and the cortege dispersed. Gallia and Praxima accompanied a weeping Axsen back to her private chambers in the palace. The fine lords and ladies of the kingdom returned to their mansions in the city. Thus ended the reign of King Vardan of Babylon, murdered by the traitor Narses.

Seven days later the coronation of Axsen took place. In the intervening time Narses had pulled all his forces back across the Tigris. Of Mithridates we heard nothing save a strange tale that Ctesiphon itself had been attacked and his frantic mother had demanded that he return forthwith to save her.

I laughed at such an idea as I sat with my father, Gafarn, Nergal, Vistaspa, Orodes and Mardonius in one of the many guest annexes in the palace. This one had been given to my father and had its own small courtyard complete with an ornamental pool with fountains in the middle. We reclined on plush couches as slaves served us pastries, sweet meats, yoghurt, bread, honey, wine and fruit. The atmosphere was very relaxed. Even my father appeared to be in a good mood.

'Where are the women?' he asked, looking at Nergal and me.

'My wife is with Axsen and Gallia,' said Nergal, 'that is the Princess of Babylon and the Queen of Dura, lord.'

191

He may have been a king himself but Nergal could never forget that he had once been but an officer in Hatra's army many years ago. He still regarded my father with awe, and perhaps a little fear.

'Ever since the funeral they have been in each other's company,' reported Mardonius. 'The Princess Axsen takes comfort in her female friends.'

'The sisterhood is a powerful force,' I remarked.

'Well,' said my father, taking a wafer from a silver plate held by a slave and dipping it in a jar of honey held by another, 'she will be a queen tomorrow. It is our job to ensure that her reign is long and prosperous. I owe that to her father, at least.'

Mardonius placed his hands together under his chin. 'Babylon has to seek an accommodation with Mithridates, majesty. We are not strong enough to withstand another invasion.'

'With the losses they have suffered,' I said. 'Mithridates and Narses will think twice before crossing the Tigris once more in a hurry.'

My father finished his honey-daubed wafer. 'Perhaps, but they can call on the resources of all the lands between the Tigris and Indus. I agree with Mardonius.' He looked at Nergal.

'And your borders may also be at risk.'

'There have been no reports of any incursions into my kingdom, lord king,' replied Nergal.

'Not yet, perhaps, but I would suggest strengthening your border defences.'

'Your friendship with Pacorus makes you an enemy of my stepbrother, Nergal,' said Orodes grimly. 'He neither forgets nor forgives.'

'Just be careful of any large-breasted women who suddenly appear at your court,' I said to Nergal. 'Mithridates prefers to send women to do his work instead of soldiers.'

'I will deploy additional troops on my southern border to assist Babylon should Axsen require it,' said my father, changing the subject.

Mardonius bowed his head. 'That would be most welcome majesty.'

'Dura will always stand by Babylon,' I added.

'That is what Lord Mardonius is afraid of,' joked Gafarn.

'This is no time for levity, Gafarn,' my father rebuked him. 'Nevertheless, my son has touched upon the one thing that may deter Mithridates and Narses and that is our unity. If Mesene, Babylon, Hatra and Dura are as one then our combined strength will be a deterrent to aggression.'

I stood up. 'I pledge Dura's allegiance.'

Nergal also stood. 'As do I.'

192

'I would if I had a kingdom to pledge,' offered Gafarn, earning him a frown from my father.

'For what it is worth,' said Orodes, 'I too offer my sword to Babylon.'

'It is worth a thousand warriors, lord prince,' answered Mardonius diplomatically.

My father clapped his hands. 'Excellent. This has been a good meeting.'

Afterwards, as we were dispersing, my father cornered me.

'Remember, Pacorus, we hold the line of the Tigris. There must be no further aggression against Mithridates.'

I held up my hands. 'Of course, father. But Dura will pay no annual tribute to the tyrant that sits in Ctesiphon.'

'That is between him and you. I doubt he would accept it anyway. Another thing.'

'Yes?'

'No more bringing Agraci into the empire.'

I smiled. 'Haytham is a true friend to Dura, father.'

My father looked very serious. 'That may be, but the presence of ten thousand Agraci warriors east of the Euphrates will have alarmed every court in the empire. I can see Assur's face now.'

Assur was the high priest of the Great Temple at Hatra and believed the Agraci to be black-robed devils that had to be kept at bay, annihilated ideally.

'Haytham is also a friend to Mesene,' I said in low voice, 'and will aid Nergal if his kingdom is attacked. As will I.'

He said nothing more but I knew that he was unhappy. He was pleased that Dura prospered and that I had made peace with the Agraci, but like most Parthians he could not see beyond his prejudice against Haytham's people. But I, who had once been a slave and had mixed with and fought beside a host of different races in Italy, had no time for such blind bias. Any man who offered me his hand was my friend, regardless of what god he worshipped or what race he belonged to.

Gafarn walked with me back to my quarters after the meeting.

'The Armenian raids against our northern borders are increasing,' he said. 'Father thinks there will be war against them soon, that is why he does not want any conflict in the south.'

'I did not realise the situation had become so bad.'

He frowned. 'It is the Romans, Pacorus, they are the ones behind it all. They covet nothing less than the whole of Parthia. Ever since Armenia became a client state of Rome there has been nothing but trouble in the north.'

'But Vata is containing it?'

193

He smiled. 'Vata is like a lion, but is a lone lion. Soon, I fear, our father will be marching against Armenia and then there will be war with Rome.'

These were ill tidings indeed. But if Hatra went to war then Dura would be marching alongside her. I put my arm round Gafarn's shoulders.

'Enough of war, tell me how your son is getting along. How old is he now?'

If a pall of sadness and misery had hung over Babylon on the day of Vardan's funeral, the coronation of his daughter transformed the city into a festival of gaiety, music and laughter. Every Babylonian lord and his family were in the city to see their princess made a queen. Their ladies dressed in brightly coloured robes, wearing enough gold and silver on their bodies to cover the entire surface of the great ziggurat that towered over the rest of city. Purple flags and ribbons hung from all the gates into the city and every building was decorated with flowers to produce a crescendo of colours. The royal guard stood on the walls of the palace and lined the route to the Temple of Marduk, while other Babylonian spearmen lined the Processional Way. Each man was armed with a long spear and knife and was dressed in purple leggings and a purple tunic that covered his arms and extended down to his knees. A turban headdress and a large wicker shield faced with leather and painted purple completed their appearance.

The city gates had been opened before dawn and by first light the streets were already thronged with a multitude of well wishers and sightseers. Jugglers, clowns, musicians and fortune-tellers plied their trade among the masses. Pickpockets too, no doubt, for the lure of rich pickings was worth the risk of losing a hand if caught.

Axsen had asked that the soldiers of her friends and allies take part in her coronation parade, and so for days smiths, farriers and squires had been labouring to get our horsemen ready for the great day. Squires worked long hours repairing and polishing leg and arm armour and smiths riveted iron plates back on to scale armour. Tunics, leggings and cloaks had been ferried to the Euphrates where they had been washed and dried by the women of the local villages. Remus and Epona had been attended to by the grooms of the royal stables and looked a handsome pair on the day of the coronation.

I wore my Roman armour cuirass and helmet, which sported a fresh comb of white goose feathers, white shirt, brown leggings and red leather boots. Gallia dressed in white silk leggings and a long-sleeved blue tunic edged with silver. Axsen had given her a gold diadem for her head inlaid with red gemstones called rubies, which had reportedly come from a distant land to the east.

194

Praxima was similarly attired in a rich golden headdress, her husband wearing a red shirt and leather cuirass on which had been attached overlapping bronze scales. Orodes outdid us all with his long-sleeved purple silk shirt, his cuirass of shining silver scales, white leggings and boots edged with silver. My father and Gafarn wore short-sleeved scale armour tunics, the metal also being silver.

We paraded on our horses in front of the place as Axsen descended the steps dressed in a simple white gown that covered her body and legs, her hair loose but immaculately groomed, her cheeks coloured with rouge and her eyelids darkened. On her fingers she wore gold rings and gold hung from her ears.

Mardonius waited at the foot of the steps by the four-wheeled carriage covered in gold leaf that would transport her to the temple. He assisted her into the transport and then sat beside her as the four horses pulling the carriage walked forward, the queen's bodyguard in their dragon-skin armour mounted all around her. We followed the royal party out of the palace and along the Processional Way to the Temple of Marduk.

I looked up at the sky. The gods were favouring Axsen today for there was not a cloud to be seen, and a pleasant westerly breeze brought fresh air from the Euphrates to blow away the stench of the city. The crowds cheered their princess as she made her way to her new life as a queen, and at the entrance to the temple she was carried shoulder high on a simple wicker chair by four of Nabu's priests through the temple and into the inner sanctum. The temple was filled with the kingdom's nobles and their wives plus the representatives of the five populations of the city. In order of hierarchy these were the original Babylonian citizens who were represented this day by the president of the city council, a small, piggy eyed man with thinning hair who had a very tall and haughty wife. The next group was the priests of the Temple of Marduk; then the Greek citizens whose descendants had arrived when Alexander of Macedon had take the city; followed by the slaves who worked in the temples and palaces. At the bottom were the so-called 'people of the land': the farmers who worked in the fields.

Axsen was escorted into the holy of holies, Nabu going before her banging a drum and proclaiming 'Axsen is queen, Axsen is queen'. This was not for our benefit but rather to alert Marduk that a new ruler of Babylon approached him. Afrand, again wearing a low-cut red robe that showed her ample breasts to full effect, stood at the entrance to the holy shrine and handed Axsen her gifts for Marduk – a richly embroidered robe, a gold bowl filled with oil and a mina of silver.

Axsen then disappeared behind the curtain with Nabu and there paid homage to the god. When she reappeared she was escorted to a gold throne on a dais covered with purple cloth that had been erected

195

in the temple for the ceremony. Nabu stood on her right side and Afrand on her left as two priests carrying felt cushions approached her, a gold sceptre laid on one, the crown of Babylon on the other. The temple was filled with the smell of burning frankincense as Nabu took the gold crown and placed it on Axsen's head.

His words echoed round the room. 'Before Marduk, thy god, may thy priesthood and the priesthood of thy sons be favoured.'

Afrand took the gold sceptre and handed it to Axsen.

Nabu's voice boomed once more. 'With thy straight sceptre make thy land wide. May Marduk grant thee quick satisfaction, justice and peace.'

Thus did Axsen become queen of the Kingdom of Babylon. As the assembled dignitaries paid homage to her, including Gallia and I, the priests burned more frankincense. I smiled to myself. This precious incense was extracted from the bark of trees that grew on the coast of Arabia. It was collected by Haytham's people who sold it to the Egyptians and Romans and even the Parthians, the merchants in Dura doing a brisk trade with the supposed enemies of the empire to acquire the precious incense.

When Axsen had received oaths of loyalty from all her nobles she was escorted outside by Mardonius to witness the grand military parade. First came her own royal bodyguard in their dragon-skin armour, followed by a thousand mounted spearmen with shields and five times that number of horse archers. Then came my father's royal bodyguard led by Vistaspa with Hatra's banner flying behind him, followed by my own heavy cavalry looking resplendent in their scale armour, steel arm and leg protection and full-face helmets. Vagharsh carried my banner and griffin pennants flew from every *kontus*. Five hundred of Nergal's horse archers brought up the rear of the column.

As the horsemen who had ridden into the city via the Ishtar Gate and down the Processional Way left Babylon through the Marduk Gate, slaves brought our horses and we journeyed back to the palace to attend the feast that was attended by four thousand people.

Two days later representatives from other kingdoms in the empire appeared at the palace to pay their respects to Axsen, nobles from Media, Atropaiene, Hyrcania and Margiana. No one came from Persis or the other eastern kingdoms in the empire, though an invitation for Axsen to attend Mithridates at Ctesiphon did arrive. The queen wrote back accepting the invitation when her present onerous difficulties had been attended to.

'You should have asked him to return to us all the Babylonians he took back to Ctesiphon as slaves after his recent visit,' remarked Mardonius dryly.

With the evacuation of Babylonian territory by Narses' army the task of rebuilding those areas laid waste by his army began. This

196

involved Axsen receiving a seemingly never-ending stream of nobles and village headmen begging for aid from the royal treasury. I attended one such meeting a week after the queen's coronation, the throne room crammed full of petitioners, guards and city officials. The intimidating figure of Nabu stood on the left side of the queen on the dais and Mardonius on the right.

The day was hot, airless and the crowded room was stuffy and began to reek of human sweat. Gallia and Praxima had taken themselves off to see a woman who lived in the south of the city who could apparently levitate off the ground from a cross-legged position. My father had already taken his leave of Axsen and was taking his men back to Hatra, a letter from Vata increasing the frown lines on his face with news of yet more Armenian incursions.

Orodes, ever the diplomat, had taken a keen interest in the affairs of Babylon and a delighted Axsen had invited him to act as an adviser with her high priest and Mardonius, and now he stood to the side of the old general listening earnestly as a headman implored the queen to send engineers to assist in the rebuilding of his village's irrigation system.

So there I was standing like a fisherman in a boat without a net, as Axsen took the burden of kingship on her shoulders. I was daydreaming when I heard someone cough behind me. Turning, I saw a young woman in a low-cut white dress standing before me. Tall and shapely, she wore delicate white slippers on her feet and her shoulders were bare. Her skin was dark brown like her eyes and her complexion was flawless. She was certainly a beauty, the wife of a prominent noble no doubt, judging by the expensive perfume she was wearing.

'Forgive me, highness, I have a message for you.'

'A message?'

She smiled, her teeth white and perfect. 'Yes, highness. I am one of the priestesses at the Temple of Ishtar and I bring a request for you to go to the temple.'

I was confused but also curious. 'Who makes this request of me?'

'A lady, highness, who asked that you come to the temple today to meet her.'

It was all very mysterious but as I had nothing better to do and was bored to distraction by what was happening in the throne room, I agreed to her request. I made my excuses to Axsen and Orodes, who appeared absorbed in it all, and left the throne room with my attractive messenger.

She accompanied me as I walked to the stables to collect Remus, smiling at me when I caught her eye, her steps delicate and silent beside me, almost as if she was gliding over the ground. The stables were like those in Hatra – large, luxurious and well staffed. A small army of stable hands tended to the horses' every need, each animal having a separate stable boy to feed him, groom him, muck out his stall and saddle him, in addition to the farriers and veterinaries who tended to their wellbeing. It was a far cry from the austere stables at Dura, not that the horses there were any less cared for, just not as indulged as they were at Babylon.

I arrived at Remus' stall and told the young men in purple livery standing around that I would be taking him out, and then was met by incredulous stares when I informed them that I would saddle him myself. They gave my escort guide lecherous glances as I dismissed them, leaving me alone with her.

The priestess stood at the entrance to the stall as I went through the routine that I had learnt as a small boy. First I brushed Remus' back to remove any dirt or grit that may cause chaffing under the saddle.

'How long have you been a priestess at the temple?' I asked, brushing him from his neck towards his hindquarters so all the hairs laid flat.

'Since the goddess spoke to me as a small child, highness.'

I inspected him to ensure there were no sores or wounds on his body.

I walked past her to fetch the saddlecloth lying on the bench opposite the stall, under my saddle hanging on the wall. Strangely the other stalls were empty of horses and this particular stable block was also deserted of people. It was suddenly very quiet and very still. As I passed her I inadvertently stared at her breasts.

I threw the saddlecloth on Remus' back, positioning it forward over his withers and sliding it back so that his hair lay flat beneath it, running my hand over the white material, a red griffin stitched in each corner.

'My body pleases you, highness?' she purred.

I could feel my cheeks flush at her words as I took the saddle from the wall and placed it gently on my horse's back, slightly forward and then settling it back.

'What? My apologies, I did not mean…'

She laughed. 'There is no need to apologise, highness. Ishtar is the goddess of love as well as war and fertility. Her servants aspire to possess her qualities.'

I checked that there were no wrinkles beneath the saddlecloth and then grabbed the free end of the girth.

'What qualities are those?' I asked, tightening the girth gently to leave enough space to be able to slide my fingers between it and Remus' body.

She moved closer to me, the alluring smell of her perfume filling my nostrils.

198

'Ishtar is the perfect woman, highness, tempting and sensual, a seductive and voluptuous beauty.' She breathed in and her breasts rose. The stall suddenly seemed very small.

She smiled as I brushed past her to fetch the bridle that had been placed on hooks beside the saddle. She stroked Remus' neck.

'Your horse is a most beautiful beast, highness.'

He moved his tail casually and adopted a relaxed stance to indicate that he was very content. I smiled as I put my right hand under his jaw and held the bit with my left, pressing it gently into his mouth and up over his tongue.

'Yes, he and I have been together a long time.'

With the bit in his mouth I gently slid the bridle's headpieces over his ears, then pulled the forelock over the brow band.

She continued stroking him, fixing me with her brown, oval eyes as she did so.

'He was sent to you, highness, so that you would not lose your way.'

I stood in front of him and ensured that the bit, noseband and brow band were level and without twists.

'No, I found him in a town called Nola in a land a great distance from Babylon.'

She stopped stroking him and smiled at me once more. 'No, highness, he found you.'

I fastened the throatash and then the noseband, running two fingers between it and Remus' nose.

She moved closer to me until her face was inches from mine, her full lips parting invitingly. She placed her hands on my hips.

'I will give myself freely if you desire it, highness.'

As my loins stirred with lust she moved one hand to behind my neck and caressed my groin with the other. She smiled.

'Your body says yes, highness.'

She moved her lips closer to mine and it was with god-like will that I suppressed my lust for her.

'My body may say yes but my marriage vows say no,' I replied, gently pushing her away.

'I am here to serve you in all things,' she persisted.

I backed away from her and held up my hands. 'You are most generous but showing me the way to the temple will suffice. We will have to find you a horse so that we may ride to the temple together for I do not know the way.'

I walked round the other side of Remus so temptation was out of view.

'He will lead you there, highness.'

I only half-heard her words as I checked that there was a width of two fingers between the brow band of the bridle and Remus' brow.

199

'All done,' I announced. 'Now, let's get you a horse and then we can ride to the temple together.'

I turned to discover that she no longer stood behind me. I walked out of the stall and looked up and down the corridor. She was nowhere to be seen. I led Remus from his stall outside into the expansive courtyard. An elderly stable hand came towards me carrying a bucket and spade, bowing his head to me.

'Did you see a young woman leaving these stables, she was very beautiful and wearing a white dress?'

He shook his head. 'No, majesty.'

He called to one of his companions nearby on the paved courtyard, who also reported not having seen the priestess. I vaulted into the saddle.

'A striking young woman cannot just disappear into thin air.'

'Do you wish for me to fetch the captain of the guards, majesty?' he said.

'No, carry on with your duties.'

He bowed his head and continued on his way, leaving me none the wiser.

'Well,' I said to Remus, 'I had better find a guide to take me to the temple so that I can resolve this little mystery.'

Without prompting Remus began to walk forward purposely, across the courtyard and out of the palace compound. He ambled past the guards at the gates and swung left to take us north up the Processional Way.

'You seem to know the way,' I said to him and sat back to enjoy the ride.

He took me to the northeast quarter of the city, along an unpaved road at right angles to the Processional Way. Away from the royal thoroughfares citizens threw their garbage and filth onto the streets, which was then covered up with layers of clay. I thus rode along a street that was significantly higher than when it had originally been constructed.

I came at last to the Temple of Ishtar, which was surrounded by a high wall built of mud-bricks. Guards stood at the entrance to the temple complex to keep the throng of worshippers at bay, spearmen dressed all in white with wicker shields painted gold. As soon as they saw me one called inside the tunnel entrance to the temple and a score of other guards appeared and roughly pushed aside the worshippers with their spear shafts to make a passage for me. Remus was unconcerned by the assembly of well-dressed dignitaries, half-naked mystics, poor people, cripples and visitors from other lands dressed in exotic robes who protested and wailed as they were shoved aside to give me access. We passed through the tunnel in the thick perimeter wall and past two guardrooms that flanked its other end to exit into a rectangular courtyard surrounded by stables, barracks and other accommodation. In fact it looked more like a palace than a temple.

'I told you he would find his way here, highness.'

I looked down to see the beautiful priestess who had tried to seduce me in the stables standing on my right side. She smiled at me.

'Shall I take him? The high priestess awaits.'

I was going to ask how she got here before me but then I saw Afrand coming towards me, like her other priestesses dressed in a low-cut white dress, white slippers on her feet and a gold diadem in her hair. I dismounted and my beautiful messenger led Remus to the stables. Guards ushered worshippers from the temple grounds. One man, obviously of some importance judging by the amount of gold on his fingers and round his neck, and the richness of his accompanying wife's apparel, was protesting loudly.

'Do you know who I am? I will tell you. I am the governor of Sippar and a member of the royal council. I have paid handsomely to enter the temple and object strongly to being treated in this way.'

His wife was making noises like the shrieks of a crow as they were unceremoniously ushered from the courtyard.

'How small are the minds of men,' remarked Afrand as she watched them go. She bowed her head to me.

'Welcome, King Pacorus, you honour us with your presence.'

I returned the gesture. 'Your servant, lady. I have to confess that I am a little confused by the message I received summoning me here.'

'Your friend was right – a tall man on a white horse with a scarred face,' she said.

'And where is this "friend" now?' I asked.

'With the goddess,' Afrand replied. 'Can I offer you refreshments?'

'No, thank you. I would like to see her now.'

'Very well. Follow me, majesty.'

We walked across the courtyard, which was now empty of people, through an arch in a stonewall that led to a second courtyard. On the roofs of the buildings that surrounded this courtyard were at least two score of dovecotes housing dozens of white doves. Afrand saw me admiring them.

'White doves are the personal birds of Ishtar. Worshippers purchase sacred cakes made in our own kitchens, which they crumble and feed to them. Thus do they hope to gain favour with the goddess.'

'And does it work?' I enquired innocently.

Afrand looked at me with her large hazel eyes. 'The goddess grants those who are worthy what they desire.'

'And how many are worthy?'

'She said that you were always full of questions,' she replied.

'Who?'

'Your friend.'

201

We carried on walking across the second courtyard to a building at the far end that had a façade decorated with niches and narrow buttresses. Two guards stood at the centrally placed entrance cut in the brickwork – two golden doors. They snapped to attention as Afrand approached and then one banged on the doors.

They opened and Afrand beckoned me to enter.

'These are the goddesses' personal quarters which only a chosen few may enter. Come, King Pacorus.'

She walked inside and I followed. We entered a windowless chamber lit by oil lamps hanging from the walls and filled with the aroma of burning jasmine. As my eyes got accustomed to the half-light I could see a white curtain hanging from a gold rail in front of me that led to another room. Two priestesses dressed in white approached and bowed to me, one holding out her hands.

'Your friend waits beyond the curtain with the goddess but you must leave your sword here. No weapons are permitted in the presence of Ishtar.'

I unbuckled my belt, handed my sword and dagger to the priestess then walked forward. I stopped and turned to Afrand.

'Are you not coming?'

She shook her head. 'Her words are for your ears only. Do not fear, you are beloved of the gods. Place the lock of your wife's hair on the altar before you ask a question. You can retrieve it once the audience is over.'

I felt a chill go down my spine. 'How do you know of such a thing?'

Afrand seemed surprised at my question. 'Your friend told me, of course. How else would I know of such an intimate item?'

I swallowed and walked towards the curtain, then pulled it back and entered Ishtar's sanctuary. This room was even darker than the other chamber; a handful of oil lamps cast a dim light. The smell of jasmine was even stronger. I strained my eyes to observe the room, which like the one I had just left was windowless but had a lower ceiling. There were no seats or other furniture, just gold stands on which incense burned. I walked forward to approach the statue of Ishtar that stood on a marble pedestal, a low altar placed before it to receive offerings. I reached inside my shirt and lifted the chain that held the lock of Gallia's hair over my head and placed it on the altar. My heart was pounding in my chest as I stared at the statue carved from alabaster and inlaid with rubies. The goddess stood naked before me, supporting her breasts with her hands. She was curvaceous and seductive just like her priestesses.

The smell of jasmine began to make me feel light-headed as I stood in front of the altar. I strained my eyes to discern any movement or sound. There was none.

202

'Pacorus.'

I was startled by my name being whispered. I looked around but could discern no one else in the room.

'You have achieved much and yet there is so much more that you must do.'

It was a woman's voice, soft yet strong, commanding yet kind. My heartbeat increased.

'Are you, are you Ishtar, lady?'

She laughed, though it was not in a mocking way.

'Oh, Pacorus, you are just the same as when I first met you. I am not a goddess. I am your friend.'

'Do you have a name, lady?'

'That is not important. What is important is that you remain strong for your task is not yet complete. Your enemies grow strong but the gods have sent you helpers who will aid you to defeat them. But they are not kings and princes.'

'I do not understand.'

'Do you not? Then I will help you see. The one born in the land of water must be given his own army, and you must journey with the one who came from the desert who will furnish you with temple gold. It is always darkest before the dawn, Pacorus. You must keep the faith, little one.'

I turned to face my celestial visitor but when I did there was nothing but an empty space. I waited for a few more minutes to see if she would speak to me again but there were no more words. I picked up the chain and replaced it round my neck and then left the sanctuary, confused. Afrand saw my confusion as she escorted me back to Remus.

'The gods speak in riddles,' I said at length.

'Your friend was not a god, she was as real as you or I.'

Now I was even more confused. 'But you sent me into the holy sanctuary of Ishtar.'

'Because that is where she wanted to see you.'

I was getting angry now. 'And you let this person, whom you had never seen before, just wander into your holy of holies? She could have been any trickster or liar.'

Afrand remained calm as I hoisted myself into Remus' saddle. She held his reins.

'All the priestesses who serve Ishtar here are chosen by the goddess for their special and unique gifts. For example, one can see things that will happen in the future. Yesterday she had a vision of a dark-haired woman walking into the temple and asking me to send a message to King Pacorus of Dura. The priestess told me that this woman would tell me of the scar on your cheek, the others on your back and leg, and the lock of your wife's blonde hair you always wear round your neck.'

203

'These things are known to many people,' I answered.

'The visitor also told me of the last time you saw each other, when you kissed her hand when she held it out to you, though she meant for you to take it, on that storm-lashed night when her son was born and you promised to take care of him.'

I looked at her and my blood ran cold.

'Did she give you her name?' I asked.

'Of course. It was Claudia.'

Chapter 9

I said nothing to Gallia or anyone else about my experience at the temple. I rode from Afrand and her seductresses with an angry heart, thinking I had been the victim of a cheap trick. But if that was so, how did she know about that night in the Silarus Valley long ago when I had indeed held the hand of Claudia after she had given birth to the son of Spartacus? And what purpose would it serve to deceive me thus? What was I to the high priestess of Ishtar? With these thoughts swirling in my mind I rode back to the palace to find Gallia waiting for me in our private chambers.

'Where have you been?' she quizzed me.

'Sightseeing,' I answered evasively.

'Well, now that you are here I wish to ask you a favour.'

She had changed from her riding gear and was dressed in a sheer, sleeveless white dress. She was standing framed in the arch that led to our bedroom balcony, the sunlight streaming into the room and highlighting her naked body beneath her dress. I let my eyes go from hers down to her breasts and then her thighs.

She glided towards me and slipped her arms around my waist, drawing her mouth closer to mine. She was wearing the most delightful perfume.

'What is the favour, my sweet?'

She drew her mouth closer to mine and kissed me tenderly, then pulled away to look at me with the eyes of a temptress.

'I want you to ask Orodes to stay here in Babylon for a while longer.'

She began kissing my neck, her hot breath on my skin, her body pressed against mine.

'Orodes?'

Her hands came to the front of my body and unbuckled my sword belt, letting it fall to the floor. She tugged my shirt from my leggings and ran her hands up my back.

'He likes it here, it would be a shame to drag him back to Dura.'

She closed her lips on mine and her tongue went deep into my mouth. My heart was racing and my loins were afire. She pulled away from my lips.

I ran my hand over her cheek. 'He is his own man. He goes where he will.' I let my other hand fall to her buttocks and gently pressed her groin into mine.

'No,' she purred, 'he does what you ask him.'

She kissed me long and hard again and ripped off my shirt, then my vest.

'I really need him back at Dura,' I whispered into her ear, pulling up her dress with my hand.

205

She tensed and pushed me backwards. It was as if a demon had suddenly taken possession of her body.

'So,' she snapped, 'you will not do this one small thing that I ask?'

I smiled and tried to pull her close. 'Gallia, this is not the time for talk.'

She would have none of it, pushing my arms away from her. 'Don't Gallia me. If you will not to accede to my desire why should I submit to yours?'

'What?'

She folded her arms and held her head high in a stance of defiance.

'Why do you need him at Dura? I thought you commanded your army.'

I was confused. 'Why do you want Orodes to stay here?'

She placed her hands on her hips and her nostrils flared. 'Do I have to explain all my actions? Am I your slave to be questioned and ordered about so?'

She turned on her heels, picked up a cloak from the bed and wrapped it around her.

'I am going to bathe. I will see you again when you are in a better mood.'

I spread my hands in exasperation. 'When I am in a better mood? Can we please discuss this like civilised people?'

But she merely waved a hand at me and stomped from the room. I flopped onto the bed and stared at the ceiling. Women were more difficult to unravel than the famed Gordian knot that Alexander of Macedon had cut with his sword. It was a complicated knot tied by King Gordius of Phrygia that the famed Alexander had severed with a swing of his sword. That knot appeared mere child's play when compared to working out my wife's emotions.

I had no idea why she wanted Orodes to stay in Babylon. Perhaps he had offended her. I discount the possibility. Still, something had obviously irked her. Perhaps Axsen was drowning under responsibilities and required assistance. Who better than Orodes, upon whose shoulders great responsibility sat so lightly? That must be it. To solve the mystery I went in search of him and was told that he and Axsen had departed the city to go hunting. I saddled Remus once more and rode him to the royal hunting grounds located directly south of Babylon. Here the land adjacent to the river was not cultivated or populated but was given over to wildlife. There were irrigation channels that had been deliberately cut to water the foliage and trees and to attract game. This great area of greenery was out of bounds to ordinary citizens and was patrolled by royal gamekeepers. I wore my leather cuirass and plumed helmet to identify myself to them as I rode through poplar, willow and date palms, which fortunately had not been despoiled during the recent siege. Narses had probably used it for his own recreation. Near the river itself were great clumps of the large Mardi reed that grew to four times the height of a man.

The land between the Tigris and Euphrates may be desert but around the waterways there was a plethora of wildlife and fauna. The rivers are full of giant barbels, soft-backed turtles, catfish and eels, while along the banks and overhead fly babblers, crows, hawks, falcons, eagles and vultures. As I followed the churned-up track indicating the hunting party had preceded me I heard the grunting of wild pigs and saw fleeting glances of gazelles. Other animals that inhabited this area included jackals, wolves, hares, river otters, foxes and the king of the beasts: the lion.

The day was hot and still as I tilted my head to try to discern the noise of the beaters who would be with the royal party. But I could hear nothing. Perhaps they had halted for a midday meal. I continued to follow the track, going over in my mind again the earlier experience at the temple and the words of Afrand. I was lost in thought when Remus suddenly stopped and reared his head in alarm, his tail twitching and his ears drawn back. He began to move sideways and then backwards, his eyes wide with alarm. Something had obviously spooked him.

I stroked his neck. 'Easy, boy.'

But my words did not comfort him. His tail was flattened between his legs; he snorted and became skittish. I looked around but could see nothing among the trees and bushes. But I knew that a threat was close. Horses are grazing animals and become agitated if they can smell or hear a predator, just like Remus was now. I scanned the terrain near me but saw nothing. I pulled my bow from its quiver and nocked an arrow in the bowstring as he backed away from a dense group of bushes about fifty paces in front of us. His ears were pinned back in fear and he snorted again. Then the animal broke cover.

Lions have little stamina and prefer to attack their prey from a close distance, usually around thirty paces, but this one was either very hungry or believed he could reach us before Remus had time to turn and flee. A big male with a great mane and huge paws, he came crashing through the bushes and bounded towards me. Survival instincts took over as I drew back the bowstring and released it as the distance between me and the lion disappeared in an instant. Remus reared up as the lion pounced. I was thrown from the saddle and my horse bolted from sight. As soon as I hit the ground I leapt to my feet and drew my sword and dagger. My helmet had come off my head and my bow lay on the ground several feet away. The arrow had struck the lion in the shoulder, fortunately deflecting his leap and saving both Remus and me, who was now fleeing as fast as his powerful legs could carry him.

The lion circled me, possessed of a rage caused by his scent of prey and the pain from the arrow stuck in him. He curled his lip as me as he limped forward, then roared. He may have been wounded but he could still pounce again using his powerful back legs. Lions usually kill by swiping the head of their prey with their forepaws, the blow being sufficient to stun their victim. If he caught my head with such a blow it would break my neck. So I decided to attack him.

I screamed and ran at him with my dagger held in front of me in my left hand and my *spatha* over my head in my right. Unfortunately he had the same idea and came at me, leaping into the air with his claws extended and his fearsome canine teeth bared. I collapsed on the ground and tried to stab up at him as he passed over me but missed. I jumped back up and faced him again as he landed, turned and gave another mighty roar. Blood was seeping from his wound but the rage that possessed him meant it had not slowed him down. He could smell blood and wanted to taste it. He roared once more and again came at me. I had not time to run or move as he ran towards me, so I gripped the handles of my weapons and prepared to meet the great lump of claws, teeth and muscle that wanted to turn me into offal.

When the arrows hit him he did not drop but just veered sideways, faltering but remaining on his feet. Another volley of six arrows slammed into his side and he gave a faint roar and then halted. Then arrow after arrow struck his side, shoulder, rump, hind legs and neck. He turned his head in the direction from where the arrows had come, grunted and then collapsed on the ground, dead.

Riders appeared clutching bows, soldiers of Babylon's royal guard in their dragon-skin armour, and then gamekeepers on foot with spears and long knives tucked in their belts, followed by a host of beaters, all looking dumfounded as I picked up my helmet, returned my sword to its scabbard and slid my dagger back in its sheath. Then Orodes and Axsen rode into view, the prince holding his bow that had an arrow still nocked in the bowstring. Their faces registered concern as they halted before me, Axsen looking at the dead lion and then at me.

I bowed my head to her. 'My thanks, lady, your party appeared in the nick of time. Another few seconds and I would have been lion kill.'

'Are you hurt, Pacorus?' she said in a concerned voice.

'No, lady, but Remus bolted and I don't know where he is.'

She swung in her saddle and pointed at an officer mounted on a grey mare in front of a dozen spearmen carrying round shields.

'Find him,' she ordered.

The man saluted and led his men back down the track I had been riding on.

'Where is your escort?' enquired Orodes.

I walked over to where my bow lay on the ground and picked it up.

'Didn't bring one.'

Axsen looked at Orodes in confusion. 'You went hunting alone?'

'Actually, I was not hunting. I came looking for Orodes.' I jerked my head at the dead lion. 'He was the one doing the hunting.'

Orodes took the arrow from his bowstring and slipped it back into his quiver. 'It is lucky for you that we were but a short distance away. I hate to think what would have happened if we had not arrived when we did.'

I brushed the dirt from my goose-feather crest and then put the helmet back on my head.

I smiled at him. 'To coin one of Domitus' phrases, I can always rely on you when I'm in a tight spot.'

The riders returned with my errant horse, and after I had checked him over I put my bow back in its case and regained my seat on his back.

'We ride back to the city,' announced Axsen, who looked very striking in brown leather boots, tan leggings and a long-sleeved blue silk shirt, her hair arranged in two long ponytails that had purple ribbons tide along their length.

She smiled at me. 'Ride with us, Pacorus.'

We rode back to the city preceded by a score of the royal bodyguard with a score more behind us. After them came the gamekeepers and the beaters carrying the day's spoils hanging from poles carried between two men: a dozen gazelles, three wild pigs, four hyenas and my lion.

'A good day's hunting?' I asked, riding on the left of Orodes with Axsen on his other side.

'A very agreeable day,' said Axsen. 'Though I would have never forgiven myself if anything had happened to you, Pacorus.'

'If it had, lady, no blame could be apportioned to you.'

'I shall have the lion's skin sent to Dura as a memento of your visit to Babylon,' she promised.

'And a reminder to take an escort the next time you go on a hunting trip,' added Orodes.

Axsen laughed. They were both obviously in a happy mood. I therefore decided to broach the subject of him remaining in Babylon for a while longer.

I cleared my throat. 'Orodes, I wonder if I might ask a favour of you?'

'Of course.'

'Well, the thing is, and with the present indeterminate situation along the Tigris, I thought it might be prudent for you to remain at Babylon with your bodyguard for a while. If you are in agreement, that is. And also if it pleases you, lady.'

'It pleases me very much,' replied Axsen.

'I would consider it an honour,' added Orodes, much to my surprise.

'Well, that is agreed, then,' I said.

The next morning, as I lay beside Gallia after she had given herself to me as a reward for carrying out her request, she stroked my scarred cheek and wrapped her naked body around mine.

'You see, it was not that difficult.'

'No, indeed,' I agreed. 'In fact, Orodes did not object at all.'

She began kissing my neck. 'Why should he? Axsen is good company and this is a great city.'

She stopped caressing my body and looked at me.

'It was rather foolish nearly being eaten by a lion, though.'

'Axsen is having the skin sent back to Dura,' I frowned. 'A constant reminder of my foolishness.'

The next day we left for home, saying our goodbyes to Axsen and Orodes on the palace steps and also to Nergal and Praxima who were taking their men back to Mesene.

'Now remember,' I said to Nergal with an arm round his shoulder, 'if that bastard Narses starts raiding your kingdom call on Yasser for help.'

Yasser was one of Haytham's fierce subordinates whose lands sat directly across the Euphrates from Mesene. Formerly he used to cross the river to burn, loot and pillage Mesene, but since my friendship with Haytham and Nergal's accession to the throne of that kingdom all raiding had stopped.

'Your father will be unhappy at such a thing,' he said.

'What he does not know will not aggrieve him,' I shot back. 'Narses will think twice about violating other kingdoms if the result is Agraci war bands sweeping across his territory, that goes for Mithridates too. We must fight fire with fire.'

He looked pensive. 'You think they will launch another invasion, Pacorus?'

'I fear it will be so, my friend. But if we keep our quivers full and our swords sharp we will be triumphant in the end, of that I am sure. But you must call on Yasser's aid if you need it. His reinforcements will reach you before mine do.'

We clasped each other's forearms and I embraced Praxima and then we all rode from the palace. My cataphracts and their squires were already on the road north before we left the city, having struck camp at dawn. We joined them inland from the east bank of the Euphrates mid-morning and maintained a brisk pace for the rest of the day. Twelve days later we rode across the pontoon bridges that spanned the Euphrates and entered Dura. The horsemen were dressed in their full battle array and Vagharsh carried my griffin banner behind me. My wife and her Amazons wore their mail shirts and helmets with their

210

cheekguards tied shut as we rode through the cheering crowds that lined the riverbanks and the route into the city.

Waiting for us in front of the Palmyrene Gate, drawn up for inspection, were Domitus and his legions. The cataphracts and Amazons formed into line behind Gallia and me as I faced them, now looking very different from the battered men who had limped home following the battle against Narses and Mithridates. Now the Durans and Exiles stood in their cohorts and centuries with clean tunics, burnished helmets and spotless shields, the points of thousands of javelins glinting in the sunlight.

Beyond the legionaries stood my horse archers arrayed in their dragons: one, two, three! There were three dragons, which meant that the one that had been sent east of the Tigris had returned. I squinted and saw Surena on his horse in front of them. I closed my eyes and gave thanks to Shamash for his and their safe delivery. Beyond them I caught sight of more horsemen. The lords' horse archers, perhaps?

A blast of trumpets rent the air and then the colour parties stepped forward, one carrying the golden griffin, the other holding the silver lion of the Exiles. I drew my sword and held it before me in salute.

I nudged Remus forward to within a few feet of Domitus who stood a few paces in front of Drenis with the Duran colour party and Kronos with the colour party of the Exiles.

'It is good to see you, my friends. The men look in better shape than the last time I clapped eyes on them.'

Domitus nodded. 'Good to have you back, as well. Sorry to hear about Vardan.' He looked beyond me to where the Amazons and cataphracts were lined up.

'Where is Orodes?'

'Staying in Babylon for a while. He sends his regards.'

Surena brought his horse to a halt in a cloud of dirt. 'Hail, lord.'

'Good to see you are alive, Surena. I trust you took care of my horse archers.'

'Yes, lord,' he beamed and then pointed to where the lords were gathered. 'I bring you reinforcements, lord.'

I was confused. 'Reinforcements?'

'You and Gallia better get yourself settled and then all will be revealed,' said Domitus.

'We heard you nearly got eaten by a lion, lord,' said Surena, grinning at me like an idiot.

'Don't believe all you hear, Surena,' I replied.

'So it's true, then,' said Domitus. 'That's what happens when you don't have me to watch your back.'

The parade was dismissed and the various contingents returned to their quarters, the legions, minus those legionaries who had been on garrison duty in the city and Citadel, to the tented camp that stood west of the Palmyrene Gate; the horse archers and cataphracts to their stables and barracks in and near the Citadel. In the days following companies of horse archers would be assigned to the mud-brick forts north and south of the city to both alleviate the need for barracks inside the city and to provide the kingdom with security. As in Hatra the forts were not designed to be major strongholds but rather to be the eyes and ears to any hostile incursions.

It was late by the time we were reunited with our children in the Citadel after being welcomed at the foot of the palace steps by Rsan and had washed the Mesopotamian dust from our bodies. I told him to convene the meeting of the council for the next day. We took our evening meal on the palace balcony with our children and Dobbai, who laid a bony hand on my arm and told me that she was glad I was back where I belonged. When the children had eaten and fallen asleep in our arms we carried them to their bedrooms and returned to the terrace as the sun set in the west and turned the desert beyond the river blood red.

I looked at Dobbai, this frail old woman swathed in black robes sitting in a great wicker chair stuffed with cushions, Gallia fussing around her and wrapping her in a blanket as twilight enveloped the earth and the temperature began to drop. Known throughout the empire as the feared sorceress at the court of King of Kings Sinatruces, I had first met her some fourteen years ago when I had accompanied my father to Ctesiphon after I had captured a Roman eagle near the Kingdom of Zeugma. Her appearance, lack of manners and conduct at that time had disgusted me, but then I was a naïve, arrogant young fool who judged people on appearances. I had seen her briefly after I had returned from Italy and again when she had appeared one day at Dura shortly after I had assumed its kingship. She had stayed ever since, becoming the confidant of my wife and the guardian of our children. And for that I thanked Shamash for her presence.

Servants brought us warm wine to drink and lit oil lamps on stands to illuminate the terrace as the sun departed the world for another day.

'You were right,' I said to Dobbai. 'I underestimated Mithridates and Narses and nearly got the army wiped out.'

'And yourself killed,' added Gallia.

I chuckled. 'If I had led the army to disaster I would have deserved to die.' I looked at Dobbai, then Gallia.

'I have my two favourite women to thank for my salvation.' I raised my cup to them. 'So I salute you both.'

Dobbai waved away my gesture. 'You have learned a valuable lesson, son of Hatra. The two vipers who rule the empire have many weapons in their armoury whereas you have but one, your sword. You think too much of your soldiers. I heard that you could have escaped with Prince Orodes but chose to stay and play with them in the desert.'

I frowned. 'What kind of king deserts his soldiers?'

She laughed. 'A living one.'

'I would rather die alongside them than do such a base thing as to save my life at the expense of theirs.'

She pointed a bony finger at me. 'And that is your weakness. Did you know that Narses murdered his own parents so that he could become king?

'By the look of disdain on your face I see that you did not. The lives of others mean nothing to him, or Mithridates for that matter. They laugh at your attachment to mere soldiers.'

'One day, my mere soldiers as you call them will destroy those two and restore the empire to its former glory.'

'Have you noticed, my dear,' said Dobbai to Gallia, 'that men always take comfort in an imagined past when truth and justice ruled the world and there was no famine, plague, war or tyranny.'

Gallia looked at me sympathetically. 'Alas, I fear there has never been such a time.'

'And nor will there be,' said Dobbai, sipping at her wine.

'Then why do we bother to fight at all?' I asked.

Dobbai drained her cup and then rose from her chair, Gallia walking over to assist her and then linking her arm in the old woman's.

'You fight, son of Hatra, because you enjoy it and because you will save the empire from a great danger. That is your destiny.'

I noticed that Dobbai took short steps and leaned on Gallia for support. She suddenly seemed very old.

I looked into my cup of wine, the red liquid appearing thick like blood.

'Vardan is dead,' I said suddenly.

Dobbai stopped and turned. 'I heard. Kings die, it is the way of things.'

'It is my fault and Axsen is alone because I asked her father for help.'

'He died saving his kingdom. I would have thought you would be pleased by such a death,' she retorted. 'Better that than a frail old wreck lying in a bed of his own piss and dung waiting for the end. As for the princess, the seed of her future greatness and happiness has been planted in the blackness of her misery.'

'I don't understand,' I said.

'Of course you don't,' she snapped. 'You are not meant to.' She smiled at Gallia. 'Help me to my bed chamber, child, and leave him alone with the riddle he has neither the wit nor wisdom to fathom.'

213

The next morning the council assembled in the headquarters building in the Citadel. It felt good to be home and among friends once again. I thanked Shamash that Dura did not have great temples such as in Babylon where powerful priests and priestesses could weave their magic and indulge in intrigues. My visit to the Temple of Ishtar still played on my mind but I still said nothing about it to anyone.

Any thoughts of the dead wife of Spartacus soon disappeared as Rsan read from a great list he had drawn up pertaining to the state of the army and its provisioning. He may have been made the city governor but his years spent as its treasurer had accustomed him to seeing everything in terms of outgoings and income. Domitus adopted his usual habit of toying with his dagger as Rsan lectured us all. Behind him sat Aaron with parchments and no less than two scribes took notes of the meeting. Rsan had clearly made these meetings his own during my absence.

In addition to Domitus, Kronos, Gallia and Dobbai attending the meeting, I had also asked Surena to be present as the commander of my horse archers so that he could give an account of his expedition east of the Tigris. But it was Rsan who spoke first.

'I have yet to receive reports from the commanders of the horsemen who returned with you yesterday, majesty, but thus far the expenditure of your recent campaign has been most costly.'

'How costly?' I asked.

Rsan looked at the parchment in his hand, then turned and held out his hand to Aaron who passed him another.

'Let me see. Well, first of all the legions,' he nodded to Domitus, 'required four thousand new shields, five hundred swords, over four hundred mail shirts, in addition to the five thousand that required repairs, four hundred and fifty wagons that were apparently left in the desert – quite extraordinary – six hundred dead mules and hundreds of other tools and utensils that have mysteriously disappeared.'

Domitus stopped playing with his dagger and looked at Rsan.

'I apologise for leaving so much equipment in the desert, as you say, but at the time a great host of the enemy was trying to kill us. Wagons and cooking pots slipped my mind when the air was filled with enemy arrows and hostile horsemen were trying to turn me into a kebab.'

Rsan's brow was furrowed like a freshly ploughed field.

Dobbai cackled and pointed at Rsan. 'The tallyman thinks it would be better if the vultures were picking at your bones and those of your men, Roman. That way he wouldn't have to open his precious treasury to pay for replacement items.'

Rsan flustered and dropped one of his parchments. Domitus pointed his dagger at him.

'Haven't you forgotten something? My javelins?'

Rsan cleared his throat and handed the parchments back to Aaron. 'The general has requested twenty thousand new javelins, majesty. Ruinous.'

'War is an expensive business, Rsan. The general must have everything he desires if Dura is to remain strong. Is not the treasury full?' I asked.

'Full is vague notion,' answered Rsan defensively.

'No it's not,' said Domitus. 'It's either full or it isn't.'

Rsan brought his hands together in front of him. 'It is a matter of income streams and outgoings, general.' Domitus went back to playing with his dagger while Kronos stared at the wall. 'Ten thousand foot soldiers and four thousand horsemen, plus their weapons and equipment, is a constant drain on the treasury, made worse when the army goes on campaign.'

Domitus sighed loudly. 'That is what armies do, Rsan: go on campaign.'

'And now we have an additional eight thousand soldiers to house and feed,' continued Rsan, ignoring Domitus.

'Ah, yes,' I said, 'which brings us nicely to Surena.'

'But what about the cost of re-equipping the army, majesty?' queried Rsan.

'Are there sufficient funds in the treasury to cover the cost of the army's refurbishment?' I asked.

Rsan nodded sullenly.

'Then see to it, that is my final word on the matter.'

Rsan blushed and then instructed the clerks to make a note of my decision.

'And now, Surena, please inform us how you came about acquiring eight thousand horsemen on your travels.'

He told his story with pride, of how the queen had sent for him on the day she brought reinforcements from Dura and told him that she was giving him a thousand men to command, and that he should lead them across the Tigris.

'I rode south and then east, lord, crossing the Tigris in Mesene. We encountered no opposition and so I assaulted the walls of Ctesiphon itself before striking southeast towards Elymais.'

That would explain why Mithridates had departed suddenly, to hurry back to his mother's side.

'Ctesiphon is protected by a perimeter wall, albeit crumbling, that is still strong enough to beat off an assault by horsemen,' I said.

'Yes, lord,' agreed Surena, 'so we quickly departed after we had shot some of the guards off the walls.'

'Did you reach Elymais?' I enquired.

Surena shook his head. 'No, lord. We continued on for another two days and then came across a great host of horsemen heading north. They carried a banner that showed a four-pointed star, the emblem of Elymais, and thus I knew them to be soldiers of King Gotarzes. I remember being taught that.'

Like many promising leaders in Dura's army Surena had attended classes as part of the Sons of the Citadel scheme. In addition to their normal lessons they were also taught the history of the empire and surrounding lands.

'I met with their leader,' continued Surena, 'who told me of a great battle between Narses and Gotarzes in which the King of Elymais fell and his army was defeated. Afterwards the king's capital surrendered and his kingdom was no more. But there are those who have stayed loyal to their king's memory and vowed to carry on fighting until their homeland is free once more.'

'Most of them young men burning with hatred for Narses and having a thirst for revenge,' added Domitus.

'I know how that feels,' said Kronos. He was from Pontus, like most of the men of the Exiles, a land now under the Roman heel, though he and his men dreamed of a time when it would not be and they could return to their homeland. He knew, as did all of us, that only a miracle would make it so.

'Dura is stronger because of such men, Kronos,' I said, smiling.

'I told them that Dura and its king would welcome them,' continued Surena, 'and so we joined forces and retraced our steps before recrossing the Tigris and heading for home.'

'Are we to bear the expense of sheltering and equipping these men also, majesty?' enquired Rsan.

'Until I have spoken to their commander and worked out what to do with them, yes,' I answered.

I saw the man who led the soldiers of Elymais that afternoon when I summoned him to the palace. I sat in the throne room beside Gallia as he stood before us. I guessed him to be a man in his early forties. He had long dark brown hair, a beard and a world-weary expression. A sword hung from his faded leather belt and he held a battered helmet in the crook of his right arm. His name was Silaces.

I ordered a chair to be brought for him as he told us his tale of woe.

'Most of us either have no family or they are dead, majesty. After the king was killed I decided to leave Elymais. I had served him too long to see his kingdom reduced to a vassal state of that bastard Mithridates.' He glanced at Gallia. 'Begging your pardon, majesty.'

'It's quite all right,' she replied, 'we loved Gotarzes too.'

Silaces continued. 'With the capitulation of the king's capital the fight went out of most people, but I gathered up those who thought like me and we headed north.'

216

'Where were you going?' asked Gallia.

'Any of the northern kingdoms – Media, Atropaiene, Hatra – that would give us refuge. After that,' he shrugged, 'we had no plans after that.'

'Well,' I said, 'it was fortunate for you and us that you crossed paths with Surena.'

Silaces laughed and the burden of worry and responsibility he carried on his shoulders disappeared for an instant. 'He is a strange one, that's for sure, and as cocky as I was at that age. He told me that he had been sent by Dura's blonde-haired queen and her witch to raise some hell across the Tigris, and that he had already attacked Ctesiphon. I had heard of King Pacorus of Dura of course, and he said that there would be a home for us in your kingdom. I don't know why but I believed him and so here we are.'

'He spoke the truth,' I said. 'You and your men are welcome here, Silaces. Welcome to stay and welcome to fight alongside us if you so wish.'

Silaces stood and bowed to us. 'You are a most gracious king, majesty.'

'I shall inspect your men tomorrow,' I told him.

When I did I found them to be in a most parlous state. They had been quartered five miles south of the city, on land that was part of the royal estates. Most of Dura's lords lived in the northern part of the kingdom, their estates extending north for a hundred miles and west into the desert. But Duran territory also extended south of the city for another hundred miles, most of it belonging to the crown and containing the royal tanneries, farms that produced food for the palace and army, and fodder for our horses and camels, mule-breeding centres and the fledgling horse herds that would be used to provide future mounts for Dura's horsemen.

Silaces had brought the equivalent of eight dragons with him across the Euphrates, but as I rode among them with Surena and Gallia I estimated that less than half of them were adequately equipped. All had their bows, for a Parthian's most precious object was the bow that he had made himself, but most of their quivers were empty. Few had swords and many of their horses were in urgent need of new saddles and shoes.

Silaces saw me screwing up my face at them. 'They are not much to look at, majesty. Most of us are survivors from the last battle when we escaped with our lives and not much else. But they are good men and brave given a chance.'

'I don't doubt it, Silaces,' I said, 'but right now they need new uniforms, new weapons and some of them new horses. It will be many months before they will be ready to take the field again.'

217

In fact it took the rest of the year to provide Silaces and his men with new clothes, weapons and full quivers, in addition to the resources that had to be devoted to bringing the legions back up to strength. Fortunately we had established a replacement cohort that was permanently stationed in the city, through which replacements could be allocated to those centuries that had suffered losses, but it was still a time-consuming business. And every week without fail I received complaints from Rsan about the high costs involved.

He had a point. The wealth of Dura came from the endless caravans on the Silk Road that passed through the kingdom on their way to Egypt. But unlike other kingdoms, where the king had his palace guard and a small number of other professional soldiers, in Dura there was a standing army to support. And now Dura was saddled with an additional eight thousand horsemen and their animals to feed and clothe. As the treasury began to empty of its gold reserves I too began to worry that the army would eventually drain it dry and ruin the kingdom.

During the next six months the armouries were restocked with weapons and equipment to replace those that had been lost in Babylonia. The foundries and workshops that produced the swords, lances, javelins, bows, arrows, scale armour, bow cases, quivers and mail shirts for the legionaries were located in the northeast corner of the city, beyond the walls of the Citadel. The buildings in that area were purchased from their owners for generous amounts and then converted into production centres. The workers had originally been housed in tents north of the city walls but now lived in permanent accommodation sited near their workplaces. There were now several hundred of them, which represented a further drain on Rsan's treasury, as he never tired of telling me.

As Dura had no access to great forests or iron ore deposits, wood and iron had to be purchased from elsewhere. Great quantities of ash, used for making shields, lances and javelins, came from the northern kingdoms of the empire, from Media and Atropaiene. The timbers were cut and loaded on carts for transport to the Tigris where they were lashed together and floated downstream on inflated goatskins. These rafts, called *kalaks*, were able to pass under the numerous bridges built by the Persians and Greeks that spanned the waterway. After reaching my father's kingdom the goatskins were deflated and carried back upstream on donkeys. I arranged for the loads to be met at the river and then escorted across Hatran territory to Dura. Supplies of iron purchased from Atropaiene arrived via the same route whereas metals obtained from Hatran mines were floated down the Euphrates.

As spring gave way to summer and then autumn the weekly meetings of the council became more and more tiring as Rsan produced endless parchments listing the army's expenditure. Orodes had at last returned from Babylon and his presence was a welcome addition to the meetings.

'We are still five thousand javelins short,' complained Domitus to Rsan.

'The funds have not been released for their manufacture,' said Marcus, rubbing a hand over his now almost bald scalp.

My governor smiled at him. 'Every one of your legionaries has a spear, I believe, and the armouries are full of additional ones.'

'That is correct,' replied Marcus.

'How many spears do the legionaries have in total, Aaron?' asked Rsan, turning to his assistant.

Aaron sifted through his pile of parchments and then stopped when he found the one he wanted.

'Thirty-five thousand, lord.'

Rsan shook his head. 'Thirty-five thousand; that is more than three spears for every legionary.'

'They are not spears they are javelins,' Domitus corrected him.

'What is the difference?' asked Rsan.

'You throw javelins, Rsan,' said Domitus.

Rsan tried to be clever. 'That would explain why your men go through so many of them. Perhaps they could refrain from throwing them away in future.'

Domitus curled his lip at him. 'Are you going to issue the gold so my men can have their javelins?'

Rsan folded his hands and intertwined his fingers. 'I am afraid they will have to wait, the royal armouries are at full capacity.'

'Doing what?' asked Domitus in exasperation.

'Well, for one thing completing the order for over a quarter of a million arrows for Silaces and his men.'

'Cannot we hire more workers for the armouries?' I asked.

Rsan shook his head. 'Majesty, more workers means more wages and more materials for them to work with, which means a great deal more expenditure. In plain language, there is more money going out of the treasury than is coming in.'

Domitus was having none of it. 'Caravans fill the road every day and the lords send their tribute on a monthly basis. There is plenty of money.'

'With respect, general,' answered Rsan, 'there is not plenty of money. If you wish to inspect the treasury records you will see it is so. Silaces and his men are proving too much of a burden, majesty.'

'We cannot just dismiss them,' said Gallia. 'Dura offered them a home and cannot now rescind its hospitality.'

'It is as the queen says,' I agreed.

During this interchange I had noticed Aaron becoming fidgety and agitated. I could tell he wanted to say something but was holding back from doing so.

'Besides,' I said, 'there is nowhere for Silaces and his men to go. Their homeland is occupied.'

'Perhaps Babylon or Mesene could make use of them,' suggested Rsan. 'I have heard those kingdoms need additional soldiers.'

'Babylon's resources are fully committed to rectifying the damage caused by the war earlier in the year,' said Orodes.

'And Mesene will not be able to support eight thousand horsemen,' I added.

'Then, frankly, they must be disbanded, majesty,' said Rsan. 'Before your treasury is emptied.'

Rsan looked smug and Orodes thoughtful, while Domitus leaned back in his chair and stared at the ceiling. Gallia looked at me and shrugged and the room fell silent.

'I know where there is gold,' announced Aaron suddenly.

Rsan was aghast. 'Aaron, you forget yourself.'

Aaron flushed and then cast his eyes down.

'Well, if he knows where he can lay his hands on some gold,' said Domitus, 'let us hear what the boy has to say.' He shot a fake smile at Rsan. 'If only to shut up Rsan.'

'Aaron,' I said, 'speak freely. Let us hear your words.'

Dobbai shuffled into the room unannounced and sat herself down beside Gallia. We had all got so used to her being at these meetings that we hardly took notice of her comings and goings.

Aaron cleared his throat, casting his eyes round the table.

'Thank you, majesty. As you all may know, I am a Jew from Judea.'

'My sympathies,' said Domitus.

'Domitus, please,' I asked. 'Continue, Aaron.'

Aaron cast a contemptuous look at Domitus who began toying with his dagger.

'My homeland is ruled by a tyrant named Hyrcanus, who was put in place by the Roman general Pompey when he captured the city of Jerusalem and deposed the true leader of the Jewish people, Aristobulus.'

The names meant nothing to me but Aaron spoke with passion in his voice. He continued.

'But the Romans control Judea. Hyrcanus is their puppet.'

Orodes and Marcus were listening intently but Domitus was clearly bored, Rsan puzzled and Gallia distracted by Dobbai whispering in her ear.

'Aristobulus and his family were taken to Rome as the spoils of war but one of his sons, Alexander Maccabeus, who is also my friend,

220

escaped and returned to Judea to carry on the fight against Hyrcanus and the Romans.'

'This is all very interesting, Aaron,' I said.

'Is it?' interrupted Domitus.

I held a hand up to him. 'But what has it all got to do with Dura and its treasury?'

'Well, majesty,' continued Aaron, 'Alexander needs weapons with which to furnish his supporters before they can rise up and throw off the shackles of Hyrcanus. Weapons that the armouries at Dura could furnish, majesty. Alexander would pay a handsome price for such supplies.'

Rsan's ears pricked up at these words and Domitus stopped playing with his dagger.

Rsan cut straight to the point. 'How handsome?'

'He has much gold to call upon, lord. He would pay whatever was asked for a plentiful supply of weapons.'

'Weapons to kill Romans,' said Domitus.

Dobbai laughed. 'What's the matter, Domitus, does the idea of Roman blood watering the earth offend you?'

Domitus scowled at her. 'I care not if it is Roman or Parthian blood, or even that of an old woman, but I do care if it is the blood of my friends seeping into the ground.'

'How so?' I asked.

Domitus pointed the tip of his dagger at Aaron. 'He is talking about furnishing weapons for an uprising against Rome. If the Romans found out that Dura was supplying its enemies with weapons, you can be sure they would send an army against us.'

'Trade is trade,' remarked Rsan, thinking only of his balance sheets.

'I'll remind you of that when you are carted off into slavery by the Romans after they have reduced Dura to rubble.'

'No Roman army will take this city,' said Gallia defiantly.

'I meant no offence, Gallia,' said Domitus, 'but the last thing we need is war with Rome.'

'War with Rome is coming whether you like it or not, Domitus,' hissed Dobbai. 'Your people covet all the lands of Parthia, just as they did Syria, Pontus, Armenia and Judea.'

'Alexander is an honourable man, majesty,' said Aaron. 'He would never reveal the source of his aid.'

'Of course he would,' said Domitus, his voice raised. 'Once they start nailing him to a cross he will sing like a canary.'

'The proposal is fraught with danger I agree,' said Orodes.

'If you were to meet with Alexander, majesty,' implored Aaron, 'you would see for yourself that he is a man of honour.'

221

Domitus was dumbfounded. 'Meet with him? Do you realise the danger of bringing a rebel leader who is fighting against Rome to Dura? Word would soon reach Syria of such a thing. It is out of the question.'

'The king could always travel to Judea instead,' suggested Aaron.

'Out of the question,' snapped Domitus.

'I think that is for me to say,' I reminded him. 'One thing that seems to have been overlooked in all this is the small matter of the gold itself. How is it that this Alexander possesses so much gold?'

'When the Romans were approaching Jerusalem,' said Aaron, 'Aristobulus, knowing that the city would not be able to hold out against Pompey and his legions, sent much gold out of the city to the eastern areas of Judea. There it was stored in secret places that only the most loyal followers of Aristobulus know of. It remains in those places still.'

'This is a fairy story, nothing more,' barked Domitus.

'It is not, majesty, I swear it,' replied Aaron.

I placed my hands together under my chin. 'Aaron presents us with a tempting offer, one that would solve our present financial difficulties. And yet, if I acquiesce then it potentially places Dura in danger. Domitus and Rsan have made their position on the matter clear, but I would hear from the rest of you before I decide.'

I looked at Orodes first. 'I would advise caution, Pacorus. We do not know anything about this Alexander. There should certainly be no correspondence that might fall into enemy hands.'

I nodded and smiled at Gallia. 'Dobbai said once that no Roman army would sit in front of Dura's walls while the griffin stood at the Palmyrene Gate. I believe her words and say we should accept this Jew's gold.'

'And you, Dobbai?' I asked.

'Silaces has been sent to you for a purpose, son of Hatra. Will you send such a gift away for the want of a few pieces of gold?'

'And you, Marcus, what is your opinion on the matter?' I said.

Marcus frowned and shook his head. 'I am with Domitus and Orodes in this, majesty.'

'You have been in correspondence with this Alexander?' I asked Aaron.

He nodded.

'And did you say to him that Dura would supply him with weapons?'

'No, majesty.'

'Quite right, for I will not decide until I have met with him face to face. Therefore I will go to the land of the Jews.'

Domitus looked most alarmed. 'You are going to Judea?'

'Yes, Domitus, and you are coming with me.'

That night Gallia questioned me on my forthcoming trip as we prepared for bed.

'Why are you going to Judea, it is occupied by the Romans? You will be in danger.'

I lay on the bed and stretched out my arms.

'I wasn't going to say anything but you might as well know.'

She laid down beside me, propping up her head with an arm.

'Know what?'

I turned to face her. 'During our stay in Babylon a priestess from the Temple of Ishtar brought me a message to come to the shrine, saying that a friend wanted to meet me there.'

Gallia yawned. 'So?'

'So I went to the temple and was taken by the high priestess to the inner sanctum of Ishtar, where I received the message.'

'A message from whom?'

'From Claudia.'

She looked perplexed. 'Claudia? How did a small child get from Dura to Babylon, did she sprout wings and fly there?'

'Not our Claudia; the wife of Spartacus.'

She sat up on the bed, wide eyed.

'How can this be? It must have been a cruel trick.'

'I stood alone in the inner sanctum and from behind me a woman's voice spoke. She told me that I must travel with the one from the desert who would furnish me with temple gold.'

She rose from the bed and began pacing up and down.

'Temple gold? The same gold that Aaron spoke about earlier?'

I nodded.

She stopped pacing and looked at me. 'Did you believe it was Claudia who spoke to you?'

'I did not want to, but the high priestess described to me afterwards what had happened to Claudia on the night she gave birth to Spartacus' son.'

'I remember that night,' she said grimly.

'As do I. And I remember what Claudia had said to me before she died. Only I heard those words. And there was another thing.'

'What?'

'The voice addressed me as "little one". Only Claudia used that phrase.'

Gallia sat back down on the bed and reached for my hand.

'I have always believed that Spartacus and Claudia watch over us, Pacorus. You must heed her advice and go to Judea.'

I was surprised by her change of mind. 'You do not think I will be in danger?'

She kissed my hand. 'Not with Claudia watching over you.'

223

We left a week later. I sent word ahead to Haytham at Palmyra that we would be visiting him on our way to the land of the Jews and another missive to Byrd informing him of our little expedition. In addition to Domitus I also took Surena and Aaron, the latter because he would arrange a meeting with the rebel leader and Surena because he had nagged me incessantly about accompanying me and agreeing to his request was the only way of shutting him up. Besides, I found his boundless optimism agreeable. We dressed in civilian robes but retained our bows and swords and carried two full quivers each. Domitus, who disliked riding and was awkward in the saddle, also insisted on taking his *gladius* hidden under his white cloak.

At Palmyra Haytham entertained us and told us that we were all dressed entirely inappropriately.

'You look like a rich king,' he said to me as we sat cross-legged on the floor of his tent, with Malik and Byrd in attendance. 'And the rest of you are similarly over-dressed.'

'These are our clothes, lord,' I said.

'Then we will have to get you some new ones,' said Malik.

Malik furnished us with long, loose-fitting tunics, sleeveless cloaks and head cloths that were held in place by heavy woollen coils. The head cloth was a most useful item as its ends could be wrapped around the face and neck as protection against the sun and wind and being recognised. Thus did we become Agraci for the duration of the expedition.

Aaron was sent ahead to organise the meeting with the Jewish leader and while we waited for his return I informed Haytham of my intention to supply the Jews with weapons, though only if they had enough gold.

'If, that is, you do not object, lord.'

Haytham was impassive. 'Why should I object? I do not know what every caravan carries on its way through my kingdom, only that it has paid its tolls in full. If some carry weapons to kill Romans it is of no concern to me.'

'It might be if the Romans come looking for retribution,' I said.

He smiled savagely. 'If they do we will not be here. We are not like you, Pacorus. We can be like phantoms and disappear into the desert. The Romans would wear themselves out looking for us. But you cannot do the same.'

'It is a risk I must take, lord.'

The next day we rode through Palmyra; a tent city around the oases that turned the desert green. Women in black robes carrying water jugs on their heads walked past us and small children scampered around, grinning mischievously as they pretended the sticks they carried were swords and spears. A long column of men with real weapons and black shields trotted past. Their commander bowed his head at Haytham as he passed the king, then at Malik who rode beside his father. He did not give me, Surena or Domitus a second glance, dressed as we were in similar attire to him. Tents covered the ground either side of us stretching out into the desert.

'One day there will be a city of stone here,' I heard myself saying.

'Not in my lifetime,' replied Haytham, 'though perhaps my son will build one.'

'Only when I am king, father,' said Malik. 'And I pray that day will not come for many years.'

Haytham waved away his son's loyalty.

'Why do you need more gold, Pacorus?' asked the king suddenly. 'Is not Dura rich enough?'

'Rich enough to pay for its own army, lord, but not wealthy enough to pay for a second one that has taken sanctuary with us.'

'You prepare to fight another war against Mithridates?' he probed.

'I take measures to strengthen my defences, lord,' I answered.

'What do you say, Roman?' Haytham said turning to Domitus.

Domitus swatted away a fly from his face. 'You can never have enough soldiers, sir, not enough trained ones, anyhow.'

'When I rode with your queen to save your foot soldiers, Roman,' Haytham continued, 'twenty thousand horsemen raised by Dura's lords rode beside the Agraci. Are they not great warriors?'

'They are a fearsome lot, sir, that is true. But they do not have the discipline and training of professional soldiers, men who do nothing other than train and drill from dawn till dusk. The lords lead farmers, I lead soldiers.'

'And this second army,' said Haytham, 'are they soldiers or farmers?'

'They are soldiers, majesty,' interrupted Surena, which earned him a scowl from Domitus.

'It is as my impertinent subordinate says, lord,' I added. 'They are the remnants of King Gotarzes' army that was defeated by Narses. Once re-equipped and fully trained they will be formidable warriors once more.'

'As well as being desirous to avenge the death of their king,' said Haytham approvingly.

'Hatred keeps a man strong, sir,' added Domitus.

'Indeed,' mused Haytham.

At length we came to the end of our journey – the tent of Byrd. When I had last been here there was a small corral behind it holding a few camels. Now there were several large enclosures that held many camels. Malik saw me looking at them.

'Byrd has become a man of substance among us, Pacorus.'

'So I see.'

225

When we had dismounted and one of Byrd's numerous herders took our horses we entered the tent and were received by Byrd and Noora. My friend, chief scout and merchant was as self-effacing as ever, merely nodding to each of us as Noora fussed and made us welcome. We sat cross-legged on the floor as she oversaw half a dozen young women who served us dates, nuts, raisins, milk, flat bread and bowls of butter. I noticed that Byrd positioned himself between Haytham and Malik when we all sat in a circle on the red carpets that covered the floor. Clearly he had some influence with the king now.

As we enjoyed Byrd's hospitality he told us about the situation in Judea. He had visited the land a few times and informed us that for nearly seventy years, following the fall of the Seleucid Empire, the Jews had been an independent people before a civil war broke out between the princes Hyrcanus and Aristobulus. Both princes appealed to Pompey who was in Syria at the time. This was the same Pompey that I had encountered at Dura's border four years ago. Pompey had subsequently entered Judea and captured and sacked the city of Jerusalem and installed Hyrcanus as a puppet ruler of Judea.

'Many Romani soldiers in Judea, Pacorus,' said Byrd.

'There are many Roman soldiers everywhere it appears, my friend,' I answered. 'What do you know of this Alexander Maccebeus?'

Byrd raised an eyebrow. 'What I hear is that he hates Romani and wants to free his homeland.'

'And become king himself, no doubt?' queried Haytham.

'He has much support in the south of Judea,' continued Byrd.

'But no weapons with which to arm those supporters,' said Domitus.

'The question is,' I said, 'does he have the gold to do business with us?'

'That I do not know,' replied Byrd.

Haytham dipped his bread into some butter. 'You trust Aaron, Pacorus?'

'He has nothing to gain by betraying me, lord.'

'Except a big Roman reward for your capture,' said Domitus, grabbing a handful of dates from a platter being held by one of Noora's servants.

I laughed. 'There is no price on my head, Domitus.'

He finished eating the dates and licked his fingers. 'Oh, I think there is. Remember you killed Lucius Furius, one of Crassus' protégés. I think he would be delighted if the King of Dura was taken prisoner and transported back to Rome.'

'That was years ago,' I said.

An evil smile crept over Domitus' face. 'The Romans never forgive and certainly never forget. Always remember that.'

226

'Malik,' said Haytham, 'you will go with Pacorus to Judea.'

Byrd nodded approvingly. 'I will also travel with Pacorus.'

When we were leaving I embraced Noora and thanked her for her hospitality.

'I hope you do not object to Byrd accompanying us.'

She smiled. 'I learned long ago not to question my husband's comings and goings, lord. He has always made it plain that if you had need of him he would answer your summons. You and he have much history.'

'Yes we do.' I laid a hand on her arm. 'I will bring him back. I promise.'

'Just make sure you bring yourself back, lord.'

I liked Noora. She was a plain-speaking and unassuming individual, not unlike Byrd in fact. Gallia was always trying to persuade them to come and live with us in Dura, and I promised that if they did a house near the palace would be provided for them. But they preferred the simple life, though it grieved me that my chief scout and friend and his wife were living in a tent in the desert.

Haytham's hard face cracked a smile as we rode back to his tent. 'Let me tell you about your scout and his wife. At the last count they possessed over two thousand camels that they hire out to the caravans as they pass through, complete with their own drivers. Byrd and Noora are among Palmyra's wealthiest subjects.'

I was stunned. 'I had no idea.'

'Just because he dresses and looks like a pauper does not mean he is one,' said Haytham.

'Perhaps we should ask Byrd for a loan to pay for Silaces and his men,' suggested Domitus.

But I did not ask Byrd for any money and when Aaron returned ten days later he also accompanied us on our journey to Judea. We did not follow the road west from Palmyra to Homs but instead headed southwest into the desert, riding across sand, flint and semi-arid steppe from oasis to oasis. Byrd and Malik were our guides, though Aaron had also become acquainted with the lesser-known paths across the vast expanse of emptiness that lay between Judea and the Euphrates.

It took us six days to reach the great Jabal al-Druz Mountains that lay south of Damascus. We gave the city a wide berth as it was no doubt teeming with Roman soldiers. But the Jabal al-Druz was stark, barren and largely empty of human life. Great volcanic outcrops towered over us as we threaded our way through narrow ravines and walked our horses across scree slopes below rock ledges and high cliffs. We saw few tribesmen and those we did see kept their distance from our ragged band.

227

Byrd and Malik took us west out of the mountains and onto the plain of Hawran, a great expanse of cultivated land dotted with villages and bisected by dirt roads and tracks. The contrast between this region and the Jabal al-Druz could not have been greater. We covered our faces with our headdresses to maintain our anonymity for we saw Roman patrols on the roads that were filled with travellers transporting goods. There were no wagons on these roads; Aaron informing us that donkeys or camels were used to move wares. He also told us that the main products of the plain were grain, olives, the vine and fruit. We passed a bearded man in his fifties I estimated, dressed in a short, sleeveless tunic leading three camels whose saddles were loaded with storage jars holding wine. He held a short stick and was tapping the side of the leading camel, speaking to it in a language I did not understand.

'It is Aramaic, majesty,' said Aaron. 'The language of my people.'

'And this man, Alexander, who we are to meet, he will speak this language?' I asked.

'Do not worry, majesty,' he replied, 'like you he has had a good education and speaks Greek fluently.'

We followed the course of a waterway named the Yarmuk River southwest until it emptied into a large river named the Jordan south of a great inland lake called the Sea of Galilee. For three days we travelled south along the east bank of the River Jordan, whose waters were deep and fast flowing. This river ran through a valley that is approximately two miles wide near the Sea of Galilee but became wider as we rode south, twisting and turning as we followed the course of the waterway. Flanked on each side by high mountains, the valley was filled with great clusters of thorns and thistles that grew to shoulder height. Aaron told me that most of the few villages in the valley were located on the eastern side of the river, near where tributaries flow into the River Jordan from the hills to the east.

There may have been few villages but there was an abundance of wildlife in and around the river, including leopards, boars and alligators. We also saw great herds of ibex and Surena used his bow to bring down a brace that we later skinned and cooked over an open fire. So far we had encountered no Roman patrols in the Jordan Valley.

'We will,' said Aaron, gnawing on a thighbone. 'There is a large Roman garrison in Jerusalem and they quarter troops in the outlying towns and villages.'

'Is Pompey still in Judea?' I asked.

Aaron threw the bone into the fire. 'No, majesty. He left soon after his soldiers had butchered their way into Jerusalem, taking most of the riches in the city back to Rome with him, along with Alexander's family.'

'And now Alexander is in hiding?' asked Domitus, propped up against his saddle and warming his bare feet on the fire for the nights were cool in the valley.

'He is in hiding, that is true,' answered Aaron guardedly.

'But you said that he had a hoard of temple gold, and now you say that Pompey captured the temple,' said Domitus. 'I hope we have not embarked on a wasted journey.'

At that moment we heard a snapping noise in the night and Domitus jumped up and drew his *gladius* from its scabbard. I reached for my bow and attached the bowstring, then whipped an arrow out of my quiver and stood with it nocked as I faced the direction the noise came from. Surena likewise stood with an arrow nocked in his bowstring, while Malik had drawn his sword and even Byrd had his long knife in his hand.

A voice called out of the darkness in a tongue I did not know and I drew back my bowstring to shoot the arrow in the direction it came from. But then Aaron called back in the same strange language.

'It is quite all right,' he said, smiling at us all. 'It is friends.'

'What sort of friends skulk around like thieves in the night?' growled Domitus.

Aaron called out again and two men about his age came out of the night. They were dressed in tunics that came down to their knees, cloaks and head cloths. One carried a spear and the other had a long knife tucked in his belt. Both had full beards. Aaron greeted them warmly and after half a minute brought them over to me. Surena still had his bowstring drawn back and was pointing his arrow at them.

'You can put your bow down, Surena,' I told him. 'They are friends.'

He did so reluctantly as Aaron introduced the ragged arrivals.

'This is Ananus and Levi, majesty, two of Alexander's most trusted officers.'

'Officers?' said Domitus loudly, still keeping a tight grip on his sword.

I raised my hand at him to be silent. 'Tell them I am glad to make their acquaintance,' I instructed Aaron.

Both Ananus and Levi nodded curtly at me and then stared at Domitus, who looked every inch the Roman he was. There was frantic whispering between them and Aaron, who managed to calm them. I did not understand what they were saying but assumed that they were surprised that a Roman was present. For his part Domitus kept a wary eye on them for the rest of the night, each of us taking turns to stand guard while the others tried to get some sleep.

Whether Domitus slept or not I did not know as I sat down on the ground next to him following my standing vigil. Thin shards of orange pierced the eastern sky to herald the dawn. The fire was nothing more than warm grey ashes now. Around it slept Malik, Byrd, Surena, Aaron and our two guests.

Domitus, his head resting on his saddle and wrapped in his cloak, observed the sleeping Jews across from him.

'I doubt if they have a gold coin between them, let alone enough to pay your armouries to supply them with weapons.'

'We do not know that,' I said. 'Aaron assures me that this Alexander has more than enough gold.'

'And you believe him?'

'We shall know soon enough.'

'Have you noticed something about the river we have been travelling along?' he said.

'What, apart from it being full of alligators?'

'There are no bridges across it. Not one.'

I was puzzled. 'I don't understand.'

'Bridges are an indication of a people's progress and wealth. You have seen the many bridges in Italy, and in Parthia are there not bridges that span both the Euphrates and Tigris? Well here there are none, which leads me to believe that these people are poor and backward.'

'So were the followers of Spartacus,' I reminded him, 'including you when we first encountered you if I am not mistaken.'

He shrugged and then nodded at Aaron and his comrades. 'Have it your own way, but I think we have wasted our time.'

With Levi and Ananus walking beside our horses we continued on south and came to a great inland lake that Aaron told me was called the Salt Sea. It looked like a huge blue carpet that had been dumped on the earth in the space between steep, rocky cliffs. The waters of the sea were most wondrous, being oily to the touch. When my hand dried after I had immersed it in the water it was covered in a thick crust of salt.

Aaron stared at my hand. 'The high salt levels means nothing lives in the lake, majesty. It is dead.'

As we continued on along the eastern shore of this great expanse of water, which was more blue than the waters of the Euphrates, I could not help but wonder why the gods had made it lifeless. I looked at Aaron and surmised that his people must have committed a great sin to be punished thus. I did not probe him as we veered away from the lake after an hour and headed east into the hills. It was midday now and the day was extremely hot, the air arid and stifling. We rode through a barren valley cut in the sandstone hills and then entered a deep, canyon-like wadi until we came to a stark promontory that rose up before us.

'This is Machaerus, the Black Fortress,' announced Aaron, 'where Alexander awaits us.'

We dismounted and led our horses up the steep, tussock-strewn slope with some difficulty, arriving at the summit to stunning views of the surrounding terrain. The peak contained the remains of a stronghold with most of the perimeter wall still standing. But the gatehouse was just a pile of rubble, the remains of the smashed gates on the ground in front of it. Two guards armed with spears stood on top of the rubble but were scanning the horizon rather than looking at us.

'This way, majesty,' said Aaron, disappearing through the gap in the wall with Levi and Ananus.

Inside were more soldiers, or at least men in threadbare clothes armed with a variety of knives, spears, bows and swords. None wore any armour or helmets and some carried only staffs. I estimated their number to be around thirty. The position had some strength, or had done before it had been assailed and great lumps knocked out of the defences. The high, rectangular perimeter wall had towers in each corner and contained a large stone stronghold at the far end with store rooms and barracks extending from it along each wall towards the gatehouse. At the entrance to the stone building stood two more spearmen.

'Alexander awaits us inside, majesty,' said Aaron as Levi and Ananus sat down on the ground among men whom I assumed they commanded and began to chat and point at Domitus and me.

Surena was most unhappy when I ordered him to stay with the horses while the rest of us followed Aaron into the building.

The stronghold was a rectangular building fronted by a colonnade and had an arched roof. I followed Aaron past the guards and stepped into a small reception area, with rooms without doors on either side. The roof, what was left of it, comprised timbers overlaid with thatched reeds, though most of it was missing, allowing the sun's rays to stream through. Damaged pots lay strewn across the dirt floor, along with broken spear shafts, a few twisted swords and a dented Roman helmet.

'Not much to look at, is it?'

I saw a man of medium height with a beard standing in the doorway of one of the rooms on the left. Dressed in a light brown knee-length tunic with sandals on his feet, he looked most unprepossessing with his unkempt shoulder-length hair. He smiled and approached me, offering his hand in greeting. Aaron told me that he was a prince but he looked more like a goatherd. I saw Domitus scowl and shake his head and hoped that we had not wasted our journey as he had said.

'I am Alexander Maccebeus and I am pleased to make the acquaintance of King Pacorus of Dura.'

I took his hand and found his grip like iron, much to my surprise. I also noticed that his brown eyes missed nothing, darting between my companions and me and registering slight surprise at Domitus, whom he no doubt recognised instantly as not being Parthian.

'I am pleased to meet you, lord prince,' I answered, 'Aaron has told me much about you. I hope we will be able to do business with each other.'

'I would offer you wine and hospitality,' he held out his hands, 'but alas my circumstances are somewhat reduced at the moment as you can see.' His Greek was impeccable.

'May I introduce my companions to you, lord prince?' I held out a palm towards Malik. 'This is Prince Malik of the Agraci, a friend and valuable ally to my kingdom.'

Malik bowed his head to Alexander.

Alexander next looked at Byrd.

'This is Byrd, lord prince, my chief scout and also a valued friend.'

Byrd displayed his usual nonchalance when in the presence of royalty.

I went to stand beside Domitus. 'And this is Lucius Domitus, the general of my army and the man who more than anyone is responsible for making Dura strong.'

Alexander's eyes narrowed as he observed Domitus.

'Lucius Domitus,' he said, 'that is a Roman name, is it not?'

'It is, for he is a Roman,' I answered.

Alexander nodded and then walked around the shattered room. He pointed at the broken roof, the debris lying on the floor.

'The Romans did this when they invaded my country and conquered it. They butchered the entire garrison here and then sacked the holy temple in Jerusalem, slaughtering thousands as they did so. They carried away much gold from the temple itself and defiled its holy sanctum by their presence. They also carried off thousands of Jews as slaves, including my father, my brother and myself. This being the case, you can perhaps understand why I am slightly uncomfortable by the presence of one from a race that has inflicted so much misery upon my people.'

'I understand your anger, Alexander,' I said. 'The Romans have also inflicted death and destruction upon Parthia and yet,' I placed an arm round Domitus' shoulders, 'this Roman I trust with my life.'

'Even though you yourself were enslaved by the Romans, for Aaron has informed me that it was so?'

'It is true,' I replied, 'but I have Romans serving me loyally, Alexander. I have learned to judge men on their individual merits rather than appraise them according to which race they were born into.'

Alexander smiled. 'Aaron has told me that you are fair in your dealings with others. Let us hope that is thus now.'

'What do you want of me, Alexander?'

He walked over to face me. 'Weapons with which to equip an army. I can raise the men but without arms they will be slaughtered.' Alexander handed Aaron a sheaf of parchments. 'These are the details of my requirements.'

Aaron quickly scanned the lists and his eyes opened wide as he did so. He briefly spoke his language to Alexander, who nodded.

'Would you care to share with us what is written on those, Aaron?' I said.

'Yes, majesty. It is an order for helmets, swords, spears, daggers, mail shirts, arrows and quivers.'

'For how many men?' I queried.

Aaron licked his lips. 'Ten thousand, majesty.'

Malik looked surprised and even Byrd raised an eyebrow. Domitus guffawed.

'Ten thousand? How are they going to pay you, in goats? These people don't have a pot to piss in. I told you we have wasted our time.'

Alexander spoke to Domitus in Latin. 'Not all that is barren is empty, Roman.'

Domitus looked confused and then bemused. 'And what does that mean?'

'It means, Roman,' continued Alexander, 'that you see only what you choose to see. Be thankful that your king has more wisdom than you.'

Domitus was a great soldier but a diplomat he was not. He jerked a thumb at Alexander. 'He's clearly been in the sun too long. These Jews are thieves and beggars and we are better off without them, Pacorus.'

'These Jews,' said Alexander slowly and firmly, 'outnumber you ten to one, Roman, so I would choose your next words carefully.'

I held up my hands. 'Let us not argue. Alexander, I must ask for your forgiveness. My general's words were intemperate. However, before I agree to supply you with the items you need I would like to see some evidence that you will be able to pay for said goods.'

Alexander smiled. 'I know that your armouries at Dura are capable of furnishing me with the weapons I desire, for Aaron has told me of your great army and its lavish equipment. Therefore I will show you that I have the means to pay for them.'

Ten minutes later, after being blindfolded, Domitus and I were being guided out of the fortress and down the steep slope that we had earlier ascended. Two of Alexander's men led me and another two behind held on to Domitus, who did nothing but complain to them.

'Careful, you sons of heathens, I could break my leg on these stones. Take off this bloody blindfold.'

'You wanted to come, Roman,' said Alexander, who accompanied us together with Aaron. 'The blindfold remains until we have reached our destination.'

'You didn't blindfold Aaron,' replied Domitus.

'That is because I trust Aaron and do not trust you, Roman.'

'Just be quiet, Domitus,' I said. 'The sooner we get there the sooner the blindfolds will be removed.'

We descended the slope and then turned right and walked along the bottom of a ravine for ten minutes or so before scrambling up another slope that was steeper than the one we had just come down. My helpers guided me along a narrow path that I assumed had either been cut in the rock or had been formed naturally. The surface was uneven and on a couple of occasions I tripped on jagged rock edges. Even in our Agraci robes it was still very hot and I could feel the sun on my face. Then the sun's heat disappeared from my head and I was aware that we had entered a cave of some sort as our footsteps echoed around a chamber.

'Take off their blindfolds,' commanded Alexander.

My eyes did not need to get accustomed to the light because we were standing some distance into a tunnel in the hillside, the bright yellow light at the entrance around fifty paces behind us. Alexander's men lit torches and then we walked further down the shaft. The cave was the width of five men and around ten feet in height, though the further we walked along it the lower the ceiling became until after a couple of minutes we were stooping.

We walked for a further two minutes, following the tunnel as it curved to the right, and came into a large chamber with a high rock ceiling. The noise of our boots and sandals scraping the rock floor echoed around it as we scrambled down a flight of roughly hewn steps and then crawled through a gap six feet wide and half the height of a man. We entered a second, smaller chamber where the air musty but not damp. As more torches were brought in for illumination I saw rows of chests along both sides, thirty in all. Each chest was around three feet high, three feet in length and two feet in width. The torches crackled and illuminated our faces as Alexander walked over to the first container and lifted the lid.

I gasped as the torchlight lit the gold coins that filled the chest. Alexander went to the next chest and the next, lifting their lids to reveal that each one was also filled with gold. Then he went over to the other row of chests and lifted their lids to reveal similar treasure. The chamber was suddenly filled with a yellow glow as the flames of the torches reflected off the hoard of bullion.

'As you can see, Roman,' Alexander said to Domitus, 'just because we appear poor does not mean that we are so. It serves our purpose to appear to all the world as though, to use your quaint phrase, we do not have a pot to piss in.'

'A truly remarkable store of treasure, Alexander,' I said.

'There are others,' he replied, 'similarly safely hidden from prying eyes. So do we have a bargain, King Pacorus?'

I walked over to him and offered my hand.

'We have a bargain.'

He took it and I felt his iron-hard grip once more.

'Aaron has the details as you know. And now I must blindfold you again.'

Back at the smashed fortress we collected our horses and with Alexander and his men descended from the hilltop and headed back west towards the Salt Sea. We made camp for the night a mile inland from its northeastern shore by a small stream that fed the huge lake. Beforehand most of Alexander's men had seemingly vanished into the hills and wadis that crisscrossed the area, leaving only the prince, Levi and Ananus for company.

'Large groups of men attract the attention of our Roman occupiers,' he explained as we sat round the campfire later that evening. 'And it is a wise precaution to ensure that the routes to the safe places where the gold is stored are watched at all times.'

'How many Romani troops in Judea?' asked Byrd.

'Fortunately not many, at the moment,' he replied. 'Most Roman troops are quartered in Syria. The local Roman troops are mostly used to support the rule of my uncle, King Hyrcanus.'

'Hyrcanus is your uncle?' queried Domitus.

Alexander nodded. 'That is so, Roman. Two brothers fought a civil war and Judea was the loser.'

'Why did Pompey support your uncle?' I asked.

'Because he is the elder brother and because he is weaker than my father and thus more easily manipulated by the Romans. He does nothing without first consulting Antioch.'

'And if you are successful in your endeavour to free Judea of Roman rule,' I asked him, 'will you kill your uncle?'

'*When* we free Judea,' he said determinedly, 'my uncle will flee with the Romans. If he stays he will die.'

'The Romans will also kill your father and brother in retaliation for your insurrection,' said Domitus grimly.

Alexander regarded him. 'I know that, Roman, and so do they. The price of freedom is often a heavy one.'

'Where did the gold you now possess originally come from?' asked Domitus.

Alexander traced lines on the ground with a stick he was holding as he told the story. 'During the civil war between my father and his brother, Hyrcanus brought a great army before the walls of Jerusalem and besieged us in the city. My father and his brother both made a terrible mistake in asking Pompey, who was at that time in Syria, to act as a mediator in their disagreement. At first my father was glad that he had approached the Romans for Pompey persuaded Hyrcanus to withdraw his army from before Jerusalem, but I had a premonition from god that this was merely the calm before the storm that would herald our doom.'

As the fire crackled and spat we sat transfixed by Alexander's tale, even the normally disinterested Byrd had his chin rested on his clenched hands and was staring at the Jewish prince, who continued to trace patterns on the ground with his stick.

'I was in command of the garrison in the city when my father left Jerusalem soon after Hyrcanus, hurrying to meet Pompey and thinking that he could out-fox the Roman conqueror of the east. While my father and his brother bickered and were fed lies by the Romans I gave orders that the temple gold was to be evacuated from the city. Aaron drew up rotas and a small band of trusted subordinates organised the loading and transportation of the gold to eastern Judea, where it remains.'

'You evacuated all the gold?' I asked.

Alexander stopped his tracing. 'Only a fraction before Pompey himself appeared before the walls of Jerusalem with his army.' He threw the stick into the fire. 'The rest you know.'

Aaron organised the guard rostra as the fire died down and we prepared for our last night in Judea. It had been a most agreeable day and in my mind I began to make plans for the coming months. With the gold that we would receive for the weapons supplied to Alexander, Silaces' men could be re-equipped to reinforce the army. With an additional eight thousand horsemen I could think once more of striking at Mithridates, this time in strength. I would ask Haytham to accompany me and once again enlist the lords and their men. I would therefore be able to raise upwards of fifty thousand men or more. Shamash had smiled on me this day and I went to sleep a happy man.

Domitus, who squatted beside me, shook me awake.

'Get up, Pacorus. Aaron has gone.'

Chapter 10

'Gone,' I wiped my eyes and slowly rose to my feet. My back ached and my mouth felt parched. 'Gone where?'

Domitus shrugged. 'No idea. The only thing I know is that he disappeared when he should have been on guard duty. That's a capital offence.'

I stretched my back and walked across to where the horses were tethered to a tree. I untied Remus and led him to the small stream we had camped by. It brought clear, fresh water from beneath the parched hills to the east before it was tainted when it entered the Salt Sea. Domitus walked with me.

'What are you going to do?' he pestered me.

The others were also stirring by now, wrapped in their cloaks to keep away the cool of the early morning.

'If Aaron has absconded there is little I can do. This is after all his country and if he has decided to stay here then that is that.'

'He should be taken back to Dura in chains and then executed.'

I let Remus drink from the stream as the others brought their horses to the water. I rubbed my stubble-covered chin.

'Aaron is not in the army, Domitus, so you cannot have him executed.'

'He put us all in danger by disappearing like he did. That alone is enough to place a noose around his neck.'

I squatted down and scooped up some water with my hands to wash the dirt from my face.

'Where is Aaron?' asked Malik.

'Where indeed?' said Domitus.

I stood up and stretched my back again. I must have slept on a stone because the ache would not go.

'Aaron has gone, Malik,' I replied.

'Deserted, more like,' added a furious Domitus.

Malik looked around at the barren hills that surrounded us. 'Deserted to where?'

'Jericho.'

Alexander had sauntered over to where we stood.

'Jericho?' I was confused. 'What's that?'

He bent down and scooped up a handful of water to drink.

'A town about ten miles northeast of here. Aaron grew up there, though his father is long dead and there is no family business now.'

'Why would he go back, then?' I asked.

Alexander smiled. 'His beloved lives there. To be so close to her was too much for him to bear, I think. I would wager all the gold I have that at this very moment he is at her mother's house in the town. The young idiot!'

'Idiot and deserter,' said Domitus.

'Why an idiot?' I asked.

Alexander looked to the north. 'Aaron, son of Jacob, is well known in Jericho, well known for being a senior figure in the faction that supported my father. There is a large reward on his head, just as there is on mine. By visiting Jericho Aaron has signed his own death warrant.'

'Well,' I said, 'we had better go and get him back then.'

Domitus, his mood already sombre when he had awoken to discover Aaron had absconded, got even more gruff and snappier when I announced that we would go to Jericho to rescue Aaron. After we had groomed and fed the horses and checked their shoes, and then eaten a meagre breakfast of hard biscuit and salted mutton, he cornered me. I was checking my saddlecloth for insects that might have embedded themselves in the material and which might be an irritant to Remus when he was saddled.

'I say we should leave him to it. These Jews are more trouble than they're worth.'

'You are being uncharitable, Domitus. Aaron was as good as his word was he not, regarding the gold, I mean?'

'Be that as it may, there is no point in getting involved in their little civil war. Look around. You have no cataphracts or horse archers to back you up if things take a turn for the worse, and my legions are back at Dura.'

I smiled at him. 'I thought they were my legions.'

He was not amused. 'Don't get smart. How are you going to fight a Roman garrison with only Malik and me? Byrd is not a soldier and I don't trust Surena.'

'He is fearless, Domitus.'

He nodded grimly. 'That is exactly what I mean. He's fearless and also reckless and headstrong and quite capable of getting us all killed.'

I laid a hand on his shoulder. 'Then it is a good job that I have worked out a plan that will get us Aaron back without having to fight, hopefully.'

'Do we want him back?' He mumbled before stalking away.

I asked Byrd and Malik to ride into Jericho to scout the town to find Aaron and bring him back before he was arrested. Alexander drew a rough plan of Jericho in the dirt using his dagger, indicating where the house of Aaron's sweetheart was located. He said he could not accompany them since his face was too well known in the area. Even though the region contained a large number of his supporters, the adherents of Hyrcanus and their Roman allies also lived in the town. We would wait until they returned, hopefully with Aaron. Surena also wanted to accompany them but I refused his request. Byrd had a talent amounting to genius for moving unseen through the countryside, cities and crowds; Surena had a habit of drawing attention to himself like a roaring lion in the middle of an empty square. Instead I sent him on foot into the hills with Alexander to bring us back some fresh meat to eat, leaving Domitus and me in camp.

For the first hour Domitus said nothing but amused himself with sharpening his sword on the stone he had brought with him. At first I occupied myself with stringing my bow to test the tautness of the bowstring and then inspected every one of my arrows. Then I oiled the blades of my *spatha* and dagger and all the while he watched me like a falcon observes its prey.

'You have something to say, Domitus?'

He stopped running the stone along the keen edge of his sword.

'You are making a mistake. We should be on the road back to Dura by now. Aaron clearly wants to stay in this land so let him. It's no great loss.'

'I suspect my dear Domitus that Aaron prefers Dura to Roman-occupied Judea and has let his heart get the better of him in this instance. I would have done the same if Gallia had been but a stone's throw away.'

He shook his head and returned to sharpening his sword, mumbling to himself as he did so. Mid-morning Surena and Alexander returned to camp with a slain gazelle Surena had shot. Alexander told me that the beast had been brought down with a single arrow at a great distance, which a gloating Surena had great delight in telling Domitus. This served only to further sour my general's mood, though he was able to take out his frustrations on the dead gazelle. The sun was high in the sky now and the day was dry and hot. While Surena and Alexander stripped off and cooled themselves in the stream Domitus gutted the dead animal away from the horses so the smell of blood and guts would not alarm them. He made a small hole in the ground and then slit the animal's throat to bleed it, the blood gushing into the depression.

He had obviously decided that discussing Aaron further was futile and only served to raise his wrath, so he brought up another topic.

'After Silaces and his men are equipped,' he rolled the carcass onto its belly, 'you will march against Mithridates and Narses once more?'

'Yes, their assassination attempt on me must be avenged lest I appear weak.'

He nodded approvingly and rolled the beast onto its back. 'Makes sense. You will always be looking over your shoulder while those two bastards are still in the world.'

He cut the animal's skin with his dagger from the tailbone to just under the chin and then from foreleg to foreleg and then hind leg to hind leg, being careful not to cut the thin membrane enclosing the entrails.

'And once they are in the same position as this animal, then what?'

He began skinning the carcass, lifting the skin and using his dagger to peel it away. He then slit its belly and turned it on its side to roll out the entrails.

'I don't understand,' I said.

He turned the animal on its skinned side and began again on the opposite side.

'The empire will need a new king of kings, that's what.'

I shrugged. 'That will not be my concern.'

'It will be if you don't have someone you think is suitable to fill the position, bearing in mind that your father is not interested. Killing kings is easy, finding their replacements less so.'

Once Domitus had finished skinning the carcass he quartered the animal and then he and I searched for wood to make a fire. By the time Byrd and Malik returned to us later that afternoon the fire was raging and the smell of roasting meat filled the air. Alas their news was not good.

They informed us that Aaron had indeed visited the house where his beloved lived in the northeast part of the town, but had been spotted and reported to the Roman authorities and duly arrested. He was currently being held in the town's jail before his execution.

'His execution!' I was horrified.

'The Romans are eager to rid Judea of any opponents to their rule, that is why most of us who are opposed to them live in the hills and other places away from the towns,' said Alexander. 'Aaron would have been on a list of political enemies to be apprehended. When is his execution?'

'Tomorrow,' replied Byrd, tucking into his portion of meat. 'He condemned by Romani council.'

Alexander explained that after its occupation by the Romans Judea was divided into five administrative districts called *synhedroi*, the headquarters of one of them being Jericho. All those arrested for political crimes were brought before each district's Roman council rather than the local Jewish religious court.

'I speak to Romani soldier outside courthouse,' said Byrd, 'he say Aaron denounced Rome as the mother of harlots, an abomination drunk with the blood of saints.'

'Well, that's him done for,' said Domitus with relish. 'They'll lop off his head tomorrow in the jailhouse and then dump his body on the rubbish heap.'

'The punishment for political crimes is crucifixion,' said Alexander, staring unblinkingly at Domitus.

'So?'

'So,' replied Alexander, 'the condemned are put to death outside the town's walls.

'Alas for Aaron,' said Malik.

'But perhaps not,' I mused, looking at Alexander. 'Crucifixions are held outside the town, you say?'

He nodded. 'That is correct. On a small hill a short distance to the east of the town. The Romans like to put on display the corpses of all those who dare to defy their rule as a warning to others.'

'What time are crucifixions?' I asked.

'Two hours after dawn.'

Domitus wore a worried expression. 'Please tell me you are not thinking what I suspect is going through your mind,' he said to me.

'No man deserves to be nailed to a cross for the crime of seeing his sweetheart. Tomorrow, my friends, I intend to rescue Aaron and see him brought safely back to Dura. I hope I can count on your assistance.'

Domitus spent the next hour trying to dissuade me, giving me a score of excellent reasons why the whole idea was folly and that we should leave Aaron to his fate and return home. But I would not change my mind and Surena and Malik pledged their support, while Byrd merely shrugged and said he cared little either way. Thus was Domitus outmanoeuvred and outnumbered and forced to accept defeat. Alexander also wanted to come along but I politely refused his offer. For one thing I did not know if he was a warrior – he certainly did not look like one – and for another he had no horse. I intended to strike hard and fast and leave even quicker.

We broke camp two hours before dawn and walked our horses for the first hour. Alexander sent Levi and Ananus sprinting ahead to ensure the road was free of any Roman patrols. Alexander had told us that the Roman garrison in Jericho numbered no more than a century, probably less – under eighty men. The main concentrations of Roman soldiers were at Jerusalem – a cohort – and Caesarea, the provincial capital, which held a further two cohorts. There were in addition numerous auxiliary units raised from locals spread throughout Judea. Alexander reported that there were a hundred such soldiers in Alexandreum, a town twenty miles to the north of Jericho. They were too far away to trouble us.

We rode along the shore of the Salt Sea and then headed northwest to Jericho, crossing the River Jordan via a ford. Alexander, Levi and Ananus stayed behind at the river to ensure our escape route stayed open. Byrd led Aaron's horse as we rode the last five miles to Jericho. It was well past dawn when I saw the walls of Jericho for the first time, a stone circuit that encompassed the town and was broken only on the eastern side – the town's sole gate. In the distance, beyond the town to the west, were mountains that looked down on the fertile plain in which Jericho was situated. Alexander told me that the fields around the town grew spices and flowers for perfumes but the main product was dates. Indeed, Jericho was nicknamed 'town of palm

241

trees'. As we approached the town gates I saw wooden poles planted in the ground on top of a small hill just off the road, some of them with crossbeams attached from which hung skeletons with grinning skulls. The Romans had planted their own unique crops in the area as well.

There was already traffic on the road, haggard-looking men leading donkeys and camels laden with wares going towards the open gates and passing others exiting the town. I halted our small contingent adjacent to the hill where the crucifixions were carried out. Giant crows were already perched on some of the crossbeams, eagerly awaiting the next batch of unfortunates who would be nailed to crosses. It could take up to five days to die on the cross and in that time the ravens would feast on the bodies of the condemned, pecking out their eyes first and then gorging themselves on their flesh.

'Domitus and Malik,' I ordered, 'stay here. When Surena and I begin to kill the escort that will be your signal to free Aaron. Byrd, you stay with Aaron's horse back up the road. When you see that he has been freed, make haste and get it to him. Then ride with him back to the ford as quickly as you can. Everyone understand?'

They all nodded and I nudged Remus forward with Surena behind me as Byrd retreated two hundred paces or so back up the road. As Remus walked towards the town there was a commotion at the gates and then a party of Roman legionaries appeared, twelve men in two files flanking a stooping figure with a heavy crossbeam across his shoulders – Aaron. His pace was slow and he shuffled his feet as he trudged towards his place of execution.

'Surena, ride on the left-hand side of the road and I will take the right-hand side. Wait for my command before you begin shooting.'

'Yes, lord,' he replied.

I saw a centurion at the head of the column with his telltale transverse crest atop his helmet. The legionaries behind him were equipped with mail shirts, shields and helmets. They carried short spears rather than javelins, no doubt for crowd control should there be any trouble. That appeared distinctly unlikely for behind the soldiers trooped a small number of civilians led by what looked like a priest in blue and white robes. He sported a black beard whose ends were fashioned into coils. He seemed to be chanting some sort of prayer. Behind him came two ashen-faced women, one of them middle aged supporting the other, younger one who was sobbing uncontrollably. Aaron's beloved I assumed.

Both Surena and I had our head cloths covering our faces as we ambled past the centurion at the head of the column and the legionaries filed past us one by one. I glanced at Aaron; his eyes cast down, and saw blood around his shoulders. The Romans had already scourged him, as was their custom, to further increase his torment once he was fixed to the cross. His arms were also spread along the crossbeam and held in place by leather straps. They made it impossible for him to struggle while hammering nails through his wrists. The Romans were above all a practical people in such matters.

Behind the wailing woman and her older friend came the usual chaff that accompanied public executions: the bloodthirsty, the sanctimonious, the curious and those whose lives were so wretched that they could only be made bearable by being witness to suffering greater than their own. These people I did not concern myself with. They would disappear faster than the crows perched on the crucifixion posts when the violence began.

Aaron was bundled off the road and onto the hillock beside it. Then he was shoved roughly by a legionary towards one of the poles. These were not high, no more than seven feet I estimated, just high enough to allow the crossbeam to be planted on top by means of a square peg of wood that had been carved from the top of the pole. There was a hole of the same shape in the middle of the crossbeam, which could easily be slotted onto the top of the pole. Simple and effective. The victim would be left to dangle and would die in agony as the weight of his body prevented him from filling his lungs with air. He would try to pull himself up but the pain in his wrists would be excruciating, and so his strength would fail and he would die of asphyxiation. Eventually.

The crucifixion party had halted now and were grouped around the waiting pole. There was a ladder propped up behind it. Once the victim had been lifted into position by two legionaries holding each end of the crossbeam, another on the ladder in a final act of cruelty would adjust the leather straps to allow the victim to sag slightly, at the same time giving him the means to breathe, if he could pull himself up with his arms.

The small crowd had gathered around the legionaries as Aaron stood with his eyes closed, his lips moving as he recited a prayer I assumed. We all seek the comfort of our gods when death is close. I looked at the young woman who was barely able to stand due to her grief, her friend supporting her as she wailed. The centurion stood and faced the crowd, a look of boredom on his face, while two of his men stood either side of Aaron and turned him so that he also faced the onlookers.

'Let it be known that Aaron, son of Jacob,' the centurion's voice was emotionless, 'has been found guilty of being an enemy of Rome and the Judean authorities and has been sentenced to death.'

A legionary threw a bag of nails on the ground at Aaron's feet. Another put his spear and shield on the ground and pulled a hammer from his belt. I looked over to Surena and nodded. I glanced at Domitus and Malik who had dismounted and moved among the

243

crowd. I reached behind and pulled my bow from its case, then extracted an arrow from my quiver. The centurion continued.

'The people of Rome condemn you. The gods of Rome condemn you.'

He turned and nodded to the two legionaries standing beside Aaron and I released my bowstring. The arrow hissed through the air and struck the centurion in the middle of his back, causing him to first arch his body and then pitch forward onto the ground. Surena's first arrow hit the legionary holding the hammer in his chest, the bronze arrowhead going through his mail shirt and into his heart. He was dead before he hit the ground. My second arrow hit the legionary who had been carrying the bag of nails in the belly, knocking him to the ground.

I strung another arrow and saw Domitus draw his *gladius* and thrust it through the neck of a legionary who had heard the dull thud of the arrows hitting his comrades and had turned to see where the noise was coming from. He never saw the face of his killer as blood sheeted from his neck and he collapsed on the ground. Malik had run his sword through the legionary who had been standing next to the one that Domitus had killed and was running towards Aaron.

Chaos erupted as people scattered in all directions to avoid being killed. They had come to witness another man die but now faced danger themselves. A legionary grasped his spear to throw at Malik, who was desperately cutting at the leather straps that pinioned Aaron's arms to the crossbeam. My arrow felled him before he could throw it.

Half the Romans had been killed by now as Malik freed Aaron and Byrd galloped down the road leading his horse. Malik bundled a stunned Aaron towards his waiting horse as Domitus, who had grabbed an abandoned *scutum*, fought the rest of the Romans single-handedly. A legionary ran at him with his spear levelled but Domitus jumped aside and went down on his right knee as his opponent passed him, then cut deep into the man's hamstring with a wicked back slash of his *gladius*. The man yelped and halted, and was knocked off his feet by an arrow shot by Surena. I killed another Roman who attempted to flee back to the town, who in his blind panic did not see the man on a white horse in front of him who calmly pointed his arrow straight at his chest and then released his bowstring. It was all over in less than two minutes.

Surena whooped with joy as he surveyed the dead Romans on the ground and held his bow aloft. He then spotted the Jewish holy man who stood like a rock in the middle of the road and who was berating me like a man possessed, his eyes wide and his voice booming as he aimed a stream of invective in my direction. What he was saying I did not know but by his tone and demeanour I assumed he was calling on his god to strike me down.

Twang.

The holy man fell silent when Surena's arrow went through his ribcage.

I trotted over to where he sat in his saddle with a smug expression on his face.

'It is considered bad luck to kill holy men,' I told him, 'lest you offend their gods.'

'I don't believe in the gods, lord,' he grinned, holding up his bow, 'only in this and the man who shoots it.'

I rode over to where Malik was shoving Aaron into his saddle. 'How is he?'

'He will live,' said Malik, 'but his back needs tending to.'

'That will have to wait. Byrd, get him out of here.'

'Thank you, majesty,' said Aaron weakly.

Domitus ran over with his and Malik's horse.

'That was easy enough. We had better get out of here.'

Suddenly the young woman who had been weeping was by Aaron's side, kissing his hand, tears running down her face. Then the other woman appeared beside her friend.

'We must take them too, majesty,' said Aaron. 'They will be in danger if they remain.'

Domitus hauled himself into his saddle. 'We must go, Pacorus. We can't take any women with us.'

'Please, majesty,' implored Aaron, the young woman still clutching his hand. The older woman looked up at me with sad brown eyes.

'Very well,' I said. 'Malik, the young woman will ride with you and Domitus can take the elder one.'

Domitus was not amused. 'What?'

'Just do as I ask,' I ordered as Malik pulled the young woman up behind him.

Domitus shook his head and did likewise, just as Byrd pointed towards the town.

'Romani horsemen come.'

I turned and saw a column of riders gallop through the town gates, about ten in number and armed with spears and carrying round shields on their left sides.

'The rest of you go now,' I shouted. 'Surena and I will form the rear guard. Move!'

They rode back towards the ford as I pulled an arrow from my quiver and followed them with Surena beside me.

'Aim for the horses,' I shouted to him.

They were closing on us fast as I tensed my thigh muscles to keep me locked in the saddle and twisted to the left to look behind me.

They were riding two abreast about fifty paces behind us. I released my bowstring and the arrow hit the right front horse, pitching its rider over its head as it collapsed on the ground. Surena's arrow was shot too high and missed the flanking horse but struck its rider. The result was that our pursuers were thrown into disorder as they swerved left and right to avoid colliding with the head of the column.

I halted and turned Remus around as the others galloped towards the ford. Surena pulled up his mount when he realised I was no longer beside him and rode back to me.

'Is Remus lame, lord?'

'No,' I replied. 'We have slowed them but we need to drop a few more to deter them from pursuing us.'

I strung an arrow and hit another of their horses, then hit a rider who was charging towards me. I kept pulling arrows from my quiver and shot them in quick succession until it was empty. Surena did the same and my gamble paid off, for the enemy riders, those who still lived, retreated back towards the town. We waited there for a few minutes to ensure they did not rally to continue their pursuit, before continuing our journey to the ford.

At the river we found a waiting Byrd and no one else.

'Others have gone on ahead, back to camp.'

I told him and Surena to ride ahead as I halted Remus on the eastern bank of the Jordan and watched and waited for any other pursuers. After ten minutes of seeing no one save a poor farmer pulling a surly donkey weighed down with a great load of firewood, I followed my companions back to camp. Alexander had posted sentries all round the campsite when I reached it half an hour later, and had also positioned lookouts on the surrounding hills.

'We can't stay here much longer,' he said, wincing as Domitus cauterised a wound on Aaron's back with his dagger that had been heated in a fire.

'How long do we have?' I asked him.

'The authorities have probably sent an urgent message to Alexandreum for reinforcements. They won't do anything until they arrive. I would say we have about three hours before they send riders to track us down.'

After leading Remus to the stream to drink I sauntered over to where the young woman was applying a bandage to Aaron's wounds.

'How's the patient?' I enquired.

Domitus wiped his dagger on a rag and replaced it in its sheath.

'He'll live.'

I watched as the woman tenderly assisted Aaron in putting on a fresh tunic, after which she kissed him on the lips. She then stood and faced me. She was dressed in a simple light brown robe, blue belt at her waist, white head cloth and sandals on her feet. She was certainly

246

a striking woman. She fell on her knees before me, took my right hand and kissed it, speaking me to in her native tongue that I did not understand.

Aaron spoke up though his voice was weak from the flogging he had received. 'She thanks you for saving the life of her beloved and asks god to be kind to you.'

I lifted her up and smiled at her. 'Tell her that she is very welcome. What is her name?'

'Rachel, majesty.'

I bowed my head to her. 'Rachel.'

The elder woman was brought to me. Like the younger one she had an oval face, dark brown eyes and olive skin. She was a tall woman dressed in a blue flowing robe that covered her arms and legs. She too wore a white head cloth.

'This is Miriam, majesty,' said Aaron, 'Rachel's mother.'

I embraced her as befitting her status. She also thanked me but kept glancing at Malik.

'I think your tattoos are alarming our guests, Malik. Aaron, tell your future mother-in-law that Malik is a great prince of the Agraci and that he means her no harm.'

To spare the women's modesty we gave them each a pair of leggings to wear under their robes so they could ride more easily. Then, an hour after I had entered camp, we mounted our horses again for the journey back to Dura. Alexander cautioned against returning via the Jordan Valley and so we headed east into the desert. Malik assured me that we could make our way from oasis to oasis while staying well clear of Judea and Syria, and the Romans. Aaron wanted Rachel to ride behind him but his lacerated back would have made his journey intolerable and so she rode behind Malik. Miriam again rode behind Domitus who protested loudly, but I think he secretly liked the idea of being a woman's champion.

Before we left we said our farewells to Alexander and his men.

'When we get back to Dura, Aaron and my governor will work out the details of our arrangement,' I said to the Jewish prince.

'How soon will you be able to supply me with weapons?' he asked.

'The first consignment will leave Dura the day the first payment in gold arrives, that I promise.'

He offered me his hand. 'I look forward to a long and mutually beneficial friendship.'

I took his hand. 'That is what I also wish for, lord prince.'

And so, with full waterskins and sacks filled with fresh provisions and fodder provided by Alexander, we rode east into the sun-blasted land of rock and sand east of Judea. Surena and I acted as a rear guard for the others, and I glanced back one last time to look at the shimmering figure of a Jewish prince silhouetted against the bleak yellow hills of eastern Judea where that kingdom's great wealth lay hidden.

We rode for three hours directly east, travelling through sparsely vegetated wadis that ran between limestone and granite cliffs. The steep-sided rock faces dwarfed us as we moved through them, the sounds of iron-shod hooves echoing around the canyons. I kept looking back to see if we were being pursued but saw nothing but a saker falcon or bustard in the sky. I also saw an ibex, a large mountain goat with magnificent curved horns, staring down at us from a precipitous rock ledge high above.

As the day waned the temperature dropped quickly but that night we lit no campfire for fear of alerting any would-be pursuers. We organised a guard rota but I hardly slept a wink as I leaned against a rock wrapped in my cloak with my knees drawn up to my chest. I must have slept a little because I awoke stiff, tired, dirty and chilled to the bone. The others in our party also appeared to have had a less than comfortable night. Rachel and Aaron, however, looked blissfully happy in each other's company.

We set out east again, following the course of a wide stream that coursed through a great wadi. People think that the desert is a barren wilderness filled with sand dunes and death, and great tracts of it are indeed so. But the desert also contains an abundance of water, animals, plants and people, if you can find them. As our horses waded through water that ran between large boulders and canyon walls rose sheer on either side of us, I was struck by the abundance of greenery in this place. Reeds and small bushes lined the banks of the stream and trees sprouted from the cliff face to resemble a great hanging garden, made green by the water springing from the rock.

The sky was clear blue and the sun beat down to warm the earth, but the cliffs shaded us from its heat. Around midday we halted in a spot where the stream filled a vast rock pool, its waters clear and cool. Surena and Domitus stripped naked and threw themselves in as Rachel and Miriam averted their eyes and Malik laughed. The Agraci prince also disrobed and immersed himself in the waters, his back and chest adorned with black tattoos that were the hallmark of Agraci warriors. I stripped to the waist and washed the grit from my body. I thought it improper that the King of Dura should show himself naked to his subjects, a notion that Domitus ridiculed.

'Gallia has told me that it's nothing to get excited about, so you might as well join us.'

'I'm glad that the general of my army retains a great respect for his king,' I replied dryly.

Afterwards, when they had washed themselves clean and dried their bodies, we watered the horses and Rachel fetched water to clean Aaron's wounds. He may have been a happy man but his back looked horrid. As he lay on his stomach on a blanket and Rachel dabbed his wounds with a damp cloth, Domitus shook his head.

'They made a right mess of him. No doubt the whip was reinforced with bone and nails to give it a bit of spice.'

'I know what it's like to be flogged,' I said, wincing at Aaron's red raw back. 'It is most painful.'

'It felt as though my flesh was on fire,' said Aaron, grimacing every time Rachel's cloth touched his flesh.

Malik looked at the trees growing out of the cliff face above us, then licked his finger and held it aloft.

'No wind; good. Time to call "the wolf", I think.'

'The wolf?'

He nodded. 'These are Lord Vehrka's lands. Vehrka means "wolf". I should announce our presence.'

Malik took a small leather pouch from his saddlebag and then began to scour the area for dry wood. I also lent a hand and was joined by Byrd, Surena and Domitus. Malik told us to make a pyre away from the campsite, on the other side of the stream. We did so and then he told us to collect the dung that had been deposited by our horses and position it so that it was in the sun. I ordered Surena to carry out this task.

'But, lord, I am the commander of your horse archers,' he protested.

'Alas, Surena, we outrank you all,' I replied. 'I am a king, Domitus is a general and Malik a prince. Byrd is a civilian and thus exempt from the chain of command. And you wouldn't expect the women to undertake such an unpleasant task, would you?'

He mumbled and grumbled as he collected the manure in his hands and dumped it on a boulder that lay in the sun. Malik assured him it was absolutely necessary for the task in hand. As a horse usually produces around fifty pounds of manure daily, there was no shortage of it to dry in the sun. When he had finished he spent a long time in the rock pool washing his hands and using the point of his dagger to clean under his fingernails.

'The Ma'adan use buffalo dung to keep away flies, do they not?' I said as he sat by the edge of the pool examining his fingers.

'They do, lord,' he muttered. 'But I thought I had left that life behind.'

'Never forget your roots, Surena. If you know where you have come from then you know where you are going.'

He was far from convinced. 'If you say so, lord.'

An hour later Malik judged the dung dry enough for his purpose and lit the great pyre that had been built. He tossed the dung on the flames and then opened his leather pouch and extracted a handful of powder.

'Sulphur,' he grinned at me, tossing it on the fire.

Soon a pillar of thick black smoke was extending upwards into the sky.

'That will be seen miles away,' said Domitus with alarm.

'Exactly,' replied Malik.

The fire burned down to ashes and the pillar of black smoke got thinner and thinner until it resembled a dark needle pointing towards the heavens and then disappeared altogether. Malik said that we should wait in this spot and so I sent Surena back up the canyon to keep watch. We had seen no sign of pursuit but if there were any Roman patrols out they would have seen the smoke and would be heading in our direction. But Malik dismissed my fears.

'Believe me, Pacorus, if there are any enemy horsemen riding in this region they will have more to concern themselves with than us.'

So we unsaddled the horses and I shot a curious ibex that thought it was safe to peer at us from a rock ledge fifty feet above our position. He moaned when the arrow struck his belly and then tumbled from the ledge onto the rocks below. Domitus skinned and gutted it and had the meat roasting over a fire by the time I relieved Surena on watch. Three hours had passed before we heard the sound of horses and men coming from further down the wadi. Surena and I immediately strung arrows in our bowstrings and Domitus drew his *gladius*, but Malik laughed and said that we had nothing to fear.

Then men in black robes on horseback filled the canyon as at least a hundred Agraci warriors rode towards us. And above us on either side I saw other Agraci horsemen on top of the cliffs, black shapes silhouetted against an intense blue sky. Like Malik the warriors in front of us carried round black shields, though these men also carried long spears in addition to the swords at their hips. Their faces were covered by head cloths, which gave them the appearance of demons from the underworld. Rachel and Miriam shrank back from the black host before them, seeking sanctuary in each other's arms.

A figure on a grey stallion at the head of the group urged his mount forward. It was a beautiful Agraci beast with a wide, flat forehead, broad nose, long, erect ears and a straight and slender neck. I assumed the man who rode on its back was Lord Vehrka judging by his horse's rich decoration: a black, beaded halter decorated with silver discs and black tassels. His wool and cotton saddle was also decorated with black tassels. The man slid off his horse's back and walked towards Malik, pulling aside his head cloth to reveal his face. I have to confess that he did not have the appearance of a wolf, being slim, of medium height and possessing a thin face with a large nose. He bowed to Malik.

'Greetings, Prince Malik, welcome to my lands.'

'It is good to see you, Lord Vehrka. I must request your hospitality.'

Vehrka bowed his head again. 'It is freely given.'

'One of our party is injured and we require additional horses for those who have none.'

After the introductions were complete Vehrka gave orders for his surgeon to attend Aaron. I watched as the man took a small jar from his bag and rubbed a blue paste onto Aaron's wounds. The man had a very light touch because Aaron did not flinch as the ointment was applied to his broken skin.

'What is that?' I asked Vehrka.

'Malachite, ground down to make a paste. It will heal his back and also keep the flies away. Wealthy Egyptian women use it to decorate their eyes but we use it for its medicinal properties. Looks like someone gave him a thrashing.'

'He was lucky,' I said. 'A few more minutes and he would have been nailed to a cross.'

'You took a great risk, lord, riding into enemy territory with so few warriors.' He looked at Rachel and Miriam. 'And two women?'

I laughed. 'We picked them up on our return journey.'

'Ah, they are your slaves.'

'Not slaves,' I corrected him. 'Guests.'

'And now, lord, you must allow me to entertain you in my camp as my guests.'

With Aaron's wounds dressed and the two women given their own horses we rode east once more to Vehrka's camp. That night we were treated to roasted goat and warm camel milk as we sat round a raging fire with the Agraci lord and his warriors. Vehrka asked me to sit beside him but said little during the early part of the evening. Malik sat across the fire from us, between Domitus and Byrd who seemed his usual distant self.

'Prince Malik will marry my daughter,' said Vehrka quite unexpectedly.

'Really?' I was shocked. I had no idea that Malik was even seeing a woman let alone thinking of marrying one.

'Her name is Jamal, which means "beauty", and even though a father will always say that his daughter is attractive in this case it is true. It will be a good match.'

'I am pleased for you.'

'One day Malik will be king and she will be his queen and they will rule the whole of Arabia. It is their destiny.'

'Malik is a great warrior,' I agreed.

'Haytham says that you are a great warrior, lord. I have heard of your many victories. But it is unwise to travel without a great number

251

of your warriors with you. I shall therefore escort you back to Palmyra.'

With our new companions the rest of the journey through the desert was uneventful. It took twelve days to reach Palmyra, the pace slow due to the frequent halts we had to make to dress Aaron's wounds and the fact that neither Rachel nor Miriam had ridden a horse before their escape from Judea. They conversed with Aaron but said very little to the rest of us, though Miriam especially was very polite to me as far as our inability to communicate allowed. She knew a few words and phrases of Latin on account of having had some conversations with the Romans in Jericho, and used them to speak with Domitus, who I think was pleased that he was no longer the poorest horseman among our group. As the days passed their conversations grew in length as they whiled away the hours in the saddle, the gaps filled in by Aaron who rode behind them beside Rachel. Domitus told me that Miriam's husband had died of a plague that had ravaged Jericho and Judea several years ago and that she had struggled to keep a roof over her and her daughter's heads, working in the fields and offering lodgings to travellers. She and Rachel slept in their small barn if they had house guests. She had frowned on Rachel seeing Aaron because she knew that he had joined the party of Alexander in the civil war. When the Romans came Aaron disappeared and unknown to her he had fled to Palmyra and then Dura. She had tears in her eyes when she told Domitus that she and her daughter would never be able to return to Judea.

'We shall have to make them welcome at Dura, then,' I told him. 'Considering the great service that Aaron has rendered the kingdom it is the least we can do.'

We bade farewell to Vehrka and his warriors and rode into Haytham's capital four days short of a month after we had left it for Judea. The king and Rasha were waiting for us at his tent, his young daughter delighted that I was paying her a visit.

'Why are you dressed like one of my people?' she asked as I slid off Remus' back and embraced her.

'I have been in disguise,' I replied.

'It was an adventure, then?'

I watched Domitus and Rachel assist a still very tender Aaron from his horse.

'For some more than others. And you, what adventures have you been taking part in, little princess?'

She smiled excitedly and turned on her heels. 'I will show you.'

She disappeared into the great goatskin tent of her father and re-emerged moments later carrying a recurve bow. It was a beautiful piece of work, with the arms and setback centre fashioned from layers of mulberry and maple with water buffalo horn plating on the inside.

The handle and tips of the bow were stiffened with additional horn. The tips had been carved into horse's heads and the wood and horn had been bound together by fish glue and tendon strings. The whole bow was covered in lacquer brought from China to keep it waterproof. 'It was a present from Gallia,' she said, holding it out to me.

I took it and admired the craftsmanship. It would have taken the armouries at least ten months to produce such a weapon, to prepare the tendons, woods and glue and then mate them all together. It was a fitting gift for a princess.

I passed it back to her. 'A beautiful bow for a beautiful princess.' Rasha took the bow, kissed me on the cheek and then blushed before taking it back inside.

'Gallia spoils her, I fear,' remarked Haytham.

'We love her as if she were one of our own daughters, lord.'

'So, tell me of your journey to the land of the Jews.'

We went inside as Aaron and the two women were shown to a guest tent where Aaron's wounds could once again be treated. He seemed to have regained some of his strength and I no longer feared for his life.

'What about your life, Pacorus,' said Haytham, 'or the lives of Gallia and your children, will you not fear for them when the Romans find out that the armouries at Dura have been furnishing their enemies with weapons?'

'I have thought of that, lord, but the Romans are already my enemies so if I can keep them occupied in their own domains then hopefully they will not trouble Dura.'

'It may be as you say. But know that Vehrka has already had several Roman incursions into his lands, mostly small patrols of horsemen. It will not be long before more will come, of that I am certain.'

'And then?'

He smiled savagely. 'And then I will lead the Agraci against them.'

'And Dura will stand beside you,' I announced grandly.

'And your father and your allies will stand beside you?'

I was unsure whether Hatra would get embroiled in a war supporting the Agraci. 'I hope so, lord.'

'And the Jews, do you think they will throw off the Roman yoke?'

I thought of the ragged individuals we had met, the shattered fortress where we had encountered Alexander and Domitus' comment about the lack of bridges across the Jordan. Then I thought of the two legions that were stationed in Syria and the others that the Romans could send as reinforcements.

'I hope so, lord, I sincerely hope so,' was all I could offer.

He pondered for a moment. 'Hope will avail them not in a battle with the Roman army.'

He was right, of course, but I had seen some of the gold that Alexander possessed. With the right weapons, the right timing and the support of the people they might just be victorious. They might just be able to win their freedom.

When we returned to Dura Aaron and his future wife and mother-in-law were settled in a house near Rsan's mansion in the city and he continued to make a rapid recovery. Rsan himself was extremely happy with the outcome of our expedition to Judea and had already drawn up a delivery schedule for Alexander's weapons. Following discussions with the chief armourer he had informed me that it would over a year to fulfil Alexander's requirements. Byrd had accompanied us back to Dura and had come to an agreement with Rsan with regard to the transportation of the weapons to the Jews. We would be using Byrd's camels to carry them west to Palmyra, then directly south into the desert and through the volcanic mountains southwest of Damascus, before heading due west again to the mountains that lay to the east of the Salt Sea. Malik and Rasha had travelled back to Dura with us and Rsan had also come to an agreement with Malik whereby his Agraci warriors would provide an escort for each camel train. The cost of hiring Byrd's camels and Malik's warriors was to be borne by Alexander, meaning Dura would make a handsome profit on each shipment of weapons. After all the sums had been done Rsan was the happiest I had ever seen him. Aaron said that he would travel with the first shipment, which would be ready in two months' time, by which time his wounds would be fully healed. The treasury would be full, Silaces' men would be fully equipped and I could begin to plan a new campaign in the east.

'The Jews are a beaten people,' scoffed Dobbai as she stood beside me atop the Palmyrene Gate a week later.

'You do not agree the Jews are beaten?' Dobbai pressed me.

'Mm?'

'The Jews. I said that they are a beaten people.'

We were standing next to the stone griffin with its unceasing guard over my city and kingdom. Dobbai was leaning against it as a column of Dura's horsemen approached the city following manoeuvres in the desert.

'Perhaps with my help they may be a free people,' I said.

'You have shown imagination in reaching an agreement with this Alexander, but it will not help the Jews.' She cast me a sideways glance. 'Though it may aid you.'

The approaching column of horsemen wheeled away from the city two hundred yards from the Palmyrene Gate to return to their quarters south of Dura. A small group of horsemen had halted to take their salute and then they about-faced and rode to the city.

'It has aided me,' I said. 'With the Jewish gold I can rearm the legions and Silaces' men and deal with Mithridates once and for all.'

The horsemen entering the city were led by Surena, who spotted me standing above the gates and drew his sword to salute me. I raised my hand in recognition. He lived in the city with Viper in accommodation befitting his rank as the commander of my horse archers. I smiled at him as he passed under us.

'You like him, do you not?'

'Of course,' I said. 'He has turned into a fine officer. He is brave, quick witted and has a brain in his head. I never thought I would find a replacement for Nergal, but Shamash has given me one.'

'His destiny and yours do not follow the same path, son of Hatra,' she said. 'You must release him.'

I was confused. 'He is not a slave to do my bidding. He serves me of his own free will.'

'That may be, but while he does so he does not serve the empire.'

'I do not understand.'

She waved her hand at me. 'You will learn that later. By the way, when were you going to tell me that Claudia had spoken to you?'

'How do you know that, has she spoken to you too?'

She raised an eyebrow at me. 'I asked you a polite question, why do you answer so flippantly?'

I had tried to erase the memory of my experience at the Temple of Ishtar from my mind, notwithstanding that the prophecy of the temple gold had come to fruition, which in many ways made it worse.

'I did not think it was of importance.'

'Really?' she said in surprise. 'And yet you thought it important enough to venture to Judea on the word of a Jew who you have known barely a moment. Clearly you attach a great deal of credence to Claudia's words, as you should. What else did she tell you?'

'Nothing,' I snapped.

'Your disrespectful reply suggests otherwise.'

I said nothing but stared at the legionary camp in the distance. She shuffled away from me.

'Have it your own way, son of Hatra. But disregard her words at your peril.'

But the words of Claudia were far from my mind as the weeks passed and the armouries operated at full capacity once the first payment of gold arrived at Dura. Aaron had travelled back to Palmyra and then south through the desert, this time with over a hundred Agraci horsemen acting as his escort, before meeting with Alexander twenty miles east of Machaerus. It had been previously agreed that Alexander would make the first payment before the first shipment of weapons as a sign of his good faith, and so Aaron brought back with him fifty large leather bags full of gold. Once it had been itemised and safely deposited in the treasury, camels were taken to the armouries and loaded with arms.

The armouries needed to manufacture per day twenty-five of each of the following types of weapon: *gladius* and scabbard, spear, dagger and sheath and helmet. Over a fifteen-month period this would be enough to equip ten thousand men. And Alexander also wanted a thousand mail shirts for horsemen. It was fortunate for Dura that the armouries were staffed by four hundred blacksmiths, each one having an apprentice that had begun his training in metal craft at the age of eight. Even so the pace of production was frenetic and the chief armourer, a squat, barrel-chested man named Arsam, made frequent complaints that the requirements of the army and the monthly shipments to 'the rich Jew' were placing an intolerable strain on his ironworks. Arsam had forearms as thick as stone pillars and his name ironically meant 'possessing the strength of heroes'. I told him to hire additional workers from Babylon and Hatra if he wished, though not from Damascus. I had no doubt that eventually the Romans would discover that I was sending weapons to Judea, but hiring workers from Syria would ensure they would find out sooner rather than later.

Domitus continued to rebuild the legions, finally receiving his five thousand 'missing' javelins. Meanwhile the horse archers of Silaces began to fill their quivers as the armouries churned out thousands of arrows. It was fortunate that the arrowheads were made of bronze and were cast rather than forged and then shaped on anvils. This way Arsam could order additional quantities from Babylon and have them transported by camel to Dura.

As a reward for his services to Dura I made Aaron the royal treasurer, as Rsan was now the city governor. As the old year waned Dura slowly became one of the richest kingdoms in the empire as the caravans on the Silk Road passed through the city and Alexander's gold arrived at the Citadel. The reports I received from Babylon, Uruk and Hatra reported no hostile activity east of the Tigris, and in the west all was quiet in Roman Syria and Judea. No doubt Mithridates and Narses were licking their wounds and preparing a fresh campaign against me, but the longer they delayed the stronger Dura became.

When the new year dawned I once again refused to pay the annual tribute demanded of each kingdom by the king of kings. I received word from Nergal, Axsen and my father that Mithridates had demanded twice the normal tribute so he could deal with the 'traitorous King of Dura'. Apparently he could not bear to even mention my name in his royal proclamation.

Hatra, Babylon and Mesene declared that they were unable to meet his demands. My father stated that he was dealing with Armenian incursions into the north of his kingdom and invited Mithridates to send an official letter to the Armenian king, Tigranes, politely requesting that he desist his aggressive actions. For her part Axsen stated that her kingdom could not afford the additional tribute as resources were being directed to repairing the damage incurred during the invasion of her lands the previous year. Though she was diplomatic enough to refrain from stating that it was the king of kings and his lord high general who were responsible for the damage. Nergal did not even bother to reply to Mithridates' demands.

The prospect of war hung over us like thick smoke on a windless day, and we prepared our forces accordingly. The men of Elymais were fully equipped now – eight thousand horse archers divided into eight dragons, each one made up of ten hundred-man companies. Silaces and his men trained every day to turn them into an effective force, though there was not the time to train them to work with the cataphracts, much less the legions. In any case I hoped that in the near future they would be in the vanguard of an army that would liberate the Kingdom of Elymais. They were quartered near the ruins of Mari, forty miles south of Dura beside the Euphrates. It had once been a great city but that was seventeen hundred years ago, and after its destruction by King Hammurabi of Babylon had been largely deserted. The remains of its mud-brick buildings provided adequate shelter for eight thousand horses, though.

Two months into the new year I had the whole army drawn up in front of the Palmyrene Gate and presented Silaces with his new banner: a great white flag upon which was Gotarzes' symbol of a four-pointed star. I could now call upon over twelve thousand horsemen and ten thousand foot, in addition to the men the lords could raise. Last year I had relied on speed and surprise to achieve success; this year I would assemble greater numbers to ensure victory.

Orodes made yet another trip to Babylon, this time to ensure that the production of arrowheads was progressing smoothly. I told him that he did not need to concern himself with such trivia but he insisted. And to speed his journey he and his bodyguard plus their horses travelled down the Euphrates on rafts.

While he was gone I had a most unexpected visit from my father. He sent word that he was visiting me and arrived ten days later accompanied by Vistaspa and his bodyguard plus their squires, who camped across the Euphrates in Hatran territory while their king and his general were lodged in the Citadel. Gallia and I greeted them at the foot of the palace steps in the company of Domitus, Surena, Rsan, Aaron and my three daughters. My father kissed Gallia and knelt to embrace his granddaughters while Vistaspa bowed his head to everyone stiffly and ignored my children. I think he thought infants were small demons sent to torment adults, a view that was not entirely incorrect.

257

We took refreshments on the palace terrace as a forest of tents began to spring up across the river as the squires of Hatra's royal bodyguard erected the shelters of their pampered masters.

My father flopped down in a wicker chair next to the stone balustrade. He looked tired. 'I wish to make a show of force against the Armenians. I grow weary of their incursions into my kingdom, and the longer I do nothing about them the bolder they become.'

To say I was surprised was an understatement. My father had always been a cautious monarch, always reluctant to seek recourse to conflict.

'I had no idea the Armenians were proving so bothersome, father.'

He smiled wryly. 'Vata holds the northern frontier but now raiders are coming from Gordyene. It has become an intolerable situation. I have asked Farhad and Aschek for their assistance and they have agreed that we should arrange a meeting with Tigranes to sort this matter out once and for all. I now ask you, my son, if you will join with me.'

'Dura stands by you, father,' I said with pride. 'When do we attack?'

Vistaspa looked at my father, who frowned. 'We do not go to make war, Pacorus, but to persuade Tigranes that his recklessness endangers Armenia.'

'You will be wasting your words.' Dobbai had walked unseen onto the terrace and took her seat, unconcerned that my senior officers and I were in conference with the King of Hatra. She waved over a servant holding a tray of drinks.

'Armenia is the slave of Rome, even I know that.' She took a silver cup filled with wine and sipped at it as my father regarded her with curiosity and Vistaspa glowered at her.

'Do you suggest I declare war on Rome, then?' asked my father, trying to out-fox her.

'War is coming with Rome whatever you do,' she replied. 'The question is, when it comes will the empire be united or divided?'

'I can see where my son gets his advice from,' said my father dryly, 'advice that nearly led to his death last year at the Tigris.'

'I told him not to underestimate Mithridates and Narses, he chose to ignore that advice,' she snapped back.

I held up my hands. 'We are straying from the matter at hand. When do you meet the Armenians?'

'I have sent a message demanding a meeting with Tigranes at his southern border in a month's time,' said my father.

'The army of Dura will be there, father, I guarantee you that; though I am surprised that Aschek and Farhad have agreed to support you.'

'Raiders from Gordyene have also been attacking Media and Atropaiene,' said Vistaspa.

'Gordyene is like an abscess,' complained my father.

'And where does the king of kings stand in this matter?' I asked. 'His empire is assaulted and all he can do is demand more money to raise an army to march against Dura.'

My father shook his head. 'Mithridates will not support me after I supported you last year.'

'And when Pacorus is away in the north, father,' said Gallia, 'what is to prevent Mithridates and Narses marching against Dura?'

'A wise question, child,' said Dobbai, looking at my father.

'Mithridates is a coward,' I said. 'He will not march through Babylonian and Hatran territory to attack Dura and thereby risk outright war with those two kingdoms having been worsted by them last year. Had he desired that he would have marched against me a long time ago. No, he will bide his time and let others do his work.'

'Mithridates will not attack you, Pacorus,' said my father. 'After all, you have Babylon and Mesene behind you, to say nothing of Haytham and his hordes.'

'Is it not curious,' mused Dobbai, 'that had it not have been for Mithridates taking the daughter of Haytham hostage when he ruled this city, Pacorus might never have forged an alliance with the Agraci. The gods weave their magic in most curious ways.'

My father regarded Dobbai guardedly. 'Well, be that as it may, I doubt that Dura will face any problems while you are away.'

He was probably right, but in the days following his departure I appointed Marcus as Rsan's deputy and instructed him to mount his smaller ballista on the towers on the city walls that faced west. Deep wadis were immediately beyond the city's north and south walls and at the bottom of the rock escarpment upon which the Citadel sat was the Euphrates. An attack against the city could only be mounted against its western wall. I thought it highly unlikely but it was better to be safe than sorry.

The replacement cohort would act as the garrison while the army was away. It consisted mostly of green recruits who received basic training before being allocated to either the Durans or Exiles. There was also the walking wounded who had received injuries in training or who were suffering from fever and similar ailments. Too sick to go on campaign, they were quite capable of undertaking garrison duty. Dobbai had told Gallia that there would no fighting with the Armenians and so she decided to stay in the city, which meant her Amazons could use their bows against any attackers.

Peace or war, training continued as usual. Each day was the same routine for legionaries and horsemen – wake, wash, attend to the horses if a cavalryman, eat breakfast, morning parade and roll-call, camp duties, such as cleaning the latrines, hours spent drilling and training, bedding down the horses, evening meal and bed. The time between evening meal and bed was usually filled with cleaning weapons and equipment, though the married soldiers usually also found time to visit their wives and children in the city. It was certainly an austere life but one that was rewarded with ample amounts of good food, regular pay, the best weapons and equipment that gold could buy and the knowledge that they were part of what I believed to be the best army in the world. And at the apex of the army was a figure feared and respected throughout the kingdom, a man who was the benchmark when it came to professionalism, discipline and fighting prowess. A man that was harder than the blade of the *gladius* he wore at his hip – Lucius Domitus.

I was in the Citadel's courtyard discussing with Rsan the licensing of brothels in the city when Orodes and Surena rode through the gates and jumped from their horses.

'The queen won't approve,' I said, 'but the fact is that thousands of young men travelling with the caravans pass through Dura each year, and when they stop here they seek the company of prostitutes.'

'It is as you say, majesty,' agreed Rsan gravely.

'So the treasury might as well benefit from their brisk trade.'

Rsan nodded approvingly. 'I was thinking of a licence for each brothel, majesty, renewable each year.'

I saw Orodes and Surena pass the reins of their horses to waiting squires and then walk towards us.

'Good, Rsan. I leave the matter in your capable hands.'

'It was actually Aaron's idea, majesty. He has proved a most useful addition to the administration here.'

He bowed and went back to the treasury as Surena and Orodes appeared in front of me.

'I think you should ride to the legionary camp immediately, Pacorus,' said Orodes.

'Grave news, lord,' added Surena.

'What is it?' I said, concerned.

'It would appear that Domitus has a woman,' said Orodes seriously.

I looked at them both, suddenly grinning like mischievous children. 'What nonsense is this?'

'No nonsense, lord,' said Surena. 'He has been spotted walking with a woman, in camp.'

'I think you should investigate immediately,' suggested Orodes.

The idea that Domitus would have a woman was a ridiculous notion. He was married to the army, unyielding, iron-hard, devoid of emotion. The whole army looked up to him; indeed, the whole kingdom held him in high esteem.

'Impossible,' I said. 'I have known that man for thirteen years and in all that time he has shown no interest in the opposite sex.'

Orodes held up his hands. 'Have it your own way, but I have it on good authority that he is in camp with her as we speak.'

'You should ride to the camp and see for yourself, lord,' urged Surena. 'Everyone is talking about it.'

'We will be marching north soon,' I said, 'and I have better things to do than indulge in idle gossip. And so do you two.'

'Actually,' remarked Orodes, 'I don't. Your cataphracts are fully prepared and Strabo has ensured that the horses, camels and men are fully provisioned.'

'As are my horse archers, lord,' added Surena, a self-satisfied smug look on his face.

'But the legions may not be,' said Orodes casually.

'Oh? Why not?'

He feigned ignorance. 'Well, if Domitus is distracted then who knows what might happen? His men might arrive in Nisibus without javelins, or helmets even.'

I decided to put a stop to this frivolity right away.

'I am riding to the camp and you two are coming with me,' I commanded.

The three of us rode from the city and into camp, leaving our horses at the stables near the workshops. Domitus was not in his headquarters tent and the sentries standing guard outside did not know of his whereabouts.

'Bad sign that, Pacorus,' remarked Orodes.

'Please be quiet,' I replied.

'Perhaps he has been kidnapped,' suggested Surena.

I turned to face them both. 'Listen you two, I hope Domitus is not out on manoeuvres and you have dragged me here for some sort of joke.'

Orodes looked most alarmed. 'Joke, Pacorus? I hardly think the corruption of the commander of the army is a joke.'

At that moment I saw Drenis striding across the parade square adjacent to the headquarters tent. He saluted when he saw me.

'Drenis,' I said, 'have you seen Domitus?'

Orodes and Surena both smiled at him but he ignored them.

'I saw him go in the griffin's tent a few moments ago.'

'Thank you,' I replied, relieved.

His eyes narrowed. 'Is everything all right?'

'Of course, thank you. How are the men?'

He winked. 'Lean and mean and itching for a bit of revenge. They've never fought Armenians before.'

'Well,' I said, 'let us hope that it won't come to fighting.'

'If that is all, Pacorus?' Drenis was not one for small talk.

I nodded. He saluted and then went about his business as we strolled over to the tent that housed the golden griffin standard of the Duran Legion. Guards ringed it and there were more guards inside to watch over what had become the religious totem of the Durans. The Exiles had their own emblem, a silver lion that also had its own guarded tent nearby. The legionaries at the entrance snapped to attention as we removed our headgear and went inside.

There, positioned in the middle of the tent and held in place by a stand, was the griffin that had been cast in gold sitting on its metal plate, bold, defiant and seemingly about to fly. The atmosphere inside the tent was still and dripping with reverence, as though the griffin was holding court. This was as it should be for it was the symbol of Dura and, like the statue at the Palmyrene Gate, as long as it existed no harm would come to the city. And there, standing before it, helmet in the crook of his arm, straight as the shaft of an arrow, was Domitus. And beside him was standing a woman dressed in a long blue robe and with a white head cloth descending down her back. He was speaking to her slowly in Latin.

'And ever since it was presented to them my soldiers believe that it has magic powers, and that as long as it remains unharmed they and the kingdom are safe.'

'They worship it?' asked the woman, whose voice I recognised.

'Some do, believing it to be sacred object; others look upon it as a good luck charm. But they would all die to protect it.'

'My religion teaches that it is wrong to worship idols.'

'Each to his own, I say,' replied Domitus whose instincts told him that there were others in the tent behind him. He turned round to see the three of us standing in a row like legionaries waiting to be disciplined. The woman also turned and I saw that it was Miriam, the mother of Aaron's future wife.

Domitus was dressed in his full parade uniform. Though he was now a general he had never abandoned the uniform of a centurion that he now wore: mail shirt adorned with silver discs, silver-edged greaves and helmet with a white transverse crest, the colour of Dura's army. His *gladius* was in its scabbard at his left hip, dagger at his right and his trusty vine cane in his right hand. He looked at us all suspiciously.

'Come to pay your respects, have you?'

I cleared my throat. 'Yes, sort of.' I smiled at Miriam and spoke to her in Latin. 'How are you, Miriam?'

She bowed her head. 'I am well, majesty.'

'I hope Domitus is treating you well.'

She smiled at my general. 'He has great civility, majesty.'

Orodes cleared his throat, drawing attention to himself. Like Surena he had been wearing a dumb smile.

'Are you not going to introduce me, Domitus?'

Domitus looked most uncomfortable, sighing deeply.

'Miriam, this is Prince Orodes of Susiana, a land to the east of the River Tigris and...'

Orodes stepped forward, took Miriam's hand and kissed it, much to her surprise and slight shock.

'And I am delighted to meet you. Domitus has been remiss in keeping you from my presence.'

Like all Parthian nobility he could speak Latin, Greek and of course Parthian, but he now proceeded to converse with Miriam in Aramaic, which clearly delighted her. Before she was stiff and formal but now she smiled and was relaxed. Orodes could charm the birds from the trees when he had a mind to. Domitus was not amused and stood in sullen silence as the two of them chatted away.

'I think we have taken up too much of Miriam's time,' I said at last.

'You certainly have,' growled Domitus. 'Don't you three have any stables to muck out?'

I was slightly embarrassed about our intrusion into their company. 'Apologies, Domitus, we did not mean to disturb you.' I turned to Miriam. 'I hope Dura is agreeable to you and your daughter, lady. Know that you are both very welcome here.'

'Thank you, majesty.'

Orodes insisted that he kiss the hand of Miriam once again as we took our leave of her and Domitus. Surena had moved towards the griffin and stretched out his hand to touch it. He stopped and looked at Domitus. The last time he had been this near to the treasured icon he had been an ill-kempt boy from the marshlands and his dirty hand had been brushed away from the standard before he could touch it. That was over five years ago and in that time the boy had become a man and a leader of other men. He had saved my life on the battlefield and had risen to become the commander of all my horse archers. And yet he still hesitated to lay his hand upon the golden creature.

'You've earned it,' said Domitus.

Surena grinned in triumph and gently laid his hand on the griffin's head, then turned and walked from the tent. Miriam looked at him leaving and then back at the griffin sitting on its metal plate. She did not understand, much less when both Orodes and I bowed our heads to it before we also departed.

During the days following wagons were loaded with food, tools, tents, spare javelins, swords, mail shirts and helmets, clothing and shields. The wagons we had lost during our battles with Mithridates and Narses had been replaced at considerable cost, and mule numbers had been brought up to strength from the royal estates. Even the stakes that were used to surround the camp each night had had to be made afresh, to be once again carried on the backs of mules.

Strabo had been at the warehouses on the royal estates every day to ensure that the mounts of the cataphracts, horse archers and the camels had sufficient fodder to sustain them during the coming campaign, and stables echoed with the sound of red-hot iron being beaten on anvils to re-shoe horses.

A week before we departed Gallia and I were invited to a pleasant diversion: the wedding between Aaron and Rachel. The ceremony took place in Rsan's mansion a short distance from the Citadel and near to the former residence of Godarz. This had remained empty since that dreadful night when our friend had been murdered. I had broached the subject of it being used again but Gallia would not hear of it and so, aside from a few gardeners to maintain the grounds and a small number of cleaners who went in each week, Godarz's mansion remained empty, a shrine to the man who had been like a father to her.

Rsan's mansion was similar to that of Godarz's with a courtyard fronting the main residence and a wall surrounding both. There were stables, a small barracks and a gatehouse. The actual wedding ceremony took place in a garden complete with fountains and fish-filled ponds positioned to the rear of the main reception hall. As well as Greeks, Parthians, Agraci and Syrians, Dura also contained a small Jewish community, and so Gallia had requested its leaders attend the Citadel to acquaint her with the wedding ritual we had been invited to.

We walked to Rsan's mansion as the sun was descending in the west and casting long shadows amid the buildings. Gallia was dressed in a simple long-sleeved blue dress and had her hair gathered on top of her head and held in place by a gold diadem.

'Guests are expected to dress modestly, Pacorus, and keep their flesh covered.'

'Malik will have no problems getting in, then,' I remarked.

Malik had been invited because he had carried Rachel to safety on the back of his horse after we had rescued Aaron outside Jericho.

'He will be one of the witnesses,' she told me. 'The other one will be Domitus, who carried Miriam to safety.'

We joined the other wedding guests in the fragrant garden as the dusk was approaching. We greeted Byrd and Noora who had come from Palmyra, Surena, who had also been a member of the party that had travelled to Judea, and Rsan. The other guests were the Jewish men and women who lived in Dura. We were asked by a Jewish man with a long grey beard to assemble under a great canopy that had been erected in the garden.

'It is open on all four sides so that all may be made welcome,' Gallia informed me. 'The old man with a beard is one of their priests, a rabbi they call him.'

As we gathered under the white canopy Aaron and Rachel appeared in the roofed aisle supported by marble columns that surrounded the garden on all four sides. Both of them were dressed in white and beside them walked Miriam, also dressed in white, and Domitus, who was wearing a fine white tunic, a rich blue cloak draped over his left shoulder and arm and held in place by a gold broach, and blue boots. I scarcely recognised him!

'The bride and groom wear white to resemble royalty and cleanliness of sin,' said Gallia. 'They will have fasted today and recited psalms together to ask god for his forgiveness for their transgressions. In this way they both enter their marriage fully cleansed.'

'And starving,' I added. She jabbed me in the ribs with a finger to indicate her disapproval of my levity.

The rabbi gestured to all of us beneath the canopy to come closer as the sky darkened and servants lit oil lamps hanging from the columns to illuminate the scene. Rachel's face was covered with a veil, which Gallia explained was a sign of her modesty, while Aaron had a prayer shawl over his head.

'It is a strange time of day to have a wedding,' I whispered to her.

'It is so the couple may see the stars and be reminded of the blessing their god gave to Abraham that his children would be as numerous as the stars.'

'Who is Abraham?'

'One of the first of the Jewish people to have lived on the earth, many thousands of years ago.'

Rachel and Aaron stood beneath the centre of the canopy and then Rachel circled him seven times.

'In the teachings of the Jewish religion,' whispered Gallia, 'it is stated that god created the world in seven days. So Rachel circling Aaron thus ensures that their god blesses their union.'

After this had been completed Aaron produced a simple gold ring and gave it to Rachel. The rabbi announced that this symbolised that the pair were now married. I looked at Gallia and thought of our own wedding and everything that had happened before and since, and reached for her hand. The world was divided into many different religions and races but whatever language people spoke or gods they worshipped, in the end everyone was on the same quest – to find someone to share their life with.

My thoughts were interrupted by the rabbi's deep voice reading the marriage contract, called a *ketubah*. This was a most curious part of the ceremony in which the rabbi read from a document that listed all the responsibilities the husband had towards his wife, after which it was signed by the groom and the two witnesses. The rabbi then recited a number of blessings that were repeated by the assembled congregation and then Aaron and Rachel, now minus her veil, drank from the same cup of wine as they held hands. The rabbi then took the prayer shawl that had been adorning Aaron's head and wrapped it round the couple's hands to symbolise their union before god.

After the ceremony we went into Rsan's banqueting room and sat at tables where we were served chicken, lamb, fruits and wine. During the meal Aaron and Rachel served us portions of Jewish bread named *challah*, which Gallia informed me was made from eggs, flour, water and yeast. The bread was braided to resemble arms intertwined to symbolise love.

I sat next to Orodes as jugglers in bright clothing threw knives in the air in front of us and musicians played in accompaniment to the dazzle of flashing blades.

'You think your father will fight the Armenians, Pacorus?'

'No. He wishes to avoid war if he can. He seeks to overawe the Armenians with a show of strength.'

'And you?'

I laughed. 'I think the way to overawe them is to destroy their army and march on their capital.'

'They have the Romans behind them,' said Orodes with concern, 'and there are Roman troops in Syria also.'

'Their general Pompey, who we met at the Euphrates, has returned to Rome and disbanded his army, I hear. He had formed some sort of alliance with Crassus and another man named Caesar, but there are reports that Rome is divided between different factions.'

He looked confused. 'What has this to do with the Armenians?'

'If the Romans are preoccupied with internal politics they will be less focused on the east. That will hopefully make the Armenians more likely to see sense.'

'The Armenians will know that the Parthian Empire is also riven with internal disputes, Pacorus.'

I pushed a piece of spicy chicken breast into my mouth. 'That will need addressing after we have dealt with the Armenians.'

'You still mean to attack Mithridates, then?'

I smiled at him. 'Naturally. He still has to pay for trying to assassinate me, to say nothing of the deaths of Gotarzes and Vardan, and your father. And then there is the matter of you regaining your rightful place on the throne of Susiana.'

He took a swig of wine from his jewel-encrusted goblet then admired it, turning it in his hand.

'No one has the stomach for such a fight, Pacorus, aside from you. Even your father shrinks back from making war on Mithridates and Hatra has one of the most feared armies in the empire.'

'And what of Babylon?' I asked him.

'Babylon?'

'Yes,' I said. 'You have been spending so much time there of late that I was wondering if Axsen had made you the commander of her palace guard.'

He blushed and turned away. 'I do not know what you mean.'

'Will Axsen support Dura if I march east?'

He quickly regained his composure. I had no idea why he had become so flustered.

'Babylon will support you but will not be able to lend you any troops for a campaign against Mithridates. Axsen has to look to her own defences first. Nergal is in a similar position, I fear.'

I nodded. 'It will be only a matter of time before Mithridates and Narses attacks Babylon and Mesene. That is why we must strike the first blow.'

It was like a great game of strategy and the whole empire was the playing board. Mithridates had the active support of Narses of Persis and Sakastan, his co-conspirator, King Phriapatius of Carmania, King Vologases of Drangiana, King Cinnamus of Anauon, King Tiridates of Aria and King Monaeses of Yueh-Chih, the kingdoms in the eastern half of the empire. Dura was but a tiny speck compared to their vastness, but I had powerful friends, if not actual allies, in Hatra, King Musa of Hyrcania and above all King Khosrou of Margiana. And there was Mesene under Nergal and Axsen's Babylon, while to the north stood the kingdoms of Media and Atropaiene ruled by Farhad and Aschek respectively.

Unfortunately for me both Musa and Khosrou were at this moment engaged in a great campaign against the wild peoples who lived on the vast steppes between the Caspian and Aral seas. They had mustered over one hundred thousand horsemen between them to stop the raids that had been increasing in intensity over the last two years. Dobbai had derided the notion that the nomads could be destroyed and thought Musa and Khosrou fools. Whether they were or not remained to be seen, but while they were occupied in the north they could not aid me.

Aschek and Farhad were old friends of my father and tended to go along with what Hatra desired, and at the present moment in time my father desired their presence at Nisibus to present a united front against the Armenians, another piece on the board of the great game of strategy that I was also a part of. And to the east, in Syria and Judea, were the Romans; while between them and Dura were Haytham's Agraci. The game was finely poised at a temporary stalemate, but soon enough the pieces would be moving again.

'They make a nice couple, do they not?'

'Mmm?'

'Are you listening, Pacorus?'

I smiled at Gallia. Of course I had not been. 'Of course, my love.'

She leaned towards me and nodded at the top table where a lean poet with a wispy beard was reciting some rather long and frankly pompous verses to the newlyweds. They did not care because they were in love. He could have been reading the list of items for the feast, which would probably have been more interesting.

'Of course they make a nice couple, they have just got married,' I replied.

'Not Aaron and Rachel. Domitus and Miriam.'

I sighed loudly. 'Not you as well. Has Orodes put you up to this?'

She looked at me in confusion. 'What do you mean?'

'I had him and Surena bending my ear about Domitus and Miriam and now you are harping on about them.'

'First of all, I don't harp on as you so quaintly put it. Harping insinuates idle and irritating gossip and I indulge in neither. On the contrary I make informed judgements on what I have observed.'

I drank some more wine. 'Then I will tell you what I told them. Domitus, who by the way must be over fifty years old, is already married to the army. He's set in his ways and that's just the way I like it. He's happy, I'm happy and that is that.'

'I don't think Domitus is happy at all,' she replied. 'He works so hard because it fills the loneliness in his life.'

'This is Domitus we are talking about, the fiercest warrior on both sides of the Euphrates.'

'He deserves to be happy,' she persisted.

'He *is* happy. He would tell me if he were not.

'You know so little about the heart, Pacorus. Do you really think he would tell you, his lord and friend, that he craves love like the most humble and simplest man in the kingdom? And he is not the only one.'

This was ridiculous. 'Don't tell me, all my centurions are lonely.'

She sat back in her chair and raised an eyebrow at me. 'Do not try to be clever; it does not suit you. Fortunately I have affairs in hand so you can concentrate on frightening the Armenians.'

She ran a finger down my scarred cheek. 'That shouldn't be too much of a problem. Is the marsh boy going with you?'

'Surena? Of course. He is a fine commander, would you not agree, Orodes?'

Orodes cupped his ear to hear above the din of the wedding feast. 'Agree with what?'

'That Surena is an excellent commander.'

He nodded enthusiastically. 'Most excellent, yes.'

'Perhaps you should give him his own army, then,' suggested Gallia.

I looked at her. 'What did you say?'

'Give the marsh boy his own army.'

268

My blood ran cold and I was taken back to the voice that had spoken to me in the Temple of Ishtar.

The one born in the land of water must be given his own army.

I said no more on the matter of Surena but as I sat there surrounded by laughter and merriment I knew that the first part of what the voice had told me, and I still refused to believe that it was Claudia, had come to fruition. I had followed Aaron to Judea and now the gold from the temple of Jerusalem was helping me to finance the army. But there was no other army for Surena to command, no kingdom of his own from which he could draw recruits. The idea was preposterous. Then again no more preposterous than a simple boy from the great marsh lands of what had been southern Mesene rising to become the commander of Dura's horse archers.

Rather than drive myself to distraction with such thoughts I pushed them to the back of my mind, drank more wine, slipped my arm round my wife's waist and enjoyed the rest of the evening. Two days later, nearly a year to the day since I had set out on the fateful campaign against Mithridates that had nearly resulted in my death, I once again led the army across the pontoon bridges that spanned the Euphrates. This time it headed north along the eastern bank of the river, a great column of foot soldiers, camels, wagons and horsemen that stretched over twenty miles. It was time to show our strength to the Armenians.

Chapter 11

It was spring once more and the days were bright but not hot, a slight northerly wind being enough to make the march comfortable and dispel the clouds of dust that always hung over our great column of iron-shod hooves and hobnailed leather sandals. Though we were in friendly territory the army assumed the usual marching order it adopted for every campaign. Far ahead of the army, in front and on the flanks, rode Byrd, Malik and their scouts – fifty hand-picked men who were answerable to those two alone and who were the eyes and ears of the army, their task to inform me of the enemy army's whereabouts and its movements. Sometimes we didn't see them for days but it comforted us all to know that they were riding far and wide to provide early warning of any threats. Most of them were Agraci like Malik though there were a few Parthians among their ranks. They dressed like desert nomads and like their horses were scrawny and unprepossessing individuals, but they could ride all day and all night and move like ghosts over any terrain and I thanked Shamash that they served me.

The advance guard of the army comprised five hundred widely dispersed horse archers who kept a lookout for any possible ambush sites on route, such as fords across rivers, woodland, canyons and the like. If they suffered any attacks they were to immediately break contact and fall back to the army where a plan could be formulated.

Next came the pioneers, a small contingent of surveyors and workmen who determined where the army would camp for the night and once at the site would mark out where the tents would be pitched, the stables sited and the ditches dug. These men were under the command of Marcus, as was the unit of engineers that came next in the order of march, whose task was to repair the roads and bridges along which the army was travelling.

The wagons and mules carrying the army's supplies and food came next, plus the oxen pulling Marcus' siege engines (though for this campaign they had been left behind at Dura) and the thousand camels and their civilian drivers of the ammunition train carrying spare arrows. This was the slowest part of the army and also the most vulnerable – any successful assault on the baggage train would destroy the food supplies and seriously damage the army's ability to continue the campaign. It was thus protected by two dragons of horse archers – two thousand riders.

Next came the senior officers of the army, which should have included Domitus and Kronos, but they always insisted on walking at the head of their legions and so the only company I had was Orodes and Gallia when she accompanied the army. Surena should have been attending me but he always found an excuse to ride with the advance guard. On this march I asked Silaces to ride with me as the banner of

Elymais was carried behind us, alongside those of Susiana and Dura, though all three flags were wrapped round their poles and covered with waxed sleeves. As we were marching through Hatran territory I thought it impolite to fly the flags of other kingdoms in my father's lands.

Behind us rode the cataphracts, their heavy scale armour and lances carried on the camels led behind them by their squires. On the march the cataphracts acted as horse archers, though they insisted that they were actually the king's bodyguard because they rode immediately behind me. Then came the legions, the men in their centuries and cohorts marching six abreast at a steady pace that allowed them to cover twenty miles a day.

Behind the legions I had placed Silaces' eight thousand horse archers and behind them the rear guard made up of the remaining Duran horse archers – five hundred men.

We marched inland from the Euphrates, away from villages and cultivated land as a thousand cataphracts, two thousand squires, eleven thousand horse archers and ten thousand legionaries can cause much damage tramping over fields and irrigation ditches. In addition to the horses and men there were the cataphracts' two thousand camels, a further thousand camels carrying spare arrows, two thousand wagons and three and a half thousand mules that accompanied the two legions. As with the camels carrying spare arrows, the drivers of the wagons were all civilians under Marcus' command.

It was only when the army was fully assembled did I realise what a massive organisation it was, and how much wealth was required to keep each part of it armed and provisioned.

We marched for four days north parallel to the Euphrates and then headed inland in a northeasterly direction towards Nisibus. It took a further five days before we made camp ten miles south of the city near the River Mygdonius, which ran through the city further north. During our march the country had changed from desert to steppe and finally to fertile plains as we neared the great Taurus Mountains that separated Hatra from Armenia.

The camp was its usual square shape, each side measuring twelve hundred yards comprising an outer ditch and earth rampart with wooden stakes planted on top. I decided that this spot would be our base until we returned home. We were near water and the area around the city itself would be crowded with tents containing soldiers from Media and Atropaiene and others from the garrison. My father's entourage filled Nisibus itself. After the evening meal I assembled the senior officers in my tent and briefed them on the course of action for the following days. Byrd and Malik had returned to us and sat at the

271

table with Alcaeus, Domitus, Kronos, Surena, Orodes, Silaces and myself. The mood was relaxed, confident.

'We will stay here,' I announced, 'as we are near water and the city and the surrounding area will be thronged with soldiers and people. I see no reason to add to the multitude.'

'The more people there are in a confined space,' said Alcaeus, 'the more likelihood of pestilence. I've seen armies reduced to nothing when sickness sweeps through them.'

'I have sent word to Vata, the commander in these parts, that we are here,' I continued, 'and will await my father's summons.'

'When do we fight the Armenians?' asked Surena with relish.

I gave him a disapproving look. 'We don't, unless they provoke us. We are here to impress them, to awe them, Surena, not to fight them.'

'I've always found that grinding an enemy into the ground impresses them,' sniffed Domitus, to which Kronos, Malik and Surena banged the hilts of their daggers on the table. I held up my hands to still the hubbub.

'We are here to support my father, and he prefers to try the route of negotiation first.'

'And if that doesn't work?' pressed Domitus.

'Then, my friend,' I answered, 'we will do things your way.'

The others cheered, even the normally reserved Orodes, and I smiled. Their morale and that of the army was excellent and I knew that the legions wanted to avenge the near defeat they had experienced not far from the Tigris last year. The fact that their discomfort was not at the hands of the Armenians was irrelevant. They sensed an opportunity to wash away the bitter taste of defeat by dipping their swords in Armenian blood.

There were sounds of horses' hooves and voices outside and the tent flap opened. One of the sentries entered and saluted.

'Lord Vata is here to see you, majesty.'

I was delighted. 'Vata, here? Have him shown in and have more wine sent to us.'

He saluted and then held the flap open to let my childhood friend enter. I hardly recognised the squat, round-face individual who strode across the carpet to embrace me. The son of Bozan had always been shorter and stockier than me, but his big round face had always worn a smile to reflect his happy-go-lucky nature, but now his countenance was severe, pitiless and also haggard. He looked more than his forty years of age; perhaps I appeared the same to him.

'Welcome, my old friend,' I said, 'take the weight off your feet.'

I poured him a cup of wine and introduced my officers to him as he drained the cup and helped himself to another. I noticed that he looked at Malik disparagingly.

272

'Your father and the other kings are in Nisibus and their forces are camped outside,' he looked at me with dark-ringed eyes. 'In two days' time Tigranes the Great, so called, will grace us with his presence.'

'Who is Tigranes?' asked Surena.

Vata cracked a smile. 'The king of the Armenians and the bastard who, for the last few years, has been sending raiding parties through the Taurus Mountains and lately from Gordyene into northern Hatra.

'Every caravan that passes through these parts I have to furnish with an escort to see it reaches Antioch safely. They already pay duties to travel through Hatra so we cannot charge them any more. So the king, the father of Pacorus, has to pay for the additional troops that garrison this region out of his own treasury.'

'You say the caravans are protected,' said Orodes.

'That is correct, lord prince.'

'Then surely they are safe from raiders.'

Vata drank another cup of wine and I noticed a nasty scar on his right hand. 'I don't have enough men, lord prince, to protect all the caravans and all the towns and villages in this area. If I provide protection to all the caravans then the villages and farms are raided and crops and livestock plundered. If I station troops in the villages then the caravans are vulnerable. So you see, lord prince, I face a dilemma.'

'One that will now be resolved,' I reassured him.

His mouth broke into a weak smile. 'Let us hope so, my friend, for the stakes are high.'

They were indeed. Northern Hatra was the richest part of the kingdom, a fertile area containing countless springs and brooks that irrigated land that produced grapes, rice, grain, olives, figs, pomegranates, apples, pears, apricots and dates. The estates of the lords who lived in the area possessed great herds of horses that supplied my father's army with mounts, while the royal estates here also raised camels and mules. The great number of villages provided troops for the army and farmers to work the land. If these resources were lost Hatra would lose a great source of wealth, in addition to endangering the Silk Road that ran from the city of Hatra north to Nisibus and then west to Antioch.

'Still,' said Vata, 'now the army of Dura is here I think Tigranes will think twice before continuing provocations.'

I looked at the others. 'I would speak to Lord Vata alone.'

They saluted Vata and filed from the tent back to their commands, my friend nodding to each of them as they left.

'You've collected a strange bunch, Pacorus. The one with the face tattoos, he's Agraci, isn't he?'

'An Agraci prince,' I corrected him.

His eyes were wide with surprise. 'And he fights for you?'

273

'Of course, he is a good friend.'

Vata shook his head. 'I heard about the scrape you got yourself in last year. When your father came back he was far from happy, as were a lot of people, that ten thousand Agraci had crossed the Euphrates.'

I refilled my cup with wine. 'Well, the Agraci helped save my neck and for that I am in their debt.'

He suddenly looked alarmed. 'You didn't bring any Agraci with you, did you?'

I laid a hand on his arm. 'Only Malik and a handful of his men, Vata.'

'Your father does not want a war,' he said gravely.

'He sent you to tell me that?'

'No,' he replied, 'but I know he is worried that a full-scale war will erupt between Hatra and the Armenians. He can't afford two wars.'

'Two wars?'

He smiled. 'How long have we known each other, Pacorus? I know you will march again against Mithridates, it is only a matter of time. And when you do Hatra will be forced to fight beside you.'

'I ask no one to fight beside me,' I said casually.

'You are wrong. You have already asked Hatra, Babylon and Mesene to fight for you, either that or meekly submit as Mithridates subdues them. I can read maps too.'

'There are debts that must be repaid,' I said slowly.

He laughed and slapped my arm. 'Same old Pacorus. Well, I must get back to the city. Your father sent me to request your presence at the palace tomorrow at midday.'

'I can't wait,' I said dryly.

He stood and drained his cup. 'It is good to see you, my friend.'

I stood and we embraced. 'You too, Vata.'

'I like your camp. Do you always construct it thus?'

'Always. It allows all those inside to sleep sounder at night.'

I stood at the tent's entrance and watched him ride down the camp's central avenue with his escort of spearmen around him. The wind coming from the north was cool and carried with it a light drizzle. I shivered and gathered my cloak around me as Vata and his men disappeared in the distance.

The next day I ordered hunting parties to be sent out to collect some fresh food that could be cooked in the evening. I had hunted in these parts as a boy with my father, Bozan and Vata and knew they were rich in lions, hyenas, jackals, wolves, wild boar and antelopes. Surena organised a competition between fifty hunting parties, each one made up of twenty horse archers, whereby the winning party would be the one that killed the most edible game and would be rewarded with a bonus of a week's pay. Marcus added a proviso that they must collect any arrows they shot that missed the target and

274

extract any others from the animals they killed. The thought of thirty thousand arrows being wasted on a hunting trip did not improve his humour. Before they left camp Surena promised instant promotion to anyone who brought back a dead Armenian. I also reminded them not to damage any farms or property, or indeed frighten the locals who might mistake them for raiders.

I took Orodes with me to the meeting of the kings, the two hundred and fifty men of his bodyguard in their scale armour riding behind us. Nisibus stands beside the Mygdonius that flows south through a huge plain located below Mount Masius, one of the mountains in the Taurus chain. The lower slopes of the mountain are covered in deciduous and conifer forests, while the arrival of spring had covered the plain of Nisibus in white roses. I took this to be a good omen signalling that the white horse of Hatra and the white tunics of Dura would overcome their foes.

It had been over five years since I had last seen the kings of Media and Atropaiene and in that time they had aged considerably.

They were waiting in the main hall of Nisibus' palace; a squat stone building that was entirely functional and largely devoid of rich furnishings. The palace was in the centre of a walled compound that also contained storerooms, stables, armouries and barracks. At this time it was crowded with horses, soldiers and the retinues of lords that waited as their masters gathered in the main hall.

Orodes and I left our horses at the entrance to the palace and walked through the reception hall. Guards stood at every pillar and a host of petitioners waited outside the closed oak doors at the entrance to the hall. We pushed our way through the throng and the guards at the entrance opened the doors to allow us to enter. They were closed behind us. The hall had plain white-washed walls and grey stone slabs covering the floor. We made our way to where my father was sitting at the head of a massive rectangular oak table positioned in the middle of the chamber. Beyond it stood a stone dais over which hung Hatran banners depicting a white horse on a red background, and around the dais, behind my father, stood the lords of northern Hatra dressed in their war gear.

My father nodded to me and then Orodes as we took our seats at the table. Beside my father, as always, was Vistaspa, his elbows resting on the table and his hands clasped together under his chin. I could tell from his demeanour that the meeting would be serious. On my father's other side was the world-weary Vata who managed a thin smile. Across the table from me sat King Farhad of Media, a lean, severe individual with dark eyes. Next to him was his son, Prince Atrax, a man I liked enormously for his courage, amiable nature and sense of honour. Unfortunately for me he was married to my sister Aliyeh, who had taken against me when Atrax had received a severe

275

leg wound as a consequence of fighting the Romans. Aliyeh had blamed me for intoxicating Atrax with notions of glory and encouraging him to seek battle, which was untrue. Anyhow Atrax had nearly died and now walked with a permanent limp as a consequence of his wound and Aliyeh never forgave me. She also disliked me for having, as she put it, lured Atrax away from her side to fight beside me during my ill-fated campaign in Gordyene, during which we had all nearly died. That was years ago but her anger towards me had not diminished. Since then Aliyeh had born two sons, the future rulers of Media. I had heard that Atrax had wanted to name his firstborn Pacorus but Aliyeh had forbidden it. The rumour was that my sister ruled both her husband and father-in-law and thus the whole of Media.

Atrax's angular face broke into a grin and I smiled back. Behind the king and his son stood Media's senior commanders, all dressed in blue tunics, grey leggings, armour and helmets. At the other end of the table sat the King of Atropaiene, Aschek. He had thick, wavy black hair and a hooked nose. Either side of him were his two sons who had inherited their father's nose and behind them were grouped Atropaiene's generals.

'These are dangerous times,' began my father, 'when all of our kingdoms face external threats. For too long now our borders have been assaulted by raiders from Armenia.'

'It is as you say, Varaz,' said Farhad. 'Ever since Balas was killed and Gordyene lost to the Romans we have had nothing but trouble.'

'Only last week,' added Aschek, 'a large party of the enemy attacked my lands from Gordyene and did a great deal of damage. It is intolerable.'

My father nodded while Vistaspa continued to look down at the table. 'Intolerable, I agree, which is why I have demanded this meeting with Tigranes.'

'It was better for us,' said Farhad, 'when Tigranes was fighting the Romans. Now he is their ally he turns his spears against us.'

'He is their client,' I corrected him.

Farhad held out his hands. 'Client, ally, what does it matter?'

'It matters a great deal, lord,' I answered. 'Armenia is a client state of Rome and Tigranes is what is called *amicus populi Romani*, "a friend of the Roman people", which means he is under Rome's thumb. He does nothing without the agreement of his Roman overlords.'

'And you think that Rome believes there is advantage to be gained in provoking us?' asked Aschek.

'Yes lord,' I answered.

'And what is that, Pacorus?' queried my father.

'What Rome has always desired, father. Control of the Silk Road.' I looked at Vata. 'These raiders that attack Hatra's villages and the trade caravans, do they include Romans?'

276

He shook his head. 'There are no Romans in these parts any more, Pacorus.'

I was surprised. 'Are you sure? I remember when I was last in Gordyene,' I nodded at Atrax, 'there were plenty of Romans there at that time.'

'There might be some in Armenia itself,' replied Vata, 'but there are none in Gordyene and no Romans raid our frontier.'

'They get others to do their dirty work,' complained Atrax.

'Gordyene is a refuge for thieves, murderers and bandits,' said Aschek, 'and a base from which our three kingdoms can be attacked.'

'Which is why I have demanded this meeting with Tigranes,' answered my father. 'It is within his power to stop these raids against us and restore peace between Armenia and Parthia. I have asked you all here so that he may see that our desire for peace is made from a position of strength.'

'What if he rejects our overtures, Varaz,' asked Farhad, 'what then?'

My father smiled at him. 'I have every reason to believe that he will not.'

'And what does the king of kings say on this matter, father?' I asked. 'For is it not his empire that is under threat from the Armenians and not just your kingdom, Media and Atropaiene?'

My father gave me a withering look. 'Mithridates wrote to me stating that he had every faith that Hatra could resolve the present difficulties with Armenia both amicably and peacefully.'

I laughed. 'The man is an ass. It is he who should be meeting with the Armenians tomorrow to demand they cease their hostilities.'

Farhad and Aschek looked at each other and then at my father, who sighed. 'I do not wish to discuss Mithridates, except to say that he would not travel to these parts knowing that the army of Dura would be camped at Nisibus and knowing that the safety of his royal person could not be guaranteed.'

'He is right about that,' I said, prompting Atrax to laugh.

My father pointed at me. 'I do not want a war with Armenia, Pacorus. You will keep your army in check.'

'Yes, yes,' said Farhad. 'No war, most definitely not.'

'Do not worry,' I told them, 'the army of Dura is also under tight control. It only does what I desire it to do.'

'That is what I am afraid of,' said my father.

The next day dawned overcast and drizzly as the legions marched north out of camp, escorted by the cataphracts in their scale armour and the horse archers. Because of the cold the legionaries, cataphracts and horse archers had their white cloaks around their shoulders and the legionaries had also been issued with leggings. I had no idea how long or short the meeting with Tigranes would be and I did not want the men to be standing for hours on end in a cold plain getting lashed by rain. The army marched along the east bank of the Mygdonius and then swung east to avoid Nisibus and the vast array of tents and animal parks that had sprung up around it since the arrival of the other kings.

A mile northeast of the city I was met by Vistaspa and a company of my father's bodyguard, while around half a mile behind him a long line of Hatra's horsemen were filing out of the city. A slight northerly breeze had picked up to make the morning even cooler. Vistaspa bowed his head.

'Good morning, majesty. The designated meeting spot is five miles north of the city. An Armenian delegation has already arrived to ensure protocol is observed. Your father would like your foot to be positioned in the centre of the line and your horsemen to their right.'

'When do our guests arrive?'

'There is no sign of Tigranes yet, though the delegation has sent word that he will be arriving before midday. In the meantime, your father wishes for all our forces to be arrayed before he appears.'

I nodded. 'Very well. Convey my greetings to my father.'

I dug my knees into Remus' flanks and rode to where Domitus was marching at the head of the Durans.

'The Durans and Exiles will deploy to the right of my father's horsemen, Domitus.'

He fell out and stood in front of me as his men filed past.

He looked towards the brooding shape of Mount Masius in the distance, its upper slopes wreathed in mist.

'Shitty day for a battle.'

'We are not here to fight a battle,' I told him.

He grinned savagely. 'If the enemy attacks I assume I have your permission to fight back.'

I frowned. 'They won't attack. They will take one look at our numbers and agree to peace.'

'Course they will.'

He raised his vine cane in salute and re-joined his men, barking orders for them to keep in step and not to talk in the ranks. He seemed happy enough.

It took two hours for the army to assemble, the Durans and Exiles arrayed in their standard battlefield formation of three lines. In the first line stood four cohorts, with three in the second and three in the third. Immediately to the right of the legions stood the cataphracts – five companies in the first line, each one two ranks deep, and five companies in the second. Deployed on their right were Dura's three thousand horse archers and beyond them Silaces and his eight thousand men.

The left flank of the army consisted of my father's fifteen hundred cataphracts and five thousand horse archers, Farhad's seven hundred cataphracts and five thousand horse archers and Aschek's one thousand cataphracts and three thousand horse archers. Immediately to the rear of the Hatran contingent were a further ten thousand horsemen that the region's lords had raised. This gave the army an impressive combined strength of just over forty-eight thousand men. In addition to this there were the five thousand men that Vata commanded to defend the region, but though he was here with my father his men were scattered far and wide providing protection for villages and the caravans on the Silk Road, garrisoning Nisibus and patrolling the borders.

When the army was finally in its positions I rode with Orodes to where my father waited on his horse at the head of his bodyguard. The breeze had picked up and his white horse head banner fluttered behind him, and was soon joined by Farhad's white dragon and Aschek's *shahbaz*. The red griffin of Dura and the eagle clutching a snake of Susiana completed the array of standards.

'A most impressive sight, father,' I said, looking left and right at the assembled troops.

'Let us hope the Armenians think so,' he replied sternly.

They appeared less than half an hour later as the clouds in the sky got blacker and blacker, a seething mass of horse and foot spewing from the tree-covered lower slopes of Mount Masius. Slowly and inexorably they filled the plain in front of us, a huge body of foot taking up position directly in front of the legions.

I sat for a full hour as the enemy host deployed into position, presenting a dazzling display of brightly coloured uniforms and hundreds of standards depicting the symbols of Armenia: the six-pointed star, eagle, lion, bull and the rosette, the eternal flower that signifies life everlasting. In front of the Durans and Exiles the Armenians placed their levy spearmen, individuals who had been raised from among the civilian population for the duration of this campaign. Like most civilians pretending to be soldiers they were poorly armed with only a spear and perhaps a dagger and a round wicker shield for protection. As far as I could tell they wore no armour and only linen caps on their heads. These spearmen were deployed in a single huge block that must have numbered at least twenty thousand men.

In front of the spearmen were positioned heavy swordsmen. These were professionals who wore mail shirts, helmets and carried oval shields faced with iron or bronze. Each man was armed with a long sword and two spears and their task was to hack through the ranks of the enemy foot standing opposite to create gaps through which the levy spearmen could sweep through like a raging torrent of floodwater. I estimated their number to be five thousand.

Either side of the heavy swordsmen were professional spearmen – men equipped with large, leather-faced wicker shields nearly the height of a man and armed with long spears. They wore leather armour and had helmets on their heads and their task was to stop the horsemen they faced. There were at least twenty thousand of these men extending left and right to oppose our cavalry. And behind them were their missile support – archers ready to release their arrows over their heads into the ranks of an attacker. Dotted all along the line were small groups of slingers, no doubt recruited from the lands that bordered the Black Sea.

Either side of this huge mass of foot were the Armenian horsemen: mounted archers carrying light axes, daggers and short swords in addition to their bows; spearmen in scale armour cuirasses, helmets and carrying round shields; and heavy cavalry riding partially armoured horses and armed with lances and swords. Impressive though they were, the Armenian horse numbered fewer than twenty thousand men.

Then the royal party appeared surrounded by two thousand fully armoured cataphracts. The horsemen in their glittering armour halted immediately opposite where we were positioned and a lone rider came from their ranks towards us. My father nodded to Vistaspa who likewise rode from our ranks to meet the Armenian representative halfway between the armies. An ominous stillness descended over the plain as around one hundred and twenty thousand men stared at each other.

After a few minutes Vistaspa returned to report to my father.

'Tigranes and his son will meet with the you and the other kings, majesty.'

'His son?' I said.

'Prince Artavasdes,' said Vata without enthusiasm. 'A treacherous snake.'

'Thank you, Vata,' my father rebuked him, 'kindly keep your thoughts to yourself.'

I rode with my father, Farhad and Aschek across the wet turf to meet the Armenian king, the first time that I encountered the man who had earned the title 'great'. At one time he had ruled this plain and Syria, but that was many years ago and since then Armenia's power had waned. As we approached and slowed our horses I saw that there were no Romans in Tigranes' party. My spirits rose in expectation of an agreeable meeting. I was wrong.

Tigranes himself was mounted on a large brown stallion with a red saddle and a great purple saddlecloth. He wore no armour but was dressed in a rich tunic striped in white and purple and a great purple cloak around his shoulders. He sat tall in the saddle, his height accentuated by a high hat adorned with diamonds and pearls. I knew he was nearly eighty years of age now and though his eyes were still sharp his face betrayed his great age, his skin wrinkled and his cheeks sunken.

Next to him, similarly adorned in rich purple robes, rode the man I assumed to be Prince Artavasdes. He had inherited his father's height though not his stature, appearing slightly diminished next to him. Artavasdes had a narrow face and a long nose that he held in the air to give him a haughty aspect. He had obviously been spending too much time among Romans!

Behind Tigranes rode two hulking cataphracts in short-sleeved scale armour and leg armour. They wore helmets and chainmail veils obscured their faces. They carried great maces in their hands but they were not here to intimidate, merely to even the numbers as four Armenians faced four Parthians. My father raised his hand to Tigranes.

'Hail Tigranes, great king of Armenia.'

Tigranes raised his hand in return as the drizzle started to turn to light rain.

'I came to this place, Varaz, because I know that you were a friend of Balas, late ruler of Gordyene, a man who I also held dear.' His voice was deep and commanding. 'Out of respect for his memory I decided to leave my warm palace to meet with you on this cold plain.'

'I am in your debt,' said my father, 'and hope that we may settle our differences today to the mutual benefit of all.'

Tigranes smiled at my father. 'Do Armenia and Hatra have differences? And I see the banners of Media and Atropaiene beside your own and recognise Farhad and Aschek before me. Do I take it that there are differences between Armenia and Media and Atropaiene also?'

'Media has suffered wrongs at the hands of Armenia's soldiers,' replied Farhad.

'As has Atropaiene,' added Aschek.

'My villages are attacked, the trade caravans are threatened,' said my father with force, 'and my people are murdered.'

'And Armenia is responsible for these depravations?' asked Tigranes.

'Raiders come though the mountain passes and from Gordyene,' continued my father. 'These regions are controlled by Armenia.'

'These are grave charges you levy against me,' said Tigranes, his eyes flashing menace. 'A king might take offence at such words.'

I saw Farhad and Aschek shift uneasily in their saddles. I knew that Aschek in particular did not want war with the Armenians, and ever since Media's defeat at the hands of the Romans and Prince Atrax's near fatal wounding, Farhad had also been reluctant to embroil his kingdom in further conflict.

'It is we who are offended,' I said, causing Tigranes and his son to look at me.

'And you are?' queried Tigranes.

'Pacorus, King of Dura Europos,' I answered.

Tigranes nodded and smiled ever so slightly. 'So you are the famed King Pacorus, the slayer of kings and the confidant of witches.'

'And the friend of slaves,' added Artavasdes, his voice mocking and slightly high pitched.

'Better than being the friend of Romans,' I answered, 'or their lackeys.'

Artavasdes bared his teeth at me and was about to rise to the bait but was stopped by a hand raised by his father.

'Tell me, King Pacorus,' said Tigranes, 'your domain lies far to the south of here. Why then would you concern yourself with matters in these parts?'

'Dura is an ally of Hatra,' I answered. 'Its problems are my problems and its wars are my wars.'

'But there is no war,' said Tigranes.

I fixed him with my eyes. 'Not yet.'

'Enough, Pacorus,' snapped my father. 'Hatra does not desire war, Tigranes, but conflict will break out if raids against my kingdom continue. This is my warning to you.'

Tigranes appeared unruffled by the threat, looking at Farhad and Aschek in turn. 'And Media and Atropaiene stand with Hatra in this?'

Farhad nodded and Aschek did likewise, though without conviction. Artavasdes saw their lack of belief and gloated.

'Dura also stands with Hatra,' I announced.

'Oh, I can see that,' said Tigranes, 'perhaps you wish for things to be settled here, today, King of Dura Europos?'

'Why not?' I replied indifferently.

'We did not come here to shed blood,' said my father, 'Pacorus forgets himself. But you can see with your eyes, Tigranes, that my words can be backed up with force if need be.'

Tigranes peered past us to where our combined forces were drawn up and smiled. 'You also have eyes, Varaz. Do they not see the multitude that I have brought with me?'

'They are but a fraction of the host that Armenia can put into the field,' boasted Artavasdes.

Perhaps Farhad and Aschek were intimidated by such threats but I had learned long ago that it was not numbers that counted in battle but training and discipline. I yawned.

'You are impertinent,' Tigranes said to me.

'And you are an old man, once called great but now a Roman puppet. Let us settle things now, on this ground, for I grow tired of hearing your words and the empty boasts of your preening son.'

Aschek sat on his horse with his mouth open and Farhad was looking in alarm at my father, who now spoke.

'You will leave us, Pacorus, so that wiser heads can resolve this problem.'

Artavasdes pointed at me. 'Do not start a war with us.'

'Or a conversation, it seems,' I retorted.

'Pacorus!' shouted my father, 'you will retire.'

I grabbed Remus' reins and turned him. 'You are wasting your time, father.' I dug my knees into Remus' sides and trotted back to where Orodes, Atrax, Aschek's sons and Vata waited.

'What is happening?' asked a concerned Orodes.

'Nothing,' I answered. 'Tigranes mocks us and we do nothing.'

I looked at Vata. 'You were right about his son. When he gains the throne things will get a lot worse for you.'

The rain got heavier as I pulled my cloak about me and waited for my father and the other two kings to return. When they did my father had a face like thunder.

'Well?' I asked.

'You made things worse, Pacorus,' he said wearily.

'Tigranes refuses to even acknowledge that his men are raiding our kingdoms,' added Farhad.

'We will just have to increase our security,' said Aschek, 'there is nothing else we can do.'

Cold, wet and drained, the three of them suddenly resembled old men. I thought of the smug expression on Artavasdes' face and the sardonic words of his father.

'There is something we can do,' I said, 'we can destroy Tigranes and his army.'

I pointed to where my legions faced the swordsmen and huge block of levy spearmen behind them.

'You see where their foot stands. If my legions attack they will shatter that screen of heavy swordsmen in front of the spearmen easily enough. Those spearmen behind may look impressive but they are just farmers and the like armed with sticks. My men can slaughter them without breaking sweat. With their centre shattered the Armenians will crumble.'

'He is right, father,' said Atrax to Farhad, his eyes alight at the prospect of glory.

I stoked his enthusiasm. 'We greatly outnumber them in cataphracts. One battle, that will settle it, and then there will be no more Armenian problem.'

'It would be good to lop that arrogant head off Artavasdes' shoulders,' remarked Vata.

Aschek peered at the Armenian host, now partly shrouded by the rain that was pouring from low-hanging black clouds.

'They outnumber us greatly, Pacorus.'

'Numbers are irrelevant,' I said. 'Farmers with sticks cannot withstand my legions, and my horsemen are well schooled in war, they live for battle.'

'And therein lies the problem, Pacorus,' said my father calmly. 'War is your constant companion. You have built your kingdom to nourish your army.'

I grinned at Atrax. 'What is wrong with that?'

'Wars are easy to start, Pacorus,' my father replied, 'but less easy to finish. You are currently at war with Mithridates and Narses, to say nothing of the armed peace you have with the Romans, and yet you seek another war here.'

'Better to die on your feet than live on your knees, father.'

Atrax whooped and Vata laughed but my father was not amused.

'If the Armenians attack we will defend ourselves. But I will not instigate hostilities.'

And so, as the rain coursed off my helmet, ran down my face and soaked my arms and legs, we watched as the Armenians, their banners now hanging soaked and limp from their flag staffs, began to slowly retreat from the field. The foot withdrew first, the damp and shivering hordes of spearmen, archers and slingers trudging back to the tree line to retrace their route back to Armenia. Then the heavy swordsmen followed them protected by the mounted spearmen. The royal party must have been the first to depart for I saw no sign of the Armenian cataphracts. Last to leave were the horse archers who formed a rear guard as the soldiers of four Parthian kingdoms stood immobile and watched them go.

It took two hours of standing before a burning brazier before the feeling returned to my soaking, cold feet and hands. As well as feeling like a drowned rat I also felt cheated. Cheated of the chance to do my father a great service.

'He doesn't see it like that,' said Domitus, holding his hands out to the red coals.

We were standing in front of my tent holding cups of warm wine that had been brought from the field kitchens. The dark and dank night was illuminated by the red glow from dozens of braziers, around which were clustered groups of men trying to warm themselves and dry their sodden clothing. There would be much rust to be removed from mail shirts in the morning.

'You start a war and he has to deal with it.'

284

I wasn't listening to him. 'We could have broken them easily. Did you see their foot? Most of them would have turned tail and run at the first opportunity.'

He rubbed his hands together. 'No point in agonising over what might have been. What will you do now?'

'Go back to Dura. What a complete waste of time this has been.'

'Pity we can't go via Gordyene,' said Domitus. 'At least we could try to destroy some of the bases the Armenians are using to launch raids from.'

'The one born in the land of water must be given his own army,' I found myself saying.

'What did you say?'

I smiled at him and slapped him on the arm. 'Of course, it makes perfect sense.'

He looked at me as though I was mad. 'It does?'

'My friend, you would not believe me if I told you.'

He eyed me warily. 'You sure you haven't caught some sort of fever?'

I went to bed happier than I believed I would and woke to discover that the rain had stopped and the sun was shining down from a sky largely devoid of clouds. It was a beautiful spring day laced with the scent of cyclamen, hyacinth, lavender and narcissus. As the men hung clothing and saddlecloths out to dry and the ground slowly warmed under the sun's rays, I sent a rider to Nisibus to invite Vata and Atrax to attend me, ostensibly to inspect the camp.

Atrax appeared at midday escorted by a hundred Median horse archers. Vata rode into camp an hour later accompanying a hundred wagons piled high with wine, fresh meat, bread and fodder for the horses.

'I thought it was the least I could do after your wasted trip, Pacorus.'

I embraced him. 'Not wasted, my friend. Come inside and take refreshment.'

After we had shared a jug of wine between us I escorted Atrax and Vata round the camp. It was the first time either of them had seen Dura's legionaries at close quarters.

'You have made good use of all those men from Pontus I sent south to you,' remarked Vata as a column of Exiles marched past to undertake two hours' drill outside the camp.

'They have made good soldiers,' I agreed.

'And the rest are all slaves?' asked Atrax.

'Some are former slaves,' I replied, 'some are free men who left their homelands because they were occupied or there was no work for them. In Dura's army they have good food and are paid regularly.'

'What will you do with them when there is no one left to fight?' asked Vata mischievously.

'There is always someone to fight, Vata, which brings me to the reason I invited you both here. I am considering a campaign in Gordyene.'

They both halted and looked at me.

'Gordyene is occupied by the Armenians,' said Vata dejectedly.

'But its people are Parthian,' I said. 'Do they not deserve to be liberated from their oppressors?'

Atrax let his head drop. 'My father would never agree to support such a campaign.'

'Neither would your father, Pacorus,' added Vata.

'I do not need their support,' I said, 'merely yours.'

They both looked at me in confusion as I led them back towards my tent. I explained to them both about the eight thousand men from Elymais who had sought refuge at Dura and who had marched north with the army.

'Gordyene lies on Hatra's eastern border and to the north of Media,' I said. 'You two could easily supply friendly forces from your respective territories. In this way the Armenians in Gordyene would be preoccupied with fighting Parthian troops instead of raiding Hatra and Media, and Atropaiene for that matter.'

Atrax was warming to the idea. 'In theory it is a good plan, Pacorus, but you know what happened the last time Parthians rode into Gordyene, they were defeated and nearly destroyed. I know, I was one of them, as were you.'

'I know that,' I agreed, 'but then we numbered but a thousand men. Eight thousand is a different matter, especially if they are regularly supplied with provisions and weapons.' I smiled at him. 'And reinforcements.'

'Waging war in enemy territory requires sound leadership,' said Vata, still far from convinced. 'Whoever commands your men must know what he is doing.'

We had returned to my tent and I gestured for them both to go into its interior.

'Fortunately I have just the man.'

I had commanded that Surena and Silaces attend us in my tent and now they both stood as we entered. After an orderly had served us wine I told everyone to sit at the table, after which I revealed my plan to Surena and Silaces.

'I would like you to be the commander of the expedition,' I told Surena, 'and you to be his second-in-command, Silaces.'

Surena clenched his fist in triumph. 'It would be an honour, lord.'

'This man was your squire, was he not?' asked Atrax, which earned him a sneer from Surena.

I laid my hand on Surena's shoulder. 'Squire, cataphract, company commander and now the man who leads my horse archers.'

I looked at Silaces. 'Before I authorise this expedition, I ask for your opinion on this matter for there is no guarantee that it will succeed or that you and your men will live to see its conclusion.'

'But lord,' interrupted Surena. I held up a hand to still him.

Silaces looked at me and then the other faces that were staring at him.

'We are the last remnants of King Gotarzes' army, majesty, and were it not for you we would no longer be a body of soldiers and he would not be remembered. You have given us back our pride and belief and kept the memory of our king alive. We are honoured to serve you in whatever capacity we can.'

Two days later Surena led eight thousand horsemen towards Gordyene, the whole army drawn up on parade to watch them depart. I sat on Remus with Orodes beside me as the men from Elymais carried the banner of the four-pointed star into Gordyene. Byrd and Malik had left the day before with their scouts to ensure they did not run straight into any large Armenian forces that had remained this side of the Taurus Mountains following our unsuccessful meeting with Tigranes. I told them they were to report back to me immediately after Surena had established a base in Gordyene.

He rode up to us as his new army trotted east, each man carrying three full quivers of arrows and leading a mule loaded with food and fodder for the horses. After they had exhausted their supplies they would receive fresh provisions from Atrax and Vata.

'Remember, Surena, resist the temptation to take anything from the local population. You have to win them over, not alienate them.'

He nodded. 'Yes, lord.'

He bit his lip, the first time that I had seen any nervousness in him. But then, this was a great leap he was taking. The responsibility for the lives of eight thousand men must be weighing heavily upon him.

I reached over and laid a hand on his forearm.

'Above all, remember all the things you have been taught these past few years. And if you believe that your presence in Gordyene is unsustainable then withdraw. There is no shame in retreat, only in refusing to see the blindingly obvious.'

He nodded, bowed his head and then moved forward to join his men.

'And Surena,' I called after him.

He stopped and turned in the saddle. 'Yes, lord?'

'Good luck.'

He smiled and then galloped away to lead his riders. Thus did Surena's campaign in Gordyene begin.

As the rear guard of the column disappeared into the distance Domitus ambled over to me.

'That's the last we'll see of them,' he mused.

'I think you underestimate Surena,' I replied. 'A friend told me that he would be very successful.'

He looked up at me quizzically.

'It's a long story, Domitus.'

I had kept any knowledge of Surena's expedition into Gordyene from my father, as I knew he would have disapproved. He took his own army back to Hatra the day after, visiting me in camp as his cataphracts and horse archers wound their way south with their accompanying squires, mules and camels. Domitus took Vistaspa on an inspection of the camp as I entertained him in my tent.

'When do you leave for Dura?'

'In a week or two,' I replied.

'Why so long?'

'I will spend some time with Vata. I have hardly seen him these past few years.

'No, he has been fully occupied.'

'You think the Armenians will continue with their raids.'

He looked at me with black-ringed eyes. 'Undoubtedly.'

'Then why did you not fight them when you had the chance?'

'I do not wish to go over that again, Pacorus. I do not seek war with the Armenians. If we had defeated them and perhaps killed Tigranes, what then?'

'Then you would have had a peaceful northern frontier.'

He shook his head. 'Then I would have had a Roman army on Hatra's northern border.'

'The Romans are preoccupied with their internal squabbles,' I reassured him.

'For the moment, yes, but once they have settled their differences they will turn their gaze towards Parthia once more.'

I smiled at him as I thought of the weapons I was supplying to Alexander in Judea. 'They might have other things to occupy themselves with other than Parthia, father.'

'You are spending too much time with that sorceress of yours, son, for you speak in riddles. How is the old witch?'

'Er, old,' I replied. 'Gallia likes her company and Claudia adores her, too much I think. How is young Spartacus?'

'He is growing big and strong and will make a fine warrior. You should come to Hatra and visit him. Your mother, Gafarn and Diana are always complaining that they do not see enough of you.'

'They are right. I will try not to be so remiss.'

It was an amicable parting between father and son as he left me to rejoin his men on their trek south back to Hatra. Later that day I rode with Orodes to Nisibus to bid farewell to Farhad and Aschek as they too took their armies home. When we arrived at the palace the courtyard was filled with hundreds of horsemen, each one armed with a spear and round, leather-faced wooden shield carrying the emblem of the white horse's head – Hatra's symbol. Each man was also armed with a bow and quiver.

A servant took our horses from us at the foot of the palace steps and we went inside the building. In the main hall we encountered Farhad, Atrax, Vata, Aschek and his sons. Vata was bidding them farewell while behind him a large knot of his officers stood in a group waiting for orders. The atmosphere was dripping with anxiety. I gripped Vata's arm.

'Problems?'

He ran a hand through his hair.

'As soon as the kings depart I have a caravan to protect. Four hundred camels loaded with spices, silk and ivory bound for Edessa and then Zeugma. You saw their escort in the courtyard.'

'Does not the caravan have its own guards?'

He smiled wryly. 'To keep away a few bandits and thieves, yes, but not enough to fend off an Armenian raiding party.'

He walked over to where Farhad and Aschek stood and bowed his head to them. I followed him and embraced them, then Atrax and Aschek's sons. Orodes, ever the diplomat, walked with them from the chamber. Atrax told his father he would catch him up as he pulled Vata and me aside.

'As soon as I get back to Media I will alert the outposts on our northern border to keep watch for Surena's men.'

'I will do likewise,' said Vata. 'I can send supplies and arrows but no men. I have my hands full as it is.'

I could see that he was agitated by the way his fingers fidgeted by his sides.

'Are you expecting the caravan to be attacked?' I asked him.

'Caravan?' enquired Atrax.

'Vata has a large caravan leaving Nisibus and fears it may be attacked.'

'I have no doubt the Armenians will try something,' he said, 'especially after the inconclusive meeting between the king and Tigranes.'

'How many men are you assigning to its protection?' I asked.

'A thousand.'

Atrax was stunned. 'That many?'

'I have no choice,' Vata replied. 'Any less and it will be too tempting a target.' He looked at me.

'I could ask my father to provide you with horsemen,' offered Atrax.

'Or perhaps we could entice the Armenians into a trap?' I suggested.

Vata was perplexed. 'Trap?'

'What would happen,' I continued, 'if the caravan had few guards?'

Vata laughed. 'We might as well take the goods it is carrying and leave them on the road for the Armenians to collect at their leisure.'

'What are you thinking?' Atrax asked me.

'Let the Armenians attack the caravan, except that it will not be a caravan, it will be a trap. Time to give the Armenians a bloody nose.'

Atrax grinned mischievously. 'Count me in.'

The headman in charge of the caravan was informed that his camels would not be able to commence their journey on account of a landslide on the road fifty miles from the city. Vata told him that he would have to remain in Nisibus for another seven days while the debris was cleared from the route.

The road to Edessa heads north from Nisibus and then west along the base of the foothills of the Taurus Mountains, running parallel to the forests that blanket their slopes. The Armenians usually established their camps deep in these forests, from which they launched attacks against the caravans. Vata often sent large parties of troops into the trees to track down and destroy these camps but it was a time-consuming business and he did not have the resources to establish outposts all along the road. I hoped that such a large caravan would attract a substantial number of Armenians.

For our trap we used four hundred of Dura's camels and strapped empty wooden chests from Nisibus on their backs. Each camel would have two attendants who would actually be a pair of Duran horse archers, their bows and quivers secured to the camels and hidden by canvas covers.

The fifty covered wagons would not be transporting highly prized items from the east but rather hand-picked legionaries, each wagon carrying eight men and their weapons and equipment. It would be a tedious journey for these men, cooped up under oilskin covers made to resemble a wagon piled high with goods. But at least they could take it in turns to be drivers. Only when the Armenians took the bait would they be able to spring into action. But then war is mostly long stretches of tedium and routine interrupted by brief periods of terror.

We left Nisibus three days later, four hundred legionaries hidden in the wagons and eight hundred horse archers disguised as camel attendants. I walked at the head of the column with my second-in-command camel herder – Orodes – while Atrax and a hundred of his Median horse archers provided the illusion of an escort. The weather was warm and mild and Mount Masius in the distance looked tall and imposing. The day after we left Vata and his thousand riders would follow us at a distance. This was to deceive the Armenian spies whom

290

he knew operated in Nisibus and who provided Tigranes with exact details of the movements of caravans. He and his horsemen would be able to close the distance between them and our caravan easily enough.

The first two days were uneventful, a pleasant enough stroll through a country seemingly at peace. We saw hares observing us warily from the long grass and antelopes peering at us from the safety of the trees that began around a quarter of mile to our right. The forest was a blanket of green, a vast covering of oak, sycamore, wild olive trees, pine, juniper, fir and cedar.

On the third day, having covered around fifty miles in total, my leg was beginning to ache from the walking and I began to develop a slight limp. Atrax, who was riding beside us, saw my discomfort.

'Ride for a while on my horse, Pacorus.'

'No, thank you,' I replied. 'For one thing your own limp will make a prolonged period of walking most uncomfortable for you, and for another it will look highly suspicious if the commander of the escort gives up his horse to a camel herder.'

'You think we are being watched?' asked Orodes, looking like a vagabond in his long beige robe and head cloth.

'Undoubtedly,' I answered.

Atrax turned and peered at the trees.

'Perhaps we could move off the road and onto the plain, to increase the distance between us and the trees.'

'I think not, my eager friend,' I said. 'We want them to take the bait. Just you make sure that you and your men desert us when they attack.'

He was most unhappy. 'I should not leave my friends to fight alone, it is dishonourable.'

Orodes said nothing but I knew he was thinking the same.

'Listen,' I said. 'The whole aim of this little expedition is to entice the Armenians from their forest abode into the open where they can be destroyed. When they appear, Atrax, you and your men will run, thereby convincing them that we are defenceless. Remember the plan.'

'I hope your foot soldiers know what they are doing,' said Atrax with concern.

I smiled at him. 'Don't you worry about them. They are led by a burly German named Thumelicus who knows what he is doing.'

'What's a German?' he asked.

'An inhabitant of a land called Germania, a great distance from these parts.' I tilted my head towards the trees. 'I have never been there, but the Germans in my army tell me that it is mostly forests filled with wild beasts and even wilder people. Even the Romans fear and respect them.'

291

Atrax looked at the forest and then behind us to the road where the wagons ambled along in two sections, each one of twenty-five wagons, one of which contained Thumelicus.

'Don't worry,' I said to him, 'we will still be here when you return with reinforcements.'

The rest of the day and the morning of the next passed without incident and I was beginning to think that we might have wasted our time. Perhaps my father's words and our show of strength had intimidated Tigranes into issuing orders that there were to be no more attacks on the Silk Road caravans. I looked up at the puffy white clouds that filled the sky and the blue in between them and smelled the pleasing aroma of mint and lavender. Atrax had fashioned me a walking stick from a branch that he had cut and now I held it in my left hand while Orodes walking beside me on my left led the camel, an evil beast with a nasty bite and a vindictive nature.

'I'm going to ask her to be my wife,' he announced suddenly. 'Even though I am only a prince and she is a queen.'

'Marry? What are you talking about?'

Orodes suddenly stopped to face me.

'Axsen, Queen Axsen. I am going to ask her to marry me.'

He wore a look of a man who had just been told he had minutes to live instead of one gripped by joy. I burst out laughing. Only Orodes could tinge such a happy announcement with severity.

'You think I have no chance, that I offend protocol by thinking a prince, a landless prince, could ask for the hand of a queen in marriage?'

I laughed even louder, which caused his face to darken even more.

I laid a hand on his shoulder. 'My friend, I think that she would be both honoured and flattered to receive such a proposal. I think the gods will smile on your union.'

He now wore the look of a man who had been reprieved moments before his execution.

'You really think so?'

'Axsen is possessed of a kind heart and noble nature. She has been looking for her prince for many years and now she has found him. I am truly happy for you.'

He grinned. 'And you and Gallia will come to the wedding, if she accepts my proposal, that is?'

'She will accept and yes, we will come to the wedding. Nothing will stop us.'

His grin disappeared as he looked past me. 'They might.'

I turned to see a great mass of men emerging from the trees, hundreds of them. So, they had come at last.

I dropped my stick and threw off my robe, then with Orodes loosened the straps that held the waxed canvas cover in place on the camel's back. We pulled our bows from their cases and then slung a quiver strap over our right shoulders so we could pull arrows from our quivers with our right hands. I glanced down the road and saw that the other archers were doing the same, each one taking up position behind the front and rear of their camels. Atrax galloped towards me.

'Go, go,' I shouted at him.

He halted, turned and then galloped back down the road with his riders thundering after him. So far, so good.

Like Orodes I wore only a shirt, leggings and boots under my robe, which I now discarded, though I also had my silk vest under my shirt. My sword and dagger were hanging from my hips. I scanned the tree line, in front of which was a great black mass of advancing men carrying what looked like round shields and spears. They were walking towards our now stationary column, the men inside the wagons still hidden from view and our 'escort' having fled for their lives. I also saw horsemen coming from the trees, no doubt tribal chiefs and their personal bodyguards – men in helmets wielding swords and carrying round, brightly painted shields. These men rode to the head of the warriors on foot and began to gallop up and down the line, waving their swords in the air as they did so. No doubt they were encouraging them with promises of loot after they had slaughtered us.

There must have been at least three thousand foot and two hundred horsemen coming at us, at first walking and then breaking into a gentle trot as they got within five hundred paces of our position. The men on horseback were trotting a few paces beyond their front ranks, shouting behind them to encourage those following. The foot soldiers were widely spaced and I could see that in addition to their spears many had axes tucked into their belts. But they wore no armour and most had nothing on their heads.

'Someone is going to get a nasty surprise in a minute,' said Orodes, nocking an arrow in his bowstring and aiming it at the oncoming mass.

When they had advanced to within four hundred paces we began shooting. In the saddle a horse archer can lose around five to six arrows a minute, but now, standing and with spare quivers, we shot one every six seconds to create an arrow storm into which the Armenians ran. We did not bother to aim but rather shot and then strung another arrow, one after another, filling the air with deadly raindrops as the arrows arched into the air and then pelted the enemy.

Within a minute eight thousand arrows had been loosed at those ragged ranks, the bronze arrowheads hissing in anger as they struck wicker shields, flesh and bone. At first the Armenians did what all soldiers do when they encountered the unexpected in battle – they halted. It was an added bonus for us that these were not soldiers but

293

hill men, warriors used to fighting as individuals around their chiefs rather than as part of a disciplined unit. So they halted as arrows dropped from the sky to thin their ranks, and when they did so more arrows fell on them to inflict further casualties. A few arrows struck eye sockets as the stupid ones looked into the sky; these men died instantly. Others struck necks and even hearts to kill their victims but most lodged themselves in arms, feet, legs and thighs to wound and disable.

I had emptied two quivers when I heard the shrill sound of whistles being blown and took a few steps back to see legionaries pouring from the wagons.

'Time to go, Orodes,' I shouted, picking up another two quivers.

The other archers shooting from behind their camels left their beasts and similarly sprinted towards where the legionaries were forming up by the side of the column of wagons and camels. The plan was for them to deploy in five centuries, each one made up of four ranks of twenty men. They had no javelins as the archers that were now running as fast as they could to take up position behind the centuries would provide missile support. I arrived sweating and panting at the left flank of our makeshift battle line, while in front of us the chiefs were screaming and cursing at their men to move forward to attack us.

The Armenians had spread out to envelop the whole of the caravan to ensure nothing escaped their greedy clutches, but now they had to compress themselves into a tight mass to attack our force that had seemingly appeared out of nowhere. As they did so I saw that the grass to left and right was littered with dead and wounded men, some of the latter crawling and limping back towards the tree line.

I heard a deep voice ahead bellowing orders.

'Keep tight, keep tight. Wait for the order to attack.'

I recognised Thumelicus' voice.

'I will be back,' I said to Orodes and then pushed my way through the century that stood on the far left of the line to see the Armenian throng around three hundred paces away. I ran over to where Thumelicus was standing a few paces beyond his front rank, *gladius* in hand. He was so big and bulky that his helmet always looked too small for his head and his shield, which normally covered three-quarters of the body, appeared inadequate to protect his great frame.

He acknowledged me and then went back to staring at one of the Armenian chiefs directly ahead, a huge man draped in a black bearskin cloak and armed with a great sword who was jabbing it at Thumelicus and shouting something, no doubt promising to send him to the afterlife.

'He's making a lot of noise,' he said calmly.

'Too much,' I agreed, then pulled an arrow from my quiver and nocked it in my bowstring.

The chief was pulling on his horse's reins to turn the beast so he could scream at his men behind, then he dug his knees into its sides to move him along his line of warriors. Then he faced front again to point his sword at Thumelicus to hurl more abuse.

'Do you think he is asking me to marry one of his daughters?' asked Thumelicus.

'I doubt it,' I replied, then released my bowstring.

It took the arrow around four seconds to strike the chief, hitting him in his right shoulder and causing him to wilt in the saddle and drop his sword.

Thumelicus beamed with delight. 'Nice shot.'

Behind us the legionaries cheered and whistled with delight.

'That will stir them up,' I said. 'Stay alive, Thumelicus.'

'You too, Pacorus.'

I left him to return to Orodes as a great roar came from the Armenian ranks. And then they charged. It was not a disciplined advance but a wild rush of enraged, feral men with axes and spears seeking only to get to grips with those they faced as quickly as possible to exact revenge for their friends who had been felled by arrows, and now their chief who had been wounded.

At a range of two hundred paces from Thumelicus' front ranks the arrows began striking them again, shot by the men standing behind the centuries. We loosed four volleys before the two lines clashed, at the last moment the front ranks of legionaries charging at the oncoming Armenians rather than waiting to be hit by the wall of axe-wielding savages hurtling towards them.

A brutal mêlée began as the Armenians hacked with their weapons at the tightly packed ranks in front of them, as more and more of their comrades behind them pressed forward and forced those in front against the Duran shields. And from below and above the latter came *gladius* thrusts, like hundreds of hornet stings, stabbing into groins, thighs, guts and through shields. I heard terrible screams as Armenian bellies were sliced open, eyes were put out and genitals were reduced to bloody messes.

I smiled when, above the horrible cries, I heard the chant 'Dura, Dura' as Thumelicus and his men turned the front ranks of the enemy into a heap of dead flesh. The enemy dead, held upright by the Duran shields to the front and the press of Armenians from behind, now formed a barrier between the two sides. The Armenians resorted to throwing their axes at the heads of the legionaries, but the ranks behind the first had hoisted their shields above their heads to form a roof of leather and wood to defeat missiles.

Some groups of Armenians, seeking to take advantage of their greater numbers, attempted to sweep around our flanks but were spotted and felled by arrows. After dozens of them were shot in a matter of minutes the rest fell back. And then, above the screams, curses, shouts and moans, I heard a new sound and then felt the ground rumble. To my right I heard horns being blown and knew that Vata had come.

The Hatran horsemen had actually been trailing the caravan on a parallel route some five miles to the south. Any Armenian scouts in the forest would have confirmed that the caravan was not being followed but would not have seen Vata's men at such a distance – and the latter were under orders to light no fires at night – thus the surprise was complete.

The horsemen swept round our flanks, one group led by Vata the other by Atrax. They did not shoot their bows but instead first used their spears to kill the Armenians. Each wing wheeled inwards to trap the Armenians and went to work with their swords, hacking left and right at men trying to escape back to the tree line. But they were too far away from the safety of the forest and were being hunted by men on horseback, and so soon the plain was covered with more dead as Vata's men, working in their companies, charged, reformed and then charged again to cut down the enemy.

The legionaries leaned on their shields and the archers unstrung their bows as the horsemen finished their slaughter at the tree line.

Not all the enemy warriors were killed, a few escaped into the forest to tell the tale of their defeat to their tribes, while those who had been wounded by arrows at the beginning of the engagement had managed to hobble into the trees. Whether those men would live depended on how quickly they reached their villages and the skill of their healers.

A quick roll call revealed that our own casualties were ten dead and fifteen wounded. Most of the camels had taken themselves off to avoid the battle and so Vata sent out patrols to get them back. It had been a very satisfactory ambush.

We burned our own dead, left the Armenian corpses to the vultures and retraced our steps back to Nisibus. That night we celebrated our victory and toasted the forthcoming marriage of Orodes and Axsen.

'But she has not accepted,' he protested as we stood round a raging fire, 'she does not even know that I am going to ask for her hand in marriage.'

I slapped him on the shoulder. 'She will know soon enough and will accept, I promise you.'

Word had spread of his intentions and soon a great crowd had gathered behind us and began chanting 'Orodes, Orodes' as the Prince of Susiana grinned sheepishly and a drunken Thumelicus nearly crushed the life out of him when he locked him in a bear hug. Atrax, having spent the whole afternoon hunting down and slaughtering Armenian stragglers to 'atone' for his having deserted us earlier in the day, was the happiest I had seen him, and even Vata resembled my old carefree friend once more. It had been a good day for them and for Hatra, and I felt satisfied that I had given the Armenians a bloody nose. Perhaps Tigranes would now think twice before antagonising Hatra.

The next morning we made our way back to Nisibus in high spirits. But our mood soon darkened when we received news that the Armenians were the least of our problems.

Chapter 12

The empire was fortunate in having an excellent courier system whereby every kingdom maintained a system of post stations along every major road at intervals of thirty miles or so. Comprising nothing more than a one-storey building with stables and barn attached, when a courier arrived he left his mount behind and rode a fresh horse to the next station. In this way letters could travel up to ninety miles a day in extreme circumstances, though it was usual for a courier to travel sixty miles a day. In this way a letter could travel the breadth of the empire – a thousand miles – in around seventeen days. In Dura it was slightly different as the forts that I had built up and down the kingdom also acted as post stations, but the result was the same. It was a curious thing that even in times of civil strife the communications system was respected by all sides and not interfered with, no doubt because couriers were an excellent way of transmitting threats and abuse.

I thanked Shamash that we had such a system, for when we returned to Nisibus I found that there had been a flurry of letters sent to the city, all of them conveying ill tidings. I also arrived to find my father had returned to the city with Vistaspa, neither of them being in particularly good moods. It was late afternoon when we rode through the city's two surrounding brick walls, between which was a deep moat spanned by several bridges. We left our horses at the palace stables. The wagons and camels carried on south back to camp. I had written a short note to Domitus informing him of our victory over the Armenians and recommending Thumelicus for promotion.

Vata had pointed to my father's banner flying over the palace when we entered the palace grounds, signalling that the king was in residence.

'Bad sign that your father is back so quickly. Something must be awry.'

I asked him, Atrax and Orodes not to say anything concerning Surena's expedition into Gordyene.

'Perhaps he knows already,' mused Orodes as we walked into the palace's main hall.

My father watched us enter and walk to the dais as the doors were closed behind us. He was sitting in a great wooden chair with the black-eyed Vistaspa standing beside him. My father had his elbow resting on the arm of the chair, his chin on his palm. He resembled a brooding wolf.

We stood before him and bowed our heads. He began tapping his fingers on the chair's other arm.

'Who rules in Hatra?' he said at length.

I looked at Vata and then Orodes in confusion.

'You do, father, of course,' I replied.

He leaned back in the chair, bringing his hands together in front of his chest.

'Are you certain of that?'

I spread out my hands. 'I do not understand, father.'

He stood up slowly. 'Do you not? Then tell me, Pacorus, what would you say of a king who allows another king into his realm to fight his own private war? How is your war with the Armenians going, by the way?'

Orodes and Vata shifted uneasily while Atrax looked shamefaced.

'I was merely trying to reinforce the safety of your kingdom, father, by sending a clear message to the Armenians,' I said.

My father looked at Vata. 'Did you not have enough soldiers at your disposal to protect the caravan, Vata?'

'Yes, majesty,' he replied, 'but Pacorus, that is King Pacorus, suggested that we might lay a trap for the Armenians.'

'I see,' said my father, 'and as the governor of the north you thought that you would obey the King of Dura instead of me?'

Vata was squirming now. 'Of course not, majesty, but we had an opportunity to inflict losses on the Armenians that would make the road to Edessa safer.'

'Whether the road to Edessa is now safer than before remains to be seen, but your decision to support my son in his folly would normally have cost you your command.'

Vata blinked and the colour drained from his cheeks.

'Father,' I protested, but he held up his hand to still me.

'I said normally because events in the east are more pressing and I cannot yet afford to dispense with his services, or yours.'

'Events in the east?' I enquired.

An ironic smile crept across his face. 'Five days ago word reached me at Hatra that a great army has passed through the Caspian Gates and is advancing west.'

Atrax cast me a concerned glance, which was spotted by my father. 'You are right to be alarmed, Prince Atrax, for a message arrived for you here at Nisibus this very morning.'

My father snapped his fingers and pointed to a servant standing by a pillar to the side of the dais. The man, who held a silver tray in front of him on which was a letter, walked briskly over to Atrax and bowed his head, holding out the tray to my friend. Atrax took the letter and opened it.

'The seal was unbroken,' said my father, 'but if I was to guess I would say that it is from your father urgently requesting your presence at Irbil.'

Atrax read the letter and looked at my father, who leaned back in his chair.

'You are correct, majesty,' he said. 'My father requires me back in Media.'

'A more serious challenge than killing a few mountain bandits I assume, lord prince.'

My father nodded to Vistaspa.

'We have received other news, though its accuracy as yet cannot be confirmed,' said my father's second-in-command flatly, 'of a great army assembling at Ctesiphon and another at Persis.'

'Three armies?' I said.

My father pointed at Vata. 'Get a map of the empire and bring it here.'

'We do not have a map of the empire, majesty,' said Vata apologetically.

One of his stewards, a gaunt man in his forties dressed in a long brown robe, stepped forward and bowed his head to Vata.

'The chief archivist may know of such a chart among his documents, lord.'

'Go and tell him to search his archives, then,' ordered Vata.

The man bowed and scurried off, leaving the four of us standing before my father and feeling distinctly uncomfortable.

'You must be thirsty after your great victory,' said my father mockingly. He nodded to another servant who brought us silver cups filled with wine, serving my father and Vistaspa first.

My father rose from his seat and held his cup aloft.

'What shall we toast? Victory, or a glorious war before Atropaiene, Media, Babylon and Mesene are all crushed, their cities reduced to ashes and their peoples either killed or enslaved?'

We shuffled on our feet and said nothing. My father drained his cup.

'Why so bashful? Pacorus, you of all people should be glad that the eastern half of the empire is now marching west. Have you not desired this war for a long time, a final reckoning with Mithridates and Narses?'

'I have only desired justice,' I replied through gritted teeth.

Our further discomfort was spared when the steward returned with a stooping man in his sixties at least who was clutching a rolled-up map. He had thinning white hair and took small steps as he shuffled towards the dais.

'You have a map of the empire?' my father asked him.

'Yes indeed, majesty,' he replied, bowing and dropping the map on the floor. My father rolled his eyes.

'Place it on the table,' he instructed.

The archivist bowed again, picked up the map and then shuffled over to the table and unrolled it, brushing away cobwebs from its edges. The hide map was intricately detailed, showing all the empire's major rivers, kingdoms, cities and mountain ranges.

'It has been in the library here for at least fifty years though I suspect it is older,' reported the archivist as he admired it. 'I believe that it was produced by a Greek whose name escapes me, though he was clearly influenced by his fellow countryman Hipparchos, who I believe lived for most of his life in Greece but who travelled widely in these parts.'

'Thank you for being most informative,' said my father, stepping from the dais and walking to the side of the table. 'You may go.'

The archivist bowed and ambled from our presence.

'Please join me,' said my father, his tone indicating it was a command rather than a request.

With our full cups still in our hands we gathered at the table to stare at the map.

My father began to speak, uttering his thoughts rather than engaging us in a conversation.

'Messages sent from Hyrcania and Margiana indicate that four kings have marched through the Caspian Gates – Monaeses of Yueh-Chih, Tiridates of Aria, Cinnamus of Anauon and Vologases of Drangiana. This host is made up of only horsemen so it may move quickly, and it is heading in our direction.'

He pointed to the area between Lake Urmia and the Caspian Sea.

'They mean to attack Media, Atropaiene and then Hatra, all the kingdoms that have supported Dura against Mithridates.'

His hand moved further south across the map.

'If the reports concerning Mithridates and Narses are true, then they are gathering another army at Ctesiphon. This can only mean that they will once again strike at Babylon.'

I looked at Orodes and saw alarm etched on his face.

'Mesene can aid Babylon, father,' I said.

My father looked at me and then at Vistaspa, who now spoke.

'Word is that King Phriapatius of Carmania is moving west with his army and has reached Persepolis.'

'Which means,' continued my father, 'that he will attack the Kingdom of Mesene, which in turn will prevent King Nergal from assisting Babylon. Thus does Mithridates gather the whole of the east to attack us.'

I looked at the map and my heart sank. I had been so preoccupied with planning and preparing my own campaign against Mithridates and Narses that I had given no thought to the notion that they might be doing the same. But now it seemed I had underestimated them once again. The silence in the hall was deafening as we stood rooted to the spot. Atrax broke the silence.

'I must return to Media, lord.'

'Let us hope, lord prince,' said my father, 'that there is still a Media to return to.'

Atrax left the next morning with his bodyguard. He came to see me in camp before his journey, promising to aid Surena when he could but fearing that the great army moving towards the borders of his father's kingdom would absorb all his time, to say nothing of Media's resources. I stood with Domitus and Orodes and watched him and his men ride from camp. I placed an arm on Orodes' shoulder.

'Do not fear, my friend, the walls of Babylon are stout and high.'

He smiled wanly. 'Even the strongest city cannot hold out indefinitely, Pacorus.'

I knew what he was thinking: that he should ride south with his men and be by the side of Axsen when the storm broke against Babylon's walls. But I needed his men with me where they would be more use rather than cooped up inside a city. That said, if he decided to ride to his beloved there was nothing I could do. I prayed that for the moment his head would rule his heart.

We went back inside the tent and took our seats at the table, an air of uncertainty hanging over us. Domitus extracted his dagger from his sheath and began toying with it.

'Well,' he said, 'are we marching back to Dura?'

'That would seem to be the most logical course of action,' added Orodes. 'If the Kingdom of Babylon falls then Nergal at Uruk will be cut off and Mithridates will be able to reduce Mesene with ease. And after that Dura will be attacked.'

He was right, but I was loathe to leave my father's kingdom knowing that a great army was marching in its direction. And yet if Babylon fell then Nergal would also be destroyed and after that Dura would feel the wrath of Narses and Mithridates. I suddenly realised that I had only one chance to make the right decision, for otherwise all would be lost. How the gods must be enjoying this.

'Hatra's army is strong,' I said. 'We will march south to aid Babylon. There may be three armies attacking our friends and allies, but only one of those is important, the one led by Mithridates and Narses. Destroy that and we win the war.'

Orodes was nodding and Domitus had stopped playing with his dagger.

'It is agreed, then,' I said. 'We march east to the Tigris and then down its west bank to Babylon, and then we will have a final reckoning with Mithridates and Narses.'

I heard the sound of horses' hooves outside and then men's voices. The flap of the tent opened and my father walked in followed by Vistaspa and two agitated sentries.

'It is fine,' I told them.

They disappeared as my father helped himself to a cup of water from the jug on the table and then sat in one of the chairs, Vistaspa standing behind him.

'This is an unexpected pleasure, father. Have you come to inspect my camp?'

'A courier arrived two hours ago with news concerning the army advancing from the east. It has divided just west of the Caspian Gates. One half under Monaeses and Tiridates is moving northwest towards Media and Atropaiene; the other led by Cinnamus and Vologases is heading directly west towards Hatra.'

'The enemy splits his forces,' remarked Domitus.

My father smiled at him savagely. 'That is right, Roman, he divides his forces, so confidant is he that he will be victorious. And by doing so he gives us a small chance, a glimmer of hope, to avert disaster.'

He drank from his cup and looked at me.

'Perhaps we may achieve more if the famed army of Dura will stay in these parts to aid me.'

'We have a chance to trap and destroy the invaders,' added Vistaspa.

'I had thought of taking the army south to aid Babylon,' I said, looking at Orodes. 'Surely Hatra can raise enough men to match the combined forces of Anauon and Drangiana?'

My father nodded. 'I can raise a host of men, yes, but they are not trained soldiers, not like those whose only task is war. I still need Vata to hold the north but will take his five thousand men with me. The lords in these parts can muster their retainers to hold Nisibus and the surrounding area. Gafarn can hold the city of Hatra with the garrison and a muster of my lords – a total of sixty thousand men, give or take. That leaves me with seven thousand horse archers and a thousand cataphracts that I will collect at Hatra, plus my bodyguard and Vata's five thousand horse archers.'

'Thirteen and a half thousand men,' said Domitus.

'How many march against you, lord?' asked Orodes.

My father looked at Vistaspa, who answered.

'We have no accurate reports, but a tally of eighty thousand has been mentioned more than once.'

Orodes' eyes widened at this great figure and even I was a little surprised.

'With your own army, Pacorus, that will give us a fighting chance,' said my father.

'Under thirty thousand men,' added Domitus.

Vistaspa looked confused. 'Do they not teach mathematics in Italy, Domitus? You marched into these parts with over twenty thousand men.'

Domitus looked at me to reply.

'I sent some horsemen away with Atrax,' I lied, 'as reinforcements.'

My father frowned. 'It would be better if they had remained. Still, we might yet prevail.'

I ordered food and drink to be brought from the field kitchens as he and Vistaspa revealed their plan to us. They had brought with them the map of the empire that the pedantic archivist had unearthed among his records, and which was now spread on the table before us. Despite the current dire situation the western kingdoms found themselves in, my father and his subordinate appeared to have been animated by the prospect of the coming fight.

I looked at the map, specifically at the course of the River Tigris, which the enemy had to cross to enter Hatran territory.

'The first question is, where will the enemy strike?'

'That is easy enough,' replied Vistaspa, pointing at the river to the east of the city of Hatra. 'They will cross the Tigris at Assur, which lies only sixty miles to the east of Hatra.'

'Even though it is now nearly summer,' added my father, 'there are only a few places that large numbers of horsemen can ford the Tigris. Assur is one such place. The water level will have dropped by now and its depth will be around six feet, perhaps less. The Plain of Makhmur lies across the river from Assur, which is flat and fertile. An army can establish a camp there prior to fording the river. Once over the river they can ride across flat land all the way to Hatra. They have to be stopped at the river.'

'They could be allowed to cross the river and advance inland,' I suggested, 'to walk into a trap.'

'I do not want eighty thousand horsemen running amok in the east of my kingdom,' replied my father. 'No, they have to be stopped at the river.'

'How far away is this place, this Assur?' asked Domitus.

'Two hundred miles south of here,' replied Vistaspa.

'Ten days' march,' mused Domitus. 'And how far away is the enemy from Assur?'

'They have halted at the city of Ecbatana, two hundred and fifty miles east of the Tigris,' said Vistaspa. 'The governor, one of Mithridates' friends, is entertaining Cinnamus and Vologases, so I have heard.'

Domitus stared at the map and counted on his fingers.

'They can reach the river in nine days.'

My father smiled. 'Do not worry, Roman, they will linger at Ecbatana a while longer.'

'We have received reports that a lavish festival has been laid on to celebrate their arrival,' said Vistaspa, 'with games, apparently.'

'We will leave at dawn,' I announced.

My father smiled and Vistaspa nodded approvingly.

'Trees,' Domitus said suddenly.

Orodes looked at him in bewilderment.

'Trees?'

'Are there any trees at Assur?'

My father frowned. 'You are a keen student of foliage, Roman?'

Domitus looked at me. 'Remember Mutina all those years ago, how we faced a forest of stakes? I have not forgotten that day.'

I nodded. 'You are right, well done. And no, as far as I can remember there are no trees in the vicinity of Assur, at least no tall ones.'

'Then we will be marching in three days' time,' said Domitus.

Having explained what Domitus was referring to, my father and Vistaspa rode back to the city to inform Vata that they would be taking his troops with them when they rode south and that he was to summon the lords and their men to perform garrison and caravan protection duties.

It took two days to recall Vata's men from the outlying villages and assemble them in Nisibus, during which time Domitus and Kronos organised parties to cut down as many trees as they could. Six cohorts were sent into the forests to fell trees and the others organised transport to ferry the lumber back to camp where it was fashioned into six-foot-long stakes. Working all day and through the night with the aid of torches and great fires made from freshly cut branches – which produced a great deal of choking smoke – in two days we must have cut down a thousand trees. After we had finished it looked as though a giant had been to work at the edge of the forest with a massive scythe.

I asked Vata to send additional wagons from Nisibus to carry the wood and eventually we filled a hundred and fifty for the journey south. The day before we left Byrd and Malik returned to us with their scouts to report that Surena and his men had entered Gordyene unseen. I told them both what had happened since they had been away and how we were marching south to Assur. That night I wrote a letter to Gallia telling her everything that had happened and adding a footnote concerning Orodes' desire to marry Axsen. I also asked her to remain at Dura. I said nothing of the army forming at Ctesiphon preparing to march against Babylon. If she got wind of the city being in peril she might be tempted to muster Dura's lords and march south to Axsen's aid. If she did they would be cut to pieces by Narses' heavy cavalry. I prayed to Shamash that He would prevent Dobbai having any visions about Babylon's predicament until I returned to Dura.

Heavily loaded with provisions and lumber the army marched southeast to the Tigris and then followed the river south to Assur. As the days passed the heat of a Mesopotamian summer began to roast our backs as the country turned from a lush green to a parched brown and then a sun-blasted yellow. The men stashed their leggings on the wagons and horsemen brought out their floppy hats to shield their necks and faces from the unrelenting sun. We made twenty miles every day, most of the horsemen walking beside their mounts for most of the journey, riding only when they were sent out on patrol. Even though we were in my father's kingdom I sent out reconnaissance patrols to scout the surrounding country, and Byrd and Malik rode far ahead, sending patrols into the villages. With eighty thousand or more enemy soldiers somewhere on the other side of the Tigris I did not want to run into any nasty surprises on our journey south.

The first five days were quiet and uneventful, the only opposition being the heat and the dust that was kicked up as we marched across the parched earth. The days were cloudless, windless and very hot; the nights clear, cooler and welcome. On the sixth day, in the early afternoon, Byrd and Malik rejoined the army after having spent the night with some of their men south of the army. They found me walking with Orodes, Domitus and Kronos in front of the Duran Legion's colour party. The sun was illuminating its golden griffin and making it appear almost molten.

'No sign of enemy,' reported Byrd.

'We have ridden to within forty miles of Assur, Pacorus,' added Malik, 'and have made contact with outriders from the garrison. They too have seen nothing.'

'It would appear that we have stolen a march on the enemy, then,' I said. 'What news of my father?'

'The king is marching from Hatra with his army, Assur's men inform us,' replied Byrd. He nodded towards the river. 'Water very low, Pacorus. Easy for horses to cross.'

He was right about that. The passing of the spring floodwaters swells the Tigris, especially when it receives the waters of the Upper Zab River that flows into it fifty miles upstream of Assur. But now summer was here the waters had subsided and the depth had dropped, the high-sided banks the only indication of the levels the waters had reached during the spring. Now the Tigris was a lazy brown monster that meandered its way south across the great plains of eastern Hatra and western Media.

We reached Assur two days later, making camp four miles north of the city and inland from the river. The city itself had been constructed on a great bend in the river so that the Tigris protected its northern and eastern walls like a giant moat. In addition, a proper moat had been dug to encompass the other two sides using water from the river so that the city was surrounded on all four sides by water in addition to its walls. There were three entrances to Assur: the Tabira Gate in the northwest, the West Gate and the South Gate, each one reached by means of wide stone bridges that spanned the fifty-foot-wide moat. And from each gatehouse flew the white horse head banner of my father.

I had visited the city several times when I had been a boy and remembered that there had always been a great deal of building work being undertaken during each visit. The city itself was three thousand years old and had been the capital of the ancient Assyrian Empire eight hundred years ago. It had been besieged and destroyed several times since then and it was only during the rule of my father's father, King Sames, that Assur's defences were significantly strengthened. It was now the administrative centre of eastern Hatra.

I rode with Orodes, Domitus, Byrd and Malik through the Tabira Gate to visit the governor of the city and the man who held the east of the kingdom for my father, Herneus. In the times of the Persian Empire he would have been titled satrap, as he had both civil and military authority over a large area and controlled the many brick-built forts dotted along the western bank of the Tigris that we had passed on our journey south. Most had been empty because Herneus had summoned their tiny garrisons to Assur.

The northern quarter of the city housed the religious district, with temples devoted to Anu, Ishtar and Shamash. The governor's palace was located next to the temple area and the garrison's barracks, stables and armouries occupied the northeastern part of the city. The southern area of Assur was where the general population lived: a sprawling collection of one- and two-storey homes, markets, businesses, workshops, brothels, stables, animal pens and shops arranged along streets that had been constructed in a haphazard fashion. It really was a city of two halves: order, power and serenity in the north; chaos, poverty and over-crowding in the south.

At the gates we were met by a mounted party from the city garrison, soldiers dressed in white shirts and leggings armed with spears and swords and carrying round wooden shields covered with leather painted red and sporting a white horse head emblem. They escorted us to the governor's palace, a single-storey rectangular building arranged around two courtyards. The palace was surrounded by a high stonewall that had round towers at each corner and along its length, with an impressive three-storey gatehouse that gave access to the compound. Our horses were taken from us and then a steward escorted us up the palace steps and into the large reception hall. Two guards tried to bar the way of Byrd and Malik, mistaking their black robes and untidy appearance for unwelcome guests.

'They are with me,' I ordered and the guards went back to their stations.

The hall had a high vaulted ceiling decorated with paintings depicting Parthian horsemen defeating eastern nomads. I took that to be a good omen. The walls were tiled blue and yellow with marble statues positioned in alcoves. We walked through the hall into the first courtyard, around which were the offices of city officials. Across the courtyard was the entrance to the royal hall where the governor held court, though on this occasion he sat on the right of my father who occupied the throne on the dais, Vistaspa seated to his left. City administrators, priests and officers of the garrison stood to one side, whilst officers of the royal bodyguard were grouped behind my father on the dais.

Beyond this royal hall lay the palace's second courtyard, surrounded by the private chambers of the governor, his family and guests.

Herneus and Vistaspa stood up when we entered for I too was a king. The assembly bowed their heads as Vistaspa gave up his seat for me. My father ordered another one brought for Orodes as befitting his position as a prince of the empire. The officers of my father's bodyguard shot disparaging looks at Malik and Byrd as my two friends and Domitus went to stand behind my chair.

My father began proceedings. 'Now that the army of Dura has arrived we can plan our strategy regarding how to defeat the army that approaches our borders. Lord Herneus, I believe that you have received information as to its whereabouts and size.'

Herneus bowed his head, stood in front of the dais and cleared his throat. He was a man of medium height with a round face and a head that was completely bald. There wasn't an ounce of fat on him. Despite the fact that he was extremely rich and powerful, having a mansion in the city and another in Hatra itself, he was dressed in a simple long-sleeved beige shirt, brown leggings, boots and a leather cuirass.

'Thank you, majesty,' he replied in a deep voice. 'The latest intelligence I have received is that the enemy is fifty miles to the east and advancing at a rate of around fifteen miles a day.'

'A somewhat tardy advance,' commented my father.

'Indeed, majesty,' continued Herneus. 'The size of the enemy host means that it has to forage far and wide for provisions.'

'And what size is it?' I asked.

'Upwards of one hundred thousand men, majesty.'

'One hundred thousand?' said Domitus loudly. 'Are you sure your scouts can count?'

Byrd and Malik laughed; the officers of my father's bodyguard scowled at them.

Herneus, to his credit, did not flinch but replied calmly.

'Quite sure. We have been receiving reports on a daily basis.'

'Against which we can muster how many?' I asked.

'I have brought twelve thousand horse archers and fifteen hundred cataphracts,' said my father, 'and you, Herneus?'

'I and the other lords have raised five thousand horse archers from our estates, majesty, plus another five hundred taken from the outlying forts.'

'And what of the city garrison?' I enquired.

'Five hundred spearmen, majesty,' replied Herneus, 'of little use against horsemen, I fear.'

'With Dura's army,' said Domitus, 'our combined forces are still outnumbered over three to one.'

'Long odds,' remarked Byrd, prompting murmurs of discontent from among my father's officers.

'Silence,' he commanded.

'Prince Gafarn could bring his horsemen from Hatra, lord,' suggested Vistaspa. 'That would give us an additional fifty thousand men at least.'

My father thought for a moment. 'And leave Hatra virtually undefended? No. I need Gafarn and his men to remain in the city. If Babylon falls then Narses and Mithridates will flood across my southern border. Who will stop them if all my soldiers are at Assur?'

The city officials, priests and officers of the garrison looked at each other, concern and fear etched on their faces.

'Well,' announced Domitus loudly, 'if you want to beat such a large army with so few men you will have to make his numbers count against him.'

'And how do we do that, Roman?' asked my father, intrigued.

Domitus winked at me and smiled at him. 'With a bit of bait and a bit more luck.'

After the meeting I rode with Herneus and my companions to the ford of Makhmur that lay immediately south of the city. Though there was a stone bridge over the Tigris near the city's South Gate, the river to the south of the bridge was shallow. Indeed, we rode our horses into the waters and walked them to the midpoint of the river where it was around three hundred paces wide at this spot. The current was very slow.

'As you can see,' said Herneus, the water lapping round his horse's body, 'it is about five feet deep, shallow enough to allow men on foot to cross let alone horsemen.'

Domitus looked back at the western riverbank that rose up from the water a paltry four feet. 'The river is this shallow for how far?'

'About four miles,' replied Herneus. 'In the spring it is deeper and faster flowing, but in the summer it is as you see it now. It will be no barrier to an army. It can even be forded to the north of the city, though the banks are steeper than here.'

Domitus nodded and then looked south.

'What are you thinking?' I asked him.

'We line up the legions over there, a short distance from the riverbank, stretching south of the city for around a mile. That should be a nice tempting target for them.'

'They will be able to sweep round your flanks,' I said.

'Not if your horsemen stand on our right flank,' he said.

We rode back to the city and went straight to the palace to consult with my father. According to Herneus' intelligence we had two days in which to prepare our battle plan, which Domitus estimated was just enough time to place the stakes we had brought from the north. Herneus provided the city garrison to assist the legionaries, Domitus stating undiplomatically that it was the least they could do as they would be useless when it came to the actual fighting. So the stakes were transported to south of the city and dumped on the western riverbank. They were hammered into the dry ground at an angle of forty-five degrees pointing towards the river, after which each one was sharpened to a point. The stakes were arranged in three rows, each one spaced every four feet to a length of a mile – four thousand stakes in total. They were positioned a hundred paces from the water's edge and presented a fearsome obstacle.

When the work was finished we both stood and admired the newly planted forest of stakes.

'Tomorrow the first line will stand in front of them to hide them from the enemy,' said Domitus. 'Then they will retire just before the horsemen hit them. Should give them a nasty surprise.'

'They will shower you with arrows first,' I said, 'to soften you up before they send in the heavy horsemen.'

'We've been under arrows before. You just make sure you hold them on our flanks. If they get behind us we're finished.'

He looked across the river towards the Plain of Makhmur.

'Keeping a hundred thousand men and their horses provisioned is a mighty undertaking.'

I shook my head. 'Many of them will be poorly equipped and trained, and the condition of their mounts will leave a lot to be desired after such a long journey. The kings and their lords will have taken priority when it comes to supplies, the rest will have had to scavenge for food and fodder.'

'That will make them all the more desperate to capture Assur,' said Domitus.

I nodded my head. 'No doubt they have looted all the villages along their route in Media. I hope the inhabitants had time to bury their possessions and reach the nearest walled town.'

I knew that was a forlorn hope. Fast-moving horsemen could raid and torch villages before their inhabitants knew what was happening.

Media would have felt the full wrath of the invading army. My father was right: it had to be stopped here, at the border.

The first to appear were the light horsemen, men without armour or helmets riding small horses and armed with two short javelins and a long knife. They carried a small oblong wicker shield for protection but their main task was to reconnoitre and harry, not stand and fight. At first there were only a few of them riding on the Plain of Makhmur across the river, but as the time passed the plain began to fill with more and more of them. These were the vanguard of the enemy army and I knew it would not be long before the rest of it arrived: the horse archers and heavy cavalry, the two kings and their entourages.

Dura's army had risen before dawn, the legions taking up position in front of and behind the rows of wooden stakes that extended south of Assur in an unbroken line, the first line cohorts standing in front of them to mask them from the enemy. The Duran Legion was deployed from the bridge south for half a mile, the Exiles arrayed next to them and also extending south for another half mile. Next to the Exiles were Dura's three thousand horse archers, the three dragons arrayed in a line that extended south for another mile. The cataphracts were positioned immediately behind the Exiles, and behind them were Herneus and his five and a half thousand horse archers.

I stood with Domitus and Kronos at the water's edge and watched the plain opposite fill with horsemen. Most were content to ride to the edge of the water opposite the legions and stare, though a few rode into the water and shouted insults in our direction, raising their shields and javelins above their heads as they did so in an act of bravado. The legionaries took no notice. They had seen pre-battle rituals many times and largely ignored them, though there was a large cheer when one of the horsemen was toppled from his saddle and fell in the water when his horse tripped while descending the low riverbank.

We all stood holding our helmets for the day was already hot despite the early hour, the sun rising into a clear blue sky. I had my scale armour on and as always before battle it felt heavy and cumbersome.

'You think they will attack any time soon?' said Domitus, nodding at the light horsemen opposite, who now lined the riverbank north and south as far as the eye could see.

'No,' I replied, 'they are just a screen for the main army.'

'Big screen,' remarked Kronos.

Domitus pointed his cane to the south where the light horsemen disappeared into the distance.

'If they have any sense they won't attack here but rather cross the river downstream and outflank us.'

I shook my head. 'The depth of the river increases substantially the further south you go. That is why this ford is so important, that and Assur. The city is full of stores and people.'

'People?' Kronos was confused.

'Slaves, my friend,' I replied. 'Many Parthian kings like to collect a great haul of slaves and gold to take back to their kingdoms after a campaign as proof of its success.'

'What about the troops under the city governor?' sniffed Domitus. 'You think they are reliable?'

'My father has great faith in Lord Herneus,' I replied. 'He will not let us down.'

'I would prefer your father's army behind us rather than his,' said Domitus, far from convinced.

'We agreed on the plan, Domitus,' I said. 'With luck we won't even need them.'

He drew his *gladius*. 'I prefer to rely on this rather than luck.'

Typical Domitus, hard and unyielding, much like Herneus in fact.

Then, in the distance, I heard that sound that I had come to loathe – kettledrums – signalling that the main enemy force was approaching. At first the drums created a low rumble in the distance, but as the time passed the accursed sound grew in intensity until it reverberated across the plain, like ground-based thunder. Without orders the men behind us instinctively rose from the ground, stopped chatting to each other and fastened helmet straps and checked their shields and swords. Kettledrums were designed to spread fear and uncertainty among enemy ranks, but the men of Dura had grown accustomed to their unceasing lament long ago.

'It won't be long now,' I said.

Domitus offered me his hand. 'Good luck, and don't let them outflank us.'

I took his hand and then that of Kronos. 'Keep safe, my friends, and may Shamash be with you. And remember, they must not break through.'

'Don't worry,' said Kronos, 'they shall not pass.'

We passed the first line of the Durans in front of the stakes, nodding to those men I knew and acknowledging the well wishes of others. Then I came across Thumelicus and stopped and saw that he still wore a centurion's crest. He grinned at me.

'I thought I had promoted you,' I said.

'You did,' he answered, 'but I turned it down.'

'Why?'

'A centurion is in charge of eighty-odd men,' he replied, 'that's about as far as I can count. So there's not much point in putting me in charge of anything bigger.'

He was probably correct: in battle you wanted Thumelicus standing next to you; in camp he was known for being too loose with his tongue, a vice that earned him many extra hours on fatigues and sentry duty. But he was greatly respected for his courage and fighting skill. The whole army knew and loved this prince of rogues, but he and I knew that he would never rise above the rank of centurion.

I slapped him on the arm. 'Keep safe. One day we will get you a bigger shield.'

'You too, Pacorus, don't fall off your horse.'

I walked to where Drenis was holding Remus and he helped me into the saddle. Across the river the light horsemen had left their position at the water's edge and were being replaced by groups of horse archers in bright tunics.

'Pretty bunch,' remarked Drenis sarcastically.

I slipped my helmet on my head and fastened the straps under my chin.

'I will see you after the battle, Drenis.'

He raised his hand as I rode back to where Orodes and the armoured horsemen were waiting, their helmets shoved back on their heads and their lances resting on the ground. The air was filled with the unrelenting din of the kettledrums, but was momentarily drowned out by trumpet blasts as the Durans and Exiles adopted their battle formation for dealing with enemy archers: every man in both legions knelt down, the first rank formed a shield wall while those behind lifted their shields to create a roof of leather and wood. Then there was a great blast of horns and the enemy's horse archers walked their horses into the Tigris and began advancing towards the legions.

At a distance of around three hundred paces they began shooting their arrows, releasing their missiles high into the sky so they would drop onto the packed ranks of the foot soldiers before them. The horsemen halted their animals in the middle of the river and unleashed a fearsome arrow storm that made a sound akin to a great wind whistling across the steppe. As each rank emptied its quivers it fell back and was replaced by another with full ones. It was impossible to identify individual arrows such was the intensity of the arrow fire being directed at the legions. I began to worry that not even Domitus and his men would be able to withstand such a battering. The expenditure of arrows was massive. And then there was another blast of horns and the arrow storm abruptly ceased.

Such a deluge of wood and bronze would normally kill and maim foot soldiers and spread fear and panic among those that still lived. Having softened up the enemy thus, I knew that Vologases and Cinnamus would launch their heavier cavalry to smash through the battered foot soldiers, which would then be cut to pieces and destroyed. And so it was.

313

The enemy horse archers withdrew from the water and filed back through the ranks of the next group of enemy horsemen who were forming up at the water's edge – heavy spearmen. These riders were not cataphracts but did wear helmets, scale armour cuirasses and carried long spears and large round shields whose faces were reinforced with strips of iron. They moved into the water in an unbroken line, rank upon rank of them until the whole of the river was filled with horsemen. There must have been at least twenty thousand of them, the sun glinting off their helmets and whetted spear points. This mighty wall of horseflesh moved slowly through the water as the first line of the legions fell back through the rows of stakes and before the first rank of the enemy reached the dry land of the western bank and briefly halted to dress its ranks. Then the horsemen charged the legions, realising too late that a forest of stakes barred their path.

As more and more enemy spearmen reached the western bank the first rank crossed the short strip of ground between the river and the legions and ran straight into the rows of stakes. No, that is wrong. The horses reared up in panic before they impaled themselves on the sharpened stakes and confusion reigned among the enemy horsemen as more and more of their comrades rode from the water and pressed in behind them. There was a mighty blast of trumpets followed by a cheer and then three thousand javelins arched into the air as the front ranks of the cohorts hurled them at the packed ranks of the enemy horsemen. Had they been cataphracts then many iron tips would have glanced harmlessly off armoured men and horses, but these men rode horses that wore no armour and the beasts were cruelly struck by iron points that hurt and maddened them. They reared up and collapsed to the ground or bolted forward onto the stakes, throwing their riders or crushing them beneath their great weight. The pitiful squeals and cries of wounded animals filled the air as another volley of javelins was launched at the stationary horsemen. More cries from injured and dying men and horses. Then another and another volley hit flesh and horsemeat. It was slaughter.

Frantic horn blasts up and down the line signalled the withdrawal of the heavy spearmen, though not before another volley of javelins had harvested a further crop of enemy dead. Those riders still in the water turned and withdrew back to the safety of the Plain of Makhmur, followed by what was left of those that had been first to cross the river. In front of the stakes was heaped a great pile of dead and dying horses and their riders.

'First blood to us, Pacorus,' said Orodes defiantly.

'They will attack our horse archers next,' I said.

While the carnage in front of the legions was taking place Dura's horse archers were sitting on their horses gazing across the river at the light horsemen who lined the opposite bank and watched them back.

314

How strange is battle when one part of the field is the scene of horror and another part is as peaceful as an empty temple. But now, having seen their heavy spearmen routed, the enemy shifted his attention to where my horse archers were positioned. With the departure of Surena to Gordyene command of Dura's horse archers had devolved upon Vagises, a Parthian and a Companion, a sober and intelligent individual who retained a sense of calm even in the white heat of battle. It was he who now sent a rider to me, an officer of his horse archers who saluted.

'Lord Vagises conveys his compliments, majesty, and sends word that enemy cataphracts are deploying in front of him, across the river.'

'How many?'

'Three dragons, majesty,' he replied.

I turned to Orodes. 'First blood may have been to us, my friend, but three thousand cataphracts can quickly weigh the scales in their favour.'

I looked at the courier. 'Give my regards to Lord Vagises and inform him that aid will be with him shortly.'

The man saluted and rode back to the horse archers.

'What is your plan?' asked Orodes.

'We will meet them in the water, otherwise their greater numbers will punch straight through us.'

I called forward the commanders of the cataphracts and told them that we would deploy in a long line to match the frontage of the enemy horsemen.

'Tell your men to leave their lances behind. There will be no charge; we will engage them at the water's edge.'

They rode back to their companies and moments later over twelve hundred men were cantering towards where Vagises' men were shooting arrows at the enemy cataphracts now entering the Tigris. The arrows would not be able to pierce the armour of the men or their horses but would hopefully slow them enough to allow us to deploy.

I shook Orodes' hand and then we galloped to the head of our men, the ground around us littered with discarded lances. I smiled to myself. Rsan would have a fit if he saw items of expensive equipment treated thus. Orodes and his bodyguard formed the extreme right of our long line, which was as thin as parchment – only two ranks. In this way we had a frontage of nine hundred yards.

As the men dressed their lines Vagises' horse archers moved further downriver to allow the cataphracts to fill the space they had been occupying and to extend our line further south. He rode up to me as we walked our horses forward to the riverbank. Ahead I saw a great mass of enemy riders walking their horses through the water towards us. They moved slowly to retain their order, red, yellow and blue flags fluttering from the end of each *kontus*.

315

'Send a rider to Lord Herneus,' I told him. 'Tell him that if the enemy horsemen break through us, he and his men are to retreat towards the city to form a screen so Domitus and his men can get inside the walls. That goes for you and your men also.'

'What of you, Pacorus?' he said with alarm.

'We will most likely be dead so you will not have to worry about us. Now go.'

He raised his hand in salute and went back to his horse archers. The camel train loaded with fresh arrows had been brought forward from the rear to replenish the ammunition expended against the enemy cataphracts, whose front ranks were now at the midpoint in the river. I looked behind me up and down the line and saw every man had armed himself with either his axe or mace. I reached down and grabbed the mace that was hanging from one of my saddle's front horns.

The mace is an extraordinary weapon – two and half feet of solid steel with four flanges on one end. These sharpened protruding edges can dent and penetrate even the thickest armour. Leather is wrapped round the other end to make a handle, with a metal ring at the base to which is fitted a leather strap that goes round the wrist. I gripped the shaft tightly and raised it in the air, a move reciprocated by every man behind me. Some of my cataphracts were very skilled in the use of the mace and used the strap to spin the weapon round their wrists before delivering a lethal blow, but I frowned on such antics.

The mace is an effective and brutal impact weapon ordinarily used after the charge, but today there would be no charge. Some men preferred to use axes, which were also solid steel instruments with a head comprising a blade and a point on the opposite side.

I nudged Remus forward and the others followed, walking to the edge of the riverbank and then down its side and into the water. In front of me the front rank of the enemy's horsemen threw their lances into the water and armed themselves with their own maces and axes. And thus began a grim close-quarters battle. There were no battle cries or thunder of horse hooves, just a great clatter as each side began hacking at the other with their weapons.

In such a mêlée the ability to avoid blows is as important as the skill to deliver them. I leaned to my left to avoid a scything blow from a man holding an axe that would have lopped my head off had it hit me. His horse stopped beside Remus as he brought the axe in front of his body then swung it up and then down to split my helmet and then my skull. I deflected the blow with my mace, forcing his axe away from me. But he attacked me with its point using a backswing that I stopped with my mace only inches from my face. I grabbed his axe with my left hand and he grabbed my left wrist with his free hand, and so we pushed and pulled each other like a pair of has-been wrestlers.

316

He was strong and the only thing that weighed our private war in my favour was the leather strap wrapped round my wrist. His axe had no such attachment and I eventually managed to wrench it from his hand and throw it into the water. I brought my mace back and then with all my strength swung it against the side of his helmet, splitting the metal and causing him to let out a groan. I swung the mace again and again at the same spot, penetrating the metal and his skull. One of the blows must have driven a steel flange into his brain, for he slumped in the saddle and then slid off his horse into the water without making another sound.

I looked left to see a horsemen coming directly at me with his mace held high above his head, ready to bring it down on my head. But before he could reach me one of my own men attacked him and they became embroiled in their own personal fight. I transferred my mace to my left hand and pulled my *spatha* as another rider attacked me on my right side. This time I blocked his overhead swing with my own mace and drove the tip of my sword into his exposed right armpit, driving the blade deep into his flesh. He gave a high-pitched scream as I forced the blade forward and yanked it back. I was prevented from finishing him off by a mace blow that dug into the steel rings on my left arm.

I instinctively swung my mace back with my left arm and felt it strike something, then turned to see a horse rear up and throw its rider into the river. I must have hit it on the head with my weapon.

And so it went on, men hacking and slashing wildly in all directions in a huge disorganised mêlée that seemed to go on forever. I do not know how long we were in the water. It seemed like hours but in reality was probably around thirty minutes. But as Remus moved back and forth in the brown water streaked with blood it became apparent that the enemy's greater weight of numbers had not achieved a breakthrough, at least not yet. But their numerical superiority meant that they could feed in more and more men against our tiring ranks, replacing their own injured and exhausted riders with fresh reinforcements. And yet it did not seem so because after what seemed like an eternity, following which my arms and shoulders ached, a gradual lull descended over the two sides. As if by mutual consent each side withdrew from each other, revealing a river filled with armoured corpses, most lying face down in the blood-streaked water. Some men had been unhorsed and these now waded towards the safety of their own lines. My arm armour was battered and dented though it had saved me from serious injury. I looked at the head and neck of Remus, then at his sides and rear. Not a mark on him; indeed, looking up and down the line it appeared that no horses had been killed at all.

Orodes came to my side, his armour missing several metal scales and his helmet's right cheek guard almost hanging off where a blow had smashed the hinge. He was breathing heavily.

'Are you hurt?' I asked.

He shook his head. 'Exhausted would be a more accurate description. I don't know if we can hold them if they attack again.'

Around us men had pushed their full-face helmets up on their heads and were breathing in great gulps of air. By contrast their horses appeared relatively fresh. At least they would be able to carry their riders back to the city if we were forced to retreat.

'They are they falling back.'

I looked at Orodes. 'Who?'

He pointed with his mace towards the enemy horsemen whose front ranks were now backing slowly away from us, the ranks behind having about-faced and were exiting the water. To the south the mass of enemy light horsemen who had been riding up and down the riverbank in preparation to cross once the cataphracts had scattered us were also pulling back.

'My father's army,' I said, grinning at him.

The army of Hatra had marched fifteen miles upstream to cross the Tigris at a shallow spot that Byrd and Malik had scouted during our march from Nisibus. My father had earlier sent horsemen to the exact same spot to ensure that the enemy did not use it to cross the river and then take us unawares. But the enemy's attention was focused on the Plain of Makhmur and its wide ford, wide enough for a great army to move across with ease. So my father had marched his horsemen north, crossed the river and then headed south while the enemy attacked Dura's army. And now Hatra's horsemen smashed into the enemy's unguarded right flank.

After the battle I heard from Byrd and Malik, who had ridden with my father, what had happened. It was mid-morning before Hatra's cavalry were safely across the river and had deployed into their battle formations – cataphracts in the centre and horse archers on the wings. They then rode directly south towards the Plain of Makhmur, driving deep into the mass of unsuspecting horsemen who were waiting to cross the river.

The initial clash cut down thousands of light horsemen, but so many were the enemy that the charge slowed and then stopped as Hatra's horsemen were literally swallowed by the hostile mass. My father was contemplating ordering a withdrawal but his unexpected arrival on the battlefield had panicked Cinnamus and Vologases, who ordered a general retreat, hence the withdrawal of the cataphracts from the river.

As the horsemen in front of us left the river and then rode away I sent a rider to Herneus with orders for him to bring his men to the

318

river. Notwithstanding that our horses still had their legs their riders were in no fit state to conduct a pursuit. Ten minutes later he arrived.

'The enemy appears to be retreating. Get your men across the river and harry them. If they reform and attack, fall back.'

'Yes, majesty. I assume your father, the king, has achieved success.'

'It would appear so,' I agreed.

He raised his hand in salute and then rode back to his men who had formed into columns and were now filing into the river, threading their way between dead horsemen floating in the water. I gave orders for a general retreat back to our initial position behind the Exiles. I stayed with Orodes and the rear guard as Vagises and a company of his men joined us.

'Some of their light horsemen got over the river,' he reported. 'We killed most of them before the rest retreated back to the east bank.'

'What are your losses?' I asked him.

'Light, although we have yet to take a roll call.' He looked at the dead bodies in the river. 'And yours?'

'It was a long fight,' I answered grimly.

Two hours later I was standing with Domitus and Kronos behind the rows of stakes that had served them so well that day. In front of us was a great heap of enemy dead – men and horses victims of the legions' javelins.

'They tried another assault after their first one,' he said disapprovingly, 'but failed to get even near the stakes, let alone us. They were limited to hurling their spears at us, so we hurled a few more javelins back.'

'After we emptied many more saddles they fell back,' added Kronos.

'What are your losses?' I asked.

'Four dead and seventy wounded,' answered Domitus.

'And yours, Kronos?' I asked.

Kronos looked at Domitus. 'Four dead and seventy wounded are our combined losses.'

It had been an amazingly one-sided fight, the consequence of well-trained men standing behind a wall of impenetrable stakes. My cataphracts had not been so lucky. A roll call revealed that a hundred had been killed and a further two hundred wounded, though at least Vagises' horse archers had suffered only fifty dead and a hundred and fifty wounded.

The sun was abating in its fury now it was late afternoon but I was still glad to take off my scale armour and leg and arm armour. Already the squires, who had been lining the walls of Assur with their bows to cover any retreat we may have had to make to the city, were stripping their masters' horses of their scale armour and loading it back onto their camels, as well as collecting the *kontuses* that had been dumped on the ground earlier. Losses among the cataphracts would be made good by promoting the eldest squires, and when we got back to Dura fresh squires would be inducted into the army.

Orodes had four squires, two for himself and two for me as he was always letting me know, and they now assisted me in unfastening the armoured suit that had protected Remus so well during the battle. As his squires packed his scale armour away, Alcaeus, who with his physicians had been treating the wounded, examined Orodes. Those seriously injured were taken back to the city on wagons where they could be treated more thoroughly.

Alcaeus gave Orodes a bandage to hold next to his wounded face. 'Nothing serious, you'll live. Just keep it clean.'

'Make sure it does not leave a scar, Alcaeus,' I said. 'His future bride won't like it.'

'Future bride?' said Alcaeus, mildly interested.

'Orodes is to marry Queen Axsen of Babylon.'

Orodes looked daggers at me. 'It is still uncertain,' he snapped.

'My congratulations,' said Alcaeus. 'I'm sure there will be no scar.'

He looked at my arm that was bleeding from where my armour had been dented by a mace, the white sleeve of my shirt showing red.

'What about you?'

'It's fine, Alcaeus, I hope to have another scar to add to my collection.'

Alcaeus nodded slightly and then looked at the piles of dead horse carcasses and bodies intertwined on and in front of the stakes and then to the bodies floating in the river.

'What about them?'

I shrugged. 'What about them? They are dead.'

He sighed and shook his head. 'Notwithstanding your god-like powers of observation, the bodies need to be collected and burned quickly to avoid sickness spreading to the city.'

'Oh, the city authorities can deal with that,' I replied casually.

Alcaeus raised an eyebrow at me. 'I would advise you to assume the responsibility. You can use those stakes for fuel. It would be a pity if having fought a battle to preserve this city, it was devastated by a plague.'

'He's right Pacorus,' said Orodes, 'I have seen with my own eyes what pestilence can do to cities.'

'Very well,' I agreed, 'I will detail Domitus to organise it, seeing that his men were responsible for most of the carnage.'

In fact the city garrison did assist the legionaries in their grim task of piling dead horses and men onto a dozen pyres that were erected near the riverbank, but not before they were stripped of anything that could be reused: spearheads, helmets, scale armour and swords.

That night I stood on the walls at the Southern Gate with my father and watched the fires burn, an easterly wind fortunately saving our nostrils from the stench of roasting flesh. Thankfully there was not a scratch on him and losses among his men had been light like my own.

'Herneus will snap at the enemy's heels,' he said, looking south at the funerals pyres that illuminated the night. 'Tomorrow I will organise the dead on the Plain of Makhmur to be burned.'

'How many dead are there?'

He smiled. 'During our initial charge we must have been killing them at a rate of a thousand every minute. There's probably around twenty thousand dead on the plain.'

'We counted ten thousand corpses,' I said. 'A great victory, father.'

He screwed up his face. 'They still have seventy thousand horsemen, Pacorus. I have prevented them from invading Hatra but they are still a threat.'

'Herneus will inflict more casualties on them.'

'Yes, he will harry them and hopefully force them further east but he will not be able to destroy them, and if he himself is under threat of being destroyed he will retreat.'

'And then what?'

He spread out his hands. 'Then we will have more war. I pray to Shamash that Farhad and Aschek still have their armies, for if they fall then Hatra is surely doomed.'

I was shocked. I had never heard him talk with so much pessimism before. But if the worst happened and Media and Atropaiene fell, then Hatra would face two great armies in the east, a hostile Armenia to the north and perhaps another enemy to the south, for Babylon was still in peril.

'I would like to stay and assist you, father, but I must try to help Axsen. If Babylon falls then so will Mesene, and after that…'

He smiled thinly. 'I know. Mithridates and Narses have played their hands well. They stand on the brink of victory. What happened here today will not matter if Babylon, Media and Atropaiene all fall.

'For myself, I must march east to assist Farhad and Aschek.'

I tried to be positive. 'The game is not yet up, father. If you can prevail with Media and Atropaiene and I can relieve Babylon then…'

'Then we are back in exactly the same position we were in at the beginning of the year. There can now never be peace between Mithridates and us. It is a war to the death. Well, so be it. I have tried to walk the path of peace and diplomacy, to respect the office of the king of kings as in the old days. And my reward? To see my kingdom threatened.'

He rested his hands on the wall and cast his head down.

'I did not know that the death of Sinatruces would presage so much misery and tyranny.'

I said nothing. Perhaps he was thinking back to the Council of Kings at Esfahan and his decision to support Phraates in becoming king of kings. Perhaps he was regretting not putting himself forward for the high crown. But then, Mithridates and Narses would have still schemed to promote their own interests. Perhaps we would have been in exactly the same situation as we currently found ourselves in. In front of us the funeral pyres burned brightly and above us the gods laughed at our discomfort.

We stayed at Assur for a few more days to allow the men to rest and the wounded to recuperate. During this time Herneus and his troops rode back to the city after their pursuit of Cinnamus and Vologases. He reported that the two kings had beat a hasty retreat east in the direction of Ecbatana, leaving a host of stragglers and wounded behind them. These he had destroyed but he had been unable to engage the main enemy army, only its fleeing rear guard. He reported that the enemy had left a trail of devastation in Media, burning villages and massacring their inhabitants, sometimes hanging their mutilated bodies from trees to spread terror. He had encountered no living Median who could tell him if Farhad was alive or not. My father sat grim faced in the main hall of the governor's palace listening to Herneus' report, and afterwards sent word to Hatra for Gafarn to march with thirty thousand horsemen to Assur. He told me that he was going to march to Farhad's capital, Irbil, to relieve the King of Media. No one said anything about Aschek but everyone feared the worst and assumed that he was dead and his kingdom conquered by the combined armies of Yueh-Chih and Aria.

The next day my mood lightened when a letter came from Gallia informing me that Axsen was still holding out at Babylon (she had obviously been alerted to the city's peril) and Nergal had thrown back the forces of King Phriapatius from the walls of Uruk with the aid of Lord Yasser and his Agraci warriors. Phriapatius was still occupying parts of Mesene but had withdrawn his army to the Tigris. I showed my father the letter and his spirits seemed to lift a little. She finished by saying that the border with Roman Syria was quiet.

'That may change,' he said, handing me back the letter, 'when the Armenians begin to complain to their masters about their recent differences with Parthia and they learn that conflict has again broken out within the empire.'

I was more worried about the Romans discovering that Dura was supplying the Jews with weapons with which to liberate Judea, but said nothing of this to him.

'With the Romans quarrelling among themselves, father,' I tried to reassure him. 'I think Mithridates presents more of an immediate threat.'

322

In camp I sat with Domitus, Orodes and Kronos as we tried to work out our course of action. The city of Babylon lies just over two hundred miles south of Assur – ten days' march following the course of the Tigris and then heading southwest for the final thirty miles of the journey. Orodes was all for reaching Babylon by the most direct route, which was understandable considering that his future bride was trapped inside it. Domitus and Kronos, however, argued that it would be best to follow the Tigris until we reached Hatra's southern border – one hundred miles south – and then swing west to the Euphrates and there link up with reinforcements that Gallia could send from Dura. In this way, they argued, we would have more men with which to relieve Babylon. However, it would add another five or six days to the journey.

'Babylon is surely hard pressed,' argued Orodes. 'The longer we delay reaching it the more likely it will fall.'

'I do not doubt it, my friend,' said Domitus, 'but Dura's army is only fourteen thousand men. What if Mithridates has an army the same size as the one that we fought a few days ago?'

'What Domitus says is correct,' added Kronos. 'We need reinforcements if we are to relieve Babylon. There is no point in fighting our way through to the city if then we are also trapped inside.'

'I cannot believe that Narses and Mithridates have mustered a hundred thousand men to besiege Babylon,' I said, not knowing if they had or not, 'so we will march directly to Babylon.'

Orodes appeared mightily relieved and Domitus and Kronos looked at me with confusion on their faces. But I merely smiled at them. Orodes had been a good friend and had remained with the army when he could have ridden to Babylon before the Battle of Makhmur, but he had stayed. The least I could do now was to ride with him to save his beloved Axsen.

Chapter 13

The march south along the Tigris was uneventful until we approached Hatra's southern border and began to encounter groups of fleeing civilians making their way north to safety, or what they thought was safety. The first to encounter them was Byrd and Malik and their men, who stopped to talk with these frightened wretches who had lost their homes and livestock, their only possessions being the clothes on their backs. It soon became clear that Mithridates was not only laying siege to the city of Babylon, he and Narses were systematically destroying the kingdom's agriculture and either forcing its population to leave or enslaving them. The ones Byrd and Malik had encountered on the road were the lucky ones for they had heard rumours of horsemen attacking villages further south and carrying off their populations, so they had fled for their lives, seeking sanctuary in Hatra.

When we progressed further south into Babylonian territory we saw for ourselves the destruction that had been visited on the kingdom – villages levelled, irrigation ditches and canals wrecked and livestock taken, no doubt to feed the army besieging Babylon. An eerie silence hung over the land that had seemingly been emptied of all life. If the enemy had laid waste to the whole kingdom in such a manner then it would take years before Babylon recovered. Orodes was appalled at the scenes that met his eyes. It not only offended his sense of decency but also his code of honour. This was not how war should be fought, not at all.

'Ha! You need to spend a few years in the Roman army to learn how war should be fought,' said Domitus as we relaxed in my tent after another day marching in the dust and heat of a Mesopotamian summer. We had covered a hundred miles since leaving Assur and were nearly halfway on our journey to Babylon.

'Lucky for Babylon,' continued Domitus, 'that Mithridates and Narses don't have siege engines like the Romans do; otherwise its population would be being marched off into slavery by now.'

Orodes shuddered at the thought of his beloved in chains.

'Only Dura among Parthia's kingdoms has siege engines,' I said, trying to allay Orodes' growing concern.

'How I would like to take those siege engines to Persepolis,' said Orodes through gritted teeth, 'to breach the walls of Narses' capital.'

'Alas, my friend,' I said, 'Persepolis lies four hundred miles to the southeast of the Tigris.'

'Seleucia lies nearer,' remarked Byrd casually.

We all looked at him.

'Seleucia?' I said.

'Great city on the west bank of the Tigris,' said Byrd, chomping on a biscuit.

'I know where it is, but we do not have the siege engines with us,' I answered. 'In any case we march to relieve Babylon, not assault Seleucia.'

Seleucia was the ancient city that stood on the western side of the Tigris, opposite the palace complex of Ctesiphon that had been built on the other side of the river. Seleucia protected the great stone bridge across the Tigris that Mithridates and Narses had used to bring their armed forces into Babylonia. Though Seleucia was actually within Babylonian territory, the kings of Babylon had always regarded it as the city that served the court of the high king at Ctesiphon and had thus made no claim upon it – a fatal strategic error.

'Mithridates and Narses not know you have no siege engines with you,' replied Byrd.

Domitus looked thoughtful. 'If we head towards Seleucia instead of Babylon then they might break off the siege of the city to secure the bridge over the river.'

Orodes was not convinced. 'And they might not. It is far too risky.'

And yet Byrd's suggestion had merit. If we could draw away the enemy from the walls of Babylon then we would accomplish what we had set out to achieve, irrespective of whether we endangered Seleucia or not. I looked at Byrd and Malik in their Agraci robes and smiled.

'Perhaps we may both frighten the officials of Seleucia into appealing to the kings besieging Babylon to march north to save them, thereby saving Axsen, and still march towards Babylon.'

The next day I sent Vagises and five hundred horse archers south towards Seleucia, preceded by Malik, Byrd and their scouts. We were only seventy miles from the city so the horsemen would reach it in two days. Vagises was ordered to ride up to the city walls and shout at the defenders that King Pacorus and the army of Dura, with its terrible siege engines, were going to breach their walls and put everyone inside to the sword. For added effect Byrd, Malik and their scouts were also to form up in front of the walls, and then Vagises would announce that they were the vanguard of a great Agraci army that was accompanying King Pacorus. Finally, if the garrison sallied from the walls Vagises and his men were to immediately retreat.

'You really think that such a hare-brained scheme will work?' Domitus was far from convinced as I walked beside him as the army made its way south once more, the Tigris on our left flank. It was another blisteringly hot day.

I shrugged. 'It does not matter what I think, it's what the authorities in Seleucia think.'

'If they think at all,' he said dismissively.

'They know that Dura is a friend of Haytham and they also know as a consequence of our storm of Uruk that I possess siege engines capable of breaching city walls. When they see hostile horsemen before their walls they will appeal to Mithridates for help.'

'Seleucia might have a large garrison, have you thought of that?'

I shook my head. 'A thousand at most. I remember from my time when I was lord high general of the empire. Like Ctesiphon, Seleucia's defences have been neglected.'

'And what if Mithridates and Narses break off the siege of Babylon and march towards us with a hundred thousand men?'

I laughed. 'They don't have that many. Remember we inflicted heavy losses on their army last year, and killed quite a few of their heavy horsemen as well.'

'You sound very certain.'

'You know, Domitus, for the first time in weeks I am. Byrd's idea is a good one, I should have thought of it.'

My chief scout and the other horsemen returned in three days, in which time we had marched to within twenty miles of Seleucia, passing by the now usual sights of destroyed villages and smashed dykes and irrigation systems. Next spring this whole area would be flooded when the Tigris would be swelled by the northern melt waters, which would breach the broken dykes and inflict yet more damage on an already wasted land.

We had already made camp when Vagises, accompanied by Byrd and Malik, rode through the main entrance with their horsemen. All three reported to me after they had unsaddled their horses and eaten, their clothes and faces covered in a fine white dust that gave them the appearance of phantoms.

'I did not shout at those on the walls,' said Vagises, 'but rather sent a messenger to the city governor with a letter I had composed.'

'Saying what?' I asked.

'Informing him that King Pacorus and Dura's army would be arriving imminently and that he was to surrender the city when he, that is you, arrived. Failure to do so would result in the destruction of the city and the deaths of its inhabitants. I also told him that King Haytham and his Agraci warriors were marching with you and that I had brought some of his warriors with me to show that I spoke the truth.'

Malik and Byrd smiled at me.

'And what was his reply?'

'That he did not have the authority to treat with kings and that he would have to consult with Mithridates first.'

'Playing for time,' said Domitus, 'an old trick.'

'Indeed,' continued Vagises, 'so I ordered the outlying homes to be torched, after which we withdrew as ordered.'

The expansion of Seleucia during the long reign of Sinatruces had resulted in many homes being built outside the city walls. No thought had been given to building new walls to encompass these dwellings.

'You did well, Vagises,' I said. 'That should stir Mithridates up, if only for the fact that his dear mother resides in Ctesiphon, just across the river from Seleucia.'

The next day before dawn Byrd and Malik rode out of camp with their scouts. I was half-tempted to attack Seleucia anyway. Its walls were old and crumbling, its garrison was small and even without siege engines we could probably scale the walls that were no higher than twenty feet in most places. Even a show of force might be enough for the governor to lose his nerve and surrender the place without a fight. But Orodes was adamant that we should make Babylon a priority and for the sake of our friendship I agreed. Most days he was with the vanguard, I think because he believed that if he rode at the very tip of the army then he was always the closest to Axsen. How curious are the thoughts of men when they are besotted!

We had not marched five miles when he rode back to the main column with Byrd and Malik in tow.

'Enemy force approaching from the southwest, Pacorus,' said Orodes.

'Looks like Mithridates took the bait,' I said to Domitus with relish.

Domitus looked up at Byrd. 'How many?'

'Not many, five thousand, perhaps.'

Domitus scowled. 'That is just the vanguard. How many behind?'

Malik shook his head. 'No, there are none following the foot soldiers.'

'They are foot soldiers only?' I said with disbelief.

'Well, we can't ignore them,' snorted Domitus.

The army was halted and then deployed into battle formation with horse archers on the wings and the legions in the centre, after which it moved slowly in a southwesterly direction. I had Byrd and Malik send their men out far and wide as I could not believe that five thousand foot soldiers were going to engage us. There must be additional forces nearby. But the scouts reported seeing nothing and the flat desert meant that there were no hills, forests of ravines in which to hide another army. The cataphracts donned their armour and the squires formed a reserve in the rear of the army, guarding the wagons, camels and mules.

We halted and awaited our foes, whose line did not even match the frontage of one of our legions as they marched towards us with their shields in front of them and their spears held at an angle of forty-five degrees. I heard the sound of drums being banged and saw many yellow banners among their ranks, indicating that these men were from Persis.

327

I rode beyond our front line to take a closer look but saw no horsemen and no foot archers. A Parthian army without archers, very strange. Orodes, Vagises, Byrd and Malik joined me as I stared in disbelief at the meagre force that intended to fight us.

'Are you certain that there are no more enemy troops nearby?' I asked Byrd and Malik as I peered ahead and to the left and right of the enemy.

'Unless they can fly,' said Malik, 'then those are the only ones we face today.'

Domitus trotted up, sweating in his mail armour and helmet.

'Straight through them, then? Shouldn't take long.'

'No,' I answered. 'Vagises and his archers will destroy them. I see no reason to commit the legionaries when we can shoot them to pieces.'

And so it was. The Durans and Exiles stood and leaned on their shields and the cataphracts roasted in their armour as Vagises' companies rode round the enemy and killed them with volleys of arrows. After an hour what was left of them threw down their weapons and surrendered. I had their surviving commanding officer brought to me as the rest were escorted from the scene of carnage and the army was stood down.

The man wore a linen tunic reinforced with bronze scales and a bronze helmet on his head, his scruffy black hair showing beneath it. He was armed with a sword though his men had carried spears and shields only and wore felt caps on their heads. He had the aroma of an old mule.

'How did you expect to defeat us with so few?' I asked him.

'My general was ordered to stop you, majesty. We were camped thirty miles south of Seleucia and received an order from the governor of the city to engage you.'

'How many men does your king, Narses, have in Babylonia?' I asked him.

He looked at me blankly. 'I do not know, majesty.'

He was probably telling the truth. He was, after all, but a low-ranking officer. I shook my head. It had been the most one-sided battle that I had ever taken part in: we had suffered fifteen casualties including one man who had grazed his arm during the act of pulling an arrow from his quiver and nocking it in his bowstring. By contrast the enemy had lost three and a half thousand dead and three hundred more wounded. Those who were not injured and who had surrendered were ordered to dig pits in which their dead comrades could be interred, as not even five thousand wicker shields were enough to burn three and a half thousand corpses. Besides, as it was now late and we had pitched camp two miles further east near the Tigris, I did not want the stench of roasting flesh filling my nostrils all night.

According to the rules of war I could have executed all the prisoners or kept them as slaves, but I decided that they should not only live but were to be set free the next day. They slept outside the camp perimeter that night, having been first escorted to the river to drink and wash the filth from their bodies. Alcaeus went among their wounded with his physicians and tended to their injuries – I saw little point in heaping cruelty upon their defeat and misery. The officer who had surrendered I had brought to my tent that evening to dine with my commanders and me.

When he first took his seat at the table he wore the look of a man who was expecting to receive a death sentence, but after a while and a few cups of wine he relaxed and became very talkative. He told us his name was Udall.

'All the royal foot guards,' he informed us as more wine loosened his tongue, 'went to Babylon with the king. We stayed behind to guard the road back to Seleucia.'

I smiled and poured more wine into his cup.

'And what do you hear about the siege of Babylon?'

He screwed up his face. 'Only rumours that things are not going well and the two kings are arguing. Can't scale the walls, you see.'

Udall finished his wine and belched.

'Pardon, majesty, too much wine on an empty stomach.'

'Rations are sparse?' probed Domitus.

Udall laughed. 'Sparse? They are non-existent. They ran out weeks ago. We have had to forage for ourselves as well as keep a lookout for enemy raiders.'

'Raiders?' asked Orodes, pouring more wine into Udall's cup.

'Yes, riders from Mesene. I spoke to a man from the garrison at Jem det Nasr who told me that some of his men had been killed by them, and he further informed me that there were Agraci among them, can you imagine that?'

He shuddered and drained his cup. His wine-soaked brain had failed to notice that Malik was an Agraci, but then like most Parthians he had probably never actually seen the feared and loathed people who lived in the great desert west of the Euphrates.

'How large is the garrison at Jem det Nasr?' asked Orodes, smiling and refilling Udall's now empty cup.

'Not sure, but the governor sent them a message that they too were to attack you, begging your pardon, majesty.'

'You were doing your duty, Udall,' I reassured him. 'You have nothing to apologise for.'

After two more cups of wine he collapsed and I had him carried back to his men outside the camp, leaving us to mull over what he had blurted out.

329

'It would appear that things are not going well for Mithridates and Narses before Babylon,' said Orodes with satisfaction.

'And it also appears that they have had to disperse their forces throughout Babylonia to keep their supply lines open,' I added.

'Lord Yasser must be aiding Nergal,' said Malik.

'If what Udall told us is true,' I said, 'then it means Nergal is raiding north of Babylon. No wonder the enemy are worried about their supply lines. It also means that the threat posed to Mesene by King Phriapatius must have greatly lessened.'

Suddenly the overall situation did not appear as bleak as a few days ago. Taking cities can be very debilitating for the besiegers as well as the besieged, and if supplies were not getting through to the army sitting in front of the city then that was good news indeed.

I was now more convinced than ever that if we stormed the city and took possession of its strategic bridge over the Tigris then we would deal the enemy a mortal blow. Babylonia had been pillaged but there was only so much a plundered country could supply to an invader.

An hour after dawn I had a bleary eyed, unshaven and dishevelled Udall brought to me, clearly the worse for wear after the copious amounts of wine he had consumed the previous evening. I told him that he and his soldiers would be deprived of their weapons but would be allowed to leave as free men. I advised him to avoid Seleucia, as the city was our destination. If he and his men were inside it when we attacked they would receive no mercy when I put the entire garrison to the sword. He asked me where they should go but I replied that it was not my concern.

'Go where you will, Udall, for that is the prerogative of a free man.'

So they trudged east to the Tigris. At least they would have access to water and might find some rafters who could convey them to the eastern bank of the river.

The army began its march south towards Seleucia once more, but the last centuries were still waiting on the site of the previous night's camp when Byrd and Malik returned with news that another enemy force was approaching, this time from the south.

'Both horse and foot,' said Byrd.

'Numbers?'

'Around five thousand foot, same number of horse.'

'This must be the garrison of Jem det Nasr that our friend Udall was talking about last night,' I said. 'Give the order to form a battle line. Domitus, send word that the wagons and mules are to return to camp. We will be staying here for another night, it seems.'

As I watched the leading centuries of the legions fall back and form into their battle positions of three lines, the horse archers taking up position on their flanks, the enemy appeared on the horizon – a long black line that shimmered in the summer heat. I did not bother to don my scale armour as Orodes would command the cataphracts this day. When Byrd and Malik returned once more and reported that the enemy horse consisted of spearmen with no armour and horse archers similarly attired, I gave the order that the legions were to deploy in two lines to extend their frontage. My scouts also told me that the enemy had no camel train carrying spare ammunition for the archers. I assembled the senior officers of the army.

'This is the disadvantage of filling an army with ill-equipped farmers,' I told them. 'Domitus, the legions will advance against them in a hollow square formation to draw their arrow fire. I have no doubt that their spearmen will launch an attack against you after their horse archers have softened you up. You and your men will be today's bait.'

He smiled grimly. 'Don't you worry, Pacorus, my boys will deal with them.'

'Vagises,' I said, 'when their horse archers have expended their arrows your men will charge and disperse them, after which Domitus will be able to destroy their spearmen.'

'What about the cataphracts?' asked Orodes, clearly annoyed that he had been left out of things.

'What about them?' teased Domitus. 'They can sit on their arses and watch proper soldiers at work.'

Orodes was most unhappy but the only role for the armoured horsemen was as a reserve. As Domitus went back to his men and the legions deployed into a great hollow square, he remained at the head of the cataphracts in frustration. I stayed beside him, my helmet heating up my head, the sweat running down my cheeks and stinging my eyes. Behind me twelve hundred horsemen roasted in their armour. Fighting in the height of summer could be a most uncomfortable as well as a deadly experience.

The enemy commander knew what he was doing in that he adopted the correct tactics to suit the soldiers he had at his disposal. His spearmen halted around five hundred paces from the legions as the latter inched their way across the hard-packed earth towards them, retaining their formation as if they were on the parade square. Then the enemy horse archers attacked from the wings, companies darting towards the dense ranks of the legionaries and loosing their arrows. But the legionaries had already halted to form a continuous shield wall to face their attackers, while the ranks behind hoisted their shields above their heads to make an impervious roof of leather and wood.

Horse archers swept around the square, riders galloping to within a hundred paces of the shield wall to loose their arrows, then retreating and then attacking again and again, the hiss and whoosh of flying arrows enveloping the Durans and Exiles. While this thunderstorm of arrows was taking place Vagises' men on both flanks actually fell back to further isolate the square and lure the enemy in. And behind them the cataphracts continued to roast in their armour.

After around half an hour the inevitable happened: the enemy horse archers ran out of arrows and withdrew to take up position either side of the spearmen, who were now banging their shafts against the insides of their wicker shields and shouting and screaming their war cries. Then they advanced against Domitus' square.

Having believed he had weakened the opposition with his horse archers, the enemy commander now committed his spearmen to deliver the mortal blow to the soldiers who had been peppered with arrows. The spearmen advanced at a steady rate, retaining their lines as they did so. These men were obviously professional soldiers, well trained and equipped, the sun glinting off their helmets and spear points. Against ordinary soldiers they would have prevailed easily enough. But they were not facing ordinary soldiers; they were facing the legionaries of Lucius Domitus. And in the next few minutes the enemy commander's battle plan and army disintegrated before his eyes.

As Vagises' horse archers thundered across the ground to attack the two wings of enemy horsemen, trumpet blasts ordered the legions to deploy from square into line, the five cohorts at the top of the square halting while those that had formed the left-hand and right-hand sides of the square fanned out to take up position either side of them. They presented a line of fifteen cohorts to the enemy spearmen who, to their credit, continued their steady advance undeterred. In the rear the five cohorts who had formed the bottom of the square closed up on the first line, ready to act as a reserve to plug any gaps that might appear. None did.

I heard another blast of trumpets followed by a mighty cheer and then the cohorts raced forward to assault the spearmen, the first five ranks in each century hurling their javelins and the first rank then drawing their swords moments before they collided with the enemy, ramming their shield bosses into wicker shields and attempting to push their owners over as they stabbed with their swords. Javelins hit flesh and bone and bent on impact as they embedded themselves in wicker shields and the front ranks of the spearmen buckled and then collapsed as *gladius* blades went about their deadly work.

I felt elation sweep through me as, above the ghastly din of close-quarter combat, I heard the chant that had graced so many battlefields – 'Dura, Dura' – and knew that the enemy had been broken. And on the flanks Vagises and his horse archers charged at the enemy horsemen who now had no arrows. At the gallop they shot arrows at the stationary ranks that within minutes had turned tail and fled the battlefield, abandoning their foot soldiers to their fate. Vagises and his men gave chase. Orodes drew his sword and raised it in the air, turning in the saddle to order his men to move forward. I stopped him.

'No, my friend, today we let Vagises and Domitus have all the glory.'

He looked disconsolate as he slid his sword back in its scabbard and slumped in his saddle, while behind him the cataphracts continued to sweat in the heat.

The last, tragic act of the battle was played out as the sun at last began its descent in the western sky and began to lose some of its heat. Fifteen cohorts of legionaries methodically destroyed the enemy spearmen, who were attacked from the flanks as the five reserve cohorts were moved to the wings to envelop what remained of the opposition. The enemy commander died with his men who formed a tight circle around both him and their standard as they were cut down. Domitus brought me the flag, a great square of yellow cloth with a leering black Simurgel stitched in its centre, and threw it at my feet.

'Burn it,' I ordered.

I stood the cataphracts down as the sweating but jubilant legionaries filed back to camp to once again pitch their tents. They would sleep like the dead tonight. Orodes and his men led their horses back to the camp's stable area, they and their horses soaked with sweat and gripped by frustration.

Vagises returned after dark and reported to me immediately. He looked tired, filthy but elated, which only increased Orodes' discomfort.

'We chased them all the way to the walls of Seleucia,' he beamed. 'They ran their horses into the ground trying to flee us.'

'Well done, Vagises, you and your men have earned their pay today.'

He took a jug of water from the table, filled a cup and then emptied it.

'One thing you should know, Pacorus. We saw lots of foot soldiers on the road, all of them heading into Seleucia, horsemen as well.'

'They must be reinforcing the garrison,' said Orodes.

'Your plan has worked,' I said to Byrd, 'they must be sending troops from Babylon in response to our presence here.'

Vagises shook his head. 'We did not stay around long enough to get an accurate assessment of what was happening, but there are hundreds of tents pitched outside the city walls. Very odd.'

'Tomorrow we will find out what the enemy is up to,' I said.

As a rule Parthians do not fight in the hours of darkness but I increased the number of sentries that night as a precaution against an attack. Acting like thieves in the night suited Narses and Mithridates and it was obvious that their attention had now turned towards us following Vagises' report. But no attack came and in the morning we struck camp, cremated our own dead and marched south once more, leaving the enemy corpses to rot in the desert. Our own losses had amounted to a hundred legionaries killed and thirty wounded, with a further fifty horse archers slain. It had been another easy victory.

The army had not marched seven miles before Byrd and Malik returned to report that their scouts had detected another force approaching, this time from the southwest. Then they rode off to gather more information. This was getting tiring! For the third day the army deployed into its battle positions and waited for yet another enemy force to present itself. Would we ever get to Seleucia?

Again the cataphracts deployed behind the legions with the horse archers on the wings. The legionaries stood or sat on the ground and chatted to each other, relishing the thought of another day's easy slaughter.

Domitus sauntered over to where I was sitting on Remus next to Orodes.

'Your turn today, Orodes,' he said.

'Depends on what they send against us,' I said.

'If it's a bunch of kitchen maids armed with spits then Orodes is your man,' beamed Domitus. Orodes was far from amused.

We waited an hour before the familiar black shape of a large group of men appeared on the southwestern horizon. Worryingly neither Byrd nor Malik had returned to us. I prayed that they had not been captured or killed. I felt a knot tighten in my stomach. I would exchange all the victories I had won for their safety. I closed my eyes and prayed to Shamash to deliver them back to me safely.

The shapes grew bigger, shimmering in the heat and appearing like black liquid. Centurions blew whistles and their men dressed their ranks and awaited the coming clash in silence. The enemy was moving at speed, heading directly towards our right flank, a great banner fluttering in the centre of their line.

'I recognise that banner,' said Orodes straining his eyes. 'It is Nergal.'

I did not believe him and stared at the approaching horsemen to identify them myself. Utter relief swept through me as I saw that it was indeed the banner of Mesene that came towards us. And beside Nergal rode Malik and Byrd, and I also saw the black-robed Yasser with them.

I clasped Nergal's arm as he eventually halted before us, smiling as ever, and then greeted Orodes.

'We found them wandering in the desert, lost,' beamed Malik.

'Glad to have your men with us, Nergal,' I said. 'Vagises told us that there is a great army gathering at Seleucia, which is now probably heading this way.'

He looked surprised. 'No army is approaching, Pacorus. Narses and Mithridates have fled back across the Tigris, taking their army with them.'

'And Babylon?' Orodes looked momentarily concerned.

'The city is safe. My horsemen made contact with the garrison yesterday.'

'The last I heard,' I said to Nergal, 'you were beset by the hordes of King Phriapatius.'

'If I can wash the dust out of my throat,' he replied, 'I will tell you our story.'

That night he revealed what had happened in Mesene and Babylon. The Carmanians under Phriapatius had indeed invaded Nergal's kingdom and had marched towards Uruk. But Nergal had called on Yasser for help and as the enemy advanced on his capital Nergal's horsemen launched a series of hit-and-run raids against the Carmanians.

'Small parties, mostly,' said Nergal, chewing on a biscuit, 'just to slow their advance. But we kept up the pressure on them day and night to fray their nerves. And you know how Parthians hate to fight at night.'

'I've never understood that,' remarked Domitus. 'War is not a game. The enemy is there to be beaten irrespective of whether it's night or day.'

'Those of us who follow Shamash believe that it is better to fight during the day when we have His protection,' I replied, 'though I would not expect a heathen such as you to understand that, Domitus.'

'Better a living heathen than a dead worshipper,' he sniffed.

'The enemy got as far as Umma, a town less than fifty miles from Uruk,' continued Nergal, 'but I had strengthened its walls and the garrison was not to be intimidated, and we continued to launch raids against the besiegers until it was they who were besieged.'

He smiled at Yasser. 'It got worse for them when Lord Yasser arrived. After five days the Carmanians gave up and fell back towards the Tigris. Two days later Phriapatius asked for a truce. So you see, there was never a battle and Uruk was never threatened.'

'I get the impression that Phriapatius is a rather lukewarm player in the grand scheme of Mithridates and Narses,' I said.

'That is why I am here, Pacorus,' replied Nergal, 'to take you to see him.'

The next day I gave command of the army to Orodes and told him to take it directly to Babylon to secure the city. Mithridates and Narses may have retreated but there were still probably roving bands of the enemy at large that had either been deliberately left behind or had deserted and were nothing more than groups of brigands. I took a thousand horse archers with me as I accompanied Nergal and Yasser

335

south. We travelled at speed through a land laid waste by a cruel enemy. Every village we came upon had been destroyed and its population either killed or carried off into slavery. The bodies of the slaughtered still lay where they had been cut down, the stench of decomposition filling our nostrils and making us want to retch. Occasionally we saw a dead dog next to a corpse where a master and his faithful servant had been killed side by side.

We rode into the now deserted Jem det Nasr and straight into a scene of horror. The enemy had obviously killed those remaining members of the population before they had fled. As we made our way to the centre of the city we rode through streets strewn with bodies, mostly the elderly, frail and children, those who were not strong enough to endure a forced march. Any able-bodied men and women and teenage girls would have been taken away as slaves, though we did come across the naked corpses of women whose breasts had been cut off, no doubt having first been raped before their mutilation and murder.

'And they say that we are savages,' remarked Yasser.

At that moment I was ashamed to be a Parthian, ashamed that Parthians could do such things to each other. It was worse than the scenes I had witnessed at Forum Annii in Italy when Crixus and his Gauls had stormed that place and butchered its inhabitants. There was literally no one left alive, in fact nothing left alive, just the usual repellent odour of death that hung over the whole city.

We reached the centre of the city where the Temple of Shamash stood, its massive twin doors shut. It fronted a large square and behind it was the governor's palace and the royal barracks. We filed into the square and Nergal organised parties to search the palace grounds to see if there were any survivors. Fortunately the enemy had not had time to torch the city.

Yasser seated on his horse looked at the shut doors of the temple.

'There are no braces against the doors, they must have been shut from the inside.'

'Perhaps there are people in there,' said Nergal.

I looked at the temple, the barred doors facing east like every temple dedicated to Shamash. They were set back from the yellow stone columns that surrounded the building on all four sides to support the high arched roof. There was a smaller entrance in the west wall of the temple but an officer reported that it too was closed.

I dismounted and walked up the dozen stone steps that led to the main entrance. There were square windows cut high in the walls allowing the rays of the sun to enter the temple. In the mornings the priests would welcome its first rays, signifying that Shamash had left the underworld to bring the sun to warm the earth once more. The sound of hundreds of horsemen riding into the square would have

336

been carried through those windows to whoever, if anyone, was inside. Aside from horses scraping at the ground and chomping on their bits there was silence. Any people inside would probably be filled with terror at the thought that their tormentors had returned. I stood in front of the doors.

'I am Pacorus, King of Dura and a friend and ally of your queen. If there are any within the temple let them come forth in the knowledge that I am here to protect you.'

There was no reply to my plea.

'I say again, my name is King Pacorus of Dura and I am a friend of Queen Axsen. The enemy has left your city. You are safe.'

I looked behind me to where Nergal was sitting on his horse beside Yasser, the latter smiling and shaking his head at me. I walked back down the steps.

'What now?' asked Nergal.

'We will break down the doors.'

I called forward the commander of the horse archers who organised an empty stone water trough to be used as a battering ram. A dozen men, six on each side, supported the trough on iron bars and rammed it against the doors, which were eventually forced open after being struck a dozen times.

The pungent aroma of dead flesh and emptied bowels met our nostrils the moment we stepped inside the temple, shoving aside the tables that had been used to brace the doors. Light was still flooding through the windows, illuminating the interior where bodies lay on the marble-tiled floor. Only Nergal, Yasser and I entered the temple, picking our way through the dead towards the altar at the far end. I knelt down and examined one of the bodies. There were no marks on it, no signs of a violent struggle and no gaping wounds. The expression on the woman's face was one of calm resignation. I went to another corpse, this time an old man in his sixties. Once again there were no marks on the body, no signs of violence. The eyes were closed and I saw an empty cup in his hand. Looking around I saw other cups scattered on the floor.

'They took poison. Hemlock, probably,' I said.

'Suicide?' Nergal was shocked. Parthians generally frowned on the taking of one's own life, seeing it as a cowardly and disgraceful act.

'The priests have also taken their own lives,' I said, pointing to the high altar where white-robed figures lay on the dais. 'They must have authorised the distribution of the poison and thus sanctioned the act. That being the case, I assume that the suicides were a way of protesting against submission to tyranny, and in the women's case a way of avoiding the shame of rape. Shamash will care for their souls.'

I ordered that the bodies were to be removed from the temple and consigned to funeral pyres along with the other corpses in the city.

That night we camped outside the city walls to sleep well away from so much death.

The next day I left the horse archers to garrison the city and rode on with Nergal and Yasser. Amazingly, as we journeyed south we encountered small groups of people who had come out of hiding and were making their way back to their homes. Some had fled from Jem det Nasr and were now heading back there, though perhaps it would have been better if they had not, such was the scene of desolation that awaited them.

As we rode from Babylonia to Mesene we left behind death and destruction and travelled through a countryside untouched by war. Nergal told me that Phriapatius had kept his men under control and his own attacks had confined them to a small corridor that extended from the River Tigris to Umma. We slept at the latter place the night before my meeting with the King of Carmania. Praxima had ridden to the city to await her husband and me, and I embraced her warmly, my face engulfed in her wild red hair. She told us that High Priest Rahim had things in order at Uruk and had delivered a sermon to thousands of people at the White Temple in the city, telling them that the retreat of Carmania's army was a miracle worked by Anu and proof that Nergal and Praxima were beloved of the gods.

'He told me that he frowns upon the Agraci being in Mesene,' she said, smiling at Yasser as we were served roasted chicken coated in a delicious sweet sauce.

'Let Rahim believe that the gods saved the kingdom,' said Nergal, washing his hands in a bowl of warm water. 'I am glad that eight thousand Agraci warriors are with me.'

'You do not believe your gods are helping you?' asked Yasser.

'The gods help those who help themselves,' replied Praxima.

'It is as my wife says,' added Nergal.

'Then the gods must look favourably upon our alliance with your people, Yasser,' I said.

'That is one way of looking at it,' he agreed. 'If I had been told that one day I would be sharing a meal with Parthian kings...'

'And a queen,' interrupted Praxima. Yasser smiled at her.

'Then I would have told them they were mad. And yet here we are, so perhaps the gods are indeed weaving their magic around us.'

'How many men does Phriapatius have?' I asked, turning to more practical matters.

'Around ten thousand,' answered Nergal.

'A few less now,' grinned Yasser. 'Nergal wants to talk but I urged him to attack them. I can smell their fear from here. They are weak and should be slaughtered like lambs.'

I smiled thinly at him. I sometimes forgot that our Agraci allies were ruthless as well as cunning. They despised weakness and

338

respected strength. Yasser did not become a lord by diplomacy and Haytham did not become a king of these fierce desert people by being merciful.

'I think we shall hear what the Carmanians have to say before we put them to the sword,' I said as Yasser screwed up his face at my words.

'When words run out the conversation is carried on with weapons,' he replied, holding a rack of lamb in his hand and tearing off a great strip of meat with his teeth. 'It has always been so and always will be.'

He pointed at all three of us in turn.

'You talk of peace but only when it suits you, and only from a position of strength. When you, Pacorus, were trapped in the desert before my king and your queen came to your aid, did you squeal like a little girl and ask for quarter? You did not. And you, Nergal, when the enemy invaded your lands did you lie down like a lamb and invite him to steal your kingdom? You are more like me than you like to think. Now that the enemy has retreated you wish to talk, but I know that you would both prefer war.'

There is an old road that runs from Uruk through Umma and across the Tigris to the city of Susa and thereafter to the east. From Uruk the road heads north into the Kingdom of Babylon and then into Hatra. It spans the Tigris between Umma and Susa by means of a multi-arched stone bridge that was built by Greek engineers after Alexander of Macedon had conquered the Persians over two hundred and fifty years ago. Ever since that time it had been maintained by engineers employed by the king of kings himself, for it was the only bridge south of the one at Seleucia and as such was strategically important. Though in summer the level of the Tigris drops considerably, below Seleucia the river is still at least twenty feet deep even in the hottest months and thus an army not in possession of the bridge would need a great number of rafts to get across the waterway.

Nergal had decided not to fight Phriapatius at the bridge but rather let him and his army cross into Mesene. Afterwards, as the Carmanians were advancing towards Umma, Nergal's horsemen attacked and destroyed those enemy forces left behind to defend the bridge. Phriapatius was thus cut off and surrounded at the beginning of his campaign. He had negotiated a truce with Nergal soon after, one of the terms of which was that he and his army would be allowed withdraw to the east bank of the Tigris. We now dismounted and left our horses at the western end of the bridge and walked across the yellow flagstones that covered its surface.

The day was hot and airless, the waters of the Tigris below us brown and slow moving. I walked with Nergal, Praxima and Yasser as Nergal's horse archers together with their Agraci allies lined the riverbank either side of the bridge. On the opposite bank the army of Carmania was drawn up to face them – a mass of cataphracts at the bridge, with horse archers and mounted spearmen carrying huge round shields on either side. Green dragon windsocks hung limply from their poles among the ranks of the horse archers but I knew that the symbol of Carmania was the golden peacock.

Four figures approached us to equal the number of our own party. As we got to within a hundred paces of each other both groups slowed as if by mutual consent, though more likely mutual suspicion. I rested my left hand on the hilt of my sword as I studied the king and his subordinates. Phriapatius himself walked a couple of paces in front of the others. He was a man of medium height with broad shoulders, a thick black beard, large nose and skin turned dark brown by the sun. He wore an open-faced bronze helmet on his head and a short-sleeved silver scale armour cuirass. Sculptured bronze plates bearing a peacock motif, the design also appearing on the sleeves of his red silk shirt, also protected his shoulders. His sword was held in a red scabbard decorated with gold and on his feet he wore a fine pair of red boots.

All of the men behind him also wore scale armour, two of them were about half the king's age while the third carried his helmet in the crock of his arm and wore red leggings edged with gold and silver greaves. By the look of his weatherworn face I guessed he was one of the king's senior commanders. We halted ten paces from each other.

'Greetings King Phriapatius,' said Nergal, holding out his hand to me. 'This is King Pacorus of Dura.'

I bowed my head ever so slightly to Phriapatius, who nodded back.

'I remember you from the Council of Kings at Esfahan all those years ago. You look older now and more severe.'

'Constant war does that to a man, lord,' I answered. 'How can I be of assistance to you?'

'Straight to the point, I like that. I can tell you have not spent any time at the grand court at Ctesiphon lately.'

'I find the atmosphere there disagreeable, lord, and the man who occupies its throne even more distasteful.'

He smiled wryly. 'So I have heard. Mithridates would pay me handsomely if I drew my sword and slew you right here, on this bridge.'

He made no movement to draw his sword but Nergal, Praxima and Yasser instinctively clasped the hilts of their swords; the three others behind Phriapatius did the same. I stood dead still and fixed his brown eyes with my own. He smiled.

'But then that would make me a worthless murdering wretch like he is, not a responsible king who desires only to be back in his kingdom.'

340

The atmosphere, seconds before tense, relaxed as he waved his hand at his subordinates to show restraint.

'I would talk with you in private, King Pacorus,' he said.

I nodded to the others who withdrew a few paces behind me, while those with Phriapatius likewise retreated. The king walked over to the edge of the stone parapet and stared at the water below.

'I thank you for coming here today,' he said, still staring at the river. 'I would not have blamed you if you had brought your army to do your talking.'

'My army has done its talking in Hatra and Babylonia, lord. Even as we stand here and talk, Narses and Mithridates crawl back to Ctesiphon with their tails between their legs.'

He looked surprised. 'Babylon has not fallen?'

'No, lord,' I answered, 'though grievous damage has been inflicted upon Queen Axsen's kingdom.'

He nodded to himself. 'Narses promised an easy victory against Babylon. He also promised those who marched with him would be richly rewarded with lands and gold at the expense of those kingdoms who sided with you. The reality has turned out to be very different, it appears.'

'You should also know that Cinnamus and Vologases were also turned back at Hatra's border. I know; I was there.'

He stared once more at the meandering waters of the Tigris. 'So the grand scheme begins to unfold.'

'Next year,' I announced, 'Dura and others will be marching across the Tigris to put an end to Mithridates once and for all. I would be honoured to have the banner of Carmania fly next to mine.'

He turned his head and looked at me. 'How many children do you have, Pacorus?'

'Children?'

'Yes, how many? One, two, a dozen?'

'Three, lord, all daughters.'

He jerked his thumb to where his three subordinates stood facing Nergal, Praxima and Yasser. 'The two young ones are my sons, Phanes and Peroz.'

'They are fine young men, lord.'

'I have two other sons, who are currently "guests" at Ctesiphon, and you will find that the other eastern kings of the empire also have their children being held hostage at Mithridates' palace. If my banner flew beside yours, Pacorus, their heads would be adorning his palace walls.'

I shook my head. Many years ago Mithridates had been the ruler of Dura and had taken the sons of the kingdom's lords hostage to ensure their fathers' continued allegiance. Now he did the same to the kings of the eastern half of the empire.

'He is a tyrant,' I said.

Phriapatius laughed. 'So are most king of kings, though I grant you this one seems blessed by particularly cruel traits. If it was a matter of dealing solely with Mithridates then I would give your offer serious consideration, but as long as he has my sons and his lord high general stands behind him then Carmania will not assist you.'

'And will Carmania fight beside Mithridates and Narses next year?' I asked.

'Next year Carmania will answer Ctesiphon's summons if you march against Mithridates.' He picked up a small stone and flicked it into the river. 'Though it will take a long time to muster its army and even longer to march it to Ctesiphon. By then affairs either way will most likely be settled.'

His strategy made sense. His kingdom sat in the southeast corner of the empire but was bordered by Persis to the northwest and Sakastan to the north. Narses ruled both kingdoms and could easily launch punitive raids against Carmania if he suspected Phriapatius of treachery.

'I understand, lord,' I said at length. 'And what will you do now?'

'Now, King Pacorus, out of strategic necessity I will be withdrawing my army back to its homeland.'

We watched the Carmanians pull back from the river and take the road to Susa, a long line of horsemen and camels carrying their tents and supplies. Phriapatius may have wanted to return to Carmania, a distance of some eight hundred miles, but Mithridates would retain his army nearer the Tigris in view of his own retreat from Babylon. As we watched the horsemen disappear on the horizon Yasser urged Nergal to ride across the bridge and attack the withdrawing Carmanians but he declined.

'I have enough men to hold my own kingdom but not enough to invade Susiana, even with your men, Yasser.'

'In any case,' I added, 'Phriapatius may be a useful ally when we cross the Tigris next year.'

Yasser threw up his hands in exasperation.

'Next year? We could all be dead by then. The time to strike is now, Nergal. Take revenge on those who have sprinkled the earth of your kingdom with blood.'

'They should pay for what they have done,' agreed Praxima, always ready to act first and ask questions later.

'My friends,' I said, 'they will pay, I promise. When we have taken Ctesiphon the royal treasury will be opened to pay compensation to those kingdoms that have suffered at the hands of Mithridates. I ask only that you show restraint now.'

Praxima shrugged and Yasser curled his lip in the direction of Phriapatius' vanishing army, but Nergal thankfully saw sense.

'We will accede to your wishes, Pacorus, but Mesene will want restitution for the outrages committed on its territory this year.'

I said my farewells to them at Umma and then travelled north to Babylon. As I had left my horse archers at Jem det Nasr, Nergal gave me a hundred of his men for an escort to Axsen's capital. When we arrived five days later Dura's army had already established its camp to the west of the city near the Marduk Gate. The scenes of devastation that I had seen on my journey to Mesene were repeated, with villages destroyed and irrigation systems wrecked. It would take Axsen years to repair the damage done to her kingdom.

In camp I discovered Vagises and his horse archers, who had returned from Jem det Nasr following the despatch of soldiers from Babylon to replace them. I called the senior officers to my tent to inform them of what had happened at the meeting with Phriapatius, though Orodes was not present.

'He's with the queen in the city,' said Domitus.

'He has taken up permanent residence in the palace,' added Kronos.

'Well, it will be his palace as well soon enough,' I remarked. 'Babylon will need a strong hand to guide it through the coming years.'

'There isn't much of a kingdom left,' said Domitus. 'Half of it has been carried off into slavery.'

'We will get them back,' I promised. 'Mithridates and Narses will be held to account for what they have done.'

'Turning to matters at hand,' said Domitus, 'it might be wise to get the army back to Dura. Near fourteen thousand soldiers, two thousand drivers, two thousand squires and thousands of horses, mules and camels will sap an already exhausted kingdom further.'

'I would concur, but for a different reason,' added Alcaeus. 'I have visited the city and it is still thronged with refugees. It is amazing that plague has not broken out in the city already. I would advise that the army leaves the vicinity of the city for fear of any sickness spreading to your soldiers.'

'Agreed,' I said. 'Make the preparations to march north immediately, Domitus. In the meantime I will visit the queen and her husband to be.'

Domitus gave me a century as an escort with Thumelicus in command. He and his men left their javelins in camp but retained their mail armour, helmets, swords and shields, and had been issued with wooden clubs in case of any difficulties they might encounter. The Marduk Gate was guarded by Babylonian spearmen and the gates themselves were open, though very few people were leaving the city. They had no doubt previously fled from the depravations of the enemy and were unwilling to leave the safety of the city without protection.

The commander at the Marduk Gate, a tall, thin man in his thirties made gaunt by the siege, reported to me when we entered the city.

'It is chaos, majesty. There are thousands of people camped on every street and in every doorway. Lord Mardonius is organising companies to escort people back to their villages but it will take an age.'

'Did the garrison lose many men during the siege?' I asked.

He shook his head. 'The enemy attempted no assault against the city. Their favoured tactic was lobbing the severed heads of villagers over the walls to try and cower us into surrender. It struck fear into those who had fled from the countryside, though.'

'What about your food supplies?'

'We went on half-rations two months ago. Another two months and we would have had to start eating those lot,' he nodded towards the crowd of filthy, starving refugees that had begun to gather around Thumelicus and his legionaries.

'They would not make much of a meal.'

'Do you want an escort to the palace, majesty?'

'No, we will make our own way there.'

I left him to his command of the gate and its garrison, whose drawn, sunken faces looked similar to those of the refugees. As I led Remus by his reins further into the city the legionaries closed around me, shoving aside individuals with their shields. As we walked from the gate the stench of a long siege: the smell of human and animal dung, rotting refuse and death entered our nostrils. The road was literally carpeted with people, both men and women, young and old, many too malnourished and weak to stand and move aside. The crowd who had gathered round Thumelicus and his men had followed us, probably in the hope that the big, well-fed soldiers in their shiny helmets and mail shirts might toss them a few morsels to eat. My German centurion soon grew tired of their imploring and clawing and hit one of them on the arm with his club, sending the wretch sprawling. This sparked angry shouting and some waved their fists at him, which on reflection was the worst thing they could have done.

'Ready,' he shouted and his men raised their clubs in preparation to attack the crowd.

A gaunt man was jabbing his finger angrily at Thumelicus, a stream of abuse coming from his twisted mouth, who then fell silent as a great German hand deftly flicked the club it was holding into the side of his face, splitting his nose and also sending him tumbling. The crowd were outraged at this and began shouting and threatening the legionaries, who faced the crowd with their clubs at the ready.

'No violence,' I ordered as a stone hit Remus' rump. 'Let us get to the palace as quickly as possible.'

'Raise shields,' shouted Thumelicus.

The legionaries in the front rank closed up and locked their shields together on all four sides of our formation, those behind raising theirs above their heads to form a roof as we were pelted with stones, dung, rotting vegetables and sticks. The smell was disgusting.

As we inched our way towards the palace Thumelicus and those beside him in the front rank clubbed some more civilians who got too close, splitting heads and cracking ribs. More and more people gathered round us as the tumult alerted others to what was going on and the pack instincts of a hungry and desperate crowd took hold. I was unconcerned about my men, who were more inconvenienced than threatened, but I did worry about the crowd's safety. My fears were confirmed when I heard Thumelicus curse and saw that he had been struck in the face by a great clump of animal dung. The crowd thought this hilarious and began pointing and laughing at him.

He threw down his club. 'Swords!' he bellowed and I heard the scraping sound of eighty blades being pulled from their scabbards.

The crowd must have numbered between three and four hundred people by now and I had visions of the same number lying dead in front of Axsen's palace.

'No violence,' I ordered again as the gates of the palace suddenly opened and horsemen rode from the royal compound, at least three score carrying shields and spears and attired in purple. They charged at the crowd, which rapidly dispersed from in front of the gates.

'Stand down,' said Thumelicus as he and the others returned their swords to their scabbards.

'It was a good job those horsemen appeared when they did, otherwise we would have sliced open a few bellies.'

'You really must try to keep your temper in check,' I told him.

He wiped his face and then smelt his fingers and screwed up his face.

'I don't take kindly to being pelted with shit. They should turf all those people out of the city. They stink and it stinks.'

I slapped him on the shoulder. 'And so do you! Get your men inside and then they and you can get cleaned up.'

The horsemen kept the crowd at bay as we entered the palace compound where Mardonius was waiting to greet me. He looked immaculate as usual, though his face wore a deep frown when he saw we had been the brunt of a hostile crowd.

'My apologies, majesty.'

'Think nothing of it,' I said as a stable hand took Remus from me. 'People do desperate things in desperate times.'

'And these are desperate times,' he agreed. 'I fear that the kingdom is ruined.'

So did I but said nothing.

'The queen is well?' I asked.

He smiled. 'Indeed, the more so since the arrival of Prince Orodes. He is a great friend of Babylon. As is King Nergal. I did not think I would live to see the day when Mesene and its Agraci allies would prove to be Babylon's allies against the empire's king of kings.'

'We live in strange times,' I agreed.

We walked towards the palace as Thumelicus and his men were shown to a barracks block to wash the filth from their clothing. Thumelicus barked orders at his men, still fuming at his treatment in the street and his frustration at not being allowed to kill a few civilians in reprisal.

'You travelled through the eastern part of the kingdom, majesty?' asked Mardonius.

I thought of the despoiled villages and the empty Jem det Nasr. 'Yes, it has suffered greatly during the recent strife.'

His head dropped. 'Mithridates has impoverished the kingdom.'

'There is gold enough at Ctesiphon to rebuild this kingdom,' I replied.

He looked shocked. 'You will march against the capital of the empire?'

'Next year, yes, and I will not be marching alone.'

We walked on in silence. Despite the kingdom of his queen having been ravaged by Mithridates I could sense that Mardonius was ill at ease with the notion of making war against the office of king of kings. Fortunately I did not share his reticence.

The palace itself was a place of calm and order and contrasted sharply to the scenes immediately beyond its walls. Well-dressed officials walked along its long corridors and among its pillars, white-robed priests talked with other in hushed tones and courtiers with neatly trimmed beards and wearing brightly coloured robes bowed their heads to us as we entered the throne room where Axsen awaited us.

She had inherited her father's full frame and in her teenage years her figure had earned her the cruel nickname 'Princes Water Buffalo'. With the passing of time, though, she had lost much of the baby fat of her younger years. And now the responsibility of ruling a kingdom alone and the recent siege had resulted in her losing more weight, and I have to say that the slimmer Axsen appeared more regal and attractive. Adversity suited her.

I took off my helmet and went down on one knee before the dais upon which her throne stood. Beside her Orodes occupied the other throne. Mardonius struggled to get down on his aged knee.

Axsen smiled, rose from her throne and placed her hands on my shoulders.

'Hail, great queen,' I said. 'Dura salutes you.'

She leaned forward and kissed me on the cheek. 'Oh, Pacorus, you are so formal. Please get up. And arise, Lord Mardonius, before you do yourself a mischief.'

I assisted him back onto his feet as he winced from the pain in his joints. Axsen retook her throne and smiled girlishly at Orodes. So, he must have proposed and she must have accepted his offer. I was pleased.

'We have news for you, King Pacorus, the liberator of Babylon,' said Axsen, to polite applause from the officers, priests and courtiers present. 'I am to be married to Prince Orodes of Susiana.'

Louder applause greeted this announcement and I nodded and smiled at Orodes. I went down on one knee again.

'This is truly great news, majesty, and heralds a new age for the Kingdom of Babylon.'

'Rise, Pacorus, my dear friend,' commanded Axsen as Orodes stepped forward and we clasped arms.

'Well done, my friend,' I whispered.

I stepped onto the dais and kissed Axsen on the cheek.

'May Shamash bless your union,' I said, earning me a glower from Nabu who stood by the side of the dais and looked as though he had just had a tooth pulled.

Later, when we relaxed in Axsen's private wing in the palace, sitting in a small courtyard with fountains and an ornamental pond in which swam large golden fish, I asked Axsen the reason for Nabu's miserable face.

'When the city filled with refugees I knew Babylon would not have enough food to feed all the people, but I also knew that the temples would be able to ease our burden and so ordered them to distribute their offerings to the people.'

'The daily tribute,' added Orodes.

Every major city had its great temples whose gods demanded daily tribute from the people. It was customary for granaries to be built near those temples to produce bread that was then sold to worshippers who laid it on altars, after which it was removed by the priests and preserved in the many storehouses built at the rear of the temples. It was then sold to bakeries in the city, and the other tributes were either eaten by the priests or sold by them. It was a very lucrative enterprise.

'High Priest Nabu,' continued Axsen, 'was most upset and declared that Marduk would punish the city, to which I reminded him that if the city fell then his temple would be destroyed by the followers of the bird god, so he agreed.'

'Reluctantly,' added Orodes.

'Each day,' continued Axsen, 'the faithful lay before Marduk over two hundred containers of beer, two hundred and forty loaves of

347

bread, fifty rams, three bulls and great quantities of dates, lambs, ducks and eggs. Enough to help feed a city packed full of people.'

'And what of the Temple of Ishtar and its offerings?'

Axsen giggled. 'I have to confess that I have made no demands upon Afrand as I do not want to offend the goddess before our wedding.'

She reached over to Orodes who took her hand in his.

'That annoyed Nabu even more.'

'I think Lord Nabu's annoyance will soon disappear now that the city is no longer besieged and his storehouses begin to fill again,' remarked Orodes.

'And his treasury,' said Axsen dryly.

'What of Babylon's treasury?' I asked.

Axsen showed her palms. 'Empty, and likely to remain so for many years to come.'

No more was said on the matter as I politely asked about their forthcoming marriage, but it made me more determined than ever to make Mithridates pay for what he had done. And after I had taken Ctesiphon then the treasury at Persepolis would also be emptied of its contents.

I stayed in Babylon for another week, though the army began its march back to Dura the day after I had arrived at the city. It travelled along the eastern bank of the Euphrates, now somewhat diminished in numbers compared to its size at the beginning of the campaign. We had suffered low casualties but Surena had departed for Gordyene with eight thousand horse archers and Orodes announced that he was staying in Babylon with his two hundred and fifty men. The latter was a grievous loss. He had become like a brother to me and I would miss his company greatly. Domitus was also sad to see him go but was happy that the army was returning to Dura in triumph following its victory at Makhmur.

'That will be another silver disc on the Staff of Victory,' he announced.

'What about our other triumphs near Seleucia?' I asked.

'Slaughters don't count,' he sniffed. 'I wonder what happened to those soldiers you let go? What was the name of that drunk who commanded them?'

'Udall,' I answered.

'You should have killed them by rights. You will only have to fight them again next year.'

I shook my head and smiled. No matter how long he remained in Parthia a part of Domitus would always remain Roman.

The day before I left Babylon, which was now returning to a semblance of normality with the gradual return of the refugees back to what remained of their homes, I rode to the Temple of Ishtar. The

348

temple guards at the entrance let me pass and I trotted into the first courtyard that was empty aside from two young priestesses who hurried out of sight when they saw me. I dismounted and led Remus to the stables that fronted one side of the courtyard where I left him in the care of a young stable hand dressed in the temple's livery. For some reason there were no worshippers in the temple grounds, the only movement being the white birds entering and exiting their dovecotes. I walked across the courtyard and through the arch that led to the second, smaller courtyard, passing the guards that stood before it. I continued towards the temple doors but the two guards who stood either side of them barred my way.

'Out of my way,' I ordered but they remained where they were and stared menacingly at me.

'Do you know who I am?'

'The whole world knows who King Pacorus is,' said a voice behind me.

I turned to see Afrand standing a few paces from me, her hair tumbling over her breasts that were barely held in place by her flimsy transparent white top.

'I wish to enter the temple,' I said.

'The goddess is not receiving guests today.'

'I wish to speak to the one who spoke to me when I was last here.'

'There are no words for you today, highness.'

I was starting to get annoyed. 'I will be the judge of that.'

'No,' she calmly, 'you will not.'

I folded my arms across my chest.

'It will take more than two guards to prevent me.'

She smiled. 'The goddess Ishtar has been kind to you, King Pacorus, and now you come to her home with threats of violence. Why would you treat her so disrespectfully?'

I suddenly felt very uncomfortable. 'I did not mean to insult the goddess, of course not. I merely wished to see if she would speak to me once more.'

She held out her hand. 'Walk with me majesty.'

She led me away from the temple doors, the fragrance of myrrh on her body entering my nostrils as I walked beside her. Her robe was slit from the waist, revealing her lithe legs, and I found it hard not stare at her voluptuous breasts. She was most intoxicating.

'Most people who come to worship at the temple are ignored by the goddess because they are unworthy. That she sent you a vision shows that you are beloved of the gods, Pacorus of Dura. But you do not command them to do your bidding any more than I do.'

She was right. 'I apologise for being so rash.'

We walked from the courtyard into a spacious hall that was rich with the aroma of lavender. A flight of marble steps before us led to a second storey of red-painted doors and walls adorned with scenes of fornication. I blushed as I found myself staring at depictions of naked couples intertwined.

'The murals offend you?' asked Afrand, noticing my discomfort.

'They are a surprise, that is all.'

She laughed. 'Ishtar is the goddess of love. Why are you surprised that her temple grounds should show depictions of that emotion?'

'Perhaps because I believe such things should remain private,' I replied.

She considered for a moment. 'The friend who spoke to you when you were here last, she is dead, is she not?'

'How did you know?'

She smiled. 'I could tell by the look on your face when you left us. Her spirit must be strong to be able to leave the spirit world to enter the domain of the living.'

I thought of Claudia, the wife of Spartacus, and nodded. 'She was strong, yes.'

'You will see here again.'

I felt my heart increase its beat. 'When?'

She cupped my face with her hand. 'Not yet, great king. Not until you have fulfilled your destiny.'

Chapter 14

I rode back to Dura in the company of Malik, Byrd and their scouts, following in the wake of the city's army, which had left a well-beaten track where thousands of hooves, sandals and wheels had trampled the earth. At the border of my father's kingdom we were met by a courier who brought news that the combined forces of Media and Atropaiene had fought a great battle west of the Caspian Sea. They had defeated the armies of King Monaeses of Yueh-Chih and King Tiridates of Aria, who had retreated back east. The victory was bought at a heavy price, though, for King Farhad had fallen in the battle and now his son, Atrax, ruled Media. In addition, my father and Gafarn had pursued the armies of Anauon and Drangiana back to Ecbatana where they had linked up with Atrax and Aschek. My father ended his note by stating that he believed the enemy would now retreat back through the Caspian Gates to their homelands. The threat to Hatra, Media and Atropaiene was for the moment over.

'Atrax will make a good king,' said Malik after he had finished reading the letter and had passed it to Byrd.

'Yes, he will,' I agreed.

Byrd handed the note back to me. 'So, the great plot of Mithridates has failed. What now?'

It was a good question and I would have liked to have announced that I was going to march straight to Ctesiphon, batter down its aged walls and remove Mithridates. But the truth was that the army had been campaigning for nearly six months continuously and needed a spell of rest and recuperation. Of my allies, Babylon was on its knees, Media and Atropaiene had both been invaded and no doubt ravaged and even Hatra had been forced to send its army far from home, and in addition still had to contend with the Armenian threat in the north. As far as I knew Musa and Khosrou were still campaigning in the vastness between the Caspian and Aral seas, so they would be unable to support any offensive against Ctesiphon. I consoled myself with the thought that our enemies were probably in a worse state having suffered heavier losses. The whole empire was exhausted.

'We go home, Byrd, that is what we do.'

It was good to see Dura again, to see the road thronged with traffic and to catch sight of the Citadel glowing yellow in the sun above the blue waters of the Euphrates. The army had received a tumultuous reception when it had returned but our small party slipped quietly into the city and rode unnoticed along the main street to the Citadel. We dismounted in the courtyard where Gallia, my children, Rsan and Aaron waited at the foot of the palace steps. I embraced my family and then sat with them on the palace terrace as Rsan gave me his report first. While he did so Dobbai slept in her wicker chair by the side of the balustrade. Servants brought us drink and food as Eszter played with her maid and Isabella and Claudia arranged their chairs beside mine.

'Notwithstanding the recent conflict, which did interrupt trade, revenues have remained largely stable, majesty.'

'And the deliveries to Alexander?' I asked Aaron.

'All is in order, majesty,' he replied. 'Deliveries are on time and payment is prompt.'

'Indeed,' said Rsan, 'though we will need the gold to pay for the costs incurred by the army during its recent campaign. General Domitus has once again put in a large request for javelins and Lord Vagises has requested a sizeable amount of arrows.'

'That is the nature of war, Rsan. Surely the gold that comes from Alexander is more than sufficient to pay for the army's requirements, especially now Silaces and his eight thousand men are no longer with us?'

Rsan nodded gravely. 'It is as you say, majesty, though it would be better to build up the treasury's reserves rather than continually dipping into them.'

Rsan was in essence a hoarder, an individual who liked nothing more than to amass ever-greater quantities of items around himself, in his case gold.

'The revenues from the caravans and from Alexander are more than enough to pay for the army and build up the treasury's reserves,' I told him. 'However, it may comfort you to know that next year your treasury will be benefitting from another source of gold.'

Rsan's eyes lit up. 'Most excellent news, majesty. May I enquire the nature of this new source?'

'The treasury at Ctesiphon,' I replied.

Rsan looked confused. 'I do not understand.'

I waved my hand at him. 'It has been a tiring day, Rsan, you may go.'

He wanted to know more but I was in no mood to explain so he bowed his head and retreated from the terrace, followed by Aaron.

'Aaron,' I called after him, 'I would speak with you.'

He retraced his steps and stood before me.

'Majesty?'

'You have been in contact with Alexander?'

He nodded.

'When will he begin his rebellion?'

'Next year, majesty, as Arsam has increased the quantities of weapons being produced by the armouries.'

'And Alexander is pleased with the weapons we are supplying?'

Aaron smiled. 'Very pleased, majesty.'

'Good, you may go.'

'Viper was most upset that you sent Surena away from the army,' said Gallia after Aaron had left the terrace.

'He is a good commander and has eight thousand men with him. He will be safe enough.'

'She wants to know how long he will be away.'

I closed my eyes and stretched out my legs. 'I have no idea but it could be a few more months yet.'

'She has requested that she be allowed to go to his side.'

'Well,' I replied, 'she is one of the Amazons so it is your decision.'

'Since Praxima's departure Viper has become one of my best warriors. I do not wish her to leave.'

'Then tell her so,' I replied.

'What did you mean when you told Rsan that the treasury gold at Ctesiphon will be made available to him?'

'He means, child, that next year the King of Dura will be marching against the king of king's capital. Is that not correct, son of Hatra?'

Dobbai had awoken from her slumbers and was now ambling towards me.

I opened my eyes. 'Mithridates must pay for the damage he has caused in the empire. I have seen what his troops did in Babylonia and attempted to do in Hatra. My father is in agreement that he should be removed, and with Hatra's army beside mine no one will be able to stop us.'

'We received word from Atrax,' said Gallia, 'that Media had also been devastated and large parts of Atropaiene.'

'There is gold enough at Ctesiphon to compensate all.'

'Not if the Romans get it first,' said Dobbai, cupping Claudia's face in her palm.

'The Romans?'

'You did not think that they had gone away did you, son of Hatra?'

'I have heard no reports of Roman activity in Syria,' I answered.

'They watch and wait,' said Dobbai, pointing at me. 'They have seen the empire tear itself apart by civil strife and they wait. I told you once that you would face two mighty armies, one from the east and one from the west. You have helped to turn back the one from the east but have yet to vanquish it, but you must act quickly so that you will be able to face the one from the west when it comes. And it will, mark my words. The eagles are gathering.'

But Byrd and Malik assured me that there was no indication that the Romans in Syria were preparing an offensive against Parthia. So, as the year faded and then died, a strange calm descended over the empire. From the Taurus Mountains to the Persian Gulf there was an uneasy peace and gossip picked up from the trade caravans informed us that the eastern kings had limped back to their homelands where they remained. Nothing was heard from Musa or Khosrou and many thought that they had both been killed in the northern wastes, while other stories spread that they and their armies had been swallowed up by the endless steppes across which they marched and were doomed to forever wander the empty vastness. Word reached us from Nergal at Uruk that Phriapatius had returned to Carmania and that Narses brooded in Persis, but no one heard anything from Ctesiphon. And when the new year began the king of kings received no annual tribute from the kingdoms of Hatra, Media, Atropaiene, Babylon, Mesene and of course Dura. The list of kings in open defiance of Mithridates grew.

Everyone knew that war would be renewed in the spring but before then the activity that preoccupied us all was far more pleasant, for there was an unexpected spate of weddings. The first to take place was that between Domitus and Miriam. Gallia was most pleased by this news and in the weeks before the actual event took every opportunity to gloat at my expense. To say that you could have knocked me down with a feather when my grizzled Roman friend informed me was an understatement.

'I've been thinking of it for a while,' he told me as we strolled through the camp one early evening, the sun turning orange in the western sky. He stopped and looked at me.

'I hope you do not mind.'

'Of course not. It is a surprise, that is all.'

'A surprise to me also,' he said. 'But I find Miriam's company agreeable and I am not getting any younger. A man should have someone to talk to in his old age, after he has sheathed his sword for the last time.'

I laughed. 'You are not that old, Domitus. You have many years left in you.'

We arrived at the tent that contained the legion's golden griffin and went inside. It rested on its metal plate in the centre of the tent as usual, the air still and warm. The guards looked like statues around the rack that held the sacred object. Beside the griffin stood the Staff of Victory, now with an additional silver disc depicting a battle by a river to celebrate our victory at Makhmur. Domitus walked up to the griffin and gently laid a hand on it, bowing his head in reverence as he did so. I did the same, then stepped back to admire it.

'When Godarz was killed I began to think of my own mortality,' he said. 'And every year there are more names on the memorial in the Citadel, a daily reminder that death stalks us all.'

I had no idea that he was such a deep-thinking man. To me he had always been Lucius Domitus, iron hard and the army's talisman, but Gallia told me that even the fiercest warrior is alone with his thoughts in the quiet of the night hours, when he has time to reflect on his life. It appeared that Domitus had done much reflecting.

'Miriam will make a fine wife,' I said, trying to lighten the mood.

He smiled. 'Yes she will. The ceremony will be according to her own religion, of course, but I do not mind that.'

He turned and looked at me. 'I would like you to come to another ceremony before the wedding, Gallia too.'

'I would be delighted to,' I answered, intrigued.

Like all soldiers Domitus was superstitious. And like me he had a routine when it came to dressing on the day of battle that he followed religiously. Though he was going to be married according to the Jewish faith, the day before the ceremony he sought the blessing of his own god. He invited a small number of the Companions and Kronos to a tent that had been erected in the desert five miles to the west of the legionary camp. We arrived in the late afternoon to find Malik, Noora and Byrd also in attendance and a score of Agraci warriors. In pens beside the tent were an ox, boar and ram.

'This is all very mysterious,' remarked Gallia as we slid off our horses' backs and tethered them next to the Agraci animals.

Domitus stood at the entrance to the tent, welcomed us and asked us to enter. He was dressed in a simple white tunic and wore sandals on his feet.

The goatskin tent was spacious and open at the far end. A white-robed individual with a veil stood at this opening beside a young boy also in a white robe holding a flute. Beside him were grouped what looked like three butchers in leather jerkins. There were no chairs in the tent and no refreshments, just a group of similarly confused individuals. I nodded to Drenis and Kronos who were standing talking to Alcaeus and Thumelicus. Gallia and I sauntered over to where Byrd, Noora and Malik stood.

'Any idea what this is about?' I asked them.

'Domitus wishes to pay homage to his god,' answered Byrd, 'to bring luck to his marriage.'

'Byrd has opened an office in Antioch,' said Malik, nodding at the white-robed figure. 'That man is a Roman priest at the Temple of Mars in the city. Byrd hired him as a favour to Domitus.'

'It was our wedding gift to him,' added Noora.

Antioch was now the capital of Roman Syria, though until fairly recently had been part of Tigranes the Great's empire. But more to the point I was intrigued by Byrd's business venture.

'What sort of office?' I asked.

'Of no significance,' replied Byrd, 'very modest. It is run by my brother-in-law, Andromachus.'

Malik laughed. 'Byrd is being too humble. Noora has a keen business mind and while our friend here is away enjoying himself as a scout she has helped to build up his business interests, and now his growing army of camels moves grain, pottery, fruits, wool and linen between Palmyra and Antioch.'

Byrd looked disinterested. 'I like to keep Noora happy.'

'Quite right, too,' said Gallia, smiling at Byrd's wife.

'I do not mean to keep Byrd away from you for so long, Noora,' I said.

'Part of him will always be a wanderer,' she replied. 'In any case he likes to know what is going on far and wide.'

Byrd smiled slyly at me. 'Andromachus also keeps me informed of developments among the Romani.'

The priest clapping his hands to get everyone's attention interrupted our conversation. Domitus stood before him and raised his hands.

'My friends, I have asked you here on the eve of my wedding to bear witness to my paying homage to the god that I have followed ever since I was a young legionary in the army of Rome.'

'Can you remember that far back?' shouted Thumelicus. Drenis told him to hush.

'Though I am to be married tomorrow before another god, I ask Mars to look kindly on me as I embark on a new journey of my life.'

We all clapped his words as the priest spread his arms and raised them to the ceiling. He then prayed to Mars in a deep voice that could be heard clearly despite his veil.

'Father Mars, I pray and beseech thee that thou be gracious and merciful to Lucius Domitus, his house and his household; that thou keep away, ward off and remove sickness, seen and unseen, barrenness and destruction, ruin and unseasonable influence from him and his loved ones; and that thou permit his harvests, his grain, his vineyards and his plantations to flourish and to come to good issue; preserve in health his shepherds and his flocks, and give good health and strength to him, his house and his household. To this intent, to the intent of purifying his farm, his land, his ground and of making an expiation, as I have said, deign to accept the offering of these suckling victims, Father Mars.'

He turned and nodded to the three butchers who disappeared and then reappeared moments later, bringing the ox, boar and ram into the tent. The priest sprinkled wine and salt over the animals' heads while the flautist played a rather pleasant tune. Then the priest picked up what looked like a small cake off the floor and sprinkled bits of that on the heads of the animals.

'That is sacred cake made from flour and salt,' whispered Byrd.

'Why the flute?' asked Gallia, fascinated by the proceedings.

'To drown out any ill-omened noises. The priest wears a veil to shut out evil influences from his eyes.'

'He means you, Pacorus,' said Malik, grinning.

The priest had been mumbling prayers as he anointed the heads of the animals and when he had finished he stepped back and nodded to the three butchers, who each held a mallet in their right hands. In a flash each one struck their beast on the top of the head with it. The animals grunted and their legs buckled by being stunned thus, then the men dropped the mallets and pulled their knives to expertly slit the animals' throats. Blood gushed on the ground as the beasts collapsed, dead. The butchers then went to work with their knives to disembowel each beast; the priest examining the entrails of each one carefully to see that there was nothing untoward.

'This is the most important part of ceremony,' said Byrd. 'Bad insides mean god not pleased.'

The smell of blood and guts reached my nostrils and I recoiled somewhat. But after a few minutes the priest spread out his hands to us once more.

'Father Mars has blessed Lucius Domitus and his marriage.'

Afterwards, as the vital organs of the three dead animals were thrown onto a burning brazier to the accompaniment of music from the flautist, we all congratulated Domitus on the auspicious omens. I had never seen him so happy, now secure in the knowledge that his god was smiling on him. I saw Byrd give a large pouch of money to the priest once he had finished consigning the vital organs of the slaughtered animals to the fire and removed his veil. Malik also saw it.

'The blessings of the gods do not come cheap, it seems.'

As the priest, his flute player and the three butchers, who had also come from Syria, took their leave us of and began the journey back to Antioch with their Agraci escort, Domitus embraced Byrd.

'Thank you for your most generous gift, my friend,' said Domitus.

'Think nothing of it,' replied Byrd. 'I glad that you are happy.'

As the tent was dismantled and packed onto a camel, Byrd, Noora and Malik joined us for the journey back to Dura to attend Domitus' wedding. We travelled with the rest of the Companions and Domitus. Thumelicus, unused to riding, jumped onto his horse's back and slid off the other side.

'Pull yourself up using the saddle,' I told him as Domitus and Kronos, both of them no masters of horsemanship, laughed at him.

After several more attempts and more laughter he eventually managed to hoist himself into the saddle and we began our journey. His large frame looked slightly ridiculous perched on the back of the medium-sized mount of a horse archer, which fortunately had a docile nature. It did not take long, though, for the mischievousness of Thumelicus to surface.

'So, Domitus, you are to become a Jew?'

'I am being married by a Jewish priest,' Domitus replied, 'but I will not become a Jew.'

'I have heard that Jewish males have the ends cut off their manhoods.'

Gallia frowned and Noora looked most uncomfortable. Domitus rolled his eyes and shook his head.

'Begging your pardon, ladies,' said Thumelicus.

'The thing is,' he continued, 'my *gladius* is very sharp and you know I am always willing to help out a friend.'

'Be quiet,' ordered Domitus.

'Imagine the shock that Miriam will get tomorrow evening.'

Domitus halted his horse. 'That's enough!'

Thumelicus held up his hands and we resumed our journey, Drenis shaking his head and Noora maintaining a stoic silence. We had not gone three hundred paces when Thumelicus continued his ribbing of Domitus.

'I can do it now if you wish, shouldn't take more than a few seconds. Mind you, a *gladius* might be too big. I'll use my dagger instead.'

He winked at Gallia. 'It's a good job that I'm not becoming a Jew, otherwise you would require the services of a two-handed axe. You know what they say about Germans, don't you?'

'Yes, their brains are in their balls,' she replied.

'Brains?' said Domitus. 'I have heard that German brains make grains of sand look large and ungainly. That is why their heads are so thick, they don't require space for anything else.'

Thumelicus looked hurt. 'What is this, gang up on Thumelicus day? That's the thanks you get for trying to help a friend.'

The next day Domitus and Miriam were married under a white canopy in Godarz's old mansion. I had discussed with Gallia what we should do about the empty residence and it had been she who had suggested giving it to the couple as a wedding gift. Rsan was now the city governor but he had his own mansion and Domitus needed his own home. Technically he was homeless as the headquarters building in the Citadel was a depository for records and filled with offices and the tent that he occupied in camp became mine on campaign, so it made sense that he should have a residence that befitted his high rank. It was a most enjoyable day, made more so when Aaron announced that Rachel was pregnant.

'You will be a granddad,' Thumelicus said to Domitus, beaming with delight.

Three weeks later Gallia and I rode with Domitus and Miriam to Palmyra to attend Malik's wedding. This was an altogether more lavish affair and was attended by all the Agraci lords in Haytham's kingdom. Palmyra was bustling and full to bursting when we arrived.

Haytham had set aside two tents for us near his as the wedding ceremony lasted for a week. The Agraci are a people that favour black for everyday wear but for Malik's wedding there was a profusion of colours as the lords dressed their best camel riders in red, yellow, orange and blue to take part in the races that took place on a daily basis.

We saw little of Haytham or Malik in the days before the actual ceremony, though Rasha took great delight in informing us what was happening. She was maturing into a beautiful young woman now and was also becoming aware of her status as Haytham's daughter. She still dressed in leggings and boots but also wore the black robes of her people on her upper body and a black headdress draped around her head and under her chin to cover her throat. She carried the bow that Gallia had given her in its hide case on her saddle with her quiver slung over her shoulder. Behind us rode a dozen Agraci warriors, her permanent bodyguard. The daughter of the king of the Agraci was too important to be allowed to travel without an armed escort, even through the tents of his capital.

She rode a magnificent young black stallion that was obviously bred from the finest stock with his wedge-shaped head, broad forehead, large brown eyes and nostrils and small muzzle. He had the distinctive bulge between his eyes that marked him as a horse of the desert people. Called a *jibbah*, it gave him additional sinus capacity to help with the dry desert climate.

'I like your horse, Rasha,' I said, admiring its compact body with its short back, deep, well-angled hips and laid-back shoulders.

'It was a gift from my father. He said that he suited my temperament.'

'What is his name?' asked Gallia.

'*Asad*,' she replied, 'which means lion.'

'Most appropriate,' I agreed.

We arrived at the tent of Byrd and Noora to discover more large camel corrals in the area behind it and many herders tending to the animals. Byrd's commercial empire was growing apace.

We spent the next few days in his and his wife's company, the excited Rasha acting as our guide to the wedding ritual.

'First Lord Vehrka and my father will sit down with each other and work out the marriage agreement. After that is concluded the bride's hands and feet will be decorated with henna.'

'To symbolise beauty, luck and strength,' added Noora as we ate *mansaf* – rice covered with stewed lamb cooked in a sauce made from dried yoghurt – with our fingers from huge metal dishes.

'One day your friends will be painting your hands and feet, Rasha,' said Noora.

359

Rasha screwed up her face. 'I am going to be an Amazon and ride beside Gallia in battle. Is that not correct, Gallia?'

Gallia smiled at her. 'Let us not talk of war at the time of your brother's marriage, Rasha.'

I leaned over and kissed my wife on the cheek. 'A most diplomatic answer.'

I knew that in two summers' time Haytham would be looking for a husband for his daughter, no doubt the young son of one of his lords. But for the moment all eyes were on his son, and with the successful conclusion of the negotiations between the two fathers the week culminated with the *Al Ardha*, a war dance performed by dozens of warriors with swords and whips, after which the guests presented Malik and his bride with gifts in celebration of their union. Dura's gift was a thousand camels that Rsan thought was excessive, but both Gallia and I believed it to be the least we could give in view of Malik's service to us.

We stood next to Vehrka as thousands of Agraci watched their prince and his new wife leave for the desert to spend some time alone together, and hopefully their intimacy would not be spoiled by the three hundred warriors, fifty camel riders and three score servants that accompanied them. Malik and Jamal rode on a pair of richly attired camels, and Jamal's had silver bells round its ankles.

'They make a handsome pair, lord,' I said to Vehrka as we watched the royal couple and their entourage ride into the desert south of Palmyra.

'Your shipments all reach their destination without harm,' he said, keeping his eyes on the long line of camels diminishing in size on the horizon.

'I am sure they do, lord, though that was not my immediate concern.'

He regarded me out of the corner of his eye. 'Of course it was. That's the only reason you came over to stand by me. Well, as I said, the shipments all reach their destination.'

I was slightly taken aback by his brusque manner, but then he was an Agraci lord and they were not known for their diplomacy.

'It is good that we aid our allies, lord.'

He looked at me with a bemused expression. 'Allies? I don't care if the Jews live or die, Parthians too for that matter. It is a business arrangement, that is all.'

'And a lucrative one,' I added.

'For you too,' he said, 'unless you are doing it out of the goodness of your heart.'

'Of course not.'

'How long will you be sending weapons to the Jews?' he asked.

'A few more months yet.'

'And you hope that they will slaughter the Romans and save you the trouble.'

He really was quite perceptive. 'I hope that they are able to win their freedom.'

He curled his lip. 'Only the strong have freedom. The weak and the vanquished do not deserve it. It has always been so.'

There was little point in pursuing this line of conversation so I went back to his daughter's new husband.

'Malik is your new son, Vehrka.'

'He is a brave warrior and will produce many fine sons. I hear that you have no sons.'

'The gods decreed it thus,' I replied.

He looked at Gallia. 'Your child-bearing years are over.'

She bristled at his effrontery. 'That is an impertinent question. I assume your balls are withered like your face.'

His eyes narrowed for an instant then he smiled at her. 'I meant no offence, lady. But a man should have sons, especially a great warrior like your husband.'

She sneered at him and then stomped off. I made to follow her but Vehrka grabbed my shirt.

'I have two more young daughters, very fertile, should you wish for a new queen.'

'A most generous offer, lord, but I could never leave my queen.'

'Women are put on the earth to bear children, nothing more. When they can no longer do that then they become worthless. Think on my offer and visit my camp some time. It would be a great honour for one of my daughters to bear the sons of a famous warlord such as yourself.'

He looked at Gallia walking away from us.

'But come alone next time.'

After Malik's departure we too left Palmyra and headed back to Dura, and a month later we were in Babylon for the wedding of Orodes and Axsen. Gallia was very happy during this time as the marriage meant that she could be with Praxima and the rest of the surviving Amazons once more. Viper had risen to be Gallia's second-in-command now, a position that never failed to amuse me, as she still resembled a teenage girl with her small breasts and lithe figure. She rarely heard from Surena, none of us did, but both Vata and Atrax sent me frequent messages that they had regularly supplied his men in Gordyene so at least he was still alive. He had been in the kingdom for nearly a year now and I was considering recalling him; after all, twelve months was long enough for a husband to be separated from his wife, and Gallia did not wish Viper to go to Gordyene and live like 'a beggar among a bunch of thieves' as she so eloquently put it. But all that could wait until after the wedding.

I was delighted to discover that the city of Babylon had been transformed since the last time I visited it. The refugees had been persuaded or coerced to return to their villages and the streets and buildings had been cleaned and repaired. The stench that had hung over the buildings had also disappeared and the spring melt waters of the Euphrates had washed away much of the debris that had clogged the river. The area around the city where the armies had conducted the two recent sieges was still largely flat and barren, but at least the replanting of crops and trees had begun. In addition, both my father and Nergal had sent additional troops to Axsen's kingdom to strengthen its garrisons. Seleucia was still occupied by the soldiers of Mithridates and pointed like a dagger at Babylon but there was nothing that could be done about that at the moment. However, Mardonius reported that there had been no hostile activity along the Tigris.

I met with him, Orodes and Nergal one morning when the old commander took us on a tour of the city's defences. Like most Parthian kingdoms Babylon had a city garrison comprising spearmen and archers, though Mardonius also commanded a large detachment of slingers. The spearmen who guarded the walls and gates of the city were dressed in purple trousers, purple tunics that covered their arms and ended just above their knees and wore turbans on their heads. They carried wicker shields, six-foot-long spears and long knives. Adequate for defending Babylon's high walls that were protected by a deep moat, they were poor battlefield troops. Still, they had defeated two sieges so I commended the commander of the Marduk Gate when we encountered him. It was the same officer I had met following the second siege. He had looked gaunt and tired then but now he was well fed and full of energy and showed off his men to me enthusiastically. All their spears had whetted points and their uniforms were spotless.

'The soldiers of the garrison appear reinvigorated,' I said to Mardonius, who was now walking with the aid of a stick. Out of politeness I did not inquire if it was the result of a wound or old age.

'We have the arrival of Prince Orodes to thank for that,' he smiled at Orodes.

'You are too kind,' replied Orodes. 'I have merely assisted when I can.'

'Word is,' said Nergal, 'that the lords in Susiana and in the kingdoms in the east of the empire are unhappy with Mithridates and his lord high general. They have lost many sons and subjects these past two years.'

'So has Babylon,' remarked Mardonius grimly.

All of us present knew that a third invasion of Babylon would probably finish the kingdom for good. Though the Silk Road ran from Seleucia through the Kingdom of Babylon the dues raised from the caravans were insufficient to pay for the rebuilding of Axsen's realm. The only way that would be possible was to capture the royal treasury at Ctesiphon, and that meant in turn taking Seleucia first, which meant plunging the empire into a fresh war.

'Well,' I said, 'at least Babylon has Mesenian and Hatran troops on its territory to reinforce its own army.'

I had sent Marcus and a contingent of engineers to Babylon at the turn of the year to assist in the rebuilding of the irrigation systems that had been damaged during the last siege. The next day I found him standing on the edge of one of the many canals that emanated from the Euphrates. He looked like a vagrant dressed in his wide-brimmed floppy hat and dirty tunic. He was surrounded by a score of workers carrying spades and picks. I waited until he had finished briefing them and then walked over when they had dispersed.

'You look like a poor farmer, Marcus.'

He raised his arm in salute after the Roman fashion. 'Yes, sir, though master dredger would be a more accurate description.'

He took off his hat and wiped his crown with a cloth for it was a hot day.

'How is it going?'

'Slowly. The damage done to the irrigation system can be repaired easily enough, but some of these canals are over a thousand years old so people tell me. The farmers and villages cannot hope to maintain such an old system efficiently. I have suggested to the queen that she establish an irrigation corps to maintain the whole system.'

He pointed at the river and then moved his arm to encompass the surrounding countryside.

'Weirs and diversion dams are what we need to create reservoirs to supply canals that can carry water far into the countryside. That and a small army of dredgers to prevent the new canals and the old ones from silting up.'

I was impressed. 'You have been busy.'

'The queen and Orodes have accepted my ideas. I like her and she's clever.'

'In what way?'

'To build a new irrigation system and raise the manpower to maintain it on a permanent basis will be expensive, so she approached her high priest.'

'Nabu?'

'Yes, that's him,' he replied. 'Face like a caravan dog chewing a wasp. Anyway, he has agreed to fund the project from the temple treasury.'

I thought that highly unlikely. 'He has?'

'Of course, more irrigation means more crops, which means more tribute for his temple. These religious types are all the same: as long as their temples are full of worshippers paying tribute they are happy enough.'

Nabu appeared to be positively beaming during the time preceding Axsen's marriage to Orodes. The city was a blaze of colour with painted statues of horned bulls along the Processional Way, purple flags flying from the temples and palace, and a great stream of people flocking to his temple to offer their gifts to Marduk. In the days before the ceremony the huge palace compound was filled by the arrival of other kings and their retinues. My mother and father arrived with Gafarn and Diana, plus Diana's young son and the boy Spartacus. Vistaspa and my father's bodyguard camped outside the city, as did the retinues of Atrax, Aschek and Nergal. I think Axsen found it all a bit overwhelming but Orodes was the perfect host, welcoming the kings and their wives and making time for all of them.

The day before the wedding my father invited Gallia and me to a family meeting in a wing of the palace that had been set aside for him. It was the first time in years that my sisters and I had been all together in one place. Adeleh was still smiling as she hugged Gallia and then me, happy in the knowledge that the next wedding she would be attending would be her own. Aliyeh, now Queen of Media, was polite, aloof, serious and icy in equal measure in contrast to her husband who was gracious and friendly. Aliyeh blamed me for the fact that her husband walked with a limp and thought me a bad influence on him. Gallia also knew what Aliyeh thought of me and the greeting between the two was uncomfortable to say the least. After their curt embrace, Gallia threw her arms around Diana.

We sat on couches as slaves served us wine and food and we smiled politely at each other. After a while, though, the atmosphere became oppressive.

'This is nice,' said my mother, trying to lighten the mood as Gallia and Aliyeh stared unblinking at each other.

'How are the Armenians, father?' I asked.

'Quiet, thanks be to Shamash.'

'We should have settled affairs with them last year, then they would be even quieter.'

'We do not need more war, Pacorus,' said Aliyeh. 'Media needs peace to repair the damage visited upon it last year, which also claimed the life of its king.'

'Of course, I meant no offence, Atrax,' I said. 'We all grieve for your father.'

My father nodded gravely and my mother wiped away a tear. They had been good friends of Farhad. My father looked at me.

'Hatra has been hearing stories from Gordyene, of an undeclared war being fought within its borders. Do you know anything of this, Pacorus?'

I felt distinctly uncomfortable. He obviously knew something, but how much?

'Gordyene is Armenian,' I replied evasively.

My father smiled knowingly. 'Then let me ask you another question. Do you know of a man named Surena, who appears to share the same name as one of your commanders that accompanied you to Hatra last year?'

I saw Atrax blush and shift uncomfortably. My father looked at him and then at me. I felt my cheeks burning.

'I see that you do. You play a dangerous game, Pacorus, and were it not for the fact that you aided me last year I would order you to recall this adventurer, this bandit, who fights on my eastern border. Hatra wants no war with the Armenians.'

'And neither does Media,' added Aliyeh, speaking for Atrax and out of turn.

Gordyene lay to the north of Media, just across the Shahar Chay River.

'If the Armenians are occupied in Gordyene they will not trouble Hatra or Media,' I answered.

'Do you not think that you should have consulted Hatra and Media before you launched your private war, and Atropaiene for that matter?'

'I quite agree,' added Aliyeh.

'Be quite, Aliyeh,' snapped Atrax.

'Can we all try to be civilised?' implored my mother. 'This is the first time we have all been together in an age. I will have no more talk of war, Varaz, and that goes for you too, Pacorus.'

So we sat picking at sweet cakes and pastries and indulging in polite conversation about children, weddings and the weather, all the time Aliyeh glaring at me, Gallia glaring at her and my father regarding me with suspicious eyes.

The wedding was an altogether more enjoyable affair, the streets full of cheering and happy people and Babylon's finest attired in bright colours and dripping with gold and silver jewellery. The road from the palace to the Marduk Temple was carpeted with flowers and garlands and on either side had been placed silver altars heaped with perfumes. Cages on wooden plinths held leopard and lions, which roared with anger as small children with sticks tried to poke them. We walked from the palace to the temple, the crowds being kept at bay by ranks of purple-clad spearmen who lined the route. The sun shone in a clear-blue sky and white doves released by the sensual followers of Ishtar flew over us as we followed the royal couple to the temple.

Axsen and Orodes both wore long purple robes as they led the procession, Nabu walking a few paces in front of them, a great white and gold mitre on his head and jewels entwined in his beard. Axsen had strips of gold in her hair and gold on her fingers, but both she and Orodes walked barefoot to the temple on a strip of rose petals that had been painstakingly laid out earlier by a host of palace slaves. The bride and bridegroom each wore a gold necklace with pendants of amethyst to protect against nightmares, thieves, hail, locusts, plagues and infidelity; red coral to ward off evil; and rubies to safeguard them against evil and the dangers of storms and floods.

I walked with Gallia, Praxima, Nergal, Gafarn and Diana. It was good to be in the company of old friends and I felt relaxed and happy. Though our time in Italy seemed like yesterday we had all aged to a lesser or greater degree, me most of all I think. Gafarn's thin frame had padded out somewhat since he had been my slave, too many palace feasts no doubt, though he certainly looked more regal with his neatly cropped beard. Diana looked remarkably similar to when I had first met her on the slopes of Mount Vesuvius and had effortlessly slipped into the lifestyle of a Parthian princess. Ahead of us my father and mother were walking with Atrax, Aliyeh and Adeleh, the young Spartacus ambling along with them, his long black hair around his broad shoulders.

'I can see his mother in him,' said Gallia.

'That is what I tell everyone,' agreed Diana, 'but Gafarn only sees his father's frame.'

'It's hard to miss,' I added. 'He must be as tall as I am now. How old is he now, thirteen?'

'He will begin his training as a squire in our father's bodyguard next year,' said Gafarn. 'Four years after that he will be a cataphract. Diana and I have great hopes for him.'

'You think he will make a good soldier?' I asked.

'He is his father's son,' replied Gafarn. 'He does not take to discipline readily, but if he can cure his headstrong nature he will make an excellent soldier.'

'What does he know of his father and mother?' asked Gallia.

'We have always told him who his parents were,' said Diana, 'but he never knew them so it is difficult for him. He does not talk about them. I think he is embarrassed that they were slaves.'

'He sees himself very much as a Parthian noble,' said Gafarn, 'which is what he is, I suppose. He seems to have inherited his father's dislike of the Romans, though. Perhaps it is a Thracian trait.'

'What news of the Romans, Pacorus?' asked Nergal.

'Crassus and Pompey and another are still dividing up Rome between them, I believe,' I said. 'So for the moment all is quiet to the west.'

'It will not remain so, lord,' said Praxima, her hair still red and wild. 'The Romans are always hungry for more land.'

'You are right, Praxima' I agreed. 'When they come I will send for you and we can fight them together.'

'Like the old days, lord,' she beamed.

'Yes, like the old days.'

As we followed Axsen and Orodes through the entrance into the temple young Spartacus turned and nodded to me. I smiled and nodded back before he disappeared into the cavernous structure whose walls were covered with gold leaf.

It may have been large but inside there was hardly any space to spare that day. The temple's vast numbers of clergy were in attendance in their robes, all gathered around their high priest as he chanted prayers before Axsen and Orodes. As well as priests the temple employed numerous musicians, singers, magicians, soothsayers, diviners, dream interpreters, astrologers and slaves. The air was pungent with the scent of frankincense as we were shown to the front of the congregation to witness the marriage ceremony, row upon row of the kingdom's nobility behind us. To one side of the altar stood a score of priestesses from the Temple of Ishtar, scanty white tops barely covering their breasts and short white silk dresses that hung from their shapely hips to above their knees, their feet bare and their beautiful young bodies oiled and glistening. I saw Afrand standing beside Nabu in front of the altar, her long hair oiled and dark make-up around her eyes that gave her a feline appearance. Her top was even sparser than those worn by her priestesses, her ample breasts threatening to liberate themselves at any moment.

The temple was decorated with flowers, plants and candles and set upon the altar was a pot of burning incense and charcoal, a cup of water, a bowl holding grain and another containing oil.

As the singers ended their rather hypnotic hymn Nabu raised his hands to the ceiling and his voice resonated over the heads of the assembly.

'Great Marduk, defender of Babylon and all things true and just in the world, we ask you to bless your servants, Orodes and Axsen, who have come to your temple to be joined in marriage in your great presence. May they be welcome.'

As one the priests and priestesses said 'we welcome you both'.

Nabu then turned to the altar and held the palms of his hands over the incense, the cup of water and the vessels of grain and oil.

'May these elements of water, fire, earth, air and ether be hallowed for this ceremony.'

He took the cup of water and dipped his middle finger in the liquid, then marked Orodes and Axsen on the forehead.

'Through this water from a holy well may true vision awaken in each brow.'

Nabu turned and took the pot of incense from the altar and handed it to Orodes and Axsen.

'Together you shall hold a pot of fire so you may use your will for good.'

Having both held the pot they returned it to Nabu.

'How long does this go on for?' whispered Gafarn. 'My knees are starting to ache.'

Diana put a finger to her lips to still him.

Nabu, holding the pot of incense before him, nodded to Afrand who took the cup of water and offered it to Orodes and Axsen. They dipped a finger in the liquid and let a few drops fall into the pot of incense.

'Water is now added to fire,' said Nabu, 'so that calm emotion can harmonise with will. Now let the element of air, symbol of the mind, combine with water and fire.'

Nabu handed the pot of incense back to the couple so that they could they hold it aloft and move it about to allow the smoke to circulate freely. Then they handed it back to Nabu.

'Strength and abundance from the fruitful earth,' continued Nabu, 'must now be added through these grains of oats.'

Afrand took the pot of grain from the altar and held it out to Orodes and Axsen who each took some and then dropped them into the pot of incense.

'Ether,' said Nabu, 'through this oil, blends water, earth, fire and air to find harmony.'

'I'll need some of that ether to revive me if this goes on much longer,' muttered Gafarn. I had to stifle a laugh and Nergal was grinning.

'Gafarn, be quiet,' hissed Diana. My father turned round and frowned at us.

Nabu placed the pot of incense back on the altar and then he and Afrand placed their hands and feet against the bare feet and hands of Orodes and Axsen respectively. Axsen then laid her head on Orodes' shoulder who now spoke.

'I am the son of nobles. Silver and gold shall fill your lap. You shall be my wife and I shall be your husband, and like the fruit of a garden I shall give you offspring.'

The priests held out their hands and were handed pairs of sandals by their subordinates. Nabu and Afrand then slipped the sandals on the feet of the royal couple, kissing their insteps.

I smiled as my friends were married and then heard a woman's voice. 'The gods are with you, Pacorus. Your faith has been rewarded.'

I turned to Gallia. 'What did you say?' I whispered. She looked at me in confusion.

'I did not say anything.'

I heard the voice again. 'We are always with you, little one.'

I glanced left and right and saw only the faces of my friends looking forward. I looked up and then behind me but saw nothing untoward. Nabu and Afrand had now risen to their feet and the former faced the congregation and held his arms aloft. Once more his deep voice filled the temple.

'May Orodes like a farmer till the fields.

May he like a good shepherd make the folds teem.

May there be vines under him, may there be barley under him.

In the river, may there be carp-floods.

In the fields, may there be late barley.

In the marshes, may fishes and birds chatter.

In the canebrake, may dry and fresh reeds grow.

In the high desert, may shrubs grow.

In the forests, may deer and wild goats multiply.

May the watered garden produce honey and wine.

In the vegetable furrows may the lettuce and the cress grow high.

In the palace may there be long life.

May the Tigris and the Euphrates bring high-riding waters.

On their banks may the grass grow high, may they fill the meadows.

May holy Nisaba pile high the heaps of grain.

O, My Lady Axsen, May he spend long days in your holy lap!

Let all here assembled know that the Great Marduk has blessed this union and that Queen Axsen and King Orodes are united in marriage. All hail to Marduk.'

The congregation replied 'hail' and then the singers began reciting another melodious song to the accompaniment of flutes and harps. Nabu gestured to the newlyweds that they should now seek the blessing of Marduk and so they disappeared into the holy of holies before reappearing to make their way back to the palace and their new life. Thus began the reign of Orodes and Axsen of Babylon.

Afterwards we attended the great feast at the palace where jugglers, acrobats, contortionists and magicians entertained us while we ate. The palace kitchens had prepared enough food to feed the thousand people who sat at the tables in the vast banqueting hall. And outside the palace the generosity of Axsen allowed her people to feast on freshly grilled goat, mutton and pork from stalls set up on every street corner throughout the city. They could also purchase roasted beef if they wished, though as cattle were usually slaughtered at the end of their lives the meat could be rather stringy. The wedding guests feasted on gazelle, duck, fish and pigeon, all seasoned with herbs including coriander, cumin, fennel, fenugreek, mint, mustard, saffron and thyme. I had to smile when slaves offered porridge with dates on

369

large silver platters, which had been considered a delicacy in Babylon for hundreds of years. The city's nobility would be taken aback if they learned that porridge was the staple diet of my legionaries.

We sat on the top table with Axsen and Orodes, the newlyweds separating myself, Gallia, Nergal and Praxima from my father and mother, Atrax, Aliyeh, Gafarn, Diana and Adeleh, and thus preventing any uncomfortableness. Young Spartacus looking bored was at the end of the table next to Adeleh. Both Axsen and Orodes wore jewel-encrusted gold crowns on their heads and during the feast Mardonius presented Orodes with King Vardan's old sword, the pommel of which was a gold *gauw*. I was pleased that he at last wore a crown for Orodes deserved to be a king and would be a just and noble ruler.

I began to relax and chat with Nergal and Praxima while Gallia giggled with Orodes and Axsen. She was very smug, believing with some justification that she had engineered their romance. Both wine and beer flowed in abundance and the level of noise increased in direct proportion to the amount of alcohol that was consumed. Wine had been almost unknown in Babylon until quite recently, the ancients preferring beer, but later generations had become acquainted with the agreeable produce of the grape following Alexander of Macedon's destruction of the Persian Empire.

I thought about the words that I had heard in the temple, or what I thought I had heard. There was so much incense being burned that my senses had obviously been dulled. A slave filled my golden *rhyton* with more wine and I leaned forward to catch Orodes' eye. I raised the vessel to him.

'To you, my friend, may your rule be long and peaceful.'

He smiled and nodded, then frowned after something else caught his eye. I looked to where he was staring and saw a scruffy looking man at the entrance to the hall. Dressed in beige baggy leggings and a dirty purple tunic, he was a soldier of Babylon's army and stood clutching something in his hand as one of the guards at the entrance pointed towards Orodes and Axsen, and then escorted him through the tables towards us. The loud chatter and laughter continued as the two threaded their way among now drunken nobles and their gaudily dressed wives and concubines. When he arrived at the top table he went down on one knee before Axsen and Orodes. My interested father leaned forward, as did Gafarn. Mardonius, seated on the table immediately in front of ours with his senior officers and their wives, stood up as Orodes commanded the soldier to rise.

'Forgive me, highness,' he said, looking left and right at us all at the table. 'I have a message for King Pacorus of Dura.'

All eyes were now upon me as Orodes pointed to me.

'You had better give it to him, then.'

The man walked over and bowed his head to me, keeping his eyes down as he extended his right hand and proffered the rolled parchment that had a wax seal. I stood and took it, going to break the seal but then stopping when I recognised that it bore the lion of Gordyene. What nonsense was this?

'Is there something wrong, Pacorus?' asked a now slightly concerned Orodes. My father also wore a look of curiosity. As I broke the seal I looked up and saw that all eyes in the hall were now upon me and all chatter had stopped. I unrolled the parchment and read the words, re-reading them as the significance of what they revealed dawned on me.

'This cannot be,' I said.

I read the words on the parchment again as Orodes and my father rose to their feet, followed by everyone else at the top table.

'The gods are with you, Pacorus. Your faith has been rewarded.'

Still clutching the letter in my hand I left the dais and walked to stand before Orodes and Axsen, both of whom were wearing perplexed expressions. I knelt before them.

'The gods have blessed your marriage, my friends, for they have sent me word that Gordyene is Parthian once more.'

I rose and smiled at them, then handed Orodes the letter. My father looked at my mother and then Gafarn, who raised an eyebrow at him.

'What is this?' asked my father.

'This,' I answered, pointing at the parchment that Orodes now handed to Axsen, 'is a letter sent from Vanadzor, the capital of Gordyene.'

'I know where it is,' he replied.

'But what you do not know, father, is that Surena now occupies the city and indeed the whole kingdom.'

'Surena has liberated Gordyene?' Orodes may have read the words but still dared not believe them.

'It is true, my friend,' I said, 'I recognise the seal on the letter. There was no way Surena could have used it unless he had possession of the palace in Vanadzor.'

My mother smiled at me and then hugged my father, then began to cry. She and King Balas had been very close and his death had upset her deeply, compounded by the subsequent conquest of his kingdom by the Romans and their handing it over to the Armenians. Atrax was similarly delighted as it meant that his kingdom would no longer be subjected to Armenian raids. He held his wife's face in his hands and kissed her on the lips, which somewhat mortified her. Around us a general hubbub arose as the news was conveyed to each table. Mardonius came up to me and bowed his head.

'Hail to you, majesty, for making this possible.'

'Yes, Pacorus,' said Axsen, 'hail to you for returning the Kingdom of Gordyene to the Parthian Empire.'

371

Orodes held his arms aloft and the commotion died away. He raised his drinking vessel.

'To King Pacorus, liberator of Gordyene.'

The guests raised their cups and toasted me, then began banging their hands on the tables and shouting 'Pacorus, Pacorus', as they acclaimed me. I turned and raised my hands to them, allowing myself a moment to bask in the glory. Then I composed myself and remembered that I had done nothing. This was Surena's victory. I raised my hands again to still to noise.

'I thank you for your kindness but this triumph does not belong to me but to another and it would be unjust of me to steal his glory.'

But they would have none of it and began chanting my name once more as I retook my seat.

'This is Surena's victory,' I shouted to Orodes above the din.

'They have not heard of him but they have heard of you, Pacorus,' he said. 'What will you do now?'

'I do not understand?'

He smiled. 'Surena has freed Gordyene but he is still under your command. Will you take the kingdom for yourself as Balas left no heirs to inherit his throne?'

It was a question that my father also wanted an answer to when he requested my presence in his quarters the day after the feast.

He was in a frosty mood as Gallia and I sat down with him and my mother, Gafarn and Diana. As slaves fussed around and cleared away the breakfast they had all enjoyed in the small garden, Diana's young son, Pacorus, played with young Spartacus, waving his small wooden sword at the elder boy and screaming with delight at the top of his voice. My father shouted at him to be quiet, earning him a rebuke from Diana and a scowl from Gafarn. My mother played the role of diplomat and asked the steward who attended Hatra's royal party to take the boys to see the animals in the palace zoo. Diana warned the boys not to put their hands near the cages and told the steward not to allow any harm to come to them.

I smiled at the boys as they were led away by the steward and two male palace slaves dressed in purple tunics and black belts. Other slaves offered Gallia and me fruit juice after we had kissed my mother and Diana and sat on plush couches arranged near the ornamental pond filled with large goldfish.

I smiled at my father. 'This is all very pleasant.'

'You intend to claim Gordyene for yourself?' he asked, his eyes boring into me.

'Straight and to the point,' I answered.

'Father is in no mood for idle chatter,' remarked Gafarn as my father brushed away a slave proffering juice in a jug.

'I can see that,' I said.

'You have not answered my question,' pressed my father.

I sighed half-heartedly. 'I have not given the matter much thought. Surena is a good man. He will hold the kingdom until I have decided what is to be done with it.'

My father clenched the sides of his couch, his knuckles turning white.

'Who is this man, this Surena?'

Gallia's answer served only to increase his agitation. 'A simple boy from the great marshlands that lie south of the city of Uruk. Pacorus found him and brought him back to Dura. He was his squire.'

My father rose from his couch and began pacing – always a bad sign.

'A squire? A squire is in charge of Gordyene?'

'Calm yourself, father,' I said. 'This squire has risen to become the commander of Dura's horse archers, and has, since I sent him to Gordyene last year, apparently managed to defeat the Armenians and expel them from Balas' old kingdom.'

'Not bad for a squire,' agreed Gafarn. 'He's not related to that sorceress of yours, is he?'

My mother shook her head at Gafarn but my father did not see the amusing side of the matter.

'The Armenians will not take kindly to this.'

'Indeed,' I agreed.

My father stopped pacing and looked at me. 'Is this what it is about, to provoke the Armenians so you can have the battle that you were denied last year?'

I too now rose to my feet. 'No, father. It is about returning the Kingdom of Gordyene to the Parthian Empire where it belongs.'

'Behind the Armenians stand the Romans, Pacorus,' said Gafarn, suddenly looking serious.

'And Hatra lies next to Gordyene,' added my father.

'If the Armenians, or the Romans for that matter,' I replied, 'attempt to retake Gordyene then they will at the very least be preoccupied with a campaign against Vanadzor. Hatra will not be high on their list of priorities.'

My father was not convinced. 'It will be if they decided to march from Zeugma across the north of my kingdom to get at Gordyene instead of via Armenia.'

'In which case, father, I will attack Syria in retaliation.'

Gallia looked at me with surprise for it was the first time that I had given any intimation of aggression against Syria. But Surena had changed everything by freeing Gordyene. No longer would the Armenians be able to launch raids against Hatra or Media using it as a base, and nor would the Romans be able to use it as a base from which to make further inroads into the empire. Better than that, Gordyene

373

itself might be used as a base to attack Armenia should the need arise, and of course my father did not know that I was arming the Jews in Judea who would rise against the Romans in the coming months. Rome would have more than enough to occupy itself with in the near future.

'Have you forgotten about Mithridates?' asked my father.

I have to confess that in all the excitement I had. 'Of course not,' I replied. 'What of him?'

'He may have been thwarted in his plans to destroy his enemies, but he is still king of kings and will be seeking revenge next year.'

I smiled. 'The liberation of Gordyene will allow us to settle affairs with Mithridates without you having to worry about your northern border.'

'And the Romans?' asked Gafarn.

'The Romans are preoccupied with their own internal affairs,' I answered. 'We do not need to worry about them.'

'You seem very certain of all this, Pacorus,' mused my mother.

'The Romans above all respect strength,' I answered, 'if they respect anything at all. Evicting the Armenians from Gordyene will send a clear message to Rome that Parthia is not weak but strong.'

My father retook his couch. 'You still have not informed us what the status of Gordyene will be now that you, or should I say your commander, has conquered it.'

'Gordyene will be under Duran control until I decide what its future shall be. In the meantime I shall visit Vanadzor to convey my gratitude to Surena for the great service he has done the empire.'

'And I shall be coming with you,' declared my father.

I stayed at Babylon for another two days, during which time I informed Orodes and Axsen of my intention to ride north. In contrast to my father they were both delighted that Gordyene was a kingdom of the empire once again, Axsen because Balas had been an old friend and ally of her father and Orodes because a Parthian Gordyene appealed to his sense of correctness concerning the status of kingdoms within the empire. Gordyene had been conquered by a foreign power and that had aggrieved him deeply. With the old molester of children Darius at Zeugma it had been different. He had become a client king of Rome in exchange for an uninterrupted supply of young girls and boys. I think Orodes was not alone in thinking that the empire was better off without such immoral individuals. Atrax was also delighted about Gordyene, not least because it meant that his kingdom would no longer be subjected to cross-border raids. He too decided to ride north with my father and me, though thankfully his wife stayed at Babylon. Gallia declared that she too would remain in the city. I think she wanted to be with Diana and Praxima for as long as possible, and she also had no interest in congratulating Surena. In all the years he had been with us she had never taken to him, tolerating him only because he was the husband of Viper.

'I shall make him governor of the province,' I told her on the morning of my departure.

She was unimpressed. 'Someone of greater status should be the governor of a province. Someone like Domitus.'

'Domitus would hate being away from Dura. In any case I need him with the army for the campaign against Mithridates.'

'What about Kronos, then? He might like being nearer to Pontus, his homeland.'

I buckled my sword belt. 'Gordyene is around four hundred miles from Pontus. Besides, I also need him to command the Exiles. You will just have to accept that Surena has exceeded all expectations. He deserves to rule the land that he has liberated.'

'He will rule it in your name,' she corrected me.

I picked up my helmet and inspected its white goose feather crest.

'A governor should also have his wife beside him,' I said casually. She spun round. 'Viper?'

'Yes, they have been apart for far too long and now it is only right that she should travel with me to be at her husband's side.'

Her eyes narrowed as she regarded me. Gallia protected her Amazons fiercely and resented any interference in their affairs. However, now Surena was going to be a governor Viper was going to be a governor's wife and could no longer be part of the queen's bodyguard.

'She is not yours to command,' she snapped.

'She cannot remain in your bodyguard while her husband is a governor, or satrap, of a province of the empire. It is a high position that I am bestowing on him and, de facto, his wife,' I shot back.

'She should be consulted at least.'

I saw no reason why I, a king, should consult a mere girl in my queen's bodyguard. But I could tell that Gallia's temper was starting to arouse itself and as I had no desire to part from her on bad terms I agreed that Viper should be consulted. And so we walked to the throne room while Gallia summoned Viper from the palace barracks. We had to say our farewells to Orodes and Axsen anyway so I suppose it made sense to kill two birds with one stone, so to speak.

Orodes and Axsen were already sitting on their thrones upon the dais as a steady stream of people entered the throne room to begin the morning's proceedings. Mardonius, dignified as ever, took his place to the right of the dais though Axsen ordered a chair to be brought for him to save his aged knees. My father, mother and Adeleh came to pay their respects and to bid the newlyweds farewell, as did Gafarn and Diana who would be travelling back to Hatra with my mother, my sister and their two boys. Next to appear were Nergal and Praxima and then Atrax and Aliyeh, the latter looking contemptuously upon the king and queen of Mesene. It was difficult for a former pampered princess of Hatra to accept that a woman who had been a slave could wear a crown like herself. I had to laugh at such a notion; crowns were nothing but pieces of metal. It was the swords and bows behind a crown that were more important.

Finally Viper appeared dressed in her mail shirt, leggings and boots. Her short-cropped hair and girlish face making her seem as though she had stolen her clothes from an adult. But she was no child and knew how to use the sword that hung from her hip. She bowed to Axsen, Orodes, Gallia and me and ignored everyone else.

'We welcome you, Viper,' said a smiling Axsen.

Viper smiled back. Axsen was a friend of Gallia's, which made her a friend of every Amazon, and my wife's warriors also liked Orodes who had fought by their side for many years.

'Before I take my leave of your majesties,' I said to Axsen and Orodes, 'I have something to say to Viper.'

My father sighed irritably. He thought the idea of the Amazons complete nonsense and was also clearly impatient to be away. My mother froze him with a stare.

'Of course,' said Orodes politely, 'we are all interested in the affairs of the Amazons.'

Aliyeh rolled her eyes but Atrax was most intrigued.

'You will have heard,' I said to Viper, 'that Surena has liberated the kingdom of Gordyene.'

'Yes, majesty,' she replied with pride.

'I intend to make your husband the governor of the kingdom, Viper.'

My father suddenly became very interested in what I was saying.

'And I would like you to accompany me north so you can be a governor's wife.'

Viper looked at Gallia who nodded.

'Yes, majesty,' beamed Viper.

'This is most excellent,' said Axsen as Viper hugged Gallia, Diana, and Praxima and then bowed to Axsen and Orodes before scampering away to prepare for the journey.

'So Gordyene becomes a part of the Kingdom of Dura,' said my father.

'For the moment, father.'

'Gordyene will need a king, Pacorus,' said Orodes. 'It was a self-governing kingdom and should be again.'

'I quite agree, lord king,' I replied. 'But until a suitable candidate is found I think it is safe under Surena's governorship.'

We left two hours later, a long column of my father's bodyguard, Atrax's two hundred horse archers and my own hundred horsemen.

Thankfully my father's bodyguard also rode as horse archers and left their camels and squires behind and so we covered around nearly thirty miles a day to arrive at Gordyene's southern border, the Shahar Chay River, ten days after we had left Babylon. Messages had been sent ahead to announce our visit and thus at the frontier we were greeted by Silaces and a thousand horse archers. There was a stiff northerly breeze behind him that showed the banner of the four-pointed star, the flag of Elymais, to full effect and I thought I saw my father nod approvingly when he saw it.

We walked our horses across the shallow river and entered Gordyene, the land of tree-covered mountains, mountain steppes and lakes, and lush, deep valleys and fast-flowing rivers. The kingdom of great forests of beech, oak, pine and peach; home to bears, deer, wild bore and wildcats. Higher on the rocky slopes were mountain leopards and white panthers. It was also an ancient land where wheat had been first been cultivated twelve thousand years ago, and where Alexander of Macedon had discovered the apricot and had sent it back to Greece. And now it was Parthian once more.

Silaces' men lined the far riverbank and he bowed his head to us as we exited the water.

'Greetings, majesties.'

'It is good to see you again, Silaces,' I said to him.

'And you, majesty. Surena waits for you at Vanadzor.'

The new governor would undoubtedly have met us at the border had he known that his wife was with us, though it took us only two more days to reach Vanadzor, the brooding city built in the valley of the Pambak River. When we arrived on the morning of the second day Surena was waiting for us. Rank upon rank of white-clad horse archers paraded in front of the city gates and he himself was mounted upon a magnificent grey horse with the lion banner fluttering behind him. Lion banners also hung from the walls and towers of the city, the battlements lined with spearmen and archers. I turned to Viper as we neared Surena and his officers.

'Go to your husband, Viper.'

She whooped with delight and kicked her mount forward. Moments later the two embraced as the kings of Dura, Hatra and Media brought their horses to a halt before Surena. He had removed his helmet to kiss his wife and now he smiled at us all.

'Hail, majesties, and welcome to the city of Vanadzor. The garrison awaits your inspection.'

He may have been only still in his twenties but the months spent conducting his own campaign had matured Surena beyond his years. As he showed us round the walls and the palace stronghold that in truth was nothing more than an ugly squat building with thick walls and tall towers at each corner, I detected a change in him. The cocky, carefree boy seemed to have disappeared, to be replaced by a more serious, calculating individual.

That evening, as we sat in the dour banqueting hall, he told us how he had reconquered the kingdom. Viper, her eyes afire with excitement and pride, sat next to him. I could tell that Atrax was delighted to be back in Vanadzor, not least because he and his father had often visited the city in his youth to participate in great hunting expeditions organised by Balas, but also because a Parthian Gordyene made his own kingdom much more secure. My father was, I think, bemused by it all. He was above all a traditionalist, a man who believed in the natural order of things. That meant kings ruled, nobles and the sons of nobles served as cataphracts and rose to be the commanders of armies and governors of cities, those who were not nobles tilled the fields, served in temples, worked in towns and cities and fought in the king's armies when required. It was a strict hierarchy blessed by the gods and was thus sacred. At the bottom were slaves who were not worthy of thought or consideration. But now, in the banqueting hall of his dead friend, King Balas, my father was forced to listen to a young man who was Ma'adan, a member of a people regarded as little better than slaves by many Parthians – marsh dwellers, individuals who lived among water buffaloes and filth. It must have riled him enormously. But then, for all the great nobles and wealth in Hatra, Media and Atropaiene, it had been Surena, a former urchin from the marshlands, who had freed Gordyene. And now he told his story. As he did so the fire in the great hearth crackled and spat for it was still cool in the northern uplands in the evenings.

'When I first came here I did not know the strength of the enemy or the dispositions of his garrisons, so for the first month we made camp in the forest and gathered information. We rode into the villages, just small parties, and gave food to the inhabitants, saying we were their friends, nothing more. We made no demands or threats, merely promised that we would return with more food. And we kept our promises.'

He looked at me and a slight smile creased his lips. 'Your tutors taught me well, lord. We did not seek battle with the Armenians but rather endeavoured to break their resistance without fighting. So we ambushed their patrols and supply columns, and when they were strong and sent many soldiers against us we avoided them and melted back into the forest. And when they followed we laid ambushes for them and raided them at night, but always avoiding battle.

'We attacked their isolated outposts and massacred the garrisons. We ambushed their reinforcements coming from Armenia through the mountain passes that we controlled, and we never gave them any rest. We were like the wolves outside these walls – invisible but always present. The villagers became our friends and eyes and ears and told us of the enemy's movements so we could attack the Armenians when they did not expect it, and avoid them when they were prepared.

'Their losses mounted and they became demoralised when no reinforcements or supplies could get through. And then we heard of a great column of horses, men and wagons leaving Vanadzor and heading north back to Armenia, and then…'

He stretched out his arms and fell silent.

'And then what?' asked my father.

Surena regarded him for a moment with his brown eyes, this famous king whose haughty bodyguard wore more silver than he had seen in all his life.

'And then, lord king, we were like a pack of hungry wolves. We surrounded them on all sides and harried them constantly, day and night, picking off the stragglers, the injured and the lost. Many thousands left Vanadzor but only a few hundred made it back to Armenia. You can follow their trail if you have a mind to; it is marked with the bones of their dead and the debris of their army.'

'What of you own losses?' I asked.

Surena smiled again. 'Less than three hundred, lord.'

'That few?' Atrax was amazed.

Surena looked very serious. 'Of course, for I was taught to regard my soldiers as my children, for then they will follow you into the deepest valleys. To look on them as my own beloved sons, and they will stand by me even unto death.'

My father looked more bemused. 'Who taught you that? Are they the words of the slave general my son fought under?'

'No, lord,' replied Surena. 'They are the words of a Chinese warlord named Sun Tzu who lived some four hundred years ago.'

Viper placed her hand on Surena's arm.

'You are to be governor of Gordyene, Surena,' I told him. He and his wife grinned at each other.

'Until such time as the affairs of the kingdom are settled,' my father reminded us.

'Since we control the mountain passes into the kingdom,' continued Surena, 'we can also use them to attack our enemies.'

He smiled savagely at my father. 'Even as we sit here groups of horsemen are travelling to Armenia to repay the atrocities that have been visited upon Gordyene.'

My father shook his head in exasperation. 'You have no authority to make war against a foreign kingdom.'

Surena leaned back in his chair. 'Lord king, the Armenians will not forget the defeat they have suffered here. We are already at war with them. This being so, it is more preferable to fight it on their territory as opposed to my own.'

'Your territory?' glared my father.

Surena smiled. 'A slip of the tongue, lord king.'

He looked at me. 'There is another matter, lord.' He beckoned over Silaces who handed Surena a rolled parchment. Surena handed it to me.

'Word also reached Mithridates that Gordyene was Parthian once more. He has demanded that I surrender it to him.'

I read the demand and then passed it to my father, who shook his head.

'This requires careful consideration. King of Kings Mithridates has a right to assume control over Gordyene, especially as Balas left no heirs to inherit the kingdom.'

'You have no need to worry, lord king,' said Surena. 'I have already replied to Ctesiphon stating that Gordyene belongs to the King of Dura and that he has no authority over it. I finished by saying that if he wants this land then he had better come and take it.'

There was a stunned silence. My father's mouth opened in shock. He could not believe what he had just heard. For his part Atrax looked most uncomfortable while Viper nodded approvingly. The only sounds in the hall came from the logs burning on the fire.

'How many men do you have, Surena?' I said.

'Seven and half thousand of those I brought with me under Silaces and another eight thousand men that I have raised in Gordyene. I will have more by the end of the year.'

'If you last that long,' remarked my father.

'We should have fought the Armenians when we had the opportunity,' I said, thinking aloud.

'Do you wish to add Armenia to your kingdom as well as Gordyene?' asked my father.

I did not answer him. I knew that what Surena had done with regard to the Armenians was correct. Better that their own lands are laid waste than Parthian towns and villages. Still, he had exceeded his authority with regard to Mithridates though I could not find it in my heart to reprimand him for doing so. In any case I cared nothing for the Armenians or for Mithridates. The world would be a better place with both of them no longer in it.

My father and his men left the next morning, which was overcast and drizzly and entirely appropriate for the mood the King of Hatra was in. I stood in the palace courtyard with Surena and Atrax and watched him go, his bodyguard wrapped in their white cloaks as the drizzle turned to light rain and then got heavier before turning into a downpour. He raised his hand to us and then rode through the palace gates and into the city.

'Your father is angry with me, lord,' said Surena, the water coursing off his nose as we stood getting soaked.

'He will be less so when he realises that Hatra is safer with a friendly Gordyene on its border.'

'The King of Media already thinks that,' said Atrax, slapping Surena on the arm. 'Now let us get out of this rain before we all catch our deaths.'

Atrax returned to Media the following morning in high spirits. Not only had it stopped raining and the sun was shining, his kingdom, severely ravaged during last year's war, had a secure border with Gordyene. Atrax also cared little for legal niceties when it came to Mithridates, who had been responsible for a full-blown invasion of his kingdom. Before he left for Irbil he told Surena that he had made the right decision with regard to the demands of Mithridates and told him that he would always have an ally in Media. I also informed Surena that he had done well as we watched Silaces and some of his officers put some new recruits through their paces on the target ranges outside the city.

'They are mostly boys or youths who have just become men,' remarked Surena as a group of six horsemen rode by and released their arrows at targets of packed straw fixed to poles and mounted six feet off the ground.

'Most of the men folk were either dead or had been taken as slaves,' he continued. 'Though a few took to the hills and lived as brigands. It was hard to persuade them to join us.'

'But they did.'

'Eventually, I sent them to the northern border to fight the Armenians. They are used to living in the mountains and after so long in the wild they are like half-savages themselves.'

He pointed at another six riders shooting at the targets. 'These boys are the future of Gordyene.'

I had to admit that I was immensely proud of Surena and what he had done in Gordyene. He was more than capable of holding the kingdom.

'Do not over-extend yourself when dealing with the Armenians,' I told him. 'Just keep them occupied so they cannot raid Hatran territory. That at least will improve my father's humour.'

'They will try to take Gordyene back, lord.'

'I know, but you have given us time to deal with Mithridates before we settle things with the Armenians.' I tapped him on the chest.

'I will need you in the south when we march against Ctesiphon, Surena, and this time we will not be marching alone.'

'And who will replace Mithridates, lord?'

The same question arose time and time again when the toppling of Mithridates was broached: who would replace him? With my father pledged to march against Mithridates the ruler of Hatra might be persuaded to take the high crown, but I doubted it.

381

'I do not know, Surena, but I know that as long as Mithridates is on the throne the empire will have no peace.'

Peace. What is peace but the interval between wars? If, when, we defeated Mithridates and his lord high general then we would have to fight the Armenians to secure peace in the north, and perhaps the Romans to secure peace in the west. And after that? Perhaps there would be no after that, perhaps we would all be dead and our kingdoms ground into dust. But perhaps it would take only one battle to rid the world of Mithridates and Narses and everything else might fall into place. Just one battle and the empire would be united against its external enemies. And perhaps then the Armenians and Romans would be deterred from launching any further invasions. Just one more battle.

I looked into the sky heaped with grey clouds and heard the low rumble of thunder coming from the mountains and smiled. How many other kings through the ages had believed that just one more victory would be the answer to all their problems? The rain began to fall and the thunder got louder as the gods laughed.

Chapter 15

'So the marsh boy has repaid the faith you placed in him?'

Dobbai was as usual sitting in her chair near the balustrade as I settled into another one a few paces from her. It was late now and so servants placed bronze oil lamps on the tables and balustrade so we could see each other's faces, though I was mischievously tempted to order them to be taken away so that I would not have to look at Dobbai's haggard old visage. They also placed stands around the balustrade that held incense sticks made from the dried flower heads of chrysanthemums and lit them. This was to keep away the swarms of mosquitoes from the river below that otherwise would have been attracted to the lamps and would have bitten us and given us the fevers that can lead to death. We also burnt oil made from the balanite tree to keep away these insects.

'He has exceeded my expectations,' I replied proudly.

Gallia flopped down in her chair beside me. 'No doubt he is more arrogant than ever.'

Servants brought us wine and freshly made pastries from the kitchens while others placed silver boxes with holes in their sides around the edges of the terrace. We used these boxes all over the palace. They contained dead insects – cockroaches, flies and ants – that had been ground up. Though they had no smell these boxes acted as repellents to living insects and thus kept our home largely insect free.

'Actually he has matured since he has been in Gordyene,' I replied.

'Good,' said Dobbai, 'he will need all his wits to fulfil the task the gods have set him.'

'I would have thought he has done that already,' I suggested.

Dobbai stopped sipping her wine and regarded me with contempt. 'What has he done? Killed a few Armenians and taken possession of a hovel in the mountains.'

'He has freed Gordyene and returned it to the empire,' I said sternly.

She cackled. 'If you are comparing your own feeble efforts in Gordyene with his, then I agree he has achieved some success. But he will achieve more. His star rises.'

'How tedious,' remarked Gallia.

'Tedious or not,' I added, 'Surena's victory in Gordyene has assisted us greatly.'

'Us? Do not you mean you?' said Dobbai.

'Me?'

'Of course, for you now rule Gordyene as well as Dura and have an army in each kingdom.' She rose from her chair and walked to the balustrade to gaze at the marble-smooth waters of the Euphrates bathed in the pale glow of a full moon.

'The recent strife in the empire has weakened all the kingdoms except Dura. The kingdoms in the west have seen their lands despoiled while those in the east have lost many sons during two years of bloodshed. Only Dura and Hatra remain unscathed.'

'And Mesene,' I added.

She looked at me and laughed. 'Mesene is poor and stands only because of its Duran and Agraci allies. Above all Mithridates and Narses wanted you dead, son of Hatra.'

'You say the most reassuring things,' I quipped.

'But they failed and now they are weaker and you are stronger.'

'Will you take Gordyene for your own?' asked Gallia.

'He already has, child,' said Dobbai before I could answer.

'It does not belong to me,' I said.

Dobbai threw up her hands. 'Then who does it belong to, Mithridates?'

'He sent a demand to Surena for him to hand it over,' I replied. 'Surena told him he would have to take it by force.'

'Ha!' Dobbai was delighted. 'A most appropriate answer. The boy obviously has some steel in him. But you have not answered my question. What are you going to do about Gordyene?'

'I will decide after the wedding.'

I was referring to the final wedding that we would be attending, that between Vata and Adeleh which would be taking place at Hatra in a month's time.

'I will be attending,' Dobbai suddenly announced.

I looked at her in disbelief. For years now she had hardly ventured beyond the confines of the Citadel, being content to shuffle around the palace and spend most of her time with our children.

'Are you sure?' I queried. 'You have not left the palace in an age.'

'I am quite capable of sitting on a wagon for the duration of the journey, unless you do not wish me to attend.'

'He course he does,' said Gallia. 'Don't you, Pacorus?'

I held up my hands. 'Of course, the more the merrier. We will have to take the children, then. Claudia and Isabella won't stay here if Dobbai is not with them.'

Gallia frowned at me. 'Then we will take them as well. Your father's palace is large enough to accommodate us all.'

'I have business to settle at Hatra,' muttered Dobbai.

I shook my head and finished my wine. What business could she possibly have at Hatra? It was sad to witness her wits slowly diminish.

As we prepared for our journey life at Dura continued as normal. Regular deliveries of weapons were made to Alexander and Aaron's treasury filled with Jewish gold. The trade caravans continued to pass through Dura and brought with them news of what was happening to the east of the Tigris. We heard that the court at Ctesiphon was riven with fear and loathing and that courtiers were pressing Mithridates to move further to the east, to Susa or even Esfahan. They feared that they were too near the western kingdoms whose kings might assault them. They were right about that at least. But Mithridates would not abandon the empire's symbolic seat of power, not least because he desired to launch a fresh attack against those who were now in direct rebellion against him. Because the kingdoms of Mesene, Babylon, Hatra, Media and Atropaiene, as well as my own, refused to pay their annual tribute to Ctesiphon, Mithridates railed against them and threatened reprisals. But we heard that the eastern kings had no stomach for another great war, especially after their recent losses.

Of the Romans we heard little save what Byrd told us when he visited Dura. He had expanded his business interests and had established new offices in Damascus. Despite his wealth and importance he still rode a shabby horse and dressed in faded robes. He told me that Egypt was now a protectorate of Rome following a series of internecine struggles and I shuddered. Though Roman Syria was quiet I knew that the caravans that traversed the Parthian Empire before entering Syria or Egypt would also tell the authorities of those two regions that the Parthians had weakened themselves through years of civil war. It would surely be only a matter of time before Rome sent its legions against the empire.

It was a blisteringly hot morning when we set off for Dura. Initially we had determined to depart a day earlier but word came from Uruk that Nergal and Praxima had also been invited to Vata's wedding. I had no idea why this should be so as Nergal had never known Vata but Gallia was delighted and insisted that we wait for them to reach Dura so we could all make the trip together. Dobbai and the children travelled in a large four-wheeled wagon on which Marcus had erected a metal frame so it could be covered with canvas to make a shaded interior. It was pulled by six mules and led two camels that carried our own tent and Dobbai's. She also insisted that there should be three hammocks inside the wagon: one for her, one for Claudia and one for Isabella, in addition to Eszter's cot. I had never seen Marcus so flustered as she ordered him around in the days preceding our departure. I think he was glad to see the back of us.

Gallia took the Amazons as her personal bodyguard. I told her this was unnecessary, as I had already organised a hundred cataphracts to escort us to Hatra. But now that Praxima was also with us it was an opportunity for her and Gallia and the rest of the female Companions to be united once more. Nergal brought a hundred of his horse archers with him, which meant our party numbered two hundred horse archers, two hundred squires and a hundred cataphracts. This number increased when we left Dura and passed over the pontoon bridge to the eastern side of the Euphrates where we had agreed to link up with the party of Orodes and Axsen who were also travelling to Hatra. The rulers of Babylon were escorted by one hundred royal guards attired in dragon skin armour. Axsen had inherited her father's penchant for taking large numbers of servants on campaign, and so in addition to her royal guards there were cooks, the queen's female attendants, grooms, slaves and farriers. I think Orodes was embarrassed by the massive entourage but seemed very happy with his new wife.

We all rode in one group as our small combined army made its way north, the Amazons riding directly behind us and a long line of horses and camels following. There must have been a thousand camels in our great expeditionary force.

Axsen found it most strange but was also intrigued. It was the first time she had ridden with Gallia and Praxima, both of them dressed in their mail shirts and fully armed, though because of the heat they were wearing their floppy hats and not their helmets. Axsen was most excited that Dobbai was travelling with us.

'Perhaps your sorceress would dine with us tonight, Gallia,' said Axsen as sweat poured down my neck and soaked my shirt. I would have to have words with Vata about getting married in the middle of a Mesopotamian summer.

'I can ask her,' replied Gallia.

'I doubt she will agree,' I said. 'She hates the heat and she hates travelling, which means she is as ill-tempered as a angry viper at the moment.'

'Is she really a sorceress?' asked Axsen.

'She is beloved of the gods,' replied Gallia.

'She predicted that you and Orodes would be married,' I added.

'And she saw Pacorus in danger when Narses and Mithridates had him surrounded and sent Gallia to rescue him,' offered Praxima.

I grinned at Nergal's wife. 'Thank you for reminding me of that.'

'I must meet her,' implored Axsen.

'Why don't you visit us when we have made camp tonight,' said Gallia. 'I fear she will ignore any invites to a feast.'

Axsen was delighted. 'We will come. How exciting.'

I was exhausted by the time we had travelled a grand distance of fifteen miles in the stupefying heat, and by the end of the day my clothes were drenched in sweat and I felt both tired and irritable. The Durans made camp well away from the large pavilion that housed Babylon's royal couple, though Nergal and Praxima pitched their tent close to ours. The squires erected our tent first, which was similar to Domitus' command tent to accommodate the children; then Dobbai's, a black camel hair affair that was like the Agraci tents; and then put up the tents of the cataphracts. As usual the latter were laid out in a neat row with the squires' own tents pitched in another row immediately behind.

Despite dozing in their hammocks the children were exhausted by the journey and fell asleep almost immediately after we had eaten a meal of salted mutton, water and biscuits. The night was very warm though mercifully not intolerably hot and a slight easterly breeze was most welcome. After the children had been settled Dobbai relaxed with Gallia and me in front of her tent. We sat on stools while she reclined in her favourite wicker chair that she had ordered Marcus to pack on the wagon. For the journey Dobbai had half a dozen stable hands from the Citadel to attend her, drive her wagon, ensure none of my children fell off it during the day and water and feed the mules. The boys walked beside the wagon during the day, taking it in turns to drive it. They were beside themselves with joy when Dobbai gave each of them a piece of red coral, an ancient talisman to protect the wearer from evil spirits.

Orodes and Axsen appeared out of the darkness an hour later with a score of guards, half of them carrying torches. Axsen was dressed in a simple purple shirt and tan leggings, Orodes in his silver scale armour cuirass and sword at his hip. Dobbai's eyes were closed as we embraced them and their guards retreated from our presence. Axsen grinned girlishly at Gallia and then looked at the seemingly sleeping Dobbai.

The oil lamps flickered faintly in the slight breeze as we all regarded the apparently dozing Dobbai, who suddenly spoke without opening her eyes.

'Cannot an old woman get any peace in this world?'

Axsen moved two steps towards her, Orodes remaining a few paces behind.

'Forgive us, lady, we did not mean to interrupt your evening.'

Dobbai opened her eyes and looked at Axsen.

'Of course you did. Why else would you bring a host of soldiers with you to make a noise like a herd of bulls if not to disturb me?'

Axsen was taken aback, not least because she was unused to being spoken to thus by anyone, least of all an old crone. Axsen ignored Dobbai's impertinence and smiled.

'Your name is known throughout the empire, lady, and I would like to make your acquaintance.'

Dobbai grunted. 'You want something from me, Queen of Babylon. What is it?'

Axsen glanced nervously at Orodes who shrugged, and then looked back at Dobbai.

'They say that the gods reveal the future to you.'

Dobbai leaned forward in her chair. 'They reveal things that will come to pass and other things that may come to pass. What of it?'

Axsen smiled at Orodes. 'I heard that you predicted my marriage to Orodes.'

Dobbai pointed at Orodes. 'Step forward, King of Babylon, so that I may see you both together.'

Orodes moved to Axsen's side and held his wife's hand. Then Dobbai looked at me and nodded.

'They have a regal appearance, I grant you that. There are worse choices you could make.'

'I do not understand,' I said.

Dobbai cackled. 'Of course not, but it does not matter.'

She looked at Axsen and Orodes again. 'You have a crown, Queen of Babylon?'

Axsen looked quizzically at her. 'Of course, I am a queen.'

'You will be leaving Babylon and will require it no longer.'

The colour drained from Axsen's face and Orodes looked most concerned.

'Is Babylon in danger?' he asked.

Dobbai frowned. 'Did I say that? All I said was that your wife will not need Babylon's crown much longer. She will have a new one to wear.'

Now Axsen was intrigued. 'What crown?'

Dobbai waved her hand at her. 'All will be revealed. Did you know that the King of Dura has no crown? Is that not correct, son of Hatra?'

'It is true,' I replied. 'I have never seen the need.'

Dobbai began to rise from her chair, whereupon Orodes walked forward and assisted her to her feet.

'Thank you, Orodes. I always knew you would make a good king and now you stand on the brink of becoming one.'

Orodes smiled at her. 'You are mistaken.'

'He is already a king,' said Axsen.

'Not until the son of Hatra makes him so,' replied Dobbai. 'And now I am tired and bid you goodnight.'

She turned and shuffled into her tent. She stopped and pointed at Axsen.

'And you will make a good queen.' And then she disappeared into the tent and closed the camel hair flap.

Axsen was confused and slightly disappointed while Orodes whispered to me that he believed that Dobbai's senses were failing her.

'She did not realise that I was the King of Babylon,' he said. 'How sad it is when old age addles us so. Alas for Dobbai.'

It took us twelve days to reach Hatra and on the last day of our journey Vistaspa, accompanied by two hundred of my father's bodyguard, met us ten miles from the city. He informed me that we were the last of the wedding guests to arrive and would we mind riding through the southern gates of the city to the palace quarter that was located in the north. My father wanted to impress the inhabitants

388

with a show of strength, and also the many merchants and foreign traders in the city, including a few Romans. In this way news would spread far and wide of the assembly of kings at Hatra.

No doubt my father also intended to send a message to Ctesiphon, Syria and Armenia of the gathering strength at Hatra, and was using Vata's wedding as a statement of intent. However, it was still intolerably hot and the cataphracts sweated in their full-face helmets and scale armour on the morning we rode towards the city's southern entrance. Pennants sporting the red griffin flew from every *kontus* and every Amazon wore her helmet with its cheekguards tied shut. Because I was the heir to Hatra's throne my cataphracts rode in the vanguard. Next came the royal party of Gallia, myself, Axsen, Orodes, Nergal and Praxima, the latter wearing her Amazon uniform. Behind us were our banners and next trundled the wagon carrying Dobbai and my children and behind that the Babylonian guard. Nergal's horse archers brought up the rear. The squires and camels remained in camp but would be relocated later that day to outside the city's northern gates, nearer to the palace quarter.

On the wooden bridge spanning the great moat that surrounded Hatra stood soldiers of the garrison, with more lining the route from the gatehouse through the streets to the royal quarter – men wearing bronze helmets with white crests, round shields faced with bronze, leather cuirasses fitted with iron scales and leather greaves. The soldiers had difficulty holding back the cheering crowds as our column made its way to the palace, Claudia and Isabella peering from the back of the wagon and waving at the multitude.

We finally arrived at the royal square that stood between the limestone palace and the Great Temple, also called the Sun Temple, dedicated to Shamash. We left the heaving crowds at the gates to the palace quarter, which like the Citadel at Dura was surrounded by its own walls. The difference was that at Dura the Citadel was squat and compact whereas the royal quarter at Hatra was grand and expansive. As well as housing the palace it also contained the mansions of the kingdom's nobility – I knew that Lord Herneus had a great house here – the royal armouries, stables, barracks and granaries. It was no exaggeration to say that ten of Dura's Citadels could easily be accommodated within the walls of Hatra's royal quarter.

Today the square was filled with the nobles and their families as the king's son and his friends came to a halt before the steps of the palace. Servants came forward to hold the reins of our horses as we dismounted. The stable hands assisted my children from the wagon and Dobbai passed a crying Eszter to Gallia and then stepped down from the rear of the wagon. The square echoed with polite applause as I walked beside Gallia to the foot of the steps, flanked by Orodes and Axsen on my right and Nergal and Praxima on our left. However, there were also murmurs as Dobbai, Claudia and a bashful Isabella clutching her hand, followed us immediately behind. I too was surprised, though not by Dobbai, as standing on the steps were several individuals I had not expected to see at Hatra. My father and mother stood in the centre of the group, Gafarn and Diana and the young Spartacus beside them. Then came Vata and Adeleh and Atrax and Aliyeh. Aschek and his wife Ona stood next to the rulers of Media and beyond them were Surena and Viper. If I was surprised to see the new governor of Gordyene I was astounded to see King Khosrou and his queen, Tara, standing on the other end of the line of royalty, alongside King Musa of Hyrcania and his wife Queen Sholeh. At the foot of the steps, to my right, stood Assur, high priest of the temple, with a dozen of his white-robed subordinates. Now in his mid-seventies, he was still tall though very thin and his beard, formerly bushy, was noticeably thinner. He glared at Dobbai as she bared her teeth at him and his priests as she walked up the stone steps.

After I had greeted my father and mother we walked with them inside the palace as our horses were taken to the stables. The voluminous palace with its marble floors and great stone columns was pleasantly cool as we made our way to our apartments, my mother continually glancing behind at Dobbai.

'You have brought the sorceress, Pacorus?'

'She insisted on coming.'

'Why?'

'I have no idea,' I replied. 'More to the point, what are Khosrou and Musa doing here?'

'All will be revealed,' answered my father.

I had nodded to Khosrou and Musa when I alighted the palace steps but I had no opportunity that day to speak to them. After our journey we were exhausted and spent the afternoon relaxing while nursemaids attended to our children. Dobbai demanded to be shown to her quarters, after which she locked the doors of her room and was not seen until the following morning.

The three days before the wedding were filled with inspections of the garrison, tours of the walls, archery competitions, banquets and visits to the mansions of influential nobles. All very tedious and which diverted me from my aim of speaking at length to Khosrou and Musa concerning their presence at Hatra. I did succeed in speaking to Surena, though, when I ordered him to my quarters on the first morning after our arrival in the city. He told me that he had received an invitation from my father to attend Vata's wedding and that not to be present would be an insult to the man who had done so much to support his war effort in Gordyene.

'The wording of the letter was most insistent, lord,' he said.

'I can imagine.'

'It is wise to keep the King of Hatra happy, lord, I think.'

I smiled at him. 'I think you are right, Surena.'

'Does Hatra wish to rule Gordyene, lord? Is that why I have been brought here.'

'You know, Surena, at this moment in time I am as ignorant as you are regarding this matter. How are the Armenians?'

He smiled. 'Still licking their wounds. I have heard that their king....'

'Tigranes?'

'Yes, lord. I have heard that he is sick.'

'He will recover,' I told him, 'and when he does he will be looking to retake Gordyene.'

'We are ready, lord.'

I did manage to avoid any appointments the morning before the wedding and took myself down to the poor quarter of the city where once Byrd had briefly lived, making a living by selling pots before I had persuaded him to accompany me to Dura. I stood before the one-roomed shop he had rented that fronted the grubby square. A wooden bench still stood before the room, though instead of Byrd's pots it was piled high with sandals. There were around fifty people in the square inspecting and haggling over the products on display around its sides. I walked over to the sandal seller, a man in his early twenties with lank hair and sores on his hands who was arranging his goods. Behind him was a woman who looked twice her early years holding a naked infant with a dirty face. I picked up a pair of sandals as the man watched me, obviously confused why someone who wore expensive leather boots would be looking at poorer quality footwear. His wife looked at me with sorrowful eyes.

'How much?' I asked.

'Three obols, sir,' he replied.

Half a drachma – the daily wage of an unskilled worker.

'I'll take them.' I took the leather pouch hanging from my belt and emptied a hundred drachmas on the table.

'A fair price,' I said.

He looked in disbelief at the pile of money on the table.

'It is too much, sir.'

I looked at his miserable hovel and impoverished family and thought of the rich food and wine that would be consumed tomorrow at Vata's wedding and of the great wealth that existed in this city, just a short distance away.

'I knew the man who worked here once. I am forever in his debt. This is a way of repaying but a small part of it. But for an accident of birth our positions might have been reversed. How strange is fate do you not think?'

'Sir?'

391

'It does not matter. Keep the money.'

The wedding of Vata and Adeleh took place in the temple, the great building packed with kings, queens, nobles and their wives, and afterwards there was a huge feast in the palace. It was good to see Vata's big round face wearing a smile again and I was genuinely happy for him and my sister. So now all my parents' children were married. I had thought that Adeleh, being in her thirties, would remain single but now she went with her new husband back to Nisibus to begin her new life as the wife of Hatra's northern governor, who had been created Prince of Nisibus in honour of his entering the royal family. I watched my mother wipe tears from her eyes as she bid her daughter farewell the day after the wedding.

With the marriage out of the way I was determined to finally speak to Khosrou at length about his campaign against the northern nomads, but I was again thwarted when Gallia and I received a summons from my father to attend him in his throne room that afternoon. My curiosity was aroused when Nergal and Praxima informed me that they had also been requested to attend my father. When we arrived I discovered that in addition to the dais upon which my father and mother sat as the rulers of Hatra, seven other temporary platforms had been erected in the great chamber in two lines extending from the permanent dais. Behind each one hung great banners carrying the symbols of the kings who would sit on each one: the red griffin of Dura, the double-headed lion sceptre crossed with a sword of Mesene, the horned bull of Babylon, the sun symbol of Margiana, the Caspian tiger of Hyrcania, the *Shahbaz*, the mythical bird of Atropaiene, and the white dragon of Media.

My father and mother were already on their thrones when Gallia and I were shown to our places along with Surena and Viper who sat down behind Gallia and me. Next to my father sat Gafarn, who nodded to me, and flanking my mother was Diana who smiled and waved at Gallia. Kogan's guards stood every five paces around the walls while others stood in front of the great doors at its entrance. As Khosrou and his wife took their seats on their dais there was a commotion at the doors and I recognised the voice of Dobbai haranguing the guards. Kogan also heard it and left his place beside my father's dais to see what was going on.

'I will have entry,' I heard Dobbai shout to the four guards who barred her way with spears.

'Get the old witch out of here,' ordered Kogan.

'No,' I shouted, 'let her pass.'

Kogan stopped and turned to look at my father. I walked across to where the guards stood before Dobbai.

'Put down your weapons and let her through,' I commanded.

They knew that I was the heir to Hatra's throne and yet they hesitated to move out of the way. They took orders from Kogan and my father, not from me.

'Do not force me to draw my own sword,' I threatened them.

I turned to look at Kogan who in turn looked at my father for guidance. A disapproving Assur leaned on his staff as all eyes in the hall fell on me. Orodes was frowning and Khosrou seemed mildly amused. My father nodded to Kogan.

'Stand down and let her through,' he ordered.

The guards moved away from Dobbai as she shuffled into the chamber and held up her arm for me to take.

'I hope the chairs are comfortable,' she said loudly enough for everyone to hear as I escorted her over to my platform. 'The conversation of kings can be long and tedious and my back is old and frail.'

I gave her my large wicker chair that was stuffed with cushions as I stood next to her and waited for another to be brought. Assur went over to my father and said something into his ear, pointing at Dobbai as he did so, but my father shook his head and waved him away. Directly opposite us sat Atrax and Aliyeh, my sister curling her lip at the ugly old woman she now had to look at during the meeting, while Aschek and Musa were busy grinning at each other and pointing at Dobbai as she rearranged the cushions and settled herself in her chair. Fortunately there was room on our crowded dais to accommodate another chair and the five of us sat and waited for my father to speak. Normally only kings would have been invited to such gatherings, but he knew that Gallia would not have countenanced being excluded and neither would Praxima, and in any case Orodes would have been loathe to exclude Axsen from the proceedings so besotted was he with her. And in any case she had been the ruler of Babylon before their marriage. Thus all the wives of the kings had been invited though none was expected to contribute.

The doors were closed and my father rose from his throne and stepped from his dais. He stood on the tiled floor and looked at each of the kings in turn before he spoke.

'My friends, I asked you here because the empire is in great peril. The days of the eighteen kingdoms under the great King of Kings Sinatruces are long gone, and with them the peace, stability and respect for the law that his reign brought and which made the empire strong. Now we have unending war: war with external enemies and war within the empire itself. Last year King of Kings Mithridates launched a war against those of us who sit in this chamber, rulers who had hitherto been loyal and true towards Ctesiphon.'

He held out a hand to me.

393

'Others among us have been banished from the empire and their kingdoms traded with our enemies like cheap goods in a market. Only because of the King of Dura's battlefield skills does his kingdom remain Parthian.'

I smiled at my father.

'Now Hatra refuses to pay any tribute to Ctesiphon in retaliation for the aggression waged against it by the high king. My fellow kings from Atropaiene, Babylon, Mesene and Media adopt a similar stance.' He tipped his head at Musa and Khosrou. 'My brothers the rulers of Margiana and Hyrcania have just returned from a long campaign in the northern wastes against the steppe nomads whom formerly they were at peace with. How bitter must have been the news that gold from Ctesiphon had paid the nomads to attack them.'

I was saddened but not surprised by this revelation; after all, Mithridates had encouraged the Romans to invade Dura. He had now done the same with the northern nomads.

My father continued. 'The mighty armies of Margiana and Hyrcania have, after more than two years of bloody and constant fighting, cowed the northern barbarians and once more their borders are quiet.

'But I ask all of you this: how long will it be before our kingdoms are once again attacked, by the Armenians, the Romans, the northern barbarians or by King Narses acting on the orders of Mithridates? An empire that is divided encourages external enemies to be bold. But an empire that is united earns respect and deters aggression.'

'What you say is true, King Varaz. But how do you propose to remedy the dire situation the empire finds itself in?' asked Khosrou.

'How, Khosrou? The removal of Mithridates,' he replied before retaking his throne.

I reached over to grip Gallia's arm.

'Finally,' I whispered.

'Stay silent, son of Hatra,' hissed Dobbai, 'lest you appear too keen on further bloodshed.'

I kept my counsel as the hall fell silent. Orodes shifted nervously in his seat and Atrax appeared thoughtful while Nergal looked solemn. It was Musa who spoke first. Everything about the King of Hyrcania was large – his round face, his frame wrapped in a great white robe edged with red and gold and his bear-like hands. He rose from his chair and spread his paws out wide.

'When I received your invitation, Varaz, I knew that I was not coming to Hatra just for a wedding feast, agreeable though it was I have to say. Hyrcania has always been a loyal kingdom to the empire but now that loyalty has been repaid by treachery. Therefore Hyrcania will stand with Hatra in this matter. Let us be rid of Mithridates and make the empire strong again.'

Musa sat down and looked at Khosrou. The King of Margiana, dressed in a simple green shirt, black leggings and tan leather boots, was the opposite of Musa in appearance with his slim frame, hawk-like nose and narrow eyes. He had a long white moustache and white pointed beard that matched the colour of his hair. He stroked his beard before slowly rising from his chair like an angry cobra.

'I agree with Varaz that the empire, much less Margiana, cannot withstand more conflict, though removing Mithridates, agreeable as it that may be, will require more bloodshed. I am prepared to draw my sword to achieve this end, but there is still one question that remains unanswered. Who will replace him? At the Council of Kings, Varaz, you stated before all the other rulers that you had no wish to wear the high crown.'

'That is still the case,' said my father.

Khosrou sat back down. 'Then what? We cannot be rid of one tyrant only for another, Narses most likely, to take his place.'

'Perhaps that issue can wait,' replied my father. 'I would first know where the others here assembled stand on the issue of removing Mithridates.'

I saw Axsen look at Orodes and nod at him. He rose from his chair. 'Babylon has suffered grievously from the aggression of Mithridates and Narses, and would support Hatra, Margiana and Hyrcania in their plans. But speaking personally I would also desire that the matter of who replaces Mithridates be settled at this assembly.'

I smiled. Orodes – ever the stickler for procedure!

Nergal rose nervously and added his support to my father's scheme. That was never in doubt as he was formerly an officer in my father's army and he still had family members living in Hatra. Atrax also pledged Media's support to my father's venture. Aschek rose from his chair and announced that he too was willing to support my father, though with the proviso that Atropaiene had suffered grievously the previous year and therefore would not be able to supply any troops to march against Mithridates.

There was only my voice yet to be heard.

'What does the King of Dura have to say for himself?' asked my father.

I began to rise and noticed that Dobbai had her eyes closed and appeared to be asleep. So much for the great decisions that were being taken in this hall! I nodded towards her, rolled my eyes at Gallia and stepped onto the floor.

'You all know my opinion of Mithridates and Narses. It is no secret that I have never accepted the former as the empire's high king. I fully support my father's plan and would march against Ctesiphon tomorrow if I could.'

Musa burst out laughing and Khosrou smiled. I went to retake my seat but Khosrou called after me.

'Wait. Why should not Pacorus be king of kings?'

I stopped dead and turned to face him, somewhat taken aback. Khosrou stood up.

'I propose the King of Dura to be the empire's new high king.'

Musa clapped his bear's paws and roared with laughter.

'I second that proposal,' he bellowed. 'The empire could do worse.'

Such a ringing endorsement!

I raised my hand to protest but then Nergal jumped up. 'Mesene also wishes King Pacorus to sit in Ctesiphon.'

I frowned at Nergal but Praxima cheered with delight, as did Viper and Gallia. Aschek then stood.

'Pacorus has proven himself to be a brave and honourable king. If Varaz does not want the high crown then I say his son should wear it.'

'I agree,' added Atrax. 'I have fought beside Pacorus and know him to be worthy of the high crown.'

I could see that Aliyeh was horrified by the idea that I should become king of kings.

But Orodes added Babylon's support to my becoming king of kings. My father looked at each of the kings in turn and then at me and smiled. My mother clasped her hands to her face, tears of joy in her eyes.

'It would appear that nearly half the empire's kings desire you to be the man to lead Parthia, my son. Very well. Hatra will support this wish.'

'It is settled, then,' said Khosrou.

'It shall not be!'

Dobbai's voice filled the chamber to still all others. She opened her eyes and stared at me.

'Sit down, son of Hatra, and stop preening yourself like a peacock.'

Assur and Kogan glowered at her interruption while Gafarn laughed at her rudeness. My mother looked at my father who merely shook his head despairingly. Dobbai pointed at my empty chair to indicate that I should sit in it as she lifted herself up and stepped from the dais. Assur pointed at her with his staff.

'This harridan has no authority to speak in this hallowed place. Her presence violates this august hall.'

Kogan made to pull his sword but I drew myself up and placed my hand on the hilt of my sword and glared at him. He stopped and looked at my father who waved him back. I regained my seat.

'I may be a harridan but I know the will of the gods,' Dobbai said to Assur. 'Can you say the same, old man?'

Assur's cheeks coloured with anger and his nostrils flared but my father stood and held up a hand to him.

'We all know who you are,' he said, 'so if you have come to this meeting to reveal what the gods desire then speak the words and have done with it.'

Dobbai bowed mockingly to him. 'Short and to the point, King of Hatra. If only you had displayed such forcefulness years ago when Sinatruces died you would have prevented the shedding of an ocean of blood.'

'We should have thrown you on his pyre,' shouted Musa.

Aliyeh laughed and Khosrou smirked.

'But you did not,' Dobbai shot back, 'and now I say to you that the son of Hatra, the king who has no crown, shall wear no crown. It is not his destiny to rule the empire.'

'If we desire him to be king of kings,' growled Khosrou, 'it shall be so.'

Dobbai bared her teeth at him. 'If you go against the will of the gods they will send the numberless hordes of the northern steppes against your kingdom to sweep you away, Khosrou, so great will be their wrath. You think you have defeated them? I tell you that your kingdom will be eradicated from the earth if you defy the immortal ones.'

He waved his hand dismissively at her.

Aschek leaned forward. 'Then, woman, can you tell us whom the gods desire to be high king?'

'The heir of Sinatruces, of course,' she replied before walking back to her chair.

Musa roared with laughter once more. 'The old crone's brains are addled. Phraates is long dead.'

Dobbai caught my eye as she eased herself onto the cushions and nodded. I understood and rose from my chair once more.

'My lords, what Dobbai has said is true. Sinatruces ruled the empire before the crown passed to his son Phraates, who was basely murdered by Mithridates. But Phraates had another son, a man who has endured exile from his own lands and who has fought by my side for many years. He wears the crown of Babylon now but I propose that we should today elect King Orodes to wear the high crown.'

Musa looked at Khosrou with a perplexed expression. My father rubbed his nose with a finger and Orodes was rendered speechless. And yet it made perfect sense. Orodes was known to all those present as a brave and honourable man who had always conducted himself with the utmost propriety.

'Can any among you think of a man with more self-restraint, honour and sense of justice than Orodes?' I said. 'I cannot. Nor can I think of anyone better to unite the empire in the aftermath of Mithridates' removal.'

397

'And what does Orodes think of my son's proposal?' asked my father.

Everyone turned their attention to Orodes, who to his credit retained his composure as Axsen grinned at him and he rose from his chair. He held out a hand to me as Dobbai closed her eyes once more.

'My friend, King Pacorus, is most gracious and magnanimous in proposing me for the high crown. May I first state that I have never coveted the throne at Ctesiphon, being content to fulfil my duties as a prince of Susiana. Furthermore…'

'Do you want the crown or not?' queried Musa, clearly becoming bored by the whole business.

Orodes smiled at him and continued, unruffled. 'If the kings gathered in this hall unanimously desire me to be king of kings then I will accept their nomination.'

I stood. 'Dura supports Orodes.'

In turn Nergal, Khosrou, Musa, Aschek and Atrax all stood and pledged their support to Orodes, which left only my father to voice his opinion. He looked at Gafarn who nodded, then stood and smiled at Orodes.

'Hail Orodes, King of Kings!'

We all gave a cheer, though I suspect Musa's cry was relief that proceedings were coming to a close. My father held up his hands.

'We shall have Orodes proclaimed king of kings in the Great Temple tomorrow before Shamash so that all the empire may know our determination in this matter.'

Everyone clapped at these words, me the loudest. Orodes held up a hand to still the noise.

'My lords, it seems we have forgotten one matter that needs redress.'

'And what would that be?' asked my father.

'Gordyene,' he answered.

I sat down as Dobbai continued to listen with her eyes closed.

Musa was most confused. 'Gordyene. What about it? Pacorus holds it.'

Orodes smiled at him. 'Quite so, King Musa, but Gordyene has always been a separate kingdom within the empire, ruled by its own king. But it is now ruled by Dura.'

Orodes turned to me.

'Do you intend to make Gordyene your own, Pacorus?'

'I do not,' I replied.

'Then it needs its own king, as in the time of the eighteen kingdoms.' Orodes nodded at my father.

'Balas left no heirs, Orodes,' said my father. 'You know this.'

'Then as soon-to-be king of kings I have the power to select a new ruler for the kingdom if my memory regarding the powers of the high king serves me right.'

Strictly speaking Orodes was not yet king of kings, but he had obviously been giving the matter of Gordyene's throne some thought and now had the opportunity to turn it into reality. The other kings, myself included, did not see the point of discussing Gordyene here but Orodes appeared insistent and so we all sat down again.

'Can we have some refreshments, Varaz?' asked Musa. 'My belly thinks my throat has been slit.'

My mother and the other queens winced at his coarse language but Khosrou and Atrax laughed. My father ordered wine and food to be brought from the kitchens and in the interlude before refreshments arrived Orodes continued to speak about the throne of Gordyene.

'Have you another brother we do not know about?' asked Khosrou.

'No, my lord.'

'Then who do you have in mind to rule Gordyene?' queried Atrax, whose own kingdom shared a border with Gordyene and who thus had a keen interest in knowing the identity of its ruler.

Orodes turned and smiled at Surena who was whispering into the ear of a giggling Viper.

'The man who conquered Gordyene and in so doing has returned it to the Parthian Empire. I propose Surena, the resent governor of Gordyene.'

'Who?' asked Musa as he gratefully took a large cup of wine offered to him by a slave.

Dobbai opened her eyes and smiled mischievously at me. 'You never saw that coming, did you?'

Indeed I did not and nor did Surena, who appeared shocked as I turned to look at him. Gallia rolled her eyes and my father seemed most surprised, but Viper grasped the significance of Orodes' words and jumped up to hug her husband and kiss him with delight. No wonder, for she had also just been made a queen!

'Surena is a man who had proved himself to be a resourceful and intelligent commander who single-handedly expelled the Armenians from Gordyene, and in so doing made the kingdoms of Hatra and Media,' Orodes held out his hand to my father and Atrax in turn as he stepped onto the floor, 'more secure. Step forward, Surena.'

For once Surena was lost for words as he hesitantly stood up and then left the dais to stand beside Orodes, who was quickly slipping into his new role.

'Does anyone here object to Surena becoming the king of Gordyene?'

Khosrou and Musa had little interest in the affairs of a kingdom that lay four hundred miles west of Hyrcania and a thousand miles from

Merv, Khosrou's capital, so they both shrugged with indifference, Musa draining his cup, belching and then holding it out to be refilled. Nergal was nodding and grinning at Surena while Praxima was smiling at Viper. It was certainly a triumph for the Amazons. Aschek looked at my father who now rose.

'King Orodes, I think you will agree that the elevation of this young man to the office of king is unusual to say the least. That said, we live in unusual times and having just elected you to the high crown I will not contradict your first decision as king of kings.'

'Nor I,' agreed Aschek.

'I have fought beside Surena,' declared Atrax, 'and know that he will make a worthy king.' He had obviously changed his opinion regarding a mere squire attaining high command, though his wife was regarding Surena with open disdain.

'That just leaves your opinion, Pacorus,' said my father.

I turned to look at Viper who had regained her seat. I smiled at her and then stood.

'Dura supports the election of Surena, one of its most valiant sons, to the throne of Gordyene, safe in the knowledge that he will be a great Parthian ruler.'

And so it was that Surena, formerly a stripling of the Ma'adan, became a Parthian king.

The following day Assur proclaimed Orodes king of kings in the Great Temple at Hatra and I began to think about the campaign to topple Mithridates. Soon he would know that his stepbrother had been proclaimed high king and would be forced to take action, and once again Narses would bring his armies west across the Tigris.

'Except that he will not,' declared my father as I sat with the other kings in the large study beside his throne room two days after Orodes was declared high king. Despite the heat outside the room was cool and well ventilated courtesy of the wind catchers on the roof of the palace. These towers 'caught' the desert wind in vents and then directed it down into the palace to keep the air flowing and thus the building cool. In the blistering heat of the summer light bamboo screens were placed over the vents and doused with water to cool the air passing into the rooms below. All the buildings in the royal quarter were equipped with these wind catchers, even the royal stables, to make living conditions more bearable.

The mood was relaxed as my father explained to all of us present the outline of his plan. As he spoke I realised that he had been thinking of this campaign for many months after it had become clear that Mithridates and Narses had declared war on him. Like the other kings my father was a man who above all believed in stability and continuity. I knew that my hatred for Mithridates and the strife that this had engendered had upset him deeply and had created a gulf between us that only now had been spanned. The kings of Hatra had always been fiercely loyal to the empire and the king of kings but now that loyalty had been thrown back into my father's face. Unlike me he had not reacted instantly and marched his army against Ctesiphon. Rather, he had bided his time, gathered allies and prepared a carefully worked-out project. This plan he now laid before us. It was ambitious in scope and aim.

The main thrust would comprise the combined might of Dura, Hatra, Babylon, Media and Gordyene striking across the Tigris after having first taken Seleucia.

'We will need your siege engines for that task, Pacorus.'

'The walls of Seleucia will fall easily enough, father, have no fear.'

'Then we will seize Ctesiphon,' continued my father, 'before marching southeast to capture Susa and then Persepolis. Before then I expect to engage Mithridates and Narses in battle and defeat them.

'At the same time Musa and Khosrou will threaten to advance from the north with their combined armies against the kingdoms of Yueh-Chih, Aria, Anauon and Drangiana. The rulers of those kingdoms have for years provided Mithridates with support and soldiers for their ventures against us.'

I was confused. 'Threaten to advance, father?'

He smiled and nodded at Khosrou.

'They have supported Mithridates and Narses, as your father has said,' agreed Khosrou, 'but my spies have told me that they have no stomach for another great war. Musa and I may achieve by diplomacy what you will have to accomplish with arms.'

Aschek was far from convinced. 'You really think they will stand aside and do nothing when Narses sends his summons to them.'

'If they don't then we will lay waste their lands,' said Musa.

'It is as my brother says,' added Khosrou gravely.

My father turned to Nergal. 'If he is agreeable I would like the King of Mesene to stand on the defensive during the first part of the campaign until we have taken Susa. With his army protecting the crossing of the Tigris near Umma, the enemy will not be able to send raiding parties across the river to strike at Mesene and southern Babylonia. Thereafter we would welcome the addition of his troops to our army.'

Nergal nodded. My father turned to Aschek.

'My old friend, your kingdom has suffered the most during the deprivations of the enemy last year, and so to you I would like to entrust the safety of Hatra, Media and Gordyene. Vata will stay at Nisibus to secure my northern frontier and,' he looked at Surena, 'I assume troops will be left in Gordyene to secure that kingdom.'

Surena nodded solemnly.

'But,' continued my father, 'I would feel more comfortable knowing that the army of Atropaiene also guards the north.'

This was a clever strategy. Unlike Atrax, Aschek was not a great warrior and had little appetite for campaigning beyond his realm. In addition, Atropaiene had been devastated the previous year and so it made sense to leave what was left of its army as a reserve upon which Aliyeh and Vata could call upon.

'Who will you leave in Gordyene?' I asked Surena.

'Silaces, lord.'

I smiled at him. 'You do not have to call me lord, Surena. You too are a king now.'

My father looked at Orodes. 'It only remains for you, highness, to give your assent to this endeavour.'

'I know that you do not undertake this venture likely, King Varaz,' replied Orodes slowly and forcefully, 'but I think it is a most excellent scheme and I fully endorse it.'

'Soon you will be sitting in Ctesiphon, my friend,' I said, 'and after that you will be able to take Axsen on an inspection of Susa and the Kingdom of Susiana.'

I left Hatra in high spirits as we made our way back to Dura. At long last the final showdown with Narses and Mithridates would take place and I was very confident that it would have a favourable outcome. Not only had a strong alliance been forged but the empire also had a proper king of kings and not an upstart murderer. Our trip to Hatra had been leisurely and had been accompanied by Nergal and Orodes, but now they hastened back south to their respective kingdoms to prepare for the forthcoming campaign. Just one more battle and then we would have peace in the empire.

The journey back to Dura was uneventful though Dobbai was unusually quiet. On the third day after we had left Hatra I was riding behind her wagon as Claudia and Isabella threw pieces of biscuit at Remus in an attempt to make him throw me off his back.

'He has had far worse things launched at him than a few pieces of biscuit,' I told them.

'Does Remus like being your horse?' asked Claudia.

'Of course,' I answered, 'because he travels far and wide and sees many new things.'

Isabella threw another piece of biscuit at his head and laughed.

'When will he be going away again?'

'Soon,' I answered. 'He will be travelling far into the east.'

Isabella smiled at me. 'Why?'

'Because I have important business there, but after it has finished I will return and Remus and I will be staying at Dura for a long time.'

Dobbai raised an eyebrow at me. 'You are pleased with the way events have turned out, son of Hatra?'

402

'Of course,' I answered. 'The final battle approaches, one that I intend to win.'

'Are you disappointed that you are not king of kings?'

I shook my head. 'No. I have never coveted that position. In any case Orodes is far more suitable than I could ever be.'

'You must take care,' she said. 'There is death beyond the Tigris, I have seen it. It would be more advisable to let Mithridates and Narses come to you.'

I dismissed the idea. 'No. For too long we have reacted to events and it has achieved nothing. Now we have a chance to take the war to the enemy and finish what should have been finished years ago.'

'Then let us hope that you return.'

'I always return,' I boasted.

The period following our return to Dura was largely uneventful save for numerous proclamations from Ctesiphon denouncing all those who had gathered at Hatra to acclaim Orodes. Mithridates banished us all and sentenced each king, his queen and children and any who supported them to death. This made me even happier as it meant there was no stepping back from the brink: Mithridates had declared war on eight kings of the empire, including the newly created ruler of Gordyene.

Dura's army was ready to march at a moment's notice but the forces of the other kings, save Hatra, required more time to prepare for the coming campaign. I was not unduly worried about this because I knew that the enemy would be in a similar position.

Therefore, as the army was going to have to wait before it set off, Domitus ordered that the legionaries put on extra weight. This was an old Roman tactic to prepare for a campaign, the reasoning being that a long offensive could be wearing on even the most physically fit body and so every man should take the opportunity to bulk up before it commenced. In addition, the most secure way to transport supplies on campaign is as fat around the waist and so the legionaries were ordered to feast like hungry wolves. Marcus organised extra food to be distributed while Domitus reduced the amount of training and drill each legionary undertook. As the garrisons of the forts in the kingdom were reduced to allow the legions to muster, vast amounts of bread, beer, wine, meat and fruit were shipped into the main camp at Dura so the men could pack on extra pounds. The horsemen complained bitterly that the legionaries were receiving special privileges but it was pointed out to them that they were carried on their horses' backs most of the time and did not require additional weight, which in any case would tax their mounts. Horse archers were required to be lithe and thin to be able to shoot their bows from the saddle in all directions, whereas cataphracts were big men on powerful horses who crushed the enemy with a charge or in the mêlée.

As usual I mustered the lords and again informed them that they would not be accompanying the army, though this time I required them to provide garrisons for the kingdom's forts that otherwise would be empty. Rsan would be in charge of the kingdom in my and Gallia's temporary absence, though Spandarat was appointed military commander and ordered to muster five thousand men to garrison the forts; Dura would be guarded by the replacement cohort. It was eight hundred miles from the city to Persepolis, and if we had to march all the way to Narses' capital to fight him then the army would be away for at least six months. Such a length of time might tempt the Romans to try their luck and seize Dura for themselves. If, however, they knew that the forts at the borders and those further inland, plus the city itself, were garrisoned they would be deterred. And every lord had his own stronghold that was also garrisoned. I called Spandarat to the palace to impress upon him the importance of his role.

'The forts must be garrisoned at all times, and you should move into the palace while I am away.'

'Can I wear your crown?' he grinned.

'I don't have one.'

He rubbed his scruffy beard. 'You know that we held this land before you arrived. Held it against the Agraci and then helped you turn back the Romans. You worry too much.'

I smiled and placed a hand on his shoulder. 'I know that, my friend. That is why I have every faith in you. But faith does not fill bellies so I have instructed Aaron that you and your men will be paid the equivalent wages of my horse archers for the time that I am away.'

He rubbed his hands together and smiled. 'Lovely!'

'Just keep an eye on Syria. I don't trust the Romans, but that does not give you licence to launch any cross-border raids against them.'

He looked hurt. 'Me? It never crossed my mind.'

Before I came to Dura its lords and the Agraci had raided each other's lands with abandon. Peace had brought stability but old habits die hard and I feared that Spandarat and the other lords might use my prolonged absence as an excuse to pillage Roman Syria.

'Just don't stir up a hornets' nest,' I ordered him.

But it was not my wild lords who provoked the Romans on the eve of the war with Mithridates and Narses. One morning a pigeon arrived from the northern frontier carrying a message that a Roman official wished to travel to Dura for an audience with me, which I thought highly unusual. Ever since my stand-off with Pompey the Romans had conspicuously ignored both my kingdom and me. I therefore had a message sent back requesting the name and rank of this Roman who was so eager to meet me, at the same time sending another pigeon to Palmyra to ask Byrd and Malik to bring themselves and their scouts to Dura.

I visited Domitus in the now heaving camp after I received a reply back that the Roman in question was a tribune named Marcus Roscius.

'What does a tribune want with you?' he asked after he had dismissed two of his own officers of an equivalent rank from his tent.

I sat down in one of the chairs. 'I have no idea but I think it would be a good idea for you to be present when he arrives.'

Half a dozen of Aaron's clerks were sitting at his table sifting through parchments.

'I need your signature, general,' said one, holding up what appeared to be a long list of items. Domitus sighed heavily as he walked to the table and signed the document.

'I have been reduced to a clerk,' he complained.

'Organisation is a necessary evil,' I told him.

He shook his head. 'Or just evil, perhaps.'

'So, you will be at the palace when the Roman arrives?'

He scratched his head. 'If I must. When does he arrive?'

'I have ordered him to wait at the frontier until I have more information about him. I will inform you when he is due at the Citadel.'

I kept the tribune waiting at the border for five more days until Byrd and Malik had arrived at Dura. I then allowed Marcus Roscius and his dozen horsemen to ride south to the city. They were escorted by a score of horse archers who had yet to be replaced by the lords' men, it being more convenient to billet the cavalry far and wide before mustering them in one spot just prior to the army marching. It also meant that there were less men and horses concentrated in and around Dura and therefore less dust hanging over the city.

Unfortunately Byrd knew nothing of our Roman visitor save that he had most likely been sent by the Roman governor of Syria, a man named Aulus Gabinius. Byrd said that the governor was a friend of Pompey who liked expensive living and saw Syria as a way of making himself rich. This alarmed me somewhat as Crassus had once coveted Dura because of the Silk Road that ran through it. Perhaps this Aulus Gabinius desired it as well to enrich himself further.

Before our guests arrived I gave strict instructions that they were to be guarded at all times and kept away from the legionary camp. Any hint that Dura's army was going to be away from the kingdom would only embolden the Romans. In addition, I told Domitus to increase the guards at the Citadel and at the Palmyrene Gate to convey to our visitors the city's strength. However, they were to be confined to one of the barracks in the Citadel after they had arrived. I did not want them wandering around picking up any idle gossip about a forthcoming campaign in the east.

The Romans and their escort arrived at noon on a sunny autumn day and were shown to their quarters in the Citadel. From the shadows of the palace's colonnaded porch I watched them trot into the courtyard. I smiled when I saw their commander, a tall, imposing individual who wore a polished metal helmet with an enormous red crest. He took the helmet off and handed it to one of his men who were all dressed in mail shirts, helmets and carried flat, oval shields and *spathas*. Their weathered appearance contrasted sharply to the peacock that was their commander. He had short-cropped fair hair and, unsurprisingly, a haughty expression. His bronze muscled cuirass inlaid with silver was magnificent, though, as were his ornate boots decorated with flaps in the form of lions' heads. His large red cloak pinned to the right shoulder and his white tunic with a narrow purple stripe completed his opulent appearance. I went into the palace as our guests were shown to their accommodation.

An hour later the tribune was escorted into the throne room where Gallia and I awaited him. I had dressed in my Roman leather cuirass, leggings and boots, Gallia in her mail shirt with white tunic. Guards lined the walls of the entrance hall, the throne room, and stood either side of the dais upon which were our thrones. Najya, my falcon that had been a gift from Haytham, rested on my gloved left hand as I fed her slivers of uncooked duck. The steward who was her keeper stood near the entrance to the adjacent guardroom while Domitus stood next to the dais on my right side.

Marcus Roscius, helmet in the crook of his arm, strode purposefully towards us flanked by four guards.

'Tribune Marcus Roscius,' announced one.

Roscius bowed to me, then to Gallia and looked in confusion at Domitus dressed in his Roman attire and then at my cuirass that resembled his in design if not in cost.

'Greetings, tribune,' I said. 'What business do you have in Dura?'

'I am here on behalf of the proconsul of Syria, Aulus Gabinius.'

I fed Najya another piece of meat. Roscius glanced left and right at the guards armed and attired as Romans. He obviously wanted to enquire why they were equipped thus but his sense of protocol would not allow him to say anything.

'What business is that?' I asked.

'It has come to the proconsul's attention that there is in your city a Jew by the name of Aaron, son of Jacob, who is wanted for crimes committed against Rome.'

I had always admired the Romans for their organisation and efficiency but now those qualities worked against me. Aaron's excursion to see Rachel and the subsequent excitement had obviously prompted a thorough investigation by the Romans and had led to them sending the tribune who now stood before me. It was unfortunate for me that it was well known that Aaron, son of Jacob, husband to Rachel, was a Jew who was also Dura's treasurer. I saw nothing to gain by denying Aaron's presence.

'What crimes?' I asked casually.

'The murder of several Roman soldiers and a Jewish priest,' replied Roscius stiffly.

I was going to say that it was in fact I, Domitus and Surena who had killed those individuals but decided against it. Roman officers were not noted for their sense of humour.

'Roman law does not rule in Dura,' hissed Gallia.

'Surely, majesty,' replied Roscius, 'the law rules in all civilised lands and the punishment of wrongdoers is the concern of all just rulers.'

I gestured to the steward to take Najya back to her aviary.

Gallia's lip curled slightly. 'Whether Roman law is civilised is a topic that could be debated at length, but the affairs of Dura are of no concern to Syria.'

'It is as my queen says,' I agreed.

'Failure to surrender this Jew may be construed in some quarters as an affront to Roman goodwill.'

Gallia laughed. 'I have seen Roman goodwill, tribune, though I doubt the peoples who have been subjugated by it would term it so. Tell me, tribune, is it an offence for a man to defend his homeland against foreign invaders?'

Roscius' cheeks coloured as he tried to stay calm. 'It is an offence to murder Roman soldiers, majesty.'

'Really?' sneered Gallia. 'Then you had better take me back to Syria instead of Aaron for I have slaughtered many more than he has.'

Domitus stifled a laugh and Roscius' nostrils flared at the insult.

'Tribune Marcus Roscius,' I said, 'it is not my intention to insult Rome or your proconsul. But I will not hand over Aaron, son of Jacob, to you, for to do so would betray the faith he has placed in me. Tell me, do you know of my background and that of my queen?'

'I know it, majesty,' he replied, a note of contempt in his voice.

'Then you must have known that your journey here would be a wasted one. I will not surrender a friend and a faithful servant.'

A thin sneer creased his lips. 'I had heard that the King of Dura was a friend of slaves.'

'And a slayer of Romans,' added Gallia.

Roscius bristled at this. 'I had also heard that he was a man of honour.'

'I like to think that he is,' I replied.

'That being the case, majesty, can a man of honour harbour a murderer?'

407

I thought for a moment. 'All those who answer the call of arms are murderers, tribune. But a man's honour will not allow him to abandon a friend. You know this.'

He shot a glance at Gallia and then looked at me. 'And that is your final word on the matter, majesty?'

'It is.'

He bowed his head begrudgingly to me, then ever so slightly to Gallia and then about-faced and marched from the hall, escorted by his four guards. The doors were closed behind him as he entered the reception hall.

'The arrogance of the Romans knows no bounds,' growled Gallia.

'Neither does their memory when it comes to tracking down their enemies,' said Domitus.

'You think they will attack Dura?' I asked.

'Not over Aaron, no. But the peace that you brokered with Pompey is effectively over. When that tribune reports back to Syria that you have refused his request to hand over Aaron the proconsul will be looking for the slightest pretext to launch a war against Dura.'

'We've beaten Romans before,' remarked Gallia unconcerned.

But on the eve of the army preparing to march against Mithridates and Narses the last thing I needed was conflict with the Romans. But now it appeared that such a conflict was a certainty.

Chapter 16

I had little time to dwell on what the Romans would or would not do as the next day a message arrived from my father informing me that he had received word that Khosrou and Musa were rendezvousing with their armies near the city of Dara, approximately a hundred and fifty miles southwest of Khosrou's capital of Merv. He had also received word from Orodes that Babylonian forces had mustered at Babylon and were now marching north, and that Dura's army should commence its journey southeast to the rendezvous point at the Euphrates, fifty miles west of Seleucia.

Vast amounts of mutton and beef had been salted for the campaign, the salt ponds that had been established south of Dura along the Euphrates producing the means to cure the meat before it was dried. Marcus had had his hands full for weeks organising the supplies for the campaign. Each individual legionary carried around sixty pounds in weight on his *furca* – a wooden pole and crossbar – which included his pack, cloak, food bowl, water bottle, entrenching tool and several days' rations, but most of the legions' supplies were carried in wagons or on the backs of mules. The soldiers of each legion consumed around eight tonnes of food a day and the legionary animals a further eighteen tons daily.

The daily requirements of the cavalry were even greater and required intricate planning and preparation. Fortunately for Dura, in Strabo I had a man equal to the task notwithstanding his insolence and foul language. Marcus took care of the needs of the legions but it was Strabo who had nurtured the army's mounted arm – organising the growing of crops for the supply of fodder for the horses, mules and camels, maintaining the corps of veterinaries and farriers and the breeding of horses, camels, mules and oxen. Despite his shabby appearance and irreverent manner he was extremely knowledgeable about the dietary requirements of our livestock. It had been Strabo who had organised the growing of so-called Greek hay on the royal estates and the ancient horse fodder of the Medians, *medicago sativa*, known to the Romans as alfalfa, one of the best horse foods available. Under his guidance the estates also grew oats, barley and wheat, though not all went to the animals, and clover which was used exclusively for horse fodder.

Every horse in the army consumed around thirty pounds of fodder a day, the camels being able to subsist on a reduced quantity of ten pounds a day (their diet also included dates and fish meat). When the army marched it did so with over six thousand horses and three thousand camels in addition the legions' mules. The horses alone required eighty tons of fodder a day and the camels thirteen tons a day and Strabo was the individual responsible for making sure they received these amounts. He did and so everyone forgave him his idiosyncrasies, galling though they were at times. The water consumption of the army was vast but as long as it stayed near a river or other major water source it was not a problem. That is why the Euphrates and Tigris were of such strategic importance and that is why most marches were nearly always conducted along their length. It was so this time as the army commenced its journey south to the rendezvous point. As usual Byrd, Malik and their scouts rode far ahead to ensure our journey was uneventful. I had worried that now Malik was married he would not wish to leave his new wife but he told me that he would not have missed this campaign for anything. Like many he sensed that it was the final showdown between myself and Mithridates and Narses. He also had a personal grudge against Narses, who had promised to rid the earth of the Agraci people. Gallia thought the same and that is why she was riding beside me with the Amazons behind us – she did not want to miss out on the downfall of Mithridates.

'It might be our downfall,' I said, thinking about how I had previously failed to defeat them.

She shook her head. 'No, this is the final war between you and them. Dobbai told me.'

'What else did she tell you?'

'Nothing. She has been unusually withdrawn of late as if something has alarmed her.'

I dismissed the notion. 'She is probably feeling her age. How old is she, has she ever told you?'

'Never. But we are all getting old, Pacorus.'

I looked across at her. Her face was still flawless and her eyes were as blue as the clearest skies. 'Not you, my sweet.'

But she was in a wistful mood. 'The world turns, Pacorus, even though we do not discern it. Have you noticed that over the years how many of our friends have left us.'

'Left us?'

She sighed and looked away into the desert on our left. 'When I first came to Parthia it was in the company of Gafarn, Diana, Nergal and Praxima. Now they are all gone.'

'Nergal has become a king and Praxima is a queen. Gafarn and Diana are at Hatra. We should be happy for them.'

But she did not hear my words. 'Godarz as well. All gone.'

'What is the matter?'

She smiled wanly. 'I suppose I want the way things were, for us all to be together again.'

'We will be, at the next gathering of the Companions,' I said.

'It is not the same.'

410

We rode on in silence, babblers and warblers flying high above us as we headed south at a steady pace of twenty miles a day.

On the fifth day out from Dura a courier arrived from the city carrying a message from Aaron that he had received word that Alexander Maccabeus had launched his rebellion against the Romans in Judea. When I told Gallia her spirits rose because it meant that the likelihood of a Roman attack against Dura was now a remote possibility. I took it as a sign that the gods were smiling on Dura and its army. Malik was also delighted because if Judea threw off its chains then the Romans would not pose a threat to Agraci lands. When I told Domitus, however, he was unimpressed.

'I give the Jews two months before half of them are dead and the other half are wriggling on crosses.'

The next day the army of Hatra linked up with us after marching directly south from my father's capital. Gallia's melancholy lifted as we greeted my father and Gafarn and rode alongside them. My father was cheerful and confident, the world-weariness that had possessed him these past few years having been banished by a desire to see affairs in the empire settled once and for all. He had thrown himself into the current venture with all his energy, organising the formation of the alliance of kings in the aftermath of Vata's wedding, formulating the plan of campaign and now in effect, notwithstanding the election of Orodes as king of kings, becoming the commander-in-chief of all the armies. I was glad that he was for it meant that the King of Hatra, one of the most respected rulers in the empire, had grown tired of the treachery of Mithridates and was now his declared enemy. His old allies, the kingdoms of Babylon, Media and Atropaiene, having also endured the aggression of Mithridates, had joined him and in the north Khosrou and Musa had taken up arms against the false high king. I was pleased above all because the distance and unease that had existed between my father and me had disappeared. We were united in a common cause and stood shoulder to shoulder as father and son once more.

It took ten days to reach the rendezvous point and when we arrived the army of Babylon was already camped inland from the Euphrates. There were surprisingly few tents in the camp, Orodes explaining that he had brought only seven hundred and fifty horsemen: his own bodyguard of two and fifty cataphracts plus five hundred of Babylon's royal guard. The rest of his army – ten thousand men – were foot soldiers armed with spears and carrying wicker shields. That was all an impoverished Babylon could spare. The horsemen and their squires had tents but the foot soldiers slept out in the open. Domitus established Dura's camp five miles inland of the river, as usual a great rectangle surrounded by a ditch and earth rampart surmounted by stakes. I invited my father to camp his own army with mine inside our

411

ramparts but he declined, instead establishing Hatra's army five miles north of the Babylonians. Vistaspa sent his own patrols east towards the Tigris as Byrd and Malik also scouted the area around Seleucia while we waited for the forces of Atrax and Surena to join us.

Their horsemen arrived two days later, those of Surena following a huge banner sporting a silver lion on a red background. Atrax flew the dragon standard of his now dead father. That night my father gave a great open-air feast in honour of the kings, the meat of four slaughtered bulls being served to us by the squires of Hatra's royal bodyguard. A nice touch I thought. I had also noticed that there was no great pavilion to house the ruler of Babylon, Orodes being content to sleep in a modest-sized campaign tent. Unfortunately there were also no half-naked Babylonian slave girls to dazzle us with their smiles and entice us with their oiled bodies.

'I left them with my wife and Mardonius at Babylon,' said Orodes, his fingers dripping with beef fat.

'I am surprised he did not accompany you, *highness*,' I said.

He licked his fingers. 'Very amusing. The truth is that he can hardly walk without the aid of a stick and so I ordered him to stay in the city and guard Axsen.'

'Soon your wife will have a new throne to sit on.' I grinned at him. 'Highness.'

He frowned. 'I wish you would stop calling me that.'

'Why? You will have to get used to it soon enough when you have all those courtiers at Ctesiphon grovelling at your feet and whispering honeyed words in your ears.'

A squire offered us more meat from a silver tray.

'I intend to get rid of most of them,' he declared, 'and have men of integrity and honesty around me.'

'Good luck with that.'

He looked at me. 'I do not suppose you would consider becoming lord high general again?'

I nearly choked on my wine. 'You are right; I would not consider it. What about Nergal? He's brave and loyal.'

'But not a great general such as you.'

I laughed. 'If I was a great general, my friend, we would not be sitting at a wooden bench in the open eating and drinking. We would be at home in the company of our wives as I would have already sent Mithridates and Narses to the underworld.'

'It was a serious offer.'

I laid a hand on his shoulder. 'I know that, my friend, but after this campaign is over I want to return to Dura and live out the rest of my days in peace with my family.'

'You think that is possible?'

412

I emptied my cup and held it aloft to be refilled. 'Anything is possible if you desire it enough.'

The next day we marched east towards Seleucia in three great columns. The northern formation comprised the fourteen thousand soldiers and squires of Dura's army. In the centre rode my father and Hatra's fifteen hundred cataphracts and ten thousand horse archers, plus Orodes and his seven hundred and fifty horsemen and ten thousand Babylonian foot. The southern column was made up of Atrax and his seven hundred cataphracts and five thousand horse archers and Surena's eight thousand horse archers. It took two days for the fifty thousand soldiers of this army to cross the strip of desert between the Euphrates and Tigris to reach the walls of Seleucia.

As we approached the city the enemy had made no moves save to shut the gates of Seleucia and line its walls with the garrison. We stayed well out of arrow range as the central column established its camp directly in front of the western gates and Atrax and Surena pitched their forces south of the city along the banks of the Tigris. Dura's army made camp five miles north of the city adjacent to the river, being careful not to despoil the villages and the surrounding fields, as they were part of the Kingdom of Babylon. Orodes had sent his own horsemen ahead of the army to reassure the villagers that they would suffer no harm at our hands. This was irrelevant to those villages located close to Seleucia itself as they had been attacked and looted during Mithridates' two campaigns in Babylon, those of their inhabitants who had not been able to flee having been either killed or taken as slaves. The empty, charred remains of these villages stood as mute testimony to the tyranny of Mithridates' reign.

Seleucia – gateway to the east. The city had been founded nearly two hundred and fifty years ago by Selucus I called Nicator, 'The Victor', one of the successors of Alexander of Macedon who had conquered the world. Selucus had gone on to establish the Seleucid Empire and the city named after him had walls that resembled the shape of an eagle with outstretched wings. Towers stood at regular intervals along their length but I knew from my short period as lord high general of the empire that those walls had not been properly maintained. In many places they were crumbling and some of the towers were also in a state of disrepair. The main road through the city ran from the main gatehouse in the western wall directly east to the stone bridge that spanned the Tigris, which was about four hundred yards wide at this point.

Crumbling they may have been, but the walls of Seleucia were tall enough to stop an army from entering the city unhindered and seizing the bridge across the river. The size of the city's population was around eighty thousand, though many had probably fled east over the Tigris upon hearing of our approach. From what I could remember

413

from my days as lord high general the garrison was around a thousand men, though this number could be augmented in an emergency to five thousand or more, and reinforcements could also be sent from the east bank of the river if need be. In theory Seleucia was very strong and its ability to receive an unending stream of supplies and men across the bridge made it a tough nut to crack. But Seleucia had one major weakness – the walls ended at the river. Because the Tigris is wide and deep at this point Selucus' engineers had thought it unnecessary to build walls on all four sides of the city. There were thus no city walls running parallel to the Tigris, though the palace that was located in the northern part of the city, near to the harbour, was fully encompassed by its own walls. But then no army could assault Seleucia from the riverside, until tonight.

In the weeks preceding the campaign Orodes had given orders that fifty rafts were to be stockpiled well to the north of the city on the western bank of the river, guarded by soldiers that he had sent from Babylon. Now these rafts were each loaded with fifty legionaries and ten dismounted archers as two a half thousand men from the Duran Legion and five hundred bowmen prepared to float downstream and assault the city from the river.

I stood on the leading raft beside Domitus as the oarsman at the rear indicated to the Babylonians to push the raft into the river. Despite being loaded down with fifty fully equipped legionaries and ten archers it moved effortlessly into midstream and then began to move downriver. The water was calm and the current mild as we floated towards our destination, the other rafts following in a long line behind. The men carried no javelins, only their swords, daggers and shields, the archers each carrying three full quivers.

Domitus looked up at a full moon in the cloudless sky.

'Unless every sentry is asleep they will spot us before we reach the city,' he complained.

'Have faith, my friend,' I replied in a hushed tone. 'They will not be looking for the unexpected.'

'Let's hope that they don't have the harbour area lined with archers by the time we get there.'

'I'm sure your god Mars approves of our plan and will aid us in our endeavour. Time for the signal, I think.'

Domitus turned to one of his men holding a small box of tinder and took it from him. Kneeling on the planks of the raft, he took a palm-sized piece of flint from the legionary and held it in his left hand with the sharp edge angled upwards and then hit it fast with a steel striker to produce hot sparks, striking the flint again and again until the tinder in the box was aflame. The legionary then held the wick of an oil lamp to the flames until it was alight. Domitus stood up and took the lamp, faced the western riverbank and moved it from side to side. The six

Agraci scouts saw the prearranged signal and galloped off inland. So far, so good.

Domitus extinguished the flames, paced to the edge of the raft and glanced upstream. He came back to my side.

'Everything in order?' I asked.

'Seems so,' he replied, his hand gripping the hilt of his *gladius*.

We were around two miles from the city, though I could not make out its shape in the moonlight. Despite the fact that there were three thousand men moving downstream it was eerily quiet, as though the world was holding its breath before the storm. The rafts were travelling at a speed of around three miles an hour, which meant that we would reach the city in around forty minutes. The time passed agonisingly slowly and it seemed as though we had been on the water for hours before the city gradually loomed into view. Ahead I could now make out the arches of the bridge across the river that linked Seleucia with Ctesiphon. Thus far our presence had been undetected. The raft inched its way slowly towards the city's northern wall. I strained to see any activity either on the battlements or on the round tower that stood in the water and marked the spot where the walls ended, but could see nothing.

Suddenly, in the distance, we heard thuds and crumps and saw the occasional red glow. I smiled. The scouts had reached their destination and now Marcus' siege engines were commencing their attack on the city. The larger ballistae were shooting huge lighted clay pots filled with sulphur, pitch, charcoal, tow and naphtha that ignited upon impact. They were being shot against the city gates and were intended to cause a lot of noise and fire. Then we heard the cheers of thousands of men – the remainder of the Durans plus the Exiles who were arrayed either side of the engines. They had been instructed to begin shouting, blowing their trumpets and whistles and cheering when the shooting commenced as a diversion. The noise rose in volume as we drifted past the tower towards the city's harbour.

The archers nocked arrows as our raft glided past the tower and then along the walls of the palace and still we had not been spotted. I was beginning to think that my plan was flawless when an alarm bell suddenly sounded in the tower and then we heard shouts of alarm from within the palace.

'Look lively,' shouted Domitus as the oarsman steered the raft past the palace towards the harbour, which comprised a long wharf in front of which were berths where shallow-draft riverboats were moored. Set back from the wharf were sheds and warehouses and immediately south was the bridge. As our raft neared the first berth Domitus leapt onto it and ran towards the quay. I followed him as the others also jumped from the raft and ran to form up beside Domitus on the quay. The other rafts were gliding into the harbour as arrows shot from the palace walls splashed into the water. Around ten rafts had made it into the harbour area unscathed but the rest would have to run the gauntlet of arrows that was now being directed at them. The centurion on each raft shouted his commands and the men instantly formed a *testudo* on each vessel, locking shields on all sides and above, ensuring that the archers and oarsman were also under the *scutums*.

On the quay centurions bellowed orders at their men to assemble in their ranks as the archers ran past them to form a defensive screen at the northern end of the quay while the centuries formed up. I stood in the centre of the line of archers as the first enemy soldiers rushed us. These men were no doubt from the palace as most of the garrison would be lining the walls in response to the attack by Marcus' siege engines. They carried large wicker shields and wore leather cuirasses with linen caps on their heads. They levelled their long spears as they charged us in a disorganised mob and we shot half of them down before they got within fifty paces. The rest stopped and then withdrew as we loosed another volley of arrows and then another and another, this time killing less of them as they formed a shield wall and continued to fall back. More of their comrades appeared behind them and then the shouts of their angry officers made them halt and reform their ranks.

Fortunately there appeared to be no archers with them as they shuffled forward warily and into our arrow storm as we emptied one quiver and then fell back ourselves. The leather-faced wicker shields could stop arrows easily enough but our volleys had allowed the rest of the rafts to disgorge their men without interruption, and now a thousand legionaries were rushing to the bridge as the other fifteen hundred marched forward to engage the upwards of four hundred enemy spearmen who faced them at the northern end of the quay.

The quay was wide enough to allow three centuries to stand in line – a front rank of thirty men – as the centurions blew their whistles and their men charged the enemy. There was a loud bang as the Durans slammed into their opponents and went to work with their short swords. The long spears of the enemy were brushed aside by the front ranks and then the shafts were grasped by those behind, preventing their owners thrusting them into the guts of the legionaries, as the front rank of the Durans stabbed the point of their swords at enemy flesh and herded the spearmen back.

While this was going on Thumelicus was leading the other centuries to the bridge where the sentries were quickly killed and both sides of the aged span were secured.

Arrows then hit several men at the rear of the column fighting the spearmen as the palace archers finally arrived on the scene. The cry of 'shields, shields' rang out as the Durans hoisted their shields above

416

their heads for protection as the front ranks continued to grind their way forward.

My archers were grouped around me and I ordered them to shoot at the enemy archers, who were at least three hundred paces away. Thus began a desultory archery contest in the moonlight as men tried to identify targets. Domitus came running over to me.

'Thumelicus has taken the bridge,' he said. 'We are herding the others back despite the archers. It won't be long now.'

An archer near to us collapsed to the ground with an arrow in his shoulder.

'Keep shooting,' I shouted at the others. 'Keep their heads down.'

The column of Durans was steadily pushing the spearmen back, hacking their ranks to pieces as they did so. Then enemy arrows stopped falling nearby as the opposition archers directed their volleys at the Duran front ranks to allow the surviving spearmen to disengage and fall back towards the palace.

The wounded were helped to the bridge where they could be cared for while Domitus reorganised his men. He allocated three centuries to shadow the retreating spearmen and left two others on the quay as a reserve for Thumelicus holding the bridge. The rest followed the archers and me as we moved into the city.

Seleucia's inhabitants were hiding indoors as we moved from the harbour along the main street west towards the city's main gates that were being assaulted by Marcus. We did not see a soul as a thousand legionaries and five hundred archers moved quietly through a seemingly deserted city. Ahead the cheers and shouts of my men outside the city walls continued, accompanied by the thud of missiles hitting the gates. And as we approached the latter the night sky was illuminated by a red glow – the gates were on fire.

As Domitus sent parties ahead to reconnoitre the city we halted on the main road that bisected the city and ran east across the Tigris. North of this thoroughfare stood the palace, temples and official buildings, south of it the area where the citizens' tiny homes were crammed.

'Most of the garrison will be lining the walls watching Marcus' engines knocking holes in the gatehouse,' I said to Domitus. 'The rest are now cooped up in the palace. But we must assault the men lining the walls so our men outside the city can get in without loss.'

'Best thing, then, is to split the boys into their centuries and allocate archers to each one. We don't have enough men to clear all the walls.

I shook my head. 'There is no need. We just need to clear the walls either side of the main gates.'

It took a matter of minutes to organise the twelve centuries and assign each one forty archers for the assault on the walls. The scouting parties returned to inform us that there were no signs of any enemy soldiers between our position and the gatehouse and so we began to move forward once more, three centuries abreast. There were no whistles or commands just the dull crump of hobnailed sandals on the stone-paved street. I could see the main gatehouse now, which was wreathed in flames, both the gates and the large square towers either side of them alight. The flames were illuminating the surrounding area and I could see that the walls either side of the gatehouse were lined with archers, who were standing well away from the heat and flames. There was also a large body of spearmen formed up in a phalanx around a hundred paces back from the burning gatehouse, ready to repel any assault once the flames had died down.

Domitus beside me cursed. 'That's the plan wrecked. We will have to deal with those spearmen first.'

I nodded. 'Hit them hard. The archers will still try to clear the walls. Good luck.'

I held my bow aloft and then ran to the right as enemy horn blasts signalled that we had been spotted. On our left flank the homes of the city's citizens went right up to the walls, but on our right flank the ground behind the walls was more open as this was the temple district. I squatted with the officers of the archers around me as ahead the commanders of the spearmen were frantically reorganising their men to assault the legionaries that had suddenly appeared behind them.

'Two companies will clear the walls south of the gatehouse,' I ordered. 'The rest will sweep the walls to the north.'

They nodded and stood up just as Domitus' men hit the spearmen. They did not have their javelins and a few were felled by the archers on the walls as they charged to reached the spearmen, but their initial impact was still devastating and buckled the enemy's formation. There was no space to manoeuvre on the left flank that was crowded with houses, but the open space to the north allowed the rear centuries to sweep around the right flank of those in front and then wheel left to hit the spearmen's right flank. Within minutes high-pitched screams were drowning out the roaring of the flames as the legionaries scythed into the enemy.

The archers on the walls tried to shoot legionaries in the rear of their centuries as those in the front ranks were too close to their own spearmen in the mêlée. They stood on the walkway on top of the walls with the battlements behind them. But from the city side they were totally exposed as they stood shooting their bows. There must have been at least a hundred archers either side of the gatehouse loosing arrows.

I released my bowstring and saw the arrow strike my target in his stomach as he went to retrieve an arrow from his quiver. He dropped his bow and then fell from the walkway onto the ground below as my men swept the walls with arrows. It took less than two minutes to clear the walls either side of the gatehouse, most of the enemy being felled by arrows. Just a handful escaped into the two towers that flanked the gatehouse, while below the spearmen's ranks dissolved.

Assaulted in the front and on the flank and with an inferno behind them, the rear ranks tried to flee as their comrades in front were cut down. Having no helmets or armour they were easy targets for *gladius* points and their thin wicker shields were next to useless in the close-quarters fight. As their ranks disintegrated I walked back to the main street to find Domitus. The flames from the gatehouse were gradually dying down as he left two of his centurions and ambled over to me.

'That was easy enough,' he reported with satisfaction.

Suddenly there was loud crash and a large piece of masonry was dislodged from the top of the wall to our right, showering debris over dead archers on the walkway.

'Looks like Marcus is having fun with his engines,' remarked Domitus as a missile shattered another chunk of wall.

'Get the men back before the gatehouse collapses,' I ordered.

But the gatehouse did not collapse and as dawn approached the fires died down and the walls of the charred gatehouse still stood. Domitus sent out patrols to ensure we were not surprised but they reported no signs of any enemy. And all the while Marcus' great ballista threw stone and iron at the walls and towers. Legionaries were sent back to Thumelicus at the bridge to keep him abreast of developments as the majority of the men fell back to a safe distance from the walls and sat down by the side of the street to rest. It had been a long night and as muscles began to ease, arms, legs and shoulders started to ache. I received a report from those men guarding the palace that the garrison was hiding behind the shut gates. Those men still manning the walls further along the perimeter would have no idea what was happening at the gatehouse, but it would be only a matter of time before their officers tried to make contact with either them or the garrison commander, so I ordered Domitus to send a party forward to signal to the army that the city was ours, and then after the ballistae had ceased shooting to clear the smouldering debris at the gatehouse to allow our forces to enter.

Another chunk of masonry was splintered from the walls by a ballista missile.

'At least Marcus is keeping the citizens cowering in their homes,' remarked Domitus as a hundred of his men trotted forward to clear the city entrance.

'I had forgotten about them,' I admitted.

'Better rouse them to let them know they have a new governor.'

'Tell your men to keep their swords in their scabbards. Use a minimum of force.'

He smiled grimly. 'You know my boys; gentle as lambs.'

419

I decided to leave the priests in their temple compounds alone while Domitus despatched half our number to bang on doors to assemble the citizenry on the great square located just south of the main street. Very soon the early morning was filled with the shrieks and wails of frightened women and children as the inhabitants were herded into the square, and then I heard a more familiar sound – a blast of trumpets. I turned to the gatehouse to see the figure of Kronos marching at the head of the Exiles as they entered the city to the cheers of the Durans who stood up to welcome their comrades. He stopped when he reached where Domitus and I were standing and clasped our forearms, his men continuing their march towards the bridge.

'Good to see you Kronos,' I said to him.

'Best get your boys to the bridge and secure it,' added Domitus. 'When the rest of the Durans enter I can use them to secure the city.'

'Is the garrison destroyed?' asked Kronos, looking back at the corpses in front of the gatehouse.

'No,' I replied. 'Half of it has shut itself in the palace and the rest is still manning the walls or in the towers. They will surrender once they realise the city has fallen.'

A part of a tower on the wall behind us suddenly collapsed in a great cloud of dust as a result of it being battered by the ballistae.

'Not anyone in that tower,' commented Kronos.

The Exiles pushed on to secure the bridge and relieve Thumelicus' men, who fell back to our location, while the rest of the Durans filed into the city to assist in the roundup of the citizens and reinforce the men guarding the palace. I was sitting on the stone pavement propped up against the wall of a bakery, whose owner had been 'persuaded' to make us some fresh bread, when the kings rode into the city. Domitus sat himself down beside me and rested his helmet on the ground. I handed him a chunk of freshly baked bread. The baker, a short fat man with oversized arms and his family, his wife who had scars on her arms from years working near the brick ovens and a teenage girl and younger boy, worked frantically to provide a constant supply of loaves. The father snapped at his wife and children to toil harder, no doubt fearing that he and his family would be killed if they invoked our displeasure.

As we lounged by the entrance to the bakery a company of the Babylonian royal guard trotted past us, their dragon-skin armour glistening in the early morning sunlight. Then came another company and another, and then Orodes appeared on his brown mare in the company of my father, Gafarn, Gallia who had Remus in tow, Atrax, Surena and Viper. Behind them were grouped Vistaspa and my father's bodyguard, and behind them the purple ranks of Babylon's spearmen.

I raised my chunk of bread. 'Greetings ladies, my lords, welcome to Seleucia.'

'Congratulations on the success of your plan, Pacorus,' said Orodes.

'A masterstroke,' added Surena.

'You have saved us much time, Pacorus,' commented Atrax.

'The first of the enemy's cities to fall,' I said.

'Seleucia will be Babylonian from now on,' remarked Orodes.

'Good idea, Orodes,' I agreed. 'Won't you all have some bread, it is most excellent?'

My father shook his head. 'We have other things to do besides eat, Pacorus. To secure Ctesiphon for one.'

I got to my feet and helped Domitus to his.

'I would not worry about that, father. I think you will find that Mithridates has fled back to Susa or further east by now.'

I knew that Ctesiphon's walls were in no state to withstand an assault and that its garrison was small – no more than two thousand men. It would take a man with an iron will and great ability to hold its dilapidated defences and Mithridates possessed neither.

I called into the building. 'Baker, come here!'

The flustered man appeared by my side rubbing his hands and squinting up as the empire's finest were arrayed on their horses in front of his premises.

'What is your name?' I asked him.

'Agapios, sir.'

I pointed at Orodes. 'Well, Agapios, this is King of Kings Orodes.'

Agapios bowed to Orodes and then looked at me in confusion.

'Is King Mithridates dead, highness?'

I laughed and my father frowned.

'No, Agapios, he is not dead. Yet.'

'Come,' said my father irritably, 'we have no time for this.'

'One moment, father,' I said. 'Do you have any gold?'

'Gold?'

'To pay Agapios for his bread. We are after all soldiers and not looters.'

My father rolled his eyes. 'I have no gold, you try my patience, Pacorus.'

I looked at the others. 'Do any of you have gold?'

They did not, which was most upsetting for Orodes who instructed Agapios to present himself at the palace the next day where he would be fully recompensed for his goods. I mounted Remus and then kissed my wife as Agapios stood staring incredulously at the kings as we made our way to the city's palace to demand its surrender.

Once we had secured the city I ordered Domitus to allow the people assembled in the square – who numbered not even half of eighty thousand – to return to their homes. Furthermore those of the garrison who were still on the walls or had taken refuge within the towers were to be surrounded but not attacked. Once the palace had fallen the governor, if he had not taken his own life, could order them to surrender.

By now the army's horsemen were moving through the city: rank upon rank of cataphracts, horse archers and squires leading camels. With the Durans having secured the city and the Exiles across the Tigris and investing Ctesiphon I had to admit that I felt immensely smug, the more so when a courier met our royal party with a message that the city governor would meet with me at the palace.

'Your fame precedes you, lord,' remarked Surena.

'Or his infamy,' remarked my father dryly.

'Perhaps Mithridates is in the palace,' said Gafarn, 'and wishes to give himself up personally to Pacorus.'

'In that case,' I replied, 'you had better find a headsman for an execution that will be taking place this afternoon.'

Sadly it was not Mithridates who awaited me at the palace gates but an individual in an ill-fitting scale armour cuirass and a bronze helmet on his head, his unkempt hair showing underneath it.

'Udall,' I uttered in disbelief as I slid off Remus' back and walked towards the great twin gates that he was standing in front of. I looked up at the walls and at the closed wooden shutters on the gatehouse.

Udall pointed up at the walls. 'No archers or sentries, majesty, just as I promised.'

I halted a few paces in front of him and he took off his helmet and bowed his head.

'How is it that you stand before me?' I asked. 'Is the governor dead?'

'I am the governor,' he announced proudly.

I had to suppress a laugh. This day was getting better and better. The enemy must be scraping the bottom of the barrel if all he could throw at us were men of Udall's calibre.

'The last time I saw you was when you were leading what was left of your men into the desert. How is it that in the time in between you were made governor of this fine city?'

A dumb smile crept across his face. 'Because out of those Narses sent to fight you when he retreated back over the Tigris last year, I was the only one to survive. And bring my men back with me.'

'Having first surrendered all your weapons to me,' I reminded him.

'But it bought him time, you see, majesty. And weapons can be easily replaced.'

'That hardly qualifies you to be made a governor.'

He shrugged indifferently. 'It does when I told him that in agreement for my surrendering my weapons you had promised not to cross the Tigris.'

'I agreed to no such thing.'

He smiled to reveal rotting teeth. 'He didn't know that.'

'You are the governor no longer,' I snapped. 'You will surrender the palace immediately and then order those soldiers still holding parts of the wall to give themselves up.'

His cocksure attitude began to crumble. 'What about me, majesty?'

I smiled maliciously. 'I should have your head, but as you have saved me the trouble of storming the palace and therefore the lives of my men I will allow you to leave.'

He looked at me sheepishly. 'Perhaps I could be of service to you.'

'I think not.'

The last I saw of him was his bedraggled figure mounted on a half-starved horse pulling a mangy donkey behind him heading out of the gates of the palace. No doubt the donkey was loaded with stolen money that he had plundered from the palace to ease the discomfort of him having lost his position. Before he departed he made a tour of the city walls with a Duran escort to order those men of his garrison still under arms to surrender. They did so and made their way to the palace where they dumped their weapons and armour in the courtyard in front of the palace, after which they were escorted to the city square until their fate was decided.

We spent three days at Seleucia, during which time Orodes had a proclamation read to its citizens announcing that he was the rightful king of kings. I suspect this meant little to ordinary people whose lives were a daily quest for survival but it satisfied his strict code of protocol.

The seizure of Ctesiphon was a major disappointment. The king of kings, his court and the contents of its substantial treasury had been spirited away to the city of Susa, a hundred and fifty miles to the southeast. Byrd's scouts reported being told by merchants on the road that a great armada of wagons and camels had left Ctesiphon a week before we had captured Seleucia.

In the vast banqueting hall at Ctesiphon slaves who had been brought from Seleucia served us roasted chicken and mutton, rice and bread. Mithridates had even evacuated his slaves to Susa so they would not fall into our hands. Mardonius had joined us from Babylon and Orodes had made him the governor of Seleucia to ensure it remained a secure base in our rear when we marched east. Seleucia had been an easy triumph but I felt cheated of victory and picked at my food as my father spoke.

'We will be marching to Susa in two days' time.'

'And after that Persepolis, no doubt,' I grumbled.

423

'There are not an unlimited number of places Mithridates and Narses can flee to, Pacorus,' replied my father. 'Sooner or later they will have to stand and fight if they are not to lose all their lands and credibility.'

I held my gold *rhyton* in the shape of a ram's head – not all the palace finery had been evacuated: someone had forgotten to look in the kitchens.

'Let us hope that it is sooner, father.'

'It makes sense that my stepbrother has fled to Susa,' said Orodes. 'It is where he grew up and is the capital city of Susiana, his homeland. Having lost possession of Seleucia and Ctesiphon he will gather his forces at Susa and await us there.'

'Where he will be joined by Narses, no doubt,' added Atrax.

'We have beaten them before,' I said, 'and can do so again. Only this time they will not escape.'

Surena had thus far remained silent, being content to pick at his food and listen to the other kings. However, by the grim look on his face he was clearly unhappy.

'You disagree, Surena?' I asked him.

He stopped picking at his food. 'Forgive me, lord, but we are marching into the heart of the enemy's territory.'

My father finished chewing on a chicken wing. 'So?'

'Well, lord,' answered Surena, glancing at Orodes. 'We will be fighting the enemy on a ground of his own choosing and at a time that also suits him. By marching to Susa do we not walk into the enemy's trap?'

My father eased back in his chair and regarded the new King of Gordyene for a moment. He probably thought that he was a young upstart, with his Ma'adan heritage and his wife who was formerly a member of my wife's bodyguard. He would normally treat such an individual with contempt, but Surena had freed Gordyene from the Armenians and for that reason alone his words deserved some consideration.

My father picked up his *rhyton*. 'You are right in what you say, young king, but having drawn my sword I cannot replace it in its scabbard until this campaign has been concluded, which can happen only when Mithridates has been removed from power and Narses has been defeated. And if that means marching on Susa, so be it.'

My father tilted his head at Orodes. 'Besides, our new king of kings is also from Susiana and his prestige would suffer if his homeland was in the possession of the enemy.'

'We have not talked about what will happen after we have defeated Mithridates and Narses, father,' I remarked.

He took a sip from his drinking vessel. 'That is for the king of kings to decide.'

Orodes frowned and looked at me. 'I know that Pacorus desires their deaths, believing that the empire will not be at peace while they still live.'

I toasted him with my *rhyton* and smiled.

'However,' he continued, 'I am not desirous of seeing the deaths of yet more of the empire's kings. I have given the matter a great deal of thought and have decided that banishment will be an appropriate punishment. I am sorry, Pacorus.'

My father was nodding approvingly and Atrax seemed to accept Orodes' decision, saying nothing, while Surena appeared more concerned with dipping a wafer into a bowl of yoghurt. I shrugged.

'That is your decision, Orodes, and we must abide by it.'

There was little point in arguing with my friend and in any case I knew that Narses would never agree to banishment, preferring death to exile, a wish that I was determined to grant him.

The surrendered garrison of Seleucia was sent west as slaves to help rebuild the Kingdom of Babylon. Those Babylonians who had been taken as slaves by Mithridates and Narses and who had been resident in Seleucia were freed and given safe passage back to their homes. Ctesiphon also received a new garrison but Axsen expressed no desire to take up residence in the high king's palace, declaring that she would leave Babylon only when the campaign was concluded and when Orodes was free to sit beside her. Thus the great palace complex remained largely empty as the army began its march into Susiana. The pace was leisurely, averaging fifteen miles a day, which meant we would reach Susa in two weeks. We were forced to hug the eastern bank of the Tigris for the first week as the terrain between the great river and the Zagros Mountains that lay fifty miles to the east was largely barren desert devoid of water. Then we left the river and advanced directly east towards the foothills of the mountains, all the while Byrd and his scouts riding far ahead to gather reports of the enemy's movements and horse archers forming a screen on all four sides of our army. But every day Byrd and Malik returned to camp with news that the terrain was empty of travellers and of the enemy there was no sign.

After four days of marching across the baked earth we came to the green foothills of the Zagros Mountains. We were now around seventy miles northwest of Susa itself and our unimpeded march had led many to believe that the city would be undefended and that Orodes would be able to march into the capital of his homeland unopposed. If that was the case then we would be able to rest in Susa before marching another three hundred miles southeast to reach Persepolis.

As usual Dura's camp was surrounded by a ditch, earth rampart and wooden palisade. The armies of Hatra, Media and Babylon, however, preferred the traditional Parthian method of pitching their tents around

425

their king in ever-widening circles, though the majority of Babylon's foot soldiers had to sleep under the stars with only a threadbare blanket. Fortunately the nights were warm and so their discomfort was minimal. Surena, however, having been tutored in the ways of the Sons of the Citadel, had his horse archers make camp after the Roman fashion. In addition to the spare arrows that the two thousand beasts of his camel train carried, they also hauled tents, stakes, food, fodder and entrenching tools to dig a ditch and rampart at the end of every day. Atrax thought it hilarious but Orodes approved and regretted that his Babylonians could not do likewise. My father believed it to be a complete waste of time but at least admired the professionalism that Surena and his soldiers displayed.

The foothills of the Zagros Mountains are covered with forests of oak interspersed with hawthorn, almond and pear trees. I saw golden eagles fly high above us and at times it was easy to forget that we were at war as we joined the ancient road that runs parallel to the mountains, and which led directly to Susa. Orodes had told us that he expected the enemy to try to halt our passage at the stone bridge across the River Karkheh some sixty miles to the east, but when we neared the bridge Byrd brought back reports that it was undefended. I rode to the river in the company of Orodes and a thousand of my horse archers and discovered a scene of peace and serenity. The simple stone arch bridge spanned the river that was around four hundred feet wide at this point, though Orodes informed me that it widened considerably a few miles further south to around a thousand feet. We rode over the bridge to the other side and I sent companies east, north and south to scout for the enemy.

'You waste your time,' remarked Byrd as we sat sweating on our horses in the afternoon heat. 'They no here. I told you that earlier.'

'I know that, Byrd,' I said, 'but better to be safe than sorry.'

Orodes was extremely happy. 'This is the Susa Valley, Pacorus, where I hunted as a boy. I remember it as if it was yesterday.'

I smiled at him. It had been years since he had seen his homeland following his banishment by Mithridates and now here he was, only a few miles from his capital and the place of his birth.

'You will be sleeping in the palace in Susa in a matter of days, my friend,' I told him.

Later I marched Dura's army over the bridge and made camp in the valley, which was actually flatland between two rivers, though as there was not enough time to bring over the rest of our troops the forces of Media, Hatra and Gordyene slept on the western bank that night. The next day the rest of the army crossed, a great press of camels, men on foot and horses that took until dusk to move over the river. We had taken possession of the northern end of the Susa Valley without a fight.

That night I invited the kings, Gafarn and Viper to dine in my command tent in the company of Domitus, Kronos and Vagises. The mood of those present was high except for Surena, who appeared to have the weight of the world on his shoulders. No one else seemed to notice, though, and so the evening passed without incident. Orodes was in an ebullient mood and kept telling Gallia and Viper how he was going to show them around Susa's palace after we had marched into the city, which lay a mere fifteen miles south of our position.

I asked Surena to stay after the others had left around midnight. The night was fresh as I said farewell to Atrax, the last to leave. He rode down the camp's central avenue with his bodyguard grouped around him. A myriad of campfires extended from the bridge east towards the eastern boundary of the Susa Valley – the River Dez – ten miles distant.

Inside the tent Gallia was talking with Surena and Viper at the table, the King of Gordyene looking decidedly nervous. I poured more wine into his cup.

He spoke first. 'You are displeased with me, lord?'

'Not at all,' I answered, 'and even if I were you are a king now and so my feelings should be irrelevant to you.'

'It is late, Pacorus,' said Gallia, 'and I am sure that Surena and Viper want to get some sleep rather than listen to one of your lectures.'

I refilled Viper's cup and then my own but Gallia placed her hand over hers.

'I would know what troubles you, Surena.'

He looked at Viper who nodded at him.

'We are walking into a trap, lord,' he replied.

'How can you be so certain?'

He swallowed a mouthful of wine. 'The enemy made no attempt to prevent us crossing the bridge because they are inviting us into this valley. And tomorrow we advance on Susa, marching further south with two very wide rivers on either flank.'

'Byrd and Malik have seen no enemy anywhere,' I said.

Surena was unconvinced. 'The forests that cover the slopes of these mountains can hide an army, lord. I did it in Gordyene.'

'What you say is true, Surena, but we go to assault Susa. If Narses and Mithridates are in the city, and we are not certain that they are, then they will have to give battle. They have already lost Ctesiphon, if they also retreat from Susa they will appear weak and their allies may desert them. They need a victory as much as we do.'

'I would still prefer to fight on ground of our own choosing, lord' he replied.

'Once,' I said, 'before we met, I fought Narses and Mithridates at a place called Surkh, on ground that had been selected by the enemy. And you know what happened?'

He smiled. 'All those who have been tutored at Dura know what happened at Surkh, lord.'

'Well, then, do not worry about the enemy. Let them worry about us. Man for man, even counting the Babylonians, we are far better than they are.'

'And woman for woman, lord,' added Viper.

'Quite right,' said Gallia.

Surena seemed at least reassured as I bid him goodnight and Gallia embraced Viper. As they rode back to their camp with a score of horse archers behind them Domitus sauntered up gripping his vine cane.

'Been beating some poor sentry?' I enquired.

'Just doing my rounds,' he replied, then pointed his cane at Surena's party trotting towards the main entrance.

'He has come a long way since you first brought him to Dura as a half-starved urchin.'

'I never thought he would be made a king, though.'

Domitus shrugged. 'Why not? You were.'

He scraped the sole of his sandal on the ground then looked up into the sky.

'I saw a vulture today.'

'Yes, they are quite common in these parts.'

He scraped the ground once more. 'He just swooped down and landed a few feet from me, hopping behind me, staring at me with his big black eyes. When I stopped he stopped, and when I continued walking he followed.'

'Perhaps he thought you were a piece of carrion,' I joked.

'It is an omen, Pacorus. A portent of great slaughter.'

Chapter 17

The Susa Valley is lush and green, especially following the heavy rainfall it receives during the first three months of the year. Despite the heat of its summers the land between the Karkheh and Dez rivers is permanently green, partly because of the rainfall but also due to the extensive irrigation systems that exist north and south of Susa. Orodes told me that the valley was the breadbasket of Susiana, producing an abundance of wheat, corn, barley, lentils, flax, pistachios, lemons and dates, in addition to supporting the great herds of cattle that grazed on its rich grasslands. Farms cover around three-quarters of the flatlands between the rivers and their produce not only fills the bellies of the populace of Susiana itself but is also exported to adjacent kingdoms.

The city of Susa itself lies around twelve miles south of the bridge that we had used to cross the Karkheh and a mile inland of the river. The villagers and farmers who inhabited the valley had no doubt sought sanctuary inside the city, along with their livestock, for we entered a land seemingly devoid of life as we struck camp the morning after crossing the river and headed south towards the kingdom's capital.

We had travelled but two miles when Byrd and Malik came galloping up to where I was riding with Gallia at the head of the Amazons. As usual they had left before dawn to scout ahead with their men as the camp was coming to life. Now they returned three hours later, the camp having been disassembled, the stakes for the palisade loaded onto the mule train and the tents packed on the wagons.

'Enemy is pouring out of Susa,' said Byrd blandly.

'How many?' I asked.

Malik looked concerned. 'Thousands, Pacorus, tens of thousands.'

'They fill the land in front of the city,' added Byrd.

I ordered an immediate halt and sent couriers to the other kings to alert them that the enemy had at last shown his face. A sense of relief swept through me as I realised that finally, the deciding battle with Narses and Mithridates was about to begin. As the army halted and I sent Vagises ahead with a thousand horse archers to act as a forward screen, Domitus and Kronos trotted over to where Gallia and I were talking with Byrd and Malik.

'We will not be marching to Persepolis, then,' remarked Domitus casually.

'By the end of this day,' I said, 'the crows will be feasting on the carcasses of Narses and Mithridates.'

I slid off Remus and slapped Domitus hard on the arm. 'After all these years of bloodshed and toil, after all the deaths and misery that those two bastards have caused, now we finally have them cornered. Men will talk of this day for a long time.'

'Have you heard of the phrase, pride before a fall,' Pacorus?' asked Gallia as she dismounted from Epona.

I held her flawless face in my hands and kissed her on the lips. 'Not pride, my sweet, belief that I have the best soldiers led by the best officers in the empire. Today we extend the limits of glory.'

'We have to beat them first,' said Domitus dryly. 'So what is the battle plan, assuming you have one? And don't say to beat the enemy.'

'Not beat them, Domitus,' I replied. 'Today we annihilate them.'

In response to my alerting the other monarchs, Orodes sent a rider requesting my and Gallia's presence at a council of war, which took place in his hastily re-erected tent in the middle of the valley. Thousands of Babylonian spearmen were sitting on the ground behind the tent, their shields and spears stacked as they rested. Soldiers of Babylon's royal guard stood sentry outside the tent and others held our horses' reins as we went inside to join the kings. Outside the temperature was bearable thanks to the breeze that was coming from the Zagros Mountains to the east, but the air inside the tent was still and stifling as we acknowledged those who were arranged on stools in a circle. Gallia embraced Viper and then took her seat beside her fellow Amazon as I sat down next to her and opposite my father.

'The enemy appears at last,' said Orodes in a serious voice, 'and intends to engage us.'

He nodded towards me. 'The reports we have received thus far indicate that soldiers are leaving Susa and massing in the area immediately north of the city.'

'Do we know their numbers?' asked Atrax.

Orodes looked at me.

'At least as many as us, probably more. We will know more when we get nearer to them. I have sent horsemen south to ensure they don't sneak up on us unannounced.'

'We will advance to meet them,' announced Orodes.

'I would advise staying close to the Karkheh,' I said, 'to anchor our right flank against the river as the enemy also appears to be keeping close to the city and the river.'

The valley was at least ten miles wide at the point we currently occupied, and though it narrowed to around seven miles at Susa itself if we maintained a continuous front from river to river our forces would be spread too thinly.

'If we do not extend our forces from the Karkheh to the Dez,' said my father, 'then we invite the enemy to outflank us on our left wing.'

'We have enough horsemen to be able to react to threats, father,' I replied. 'Besides, the enemy won't be thinking about their flank when we are grinding their centre into dust.'

Surena and Atrax smiled and Gafarn rolled his eyes but my father did not protest and so an hour later the various contingents were repositioning themselves for the march south to engage the enemy. Byrd and Malik had departed with their scouts towards Susa once more and around mid-morning Vagises returned with a more accurate assessment of the enemy's dispositions. Beginning on their left flank, which was anchored on the Karkheh, and extending inland from the river were two great bodies of spearmen, next to which, to their right, were formations of horse archers. Vagises estimated that the entire enemy army occupied a frontage of around four miles. They had halted two miles north of the city and showed no signs of advancing any further.

When we recommenced our march south the Duran Legion was on the end of the army's right flank, moving parallel to the river, with the Exiles beside them and ten thousand Babylonian spearmen on Kronos' left flank. Vistaspa argued most forcefully that all the horse archers should be grouped together on the left wing of the army, both to extend our line towards the Dez and to respond quickly to any threats that may materialise, and so I sent Vagises and his three thousand horse archers to serve under him. Dura's contingent was the smallest, being outnumbered by Surena's eight thousand horsemen, Media's five thousand and positively dwarfed by Hatra's ten thousand horse archers. There was a brief command crisis when Vistaspa discovered that Surena was leading his own horse archers and offered the King of Gordyene the leadership of the horsemen, but Surena declined out of respect for Vistaspa's far greater experience.

Between the foot and the horse archers rode the cataphracts and the kings. It was now midday and very warm, the heat made worse because I was wearing my scale armour. The sky was devoid of any clouds and the sweat was running off my brow into my eyes. My legs and arms were also cooking in their tubular steel armour. Behind me in a long column were Dura's heavy horsemen with their helmets pushed back on their heads and their lances resting on their shoulders. Gallia rode on my right and on my left was Orodes, behind him his bodyguard of two hundred and fifty men and Babylon's royal guard. Beside Orodes rode Atrax leading his seven hundred cataphracts, and beyond him was my father in charge of Hatra's fifteen hundred heavy cavalry. Twenty thousand foot and nearly thirty thousand horsemen were on the move, while seven thousand squires and thousands of civilian camel and wagon drivers brought up the rear.

I looked at Orodes whose face was a mask of steely determination.

'Not long now, my friend, and soon you will take possession of the capital of your homeland. And then we will have peace in the empire.'

He pursed his lips. 'Let us hope so, Pacorus, let us hope so.'

431

After we had travelled five miles the enemy at last came into view – great blocks of black shapes stretching from the river eastwards. As we got nearer to them I could see the sun catching the whetted tips of the spearmen's main weapon. In front of their army rode parties of horse archers, who halted to observe us before trotting back to make their reports. The atmosphere was relaxed, almost soporific, as we ambled towards the enemy, but any drowsiness was shattered by a mass of trumpet blasts that erupted from the ranks of the legions, followed by shouts as officers barked orders at their men. I nudged Remus forward and then wheeled him right to take me across the front of the Babylonian spearmen to reach the first-line cohorts of the Exiles, Vagharsh following with my banner, the men cheering and banging the shafts of their javelins on the insides of their shields as I passed. I raised my *kontus* in acknowledgement.

I found Domitus and Kronos with their cohort commanders standing slightly beyond the first line of the Durans, on their extreme left. Domitus was pointing at the massed ranks of the spearmen directly opposite. I also noticed that Marcus was present.

'You see those trees, Pacorus?'

Domitus was alluding to a large grove of date palms that stood directly behind the enemy spearmen opposite us. The trees can grow up to seventy-feet high and these ones certainly seemed to be around that height at least, all planted in neat rows.

'The date palms, what of them?'

'Bit strange that they have so many men in front of them. If they are pushed back into the trees they will be become disorganised. They must be confident that they can stop us. They are Narses' men, aren't they?'

I looked at the mass of large wicker shields, helmets and yellow tunics showing between the walls of shields. Then I spotted a phalanx of spearmen with large yellow shields and wearing plumed bronze helmets – Narses' royal spearmen.

'Yes.'

Their frontage was very wide and encompassed the extent of both the Durans and Exiles combined. Beyond them, on their right flank, stood another huge mass of spearmen with white-painted shields – Mithridates' soldiers – who were grouped opposite the Babylonian foot.

Domitus nodded at Marcus. 'I thought we would let Marcus and his men practise using their smaller ballista, see if we can thin out the enemy's numbers a bit.'

'Wait for the order until you launch an attack,' I told him. 'I do not know what Orodes is planning yet.'

'Of course,' he replied, 'but if that lot opposite begins to move I will have no option but to attack.'

At that moment the low rumble of kettledrums echoed across the battlefield and I knew that hostilities were about to commence. I bade them farewell and then rode back to where Orodes waited on his horse with the other kings, their banners fluttering behind them in the stiffening breeze. The headache-inducing din of the kettledrums coming from the enemy ranks was increasing and almost directly opposite us enemy cataphracts had begun to form up.

'They have obviously seen our banners,' commented my father, 'and intend to assault our position.'

'They intend to kill the kings in revolt against Mithridates,' remarked Orodes.

I peered across no-man's land at the heavy horsemen moving into position and thought it most odd. A dragon of cataphracts – a thousand men in three ranks – occupies a frontage of around a third of a mile, but the horsemen opposite filled a space equivalent to two-thirds of a mile, if that. That meant there must be at most around two thousand horsemen. There could have been more, of course, but a heavy cavalry charge was more devastating with a frontage as wide as possible. It made no sense to increase the number of ranks at the expense of narrowing the frontage because the riders in the rear ranks would not be able to use their lances in the initial clash.

I looked at Orodes and then my father and knew they were thinking the same. We had nearly three and half thousand cataphracts – more than enough to defeat the enemy horsemen opposite. Our minds were made up when we saw a rider in scale armour ride to the front of the enemy horsemen followed by another holding a great yellow banner showing a bird-god symbol – Narses. In his arrogance the King of Persis believed that he could destroy us with one charge of his heavy horsemen.

Horns blew frantically as our heavy horsemen walked their horses forward to deploy into line. The sound of the kettledrums increased as Narses raised his *kontus* and pointed it at our assembling ranks. I held my hand out to my father.

'Good luck, father.'

He smiled and took it.

'Shamash keep you safe, Pacorus.'

Then he rode off to take his position in the front rank of his bodyguard. Atrax also came over to me and wished me luck, as did Orodes, before both of them galloped off to be at the head of their own men.

'Narses is mine,' I called after them.

Despite my desire to get to grips with my mortal enemy it took at least twenty minutes before we were ready to attack, the enemy also requiring time to arrange their ranks. My thousand men, deployed in three ranks, formed the right wing of our formation of heavy

433

horsemen, with the centre comprising Orodes and his two hundred and fifty men, Atrax and his seven hundred and my father and his five hundred-strong bodyguard. The left wing was made up of Hatra's other thousand cataphracts. Horses shuffled nervously in the ranks as the two wings closed up on the centre to present an unbroken line of armoured horsemen that extended for over a mile.

I turned to Gallia.

'Take your Amazons to the rear and link up with Babylon's royal guard. They and you will be our reserve.'

She nudged Epona forward, her face enclosed by the fastened cheek guards of her helmet, her hair plaited behind her back.

'Take care, Pacorus.'

I smiled and laid my hand on hers. 'It is Narses who should take care. This will not take long. Tonight we feast in Susa.'

She nodded, wheeled Epona away and the Amazons followed. I rode through the ranks of my men with Vagharsh carrying my banner behind me. I halted Remus in front of the first rank and faced my men.

'Soldiers of Dura,' I shouted. 'We have come a long way together these past few years, shared hardships and won many great victories. Now we must win one more battle to rid the world of Mithridates and Narses who stand but a short distance from us. Show the enemy no pity, no mercy, just as they have shown no mercy to you in the past. Remember those friends you have lost and remember Godarz. Above all remember that victory today will bring peace to the empire and unite it under Orodes, the rightful king of kings. Today we fight to liberate Parthia from tyranny. I know you will not fail me, my brothers. So let us fight for our friends, our families and for Parthia.

'Death to Narses.'

They raised their lances and began cheering and chanting 'death to Narses, death to Narses,' and then across no-man's land I heard massed horn blasts and turned to see that Narses was advancing.

Vagharsh retreated to the second rank as I took my position in the middle of the first line and then we also moved forward. We were around five hundred paces from Narses, perhaps more, the distance rapidly decreasing as both sides walked their horses forward and then broke into a trot. My men pulled their helmets down to cover their faces and then levelled their lances as the horses broke into a canter, the men maintaining their lines just as they had done a hundred times on the training fields.

In the charge the distance between the two sides closes alarming as both sides move into a gallop and then the final charge, riders screaming their war cries as they attempt to skewer an opponent with their lances. So it was now as both sides hit each other to produce a sickening scraping noise as *kontus* points were plunged into targets. When two lines of heavy cavalry charge each other both sides are equally matched in terms of momentum, armour protection, weaponry and length of lances, but the side that holds its nerve and is better trained will triumph. In such an armoured clash every Duran cataphract was taught to ride directly at the head of an enemy horse, and at the moment before impact to direct his horse to the right so the animal would pass by the right-hand side of the hostile rider, the opposite side on which an enemy soldier held his lance, at the same time raising his own lance to shoulder height before plunging it into the torso of the enemy horseman. In such a way Dura's finest would spear their opponents while at the same time avoid being skewered themselves. Such a manoeuvre took many months for even an accomplished horseman to perfect, but Dura's cataphracts were unequalled in the empire when it came to training, discipline and battle experience. Train hard, fight easy.

I directed Remus against a horseman, veered him right, brought up my *kontus* and then plunged it into the target, the long point easily piercing the man's scale armour. Remus' momentum meant the shaft continued to disappear into his chest half its length, swatting him from his saddle before I released. I grabbed my mace to swing it at a *kontus* that was being aimed at me by a rider in the enemy's second rank. I managed to deflect the blow as the horseman passed me and I swung my mace at his helmet, but he ducked, released his lance and in one slick movement drew his sword and directed a backswing at me that glanced off my leg armour. Then I was behind the enemy lines, which appeared to have been two ranks only.

I wheeled Remus around and rejoined the mêlée – a frenzied maelstrom of mace, axe and sword blows. Out of the corner of my eye I saw the great yellow banner of Narses to my right and so I dug my knees into Remus who bolted forward. I raised my mace above my head as I closed on the figure of Narses who was finishing off a horseman with his sword, driving its point through the victim's exposed neck. He whooped in delight as the man fell from his horse and had just enough time to turn to see me attack him, striking his armourless left arm with my mace. He yelped in pain as I passed him, brought Remus to a halt and wheeled him around. As I did I was surprised to see that Narses had followed and now swung his sword at me, the blade striking my arm armour and denting it. Then he was beside me and we were attacking each other with a superhuman rage, oblivious to what was happening around us. He moved his sword with the deftness of a juggler throwing a ball, one horizontal cut knocking the mace from my hand. I drew my sword and swung it at his head but missed. He kept his horse moving around Remus, aiming a series of downward swinging cuts with his sword at my neck and face, the only exposed parts of my body.

But by now the yellow sleeve of his left arm was soaked in blood and his movements were more laboured as I aimed a vertical cut at his helmet in an attempt to split it. He brought up his sword to stop the blow and then flicked his wrist to swing his blade horizontally at me. The point of his sword nicked my neck as it passed in front of me, but before he could aim another blow I instinctively thrust my sword forward and drove it through his neck. I yanked it free and he toppled onto the ground. Narses was dead!

'Narses is dead, Narses is dead!' I screamed, holding my sword aloft in triumph.

No one heard me as I looked around to see hundreds of men engaged in their own personal combat, hacking and stabbing at each other, trying to find weak spots in their opponent's armour. As I sat on Remus panting and soaked in sweat I saw small groups of horsemen with yellow sleeves leaving the mêlée and falling back. The enemy was breaking; victory was ours.

Vagharsh came through the fighting with an escort of my men and rode up to me. I pointed at the dead body of Narses lying on the ground and spat at it.

'Behold, the King of Persis and Parthia's lord high general.'

More and more enemy horsemen were now fleeing and around us horns were sounding to reassemble the ranks.

'Congratulations, lord,' beamed Vagharsh, who also spat on the body of Narses.

Then Orodes appeared, his leg and arm armour looking as though it had been struck many times by a large hammer. He stared at my bleeding neck with alarm.

'You are hurt, Pacorus.'

The elation of killing Narses had blocked out all other feelings, including pain, so I slid my sword into its scabbard and felt my neck. The wound was not deep and I felt nothing, though my neck was smeared with blood. It obviously looked worse than it was.

'Just a scratch. Narses is dead, Orodes.'

He looked down at the corpse on the ground, slid off his horse and knelt beside it. He turned it over, ripped off its helmet and sighed.

He looked up at me. 'It is not Narses, Pacorus; it is his eldest son, Nereus.'

The energy drained from me and suddenly my neck ached with a vengeance.

'Are you sure?' I said, but looking at the blood-smeared face I knew the answer before he spoke. Despite its fair hair, broad forehead and powerful frame I could see that it was the face of a young man.

He stood up and I helped him regain his saddle.

'I'm afraid Narses is elsewhere on the battlefield,' he said.

'Perhaps with those,' offered Vagharsh, who was looking south at a great mass of horsemen approaching our position. They were around six or seven hundred paces away and moving at a steady pace as the remnants of the enemy's heavy cavalry passed through their ranks. We may have defeated the opposition's heavy horsemen but now faced being assaulted by a great many more mounted spearmen. These riders were Mithridates' men judging by the huge banners fluttering among their ranks showing an eagle clutching a snake in its talons. Carrying round, red-painted shields and protected by leather armour around their torsos and helmets on their heads, at close quarters they were no match for cataphracts. However, we had lost our lances in the charge, had suffered losses and they outnumbered us by at least two to one.

As the men reformed their ranks behind us in preparation for another charge my father appeared with his bodyguard, Atrax alongside him.

'Greetings, father, it is good to see you safe.'

He noticed my wound. 'You are hurt.'

'It is nothing.'

He then pointed with his sword at the approaching spearmen.

'We must advance to meet those horsemen otherwise they will infiltrate our centre.'

'I agree,' said Orodes.

The kings dispersed and took up our positions in the front ranks of our men once more. We began to move forward but then a great mass of horsemen appeared on our left flank, moving across our front towards the enemy. In front of them fluttered the banner of a silver lion on a red background – Surena. We called a halt as his archers began shooting arrows at Mithridates' men. The latter may have been wearing protection on their heads and torsos but they were wearing green tunics and brown leggings and thus their arms and legs were completely exposed. Their horses were also unarmoured and within minutes men and animals were hit and falling as Surena's riders unleashed an arrow storm against them. Each rider was shooting up to five arrows a minute and there appeared to be at least three thousand horsemen under Surena's command: two hundred and fifty arrows a second were being shot at the enemy.

The missile deluge immediately halted the advance of the spearmen, the front ranks being thinned considerably before they about-faced and retreated out of arrow range. Surena's companies kept their cohesion and also fell back to a position around four hundred paces in front of us. He galloped across to me and saluted. I laughed.

'You don't have to salute me. You really must get used to being a king, Surena, but your presence is most welcome.'

437

'Thank you, lord.'

'What is the situation on the left?'

'Lord Vistaspa has the measure of the enemy. We have more men than they do so when we advance they retreat, and when we fall back to entice them into a trap they advance but do not take the bait. Lord Vistaspa sent me to support you when he saw the spearmen advance.'

Once more the kings gathered around me to assess the situation. Dead horses and their riders lay around us as the order was given to fall back to our initial positions.

My father slammed his sword back in its scabbard. 'Stalemate!'

He turned to me. 'What is happening on the right wing?'

I had no idea, so after thanking Surena for his assistance I decided to ride over to where the legions and Babylonians were deployed to see for myself.

Judging by the sun's position in the sky it was now late afternoon and in the centre and on our left wing the opposing armies remained in approximately the same position they had occupied before the fighting had begun. As I galloped across to the right wing I discovered a similar situation. The Durans and the Exiles were now each deployed in two lines, extending from the river inland, the Babylonians having withdrawn to take up position behind the Exiles. I could see arrows being shot from the ranks of the two huge blocks of enemy spearmen opposite the legions, the missiles arching into the sky before falling on the locked shields of the legionaries. And from within the ranks of the latter Marcus' ballista were hard at work.

I found Domitus a hundred paces behind the second line of cohorts in conversation with Kronos, Marcus and a group of Babylonian officers, the latter trotting past me back to their men as I slid off Remus' back in front of my senior commanders.

'What is happening?' I asked.

Domitus pointed at the Babylonians. 'We had to pull their men back behind the Exiles when the enemy opposite began hurling arrows and sling shots at us. They took a fearful amount of punishment before we managed to rearrange our lines, though.'

'The Babylonians have lost over a thousand men,' added Kronos.

'That many?' I was amazed.

Domitus spat on the ground. 'The enemy are no fools. They brought forward their archers and concentrated their arrows against the Babylonians, hardly gave us any attention at first. Just poured volley after volley at the Babylonians, knowing they would not be able to lock their shields as we do. Within minutes hundreds had been killed or wounded.'

'We had to pull them back behind our lines and extend the front of the legions to prevent them being destroyed,' added Kronos.

'After that most of the enemy archers and slingers pulled back behind their own spearmen,' said Domitus, 'though as you can see a few are dispersed among the front ranks.'

I glanced over to where the cohorts stood in their ranks and saw arrows dropping onto their shields. The volume of arrows being discharged by the enemy was not intense but rather desultory.

'Without the Babylonians we are spread a bit thin,' continued Domitus.

'Why don't they attack?' I asked.

'They too have lost a lot of men,' replied Kronos. 'I doubt they have the will to get to grips with the legions.'

I was confused. 'How so?'

Domitus nodded towards Marcus who had a self-satisfied grin on his face.

'After their arrow storm and our reorganisation we brought forward Marcus' machines and placed them in the front line and allocated them their own details of shield bearers for protection. They have been shooting for over an hour now.'

'And doing very nicely,' added Marcus.

His smaller ballista usually shot iron-tipped bolts that were three and half feet long or small stones and iron balls, but during the past few months Marcus and Arsam had been working on new missiles for the machines. This was the first campaign in which they had been used and the results were most promising. Marcus called them 'shield piercers', these eighteen-inch long arrow darts that were made from ash and had iron tips. Designed to punch through shields and armour, they had thinner fore shafts to aid penetration and short, stubby fins made from maple that were glued into grooves cut in the rear of the ash shaft. Light and compact, they had a range of around four hundred yards and their great velocity meant they could punch through wicker shields with ease. Each of Marcus' dozen ballista could fire up to four darts a minute and thus far had fired nearly three thousand of them at the packed ranks of the enemy, though he had now reduced each ballista's rate of fire to one bolt a minute to conserve ammunition.

'And they are standing in their ranks and taking such punishment?' I asked incredulously.

'Narses does not care about the lives of his soldiers as you do,' said Domitus. 'The problem we have is that even with three thousands of them dead and wounded...'

'Oh, they will be dead,' interrupted Marcus.

Domitus tilted his head at him and continued. 'Even with three thousand of them dead I reckon there are still a few thousand left, to say nothing of their slingers and archers.'

'What about Duran losses?' I asked.

'Four wounded thus far,' replied Kronos.

439

I was tempted to order an all-out attack by the legions against Narses' spearmen but it was getting late and the men had been standing in their ranks for hours and would be fatigued. So I commanded Marcus to order his machines to halt their shooting to see what reaction it would have on the enemy. The result was that their archers and slingers also stopped their activity and so the legionaries were at last able to rest their shields on the ground as both sides observed each other warily across no man's land. Parties were sent to the river to fill water bottles as the enemy spearmen inched back towards the date palm grove to increase the distance between them and Marcus' killing machines.

Thus did a cessation of fighting take place across the whole battlefield. It had been a disappointing end to a day that had begun with so much promise.

Dura's camp was sited some five hundred paces to the rear of the legions' battle line. While archers and slingers were shooting at the legionaries the squires and civilian drivers had been busy digging a ditch and using the earth to erect a rampart immediately behind it. As the legions marched back to camp they were finishing driving stakes into the rampart to create the palisade. The legionaries erected their tents as Strabo oversaw the stabling of the horses and camels within the camp's perimeter. The camp's western entrance was located next to the river and so Strabo organised the watering of the animals while Marcus assigned parties of legionaries to fetch water for human consumption further upstream from where the animals were drinking, pissing and spreading their dung.

I sent couriers to the other kings inviting them to bring their own men into camp but they declined.

'Probably for the best,' remarked Marcus as he sat in a chair in my command tent. 'It would be a very crowded camp with the forces of the other kings inside.'

After Alcaeus had bandaged my neck I had called a council of war to take stock of our situation after the day's inconclusive fighting. At least the reports were heartening. Vagises and his horse archers had seen almost no fighting though much riding to and fro as Vistaspa sought to outmanoeuvre the enemy's horse archers. The only casualties he suffered were a handful of men with broken legs as a result of being thrown from their horses. Gallia had, mercifully, spent the whole day immobile, sweating in her armour and helmet along with the unused reserve of her Amazons and Babylon's five hundred royal guards. I already knew that casualties among the legions were insignificant and so the heaviest losses were among my cataphracts – fifteen dead and twenty wounded. Normally these figures would be a cause for celebration after a battle but all the faces round the table wore expressions of indifference, with the exception of Marcus, who was delighted with the success of his 'shield piercers'.

'Mithridates and Narses will be happier than we are,' said Domitus, yawning. 'They have essentially fought us to a standstill.'

'But have lost most of their cataphracts in the process as well as Narses' own son,' I said.

'They still have a lot of horsemen left,' remarked Vagises.

'The legions should attack first thing tomorrow, Pacorus,' said Domitus. 'That might stiffen the resolve of the Babylonians. I doubt they will be able to withstand another day of being pelted with arrows and stones, and we cannot protect them and fight the enemy at the same time.'

It made sense. In terms of equipment, training and tactics the Babylonian foot were second rate compared to the legions.

'How many enemy spearmen did you face today?' I asked Domitus.

He shrugged his shoulders. 'Thirty, forty thousand.'

I was surprised. 'That many?'

'Plus archers and slingers,' added Kronos.

'After we get to grips with them at close quarters numbers won't matter,' said Domitus. 'But what we don't want is another day standing around under a hail of arrows and stones.'

Kronos nodded in agreement and Marcus looked disappointed, no doubt eager to unleash his new invention against the enemy once more.

'Very well,' I said. 'Tomorrow we attack.'

Two hours later I received an invitation from Orodes to attend a meeting of the kings in his camp. It must have been nearly midnight when I left my tent to ride to the Babylonian camp located next to Dura's army, a vast, disorganised sprawl of tents, corrals, wagons and temporary stables that stretched into the distance. And beyond the Babylonians were the tents of Hatra, Media and finally Gordyene, the latter encompassed within a square earth rampart like my own. To the south the campfires of the enemy dotted the landscape to resemble a multitude of stars that had fallen to earth. It was clear that the enemy was also determined to fight on the morrow.

When I arrived at Orodes' tent I found the other kings already there. Atrax nodded to me as he filled a cup with wine and then limped back to his chair. My father looked angry and Surena tired as I greeted them. Orodes held out a full cup for me to take. He appeared to be his usual unruffled self. We sat in a circle as Vistaspa, who appeared remarkably fresh considering his age, recounted the day's events. His horse archers on the left wing had achieved little save stopping the enemy horse archers directly opposite influencing the battle. Surena's intervention had halted the charge of the enemy's

441

mounted spearmen against our cataphracts, who had engaged and destroyed the enemy's heavy horsemen, the son of Narses having been killed in that particular engagement. Vistaspa smiled at me as he relayed this news. To complete the debriefing I informed them that my legions had initially been subjected to an enemy missile storm that had proved ineffective.

'Though at a cost of over a thousand Babylonian dead, I am sorry to say,' reported Orodes.

Fortunately the other kings reported minor losses among their contingents, which meant that hostilities could be continued with the coming of the new dawn.

'We must attack the enemy along the whole line tomorrow,' I stated.

'I agree,' said my father. 'We must finish this once and for all.'

'Then my suggestion,' I continued, 'is for the legions to attack on the right to shatter the enemy's left wing. After Narses' foot soldiers have been destroyed my men will advance on Susa.'

'The cataphracts will drive through the enemy's centre,' added my father, 'with Vistaspa once again deployed on the left with the horse archers.'

'With their left and centre destroyed,' I continued, 'the enemy's horse archers will either have to intervene or flee.'

'It is strange that the enemy remained on the defensive despite their superiority in numbers,' mused Surena.

'Narses is obviously not the great general he thought he was,' was my father's only comment.

By the time I had ridden back to camp, unsaddled Remus and walked to my tent there were only four hours of the night left. The tents were filled with sleeping men and it was ominously quiet. I slipped into my tent's bedchamber and lay beside a sleeping Gallia, then stared at the ceiling and heard Surena's voice. Why had the enemy remained on the defensive? I dismissed them from my mind.

When the dawn came the armies once more marched out to take up their battle positions, the legions deploying in two lines to extend their frontage, their right flank again anchored on the river and the Babylonians once more massed on their left. It took two hours before the latter were in their positions, during which time the two great masses of enemy spearmen once again filtered through the neat rows of the great date palm grove to face the Durans, Exiles and Babylonians. In the centre armoured riders gathered around the kings once more, while on the left Vistaspa gathered his contingents of horse archers.

The day was again dry and sunny, though there was no wind and the temperature was already rapidly rising despite the early hour. The area presented a grisly spectacle as the dead from yesterday's fighting still lay on the ground where they had fallen, the deployment of the two armies at first scattering the hordes of crows, buzzards and vultures that had been having a feast for breakfast, who then returned to their meal as both sides halted and dressed their lines. The birds pecked at the skulls of fallen soldiers and tore at the flesh of slain horses as they gorged themselves on the dead flesh in no man's land.

Once more I sweated in my scale armour as Gallia and I joined the other monarchs. In the centre of the battle line I could see small groups of enemy cataphracts directly opposite, perhaps five hundred in total, in between the mounted spearmen who now made up the bulk of the enemy's centre. And once again the opposition's horse archers flooded the valley to face Vistaspa's horsemen on our left wing.

Again the infernal din of kettledrums began to fill the air as the enemy spearmen opposite the legions began cheering and banging their spear shafts against their wicker shields.

'They attempt to intimidate your foot soldiers, Pacorus,' remarked my father.

'It will take more than a bit of noise to frighten them, father.'

'They outnumber your men, Pacorus,' said Atrax with concern.

He was right. More and more spearmen were gathering in front of the Durans and Exiles and the purple ranks of the Babylonians grouped on their left. Most of the enemy spearmen were wearing the yellow of Narses, the soldiers who faced the Babylonians carrying white shields and wearing black uniforms – the troops of Mithridates.

I smiled at Atrax. 'It is not the size of the gladiator in a fight, Atrax, but the size of the fight in the gladiator.'

Gallia laughed and Atrax looked confused. My father shook his head.

'You are certain your foot soldiers can defeat the enemy's?' he asked.

'Quite certain, father.'

'They have done so on many occasions,' added Orodes.

My father tilted his head at Orodes in recognition of his high status. It was now the turn of the king of kings to speak.

'When Domitus begins to push them back, Pacorus, we will shatter their centre. With their left wing and centre destroyed the enemy will be forced to withdraw back to Susa.'

He looked at Gallia and smiled.

'I would ask you again to lead the reserve this day, Gallia.'

She smiled at him and nodded, and then came a great cheer came from the right and I was astonished to see the enemy spearmen advancing to attack the legions, their great wicker shields presenting a long wall of yellow and white as they marched at a steady pace towards my men.

443

'Looks like the enemy has a death wish,' remarked Gafarn casually as we all watched transfixed by the great drama that was about to take place on the right flank.

Trumpet blasts sounded from the ranks of the legions and then the whole of the first line – ten cohorts of Durans and Exiles – ran forward, the first five ranks hurling their javelins at the oncoming spearmen. The latter also charged and seconds later a sound like the splintering of wood reached our ears as both sides collided. From our viewpoint it appeared as if time had frozen as the great press of soldiers suddenly became immobile, but the sounds of cheers and screams revealed that in the centre of the great mass slaughter was being done. The wicker shields of the enemy were large and thick, capable of withstanding an arrow and spear strike, but they were unwieldy in the mêlée and became more so when a javelin was lodged in them, further adding to their weight. And the legionaries could use their shield bosses to barge aside enemy spears to stab at enemy faces and necks with their short shorts.

The front ranks of the enemy spearmen had been thinned by the storm of javelins in the first charge, the survivors subsequently being cut to pieces by *gladius* blades. Soon the legionaries were stepping over the bodies of dead spearmen to get at those behind as the enemy started to crumple. We sat on our horses like members of the audience in the best seats at a play as the tragedy of the enemy's spearmen was enacted. And above the grim sounds of battle could be heard a rhythmic chant, one that I had heard many times before but which never failed to set my pulse racing. We heard 'Dura, Dura' as the legionaries herded the enemy back, back towards the date palm as they chopped the wicker shields in front of them to pieces. The enemy was faltering now, and then I heard fresh trumpet blasts and the first line of the Durans began to wheel left as the cohorts in the second line behind began to form into columns. The Exiles halted their advance as the Duran front line continued to turn like a great door swinging open towards the river, and into the gap created by this turning movement flooded the columns of the second line. Only the best-trained soldiers in the world could attempt such a manoeuvre in battle as the front-line cohorts shoved the spearmen before them towards the water. Around a quarter of the enemy spearmen were being forced into the deep waters of the Karkheh.

Hundreds drowned as they were pushed into the river, unable to flee because of the dense press of men around them. Groups of spearmen in the rear ranks began to run away as the enemy's cohesion began to crumble, but for those in front of the Durans there was no escape as they were either cut down by swords or pushed into the river and drowned. It was marvellous to behold.

We all cheered and my father turned and gave the signal to his horsemen deployed a hundred paces behind us, who began to walk their horses forward. Behind them the Duran and Median heavy horsemen also began to advance preparatory to the charge while Orodes' bodyguard closed around him. I also gave the signal to my men to move forward. All that remained was for the enemy horsemen opposite to be scattered and the day would be ours.

And then the Babylonians broke.

Having lost a thousand men the day before the morale of Babylon's foot soldiers was shaky at best. I had hoped that the guaranteed success of the legions deployed on their right wing would stiffen their resolve but I was wrong. In the initial clash they again suffered heavy casualties and began to falter, then were forced back as the Exiles next to them advanced. Within no time they were fighting their own private battle and losing it, made worse by the deluge of arrows and stones that was being directed at them by enemy archers and slingers whose commanders, learning from the previous day, realised that the missiles of their men would be more effective against the Babylonians rather than the legions. Then enemy spearmen began to envelop them to attack their flanks and so they broke and fled to the rear. Fortunately Kronos had been alert to the danger and had turned the cohort on the extreme left of his second line through ninety degrees to provide protection for his now exposed flank. Frantic trumpet commands and whistles brought the Exiles to a halt, which were reciprocated among the ranks of the Durans as Domitus also realised that something was awry. The advance stopped and then the legions disengaged and began to inch backwards.

'Gallia,' I said, 'you and your reserve are with me. We must assist the Babylonians.'

Small groups of the latter were attempting to make a stand but were being methodically surrounded and cut down by enemy spearmen who, I had to admit, were maintaining their discipline. Nevertheless there were around five thousand enemy troops advancing towards our rear where our camps and all their supplies were located.

'Do you need your cataphracts, Pacorus?' asked Orodes, pained by the plight of his foot soldiers giving way.

I shook my head. 'No, I can stabilise the situation long enough for Domitus to seal the gap in the line.'

'There is little point in assaulting their centre now,' said my father.

He was right: the enemy's left wing was still intact albeit sorely depleted. Archers had now come forward to pepper the withdrawing legions with arrows, though they inflicted few casualties. As Dura's foot soldiers fell back they revealed a ground that was literally carpeted in dead. How many soldiers did Narses have?

445

I pulled my sword from its scabbard just as Byrd and Malik brought their horses to a halt behind the kings.

'Second army come,' announced Byrd.

My father turned in his saddle. 'What did you say?'

'It is true, lord,' said Malik. 'Another army is approaching from the northern end of the valley. Horse archers leading a great number of tribesmen.'

'How many?' asked Orodes.

Byrd looked at him. 'Tens of thousands.'

The valleys of the Zagros Mountains were dotted with villages and smaller settlements that had existed since before the empire. Ruled by tribal chieftains, these villages owed allegiance to no king in a faraway city and their inhabitants spent most of their time raiding other villages and settling blood feuds. The Persians and then the Greeks had tried to subdue them and failed, and it had been the same with the Parthians. However, all these races had discovered that the hill tribes could be enlisted as allies easily enough if they had enough gold to pay them. Mithridates had obviously used some of the gold he had shipped from Ctesiphon to recruit these wild people to his cause. Armed with an assortment of axes, spears, clubs and knives they usually wore no armour or head protection, their only defence being a small shield.

'The Babylonians still need our assistance,' I said.

'Hatra's horsemen will deal with the hill men,' stated my father.

'You do not know how many there are, father.'

He smiled. 'As you yourself said, Pacorus, it is size of the fight in the man that counts.'

The next few minutes were organised chaos as a rider was sent to Vistaspa ordering that Dura's and Hatra's horse archers to redeploy north of the campsites to form up with my father's armoured riders to assault the approaching enemy. Meanwhile Orodes would lead the rest of the cataphracts against the horsemen in the enemy's centre and Gallia and I would assault the spearmen who had routed the Babylonians. Surena and Media's archers remained on the left wing to contain the enemy's horse archers. I reached over and shook my father's hand and then Gafarn's as the Amazons and Babylon's royal guard began trotting towards our right wing.

Gallia rode beside me, the Amazons in a long line behind together with Vagharsh carrying my banner, as we broke into a gallop and headed towards the phalanx of enemy spearmen that was advancing towards the Babylonian camp. Most of the Babylonian spearmen had either been killed or had sought refuge in Dura's camp, whose ramparts were at least guarded by squires and their bows.

The enemy spearmen had spotted the body of horsemen coming towards them and had halted to assume an all-round defensive posture

– shields rested on the ground and spears pointed at us at an angle of forty-five degrees. The Babylonian horsemen slowed and then halted as the Amazons deployed into five widely spaced columns that galloped to within a hundred paces of the densely packed square of spearmen, before each rider shot her bow before wheeling sharply right and right again to ride to the rear of the column. In this way a steady volley of arrows was unleashed against the spearmen, the arrows arching into the sky before falling among the spearmen. It was useless to strike the shields because the wicker and leather facing was too thick, and so the arrows were shot upwards to fall out of the sky and hopefully strike necks and faces. A hundred archers did not have enough arrows to cause many casualties among so many spearmen but they were numerous enough to bring them to a halt.

As the Amazons amused themselves with target practice, the Babylonian horsemen deployed around my wife's fighters acting as a guard, I rode across the field to where the legions had pulled back to their original positions. I had to take a wide detour to reach them as the phalanx of enemy spearmen was actually behind the left wing of the Exiles.

I saw a cohort of the Durans running back to camp as I rode up to Domitus who was speaking to Kronos. They raised their hands when they saw me.

Domitus pointed over to where the block of enemy spearmen stood. 'You stopped them, then?'

'Gallia and the Amazons are keeping them entertained.'

'I've sent to men to fetch Marcus and his machines,' said Domitus. 'They can finish them off.'

'There has been an unfortunate development, my friends,' I told them. 'Another enemy army is approaching from the north.'

Kronos and Domitus looked at each other.

'My father's takes his army to deal with it,' I reassured them. 'In the meantime remain on the defensive here.'

I looked to where the legions had battled the spearmen. Not only was the ground blanketed with bodies but there also were enemy dead floating in the river.

I nodded towards the grim harvest. 'Excellent work.'

'We would have been in Susa by now if the Babylonians had not collapsed,' remarked Kronos bitterly.

'Can't help that,' I replied. 'We may still win the day.'

I saw wagons leaving the camp and heading towards us – Marcus and his ballista.

'Make sure none escape,' I ordered. 'The more enemy we kill today the less we have to face tomorrow.'

Kronos was shocked. 'You think the battle will extend into a third day?'

'I'm sure of it. The enemy seems to have an inexhaustible supply of soldiers.'

'Whereas we do not,' said Domitus grimly.

I did not bother to ask about the size of our losses as I raised a hand to them and rode back to Gallia whose women had ceased their shooting.

'We are out of arrows,' she said frustratingly.

I looked at the phalanx of spearmen that were now rooted to the spot.

I smiled at her. 'Do not worry. Marcus brings his ballista to thin their ranks. You have done what was required.'

I heard horn blasts and the low rumble of thousands of hooves churning up the ground and turned to see Orodes and the cataphracts smashing into the enemy's centre, followed by a loud crunching noise as the heavy horsemen struck.

I smiled. The day may still be ours.

With the Babylonian guards we rode back to where the camel trains holding spare ammunition were located to the rear of our left wing. When Orodes had charged Surena had launched the horse archers against those on the enemy's right wing, inflicting many casualties but his men also suffered significant losses. Now he too rode to the camels with his men to acquire fresh quivers. Meanwhile, to the north of our camps, my father and Vistaspa led over eleven thousand horsemen against the Zagros hordes.

Surena's lion banner fluttered behind him as he rode over to Gallia and me, his men being handed full quivers by the camel drivers whose beasts were sitting on the ground.

'The Medians holds the line while we restock our quivers, lord. The enemy has suffered many losses and falls back.'

'What losses have you suffered?' I asked him.

He looked pensive. 'We also have many empty saddles, lord. Atrax's men charged most valiantly and suffered the most.'

Gallia and the Amazons received fresh quivers from Dura's camel train as a lull descended over our left wing. After we had replenished our stocks of arrows she and I rode with Surena to where Media's horse archers were deployed in their companies in a long line that extended for at least half a mile eastwards. In front of them stretching south the ground was littered with dead men and horses, many of the corpses resembling pin cushions so many arrows did they have in them. In the distance, well out of bow range, enemy horse archers were being attacked by Orodes' companies who were wheeling left to strike the enemy horsemen's right flank.

I nodded. 'Orodes has destroyed the enemy's centre.'

Now it was time to send forward Surena and his horse archers to support Orodes to complete the rout of the enemy's centre and right wing. After that the legions could attack once more to finally destroy the enemy foot soldiers in front of the date palm grove. We finally had victory within our grasp.

'Can you hear that?'

I looked at Gallia who was sitting up in her saddle trying to look over the heads of the Amazons behind her. Then I heard the sound, an ominous rumble of thousands of cheering voices. Remus stirred nervously and I also became aware that the ground was shaking. Surena looked at me with concern and I knew that the battle was about to take another twist.

All thoughts of reinforcing Orodes disappeared as Surena, Gallia and I led Gordyene's horse archers through the camel train to where my father's men were battling the hill men. What I saw took my breath away.

As we halted and the horse archers formed into their companies behind us the land to the north of our position was filled with hill men being led by groups of horse archers. Directly ahead of us my father's horsemen had driven deep into the enemy ranks and were now scything down the hill men around them. My father and Gafarn led over eleven thousand men against these heathens, but were vastly outnumbered by an enemy that now seemed certain to overwhelm them. Looking left and right I estimated that each formation of enemy horsemen numbered around a thousand men, and behind them came more than that number of hill men on foot.

Either side of my father's army I counted ten such groups of horsemen – twenty thousand horse archers – not counting the ones that the Hatrans were fighting. If each one was accompanied by three times that number of hill men then there were at least eighty thousand enemy troops heading our way!

I turned to Surena. 'We must aid my father else he will be surrounded.'

'Yes, lord.'

He gave the command to his officers to prepare to charge as I passed word to the Babylonians to move forward as my father's horsemen disappeared among an ocean of hill men. The enemy now surrounded them. Something caught my eye on the right and I saw two enemy groups peeling off to head towards Surena's camp.

'Surena,' I called, pointing towards his camp, 'who is still in your camp?'

'Farriers, grooms, veterinaries, the wounded; four hundred or so.'

The enemy, who would butcher all those inside, would soon overrun his camp. Surena's camel train and its drivers were located behind us, along with the camels of Hatra and Dura. The only chance of saving those inside the camp was to evacuate them via the western entrance and get them inside Dura's camp, whose ramparts were manned by squires armed with bows.

'Send a thousand of your men to intercept those soldiers heading for your camp,' I ordered him, forgetting he was a king, 'otherwise they will be slaughtered.'

He nodded and called forward one of his officers who then rode back to his men. Within minutes a thousand riders were galloping to intercept the enemy before they reached the camp.

'Gallia,' I shouted, 'get the camel trains back to our camp. Take the Babylonians with you.'

She pointed her bow ahead. 'I would rather fight that horde.'

'Do as you are told,' I shouted. 'The battle hangs in the balance and I don't have time to argue with you.'

She did not respond but tugged savagely on Epona's reins to wheel her away, followed by the Amazons. I nodded at Surena who dug his knees into his horse to urge it forward. Behind us seven thousand horse archers from Gordyene galloped forward to save my father.

The air was thick with arrows as we charged among the enemy masses. The enemy horse archers broke left and right to avoid our arrowhead formation but the hill men were not so lucky. As we galloped forward the front ranks shot arrows in quick succession at those men on foot before us. The hill men had little discipline and fought as part of a rabble, relying on weight of numbers to overwhelm an opponent. Against disciplined soldiers in formation they were easy meat. Most tried to get out of our way, scattering left and right, though others attempted to make a stand and formed a ragged shield wall in front of our charge. Loosing up to seven arrows a minute we shot their flimsy defences to pieces before we reached them, and then we were through them to reach the Hatrans.

Surena rode off to order his men to deploy left and right behind my father's troops to create a corridor of horsemen along which the Hatrans could withdraw.

I rode forward past companies of Hatran horse archers who were darting at the hill men with their swords drawn, obviously out of arrows. The enemy horse archers deployed behind the seething mass of hill men still had ammunition, however, and were thinning Hatran numbers with their accurate shooting. Fortunately this ceased abruptly when Surena's companies began to shoot back at them, forcing them to retire.

I rode on to where a group of my father's bodyguard was standing, my father's banner being held by a dismounted cataphract next to them. I felt a knot in my stomach and knew something was terribly wrong. Other members of my father's bodyguard faced outwards on their horses to form a cordon around this group, and beyond them the rest of my father's heavy horsemen were keeping the enemy at bay with their swords, maces and axes, launching short, disciplined charges against the hill men, riding among them to split heads and pierce unarmoured bodies, before withdrawing to reform.

I rode up to the group of men on foot and slid off Remus' back. They recognised me and parted, bowing their heads as they stepped aside, and then my knees nearly gave way. Lying on the ground in front of me, being cradled by Gafarn, was the bloodstained body of my father. I fell to my knees beside him and looked in despair at the ashen-faced Gafarn.

'He was pulled from his horse and injured,' my brother said quietly.

I looked at the blood seeping through the bandages near his left shoulder and realised that his attacker must have delivered the strike under the arm.

My father opened his eyes. 'Ah, Pacorus.'

His voice was very weak.

I held his right hand, the tears coming to my eyes.

'I am here, father.'

'You are king now, my son.'

I felt grief grip my insides. 'Nonsense. We will get you back to camp, father, to tend to your wound.'

He smiled faintly. 'Take care of your mother and tell her that I have loved her always and will wait for her.'

He looked at Gafarn, who stared unblinking at our father. 'You must take care of your brother, my son, for he is apt to get himself into trouble.'

'I shall, father,' Gafarn replied, tears running down his cheeks.

'All will be well,' my father's voice was very faint, 'Shamash be with you.'

My father's eyes remained open but they were lifeless as they stared into the blue sky. As tears blurred my sight I closed his eyes with my hand and kissed his forehead. I had been unaware of Vistaspa's presence but now I saw him standing at my father's feet holding his head in his hands, sobbing like a small child. Thus died Varaz, King of Hatra, and son of Sames. The others around us stood with their heads bowed in stunned silence as Gafarn gently laid my father on the ground and covered his body with his cloak.

With difficulty I rose to my feet and took a few paces to be by Gafarn's side. I took his arm and raised it aloft.

'The king is dead. Long live the king, Gafarn, King of Hatra.'

As one they shouted. 'Hail King Gafarn.'

Gafarn looked at me with tears still coursing down his cheeks. 'What madness is this?'

'No madness, brother. I relinquish my claim to Hatra's throne. You are now its king. Rule long and wisely.'

451

An arrow slammed into the ground at our feet and I became aware once more of the sounds of battles raging all around us.

'Our grief will have to wait, Gafarn. We must get out of this death trap.'

Hatra's cataphracts, largely immune from the enemy's arrows, were tiring under the relentless onslaught of the hill men, their dead piled high around the ring of Hatran steel. A stretcher was fashioned from lengths of broken *kontus* shafts and then four of my father's bodyguard carried their king's body back to my camp. His heavy cavalry formed a rear guard as Surena's horse archers poured withering volleys into the enemy mass. Mercifully the enemy horse archers had stopped their shooting, having expended their own supply of arrows, thus enabling us to escape relatively unscathed.

I rode in the rear guard alongside Vistaspa, who in his grief seemed determined to get himself killed. As companies of heavy horsemen formed into arrowhead formation and charged at groups of hill men, riding among them, slashing at them with swords and maces, moving at all times to prevent the exposed legs of their horses being cut by enemy blades, before turning and withdrawing, Vistaspa rode at an enemy group on his own.

There were a dozen of them, great hairy brutes stripped to the waist and carrying two-handed axes that they swung as though they were feathers. He rode straight at them, initially scattering them and then splitting one of their skulls with a back slash of his sword as he passed. But they chased after him and when he attempted to turn around when another group barred his way, a heathen in the first group grabbed the reins of his horse. Vistaspa severed the man's hand with a downward cut of his sword but another axe man swung his weapon into his leg armour, denting the metal and causing Vistaspa to scream in agony and drop his sword. At that moment Surena released his bowstring and shot the man who had tried to sever Vistaspa's leg, then killed another standing beside him and kept on shooting arrows at his assailants as I rode towards him.

Half of them were dead by the time I reached his side.

'Lord Vistaspa, I order you to fall back.' I looked at his dented leg armour that was now covered in blood.

'Move!'

He nodded and rode away as a crazed hill man, all hair and muscles, ran at me with his giant axe held over his head. I charged and swung my sword at him, lopping off his head with a single stroke. As half a dozen cataphracts rode in front to give me cover, my would-be killer's headless body lay twitching on the ground.

The enemy halted their attacks and withdrew sharply when Orodes appeared with his companies, having ridden to assist us when word reached him about what had happened. The fighting ceased abruptly as a great column of his men rode north to form a screen to allow the battered soldiers of Hatra to escort their dead king in peace. I dismounted and walked beside his body as it was carried back to camp, Gafarn beside me but saying nothing as we trudged disconsolately along. We were joined by Orodes who was likewise grief stricken.

We walked across ground that was strewn with dead: men, horses and camels, their bodies either ripped open by metal blades or pierced by arrows. Orodes answered the questions that were going through my mind.

'The hill men sacked Surena's camp after those inside had been evacuated. Gallia also managed to get many of the camels carrying spare arrows back to your camp, Pacorus, but not all. I am afraid to say that the Hatran, Median and Babylonian camps were also overrun before we forced the enemy back.'

'There is room in my camp for everyone,' I said without emotion.

As the long column of horsemen and their exhausted mounts walked to the eastern entrance to the Duran camp the sun began to set in the west, a great yellow ball of fire set against an orange background. I closed my eyes and prayed to Shamash that He would welcome my father into heaven and that he would be granted a place of honour at His table, for such a great and wise king deserved it. I opened my eyes as the sound of kettledrums once more sounded in the south.

453

Chapter 18

They hit us at twilight, when the last vestiges of light were disappearing from the world, a demented rush of feral men who hurled themselves against all four sides of the camp. Having flooded Surena's camp and destroyed the tents of the Medians, Babylonians and Hatrans, the hill men now concentrated their fury against my own camp, thinking that it too would easily succumb to their savage attacks. But they had reckoned without the skills of Marcus Sutonius.

The squires and civilians had originally erected the camp but Marcus had subsequently strengthened it further. The surrounding ditch was eight feet deep on all sides, having a width of four feet at the bottom and twelve feet at the top due to its sloping sides, and the bottom of the ditch was lined with blocks of wood fitted with iron spikes to impale anyone who fell on them. Behind the ditch stood an eight-foot-high earth rampart surmounted by a wall of stakes, with additional stakes set in the rampart pointing outwards at an angle of forty-five degrees to make it difficult to scale.

As the last horsemen rode into camp and the eastern entrance was barred with wagons and logs covered with many long iron spikes positioned in front of them, the Zagros tribes gathered in their war bands and then charged our defences. The ramparts were initially defended by squires before the horse archers dismounted and sprinted to reinforce them, Domitus also assigning legionaries to use their shields as a barrier against the hail of light axes, javelins and arrows that was being hurled against those standing behind the stakes. Fortunately there was a distance of one hundred paces between the tenting area and the perimeter rampart all round the inside of the camp, but even so missiles still landed among tents and animals to inflict wounds, some fatal.

I ran to the northern wall where the attack was heaviest, the air filled with screams and shouts as I neared the rampart. I had ordered Gallia to stay with Domitus, who with Kronos was organising reserves of legionaries to be deployed all round the inside of the perimeter, to the rear of the rampart, in case the enemy broke through. She ignored my order and led her Amazons behind me as I ran up the bank of earth to join those fighting on its summit. The area beyond the ditch was heaving with the enemy, many of whom had been felled by arrows before they reached the ditch. The latter was now choked with the twisted bodies of the dead and dying as archers around me poured volley after volley into the seemingly endless mass of hill men that stretched far into the distance.

Legionaries were holding their shields above the stakes on the rampart as the enemy archers on their stationary horses shot at us from a range of around four hundred paces. As more and more of our own horse archers came onto the wall parties of squires were ordered to fall back to bring more ammunition to the rampart.

I dumped my quiver on the floor and stood beside a legionary whose shield had been struck by two arrows. A squire beside me released his bowstring and then beamed with delight when he saw me.

'We are holding them, majesty.'

'You are doing well,' I told him.

I bent down to pull an arrow from my quiver and heard a dull thud and then a groan, and turned to see an axe imbedded in the squire's skull. He collapsed on the ground, dead.

Despite their furious efforts the enemy could not breach our defences because the ditch was too wide and they had no scaling ladders to climb up our wall of earth, so they brought forward those carrying light javelins and throwing axes and launched them at us, reinforced by the arrows of horse archers positioned to the rear. I gave the order for everyone on the wall to kneel to present a smaller target to the enemy as we had already lost too many squires, who wore no armour on their bodies or heads. More legionaries came to the wall and formed an unbroken wall of shields along its top, behind which we could shoot our own arrows at the enemy below. The hill men had suffered enormous casualties by now and their bloodlust was starting to abate, especially when the archers on the walls poured volley after volley against the javelin throwers standing just to the rear of the ditch. The latter, half-naked, were slaughtered and so the rest of the hill men withdrew into the night, leaving their dead behind them. The assault against the northern wall had failed.

I heard my name being called and saw Domitus standing behind the rampart with Kronos and Marcus. I slapped the shoulder of the legionary whose shield had protected us both and then walked down the earth slope.

'The southern wall is being assaulted,' said Domitus.

'More hill men?' I asked.

He shook his head. 'These are professionals and they have killed quite a few of our men.'

'They are standing behind shields the height of man,' added Kronos, 'and wear scale armour, helmets and mail face masks.'

'Royal foot archers,' I said. 'How many?'

'About two thousand,' said Domitus. 'Do you want me to send out some cohorts against them?'

'No,' I replied. 'Marcus, this is a task for your shield piercers, I think.'

He nodded and scurried off.

'I will get some of my men to assist him,' said Kronos, saluting and then following Marcus.

455

'Pull as many men off the wall as is safe,' I called after him. 'Don't give them any easy victories.'

Gallia joined us as the bodies of two horse archers were carried from the wall.

'I heard about your father,' said Domitus. 'I grieve for you.'

Gallia embraced me. 'He was a great man, Pacorus. We will miss him.'

I had no time for grief, though, not with what was left of the army penned in camp and surrounded on all sides.

'Where are the kings?' I asked.

'With their men,' replied Domitus.

'Go and see that the threat against the southern wall is dealt with. I will gather the kings so we can decide our plan for tomorrow.'

I pointed at Gallia.

'You are with me.'

Domitus paced away as I began to walk towards the command tent. My father's body had been placed in the tent that usually housed the griffin standard, which had been temporarily relocated to stand beside the Exiles' lion.

'Surena warned us about this,' I said.

'What?'

'That we were walking into trap. Narses has out-foxed us once again.'

'What will you do now?'

I shrugged. 'That will be for Orodes to decide.'

'And how are you, Pacorus?'

I stopped and faced her. 'My father is dead, our army is half-beaten and the enemy appears as strong as when we first engaged them yesterday. I cannot believe it has come to this.'

Her expression hardened. 'You must remain strong. We can still achieve victory.'

'You really think so?'

'I have never doubted it.'

Fortified by my wife's certainty that we would emerge victorious I decided to conduct a tour of the camp before I met the kings, which unfortunately served only to dampen my spirits once more. In the hospital Alcaeus and his medical staff were working tirelessly to stitch wounds, bind broken limbs and extract arrows from flesh. Gallia went among the wounded and tried to comfort them with soft words. We came across one of the injured, a squire lying in a cot, a blood-soaked bandage wrapped round his stomach.

'Javelin in the stomach,' remarked Alcaeus. 'He won't see the dawn.'

This boy had barely begun his life and now it was to end in a few hours, far away from his family, alone and in pain.

'No,' said Alcaeus, 'not in pain. He has been given morphe to ease his journey.'

On the royal estates in Dura Alcaeus oversaw the cultivation of herbs and flowers to make medicines for his corps. The most remarkable was the milky liquid of the unripe fruit of the green poppy. Mixed with wine it produced a drink that could take away pain, the liquid being named after Morpheus, the Greek god of dreams and sleep. It had the power to numb even the most severe pain and could also be used to hasten the end of those who would not survive their wounds. It was so now as Gallia knelt beside the cot and gently stroked the face of the youth with the far-away stare, taking his hand in hers while I stood with Alcaeus watching the scene.

'It will not be long now,' he said softly as Gallia spoke to the boy.

'How many squires have you treated?'

'Dozens,' he replied, 'most with arrow or javelin wounds.'

'They saved the camp. One day bards will write about how a few boys held off an army of barbarians with their bows.'

'Let us hope we all live to see that day.'

Gallia, pale and downcast, came to us. 'He's gone.'

Alcaeus signalled to one of his orderlies to take the body to where the others were laid out in neat rows behind the hospital, nodded to us both and continued with his duties. The low moans and occasional screams added to the overall frightfulness of the scene and though I thanked Shamash for Alcaeus and his healers, I was glad to leave them.

In contrast I was delighted to see Domitus two hours later when he informed me that Marcus and his ballista had forced the enemy's royal archers to retreat, the latter having discovered to their cost that their shields offered no protection against his 'shield piercers'. With their retreat the enemy's assault against the camp finally ceased. It was now two hours past midnight and still the kings had yet to meet. Dawn was four hours away.

We finally gathered in my tent half an hour later, all of us tired, dirty, unshaven and listless. None of us had slept much over the last two days and now we faced yet another day of combat. Even Domitus appeared drained. We drank water out of fear that consuming wine would induce sleep, chewing on salted mutton and hard biscuit as we considered our parlous position. Only Marcus appeared jovial, once again delighted that his machines had exceeded all expectations.

'Well, Marcus, perhaps you would give us a summary of our present condition.'

He rubbed his hand across his scalp and began reading from a parchment of his notes.

'There are in camp two thousand, two hundred cataphracts fit for duty, sixteen thousand horse archers, two hundred of Babylon's royal guard,' he bowed his head to Orodes, 'nine and a half thousand legionaries and two thousand Babylonian foot soldiers. Plus three thousand squires and the camel and wagon drivers, medical staff and so forth.'

No one said anything but all realised the sobering nature of these figures. In two days of fighting our combined forces had lost over eight thousand foot soldiers killed and wounded, over a thousand cataphract dead and casualties of eight thousand among the horse archers, to say nothing of Babylon's three hundred royal bodyguards killed and three thousand squires slaughtered when the camps had been overrun. The only ray of sunshine was that the legions' losses were light.

'At least the enemy's losses are greater,' offered Surena in an attempt to brighten the mood.

'We must march out of camp when it is light to fight the enemy once more,' said Orodes. 'Either that or withdraw north back to the bridge and return to Ctesiphon.'

'I would advise against withdrawing, Orodes,' I said. 'The hill men may have gone but the remnants have probably fallen back to the bridge, which means we may have to fight our way across while conducting a rearguard action at the same time.'

'I also do not wish to retreat,' added Atrax. 'It is dishonourable to flee thus before the false high king.'

Gallia rolled her eyes at his notion of honour but Surena was nodding his head in agreement.

'The enemy will think that we are almost beaten,' he said. 'As such they will not be expecting us to attack, which may give us an advantage.'

Domitus was more sobering in his assessment. 'Whatever the decision taken here, you all should know that this army has only one fight left in it.'

'There is something else,' remarked Marcus, 'we are running short of arrows.'

I was astounded. 'How can this be? Dura has its own camel train carrying spare ammunition, as does Hatra, Gordyene and Media.'

'I am sorry to report that during the last two days of fighting we have expended a great many arrows and we also lost a great many camels carrying ammunition when the camps were attacked.'

Orodes looked at him with weary eyes. 'How much is left?'

'Two quivers for each horse archer, more or less.'

'That will last about ten minutes,' said Gafarn.

'Our odds lengthen,' remarked Atrax flatly.

We fell silent as each of us mused over the possibilities in our minds. Retreat was out of the question. We had come this far and to crawl back to Ctesiphon would not only embolden the enemy but would deal a fatal blow to our cause. We had no idea how Musa and Khosrou were faring, but if we were defeated here then Narses and Mithridates would surely pursue us as we fell back west while the other eastern kings marched against our allies in the north. And when news of our defeat and the death of my father reached Hatra the Armenians would surely launch a full-scale invasion of Gafarn's kingdom.

'I have an idea.'

I stopped thinking of nightmares and looked at Surena, upon whom all eyes were now fixed.

'Please share it with us,' said Orodes, smiling faintly at him.

Surena cleared his throat.

'We must use Dura's legions to attack the enemy frontally to focus the enemy's attention, while we use our one remaining advantage – our cataphracts – to make a wide detour to envelop Narses' right wing. Then we can roll up his whole army. The horse archers can deploy on the left of the legions to support their advance with what little ammunition they have left, but the decisive force will be the armoured horsemen.'

'You will split the army,' I remarked.

'That cannot be helped, lord. We must do the unexpected to confuse the enemy.'

'Makes sense,' said Domitus, 'though what about the hill men? They may return.'

'Babylon's foot and horse can act as a reserve to deal with any threat from the north. In addition, half the horse archers should also be deployed towards the north to form a defensive screen to cover our rear.'

'You dilute our depleted forces even further, Surena,' said Orodes.

'It will make no difference with regard to missile power, lord,' he replied, 'the Babylonians are...'

He suddenly remembered that he was addressing not only the king of kings but also the King of Babylon and so stopped his words.

Domitus laughed gruffly. 'He's too polite to say that the Babylonians are finished as a fighting force.'

Orodes frowned but what Domitus said was true. The Babylonian foot had suffered eight thousand casualties and were demoralised, and even the royal guard has lost over half their number. It made sense for them to stay out of the front line.

Orodes smiled at Surena. 'Please continue with your battle plan.'

Viper smiled at Surena who spoke once more.

'The horse archers deployed to the north will carry no ammunition. Those who are supporting the legions will have all the arrows.'

Atrax stared in disbelief at his fellow king. 'What use are horse archers without arrows.'

'They will give the illusion of strength,' replied Surena.

Surena's plan had merits but it was also a gamble, and if it failed the army would face certain destruction. And yet it was audacious enough to succeed against an enemy who had also suffered high casualties but who must have believed that we were on our last legs. Whether we opted for Surena's plan or not we had to do something this day. Inactivity was not an option.

'I think we should decide what we are going to do,' said Orodes. 'Pacorus, I would hear your views on the matter.'

I could think of no alternative. 'I agree with Surena.'

Orodes looked at Atrax. 'And you, lord king?'

'Let us finish this business,' he replied.

'And what of you, Gafarn?' enquired Orodes.

Gafarn wore a mask of steely determination. 'I have a debt to settle with Narses. I say we attack.'

Orodes nodded his head. 'Very well. We march out at dawn.'

That was three hours away and so everyone left my tent to go back to his forces to brief their officers. Before they left, though, Alcaeus appeared with jugs full of a bitter-tasting liquid that he insisted we all drink. He told us that it was water mixed with an extract from a Chinese plant called Ma-huang that was a stimulant and would sharpen our dulled senses during the coming fight. He made sure that we all drank a full measure before retuning to his hospital as we went to rouse our sleeping men.

As aching and fatigued bodies were shaken awake a thorough search of the camp was conducted for arrows, including those that had been shot by the enemy during the previous day and night. In this way enough ammunition was found to equip each horse archer who would be fighting alongside the legions with three full quivers. These men would be drawn from the contingents of Dura, Media and Hatra and would be commanded by Vagises, while Surena would use his own horse archers from Gordyene to form the defensive screen immediately north of the camp. Gallia would remain in camp with the reserve.

'I do not wish to remain in camp,' she complained as she assisted me in putting on my scale armour.

Having already lost my father I was gripped by a desire to protect her at all costs.

'If the hill men return then Surena will not be able to hold them with horsemen armed only with swords. Your reserve will buy us more time.'

She was unconvinced. 'More time for what? If more hill men return then my Amazons and a few hundred demoralised Babylonians will not be able to stop them. I would prefer to fight by your side today.'

She looked at me with sad eyes. 'In case we do not see each other again.'

I grabbed her shoulders. 'Do not think such thoughts. Thinking them may make them come true. Think instead of Narses skewered on the end of my lance.'

She handed me my helmet. 'A pleasing enough thought. Just ensure you are not hurt yourself.'

I tried to ruffle the battered crest on my helmet, to no avail. 'That is in the hands of Shamash.'

She shook her head. 'You and your gods. There are so many of them with so many names, but I have often thought that perhaps there is only one, like Aaron's people believe.'

I looked aghast at her. 'Only one god?'

She shrugged. 'Shamash is your lord of the sun, but the Gauls also have a god of the sun called Lugus. I wonder how many other peoples have a name for the sun god? But there is only one sun, so perhaps there is only one god.'

I held her face and kissed her on the lips. 'What a strange idea. I'm sure the Gauls have many gods.'

'Nearly forty as far as I can remember.'

'Well, then, wouldn't you prefer to have them all on your side instead of just one?'

She was clearly in a reflective mood. 'I suppose.'

We walked from the tent towards the stable area, around us hundreds of men putting on armour and checking their weapons before mustering in their companies and centuries.

'You know,' I said, 'Surena doesn't believe in any gods at all.'

She smiled wryly. 'I can believe that. He's so cock-sure of himself he probably thinks he is a god.'

'But very able. It is gratifying to know that one of the Sons of the Citadel has become a king. It should act as an inspiration to others.'

She gave me a sideways glance. 'Let us hope that he is as talented as he thinks he is.'

The sun was a perfect yellow ball surrounded by orange hues as we rode east from the camp's entrance, the banners of Susiana, Babylon, Media, Hatra and Dura fluttering behind us, and behind them twenty-two hundred men going forth for the final clash with Narses and Mithridates. Immediately after leaving camp we swung north to avoid the wreckage of the Babylonian camp that had been thoroughly pillaged and set alight by the hill men the day before. The temperature was already warm and there was no wind and so the putrid stench of death met our nostrils as we skirted the northern side of the Hatran camp and then the charred remains of the encampments of Media and Gordyene. The camps themselves and the ground to the south, where much of the fighting had taken place, were covered with thousands of

461

dead men and slain horses and camels. Some of them had been lying on the ground for two days and already were starting to rot in the heat. The smell of death is an aroma that could only have been concocted in the underworld – an odour akin to mixed dung, urine and vomit. That is what I smelt now as we cantered east towards the rising sun.

The legions followed us out of camp and after them came the horse archers who would fight on their left flank. The last to leave would be Surena and his men to form our northern screen, while inside, straining at the leash, would be Gallia with the meagre reserve. I felt pity for Domitus and his men, who would have to march across a carpet of dead flesh to get to grips with the enemy, unless the enemy decided to assault them first.

On we rode, leaving the harvest of dead behind as we cantered further east and the sweet smell of grassland entered our nostrils. The black smoke that still hung in the air over the torched camps had fortuitously masked our exit from camp, increasing our chances of achieving surprise when we struck the enemy's flank. After five miles or so we headed south and then west before Orodes called a halt so we could deploy into our attack formation – three ranks of cataphracts spread over approximately two-thirds of a mile. Due to losses in both men and equipment over the preceding two days only the front rank was fully equipped with the *kontus*. Only around half of the second rank had lances and the third rank carried none at all. Much of our leg and arm armour was dented and many scales had been torn from their thick hide suits, but at least every man and horse was wearing some sort of armour protection.

It took only a matter of minutes for the contingents to deploy into formation. On the right flank of our depleted formation was Orodes' bodyguard – two hundred men – in the place of honour. Next came my seven hundred Durans and to the left of them nine hundred and fifty Hatrans, now led by Gafarn as Vistaspa was lying in a cot in the hospital. Finally, on the left flank, were Atrax's three hundred and fifty men. As they had done many times before my men had their helmets pushed back on their heads as they waited for the signal to advance, many sharing jokes with their comrades, others checking their weapons, their reins wrapped round their left wrists.

We had gathered a hundred paces in front of the centre of the line as the final preparations were made, the sky once again an intense blue.

'I wanted to thank you, my friends,' said Orodes, 'for your support and faith in me. Our journey has been a long and difficult one and now it comes to an end, for good or ill.'

'It is just the start of your journey as the high king of Parthia, lord' I said.

'A new dawn for the empire,' stated Gafarn.

'And an end to tyranny,' added Atrax.

Orodes raised his lance. 'A new dawn.'

'A new dawn,' we replied in unison.

We then shook hands and wished each other well before rejoining our men.

'Time to avenge our father,' I called to Gafarn as he veered away to join his Hatrans. He turned round and raised his left hand in acknowledgement.

Horses scraped at the ground and men pulled their helmets down over their faces as Orodes raised his *kontus* to signal the advance. Horns were sounded and a wall of horseflesh moved forward into a walk.

Whatever was in the drink that Alcaeus had given us had worked for I felt invigorated, intoxicated even, my senses heightened to make me aware of every small detail around me – the heavy breathing of my horse, the clattering of maces and axes hanging from saddle horns against scale armour, the thud of Remus' iron-shod hooves on the turf. But he and the other horses were tired from the previous two days of battle and their advance was laboured. To conserve their strength we trotted in the direction of our target for a distance of around three miles, maintaining our formation, before breaking into a canter. We cantered for a further ten minutes to bring us within striking distance of the enemy's right flank.

I could see them now: two great blocks of horsemen, one behind the other, the front one seemingly expanding and contracting – horse archers. The front ranks were obviously advancing to shoot their arrows before retreating to allow the rear ranks to ride forward and shoot their missiles. And once they had used up all their ammunition they would be replaced by the second formation massed behind them, waiting patiently to take their turn in the front line. And on the extreme right of the scene being played out before my eyes there was another group of horsemen – Dura's horse archers – locked in a duel with their adversaries.

Orodes rode out in front of our formation and signalled a halt, horns blasting to convey his command through the ranks. I slowed Remus to a trot and then a walk and then rode forward to join Orodes, Atrax and Gafarn who had also left their men.

Orodes was highly animated. 'We must destroy those horse archers on their right wing but it will not require all out forces. Pacorus, your men will combine with mine to attack the horse archers. Atrax and Gafarn, take your men around them to attack the rear of the enemy's centre.'

They both saluted Orodes and rode back to their men.

'One more charge, Pacorus,' shouted Orodes, 'one more charge and they will break.'

463

Obviously Orodes had had a double measure of Alcaeus' magic liquid.

I raised my *kontus*. 'Let us crush our enemies, see them scattered to the four winds and hear the lamentations of their women.'

He screamed at his horse so she rose up on her hind legs and then bolted forward. I laughed and dug my knees into Remus and he too raced ahead. Behind us nine hundred heavy horsemen broke into a gallop. We were around a mile from the enemy and it took ninety seconds to cover half that distance before we levelled our lances to break into the charge. The enemy spotted us but had less than a minute to act before we struck them – hundreds of cataphracts hurtling headlong at the right flanks of two blocks of horse archers, while Atrax and Gafarn thundered behind them. They ran out of time.

We did not so much hit the enemy but rather gouged a great chunk out of them when we smashed into their flank. I drove my *kontus* into the side of a rider's horse and then drew my *spatha* to slash left and right at heads and torsos that wore no armour, killing and maiming with wild abandon as I screamed at Remus to keeping moving. It was carnage as hundreds of men began a killing frenzy. The enemy horse archers had only one aim – to flee – but there was no escape from the steel-clad demons in their midst.

Orodes and his horsemen scythed their way into the front block of horse archers, those who were fighting Vagises' men, while my heavy horsemen lanced into the rear group.

The initial impact took us deep into the enemy's formation, those riders in our path trying desperately to get out of the way but most failing as maces split unprotected skulls and swords lacerated bodies. I held my new mace in my left hand and my *spatha* in my right. They felt weightless as I swung them at any enemy flesh that came within range. I ran a horse through the neck with my sword, smashed a man's nose with my mace, and then severed a rider's arm with a downward cut of my *spatha*. Arrows hit my body and horse and bounced off – Dura's horse archers were still shooting into the enemy's ranks – and Narses' horse archers tried to slash me with their swords, the blades glancing harmlessly off my leg and arm armour. I was suddenly gripped with merriment and began laughing hysterically as I slashed, hacked and clubbed with my weapons, my face and armour being splattered with enemy blood.

On we fought, now herding the defeated horse archers before us. The din of thousands of men locked in combat filled the air, a great roaring noise that engulfed the battlefield and blotted out all other noise. I was screaming at the enemy but could not hear my voice as the ranks of the horse archers thinned and suddenly disappeared. We had ridden straight through them. I looked left and right and saw other riders coming to a halt with blood-smeared weapons in their hands. I turned and saw Vagharsh with my banner and nodded to him. He smiled grimly and then pointed ahead. I turned and saw a great mass of archers on foot loosing their missiles over the heads of the dense ranks of spearmen arrayed in front of them. He looked exhausted but I felt elated. I caught sight of the tall trees of the date palm grove in the distance and realised that the legions must have pushed the enemy spearmen through it and out the other side. Behind the latter enemy archers were shooting volley after volley to support the hard-pressed spearmen in front of them.

More and more riders grouped around me as we reformed our ranks to attack the foot archers. As we did so I looked to my left and saw the heavy horsemen of Media and Hatra envelop of formation of foot soldiers, though from this distance I could not tell what or who they were. And then, in the same area, I saw a brief glimpse of a large yellow banner. Narses!

Orodes came to my side, his armour battered and his sword covered in gore. I pointed at the archers in front of us attired in yellow tunics, red felt caps, brown leggings and carrying only bows and long daggers.

'They are shooting at the legions over the heads of their spearmen.'

Orodes wore the expression of a man possessed. 'We will destroy them, my friend.'

'You will destroy them,' I told him. 'I have a personal debt to settle.'

'Debt?'

I pointed to the south, to where Gafarn and Atrax were battling the enemy. 'Narses is there. Vengeance is mine.'

'Go, then,' he said. 'And may God go with you.'

I nodded to him and turned in the saddle.

'First company of cataphracts, with me.'

We galloped across ground carpeted with the corpses of dead and dying men and horses, Vagharsh and seventy men behind me, as I went in search of retribution.

Gafarn and Atrax were now assaulting the palace guards of Narses and Mithridates: spearmen wearing bronze helmets with large cheekguards, leather cuirasses and large round shields faced with bronze and carrying the symbols of Persis and Susiana. I shouted with joy. Finally, after the oceans of blood that had been spilt and the years of fighting, we had the last reserves of the enemy cornered. The heavy cavalry were lapping round the solid phalanx of the spearmen, which appeared to number around four thousand, trying to work their way in. But the guards were holding firm and presented an unbroken square of spear points. I would have swapped my kingdom for Marcus' machines at that moment.

I saw the banners of Media and Hatra and headed towards them. I found a frustrated Gafarn and Atrax with their senior officers.

'We failed to break them,' said Atrax bitterly.

'Palace guards, the best the enemy has,' remarked Gafarn.

Their cataphracts were already beginning to disengage from the spearmen and were falling back to our position around four hundred paces from the enemy, when from behind I heard a great rumbling noise, like distant thunder.

'What is that?' asked Atrax.

Gafarn appeared drained as I turned to face the direction the noise was coming from. My heart sank as I saw a yellow flag and a great wave of horsemen riding towards our position. Their frontage must have covered at least half a mile.

'It is Nergal,' exclaimed Atrax.

I could still not identify the banner. 'Are you sure?'

He laughed out loud. 'Quite sure, Nergal has come.'

My eyes then focused and I saw that the banner was yellow and sported a double-headed lion sceptre crossed with a sword – Nergal had brought his army. Wild cheering began to erupt around me as word spread that reinforcements had arrived.

As Nergal's horse archers flooded the area immediately south of our position the king and queen of Mesene rode to my side. I reached over to hug Praxima and gripped Nergal's forearm, and then saw with surprise that Gallia and the Amazons were also with them.

'Your presence is most welcome, lord king,' I said to Nergal. 'As is yours, lady,' smiling at Praxima beside him.

Gallia came to my side. 'I thought you were supposed to be guarding the camp.'

She waved away my admonishment. 'Surena guards it with his horse archers that have no arrows, him and the squires.'

She looked at the square of enemy spearmen. 'What is happening here?'

'It is quite simple,' answered Gafarn, raising his hand to Nergal, 'they stand in rock-like defiance of us. We cannot break them.'

Gallia nodded thoughtfully and then smiled at Praxima who pulled her bow from its case. 'Like old times, Gallia.'

Gallia grinned in delight. 'Like old times. Amazons!'

She then pulled her own bow from its case and dug her knees into Epona's sides and bolted forward followed by Praxima and the Amazons. I shook my head.

I looked at Nergal. 'I would greatly appreciate it if your archers would assist our two wives.'

He grinned, raised his bow and then he and hundreds of his horse archers galloped after the Amazons.

466

The cataphracts sat and cheered as the Amazons and Nergal's horsemen rode at the enemy in continuous circuits, loosing their arrows and slowly eroding the number of spearmen. Fortunately Nergal had brought his own camel train with spare arrows so the destruction of the enemy spearmen was now assured. Then I saw the yellow banner of Narses and knew that the battle was not yet over.

The King of Persis was riding at the head of a line of armoured horsemen that was moving at speed towards the surrounded spearmen in an attempt to relieve them. I saw more spear points behind the cataphracts stretching into the distance and realised that a great number of horsemen were bearing down on my wife and friends.

'We must head them off. Line and column to deceive them,' I shouted to Gafarn and Atrax.

They gestured to their officers and seconds later horns were sounded to signal the advance. Moments later over twelve hundred riders were cantering towards the enemy horsemen, without lances and riding tired horses. But if we did not intercept Narses and his men they would swat away our horse archers and save the spearmen. So we broke into a gallop and extended our line to cover half a mile as the gap between the two sides shortened by the second. Five hundred paces from them our formation divided into two columns, the riders at the extreme ends of each flank forming the head of a column as cataphracts suddenly veered left and right to fall in behind them to create a space into which Narses and his heavy horsemen charged, to hit thin air.

There is no point in tired horsemen that have not a *kontus* among them charging headlong at riders who are fresh and armed with lances, unless they wish to become a kebab – a *kontus* will go straight though the thickest scale armour. So we flanked right and left to become columns as Narses and his men hurtled past us and we wheeled inwards to strike them in their flanks. The enemy slowed and then halted as the horsemen in front of them parted but in doing so their momentum was lost as we once again drew our weapons and moved into the enemy mass.

Most of the horsemen we faced were spearmen wearing helmets, leather cuirasses and carrying round shields. They jabbed their spears at our bellies but from a near stationary position we could break the spear shafts with our axes and maces. A spear point glanced off the steel on my left arm. I brought my *spatha* down to splinter the shaft and then brought up the point to thrust it at the rider as he closed on me, the blade going through his larynx. Once more I had my mace in my left hand as I swung it against the side of a man's helmet, the flange denting the metal and knocking him from his saddle.

Then the Amazons and Nergal's archers were by our side, shooting arrows at the enemy who were now beginning to slowly fall back. I continued to slash and hack with my weapon and then saw a helmet with a red crest and a fleeting glimpse of a yellow banner. A spearman fell from his saddle under my blows. Then I was before Narses himself.

Dressed in an armoured cuirass covered in silver scales, he directed his horse straight at me and hurled himself from his saddle to grab me as we both tumbled to the ground. My sword was knocked from my hand though my mace's leather strap was still wrapped round my left wrist as I lay winded on my back. Narses wore no scale armour so he was able to spring to his feet to stand over me, ready to plunge his sword into my chest. I rolled onto my left side as he missed and thrust the blade into the earth beside me, grabbed the handle of my mace and swung it to the right with all my strength. Narses emitted a roar of pain as a flange bit into his leg just above his right knee and he staggered back.

I used the mace to hoist myself onto my feet as he attacked me with a series of savage downward swinging cuts with his sword. One glanced off the side of my helmet to produce a ringing in my ears as I tried to fend him off. I was tiring now and several of his strikes managed to get through my defence, striking my shoulders, knocking off iron scales and biting deep into the hide underneath. I was breathing heavily, desperately trying to fill my lungs with air to alleviate the burning sensation in my chest.

There was blood showing on his right leg but it seemed to have no effect on him as he aimed a horizontal cut against my left shoulder that I stopped by holding my mace with both hands to deflect the blow. I was aware of nothing around me as I transferred the mace to my right hand and threw it at his face. He did not expect that as he ducked to avoid it and I ran at him with all my strength, knocking him to the ground and the sword out of his hand. I held his neck with my left hand and frantically punched his face with my fist, screaming insults as I did so. But he managed to grab his sword and rain blows against the side of my helmet with its pommel, finally knocking me aside.

He staggered unsteadily to his feet, dazed, and with difficulty grasped his sword with both hands to drive it into my prostrate body before him, as I grabbed my own sword lying between his feet and thrust it upwards into his groin.

He winced fiercely, his teeth locked together as I took what seemed like an eternity to haul myself to me feet. Narses dropped his sword and looked at me pitifully, but there was no pity in me this day. I ran my *spatha* through his cuirass and into his belly, gripping it with both hands as I did so.

'That is for my father.'

I yanked the blade free and he fell to his knees, still staring at me with disbelieving eyes, blood gushing from between his legs. I reached forward and ripped the helmet off his head, then brought my blade down on his head, splitting his skull.

'And that is for Farhad.'

He pitched forward to lie face down on the ground. I stood over him, clasped the hilt of my sword with both hands and rammed it down hard, driving it through his body.

'And that is for Vardan.'

I held up my arms and screamed in triumph and then saw the figure of Mithridates gallop away with a score or more of other horsemen behind him. I pointed at him.

'Kill him, kill him. Will someone kill him?'

But no one heard me as I stood and watched the snake ride away and then disappear from view.

Vagharsh was the first to arrive where I stood like a guard dog watching over an old bone, escorted by the men of my first company of cataphracts. He looked at the dead body.

'Who is that?'

'King Narses, Vagharsh. He is finally dead.'

Vagharsh nodded and then looked at the scene of carnage all around. 'Him and a lot of others.'

I was suddenly afraid for Gallia. 'Where is the queen?'

'She is safe,' he assured me. 'She is with the kings.'

He nudged his horse over to where Remus had been calmly standing next to Narses' horse and brought him to me, then assisted me into the saddle. I ordered horsemen to mount a guard over the body of Narses to ensure it was not taken away and then rode to join my wife.

When I found her she was with Nergal, Atrax and Gafarn as Vagharsh had said, and after embracing her and the others I told them that Narses was dead. I also informed them that I had seen Mithridates flee, back to Susa I assumed.

The battle was now petering out. The phalanx of enemy guards had been decimated by arrow fire and the survivors had given themselves up after Narses' relief charge had failed. A courier brought news from Orodes that he had destroyed the enemy's horse and foot archers and had linked up with Vagises, while the legions, despite being under a hail of arrows and sling shots from the start of the fighting, had managed to inch their way forward into and through the date palm grove, forcing enemy spearmen back as they did so, until the remnants of the latter had simply dissolved as the survivors fled south.

The Battle of Susa was over.

469

Chapter 19

There was no pursuit, no triumphal gatherings or after-battle boasting and bravado. Both men and beasts were at the limits of their endurance, having expended their last reserves of energy. We forgot that we had won a great victory as all our attention was diverted to the welfare of our horses. Dehydrated, sweating in the heat and many encased in scale armour, they were in dire need of water and rest. Horse archers slid from saddles and collapsed onto the ground, totally exhausted, their horses stumbling and wandering round them in a similar state.

I slid off Remus' back and called to Gallia. 'Help me with his armour.'

I felt queasy and lethargic myself now that Alcaeus' magic concoction was wearing off and found unbuckling the straps that held his armour in place difficult.

Gallia walked over and assisted me as I felt the last reserves of strength drain from my body. I could not focus my eyes and my breathing was laboured.

'You rest,' she said. 'I'll take care of it.'

Praxima came over to assist her friend heave the heavy hide suit off Remus' back and onto the ground. He was breathing heavily and matted in sweat. Around us the cataphracts were also stripping their horses of their armour before discarding their own hide suits.

I unfastened my leg and arm armour and then with difficulty pulled my scale armour suit over my head and dumped it on the ground. My arms felt like lead and I could barely stand. I glance over to Orodes and Gafarn who were in a similar state.

'He needs walking to the river,' I said to Gallia weakly.

She also looked drained, no doubt suffering similar effects.

'I will take him, lord,' said Praxima, 'have no fear.'

'Thank you Praxima.'

They were the last words I remember saying before passing out.

I awoke in a cot in the hospital section of the camp, the first thing I saw being the crystal clear blue sky above me in the gaps between the canvas roof and then my wife's pure blue eyes gazing down at me.

'You are awake, then?'

'What time is it?'

'Mid-afternoon,' she said.

I was confused. 'That cannot be. How did I get here in so short space of time.' I tried to rise. 'How is Remus? He was exhausted.'

She placed a hand on my shoulder. 'The battle was yesterday, Pacorus, and you have been asleep for nearly twenty-four hours. And unlike you, Remus is fine.'

Alcaeus appeared beside her.

'Ah, so Hypnos grew tired of your company and sent you back to us, did he?'

'Who's Hypnos?'

He feigned surprise. 'The Greek god of sleep, of course. How are you feeling?'

'Drained.'

He nodded. 'Yes, Ma-huang can do that. Still, kept you awake during the battle. Drink plenty of water, not wine, eat regularly and get plenty of rest and you will be fine.'

I looked at Gallia. 'How is it that you suffered no ill affects?'

'I did,' she replied, 'but unlike you I had not gone without sleep for three nights.'

After drinking copious amounts of water and eating some fruit I was strong enough to walk back to my tent, though not before I had visited the stables to ensure that Remus had recovered. Awnings had been erected over the temporary stables to provide shade for the horses and as I entered his stall he walked over to me and nuzzled his nose in my chest. I stroked his neck.

'Good to see you, old friend. I was worried about you.'

'He's fine now, though when he was brought in yesterday he was done in.'

I recognised the coarse voice of Strabo behind me.

'No riding him for at least a week. He's not as young as he was despite what you think.'

He leered at Gallia and bowed his head at her.

'Majesty.'

She frowned back as he stood beside me.

'We lost five hundred horses yesterday to fatigue; their hearts just gave way.' There was great sadness in his voice.

I was astounded. 'That many?'

'That is just Dura. The other kings must have lost more, to say nothing of the hundreds of camels that have also been slaughtered. It is a right mess that will take a while to sort out.'

'Do you think you will lose any more horses,' asked Gallia with concern.

Strabo faced her and stared at her breasts. 'If all the fighting's done then only a few. Those that are down probably won't get up. But another battle will kill hundreds more, perhaps thousands.'

'There will not be another battle,' I reassured him.

Domitus had been right: there had been only one more fight left in the army. It had been a close run thing but we had triumphed, but at a heavy cost. In my state of exhaustion Domitus had handed over control of the camp to Alcaeus and Marcus who set about their new responsibilities with gusto. The first thing the former did was to organise burial details to scour the battlefield to search for Duran dead. The morning roll call after the battle had revealed the names of individuals who were missing from the ranks, and once it had been established that they were not lying in hospital, parties were despatched to find their bodies. It was a grim business but in Dura's army every man deserved to have a proper cremation if humanly possible. And so thousands of men picked through the dead to retrieve their fallen comrades, who were then consigned to huge pyres that sprang up on the plain.

I gave orders that the body of Narses was to be dumped in the Karkheh, though not before the head was hacked off, taken south to Susa and then stuck on the end of a spear in front of the city walls. When word reached Orodes he immediately countermanded my desire, sending an officer of his bodyguard to explain to me that Narses deserved a cremation according to his high rank and that his men would take the body and deal with it. I was too drained to argue.

The ditch on the eastern and northern sides of the camp was filled with dead hill men whose corpses were already starting to rot and stink, and so Alcaeus ordered that the earth from the ramparts behind these sections of the ditch be used to cover the thousands of corpses. Thousands more dead hill men lay scattered on the ground around the camp so these had to be collected and cremated.

Later that day, in the early evening, Orodes called an assembly of the kings to take stock of our situation. Alcaeus had suggested that we relocate the camp to the River Dez seven miles to the east and I had agreed. To be in such close proximity to huge numbers of dead men and animals was to invite pestilence. There was little point in winning a victory if our army was subsequently wiped out by plague.

'It does not seem like a victory,' remarked Orodes, black rings round his eyes and his face dirty and unshaven. He looked as though he had not slept for a week.

Gallia, Atrax, Surena, Viper and Gafarn also looked tired and drained, though Nergal and Praxima were both fresh faced. Orodes had also requested the presence of Marcus, Alcaeus and Domitus at the meeting.

'The final victory, Orodes,' I said.

Orodes smiled thinly at me and looked at Marcus. 'And what is the cost of our victory?'

Marcus stood, cleared his throat and kept glancing at a parchment he held in his hand. 'Well, sir, I have consulted with the other quartermasters and have arrived at the following totals. Of the foot soldiers, eight thousand Babylonians and a thousand legionaries were killed. Losses among the horsemen total fourteen hundred cataphracts and three hundred Babylonians killed and thirteen thousand horse archers slain.'

'Thirteen thousand?' exclaimed Surena with astonishment.

472

'I am afraid so,' remarked Marcus. 'In addition, nearly four a half thousand squires were killed during the course of the battle. Finally, among the animals we have lost a combined total of eight thousand camels, ten thousand horses and four hundred mules.'

There was a stunned silence. Losses of twenty-eight thousand killed, to say nothing of the hundreds more with serious wounds and thousands carrying minor injuries, represented a staggering number. Domitus had already informed me that a thousand legionaries, three hundred cataphracts and six hundred horse archers of Dura's army had perished in the fighting. Among these were seventeen Companions whose names would be carved on the memorial in the Citadel to add to the list that was steadily filling the granite tiles. Seven Amazons had also fallen.

'What about enemy losses?' asked Atrax.

Marcus picked up another parchment. 'Well, sir, obviously we do not have access to the muster lists of the enemy. However, we have managed to carry out a rough calculation of the enemy's losses based on the density of the dead in various parts of the battlefield combined with the area that the corpses cover, including the dead in and around the ditches surrounding the Duran camp. This equates to over eighty thousand killed.'

Orodes looked appalled. 'Eighty thousand?'

'Yes, sir,' replied Marcus without sentiment. 'We are burning and burying the bodies as fast as we can but I would recommend moving all your camps east to the Dez as Alcaeus has said.'

The other kings nodded their heads in agreement. I could see that Orodes was still shocked by Marcus' revelations. Nearly one hundred and ten thousand men and boys had been killed over the course of three days – nearly thirty-five thousand a day! I had never taken part in such a bloody battle and prayed that I would never do so again.

'When do we assault Susa?'

Thus far Domitus had remained silent, but ever the professional he was thinking about our next course of action. Susa still remained to be taken, which meant yet more bloodshed.

'My machines can effect a breach of the walls,' said Marcus, 'to enable the city to be entered.'

'We need at least a week to recover our strength before any further fighting can take place,' I said.

Domitus smiled maliciously. 'Well, the city is not going anywhere. Let them stew while we surround the walls. Perhaps we could starve them out if you want to save more casualties.'

'That is my city,' said Orodes sternly. 'I do not wish to starve my own people into submission.'

Domitus shrugged. 'An assault it is, then.'

473

But Orodes deferred making any decision and then pointed out that our first priority was the funeral of my father.

It took place later at sunset, the flames consuming his body as the sun descended in the west and Shamash prepared to leave the world at the end of another day, but not before my father's spirit ascended to be welcomed into heaven by the sun god. I stood next to Gallia in the company of thousands as the fire roared and burned with a white-hot intensity to cast a red glow on our faces. I looked at the iron visage of Vistaspa, his injured leg supported by splints, as he stood without showing any emotion as the lord he had devoted his life to was cremated. Next to him stood my brother, the new King of Hatra. He had already sent a letter to my mother and sisters informing them of our father's death. I thanked Shamash that Diana would be by my mother's side when the news reached her.

The next day Dura's army moved to be beside the Dez and the forces of the other kings followed, and as the new camp was marked out and the surrounding ditch was dug Marcus and his Romans began checking the component parts of the large ballista that would be used to batter Susa. Parties were despatched to the site of the battlefield to continue consigning the dead to the fires, which included sections of enemy soldiers that had surrendered. The date palm grove was cut down to provide more firewood and companies of horse archers escorting empty wagons were sent north to the foothills of the mountains to cut down trees for more firewood. When they returned they reported seeing no parties of hill men.

After a week a delegation arrived from the city in response to Orodes sending a demand to the city that it open its gates to him: four well-dressed individuals including the city governor with an armed escort. They were made to wait as he sent couriers to the other kings to request their presence to hear what these city dignitaries had to say. As they were no doubt creatures of Mithridates I had no interest in hearing their words but Gallia pestered me to go.

'You know what Orodes is like when it comes to diplomacy and protocol,' she said. 'He will only be upset if you fail to attend.'

'I would prefer to storm the city and hear what they have to say when they are on their knees before me.'

She rolled her eyes. 'Just go, Pacorus.'

It was the first time I had ridden Remus since the battle and he appeared to have fully regained his strength, though sadly we had lost another three hundred horses in the interim. Strabo had told me this news earlier, which did nothing to lighten my mood. I wore my leather cuirass, white silk shirt and helmet for the meeting, the latter now sporting a huge white goose feather crest.

The governor was a tall man with a long face, high forehead and a ridiculous moustache, the ends of which reached down to almost his shoulders. He wore a rich blue silk shirt adorned with gold round the neck and at the wrists. His brown hair was thinning in contrast to the others in his party, two of whom had thick black curly hair and beards while the fourth had straight brown hair. I was the last to arrive at Orodes' tent as the other kings stood slightly behind him as he faced the nervous officials. The day was very hot and beads of sweat were showing on their faces. Orodes himself was dressed in his silver scale armour, purple shirt, white leggings and black boots. His hair was immaculate and he no longer had rings round his eyes. He looked every inch the high king of the empire.

'Where is King Mithridates?'

I smiled to myself. I would have used traitor, upstart, maggot or filth instead of the word 'king', but Orodes stuck rigidly to propriety at all times.

The governor bowed his head deeply. 'He left the city with his mother six days ago, highness.'

'And you thought fit not to notify me of this immediately?' snapped Orodes.

The individuals behind the governor cast their heads down and perspired some more.

'Forgive me, highness,' pleaded the governor with a faltering voice, clasping his hands in front of him. 'King Mithridates ordered us not to treat with you, on pain of death, saying that he would return with reinforcements. But no one has heard from him since.'

'No surprise there,' I said, earning me a frown from Orodes.

'You will surrender the city immediately,' he demanded, holding out a hand towards me, 'otherwise I will let King Pacorus unleash his machines against your walls.'

'You will have heard of my attack against Uruk a number of years ago,' I remarked casually.

The governor nodded his head gravely. 'The city gates will be opened to you, highness, of course. And you will wish to inspect the treasure that was transported here from Ctesiphon several week ago, highness?' Orodes turned to me and smiled. At least Mithridates had not absconded with all the wealth of the empire.

Orodes rode into the city that afternoon at the head of a thousand fully armed cataphracts accompanied by the governor. Marcus was disappointed but I was delighted: having lost one in ten men in the army I had no appetite to suffer more losses.

Thus ended the campaign that killed Narses and toppled Mithridates. I sent Byrd and Malik on a hunting expedition to track down Mithridates who we learned had absconded with several wagons loaded with treasure, but they returned a week later to report that he had seemingly vanished into thin air. This was bitter news, but the next day more palatable information arrived from Khosrou and Musa.

Their march south had been more like a victory parade, with the kingdoms of Yueh-Chi, Anauon and Aria agreeing to recognise Orodes as king of kings in exchange for peace with Hyrcania and Margiana, especially after they had learned of our victory at Susa. Khosrou had written that these kingdoms had suffered many losses during the previous year's campaign and above all desired peace. The return of the sons of their kings, who had been taken to Susa when Mithridates had fled Ctesiphon, also endeared Orodes to them. With Nergal having renewed his non-aggression agreement with Carmania, which allowed him to march to our aid, only the Kingdom of Drangiana remained as a potential enemy. However, King Vologases sent an urgent embassy to Susa declaring his unwavering support for Orodes. And so peace at last returned to an empire that was totally exhausted by years of internal strife.

Orodes stayed at Susa to await the arrival of reinforcements sent by Mardonius to augment the new garrison of the city. His bodyguard, a thousand of Mesene's horse archers, his two thousand Babylonian foot soldiers and what remained of Babylon's royal guard stayed with him. Nergal would send more troops to escort the gold to Ctesiphon when Orodes decided to move the treasure back to the empire's capital.

After we had said our farewells to Orodes the kings took their depleted armies back to their homelands. Nergal travelled back to Mesene and Gafarn, Atrax and Surena rode north together two days before Dura's army departed. It took us six weeks to march back to Dura, first catching sight of the Citadel late one afternoon after being buffeted by a sandstorm that had lasted for five hours. The population poured out of the city to welcome us back, young boys racing up to the column to search for their fathers among the legionaries or horsemen. I remembered another return to the city after the Battle of Surkh when mothers had held up their babies for their fathers to see. Those babies were now boys as we returned from yet another campaign. I also saw young mothers holding infants aloft and prayed to Shamash that these babies would not spend their childhoods anxiously waiting for the return of their fathers from war. Dura deserved peace; I deserved peace. I was done with fighting.

The day after we had arrived back in the city I sat with Gallia relaxing on the palace terrace in the company of my daughters. Claudia told me that I looked old and haggard, while Isabella just grinned at me and Eszter ran around the terrace like a child possessed. Dobbai waved a hand at us as she took her seat and the nursery maids took charge of our daughters. Dobbai was too old for their boundless energy and one of my chief stewards told me that she spent most of her days on the terrace watching the traffic on the road and boats on the river, though she always made time for Claudia, telling her tales of

476

the empire and the gods that protected it. To provide shade a pergola had been erected on the terrace made of vertical wooden posts and crossbeams with a canvas cover. I had suggested growing grape vines over it to provide shade but Dobbai had told me that when the fruit was ripening it would attract bees and she had no desire to be stung to death.

After my two eldest daughters had departed to take their daily pony ride, and Eszter was taken off to the nursery, servants brought us fruit juice and pastries. A young serving girl gently touched Dobbai on the shoulder to wake her. Gallia smiled.

'This peaceful setting makes a change to the carnage we have witnessed these past few weeks,' she said.

I raised my goblet to her. 'Now that Orodes rules the whole of the empire we can look forward to many such days, my sweet. Here's to peace.'

I heard a low cackle. 'Peace, son of Hatra? And how will a great warlord amuse himself if there are no enemies to conquer?'

'He will watch his daughters grow up and inherit his kingdom, that is how.'

Dobbai focused her black eyes on me. 'Have you forgotten my words?'

I had. 'What words?'

She closed her eyes and shook her head. 'I don't know how you put up with him, child,' she said to Gallia. 'His mind is like a great steppe: vast in its emptiness. I once told you, son of Hatra, that you would face two great armies, one from the east and one from the west, and so you will before you hang up your sword.'

'I have faced these two hosts,' I replied smugly, 'the Armenians in the west and Narses and Mithridates in the east.'

'Your infantile attempt to trick me has failed,' she snapped. 'You did not fight the Armenians, but you will have to fight the Romans.'

I laughed. 'The Romans? They are preoccupied with fighting the Jews. They will not be troubling Parthia for a long time.'

But a month later, at the weekly council meeting, I was disabused of such notions when Aaron informed me that Alexander's forces had suffered a crippling defeat in Judea and had been scattered. Byrd and Malik had also ridden to Dura to attend the meeting and they conveyed worse news.

'My office in Antioch,' said Byrd, looking at me apologetically, 'reports that Mithridates and his mother are in the city.'

These were ill tidings indeed. 'What is he doing there?' I asked, hoping that the answer would be that he was preparing to leave for exile in Rome.

'He and Romani governor plan to invade Parthia,' replied Byrd.

477

'Your failure to kill Mithridates returns to haunt you,' remarked Dobbai idly.

'Is Alexander dead?' I asked Aaron.

'Not as far as I know, majesty,' he replied.

'Roman patrols are entering Agraci territory, Pacorus,' said Malik. 'Lord Vehrka's men are encountering them on a daily basis.'

'I am certain Alexander will continue his war against the Romans, majesty,' said Aaron, probably trying to convince himself in addition to me.

'The Jews will soon be crushed,' said Dobbai, 'and then the Romans will turn their attention towards Parthia. You have little time to prepare, son of Hatra.'

I looked at Domitus. 'Has there been any activity on our northern border.'

He shook his head. 'None'

'Well,' I said, 'even if the Jews fail there are still only two legions in Syria that we can match with our own two, and we far outnumber them in horsemen.'

Domitus looked at Byrd. 'Tell him.'

An icy feeling went down my spine. 'Tell me what?'

'I have heard other rumours, Pacorus, reports that have come from captains of merchant ships. They say that Marcus Licinius Crassus will soon leave Rome to make war against Parthia. They say he will march at the head of seven legions.'

Now I was alarmed. Seven legions plus supporting horsemen added to the other two legions in Syria would pose a serious threat to the empire, not least to Dura.

'How confident are you, Byrd, that these rumours are accurate?'

He frowned. 'My sources are reliable.'

'We must inform Orodes at Ctesiphon,' I said. 'Perhaps he can persuade the Romans not to commence hostilities against Parthia.'

'Mithridates wants his crown back,' remarked Dobbai, a hint of relish in her voice.

'If the Romans put him back on his throne then he will be nothing more than a puppet ruler,' said Gallia.

'Better a puppet ruler than no ruler at all,' replied Dobbai.

'How long before Crassus gets here?' I asked Byrd.

'He has not left Rome yet. We have many weeks to prepare.'

I was unconcerned regarding Mithridates. He had no army behind him and little money with which to raise a new one. But his presence at Antioch provided the Romans with a pretext for starting a war with Parthia. Once Crassus arrived in Syria they would have nine legions on Dura's northern border, in addition to cavalry.

'We could always strike first,' suggested Domitus casually.

478

Everyone looked at him. 'If the Romans are going to invade then why not strike the first blow? We can be across the border with fifty thousand men and capture Antioch before Crassus and his legions set foot in Syria.'

I had to admit that I was tempted. I trusted Byrd and knew he would not reveal any information to me that he did not think was accurate. Still, to launch an unprovoked war against the Romans was no small thing, and would mean that I would not have the support of the other kingdoms in the empire. I also knew that Orodes would take a very dim view of such a measure. If, however, the empire was attacked then Dura would have the support of the other kingdoms. That said, if Mithridates was accompanying the Romans he would insist on marching via Dura to storm the city. But Dura's walls were thick and its defences strong. A Roman army would have to conduct a lengthy siege to take it, during which time Orodes would be able to rally the empire against the invaders. And I knew that I could also rely on Haytham for support.

'No,' I said, 'we will not launch an attack against Syria. I have no interest in conquering that province, which I would have to do if we invaded it.'

'You don't need to conquer it, just capture Antioch and kill Mithridates,' argued Domitus.

'And after we have done that,' I replied, 'what then?'

Domitus shrugged. 'Then we withdraw to Dura.'

'And when Crassus arrives with his army he will still march against us.'

'But at least he won't have the two Syrian legions if they have been destroyed,' retorted Domitus.

I was unmoved. 'No, we await developments. Having just finished fighting one war I have no desire to immediately embark upon another. The army needs time to rest and rebuild its strength.'

Rsan looked visibly relieved by my decision while Aaron looked disappointment. Alexander's rebellion had always been a gamble. It was one thing supplying rebels with weapons, quite another for them to defeat the Roman occupiers. Well-armed bandits with excellent local knowledge would always be able to achieve success against isolated outposts and small garrisons, but Alexander aspired to be a general and to defeat the Romans on the battlefield, something that was very different and much harder to achieve.

That night I wrote to Orodes and Gafarn informing them of Byrd's information and the whereabouts of Mithridates. Gallia had increased the number of guards on the city walls and in the Citadel, fearing that the former high king would again send assassins to kill me, and after the council meeting Dobbai had advised me to send my own assassins to Antioch to rid the world of Mithridates. I told her I would do no such thing. When I had finished writing it was late and the oil in my table lamp was burning low. The night was warm and there was no wind to stir the linen nets at the entrance from our bedroom to the balcony.

I looked at my sword in its scabbard propped up against the desk. It was eighteen years since Spartacus had given it to me when I had been a fresh-faced young man. Now I was forty years old and had known nothing but constant war during the intervening years. But I cheered myself with the thought that at least now the empire was united against its external enemies. If it came to war then I would not be fighting the Romans with one hand and Mithridates with the other.

I heard a rustle coming from the balcony. I drew my *spatha* from its scabbard and used it to ease aside one of the linen nets to see a huge black raven perched on the balustrade. He noticed the movement and turned his shaggy feathered neck to stare at me with his soulless eyes. I held his gaze and then he ducked his head forward and made a low, throaty rattling sound before spreading his wings and flying away.

The next day I sent the letters to Hatra and Ctesiphon and told Gallia about the visit of the raven while we sat on the palace terrace taking breakfast with our girls and Dobbai.

'It is an omen foretelling the coming of war,' remarked Dobbai.

I was unconcerned. 'We know all about the Romans.'

'The omen does not allude to the Romans,' she said. 'Another threat arises.'

'You mean Mithridates?' asked Gallia.

Dobbai shook her head. 'No, child, something more dangerous.'

I dismissed her ramblings. There was no greater threat than the Romans and we would be fully prepared to meet them when they attacked. Dobbai saw omens everywhere.

After breakfast I went with Gallia to the stables to collect our horses prior to riding to the training fields to hone our archery skills. I was just about to hoist myself into the saddle when a rider trotted into the courtyard. A guard held his reins as he slid from the saddle and reached into his saddlebag. I watched as he said something to the guard who pointed at me, then strode across the flagstones before halting in front of me and bowing his head.

'A letter from King Gafarn, majesty.'

He held out a rolled parchment with a seal bearing the horse head crest of Hatra. Gallia stared at it as I broke the seal and unrolled it. I read the words, sighed deeply and closed my eyes.

'What is it?' she asked.

I opened my eyes and handed her Gafarn's letter. From the top of the palace steps I saw Dobbai looking at me and my blood ran cold. She had been right: the raven had been an omen.

'The Armenians have declared war on Parthia.'

Epilogue

Aulus Gabinius was far from happy. Until fairly recently things had been going very well for him. Having helped to propel Pompey to power in Rome he had been made proconsul of Syria as a reward, a position from which he had profited enormously. In addition to destroying Pontus and reducing Armenia to a client kingdom of Rome, Pompey had crushed what was left of the Seleucid Empire to create the Roman province of Syria and as a bonus had also conquered Judea. When Gabinius had arrived in Syria to take up his new position he had been pleasantly surprised to discover that most of the towns and cities in his province had been accustomed to paying some sort of taxation for hundreds of years, and that in addition there was already in situ a network of local administrators to maintain the rule of law and collect said taxes. As a result money soon began to flow into the treasury at Antioch, the capital of Syria, from which Gabinius extracted a very large amount each month. It was a most satisfactory state of affairs.

Like most senior politicians and high-ranking soldiers of the Republic, Gabinius dressed and lived modestly, though they all endeavoured to accumulate large amounts of wealth to buy favours and influence in Rome. In this Gabinius was no different and had, since his arrival in Syria, amassed a fortune from the taxes levied on Syria and Judea. But now his extremely lucrative position was under threat.

First there had been a letter from his sponsor Pompey in Rome informing him that Marcus Licinius Crassus had been given the province of Syria for five years and an army of seven legions with which to fight a war against the Parthians. This meant that when Crassus arrived Gabinius would be replaced as governor of the province and recalled to Rome, which meant he had only a few months to profit from the province's generous tax returns.

Then there had been the Jewish uprising in Judea, which had been totally unexpected and had at first threatened not only the entire Jewish kingdom but also the towns in southern Syria. Fortunately his very able cavalry commander had acted quickly to bring the rebels to battle and defeat them.

It was this young general who now awaited Gabinius in the atrium of his villa nestled in the hills at Daphne some five miles from Antioch, a delightful location that was home to the city's wealthiest and most powerful citizens. It was also reputedly the spot where the god Apollo caught up with Daphne, a nymph he had fallen in love with, whereupon Daphne's father, the river god Peneus, had turned his daughter into a laurel tree to prevent her losing her virginity. As a result of this myth there was an ancient law forbidding the cutting down or harming of any of the laurel trees that grew in the area.

481

Gabinius was sceptical about the place being the playground of gods but he had to admit that it seemed a most blessed place, filled with natural springs, waterfalls, citrus orchards, orchid gardens, laurel trees and myrtle. A man could be at peace with the world in such a paradise. But not today.

'The *Praefectus Alae* Mark Antony awaits you, governor,' the villa's head steward announced as Gabinius strode into the dining room and reclined on one of the couches.

'Show him in,' he ordered, nodding to slaves who brought him dishes of fruits, meats and bread to eat, though he really had little appetite for food.

Moments later his ebullient cavalry commander marched into the room and saluted.

Everything about Mark Antony was big: his thick neck, his round face and his solid frame. And the same could be said of his personality, which made him enormously popular among both the soldiery and Antioch's nobility, especially their wives.

Gabinius pointed at an empty couch. 'Can I offer you something to eat, Mark Antony?'

Mark Antony reclined on the couch and gestured at the slaves to bring him food.

'You are very kind, governor. Our new guests are eager to meet you.'

Gabinius groaned. As proconsul of Syria he had better things to do than waste his time playing host to a group of Parthian exiles who had suddenly descended on him. Mark Antony noted his lack of enthusiasm.

'You do not wish to see them, governor?' he asked, nibbling on a grape.

Gabinius handed his plate to a slave. He had suddenly lost any appetite he may have had.

'Not particularly. No doubt they wish to borrow money from me to maintain their lavish lifestyle, either that or drag me into their internecine Parthian squabbles. I have little interest in either. What is the situation in Judea?'

'The rebels have been confined to an area in the southeast of the kingdom, around Alexandreum and Jericho. Soon we will have destroyed all of them.'

Gabinius nodded approvingly. He had spent a considerable amount of money on Mark Antony, who had at first refused an offer to serve under him in Syria. The young man had been in Athens at the time studying rhetoric and philosophy, as well as seeking refuge from his many creditors in Rome, but the incentive of a commission as the commander of all the Roman cavalry in Syria had changed his mind. The fact that none existed in Syria at the time had required Gabinius to pay for the raising of a full *ala* of cavalry – a thousand horsemen – to satisfy Mark Antony's vanity, but the governor considered the expenditure an investment. For one thing his young commander was a member of the Antonia clan, one of Rome's most influential families, whose support would be useful when Gabinius returned to the city, which unfortunately would now be sooner rather than later.

Some of Mark Antony's horsemen rode behind the governor and his cavalry commander as they later made their way from the villa to the city of Antioch, the 'Athens of the East'.

'It is perhaps fortuitous, governor, that these Parthians have appeared at this time.'

'Fortuitous is not a word I would use,' muttered Gabinius.

'You may be interested to know that I captured a number of Jewish rebels some days ago and had them all tortured before they were crucified.'

'My congratulations,' remarked Gabinius sarcastically.

'But what they revealed before they died,' continued Mark Antony, 'was most interesting.'

'And what was that?'

'The weapons that armed the Jewish insurgents came from Parthia.'

Gabinius halted his horse. 'Are you certain of this?'

'Quite certain, governor. It came from the mouths of more than one of the condemned. I think they were so forthcoming with information in the hope that it would save their lives.'

'And did it?' asked Gabinius.

Mark Antony shook his head. 'No. There can be no mercy for the enemies of Rome.'

Gabinius urged his horse forward. 'Quite right. Well, perhaps our Parthian guests can shed more light on this matter.'

The pace of their journey was slowed as they rode through Antioch's wide streets crowded with caravans, travellers, worshippers and citizens. Founded nearly two hundred and fifty years ago by Seleucus Nicator, one of Alexander of Macedon's generals, it was still populated mainly by Greeks, though it also contained a host of other races, a teeming mass of tens of thousands of people. Built beside the River Orontes, Antioch grew rich from the trade between the Mediterranean and Mesopotamia and the produce of the surrounding fertile valleys. Its many theatres, temples, libraries and public baths were testimony to the city's great wealth. And the promise of riches attracted people from far and wide, its great squares always thronged with poets, philosophers and out-of-work actors entertaining the public with varying degrees of success. Gabinius had done little to stamp Roman influence on the city apart from ordering the building of an aqueduct to being fresh water from nearby Mount Silpius and paving the city's gravel roads.

The Parthians had appeared a week ago. The first Gabinius knew of their impending arrival was the appearance of a fat courtier at his headquarters; a man with pale skin, a wispy beard and small piggy eyes whose grovelling servility he had found distasteful. The Parthian nobles had subsequently sent the governor a sizeable amount of gold as thanks for his offer of sanctuary in their time of strife (though in reality they had invited themselves), which had been far more satisfying. Gabinius had given them rooms in Antioch's palace, a vast edifice built on the island formed by two branches of the Orontes. This complex was also Gabinius' headquarters but was so expansive that it allowed him to avoid them and ignore their requests for an audience with him, but today he had agreed to meet them, if only to end the constant fawning messages they sent him and his senior officers.

The same fat courtier that Gabinius had met a week ago greeted him and Mark Antony at the doors to the chambers in the west wing of the palace where the Parthians had been housed. The courtier bowed to them and then opened the doors to allow them to enter. Gabinius had his helmet in the crook of his arm and he looked disapprovingly at Mark Antony and then down at his own helmet, indicating that his subordinate should also remove his headgear.

The room was spacious and airy, with red marble columns supporting the ceiling and green marble tiles covering the floor. The tiles came from the local quarry that produced the same coloured marble that furnished local villas and was also exported to Greece and Italy. The courtier took short steps as he led them to the far end of the room towards two high-backed chairs occupied by a man and woman.

The courtier halted around five paces in front of the seated individuals and bowed deeply to them.

'The Proconsul Aulus Gabinius and *Praefectus Alae* Mark Antony, highnesses,' he announced in a high-pitched voice. He turned to the pair of Romans and bowed again.

'My I present King of Kings Mithridates, high king of the Parthian Empire, and his mother, Queen Aruna.'

Gabinius nodded his head at them both and Mark Antony flashed a smile at the full-bosomed woman wearing a sour expression. The Romans' seeming lack of deference earned looks of disapproval from the gaudily dressed courtiers assembled either side of the royal pair. One individual caught the governor's attention: a young man in his early twenties, tall, broad shouldered, clean-shaven and with a fair complexion and shorter hair than the other men. He had a handsome face, or would have had it not been for the hateful expression it wore. He seemed to be positively bristling with animosity.

Regarding the king, the proconsul thought that the wide cheekbones and long, pointed jaw line of this Mithridates made him look like a snake, an image reinforced by his dark brown, almost black eyes and slim frame.

'I trust your quarters are agreeable.'

'We do not intend to stay here long,' the king shot back.

Gabinius was pleased by this good news. The last thing he needed was a landless, ungrateful king and his hangers-on in his province.

'Though we are grateful for your hospitality,' smiled the queen, who Gabinius noted was dripping with gold and diamond jewellery. Indeed, he observed that all the courtiers appeared to be wearing gold rings and necklaces, while rich stones dangled from the women's ears.

'It is my intention to return to Parthia,' said Mithridates, 'to punish those who have rebelled against me and conspired to steal my throne. I requested this meeting to propose an alliance between our two great powers to achieve this end.'

Gabinius was already bored. The information he had received concerning this Mithridates had revealed that he was the loser in a Parthian civil war and therefore had no power with which to reclaim his realm. The governor smiled politely and was about to say that it was not within his power to make alliances with foreign powers.

'You would be richly rewarded for such assistance,' added Mithridates.

Gabinius smiled again and suddenly became much more interested in what this foreign king had to say.

As a proconsul he had the authority to raise troops and make war on Rome's enemies, though he had no interest in his own treasury funding such endeavours. Wars could be ruinously expensive. However, if the funding came from elsewhere then he might consider conducting a campaign in the east. It was true that he had already made plans to capture the oasis of Palmyra, both to put an end to the troublesome Agraci threat and to take control of the lucrative trade that passed through the oasis settlement, but that expedition would more than pay for itself when he had control of Palmyra. He was wary of other adventures that might be expensive for very little reward.

'Why would I make war on Parthia?' queried Gabinius.

'To ensure its ruler is a friend of Rome,' answered the queen.

'Who is the current ruler of Parthia?' asked Gabinius.

Mithridates' eyes narrowed. 'Orodes, my stepbrother.'

'No friend of the Romans,' added the queen.

'His main ally is a traitor named Pacorus, a man who was a slave and fought against the Romans,' Mithridates spat the words with venom.

'I have heard of this man,' said Mark Antony, rubbing his aquiline nose with a finger.

'Man?' said Aruna dismissively.

'As have I,' said Gabinius. Pompey had spoken of him admiringly when he had returned to Rome, and of the peace they had both agreed, though the governor had an altogether different opinion of this foreign king who had refused to hand over a killer of Roman soldiers.

'But did you know that he is also a friend of the Agraci,' said Mithridates, 'the scourge that torments both our peoples?'

'I did not,' admitted Gabinius, whose opinion of King Pacorus was lowering by the minute. 'Though I do know that he is a friend of Jews who kill Romans.'

Gabinius went on to inform Mithridates about a man named Aaron who was the treasurer at Dura Europos and who was wanted for the murder of several Roman soldiers in Judea.

'I have also heard rumours that this Aaron is a friend of a Jewish prince named Alexander,' remarked Mithridates.

'Alexander Maccebeus?' asked Mark Antony.

'I do not know,' replied Mithridates, 'but other rumours tell of the armouries at Dura Europos sending weapons to this Alexander with the assistance of the Agraci.'

'You said that Rome would be richly rewarded for its assistance,' said Gabinius, changing the subject.

Mithridates smiled at the governor. 'Assist me and I will reward you from the great royal treasury at Ctesiphon, the seat of Parthian power and only three weeks' march from Syria. Once I am reinstalled on my throne I will give you three thousand talents of gold for your support.'

Gabinius tingled with excitement. Three thousand talents amounted to a hundred tons of gold. He licked his lips. A campaign in the east was suddenly very appealing.

'I think, King Mithridates,' replied Gabinius, 'that you can look forward to being back on your throne very soon. All that remains is to finalise the details. I will send one of my officers to inform you of the date of our departure when all the arrangements have been made.'

The couriers broke into applause at this news while the queen laid a hand on her son's arm and smiled at him. Mithridates raised a hand to still the noise.

'You will not forget about King Pacorus?' he said.

'No, sir,' replied Gabinius, 'you can be certain that he is high on the list of my priorities.'

'He needs to be dealt with,' said Aruna.

'He has a sorceress,' added Mithridates seriously.

Mark Antony laughed and Gabinius bit his lip trying not to. These eastern types! How ridiculous they were in their brightly coloured robes with their long hair, beards and effeminate ways. No wonder Pompey had conquered this area with such ease.

The same fat courtier who had shown them into the room fussed around them as they took their leave of the royal guests. In the corridor outside Gabinius halted to question him.

'What is your name?'

'Ashlen, highness,' replied the fawning courtier.

'Who was that sour-faced young man dressed in the yellow tunic? He appears not to like Romans.'

Ashlen looked momentarily alarmed. 'No, highness, not all at. That is Nicetas, highness, the youngest son of King Narses who was most tragically recently killed at Susa. He thirsts for revenge against King Pacorus.'

'That is the second time we have heard that name today,' commented Mark Antony.

Later that afternoon, after Gabinius had returned to his spacious villa, he relaxed on the balcony taking wine with his cavalry commander where they were joined by the tribune Marcus Roscius, one of the rising stars among his legionary officers. The mood of the proconsul had brightened considerably since earlier.

'So this King of Dura Europos, this Pacorus, has been supplying weapons to the Jews,' said Mark Antony.

Gabinius nodded. 'It would appear so.'

'Such a thing cannot go unpunished.'

He looked at Mark Antony, who was anticipating the prospect of war and glory with relish.

'Before we embark on a war with the Parthians,' said Gabinius, 'we need to know more about our enemies. Marcus, you have travelled to Dura and met with this Pacorus. What are your impressions of him and his kingdom?'

'The walls of his city are very strong, governor,' replied Marcus.

'Walls can be breached,' sniffed Mark Antony dismissively.

'He also has soldiers equipped like our own and there appear to be many of them,' continued Marcus.

'And what of the king himself, this Pacorus?' pressed Gabinius.

'We know that he was taken as a slave and shipped to Italy where he fought alongside Spartacus during the slave revolt,' replied Marcus, 'and that since his return to Parthia has won many battlefield victories. Many talk of his army with awe.'

Mark Antony waved a hand in the air. 'Idle gossip for old women. We must bring him to account. The fact that has he been aiding the Jewish rebels is itself a declaration of war against Rome.'

Gabinius nodded. 'It is as you say, Mark Antony. We cannot allow a foreign power to interfere in Rome's affairs without punishment. As I was planning a strike against Palmyra anyway we will expand the area of operations to include the domain of King Pacorus, which with Palmyra will be absorbed into Roman Syria.'

'And what of Mithridates, governor?' asked Mark Antony.

'I think we may be able to turn his appearance at Antioch to our advantage. After we have captured Palmyra and Dura there is no reason why we cannot cross the Euphrates and reinstall Mithridates back on his throne.'

'As a client king,' said Marcus.

Gabinius smiled. 'Naturally. I intend to do to Parthia what Pompey did to Armenia and Pontus.'

No Roman had attempted to subjugate the Parthian Empire, but Gabinius knew that there would never be a better opportunity to conquer it. Parthia was exhausted by years of bloody civil war and he had received word that Armenia was about to commence hostilities against the Parthians on their northern borders. He knew that Crassus aspired to conquer Parthia and extend Roman rule as far as the Indus, but Crassus was not here and it would take him months to march his army overland from Italy. Gabinius' two legions, thousand horsemen and the auxiliaries he would raise would be more than enough to deal with a motley band of Agraci nomads and the decadent troops of Parthia. He remembered reading the reports of the war waged by Lucullus in the Parthian Kingdom of Gordyene and the ease with which Roman troops had defeated the enemy.

By the time Crassus arrived Gabinius would have defeated the Agraci and the Parthians, installed Mithridates as a client king of Rome and emptied the royal treasury at Ctesiphon of its contents. By doing so he would become as rich as Crassus himself and a grateful Rome would shower him with further gifts when he brought the Silk Road under Roman control. Circumstances had conspired to give Aulus Gabinius the opportunity to conquer both the Arabian Peninsula and the whole of the Parthian Empire in one fell swoop.

31548709R00272

Made in the USA
Middletown, DE
04 May 2016